VAUDEVILLE

– THE STRUGGLE CONTINUES

Stephen P. E. Lees. LL. B.

Other books by Stephen Lees

Visions of Architecture
Published by Bloomsbury in New York and London.
ISBN No. 978-1-4081-2881-7
A fascinating study of the development of western architecture focusing on a unique selection of 54 buildings, examining why they have been designed in a particular way, the method and materials used to construct them and their impact on the *Construction Process*.

Construction Process in Architecture
ISBN 978-0-9571629-9-0
A sequel to **Visions of Architecture** foscusing on the *Construction Process* which comprises causational links explaining why architecture developed the way it has.

Volume I *The Iron Mausoleum* - A case of Sherlock Holmes and the Titanic.
ISBN No. 978-0-9571629-0-7
Volume II *The Iron Vault* - A case of Sherlock Holmes and Professor Moriarty.
ISBN No. 978-0-9571629-1-4
Volume III *The Iron Soul* - A case of Sherlock Holmes and the
Napoleon of Crime. ISBN No. 978-0-9571629-2-1
Volume IV *The Iron Titan* - A case of Sherlock Holmes and the
Invisible Presence. ISBN No. 978-0-9571629-3-8
Volume V *The Iron Metropolis* - A case of Sherlock Holmes and the
Titans of Valhalla. ISBN No. 978-0-9571629-4-5

All five novels are brand-new adventures set in a fog-bound London. During the course of the stories, Holmes and Watson visit numerous places in their quest to find an explanation for the continuing mysteries surrounding the apparent sinking of the *'Titanic'*. As Holmes and Watson progress through their investigation they encounter numerous characters from different backgrounds and find themselves in various interesting locations throughout a fog-bound London, creating an atmospheric tension throughout all five volumes.

The Première - A case of the Ridiculous and the Sublime.
ISBN No. 978-0-9571629-5-2
An informative and humorous account of a series of incidents, including a chance meeting in the Café Royal with Oscar Wilde and Gustav Mahler, during the London première, in 1910 of the mighty Eighth Symphony.
The Finalé - A further case of the Ridiculous and the Sublime
ISBN No. 978-0-9571629-6-9
Follows on from The Première, and examines the shifting attitudes by artists, composers, painters, writers and architects, all of whom are eager to establish a more real expression of the arts. Especially, in a world they perceive as, spinning out of control and into the inevitable cataclysm generated by the First World War.

Royal Aq - Queen of Music Halls
ISBN No. 978-0-9571629-7-6
A brilliant book, with an extensive index, about the history of London's varied Music Halls and their itinerant performing artistes whom the author brings to life, in a fascinating way by exploring facts which are not well known making the Royal Aq highly enjoyable, informative and humorous.

Music Hall - The Saga goes on
ISBN No. 978-0-9571629-8-3
Is the sequel to the Royal Aq and continues the saga of Music Hall and their performing artistes with further facts and drama – on and off stage, to delight fans of Music Hall. Complete with extensive index, this book remains humorous and enjoyable.

All books by Stephen Lees are available via:
http://www.amazon.com/Stephen-Lees/e/B007TWUUBG

This book published November 2015 by SPEL Publications
prodev@globalnet.co.uk

ISBN No. 978-1-5262-0271-0

A CIP catalogue record of this book is available
from the British Library.

Book and Cover design by SPEL
Typeset in Garamond

Printed and bound in the United States

SPEL Publication acknowledges kind permission from Bloomsbury
Publishers to reproduce some images from *Visions of Architecture* also by
Stephen Lees ISBN 978-1-4081-2881-7.

SPEL Publication further acknowledges kind permission from
The Calderdale Museums to reproduce the painting
entitled *Briggate* by John Atkinson Grimshaw on this book cover.

Contents

Introduction

Vaudeville - The Struggle Continues is the third in the sequel, starting with **Royal Aq. - Queen of Music Halls** and then **Music Hall - The Saga Goes On,** continues to chronicle the hilarious exploits of two Vaudeville artistes. Jack Mitchell and Theo Houston, both out of New York City accompany the impresario, Michael Lodge back to England to perform in various London Music Halls. They do so in the erroneous belief that Music Hall in England is the same as Vaudeville in America.

What they do not understand is that Vaudeville in America is not the same as Music Hall in England. And what in England might be considered Burlesque would, in America, be termed Vaudeville! What they have come to understand are the various characters and influences which make up Music Hall *acts* or *turns*. Including those based on the operas of Richard Wagner, such as *Das Rheingold, Die Feen, Die Valküre* or even *Parsifal* producing disrespectful parody or pantomime and embarrassing moments even in the well appointed red plush Music Halls!

Vaudeville – The Struggle Continues, with an extensive index, chronicles the on-going saga of Music Halls and their intrepid performing artistes, with more drama – on and off stage – making this third book again, informative, humorous and enjoyable. Complete with original line drawings of Music Halls and other buildings drawn by the author.

This book is dedicated to
Caroline Monk
affectionately known as
'Monkey'
who introduced me to Judd
the over confident
Ventriloquist's Dummy

Chapter 1

The Début at Daly's Music Hall

We had some time to go before Jack Houston, my Vaudeville partner of thirty one years, and I were due to hit the stage at Augustin Daly's Music Hall in Leicester Square in London's theater district. Michael Lodge, an accomplished impresario, had just left us to take his seat in his red plush, private box on the first tier balcony. It was he who had invited us to tread the floorboards in London, after a meeting with him when we were performing at the Majestic Theater in Chicago. Whilst relative new comers to the London Music Hall scene, we were learning new skills almost daily, as well as developing a greater understanding of this virulent, if affectionate, form of entertainment, especially in London.

Whilst waiting in the stage wings, I decided to peep through a gap in the purple velvet safety curtain, in order to get a feel of the mood of the audience. Having done so, I ascertained immediately that the audience, this evening, was lively and made up, in the main, of costermongers, who were clearly out for a good time. This vital set of individuals is guaranteed always to liven up any evening on or indeed off the stage.

The first act on the stage now being performed, was by a fellow, name of George Grossmith, playing the pianoforte. He did so whilst reciting a series of continuous anecdotes and witty observations. Typically Grossmith asked the audience a question.

"Of the two diseases to be afflicted with when drinking alcohol, which is the more preferable to have; Parkinson's or Alzheimer's?"

He gave his audience a few moments with which to try and understand this general inquiry, whilst at the same time, creating a series of sublime triple A's and and sensuous musical arpeggios on his pianoforte.

"And what would you know about such afflictions?"asked one of the costermongers in the front row of the stalls.

"But sir," replied Grossmith, "of the two diseases to contract, Parkinson's would surely be the more preferable to be afflicted with?"

"How can that be so?" asked another costermonger.

Grossmith continued unabated.

"Because it is preferable to spill part of your drink due to having Parkinson's disease of nervous shakes, than forget where you placed your drink due to memory loss as in Alzheimer disease!"

"Oh Parkinson's disease" said another costermonger embedded in the stalls, "I have got that disease; but do not worry. I will soon shake it off!"

This anecdote did elicit a limited applause. Though I suspect the audience were really clapping for themselves as a rsult of their participation in that exchange with the pianoforte playing wit.

However, be that as it may, Jack and I were also performing on stage later. This will be our stage début at Daly's Music Hall. To reassure myself, yet again, I looked at the billposter affixed to the stage sidewall. It listed the order of appearance of the various acts or turns to be performed this evening. We were on third, after the interval.

Daly's Music Hall

GEORGE EDWARDES - MANAGER

GEORGE GROSSMITH - COMIC PIANISTS
GILDA GRAY - DANSEUSE
PROFESSOR ALEXANDER - MENTALIST
INVINCIBLE - 'STRAIGHT-JACKET' - ACT
LITTLE BO PEEP & HER LAMB

INTERVAL

SHADOW PUPPET ACTS
DAN LENO
HOUSTON & MITCHELL
Marmeduke - THE Ventriloquist's Dummy

Reverting back to Grossmith's musical act on the stage. What I did find incongruous during his recital of anecdotes and witty remarks, was the accompaniment of the type of music he was playing. Profound music, such as that taken from sections of the massive and daunting Liszt's, *'Sonata in B minor,'* for pianoforte. Heavily laden as it is with counterpoint, [1] inter-dispersed with Grossmith's continuous attempted witticisms and humorous observations.

The counterpoint I knew would be lost totally on the costermongers. Other works he played on the pianoforte comprised equally serious and ponderous musical pieces.

These included an introspective piece of music by Robert Schumann called, *'Faschingsschwank aus Vien.'* Other works included another sonata, the one in B flat minor by Chopin, his opus 35 which I certainly recognized, containing as it does, the famous *Marche Funèbre,* suitable music to accompany a cortège to the grave side; but not in a Music Hall.

"Is it possible that Grossmith is playing to the wrong audiences and in the wrong place?" I said to Jack, standing next to me, "his act would be more appropriate at the Beckstein Hall 2 rather than this Palace of Entertainment, as Daly's is affectionately known."

"I agree. But what surprises me is that the music he is playing, complex as it is profound, and you know me Theo; I too can play the pianoforte quite well. But it is the anecdotes which remain beyond my comprehension, unless they are esoteric for the benefit of others who do understand them," replied Jack.

"Well, that may be the case;" I responded, "but let us hope that by the time he has lulled the costermongers into oblivion, they will be more receptive to our turn on stage. Better make sure we are full of energy and humor! But hold up; he is saying something else."

Grossmith stopped playing his pianoforte and turned to the audience and said.

"I slept like a log last night..."

"Where," interrupted one of the costermongers, "in the fire place?"

"No, but I looked *grate!*" replied Grossmith.

Jack and I just looked at each other. It was Jack who enuciated his thoughts on the matter.

"Theo, we cannot do worse than what Grossmith is doing right now!"

"A toff goes into a bar and asked for a gin and tonic

with a slice of lemon," continued Grossmith unabated.

"What do you think this place is," inquired the bartender, "a grocery store?"

After an interminable time, Grossmith completed his act, stood up and bowed to the now totally bewildered audience and then abandoned the stage to the next act. At that moment the compère got up and introduced it for the delectation of the audience, some of which were making their way out of their red plush seats and heading off almost as a controlled stampede to the nearby Crush Bars located strategically just outside the auditorium.

The fact that some of the costermongers had abandoned their seats in the auditorium in preference for the Crush Bars, in no way detracted Gilda Gray from her dance routine which she commenced in an energetic and agile manner, as she leapt on to the stage.

We had witnessed her before when Jack and I were playing Vaudeville to packed theaters in New York. She is famous, or infamous, for her dance ritual called the *Shimmy*. This routine involves shaking her hips in an overt and very suggestive manner designed to capture the attention of the audience in a mesmerizing way. It usually did, and this evening's performance, thus far, was no exception; for it had the effect of persuading several patrons to return to their seats and abandon their pilgrimage to the Crush Bars!

She was obviously on tour because she usually plays the Palace Theater on Broadway and 47th. Street in New York, where I had seen her on numerous occasions in the recent past. After some time leaping around the stage in her suggestive manner she too vacated it, in one last routine of shaking her hips in a reckless and abandoned manner. And in her so doing, I could determine from where I was standing at the side of the stage whether she had indeed captured the attention of the audience in a mesmerizing way. She always did.

Again the compère got up from behind his desk located at the side of the stage in front of the proscenium arch and introduced the next act.

"Ladies and gentlemen," he began, "for your unadulterated pleasure and delectation, please welcome the incomparable and unique Professor Alexander, whom, of course, we all know as the Mentalist to end all Mentalists. He is especially famed for his astonishing feats of memory in being able to mentally *see* whilst blindfolded. He will be assisted by the delectable Rachel D'Arcy with her ukulele!"

Jack and I looked at each other. We had heard of such persons performing acts of the incredible or incredulous but never had actually witnessed one on stage. We did know that such an act involves a mentalist, in this case Professor Alexander and his female assistant, a certain Miss D'Arcy. It was her rôle to make her way through the stalls collecting objects such as, hats, watches, such as gold Hunters, keys or canes from members of the audience.

The blindfolded mentalist, looking away from the audience, would identify each object selected, by so called *reading* his assistant's mind. I remain uncertain just how this feat, in identifying an object, is actually performed by the mentalist. Since there is clearly no visual communication between them, I imagine it must be by verbal hints or codes that are submitted to the mentalist by the assistant. This act may indeed prove interesting, I thought.

Certainly the audience had settled down after the *Shimmy* hip-shaking antics of Gilda Gray the danseuse, and an atmosphere of hushed expectation descended over the auditorium. Even the costermongers in the stalls, and they were legion, had become quiet and displayed a subdued respect in anticipation of the Mentalist's proposed astonishing act.

In the gloom of the auditorium, a yellow shaft of limelight illuminated the center of the stage gradually, followed by the footlights being increased in brilliance. Into this arena of light walked one of the most peculiar characters that I have ever seen. That he was tall and slender could never be doubted. That he walked with a stoop, almost bending forward, too was beyond doubt.

That his gray hair was lank, greasy and thinning was irrefutable. His opened black frock-coat was made of a herringbone-patterned broadcloth that matched the trousers he wore with a black silk strip down the outside of each leg. Around his waist, he had secured a flaming red satin sash. His shirt was of an indeterminate color due to the glare of the limelight reflecting off it; but it looked to be possibly mauve.

However, it was not his sartorial preferences or choice of attire which caught my, and I suspect the audience's attention, rather it was his face. Without doubt it was a face of such repellent aspect as to defy description but, there it was, and fully illuminated too by the shaft of limelight! It was pockmarked to such a severity, that life must have been despaired of during the illness of some dreadful contagion he had evidently suffered previously.

Sunk deeply into this face of dents, scars and disfigurement, either side of a large aquiline nose, were two piercing blue eyes, one of which was off set to the other eye. This had the unnerving or disconcerting effect that when he looked at one with his face forward, his eyes were at an angle looking elsewhere.

Still we were here to witness his feats of mentalism and not judge his facial condition, however repugnant it was.

After much exaggerated bowing and general ostentatious behavior to the audience, his assistant, D'Arcy, who had been prancing around the stage, with her arms in the aëther and plucking her ukulele, led Professor Alexander to the back of the stage and sat him down in a straight-backed cathedral chair. Whilst sitting in this chair, with his back to the audience, the Mentalist was then blindfolded, probably much to the relief of a grateful audience.

D'Arcy then approached the front of the stage and curtsied in an exaggerated manner, whilst plucking her ukulele.

"Ladies and gentlemen," she said in a squeaky voice, "for your delectation, Professor Alexander will, using his incredible mental powers, describe any object that I will hold up with my hand, belonging to a member of this august audience."

After more curtseying, D'Arcy continued exhorting the audience.

"And, without any trickery and in full sight of you, the audience, the Professor will describe that object accurately. And do so whilst blindfolded and facing away from the audience. As you can see for yourself," she said, whilst pointing to the hapless person sitting on the cathedral chair

A drum roll was heard emanating out from the orchestra pit.

"May I have the first person who would like to pit his wits against those of the Professor's and offer me an object? You sir, yes you sir, what have you for me?" inquired D'Arcy, whilst leaping off the stage into an aisle separating the sections of the stalls with surprising agility for one still holding a ukulele.

A gentleman, of dubious demeanor, handed D'Arcy

a gold Hunter taken from the end of his gold Albert chain.

"I have in my hand here a very beautiful object," started in D'Arcy, whilst plucking a few chords on her ukulele, "and it will last forever if looked after."

"I have it," said the mentalist, "it can only be a pocket watch, in fact a gold Hunter to be precise! Am I correct Rachel?"

"You are as usual, correct Professor," replied Rachel D'Arcy, to the simultaneous gasp from the audience.

"Can the Professor describe this object?" asked another member of the audience, as D'Arcy, plucking her ukulele, made her way through the audience to the gentleman in question.

"I am holding this object high in the aëther for all to see, except the Professor of course," announced D'Arcy, whist still plucking her ukulele.

"Is it a comb, a metal comb?" inquired the mentalist.

"It is indeed," confirmed D'Arcy, to a stunned audience.

This act went on for a few more minutes and on each occasion, the Professor was able to describe with unerring accuracy each object offered up to D'Arcy by members of the audience.

"Here miss, let me offer this glove to you for the Professor to describe," shouted a person, who instantly blushed at the realization of his faux pas.

Another personal item, a knife, was given to D'Arcy.

"It is a beautifully fashioned item, but the point I am making here is that it is a long gleaming object," said D'Arcy.

Within seconds of doing so the mentalist described the object as a knife.

Almost inaudible at first, but becoming louder, were

murmurings from the costermongers assembled in the stalls. Some were pointing to D'Arcy's ukulele as being in some way implicated in giving hidden signals by her playing various chords or different keys.

"I assure you my ukulele is for your gratification and entertainment only and is in no way used to divulge or hint at the object offered up. Professor Alexander really is an incredible mentalist and can read my mind when I am holding an object in my hand. Look, I shall prove it to you," she said, whilst handing her ukulele to the orchestra conductor.

It was thus without her ukulele that D'Arcy accepted the next object from a skeptical looking individual.

"I am seeing with my eyes a finely wrought object," announced D'Arcy to the mentalist. This time his reply was not as instantly forthcoming as replies had been previously.

"It can only be, only be, ah yes I can see now…"

"Yes Professor," interrupted D'Arcy.

"They are a pair of pince-nez.[3] Am I correct Rachel?" asked the mentalist.

To which D'Arcy replied in the positive.

Another object, a small leather hand-bag was accepted by D'Arcy, who made the following announcement.

"I have in my hand an object which should never leave one's side."

The mentalist appeared to be having difficulty in describing this object, but having kept the audience in suspense for a minute or two, did eventually describe, accurately, the object as being a hand-bag.

It would seem that Professor Alexander really was invincible and his act and mental abilities true and sincere. But then what followed was in itself, quite revealing and a lesson to be learned when dealing with the costermongers, especially when en-mass and in a Music Hall. The next object offered was in fact a bonnet given by a woman to D'Arcy who looked at it. Before she was able to accept the hat, a lone voice embedded in the audience spoke.

"I have in my hand here a round object which the owner treasures."

The mystery voice was an exact imitation of D'Arcy's squeaky voice!

D'Arcy instinctively searched the auditorium for the rogue voice and then looked at the mentalist who appeared to be struggling to find an answer, but at length suggested, without the confidence of previous answers, that the object might be a wedding band, a gold wedding band.

"No you are not correct," said the woman who had offered up her hat to D'Arcy, "It is my bonnet, and a very pretty bonnet it is too and I wear it on my head not finger."

This occasioned jeers and shouts from the costermongers, who by now, had detected a fatal weakness in the Professor's act.

D'Arcy looked about the auditorium furtively as another member of the audience handed her an object. It was a fan made from ostrich feathers.

The mystery voice imitating D'Arcy's spoke out again from the depths of the auditorium, much to D'Arcy's visible annoyance and consternation.

"In my right hand I am holding a long object…"

"A pen, a writing pen; am I correct Rachel?" asked the mentalist.

"No you are not," replied the costermongers in spontaneous unison, "it is an ostrich feather!"

At that point the compère was compelled to intervene,

by thanking Rachel and the amazing mentalist in the person of Professor Alexander.

As it was, D'Arcy grabbed her ukulele, marched up the side steps to the stage and led the still blindfolded Professor off the stage and into the wings.

I looked at Jack and Cinderella, dressed in her Little Bo Peep attire.

"Is this normally how mentalist acts are conducted?" I inquired of Cinderella.

"Sometimes," replied Cinderella, "it depends who of course is in the audience. It is an old trick in describing the object. Everybody thought that the Professor's assistant, Rachel D'Arcy, was giving away clues with her ukulele. She was not. And after she had put down her instrument, she continued to give the correct descriptions for the benefit of the blindfolded mentalist."

"Obviously the Professor could not see the objects that the assistant was holding. So how was the information relayed to him?" asked Jack.

Well as you saw," answered Cinderella, "the act began to fail when one of the female costermongers in the audience was able to effectively sabotage the coded hints to the mentalist by imitating D'Arcy's squeaky voice and..."

However, before Cinderella could complete her answer, the compère banged his gavel and commenced introducing the next act. All was quiet again in the auditorium. I also noticed Cinderella slip away from the stage wings in which we were standing watching the various acts or turns being performed out there.

The next act on stage, so the billposter affixed to the stage sidewall informed me, involved an escape artiste strapped up in a straight-jacket.

Within seconds of being announced by the compère,

a hapless individual wearing a straight-jacket and strapped to a wooded cathedral chair was carried on to center stage by two stage hands, and placed in the soft yellow limelight which illuminated his struggling person. He sat there for quite some time wriggling away but apparently seeming to make little progress in escaping from his sartorial confinement.

Minutes went by without any noticeable improvement to his potential emancipation and the person was still effectively strapped to the straight-backed chair whilst still captive by his straight-jacket. The audience, in particular the costermongers in the cheap seats, fearing his plight might go on indefinitely, resorted to entertaining themselves with impromptu gambling and arguing with each other.

A full fifteen minutes had elapsed and still our escape artiste had still not in fact escaped from his bonds. He wriggled continuously, but was still unable to free himself. The audience were, naturally enough, becoming restless at the lack of activity on the stage. So was the compère, who looked askance at our ineffective escapee.

He continued to wriggle but to no avail. I did however, notice that his face was assuming a purple tint as he struggled desperately to gain his freedom from the straight-jacket. The escape artiste trapped in the straight-jacket was still confined and unable to gain his freedom. But more alarming was the fact that he was becoming rapidly apoplectic and that desperation in his purple face showed quite clearly this was the case.

All of a sudden there was some action on the stage. The forlorn straight-jacketed escape artiste's struggling was of such ferocity that he and the cathedral chair to which he was strapped keeled over on to its side. His desperation was made all the worse now by the fact he was lying on his side, a position which must have made his plight all the more difficult. The audience continued to ignore him and entertain themselves with arguments and gambling.

Then it happened, Little Bo Peep, carrying her shepherdess' crook came wandering on to the stage looking lost and bewildered. At one point she looked down, with a questioning expression upon her pink plump face, at the straight-jacketed struggling escape artiste wriggling about on the floor of the stage.

Po Beep then turned fully around to face her audience. But in so doing, her sweet rosy face moved into the beam of bright limelight shining down on to the stage and she became momentarily blinded by the direct light in her eyes. Unable to see clearly where she was going she stumbled around the stage but tripped over the escape artiste's kicking legs as he struggled to free himself.

Bo Peep fell to the floor with such a force, the noise could be heard clearly throughout the auditorium. A deathly silence immediately descended upon the audience. Then the weeping began as Bo Peep and the audience realized that she was bleeding from a gash she had sustained by the sharp fall to the stage floor. People gasped simultaneously in horror as the full implication of the accident became visibly apparent. Only the struggling escape artiste was oblivious to Bo Peep's desperate plight; though, not as acute as his on-going predicament.

The apotheosis of melodrama had been reached and was now being played out in front of our very eyes, as Bo Peep rolled around on the stage floor clutching her blooded knee. And the hapless escape artiste was still struggling on the floor of the stage. Looking at my steel case watch, I figured he had by now been wriggling away in his straight-jacket for at least twenty five minutes.

On one occasion Bo Peep tried to get up but because her crook was out of reach, she had to drag herself across the stage floor. It was all a little too pathetic, but the audience welcomed this live entertainment, as opposed to the still purple faced struggling straight-jacketed artiste, who, in after thirty minutes of endeavoring to release himself, had failed to do so. And, clearly was not going to succeed now. Accordingly, the compère ordered a couple of stage hands to remove wretched escape artiste lest we all witnessed his death on the stage.

In the meantime Bo Peep had gotten herself up from the floor and leaning on her shepherdess's crook for support, attempted to limp off stage. At that moment a lamb came walking onto the stage bleating loudly whilst looking around the platform on which it found itself. Presently the lamb walked towards Little Bo Peep who then attempted to pick it up, but because of her weak injured leg was unable to steady herself and fell over again. This time she fell on to the lamb, which let out a loud bleat as it scampered off the stage, abandoning Bo Peep to her fate and misery.

Again, she managed to haul herself up whilst still crying her eyes out with such a sustained intensity that I feared she may have seriously hurt herself. But then she looked again around the auditorium in a wide sweeping arch with her wet, glistening tearful face so that all would see her predicament. When she had completed that manœuvre, to the accompaniment of an anæmic smile and gushing tears, she curtsied to the audience and limped across stage to her exit.

As she did so the thunderous and sustained applause from an appreciative audience was truly tumultuous with continued calls of, '*again, do it again my sweetness!*' One of the costermongers, acknowledging the apogee of her act was even moved to throw a rolled up bank note at Bo Peep which she instinctively caught with one hand!

Little Bo Peep's exit stage right also triggered off what can only be described as a stampede of blind panic proportions as the costermongers and others made their way to the several Crush Bars located strategically around the theater. A few minutes later Jack and I made our way from the stage wings and along a whitewashed corridor to a nearby bar for much needed sustenance. On arriving we realized our decision to do so was in no way unique.

At the bar buying drinks with the recently acquired banknote, was Little Bo Peep. We accepted gracefully her offer of two whiskies. Also at the Crush Bar was the escape artiste, now mercifully released from the confines of his straight-jacket, but looking as though contemplating seriously, with a large drink in his hand, the practical viability of his erstwhile escape act.

Lodge was there in the corner of the room talking furtively with some odd-looking individual. So was Rachel D'Arcy, with a drink in one hand and her ukulele in the other, berating a somewhat confused looking Professor Alexander the mentalist. Not for the first time have I thought that there is infinitely more theater in the Crush Bars than out on the stage. We complimented Cinderella on her Little Bo Peep turn and mentioned that while we knew it was an act, one was never actually certain that the injury on any such occasion might just be authentic and for real.

"That is why the audience appreciates my act, because they are secretly hoping. Hoping that one day they will be present when I suffer a real injury!" said Cinderella, with a cheerful smile upon her lips, before pouring the entire contents of her glass down her throat.

We stayed on in the bar since we none of us had any

real wish to witness the Shadow Puppet Acts just about to start on stage, even though we knew we would be on stage in forty-five minutes, after Dan Leno. Those precious minutes soon went by quickly and before long I found myself looking at the center stage from the left wing with Jack standing in the right wing.

Clearly the costermongers had been worked up into belligerent mood as a result of Leno's performance. However, the compère brought his gavel down onto the block with such force that the action succeeded in gaining the complete attention of the audience.

"Ladies and gentlemen, please put your hands together and welcome to Daly's Music Hall two Vaudeville artistes from New York; Mr. Jack Mitchell and Mr. Theodor Houston."

Right on cue, Jack and I both marched on to the stage from either wing and met in the middle, beneath a shaft of limelight which bathed us in an ethereal light, we hoped. We shook hands waved to the audience and Jack sat down at the pianoforte. I stood just in front of the footlights and got myself organized to sing for my supper. After Jack's introductory bars, I launched into an old favorite, '*Alabama in the Morning,*' as Jack tinkled the ivory keys in accompanying me. After an exchange of witticisms and anecdotes with which we regaled the audience, I began the slow build up to another song called, '*That Girl from Oklahoma.*'

I had in fact sung this song recently at the Criterion Theater in the presence of their graces Frank, Duke of Teck and George, Duke of Cambridge sitting in the Royal Box looking very imperious, but the song had been reasonably well received. Though I remember at the time it did not fit in with the other acts or turns on the stage that evening, which included the infamous Choral Anthem Symphony. Somehow the deep misgivings I had experienced during rehearsals earlier, came back into my mind like a cataclysmic torrential flood of biblical proportions.

I simply could not envisage that my song, *'That Girl from Oklahoma,'* was in any way going to go down well. Especially so since the audience had had their spirits raised to such empyreal heights, if not to the sublime, by the invocation offered by the soprano Katie Lawrence at the time when she sang the words taken from the Choral Anthem Symphony;

> *'With wings which I have gained,*
> *Shall I soar aloft into the aëther,'*

whereas my offering that particular evening in my attempt to match that transcendental and divine was with such profound lyrics as these in our new song, *'That Girl from Oklahoma,'* [4] which I now began to sing at. I did so following the creation of arpeggios by Jack at the pianoforte.

> *'That Girl from Oklahoma,*
> *My God you should have known her,*
> *With a ukulele she would often sing*
> *Verses to gain her wedding ring!'*

> *'Whilst riding though Missouri,*
> *She met a handsome attorney,*
> *Who upon seeing her ukulele*
> *Abandoned her surely!'*

> *'Though now bereft and full of woe*
> *Has concluded what she needs to know*
> *As she walks and searches the land*
> *Still looking for her wedding band!'*

On this auspicious occasion I was able to complete all three verses of the song without interruption or hindrance from hecklers or Nihilists [5] of the kind I had experienced at the Criterion Theater. At the end of my song I bowed and abandoned the platform to a developing gloominess as the lights on both the stage and in the auditorium were dimmed.

I retreated to the side of the stage. From my vantage point I could just see two stage hands placing at the back of the stage, next to the backdrop, what looked like a pile of rags. Jack was sitting at the pianoforte waiting to play the introduction cue for the next act which involved Cinderella in the guise of Marmaduke, the living Ventriloquist's Dummy.

Jack had agreed to play for her on this occasion on the basis that we might soon formalize our stage relationship with Cinderella, since we had in the past discussed the possibility of our working together as a double act. It is also to be remembered we had discarded Judd our ventriloquist's dummy, on account of his getting above himself at the Criterion Theater causing acute embarrassment to Jack and myself. Cinderella, however, had assumed Judd's ventriloquist personality in a new stage act called Marmaduke.

In the meantime, the silence in the auditorium was deafening together with a hushed expectation as the audience waited for the next act to commence.

Jack then began playing the introduction bars on the pianoforte based upon Robert Schumann's piano work called, *Waldszenen.* [6] These created a magical tinkling sound of triple fifths forming arpeggios and evolving into a sublime sonority of sound which expanded out into the auditorium.

Gradually the footlights increased in intensity, as did

a shaft of weak yellow limelight that was trained on the pile of green colored rags lying on the floor of the stage. The illuminated stage backdrop now depicted a scene of a clearing in a forest at twilight below a silver colored full moon. Moments went by, but then the limelight appeared to increase in its intensity sufficiently to illuminate further areas of the stage, including the pile of rags next to the backdrop scene of the forest.

Suddenly the pile began to move as though beneath them something was stirring. Then as if by magic, green colored rags began to rise up. Ascending from this pile the back of a head appeared and gradually we could make out a body rising up as if being hauled out of the pile by hidden wires. Presently a person emerged from what I took to be a pile of dead leaves under which this individual had been sleeping

In the subdued light, I could just make out that the fellow was wearing a loud Prince of Wales yellow and brown check patterned suit and an outsized red Derby hat, pulled down low over his eyes. This however, did not conceal his blond hair, tuffs of which were visible protruding out below his red Derby hat. On his small feet he wore a pair of scuffed boots, which were neither of the same style or indeed color!

As the limelight increased gradually, one could make out the features upon his face which were now becoming clearer, particularly his nose which looked like it had been stuck on as an afterthought to the general facial assembly. His face was peculiar too, in that it had an unnatural color to it; almost pure white with a visible painted area of rouge to the cheeks. His eyebrows were bushy and partially concealed his deep sunken black eyes.

These obvious features however, paled into insignificance when compared with the glaring manic expression he made with his open lips revealing two rows of closed teeth.

He then walked slowly in a measured step to the front of the stage. In so doing the footlights from the floorboard level below illuminated his face, creating a myriad of shadows coming up from his chin. These long dark shadows had the effect of turning his manic expression into one of an exaggerated grotesque image. He stood at the very precipice of the stage, swaying as though in a breeze. His arms merely hung loosely at his side whilst his head assumed a circular motion with the occasional flash of teeth reënforcing that unnerving manic expression.

His hands, from what I could see in the twilight, were peculiar, in that they appeared rigid and tinted to a grey hue. Gradually he lifted his face upward to the Dress Circle immediately in front of him. He then turned his face from right to left in an arc across the auditorium and finished by looking out into the auditorium as though staring into oblivion.

Then, as though he were being lowered by unseen supports, he knelt down on one knee. He did so as if in genuflection and began with a low murmur to enunciate his inner thoughts to the accompaniment of Jack's playing the pianoforte. These low sounds soon developed into a plainchant about how, as a baby in the forests, he was taken from his home beneath a leaf, lying on the forest floor. He sang about his being stolen from the woods and placed into bondage. Marmaduke related with moist eyes of how he was only fed just enough to ensure that he did not fade away.

He paused at this point and again with his manic expression caused by baring his teeth, turned his head in a wide sweep for all in the auditorium to see. He then got up, and walked about the stage in a loose-limbed manner, as though he were a puppet being controlled by hidden wires. Marmeduke then proceeded to sing one pathos-ridden song after another, about his fervent hope of release from servitude, about being manipulated or controlled by others, and about his wishes of being given his emancipation.

He included in his lyrical repertoire, songs about the Metropolitan Board of Works, [7] the Lord Chamberlain [8] and Mrs. Ormiston Chant, [9] to which the costermongers, or *costers*, as we are now obliged to call them, erupted like the volcano Vesuvius into ecstatic applause and shouts of approval.

Audiences in both the the stalls and Dress Circle erupted into unbridled clapping with some banging their feet on the floor, and others becoming evidently delirious in their re-action to this new act by Marmeduke. Indeed the clapping was as loud and sustained in the Dress Circle as it was in the stalls. They clearly had taken to this living ventriloquist's dummy strutting around the stage. Bowing to the audience and waving his red Derby hat, especially at the costermongers in the stalls and *Undeserving Poor* concentrated in the cheap seats at the back of the auditorium.

Eventually, Marmaduke lifted his hands above his head and with the palms facing out, brought his arms down slowly as a sign for the audience to now be hushed. They obliged, though not for long. Embedded in the ranks of the *Undeserving Poor*, located in the cheapest seats came murmurings of discontent. These murmurings became louder as they vented their re-action to Marmeduke.

"Come down to the poor house and see how the other half live," one of them was heard to say.

Another unexpected loquacious member of this *Undeserving Poor* also felt the imperative need to express himself forcefully.

"You sir, yes you," said another, "you denigrate the Metropolitan Board of Works and the Lord Chamberlain and yet you are nothing but timber at best or driftwood at worst. You appear to possess all those privileges we, the *Undeserving Poor*, can only dream of in our merciless and unceasing servitude."

The sustained and spontaneous cry of, *'come work the streets for naught,'* erupted repeatedly from the back of the auditorium in the cheaper seats, which comprised elm benches.

"I do not need to go to the street to work for naught, sunshine," responded Marmeduke, "working the Music Halls is the just the same!"

Marmaduke then turned to Jack at the pianoforte.

"Maestro, the, *'Burlington Bertie,'* song please and as for that Metropolitan Board of Works or the Lord Chamberlain," Marmaduke said, looking into the back of the auditorium to where the *Undeserving Poor* were concentrated, "both are intent on regulating our precious Music Halls, especially in what we can sing or perform, as well as trying to control what we do on our streets!"

The costers did not need to be told twice and erupted into sustained applause. They instinctively understood what Marmaduke was alluding to.

"And with regard to the pettifogging interfering clerkdom that the Metropolitan Board of Works is and its insatiable desire to issue a continuous avalanche of superfluous regulations, they would be better employed digging deep level sewers, for which they have an unbridled talent, and with no equal! And as for that Lord Chamberlain, surely he should stick to cleaning the king's palaces and not be trying to wash us down!" concluded Marmeduke.

The costermongers were now in their element,

standing up and clapping whilst banging their hobnailed boots down on to the wooden deck of Daly's Music Hall with such a thunderous noise as to make Jack's playing the pianoforte almost inaudible.

"Are there any more pieces of advice which you feel like off-loading to us here tonight dearie?" Marmeduke was heard to say, whilst pointing directly at elements of the *Undeserving Poor.*

None replied but rather kept their counsel, especially since the smouldering dark eyes of the mass ranks of the costermongers were viewing them.

Marmaduke completed his rendition of, *'Burlington Bertie,'* [10] to resounding applause, assisted ably by the massed chorus of the costermongers.

1. To emphasize by contrast a music idea played against another
2. Now the Wigmore Hall in Wigmore Street
3. Eye glasses which lack ear pieces but rest on the nose by means of a spring clip
4. Lyrics by Edward Plesse
5. A group who are by way of being disaffected revolutionaries sworn to disrupt concerts attended by the bourgeoisie.
6. Forest Scene - Nine pieces for piano-forte, Opus 82.
7. The Metropolitan Board of Works tries to control costermongers' street trading activities
8. Government censor of Music Hall and theater
9. Endeavors to close down Music Halls as immoral places
10. Composed by Harry B Norris and first sung by Vesta Tilley

Chapter 2

The Search for the Third Grace

The next morning, Lodge joined Jack and me for break-fast in the elaborate appointment of the Grand Dining Room in the St. Pancras Hotel. Jack and I, of course, have been staying here since we arrived from New York some weeks earlier. We had entertained the thought of quitting the hotel for more modest quarters, but elected to stay on in this opulent establishment. Now, sitting opposite us at our break-fast table was the inscrutable, but accomplished impresario in the person of Michael W. Lodge. Our being here, of course, was as a result of his invitation to Jack and me when we were playing the Majestic Theater in Chicago actually on Chicago Day, during the World's Columbian Exposition held in that city. [1] Accordingly, we had accompanied Lodge here to London, or rather *Loge*, as he prefers his close acquaintances to address him by. He does so on the flawed basis that he is deluded into believing that the fictitious rôle of '*Loge*,' apparently is the only noble character in Wagner's grand opera called, '*Das Rheingold*,' which emanates from the cycle of four linked operas, together called, *"Der Ring Des Nibulungen.'* [2]

I distinctly remember Lodge informing us on first meeting him in a bar why this was so. 'A rather amusing little tale, I recall,' Loge had informed us, 'the libretto

World's Columbian Exposition –Chicago Day Ticket

from which is based on those interminable Teutonic-fuelled legends called, the *Nibelungenlied* and the *Völsunga Saga*.

This is a titanic saga of Teutonic gods and mortals, including our erstwhile female warrior friends, the Valküre,[3] together with an assortment of heroes plotting, in the depths beneath the Nibelheim mountain, on how to get their grubby little hands on an ill-fated golden band. In addition there is a demented woman, Brünnhilde, another Valkürian, no less, who insists on throwing herself onto a flaming funeral pyre, for the sake of self-immolation in order to be re-united for all eternity with her burning dead lover, a hero-type, name of Siegfried!'

The fact that the operatic rôle of '*Loge*,' in reality is portrayed as a venal and devious character during the opera, seemed to have totally eluded Lodge, who continued to bask in this questionable sobriquet.

I recalled our first meeting with Lodge in Chicago. We had just been playing the Majestic Theater on West Monroe Street in that city. That particular evening was a monumental disaster for us and other Vaudeville artistes performing there. The reason was simply that a radical group of hecklers and Nihilists, who then considered themselves to be by way of revolutionaries, had combined to cause major disruptions throughout the evening. They had succeeded beyond their wildest expectations.

As a result, Jack and I left the Majestic Theater in disgust and had repaired to a nearby bar in North Michigan Avenue in south central Chicago, in the shadow of the huge Gothic Water Tower to endeavor to drown our sorrows. Instead we met up with Lodge.

We later learned from Cinderella that she too had attended the World's Columbian Exposition on Chicago Day and actually saw us performing later at the Majestic Theater. She had also witnessed the disruption caused by the hecklers and Nihilists.

Cinderella, of course, is an accomplished Music Hall artiste, of the very highest calibre, and performs three distinct rôles or defined characters on stage. They are Cinderella, Little Bo Peep and Marmaduke - a living ventriloquist's dummy.

Lodge is totally unaware of Cinderella's flexible rôles in this respect.

"Well what did you think of last night's performances at Daly's Music Hall Loge?" asked Jack.

Jack will insist on calling Michael Lodge by his sobriquet *Loge,* as indeed Lodge had invited him to do so previously. I prefer to just call him *Lodge* and dispense altogether with the idiocy surrounding the name *Loge* from Wagner's opera.

"As it happens I thought it went well," replied Lodge, "especially that Marmeduke fellow; he has quite an interesting act. Cannot say that I have met the artiste before or indeed know of him."

Jack and I exchanged glances. We both knew that the same person portrayed Cinderella, Little Bo Peep and Marmaduke on stage. Cinderella played these separate

Gothic Water Tower

rôles in order to get over the provisions in the so-called *Exclusivity Clause*, which then prevented artistes from appearing in Music Halls, in order to perform their act in the same district on the same evening.

Typically an artiste appearing at the Alhambra Music Hall would be prevented from appearing at the Empire Music Hall even though both are located in Leicester Square. Cinderella got over this restraint by having three secret personalities which she performed in the same Music Hall during the same evening. Lodge was unaware of this bold stratagem by Cinderella.

The conversation over break-fast drifted on to more neutral subjects, including Jack's recent lukewarm relationships with other Music Hall artistes such as Marie Lloyd and mine with Queenie Leighton.

"Well Jack, Theo, we all seemed to have met our Nemesis, in one form or another," offered up Lodge, "I did try to advise the both of you previously about those faded Music Hall artistes. Marie Lloyd and Queenie Leighton, or the *Woman in Red*, as you fancifully called her and with whom you were, or seemed, besotted. Believe me, Theo, Jack, I know both of them. And therefore knew it would end in tears. I assure you both. You are better off without them, for they could only bring perpetual misery upon you."

"Before you say anything about Marie Lloyd and my misguided affections for her, I admit, you were not wrong. Marie is her own person and I guess I did not fit in with her expectations," Jack acknowledged, contritely.

"You yourself Lodge have not fared any better," I remarked, "in that we understand that you have decided not to hire that singer from New Jersey, Elizabeth Firth, as a replacement *Third Grace*, following the dreadful murder of the late Bella Elmore by her husband, the infamous Doctor Crippen, [4] on account of his ceasing to be besotted with her. Though I do recall hearing Firth sing in Jersey City, and, in my opinion, she did so then quite well."

"Theo, the truth of the matter is, Elizabeth could not reach those sublime vocal ranges needed to do justice to my noble and elegiac Choral Anthem Symphony. I suppose my quest for the *Third Grace* continues without end!" answered Lodge, with a look of forlorn resignation in his eyes, as he stared into the middle distance of the opulent Grand Dining Room.

"When you told us of the unfortunate death of your favorite soprano, Bella Elmore, to my remark about engaging a contralto you merely replied that contraltos were as cheap as life itself; and that it was a soprano with a wide tessitura and the ability to moderate and sustain her vibrato, that you really needed, even a mezzo-soprano, would suffice if only temporarily," I reminded him.

"That is true Theo," replied Lodge, "but alas, as you know we are holding auditions this morning. To that end I have hired the Oxford Music Hall, at considerable expense to my purse. But find a soprano, I must!"

"Out of interest Loge, why have you asked Theo and me to join you in helping select a suitable candidate for the replacement rôle of soprano, since we are no longer part of that Choral Anthem Symphony?" inquired Jack, in his usual forthright manner.

"Because I have come to rely upon both your and Theo's inclination for the right judgment in these matters; but if you do not feel equal to the task, you have only to intimate," replied Lodge.

When Lodge reverted to his catachresis, [5] in being overtly complimentary. It was because he had been caught off-guard, as it were, and invariably resorted to this type re-action, in order that he might confuse his perceived antagonist. And thus afford himself time to retort with a considered, but correct reply.

"More importantly gentlemen," said Lodge, "I came to join you at break-fast. Not only to talk of auditions and sopranos, but to congratulate you on your début performance last night on the stage of Daly's Music Hall in London's Leicester Square. Indeed the both you are to be applauded".

"We were, by the audience," responded Jack.

"It is a very ornate building," I offered, "very elegant with swathes of crimson plush and brass fixtures everywhere. It was a pleasure to perform there. Am I not right Jack"?

"Did you notice the columns rising up from the stall into the tiers?" asked Lodge.

Jack and I looked at each other, shrugged our shoulders and turned to study Lodge's bemused expression.

"Precisely, there were no columns rising up from the stall, none at all. Because Daly's Music Hall was one of the first in London, as is the Palace Theater, the one at Cambridge Circus here in London, not Palace Theater on Broadway in New York, to be built using the innovative cantilever system. This principal method of constructing involves the balconies or tiers being supported from metal girders anchored into the back structural walls of the balcony. A very ingenious solution to providing the audience with an uninterrupted view of the stage from anywhere in the auditorium," said Lodge.

"I liked the classical exterior because it suggested further opulence inside," said Jack," and we were not disappointed".

"Daly's Music Hall cost sixty-thousand pounds,"

continued Lodge, "and was designed by the architect Spencer Chadwick applying the cantilever system together with Italianate Renaissance to its neo classical façade. It was built for the American theater producer Augustin Daly's then manager, Mr. George Edwardes. Alas, things went wrong and in 1894, Edwardes took over the total management of the Music Hall, removing Daly in the process.

I remember when the theater opened on October the 30th, 1891. A memorable day for all concerned, which included an opening address by the renowned Ada Rehan, the National Anthem, sung by Lloyd Daubigny and chorus. And concluding with a raucous rendition of your patriotic hymn, *'The Star Spangled Banner,'* which was sung by Lena Loraine and Percy Haswell again, with chorus and orchestra."

"Daly's, of course, as you know, is an American company and well known throughout the United States," I informed Lodge, whilst handing to him the previous night's handbill for our début at Daly's Music Hall. "And both Jack and I agree that our presence on stage last night was an important watershed for us, as you yourself witnessed from your red plush private box. Our *Vent* act [6] was such a resounding success that we are to appear again pretty soon. This will be in place of a cancelled turn by an over-enthusiastic Fire Eater, who thought, mistakenly, that she was swallowing glass and not razor blades, and now is temporarily incommoded!"

"We are now getting into our stride playing the London Music Halls," said Jack, "and I think last night's performance showed that, especially since we were on after Dan Leno and we all know what an extremely hard act his is to follow. And let me tell you Loge, it was."

"I do not doubt that, Jack, but if I may venture a little criticism..." said Lodge.

"Go on," interrupted Jack.

"If I may venture a little criticism," continued Lodge, "your act would benefit from the presence of Judd, the ventriloquist's dummy. Somehow he makes your act or turn on stage more complete."

"Are you saying Loge, a wooden doll, for which we speak as the ventriloquist, improves our act?" asked Jack, with asperity, whilst laying down his knife and fork on to the crisp white linen tablecloth.

"No Jack, I am not intimating that. Clearly a wooden mute dummy could never upstage you or steal the limelight; how could it?" inquired a phlegmatic Lodge.

Jack chose not to reply, but instead returned to his Brätwürst on rye bread, a New York style of break-fast he has reverted to.

"What I am saying gentlemen," said Lodge, helping himself to my toast," is that your knowledge of English Music Hall, though admirable, is not complete. This completion necessitates a thorough understanding of the evolution of Music Hall. From the *Pleasure Gardens,* such as those at Marylebone, Vauxhall, Ranelagh or Cremorne in the distant past, to present day expectations of audiences and new daring acts and songs.

"Singing, as we know, is essential to Music Hall and those singers, especially comic singers are now famous box office attractions. The songs they sing inevitably reflect working class life and conditions, especially in London. Typically; Gus Elen's, *'If it Wasn't for the Houses in Between,'* sings about over-crowding and bad living conditions in our big cities, especially in areas such as Whitechapel or Wapping here in London. Or, as in the lyrics of, *'My Old Man Said Follow the Van, and Don't Dilly-Dally on the Way,'* sung by that Marie Lloyd, describes doing a *moonlight flit* in order to avoid having to pay the rent which was due.

"You can take it from me Jack, Theo, if singing in our Music Halls about daily life is essential; then jokes are even more so! They take as their basic material topics of such a diverse range, from mothers-in-law to debt, patriotism to the sentimental, unfaithful wives to overdue rent, lodgers to drink, bailiffs to death and general adversity to true love.

These songs continue to attract audiences to the Music Halls repeatedly in order that they may hear their favorite song being sung. That is why I invited you two to come to London and introduce new songs and acts. Thus far my decision has proven to be the correct one," Lodge said, pretentiously.

In response Jack looked at Lodge with a seasoned eye.

"This brings me on to the so-called, *speciality* acts, such as yours" continued Lodge, "or '*Spesh*' as we call them in the business. Without doubt the singer-comedians with their songs, anecdotes or risqué jokes are the fovorite performers among Music Hall audiences. However to provide contrast in between those turns would be the *Spesh* acts and would include a diverse range from magicians, cyclists, one-legged dancers, aërial trapeze artistes, or ventriloquists – such as your Judd used to be, or acts involving electricity.

"*Electric* acts, as they are known, involve playing with electricity and still remain popular in the Music Halls, as novelties. There, performers electrify themselves and then with their fingers tips set fire to handkerchiefs by touch or more dangerously, ignite gas jets. A dangerous performance, I think, given the number of Music Halls and theaters which regularly are razed to the ground by fire.

"There are several kinds of *Spesh* acts, some often bordering on freak shows or exercises in the grotesque, but which might include aërial acts, essentially of the sort act one could expect to witness at the circus. The Sisters Onger are dab hands in this area, so too are Jules Léotard and Blondin. These aërial acts pull in the crowds, especially when they involve some daring manœuvre taking place in the actual auditorium above the audience, and not confined to the safety of the stage.

"The great Léotard, the flying trapeze artiste, recently set up a system of ropes immediately over the stalls at the Alhambra Music Hall, where he continues to cause a sensation by swinging from frame to frame directly above the audience with no safety net. This reckless act was later immortalized in a song called, *'The Daring Young Man on the Flying Trapeze.'* Similarly, in the Canterbury Music Hall, Blondin, the tightrope walker, regularly walks across the auditorium from one balcony to the other directly above the audience!

"Of course during these *Spesh* acts, fire eaters and other eating acts, abound such as those eating live goldfish, pieces of broken glass, razor blade and other sundry items, all for the delectation of an undiscerning audience. Knife throwing, on stage that is, and sword swallowing remain as popular today as when they were first introduced to the audience and are always in demand. Including the most spectacular of which is the renowned and famous Victorina Troupe of sword swallowers, one of the members of which would swallow a bayonet fitted to a rifle whilst another in the troupe swallowed an illuminated electric light bulb, the light from which shone through her flesh.

"Feats of strength by both strongmen and strongwomen are a regular feature and often the infamous Vulcana [7] will make an unannounced appearance challenging all, both on the stage and in the audience, to a duel of strength. Often she is supported by another strong woman, by the name of Maud Atlas or yet another called Madame Heculine and also known as Lady Samson.

"A famous *Spesh* act artiste, is Paul Cinquevalli, who is known as the *'King of the Jugglers,'* and is able to catch a cannon ball on his neck. Such is his act that he was recently invited to perform his, 'Human Billiard Table' trick in front of King George V[th.] during the first Royal Variety Performance. His popularity, in Music Halls, is such that he often tops the bill above Marie Lloyd.

"But all this fades into oblivion when one experiences magic and illusion acts, especially those performed by the acclaimed Maskelynes double act involving father and son operating in the Egyptian Hall in Piccadilly.

"Their acts are a treat to watch and they particularly specialize in *magical visuals,* including sawing a woman in half or the so-called, *'Vice Versa Illusion Act.'* This act, perfected by David Devant, involves changing a man into a woman, or vice versa." concluded Lodge.

"Is that not called cross-dressing, as practiced by Vesta Tilley, Barbette and a whole host of others artistes including Hetty King, Fanny Robina, Nellie Power, Bessie Bellwood and Ella Shields?" asked Jack.

"True, but one should...," said Lodge.

"But the greatest magician and escape artiste," interrupted Jack, "is Harry Houdini, from New York. His feats of escape are legendary even in England. And, if I remember correctly, he appeared here in London at your Alhambra Music Hall way back in 1900, escaping from handcuffs provided by the cops at Scotland Yard.

Theo and I have seen him on numerous occasions in New York and Atlantic City doing his party tricks. Including releasing himself from a straight-jacket while suspended from a rope. Or film of his escaping within

Egyptian Hall, Piccadilly

thirty seconds, from a high security prison cell, at the state penitentiary up the river at Sing-Sing. If not doing that, then escaping from inside a burglar proof, steel built safe within twelve minutes!" said Jack

"Is there anything from which Houdini cannot escape?" I inquired.

"Death, taxes and woman," answered Jack, "and in that order!"

"However, gentlemen, "continued Lodge, slightly put

out by Jack's interruption and pushing his chair back from the break-fast table and standing up, "time waits for no man and we do have our work before us. I suggest when you have completed your break-fast, or whatever it is you are eating, that we meet in the foyer in say fifteen minutes, and avail ourselves of my Barouche carriage which will be waiting for us outside beneath the ornate stone porte cochère ready to convey us to the Oxford Music Hall."

Lodge then made his way through the Grand Dining Room, bowing to the occasional diner and waiving extravagantly at others. Eventually he left through the large, varnished, mahogany, double-leaf doors leading into the purple flocked, silk wallpaper covered walls of the main hall of the St. Pancras Hotel.

Sometime later when Jack and I had completed our ablutions, we descended the helix shaped Grand Staircase and progressed into the foyer. Upon seeing us Lodge looked at his gold Hunter attached to his Albert chain, with a look of impatience upon his face. That is, what there was of it, for he was wrapped up as a valetudinarian [8] might, with his shiny silk top hat pulled down to his eyes and a white silk scarf secured tightly around his lower face and neck. Complementing this, Lodge also felt obliged to wear a heavy black over-coat with luxuriant collar of Astrakhan fur pulled up around his neck.

"Sometimes I cannot bear the acrid, clammy fog upon my face or person, so here is for safety," muffled Lodge, through his silken scarf in response to the look of incredulity upon Jack's face.

"It is more than likely that such a tight fitting scarf around Loge's neck might at least reduce his monomania, [9] if only temporarily!" Jack whispered to me, whilst Lodge was distracted trying to re-button-up his heavy overcoat.

After some adroit manœuvring of Lodge's person, both Jack and I succeeded in manhandling him into the open Barouche carriage. It was driven, as usual, by Lodge's truculent man-servant, a peculiar individual called Aloysius, still wearing his ostentatious powder blue uniform complete with gold braid and epaulettes and powdered grey horsehair wig, irrespective of the fog.

Immediately Aloysius flicked his two chestnut horses that responded by hauling our Barouche into the yellow fog. In this respect, if nothing else, Lodge was right about the discomfort acrid fog can produce on one's skin and around the eyes. Within minutes, I was rubbing my eyes due to the acridity in the fog-laden aëther through which we were traversing.

At length we arrived at our destination, the Oxford Music Hall in Oxford Street. Looking up at the Music Hall, one could see it exuded all the dignity and grace one came to expect in a building clad with an ornate classical façade.

Jack and I spent some considerable time in helping Lodge down from the Barouche carriage to the sidewalk. Especially since he insisted upon wearing his conspicuous Astrakhan coat, which, due to its capaciousness had the extraordinary effect of making him appear more bulkier than usual. Lending him, as it were, an image of gravitas. However, he seemed put out by this instinctive offer of assistance from both Jack and me. Almost as though we had relegated him to the status of valetudinarian.

"Unhand me! I shall not be manhandled in such a fashion," he insisted, "it is not for you two to behave in such a confident manner regarding my person. I tell you, I simply will not be manhandled in this inelegant way."

"Well, how would you like to be?" asked Jack.

Oxford Music Hall, London

Nonetheless, having dismissed Aloysius, we all three of us proceeded into the Oxford Music Hall and were advised by a liveried flunky that the manager, a certain Mr Blythe Pratt, would meet us in a few minutes at the front of the stage. Accordingly, we made our way in to the auditorium. We, of course, had met this gentleman, Blythe Pratt before, just after his Music Hall had caught fire. This was due to an over exuberant performance by a danseuse during her bawdy rendition of scenes from Stravinsky's new ballet, *'The Fire Bird.'*

On that occasion, the hapless danseuse got carried away in a reckless trance brought on by the ecstatic and rapturous applause she had generated from an appreciative audience consisting in the main of costermongers. As is often the case, in her dancing delirium, she bowed too near to the blazing footlights and in so doing, her protruding starched taffeta costume made contact with the flames causing it to catch fire instantly!

The applause increased as she ran about the stage in a blind panic, which the costermongers mistook as being part of her original *Fire Bird* act. It was not so much as what happened to the blazing taffeta-wearing danseuse, as to what her flaming taffeta costume did to the stage scenery, into which she kept colliding. Not surprisingly, that too was ignited and went up in flames. However, in a remarkably short time, the manager, Blythe Pratt, had re-opened his Music Hall, having undertaken substantial decorative repairs. It was into this recently decorated auditorium that we now headed, lead by the flamboyant, if valetudinarian, Lodge.

1. The World Columbian Exposition was held in 1893
2. The *'Ring of the Nibelung'* is a series of four sequential operas, see Chapter 22
3. Winged warrior daughters of Wotan

4. Cora Elmore was done in by the good doctor
5. Incorrect use of words
6. Acts or turns involving ventriloquists
7. Katherine Williams
8. A person who is habitually anxious about their health
9. Lodge is afflicted with the monomania habit of looking over his shoulders for no reason

Chapter 3

The Auditorium at the
Oxford Music Hall

Our arrival into the auditorium of the Oxford Music Hall in Oxford Street, in the West End of London, did little to quell the general scene of chaos evident throughout the auditorium and stage. Musicians, singers, stage hands, theater staff, cleaners and others engaged in the running of the place, were all amiably chatting amongst each other and in so doing were oblivious of the presence of the impresario, Michael W Lodge, to whom the auditorium was available.

Lodge stood there motionless, as though expecting an ovation; none was forthcoming. A few moments later Blythe Pratt came marching from the other end of the proscenium arch towards us.

"Lodge, good to see you again," said Pratt, with his arm outstretched, "we all of us are at your mercy, sorry I mean disposal!"

"My good friend Blythe," replied Lodge, shaking Pratt's hand, "you remember Theo Houston and Jack Mitchell, both Vaudeville artistes out of New York?"

"I do indeed," responded Pratt.

After we had all exchanged mutual pleasantries, Pratt suddenly announced that perhaps we might like some refreshments to sustain us during the ordeal of our auditioning several hopeful sopranos.

Lodge again consulted his gold Hunter, and with a look of total distain upon his face. No doubt brought on by Pratt's suggestion that we indulge in the consumption of alcohol within an hour of having taken break-fast. he then raised his eyes upward to the heavens.

"Very well, let us do this thing," said Pratt, as he beckoned us to the center crimson plush seats of the stalls. After we had made ourselves comfortable, Blythe Pratt marched off quickly, presumably for his morning libation.

Lodge was now in control, in total control and we felt it, but he did address those standing idly about the auditorium.

"Ladies and gentlemen, attend me," he began, "we are gathered here on this day in our noble quest to seek, no discover, a new soprano. A soprano who will be able to do justice to the extremely taxing vocal demands that will be made upon her when performing the revered Choral Anthem Symphony, especially when she attempts to do justice in that rôle of *Courage*.

Katie Lawrence and Dot Hetherington of course sing the other rôles of *Aspiration* and *Hope* respectively. The vacant rôle of *Courage* has come about due to tragic circumstances compelling us to replace the irreplaceable Bella Elmore, who sadly was taken from us recently, murdered by her husband. It is into those small hands of the successful soprano that we shall commit our destiny and therefore fortune, by way, of course, of the all important box office receipts!"

After which Lodge gave an arched bow.

Both Jack and I noticed that a few persons standing out of Lodge's vision, put handkerchiefs to the mouths to suppress sustained bouts of giggling.

After an interminable time the first soprano walked onto the stage and peered out into the middle distance.

The acetylene gas fuelled footlights illuminating her and the stage on which she stood nervously, enlivened the features on her face.

When she had finally located where Lodge was sitting and focused on his position she curtseyed.

"My name is Dora Barton and I am thirty two years of age." She then looked expectantly at Lodge.

Eventually Lodge got up out of his seat.

"Sing woman, sing!" he exhorted.

"Sing what?" Dora replied.

"Your rôle of *Courage* or *Aspiration* which ever," retorted Lodge.

"I do not have a score," replied Dora.

It became apparent that no scores had been printed and that this oversight was to be laid clearly at the feet of the impresario. The expression upon his face indicated this to be so. Lodge then bounded out of the auditorium with a speed and agility one would not expect of a confirmed valetudinarian.

"I thought we had heard the last of this Choral Anthem Symphony for orchestra and soprano," said Jack.

"I think not, after all it is a work close to his heart…" I replied.

"It is nothing of the like," interrupted Jack, "Loge did not compose the symphony anymore than you or I did. He merely got the eminent composer Gustav Mahler to score up a few ideas he had obviously come across in his varied sojourns into the rear of those Music Halls he frequents! The work is full of allegorical references and meanings, which are certainly beyond Loge's imagination. You and I have heard the sublime symphonic works of Mahler at the Carnegie Hall in New York. And we know this to be the case"

Lodge appeared on the stage clutching a sheaf of

papers, one of which he handed to Dora. Then, again with the same unexpected agility, he leapt down from the stage into the orchestra pit. After some muffled words had been exchanged between him and the conductor, he rejoined us in the stalls.

Before resuming his seat next to us, he addressed Dora standing on the stage.

"Dora, you are representing the concept of *Courage*. Do try to create that ethereality in your delivery of those precious lyrics. Maestro, begin," instructed Lodge, with a nonchalant wave of his hand.

The conductor obliged and pointed his baton at the pianist seated at a seven octave pianoforte with mahogany panelling, who began playing a series of triple A's and arpeggios. The rest of the orchestra took up the major thematic theme of the symphonic section in which Dora joined in with the words devoted to *Courage*.

'Look down upon us from your majesty,
That we may, with your light, see your greatness;
And though we know we are but mortal,
Live in hope to be with you for all eternity.'
'With the eternal light from thy saving grace,
Radiate down upon our parched souls;
And with it give us strength to gaze upon thy face,
With renewed faith our hopes with you embrace.'

It became apparent not only to me, but others too, that Dora, whatever else she could do, and it is quite feasible that she may have been a good cook, but alas could not sing; at least not for her supper. This fact was made abundantly and unequivocally clear to all but the deaf during the first of a series of auditioning contestants.

Ironically the dignity inherent in the words and lyrics of the verses could at times express a profound significance to those who might appreciate them. And indeed they were to be applauded, especially with such sentiments as;

'With renewed faith our hopes with you embrace.'

The absurdity of the undoubted majesty of the verses or such profound lyrics being sung in the confines of a Music Hall was not lost on either Jack or me. But according to Lodge, its contrivance was deliberate in moving from the absurd to the ridiculous. And by this method, which involved the mass delusion of an entire audience with his esteemed Choral Anthem Symphony. Lodge hoped to take Music Hall audiences by storm and sweep all before him on his relentless striving to achieve maximum box office receipts.

This necessity for the mass delusion of an audience, involves, as it were, perpetrating a colossal fraud, the dimensions of which are even now mind boggling, for such was the labyrinthine complexity of Lodge's Machiavellian thinking.

With no encouragement from Lodge, Dora retreated from the stage and was replaced by Ruth Vincent. Upon reaching center stage, she announced, in a squeaky voice, to everybody that she was thirty seven years of age.

Her performance was a disaster and I think she knew it. In the meantime both Jack and I conferred and concluded there was a possibility that Lodge may indeed be denied finding his precious soprano.

The next to take the audition was a Winifred Barnes. She started off quite well in a forced manner. Her singing was controlled and her diction clear. Lodge made a few notes in his green commonplace book and asked her to remain in the wings.

Then there seemed to be what sounded like an argument or a commotion at the side of the stage, in the wings, with some partition walls being shaken forcibly. We all looked expectantly at the stage wing in question.

Presently a person staggered on to the stage trying desperately to shrug off those stage hands endeavoring to prevent her from making an appearance in front of the footlights.

This person needed no introduction, as her reputation more than preceded her. Both Jack and I merely looked at each other and shrugged our shoulders.

She walked up to the edge of the stage and then, looking out into the abyss of the auditorium and with a rising C sharp, commenced her recital. The person had only gotten into a few bars before Lodge leapt up out of his comfortable crimson colored velvet seat and began throwing his arms about in an abandoned manner and shouting at the singer.

"No, no! This will not do! You must vacate the stage this instant! I will not tolerate such impertinence from you, madam!"

"Why not?" came the singer's riposte, looking at Lodge with a questioning look upon her face.

"You know very well why. I do not wish to hear your voice, let alone engage you," replied Lodge, who by now had walked to the stage edge and was looking up at the erstwhile singer.

The singer, in turn now looked down on Lodge with her arms akimbo and hands resting on her hips, indicative of a confident attitude.

"I will not be spoken down to from you up there," Lodge continued.

"My singing the rôle of *Courage* in your precious Cholera Anthem Symphony in the key of C major is pitched perfectly. As indeed you would recognise if you Theseus, [1] knew anything about singing," replied the singer.

"I have stated my view in this matter. I shall not stand here, looking up at you on the stage, and argue. I have no wish to engage you. Good day madam," said Lodge, dismissively.

"I could make Judd, that ventriloquist's dummy sing the part of *Courage* with more sublime dignity and heartfelt sincerity better than that Bella, or anybody else for that matter, could ever hope to do," replied the singer on the stage.

"How dare you madam," answered Lodge, "how dare you be confident with me! My sacred Choral Symphony is a work of sonorous ethereality and nobility of purpose fit only for the *Three Graces* to perform; not some travelling circus which comprises freaks, impersonators and traitors to the cause." [2]

"Oscar Wilde once applauded my singing," said the singer looking down at Lodge, "intimating that I possessed those rare qualities of a great depth of warmth and ability to understand intuitively the meaning of my song."

"Enough woman!" exclaimed Lodge, now in a fit of pique "my decision is irrevocable as it is final. I shall not tolerate such impertinence from one so arrogant and inexperienced, but with such inordinate confidence in her doubtful abilities."

"Lodge's decision may be final; so was mine," I whispered to Jack, "We are going to make her acquaintance again. And do so before we leave this Music Hall. I am going to propose that we join forces with her and really take the London stage by storm."

"Do you really think joining forces with Cinderella could work for us?" Jack asked.

"We could hardly fail," I replied, "between the four of us, including that Judd, the ventriloquist dummy, we possess unbridled talent!"

The next soprano to demonstrate her vocal range within soprano was Anna Held. I felt she had presence and ability, but Lodge's response to her singing indicated otherwise. She was succeeded by a Mabel Green, aged twenty-two.

This woman could sing, but in a peculiar way, and in a style which I had not heard before. She too was not beyond looking rather odd. Her face, one might describe as being bovine and hard and not in any way feminine. She had applied a generous layer of make up to her face, combined with daubs of rouge to her cheeks and vibrant red varnish to her lips. Indeed her face, made more garish by the footlights pouring out their harsh lights, was partially obscured by cascading locks of dark curly hair, the kind of which one might expect to see on a portrait of a seventeenth century cavalier.

Jack too looked intently at her whilst she graduated through the scales, almost as a nightingale might. Lodge too was becoming more interested in her and rubbing both hands together and his beaming facial features indicated this was so.

Her dress was lavish and appeared to be made up of layers of purple silk and red velvet, creating a bellowing effect. The upper part of the dress reached up to her neck and was finished off with a brooch containing a sparkling stone of lapis lazuli

When she concluded her recital, Lodge asked ingratiatingly what she had sung before.

"Oh you are so kind sir," she replied, whilst curtseying,

"for I have been these months past with such illuminating troupes as the *Cremorne Belles* and the *Gay Gordons*. I also featured in the, *'Balkan Princess,'* at The Prince of Wales's Theater, by Frank Curzon and Frederick Lonsdale with music by Paul Rubens I will have you know."

For some inexplicable reason, her reply elicited giggles from the orchestral players and others ranged around the auditorium, including loitering stage hands.

Lodge, oblivious to this re-action by others present, asked her to stay. Accordingly, she withdrew from center stage with a grace of deportment and dignity. Lodge settled down again in his seat and witnessed Eleanor Robson take the stage and within minutes she had vacated her place for Ada Reeve who was thirty five and quite clearly drunk.

To the surprise of both Jack and me, the next contestant to audition for the rôle of soprano was May de Sousa. She was a native of Chicago and played in the stage show, *'Girls of Gottenberg.'* Jack and I had met with her some weeks back when were playing the Majestic Theater in that windy city.

"This thirty year old singer's cute face and demeanor is bound to impress Lodge," I told Jack.

"That and the fact she has quite a wide tessitura [3] for I heard her arguing with another artiste whilst waiting in the ante chamber for her audition!" replied Jack.

Immediately after de Sousa had completed her recital, Lodge got up from his seat and asked that Mabel Green be sent for. When after some time Green re-appeared on stage Lodge asked her to sing the verses appertaining to another rôle, that of *Aspiration*.

Again, whilst she sang, I had another opportunity to look at this singer. Her singing was admittedly quite powerful and accomplished, but there was something about her voice that thirty odd years of being on the Vaudeville stage somewhat grated against. Still, I thought, it is Lodge's decision not mine. Looking at Jack, I think he was contemplating similar thoughts to mine.

Lodge asked her to recite another verse to the accompaniment of the pit orchestra.

She did so flawlessly, like the songbird she was and in so doing instantly ingratiated herself into Lodge's affections, who, it was evident for all to see, was becoming infatuated by her with each passing minute, much to the disgust of the other contestants. They must have known in their hearts what Lodge then confirmed, as he stepped up on to the podium.

"Ladies and gentlemen, attend me, for our search, indeed our quest is at an end! We have this day, found our paragon of virtue, in a new soprano to replace the late Bella Elmore who sadly has passed over. Introduce yourself Mabel, introduce yourself Mabel Green to the world as the new soprano and fulfil your destiny in the Pantheon of the *Three Graces*! 4 And, hopefully continue to ensure adequate box office receipts," said Lodge, under breath, as he eased himself down from the podium.

The decision to engage Mabel Green, who clearly was no ingénue,5 came as an unexpected shock. Not only that, but Lodge's announcing his decision was met with a stunned silence and looks of incredulity on the faces of the musicians, stage hands and other contestants assembled in the auditorium. Even the drunken Ada Reeve, reclining in the stalls, appeared surprised.

"Come on Jack," I insisted, "we have got to meet with Cinderella!

1. Another name for Lodge, based on his complex strategies equal to Theseus negotiating a way out of the Labyrinthine maze

2. Lodge considers Cinderella a traitor to the cause, because she found away round the *Exclusivity Clause*
3. Vocal range
4. The other two are Katie Lawrence and Dot Hetherington
5. A young woman who is endearingly innocent, virtuous and candid, but lacks sophistication or cunning.

Chapter 4

The Return of the
Ventriloqist's Dummy

As Jack had intimated to me on numerous occasions, the fate of the noble Choral Anthem Symphony and the *Three Graces* needed to perform it were no concern of ours. Instead we should be concentrating on our Vaudeville act finessed to please and entertain the London audiences. To this end, I totally agreed and it was why we were then making our way down to the dressing rooms with the express intention of meeting with Cinderella. It was alas, she who was removed from Lodge's audition for the replacement rôle of soprano in the *Three Graces*.

"In some respects, I do not rue the day we let that Little Bo Peep or Cinderella hijack Judd,[1] our erstwhile, if insolent, ventriloquist's dummy. Our meeting with Cinderella to join forces will involve our having to deal with that Judd again," said Jack as we made our way through the foyer of the Oxford Music Hall and down into the dressing rooms located in the basement.

"Jack, what Lodge said to us at the break-fast table earlier today about Judd having an opinion, kind of made sense and ..." I said.

"Theo," interrupted Jack, "Loge was being facetious; Jeez, Theo, Judd is a wooden doll, a ventriloquist's dummy, a prop. It is not a person with intelligence or a mind to think with; it is nothing more than shaped piece of painted timber!"

"I realize that Jack and I know Judd could get above himself occasionally, as he did in the Criterion Theater, an experience I shall not forget quickly. I remember the occasion all too vividly.

Judd was playing the pianoforte with you and he skipped a song in the order leaving me stranded on center stage singing out of tune to the pianoforte. I turned around to Judd who responded by beaming that fixed grin on his jaw to me. Still we got under way again and for the first time that evening, when doing our turn on stage, the audience genuinely looked as if they were enjoying our new song.

Then that Nihilist got up from his cheap seat in the stalls and asked, at the top of his voice why we were enslaving Judd by making him perform remorselessly at the pianoforte without respite, sustenance or pay.

I know the both of us were astounded by this outburst by the heckler. Even more so when Judd, the dummy, turned his head around and agreed with the Nihilist! Adding that his life was not only a misery, but that he constantly yearned for emancipation and freedom back to his wooden folks in the forest.

'You are exploiters of the mindless and underprivileged!' one bearded heckler was heard to say, and demanded that we release Judd forthwith.

At the time we were both uncertain as to whether Judd agreed with his being called mindless, but there it is!

"He, or rather Judd, is a wooden dummy, a ventriloquist's dummy" I responded to one heckler, flabbergasted at the absurdity of the situation.

At which point Jack, you abandoned the pianoforte and carrying Judd in your arms marched up to the very edge of the stage to engage a particularly vocal heckler. But unfortunately at the same time our ventriloquist's dummy, Judd, appealed to the audience for his release. To which they demanded that Judd be given his freedom at once and without condition.

Judd mischievously responded by moving his head in a wide sweeping arc of the auditorium wearing upon his wooden painted face that manic fixed grin in front of his closed teeth.

What then happened of course was unfortunate for all concerned and could not have occurred at a more inconvenient a moment. Whether you, Jack, had failed to securely fasten Judd's head to his shoulders I could not be certain. But at that instant, Judd's head departed from his shoulders and fell to the stage floor, bouncing for several moments around the stage during a deathly silence. Of course, it finally rolled off into the orchestra pit!

This action had a salutary effect on the audience who responded with gasps of horror as people and hecklers in the audience looked away in disgust, visibly shocked at what they considered to be an unmitigated act of wanton cruelty of truly grotesque proportion. Presently, it was the compère who intervened by clearing you, me and a decapitated Judd off the stage," I concluded.

"It still gives me shudders thinking about it Theo," said Jack, looking visibly shaken.

"Jack, you recall that I attended Bella Elmore's Wake of Remembrance back stage at the Vaudeville Theater in the Strand, after that botched funeral at Highgate Cemetery? Well I had a remarkable conversation with Bo Peep during the wake, during the course of which I informed her of what Judd had got up to on the stage at the Criterion Theater, demanding his release from servitude," if you can believe that!" I had said to Bo Peep.

She most certainly could, was her reply and that is why she went down to our dressing rooms, where she found the headless Judd, bound up and discarded. She decided there and then, having found his head, to rescue him. Bo Peep has re-christened him with the name of Marmaduke.

"'Is that not correct my precious?' asked Bo Peep of Judd, the erstwhile ventriloquist's dummy, that she produced out of her voluminous carpet bag, whilst talking to me at the same time.

To my horror, Judd opened his mouth and replied to Bo Peep's inquiry of him.

"'It is an axiom of life, I have always maintained," I heard Marmaduke reply, to my utter astonishment, "that I shall not be consigned to oblivion, for I too have my rôle to play on the world's stage. Indeed, for what is Soho but one large stage; upon which we are all invited to do our turns or acts? I may well be fashioned from the finest woods, but I have feelings and expect, no indeed I demand, dignity!'

"We used call him Judd…" I had said, to Bo Peep.

'Not anymore. He is now called Marmaduke, a name much more befitting his expansive character and sensitive personality,' Bo Peep had informed me.

"Marmaduke is a wooded doll, a ventriloquist's dummy, or an ex prop," I replied.

'No, I am not!' insisted Marmaduke.

'That is right,' confirmed Little Bo Peep, 'aside of which he has a lovely genuine smile and is altogether quite cute, is that not the case my precious Marmaduke?' asked Bo Peep.

Marmaduke on this occasion deigned not to reply, but stared manically into space.

"'You like his smile?" asked Bo Peep.

"What, you mean that expression of a manic grin he is wearing?" I replied.

'I do not think Marmaduke is very impressed with you Theo,' replied Bo Peep, 'and anyway, I had better take Marmaduke home now, as I think he looks quite exhausted and more than a little piquéred.'

"Does that give you some indication of how Bo Peep's mind works Jack?" I asked.

"Yes it does," replied Jack.

"Irrespective of Judd, being a wooden dummy Jack," I continued, "I was thinking more in terms of resurrecting him by hooking up with Little Bo Peep in her rôle as the irascible Judd. Remember when Queenie, Marie Lloyd, and we saw her the other day here at the Oxford Music Hall imitating Judd whom we had abandoned for good in our changing room when we were playing the Criterion Music Hall? Bo Peep's act on that occasion was very accomplished, as indeed so is she. We could benefit by being with her.

"On the stage at the Oxford Music Hall, you and I, Jack, were much impressed by the way Bo Peep had assumed Judd's character. She did so as her new act and introduced him in a convincing and affectionate way. We both know that this person also separately plays Bo Peep and also Cinderella on stage. She now has three distinct characters; Cinderella, Little Bo Peep and now Marmaduke, our former ventriloquist's dummy and plays them all extremely well. She is a very accomplished actress and we should involve her in our act.

"Just recall how she established Judd's character as being one which deserved sympathy. What did Bo Peep do when she walked on to the stage at the Oxford Music Hall some time back, dressed as Judd in a Prince of Wales checked suit and wearing a deep red good luck Derby hat? Remember when we first saw Cinderella's act in the company of Queenie Leughton and Marie Lloyd?

"Cinderella, dressed as Judd the ventriloquist's dummy, introduced for the first time her act, which we again saw last night at Daly's Music Hall.

"Judd stood at the very precipice of the stage, swaying as though in a breeze. His arms merely hung loosely at his side whilst his head assumed a circular motion with the occasional flash of teeth reinforcing that unnerving manic expression. Then as if he were being lowered, by unseen wires, Judd knelt down on one knee, as though in genuflection and began with a low murmur to enunciate his inner thoughts.

"Those low sounds soon developed into a plainchant about how, as a little twig in the forests, Judd was taken from his home beneath a leaf, resting on the forest floor, and put into bondage. How Judd was only fed just enough to ensure he did not fade away. Judd then paused at that point and again with his manic expression caused by baring his teeth, turned his head in a wide sweep for all in the auditorium to see.

"He then got up, and walked about the stage in a loose-limbed manner, as though he were a puppet being controlled by hidden wires. He then proceeded to sing about his fervent hope of release from being manipulated or governed by unseen hands. To this lyrical sentiment the costermongers in the cheap seats and, indeed some in the Dress Circle, finally failed to control themselves and spontaneously erupted into unbridled applause.

"Some members of the audience were driven to deliberately induce themselves into a mild form of delirium. Such was their re-action to Judd on the stage. The applause was tremendous as it was sustained in response Bo Peep's performing Judd in front of the gas-powered footlights illuminating the manic features upon his face.

"The enthusiastic applause was thunderous and in response, Judd removed his good luck red Derby hat as he bowed to an appreciative audience. The instant reaction in our private box was not limited to just me; it also involved you too Jack. We were both mesmerized by what we had witnessed, including the awful realization that the person on the stage below us was nothing more than a re-incarnation of our erstwhile, if discarded, ventriloquist's dummy, Judd! It was none other than Judd, come to life, as a new stage character by Cinderella, as yet another one of her guises! However, the prospect of Judd having an independent life on the stage filled us both with a nameless foreboding.

"It was Queenie Leighton, watching Cinerella's performance, who gave expression to what we were all thinking.

'Cinderella,' Queenie had said, 'Bo Peep; call her what you will. She really is the mistress of the guise!'" I reminded Jack.

A few moments later, we found ourselves walking down a white painted brick lined corridor leading to various dressing rooms. Presently, we detected a faint sound of singing emanating from one of the rooms. It was the unmistakable voice of Cinderella. We approached her door and tapped gently upon it. She turned around and motioned us to enter.

Cinderella, who was smoking a Trichinopoly cigar, looked at us and smiled.

"Ah, Theo from New York; and Jack; I think we did well last night at Daly's Music Hall in my new rôle as Marmaduke, the ventriloquist's dummy. Even though the *Undeserving Poor* tried to make a scene, we survived, did we not?" said Cinderella, after which she drank deeply from her large glass of whisky, and then breathed out noisily.

Both Jack and I held out our hands and re-introduced ourselves. I noticed when shaking Cinderella's hand that her clenched grip was quite hard and in fact painful.

"Can I fix you two gentlemen a drink?" she offered.

"Rather," came Jack's instant response.

After we had all gotten our drinks and made ourselves comfortable in various chairs, I started in.

"Cinderella, we appreciate your giving us a few minutes of your time. As you pointed out earlier, both Jack and I are from New York and have been playing Vaudeville for the last thirty one years, mainly on the eastern seaboard or recently in Chicago where we were performing to the large crowds attending the acclaimed World Columbian Exposition. Of late though, we, as with other Music Hall artistes, were plagued by Nihilists and organized hecklers embedded in the audience. Things came to a crescendo when we were performing in the Majestic Theater on West Monroe Street in Chicago.

By fortuitous chance we met with the acclaimed impresario Michael Lodge in a bar on North Michigan Avenue..." I continued,

"You mean Theseus?" interrupted Cinderella, "to some of us that is his name. Given to him on account of the fact he could negotiate his way out of any situation as the ancient classical hero Theseus found his way out of the labyrinthine maze of tunnels with ease!"

"Well we met with Lodge, Theseus, in this bar on North Michigan Avenue," I continued, "and in effect he offered us a proposition which involved our accompanying him back to London to work the Music Halls here. We have been here for some weeks now and have gotten in to the ways of how one performs in Music Halls in London. However, as you probably realize, we abandoned any pretence of being involved with the Choral Anthem Symphony as being totally inappropriate to what we are, Vaudeville artistes.

"We also dropped Judd our ventriloquist's dummy, primarily because he has recently been getting above himself, culminating in his disgraceful behavior at the Criterion Theater, where he actively encouraged the Nihilists and hecklers among the audience to agitate for his immediate emancipation from servitude to us, his masters."

I stopped, observing the expression of incredulity upon Cinderella's face.

"Theo, you talk as if Judd were a real person. He is a ventriloquist's dummy made of timber, that is all he is," advised Jack.

"Jack is correct Theo," rejoined Cinderella, "that is why I abandoned Judd, or rather Marmaduke, as a hand held ventriloquist's dummy. You may recall the other evening when I first introduced Marmaduke upstairs in the auditorium at this very Music Hall, when you were sitting with Queenie and Marie Lloyd. He was uncontrollable and rude to me when I invited him to say hello to the audience.

"'I do not want to and I hate you, put me down this instance,'" he replied, "'put me down, now.'"

"I most certainly will not," I responded, "you are a naughty boy Marmaduke for disobeying me."

'And you are a horrid, ugly girl and cannot even look after docile lambs without losing some to a fox obviously cleverer than you,' Marmaduke had said, 'and not only that, this silly girl has kidnapped me. There I was, sleeping in my cardboard box after a particularly exhausting act on the stage at the Criterion Theater, when this fat ugly girl you see here before you, stole me and refuses to let me go home!'

"That is not true; I rescued you from oblivion and certain obscurity or probability of being sold as matchwood!"

Cinderella paused to refill our glasses with neat whisky.

"As you will appreciate gentlemen this situation could not be allowed to continue and decisive action had to be taken. I was pondering this dilemma, when a solution came to me. Abandon the ventriloquist's dummy turn. And instead act the part of Marmaduke, a ventriloquist's dummy, actually in person!"

"That is the reason we came down to see you, Cinderella or Bo Peep. By the way, which do you prefer to be called?" asked Jack.

"Think about it Jack! In your company and Theo's, I would obviously have to be called Marmaduke," answered Cinderella, "especially if we are to work together!"

Both Jack and I looked at each other. There was nothing else to say. Cinderella had read our thoughts and intentions correctly.

"One question," asked Jack, "you surely did not want the part of the *Third Grace* singing the rôle of *Courage* in that Choral Anthem Symphony?"

"Certainly not Jack; I simply wanted to irritate Theseus!" replied Cinderella, draining the last of her whisky.

We left Cinderella, shaking hands again and agreed to meet with her in the Café Royal in the Regent's Street near Piccadilly to discuss our new routine on the stage.

As we made our way from the dressing room along the white painted, brick lined corridor, I stopped and looked at Jack.

"What an unadulterated pleasure it is," I told him, "to

be in the company of clever people who can think quickly and clearly. It cannot come as any surprise to know that Cinderella, Bo Peep or Marmaduke is without doubt a very successful and accomplished Music Hall artiste."

Moments later we reëntered the Music Hall foyer. Lodge upon seeing us made a big show of pulling out his gold Hunter and looking at it.

"I thought you had deserted me," he said, with clear asperity in his voice echoing slight annoyance at his having to wait on us.

"We would not dream of deserting you Loge," replied Jack.

"Well gentlemen," continued Lodge, "all this excitement in auditioning for a new soprano, to join my *Three Graces* has given me a sharp appetite, quite! I suggest we take luncheon at the Criterion Restaurant and celebrate our discovery. That is when Mabel joins us from her dressing room."

Presently Mabel did join us, looking even more luscious wearing a full length, red velvet coat tied up around her neck with collar of black mink fur. On her head she wore an inordinately large bonnet, complete with a green feather of some indeterminate bird sticking out at an acute angle. She approached us hesitantly as if uncertain of her welcome.

"Mabel, Mabel," said Lodge, whilst blowing exaggerated kisses from his lips into the aëther with open fingers, "please meet two Vaudeville artistes from New York; they are Jack Mitchell and Theo Houston."

I put my hand forward which Mabel shook with a grip I should not have expected from a woman. Jack too realised this, when having taken her hand, immediately commenced rubbing his own hand whilst opening and closing it.

"Mabel, I suggest we repair to the Criterion Restaurant for luncheon. Does that meet with your approval?" asked Lodge.

"Oh you are too kind sir. And yes, it does meet with my approval admirably," answered Mabel, "I have dined at the Criterion on numerous occasions, I will have you know. And, I have always been impressed, not only with the impeccable table service, but also the opulent appointment of the establishment in which I have been so fortunate to have been fed and watered."

Jack looked at me and then walked past Lodge and into the Oxford Street to hail a carriage.

Chapter 5

The Criterion Restaurant

Cinderella in the guise of Marmeduke has agreed to join up with us in forming a new double act. She will play the rôle of Marmeduke, our erstwhile emancipated ventriloquist's dummy, to the background of Jack's sublime playing of the pianoforte. By this new and innovative confederation of talent, as it were, unleashed on the London Music Hall audiences, we hope to carry all before us. In the intervening time we were headed to the Criterion Restaurant as guests of Lodge to join him in celebrating the discovery of a soprano in Mabel Green as his new third member of the highly acclaimed *Three Graces*.

Mabel escorted by Lodge and I, followed Jack out of the Music Hall and into a fog-bound Oxford Street, the flag stones of which glistened as they reflected the weak light radiating from the yellow gas lamps. Presently a Landau came lumbering out of the dense fog. But, before Lodge could step into the carriageway to hail it, Mabel put her two index fingers in to her mouth and let out a shrill whistle which pierced my ear drums causing an immediate sharp pain.

The Landau carriage driver heard Mabel's shrill summons too and accordingly reined in his chestnut horses to the kerb of the side walk on which we were standing. We all of us clambered aboard and made

Royalty Music Hall, Soho

ourselves comfortable on the buttoned down green leather upholstery.

Our carriage, driven by a liveried coachman, progressed along Oxford Street in an easterly direction but our progress was slow due to the fog, which had the effect of reducing to a crawl all the wagons, creating a traffic block. At length though, our coachman reined his horses in to a right turn and continued into Dean Street. It was in this street of course where we first rehearsed the Choral Anthem Symphony in the Royalty Music Hall just down the road on our right.

I looked out for the Music Hall. It was not very long before we clattered past it. A few moments later, Lodge, with his gold capped ebony stick, beloved of impresarios, pointed with it to a faint light, made pink by the presence of the fog emanating from a window on the piano-nobile of a Georgian building.

"This is where it all started," Lodge informed us "and, I have spent many an interesting hour in that green and pleasant place. It was in there that I introduced Gustav Mahler to the members of that august establishment. Later, I recall, after we had enjoyed several drinks in order to revive our strength, that I commissioned Gus, sorry I mean Gustav Mahler, to compose the music to the ethereal and elegiac Choral Anthem Symphony.

Of course the work was based on my ideas, which came to me after I had undergone what could only be described as an inspiration of particular profundity, [1] whilst within the precincts of the establishment!"

"Loge, is that the famous Colony Room Club?" inquired Jack.

"It most certainly is Jack, a place of treasured moments," replied Lodge, "and, let me say without fear of contradiction, never has so much gone on in such a small room, which affected so many."

As we clattered past the building, I noticed Mabel turn her face away from the club. She feigned interest in an innocuous, but gaudy advertisement affixed to the wall of building opposite on the corner of Bourchier Street and Dean Street.

"Are you familiar with the Colony Room Club Mabel?" I asked her, deliberately.

"I should say not, I will have you know," answered Mabel in an audibly higher pitched voice, which even

Colony Room Club, Soho

Lodge detected, "but this fog, this acrid fog does get into one's larynx."

She then opened her not inconsiderably large handbag, in which I saw quite clearly a Penny Dreadful. 2

Eventually having negotiated our way through the streets of Soho, we emerged finally into the Shaftesbury Avenue. We progressed down this Avenue of the Theaters, until we came to a circus, in the middle of which was, according to Lodge, Alfred Gilbert's recently erected large aluminum sculpture of the Angel of Christian Charity. 3

At length we pulled up outside the Criterion and had again to assist Lodge in climbing down from the Landau due to his fastened up bulky overcoat, worn as a result of his becoming a confirmed valetudinarian. Again he responded indignantly to the assistance Jack and I offered, especially as our helping him was done in front of his new protégée, Mabel Green.

"Unhand me, I say this instant, unhand me. I can manage and am perfectly capable of descending from an open top Landau carriage without assistance from you or anybody else. I am not infirm I tell you, but rather in the prime of my life!" He kept muttering this exaggeration repeatedly.

Irrespective of Lodge's protests, Jack instinctively put his hand under Lodge's elbow to lend his support in assisting the latter to ascend the steps up to the building's entrance.

Presently we made our way through the entrance leading into the Criterion building in which are located the famous bar, restaurant and adjacent theater. As we did I noticed in the corner of my eye and clearly discernable in the fog, a substantial concentration of fanatical Nihilists, 4 furtive and sporting full black beards.

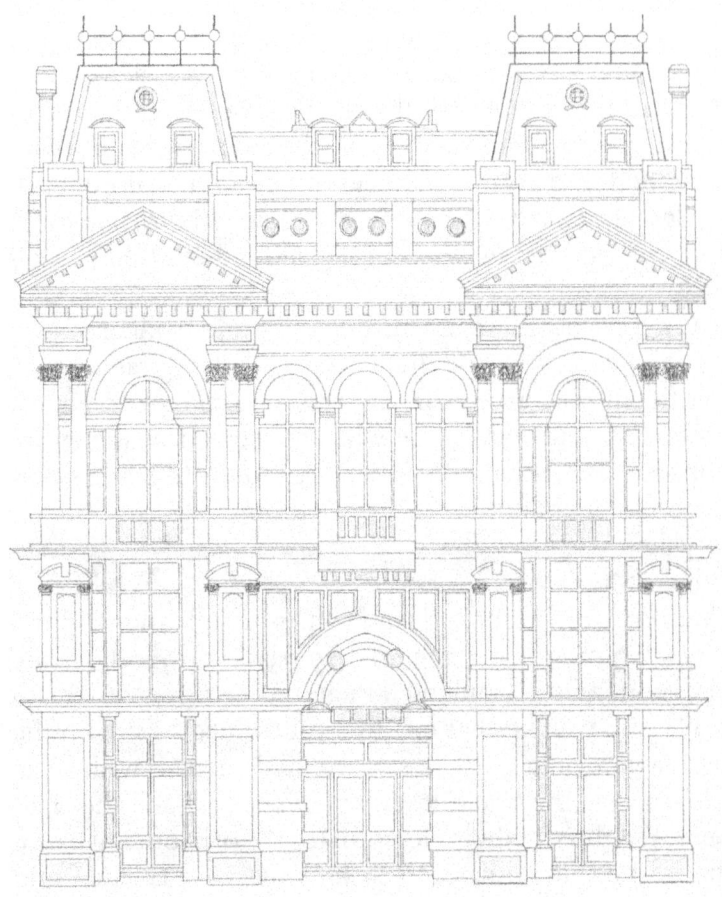

Criterion Building, Piccadilly

They viewed anyone privileged enough to be able use the Criterion with hostility. And they certainly viewed us through their dark, venal eyes, as they chanted their contempt at us and other patrons.

I recalled these Nihilists agitators on previous occasions as they had attended theaters both in Chicago and London with the express intention of heckling the performers on stage and causing general disruption throughout the auditorium. Apparently, they considered us, ordinary Music Hall artistes not only arrogant, as we imitated the manners of the privileged classes, but slaves to the feckless affluence of the upper classes who exploited us mercilessly. What therefore they thought of Lodge, as an impresario, was beyond my imagination. But, suspect that he was still beyond redemption in their eyes.

On this occasion unfortunately, their concentration was considerable and they were clearly agitating in a confident manner, for another final reckoning. A reckoning with whom or what, it seemed, was neither apparent to them, or indeed to us. However, that uncertainty did not in any way deter them from shouting out their dreadful chant; *'Be it now or never'* or *'Dispatch forthwith the dreadful upper classes to their oblivion.'* Whilst they chanted they clenched their fists at all and sundry, including members of the public passing by and on one occasion, a horse, pulling a Phäeton carriage.

It was a well known fact that the Nihilists were on the rampage because of Oscar Wilde's play,[5] with Ada Leverson in the title rôle, and in which they felt they had been slighted, their legitimate revolutionary cause diminished and turned into an object of ridicule and derision. As a result of Wilde's deprecating their cause, they had turned from being an ineffective lower middle class concern. And now have become a concentration of Nihilists, who considered themselves to be by way of being revolutionaries, and with a cause.

Notwithstanding this potential inconvenience to our persons, we stepped into a brilliant incandescent light emanating from large lanterns of glass and crystal chandeliers suspended from the ceiling which illuminated the plush red silk carpet below. The whole effect was to create a crescendo of light, a euphoric sensation of ecstasy and warmth, in direct contrast to the clammy acrid fog-laden aether through which we had just journeyed in our open top Landau carriage.

Presently we found ourselves inside what I took to be the salon, which was large, noisy and decorated extravagantly and exuberantly. It combined Queen Anne and Baroque styles featuring highly polished mahogany woodwork with brass fittings, handrails, marble surfaces and ostentatious acetylene gas-fuelled globe lanterns. Complementing these style were touches of generous Neo-Byzantine opulence in the form of mirrors and mosaics on various walls and surfaces.

There were rich brocade and red velvet drapes framing engraved windows and decorative glazed panel openings in the internal timber partition walls. The ceilings were of painted and gilded moulded plaster, looking down on elaborately patterned carpets with fleur de lys, upon which were positioned several indoor palm trees in glazed urns positioned on top of sandstone jardinières. The back of the bar, set in front of a mirrored wall, displayed decorated bronze stands on which were fixed curved glass globes containing various liquors.

In between them, and dominating the whole bar, was an enormous brass till of such intricate and ornate raised design as to be almost a work of art, rather than a cash depository. The lavish appointment of the bar was one of an opulent, sumptuous, if meretricious, establishment clearly patronized by a wealthy clièntele, resembled more the *Folies-Bergère*, in Paris. This depiction of ambience is captured in Toulouse-Lautrec's painting, *'At the Moulin Rouge,'* both complete in their expression of unbridled affluence and obvious ostentatious behavior.

We pushed past a variety of patrons and at length we managed to gain the pale green *Emperador Chiaro* marble covered bar, whereupon Lodge approached a jovial red-faced bar-tender, wearing a white apron and sporting a large handlebar moustache.

"A bottle of your finest Canard- Duchêne Grande Cuvée Charles VII champagne, my good man,"instructed Lodge, as he offered us his red leather cigar case containing the finest Trichinopoly cigars.

To my surprise and that of Lodge and Jack's, Mabel helped herself to one of the cigars spontaneously and without the slightest hesitation.

Whilst standing at the marbled covered bar, the bar-tender poured out the cuvée champagne into four fluted glasses. When the bar-tender had finished, he handed a glass to Mabel, who without waiting for the rest of us, took a sip from her glass. Upon doing so, she immediately screwed up her face and turned to the bar-tender.

"Do you have any of that new fashionable drink called the Coca~Cola?"

"Yes of course ma'am," replied the bar-tender.

"Please be so good as to fetch me some, my good man," instructed Mabel.

A few moments later the bar-tender produced the distinctive curved bottle and removed the metal cap.

Upon this, Mabel picked up the bottle and poured some of the Coca~Cola into her Canard-Duchêne Grande Cuvée Charles VII champagne. She then put the glass to her lips and drank deeply from it. After which she breathed out noisily.

"Ah, that is much better; takes the edge off the champagne," she informed us.

The look of horror upon Lodge's face, as Mabel desecrated this expensive champagne, was indescribable. Jack merely clinked his glass with Mabel's and toasted her.

Presently a waiter approached Lodge and advised him that our luncheon table was ready and would we follow him and like to walk this way.

"Why, what is wrong with the way we walk already?" asked Mabel, in all innocence.

Lodge, ever the chivalrous type, offered Mabel his arm as he escorted her to the table. Jack and I brought up the rear of our group.

Eventually we reached our circular table and sat down on elegant Chippendale chairs with seats covered in pale green moiré silk. I sat opposite Lodge with Mabel to my left.

"A magnum of your vintage Perrier-Jouët champagne and four large glasses," instructed Mabel, to one of the hovering waiters attending our table.

"And will you be wanting your usual, the Coca~Cola in yours Mabel?" asked a surprised Lodge, with deliberate asperity in his voice.

"Yes," replied Mabel instinctively, without averting her gaze from the gold tasselled menu card, which she studied with an intense blankness to her face.

Moments later the champagne was delivered to our table and Mabel was the first to start drinking it whilst perusing the menu with a questioning look upon her face.

"Perhaps you wish that I should choose from the à la carte menu for you Mabel?" inquired Lodge, seemingly coming to her aid.

"Michael," she said, laying down the menu and taking a deep draft from her fluted glass of champagne and the Coca~Cola, after which she again breathed out noisily,

"I am quite, quite capable of reading from an à la carte menu and ordering my London Particular, 6 I will have you know!"

Somewhat taken aback by this overt, if unexpected, demonstration of self-determination in her reply to Lodge, I asked her, motivated by diplomacy, what she had been doing on stage recently.

"I believe you mentioned earlier that you were in a production of the, 'Balkan Princess'?"

"Cor bless you sir; for you do have a good memory," she answered, slightly giggling, as she did so, "I did not think anybody from the auditions would remember. But you are quite correct, I did play a not inconsiderable rôle in that particular production by Frank Curzon and Frederick Lonsdale with music composed by the indefatigable Paul Rubens. We opened at the Prince of Wales's Theater, in the February of 1910 and, to great acclaim, I will have you know."

I remember reading a review of this comic opera in *Variety*, which itself had been syndicated by a review in *Lloyds Weekly News*, London edition. From what I remembered, the plot was of labyrinthine complexity, the kind of which, Lodge could with ease, construct whilst waiting for a drink at the bar. Not surprisingly, the plot involved cross-dressing and persons in the wrong clothes, a princess played by Isabel Jay, a duke played by Bertram Wallis and gross misunderstandings throughout with predictable consequences accompanied by regular outbursts of songspiel or sometimes, actual singing.

I also recalled Max Hein was cast in his usual rôle of a scoundrel and the two thieves in question in the persons of Charles Brown and Lauri de Frece. The name de Frece, for some reason, I linked with Vesta Tilley, but at the moment could not think why. I think the part played by our luncheon guest, Mabel Green was without distinction, as the companion to the duke whilst in a Bohemian restaurant, in Act II.

"And, let me tell you," Mabel continued, "my unbridled success continued in the production of the *Little Michus,* which was performed at Daly's Theater in Leicester Square. You may possibly know that venerable establishment to the arts? All who witnessed this musical play by Henry Hamilton with music by André Messanger hailed it as an unmitigated triumph for the West End! In particular, one review went on to say, were the stunning performances by Huntley Wright, Miss Mabel Love, Robert Evett and by no means least, Miss Mabel Green."

"You appear to be quite a dab hand at getting into various costumes according to the rôle created for you. You certainly appear to be very adept," said Lodge, before throwing the contents of his fluted glass down his throat in one go.

With his head tipped back Lodge was unable to see the look of surprise upon Mabel's facial features, after Lodge had uttered those innocent words.

However, in the next moment, Mabel was off on a lengthy discourse about the rôle of Music Hall in society; its duties, obligations and moral crusade in educating the *uneducatable,* as she described them. Shortly after which Mabel lapsed into a morose inactivity and concentrated on her drinking instead.

Presently Mabel came to again, but by now she was into her fourth glass of champagne with the Coca~Cola and was beginning to slur her words.

"I will have you know," she continued, "a critic was moved to describe me in this review thus;

'Miss Mabel Green,' me, 'has made quite a hit

as the other of the two Little Michus - a fact which speaks well for manager, Mr. Edwardes' foresight in promoting her from the chorus.'

Having quoted this review, Mabel's incapacity did in no way however, deter her from rummaging around for several minutes in the handbag she had opened. And then, with a flourish, Mabel retrieved what she had been searching for.

It was a stained and battered cutting from the *Daily Mail* newspaper dated 5 April, 1905. She handed it to me, presumably to read out aloud for the benefit of those sitting at our table and for others in close proximity. I did so, including the date. This fact, I noticed, in no way concerned Lodge given that the newspaper cutting was of a review seven years old!

'THE LITTLE MICHUS'

CHARMING COMIC OPERA AT DALY'S THEATER

'The complete success of *'The Little Michus,'* the delightful comic opera produced by Mr. George Edwardes at Daly's Theatre on Saturday night, deals another deadly blow at that farrago of rubbish known as musical comedy. The joyous reception given by the public to, *'Veronique,'* by the same author and composer, has shown Mr. Edwardes that his patrons have learned to expect something better than trite tunes, witless jingles and broadly farcical humour.

Artistically, 'The Little Michus,' is an advance on, 'Veronique,' for the theme of the store is more natural and human, the comedians are compelled to keep in the picture, and the music is on a higher plane. There are not, perhaps, so many mellifluous numbers in, 'The Little Michus,' as in its predecessor, but the score throughout is instinct, with poetic grace and an irresistible sense of melody. We have no one in this country who can approach M. André Messager as a composer of light operatic music.

Miss Adrienne Augarde and Miss Mabel Green as the, 'Little Michus,' play together very brightly. The performance of Miss Augarde, in particular, is a very clever, refined, and altogether notable piece of work. Miss Green is full of fun and vivacity. Her singing was sometimes rather too loud and her actions a little overdone, but with experience she will certainly develop into a favorite of comic opera.'

This review failed to make an impact on Jack's or my sensibilities and I suspect on Lodge's too, who now appeared to trying to deal with a recalcitrant piece of braised veal. But, on the basis that to be in a show – comic opera with glowing reviews about other actors in it, I suppose could lend credence to other minor participants. This was clearly the case with Mabel, who now was somewhat oblivious of any review or criticism.

Moving the conversation on, I offered an opening for her. After all we were supposed to be assisting Lodge in making an acquaintance of Mabel, or at least in our endeavoring to get to know a little more about her. Hence Lodge's inviting Mabel to join us for luncheon at the Criterion restaurant.

"I understand Mabel, from what you imparted earlier, that you were indeed part of that esteemed troupe called the *Cremorne Belles?*"

Mabel gave me a searching sideways glance and squinted her eyes. Then she reverted to her glass, from which she again drank deeply.

"We have," I continued, "had the pleasure of seeing the *Cremorne Belles* perform at the Alhambra Music Hall and also at Wilton's Music Hall, when we were last there as guests of the manager, Mr. Thomas E. Clay. On both occasions, I have to say, both Jack and I were mightily impressed, especially at Wilton's when your dance troupe, I believe called properly, the *Inexhaustible Cremorne Belles,* burst onto the stage singing, *'It is the limelight for us or nothing,'* and, I might add,to great acclaim.

"Jack and I and in fact with Lodge here, certainly remembered their dancing; it was very vigorous as the troupe sang popular songs from light operetta. You all appeared very energetic and accomplished as you carried out complex formation dance rituals and manœuvres with a remarkable coördinated precision. In so doing, I recall the *Cremorne Belles* caused fleeting shadows, created by the incandescent footlights, to appear on the stage backdrop, which in turn, depicted a classical Greek pastoral scene.

In my opinion, the choreography was accomplished yet at the same time very effective, especially that ethereal scene of wood nymphs dancing gaily with trailing ribbons intertwined about their hands, made more real by the interplay of shadows and different hues of lights fleeting across the stage backdrop. The dancing skills and abilities of the *Cremorne Belles,* were a pleasure to experience!" I said, hoping for a response from Mabel.

"Oh, you are so kind sir!" she said, and then launched into a monologue about her crucial rôle in anchoring the dance troupe in what was a very complicated series of coördinated choreographic manœuvres. Whatever else Mabel possessed in terms of personal attributes, humility was not amongst them, I thought.

It was Jack who continued with a polite inquiry as to her recent début with the *Gay Gordons* review show.

I got the impression Mabel definitely did not much feel like expanding on her involvement with the *Gay Gordons.* So we let that pass, at least for the present.

After we had consumed our brandies and smoked our Trichinopoly cigars, Mabel of course taking her brandy with the now de-rigueur infusion of the Coca~Cola, a concoction she clearly is used to, we made our excuses and took our leave. We left Lodge struggling not only with the luncheon bill, but with his new paragon of virtue; an inebriated Mabel and her loud, remorseless and unstoppable self praise, much to his chagrin.

As we made our way into the foyer of the Criterion Restaurant, Jack stopped me. He then looked at me with concern in his eyes.

"Theo, my old friend, whatever Loge has gotten himself into? I suggest we distance ourselves from Mabel and her new found rôle of being the *Third Grace* and that wretched Choral Anthem Symphony. The reason being Theo, I entertain grave misgivings about Loge's new venture. And aside of which, we are supposed to be acclaimed Vaudeville artistes and not itinerant extras to a choral oratorio or philharmonic concert or adjunct to any other pantomime which

might erupt unexpectedly – on stage – or indeed off
it!"

Jack knew me well enough after thirty one years to
realize his intuition would not be questioned by me.
Instead, we both walked out quietly into the yellow,
swirling fog and hailed a passing Brougham and headed
home to relax and rehearse our act. For the next evening
we had our début on the stage at the Empress Music Hall,
wherever that was.

1. Almost certainly alcohol induced
2. Penny Dreadful, a disparaging term implying the book is a cheap
   sensational novel costing one penny to purchase
3. The memorial is of the Angel of Christian Charity based on the Greek
   god Anteros, not Eros
4. Nihilists – those who are by way of being revolutionaries and
   sometime in league with the Futurists when the sworn aims coincide
5. The play, *Vere or the Nihilists*.
6. Pea Soup

Chapter 6

The Café Royal

Our previous meeting with Cinderella at the Oxford Music Hall had been successful and we were looking forward to meeting with her again to agree a stage routine. Jack and I both had some ideas we wished to put to her. But knowing Cinderella's character, I suggested it would be prudent to listen to her first, rather than the both of us bamboozle her with our ideas. Jack agreed with me in this matter.

In the meantime our Landau carriage driven by our liveried coachman had delivered us to the Café Royal. Jack and I entered the foyer of the famous, or rather infamous, Café Royal, the last word in opulence, located conveniently between Soho and Mayfair. Here, it seemed, the English were trying their best to be French, but the only thing French about the place was its interior décor, which was that of French Second Empire in design.

We continued into the main salon and looked around the well-appointed establishment. The place was a wild, eclectic mix of opulence and extravagant, Bohemian tastes, with drawing rooms in one area and a small hall for music in another. Accordingly, it attracted the rich and infamous, intent, at least so it seemed from my observation, on trying to imitate each other.

My first impression of the salon at the Café Royal

formed readily in my mind. The place resembled nothing more than an interesting combination of a scene depicted famously in Manet's painting of the reflections of the brasserie at *the Folies-Bergère*. And, the vision of ambience captured in Toulouse-Lautrec's painting of the *Moulin Rouge*, both complete in their expression of unbridled affluence and obvious ostentatious behavior.

Except perhaps here in London; the atmosphere was altogether more of a restrained English interpretation of European café society, rather like the Criterion Restaurant, albeit with its attendant general indulgence in wild pleasures and verbal recklessness with courtesans.

Members of the aristocracy were easily recognizable; not by their expensive sartorial arrangements, but rather by their arrogance and unbounded confidence. That they knew each other was beyond doubt, that they would come to know others amongst them, was equally so! The English, trying their best to be cosmopolitan. So I seem to remember some person once said. [1]

The salon, as fine an example of any opulently appointed interior one might expect to find in a Viennese konditorei or a Parisian brasserie, comprised walls which were covered in glazed panels with acid etched, intricate designs impressed on to those polished surfaces. They, in turn, reflected a myriad of light cascading down from numerous acetylene gas fuelled crystal chandeliers suspended from various cream-colored stucco ceilings, all of which were finished in an extravagantly ornate raised Baroque design with raised, gilded filigree patterns. The dazzling effect of the crystal chandeliers was to create a sumptuous, brilliant light that illuminated every aspect of this large spacious salon, including reflecting off highly polished carved mahogany timber finishes.

Occasionally, the light sparkled on ornate brass railings

or fittings on various surfaces and augmented the extravagant décor which prevailed throughout the room. The Café Royal was built in the late exuberant Victorian style of architecture that expresses opulence at every opportunity as interpreted through the décor of French Second Empire.

Not one square inch of the salon's walls or ceiling surfaces had escaped the architects' designs for the interior finishes. Very beautiful, but it was as though the Baroque and Victorian styles had collided to create a grandiose, though overpowering ambience, within the spaces afforded by this huge salon.

Various marble columns, reaching up, terminated in arches supporting other ornate stucco ceilings complete with raised tracery designs. Some pilasters, flat columns set flush against the walls, were performing the same rôle in creating a vaulted ceiling decorated with figurines and gold leaf. Statues looked down upon to us as we walked through on a deep-pile red carpet. Heavy, red flocked silk wallpaper lined some of the walls, which intermittently gave way to mirrored panel and highly polished mahogany doors, set in wide door frames leading to other areas of the building, with promises of even more lush splendor within.

At last we threw open two massive double-leaf doors, which were clad in varnished walnut, that gave us entry into a sumptuous salon proper, the tables in which were covered with purple *Fior Di Pesco Classico*, the only marble on which to place one's drink in style. We also noticed a very well appointed bar. Ranged upon this marble bar were huge gasogenes dispensing aërated water on an almost industrial scale. Competing for space on a long bar, were large, bronze candelabras with bundles of lit candles giving out myriad points of light. The whole effect was of dazzling opulence. Again this salon itself had not escaped the designer's meticulous attention.

Suspended from the high, white, ornate stucco ceiling were acetylene-fuelled crystal chandeliers, radiating out a powerfully brilliant light, which illuminated the whole of the salon. Laid out on the floor was a purple silk, broadloom carpet with gold stars woven into its pattern, and upon it were large sofas covered in a deep red moiré silk. Next to each sofa, very much in evidence, were ubiquitous limestone jardinières supporting palm trees, rising out of polished glazed green urns. The whole place had an ambience of luxury, where money was not a real impediment but imperial splendor was!

Various surfaces and walls were decorated with ornate carvings. There were statues, bronze or nickel metal fixtures, including window and door frames, emblems and signage. Red, green and purple velvet curtains covered the various windows to the outside world that most patrons were eager to forget. All created a sense of magnificent Victorian red plush ambience of the vernacular type so beloved by the English, adding to the general ostentatious paraphernalia ranged around the room all designed to create an impossible ideal of grandeur.

Huge panels of mirrors, the sides of which were supported by gilded Caryatids, adorned the walls, and it was from such looking glasses that patrons refined their reflected image, but also through such reflections persons espied one another. Whilst Jack, with keener eyesight, surveyed the spacious room for Cinderella, I took the opportunity to look around and absorb the opulent and luxuriant appointments which comprised fantasies of gilded ostentatious ornamentation and opulence.

The salon, I noticed, was also filled with hopeful femme fatales in the making, mingling with actors of no great acclaim. The actors in turn were imitating aristocrats. The same aristocrats, one could detect, wished to be taken for jockeys. Demi-mondaines were dressed in the fashionable garb of bi-cycling costumes, sporting white and black vertically striped shirts. Gliding amongst these characters, with the ease of Proteus, were the seasoned blackmailers, with their breast pockets bulging with evidence of compromising indiscretions.

The Café Royal, though undoubtedly impressive, looked like an anæmic version of the *Folies-Bergère* captured by Manet in his painting of the same name. There was also that pervasive and distinctive sound of various glasses being continually replaced on white *Carrara* and *Fior Di Pesco Classic* marble table tops, creating a crescendo of clinking sounds, as though a cascade of diamonds were ricocheting off those marble surfaces.

Several Bohemian painters and writers were sipping away at their absinthe in the vain hope of achieving oblivion just before penury was reached. We made our way gradually through the salon, looking for Cinderella. At last we located her sitting at a red damask covered oval table in an alcove. She rose to greet us. We shook hands again and sat down and in so doing, I felt as if we were on the threshold of eternity. Having filled our fluted glasses with champagne Cinderella sat back and looked expectantly at us. Jack started in.

He explained why we had abandoned Judd, our over confident supercilious ventriloquist's dummy, as not being relevant to our stage act in London. Also he explained that we did not wish to be involved with the Choral Anthem Symphony any longer, since we felt it was at variance to our personalities and not really applicable to our established Vaudeville act and expectations in London.

"We are Vaudeville artistes Cinderella," stated Jack, categorically, "and not some innocuous adjunct to some highfaluting choral symphony or oratorio-based pantomime!"

I nodded my head at suitable intervals to indicate that Jack was speaking on my behalf too.

Within minutes he had outlined a routine we had put together previously and presented it to Cinderella. She endorsed it immediately, but insisted that she would go on to present her version of Judd, the ventriloquist's dummy, but portrayed as Marmaduke.

"Go ahead," said Jack, "be our guest."

"Good," replied Cinderella, "the sooner we get our act together, the quicker we can take an unsuspecting London audience by storm and sweep all before us."

"Where have I heard those words before," I conjectured.

"From Loge!" said Jack.

1.   Oscar Wilde

Chapter 7

The Charing Cross Theater

Our meeting with Cinderella in the infamous Café Royal proved to be extremely useful and productive. During our discussions we had resolved a few concerns and doubts. We even managed to agree a stage routine we felt confident would benefit all three of us. As for myself, for the first time since arriving in London a few weeks previously, I actually thought that we had made the right decision in hooking up with a seasoned performer in Cinderella and that we were engaging with destiny. In the meantime, we were intent on attending a matinée at the Charing Cross Theater, since we knew an old friend of ours, Elizabeth Firth, from New Jersey, would be performing there that afternoon. Jack, is from Jersey City, on the other side of the Hudson River, west of metropolitan New York, and knew her quite well. She was of course, for a while the substitute soprano in the *Three Graces*, following the untimely murder of Bella Elmore, at the hands of her loving husband, the good Doctor Crippen.

"Well Theo, that is one deal we have managed to secure without the intervention of Loge or being guided by him," said Jack, whilst we were standing outside the Café Royal in the Regent's Street waiting for a cab.

Presently a Brougham four-wheeler carriage did come clattering out of the fog towards us. Jack hailed it.

"Charing Cross Theater, and step on it," he said,

"I agree with you Jack," I replied.

"What, stepping on it?" retorted Jack.

"No, I mean your comments about securing a deal with Cinderella without the intervention of Lodge," I answered.

"And something else Theo," continued Jack, "I feel that we have turned a corner, in that we have gotten somewhere at last that reflects our innate abilities. It is like the old days back home in New York where we did not have agents, impresarios or whatever getting in the way. We organized ourselves, just you and I. We did what we thought was right and profitable. I really do now feel as if we are back in control of our own destiny, for better or for worse."

"We have a lot to be grateful to Lodge for," I replied, "given what he has done for us, especially the influential people he has introduced us to. But, I do recall what you said to him when we were just bemoaning our fate at the bar on North Michigan Avenue in Chicago, as a result of being forced off the stage at the Majestic Theater by hecklers and Nihilists. On that memorable occasion, I remembered a suave looking person wearing a black silk coat with a collar of luxuriant Astrakhan fur and black silk top hat approached us at the bar. He then introduced himself to us."

"'The name is Lodge, Michael W. Lodge,' came his resounding reply to your inquiry. He then handed to each of us, one of his expensive and obviously ostentatious *cartes de visites*, [1] upon which was his daguerreotype image and title.

'My close acquaintances however do call me *Loge*,' he had told us. Apparently, this nick-name was based on a rather venal character in Wagner's opera, '*Das Rheingold*,' from his cycle of four operas called, '*Der Ring Des Nebulous*'[2] as Lodge described the last word.

But at the time Jack we both of us were impressed with this Michael W. Lodge and he did seem affable enough, though he was obviously English, with all the mannerisms and affectations which attend that lot. He was dressed smartly and wore spats over his highly varnished black patent leather boots. His silk necktie was ostentation, being the color of pale mauve. But more importantly Jack, that he was quite obviously well-to do was not in any doubt here and, more importantly, his liberal purse at the bar showed no signs of fatigue.

And Jack, his generosity continued unabated and it was only after the fifth round of drinks that he told us that, having seen our double act which he thought to be successful, he, as an impresario, wanted to put us both into London Music Halls. But it was your blunt reply to Lodge which I still find humorous even now. What did you say to him Jack?"

"I replied that we are not interested in your offer *Loge*, or whatever your nick-name is. We have been managing ourselves successfully for over thirty years. You, Loge, yourself said to us that you knew us to be a successful double act, so tell me, why is it that we should need you?"

We both of us allowed ourselves a giggle.

"But the question still stands Theo, why is it that we should need him?" asked Jack, as we continued down the Regent's Street, with Vigo House looming up out of the fog.

"I also recall too what Lodge had to say about this odd looking building we are approaching," I said to Jack, pointing with my cane at a building just visible in the fog.

We all remember what odd pastimes happened there, especially, the peculiar activities which went on inside at night, that were unchecked by the owner of the building.

Vigo House, Regent's Street

Indeed Jack and I were vaguely aware of the story when it was reported in various newspapers including the *New York Times* some time back. I recall the whole of polite society was shocked to the core, not only in London, but America too, at the revelation of the bizarre and peculiar practices which took place in the circular domed structure on the roof of this building at night.

Even then, just looking at the building, it retained a peculiar aspect in its presentation to the street, albeit a fog-bound street. The designs in the façade to this building, from what I could make out through fog, were based on a Neo-Classical motive with strong references to a repressive monumental style, expressed in the building's design and especially in the entablature, progressing upward from the roof line architrave. Indeed, there were features of a masked human face in the façade of this edifice, extenuated by the horizontal deep recessed openings cut into the building's upper section.

It was this pertinent fact, that of the building resembling a human face, which attracted several individuals to it at night. They would meet, on an all too regular basis, in the dome, located on the roof, so various newspapers alleged. And then commit the most bizarre of practices or outré diversions, rather than appreciate the intricacies of the designs in the façade of the building and its innate serious architecture!

Our progress in the fog was slow despite Jack's original injunction to our Brougham four-wheeler carriage coachman. So to pass the time away I read from my programme about the Charing Cross Theater, in which our friend, Elizabeth Firth, is to perform.

"Listen to this Jack, it is about the Music Hall we are headed to. The original building, in King William IV[th.] Street, Charing Cross in which Toole's Theater is housed, started out as a Chapel for the Oratorians, whoever they were. Later the building was converted, by a certain impresario, name of William S. Woodin, into the Polygraphic Hall. In 1869 the Polygraphic Hall was rebuilt and named the Charing Cross Theater. A few years later in 1876 it was again rebuilt to the designs of the famous Music Hall architect, Thomas Verity for Alexander Henderson who at the time was the proprietor and who called it the Folly Theater. In 1879 a certain John Laurence Toole bought the Music Hall and later in 1882 named it for himself, calling it Toole's Theater.

Later, after extensive rebuilding it reverted to the earlier name of the Charing Cross Theater. As with all Music Halls, the attendant risk of fire was ever present and therefore approaches to the auditorium and staircases were of stone which led from two fireproof entrances, one of which gave access to the Dress Circle and the stalls; the other to the upper boxes or pit areas, with other doors and stairs provided in case of the need to evacuate the Music Hall if necessary.

As expected the interior of the place was in keeping with most West End Music Halls in general with a combination of extravagant décor and ostentatious opulence, designed invariably to impress or at least lend verisimilitude to the establishment. In particular the proscenium arch framing the stage held suspended cloth drapery instead of the usual painted on type and complemented by allegorical illustrations of the serious and comic muses. An ornamental dome, finished in white, dominates the auditorium and gold with light tints emphasising raised filigree designs in the stucco work by Signor Emilio Marolda. The seating is covered in a swathe of scarlet velvet upholstery punctuated by gleaming brass railing.

Your dame, that Elizabeth Firth, is in good company this afternoon," I said, pointing to my handbill listing the artistes appearing at the Charing Cross Theater.

"I look forward to hearing her Theo, that is, provided we get through this acrid fog," said Jack.

"Little Tich is up there too, doing his turns with his outsized boots. So is Nellie Power [3] with her ever popular impressions of the impresario and manager George Leybourne," I said to Jack.

"I quite like Nellie Power. Especially since we have met with Leybourne [4] in the Colony Room Club and therefore can appreciate her successful imitation of him and his immediately observable mannerisms. The audiences too adored her particularly when she would satirize dandies, expressing them in a series of impudent acts and songs including, 'La-di-la,'" retorted Jack, with a smile.

"But this did allow Nellie Power to progress from pantomime up through to the Vaudeville Music Hall in the Strand playing Burlesque rôles. Returning to pantomime in 1881 she played the title rôle in, 'Sinbad the Sailor,' at Drury Lane opposite Vesta Tilley who played Captain Tralala," I replied.

"Ironically I remember Loge telling us that it was Nellie Power, not Marie Lloyd, who was the original singer of the ballad, 'The Boy I Love is up in the Gallery,' which was written for her by George Ware," Jack informed me.

"That is something I did not know," I admitted,

"I see Irène Bordoni, out of Paris, France," said Jack, looking at my hand bill, "is an accomplished chanteuse who I think from memory débuted in the chorus at the Théâtre des Variétés in Paris. When she came to New York, we saw her in various Vaudeville theaters; often appearing on the same bill at different Music Halls in New York. Though I must confess I thought she had joined the Orpheum Circuit appearing with that accompanying pianist of hers, Melville Ellis."

"Speaking of Vesta Tilley I see she is making an

appearance the Charing Cross Theater too Jack," I said, "and what I have always found intriguing is the name, Vesta. Even I know that Swan *Vesta* is the name of a brand of phosphorous matches popular in England. And I had always assumed that Vesta Tilley named herself after that brand to imply her character as being fiery, as in firebrand..." I said.

"Well, I guess she is a bit of a firebrand," interrupted Jack.

"Indeed I believe she is known as the Goddess of Fire, principally because of her being associated with Swan Vesta matches I was therefore amused and surprised to be informed by Lodge some time ago, that in fact Tilley name herself after the Roman goddess of the hearth in addition to whose temple was tended by six virgins, six *vestal* virgins!" I said.

"Surely she should be known as the *God* of Fire or Roman *God* of the hearth! Given the fact she is more than delighted to perform in men's clothing, for which she has an insatiable penchant. She too will be in good company for I can see on your hand bill that Ray Bourbon, the acclaimed female impersonator, is also making his presence on the stage. Will there be, I asked myself, enough room on the stage to accommodate these divas or dilettantes," asked Jack with a smirk on his face.

"Do tell me Theo," said Jack, "you are a hero-type. If one imitates a person, for example, a person who is well known in Music Hall circles, such as George Leybourne obviously is, could that act of imitating him be considered defamatory?"

"If in that act of imitating him," I replied, "you knowingly parody or traduce or make him out to be something he is not, then yes, I guess you could be cited for defamation. I think the act of defaming someone is not limited to doing so in writing or verbally. It can be done in a drawing, a cartoon. Therefore it must be so in acting, if one were to imitate a well-known person, such as Leybourne, as you have suggested. And one portrayed him as an imbecile, incompetent or dishonest, so that people believed I was expressing a true representation of his character, then yes I would say that would be defamation, certainly back home in America. Why do you ask Jack?"

"No reason especially, other than the fact has just occurred to me that a lot of Music Hall artistes make a living out of impersonating not just one class of people. For example, Vesta Tilley impersonates soldiers, judges or sailors. But some artistes such as Nellie Power will actually impersonate a real person, in this case the impresario George Leybourne, or at least doing impressions of him," Jack answered.

"May be that is why he is called an impresario; because people do impressions of him!" I conjectured.

We both fell into silence, probably as a result of my impromptu witticism. I looked out from our Brougham to determine just where we were in our journey. I noticed to my left that we had just passed the Criterion Theater, meaning we had only gotten to the Regent's Circus [5] and that we had some distance to go before reaching our destination at Charing Cross. I consulted my steel case pocket watch.

At length we traversed down the Haymarket and turned left into a narrow lane, name of Orange Street. Eventually we arrived at the Charing Cross Theater, and having gotten our tickets, marched straight into the auditorium just as the curtain was coming down on the first act. I asked my neighbor sitting next to me in the Dress Circle, what was the act we had just missed.

He turned to me and informed us that it was a singer, an American singer, name of Elizabeth Firth, but that we had not missed very much as she was not all that good. Jack and I decided to abandon our seats to head off to the Crush Bar for a while. As we did the curtain was raised, revealing a rather bumptious Vesta Tilley strutting around the stage in the uniform of a soldier, looking every bit like a belligerent sergeant major.

1. An early prototype of business card
2. Correctly called 'Nibelung' – but a good example of Lodge's affliction with catachresis
3. Nellie Power died 1887
4. Leybourne died in 1884
5. Correct name for Piccadilly Circus

Chapter 8

The St. Pancras Hotel

Our visit to the Charing Cross Theater to see an old friend of ours, Elizabeth Firth from New Jersey, performing at a matinée there, was effectively a waste of time, though we did see other acts. We had gotten there too late to see her perform, due to the vicissitudes of the fog which continues to hold London in its grip ever since Jack and I arrived some several weeks previously and still shows no sign of dissipating. It can be an inconvenience and a considerable encumbrance, and that day it certainly was and irritatingly so.

The following morning I rose early from my slumbers and decided that rather than stay in my bedroom, I would head off down to the Grand Dining Room for break-fast and perhaps peruse the newspapers. However, I found myself looking through the stone framed quatre-foiled window reveal looking out into the swirling fog, the same fog which had incommoded us the day before en-route to the Charing Cross Theater. Would it ever lift? I wondered.

I got to thinking about this accursed fog. Indeed Lodge had told me only a few days before never to expect the fog, to lift or disperse. It could descend in a couple of hours and it could equally disperse in as many. Or, more alarmingly; it could last for months. Lodge then

99

proceeded to describe in graphic detail aspects of the fog and one such instance of its lasting for several months!

Fog is an attendant feature of cold and damp low lying areas, Lodge had informed me, 'especially in the proximity of water. London is laid out in the flat alluvial valley of the River Thames, and is subject to intermittent periods of fog, light or dense. What makes the London fog unbearable, long-lasting and capable of killing people, is the fact that it mixes with the soot and smoke from countless chimneys ranged across England's huge metropolis, the largest on earth.

The acridity is due to those thousands of coal and wood burning chimneys ranged around London. The smoke from these chimneys is infused into the fog, which in the obvious absence of wind to disperse the fumes, lingers in the aëther. Essentially one is breathing in to one's lungs the smoke and fumes from burning coal and wood. In addition to the acridity getting into one's lungs, it causes severe irritation to one's eyes and results in untold misery.

And, accordingly, it is this combination that makes it unpleasant at best or deadly at worst. It can irritate the eyes mercilessly and infect the lungs with dreadful effects. Dense fog can often a mild claustrophobic feeling of being trapped, enclosed or unable to escape in people of a nervous disposition; escape quite into what, one does not know, but there it is.

One instance of a very bad fog, which lasted for some time, was the one from November 1879 to March 1880. During that dreadful period, several hundreds of persons lost their lives and a dense London fog got a new name as a result. [1]

But, do not be too despondent; some of our greatest poets have immortalized its atmospheric and inherent

mysterious romanticism! Lodge had once informed me.
  He then, quoted verbatim, to my surprise, from Oscar
Wilde's fog-praising poems one of which was called,
Symphony In Yellow and the other; *Impression du Matin.*

Symphony In Yellow.

An omnibus across the bridge
Crawls like a yellow butterfly,
And, here and there a passer-by
Shows like a little restless midge.

Big barges full of yellow hay
Are moored against the shadowy wharf,
And, like a yellow silken scarf,
The thick fog hangs along the quay.

The yellow leaves begin to fade
And flutter from the temple elms,
And at my feet the pale green Thames
Lies like a rod of rippled jade.

Impression du Matin.

The Thames nocturne of blue and gold
Changed to a harmony in grey;
A barge with ochre-coloured hay
Dropt from the wharf: and chill and cold.

The yellow fog came creeping down
The bridges, till the houses' walls
Seemed changed to shadows, and St. Paul's
Loomed like a bubble o'er the town.

Then suddenly arose the clang
Of waking life; the streets were stirred
With country wagons; and a bird
Flew to the glistening roofs and sang.

But one pale woman all alone,
The daylight kissing her wan hair,
Loitered beneath the gas lamps' flare,
With lips of flame and heart of stone.

"Atmospheric and mysterious romanticism! The fog would appear to be a pervasive harbinger of misery and discomfort, irrespective of its *crawling like a yellow butterfly,"* at the time, were the only words I could summon up and with which to reply to Lodge's poetic rendition of the fog.

I came out of my reverie of the fog and concentrated on getting ready to go down to the Grand Dining Room to take break-fast. It then suddenly occurred to me that whilst Jack and I had been staying at the St. Pancras Hotel, over the few weeks past, we had never actually ventured beyond certain corridors leading to the upper floors of the hotel.

Since I had some time before my scheduled meeting with Jack at the break-fast table, I decided not to take the hydraulic Ascending Room 2 to the ground floor, but instead to wander around the building. I left my room and stepped in to a thick red Axminster carpeted corridor, the panels of which were decorated in cream colored paint with exquisitely gilded raised filigree patterns to the wall surfaces, creating a sumptuous feel of opulence and extravagance, for which this hotel is justly famous. Along the corridor at regular intervals were red damask upholstered sofas.

Despite this evident beauty, I ambled along the corridor and made my way down a curved side staircase to the floor below. In so doing I past two chambermaids, bearing vessels of hot water and clean linen. I then found myself in a wide gallery I had no idea existed.

This place is full of hidden treasures, I thought to myself. It was difficult to assimilate. It was as though one had encountered something new in one's life and had not the experience to fully appreciate or understand its significance. This hotel clearly remains a magnificent structure to ostentatious Neo-Gothic excess, the vernacular of which was a very English trait. However, nothing could have prepared me for the sheer vision of beauty emanating from the gallery's lavish décor or opulence, including murals, which adorned the surfaces of the walls, beneath several bright and glittering acetylene-fuelled crystal chandeliers tinkling with cut glass radiating their myriads of light.

I made my stately progress through this gallery and its decorative extravagance, disturbed by no other soul. Indeed I had the place to myself, and was thus able to admire the pervasive beauty of the gallery in splendid solitude. The interior décor was such that it reflected that understated beauty which is so often the hall mark of a confident and high level of finish creating an elegance of appointment so evident throughout.

Eventually I made my way to the end of the gallery which continued on to the impressive double-winged cantilevered Grand Staircase, which I knew progressed dramatically from the foyer up to the vaulted decorated ceilings of the fifth floor of the hotel.

I made my way down this ornate Grand Staircase to the foyer, the walls of which were covered with maroon colored silk flocked wallpaper, punctuated with golden

St Pancras Hotel

fleur de lys. Also on display, were several wall-mounted, gilt-framed, elaborate murals, including one I recognized by Thomas Wallis Hay, impressed into the plasterwork with which some of the walls were lined. The ubiquitous indoor palm trees rising out of large green glazed urns placed on top of limestone jardinières were, of course, being in England, very much in evidence.

The spacious feeling of the hotel was due to the method of its construction. I recalled talking to one of the bar-tenders in the well appointed bar here in the hotel. He informed me then, that the hotel was built on to an iron frame, quite an innovation at the time, and which allowed the creator of the building, Sir Giles Gilbert Scott, to form large rooms and span spacious openings within the structure.

I have always been impressed with the interior appointment of this hotel, which reflects an understated elegance, normally associated with the early Victorians, especially during their embrace of Italianate styles. The ground floor salon and Grand Dining Room were spacious and yet intimate and together demonstrated quite unequivocally that the late Victorians were able to create naturally pleasing interiors devoid of any clumsiness one might easily associate with Neo-Gothic interiors.

I could appreciate this fact fully, for there was a sense of space which was all pervasive within the building. Neo-Gothic buildings can by their very style and design be sometimes gloomy places confined by evident masonry such as columns, walls or arches. Neo-Gothic structures such as Hilldrop House next to vast expanses

Hilldrop House, Hampstead

of Hampstead Heath in which we stayed with Bella Elmore and the murderous Doctor Crippen, can be typical of this style.

The St. Pancras Hotel is very much the exception, as it is light, airy and very spacious. The whole establishment remains a delightful example of High Victorian architecture one would normally associate with a country mansion rather than with a hotel, but irrespective of this fact the building still retains an innate and intimate romantic charm.

This fact is almost certainly as a result of it exterior Romantic mannerism, the style of which is expressed in the architecture of the hotel and the outline of the building only augments this appeal, complete with barley-twist chimneys, quatre-foil stone-framed arched windows, tile roofs with intricate raised apex designs, embellished gable ends and a decorated archway all dominated by a substantial clock tower, which even the all-pervasive fog appeared powerless to shroud in its clammy acrid grip.

I had by now somewhat lost my sense of time and realized, having consulted my steel case pocket watch, that it was just a few minutes to eight o' clock. I accordingly, made my way to the Grand Dining Room to join Jack for break-fast.

1. The *London Particular* - as thick as pea soup.
2. Hydraulically operated elevator carriage

Chapter 9

The Metropolitan Music Hall

As I entered the Grand Dining Room through the large double-leaf doors, which comprised exquisite walnut panelling, a thought crossed my mind. Typically, the name Grand Dining Room, in which I was to take break-fast, was in fact highly appropriate and in keeping with the hotel's general elegant appointment, as I had experienced earlier whilst walking about the upper floors of the building. For this was a room of such generous and expansive proportions that it could, with ease, subjugate any person standing within its precinct. The room was quite impressive, the proportions of which were based not on a regular rectilinear shape, but on a curved style. One curved wall, that overlooked the front of the hotel, comprised a series of Gothic pointed quater-foil arches, creating stone window reveals and into which were set large windows at least twenty feet in height. However, due to the fog, no clear vision through them was possible and the windows merely took on the appearance of white opaqueness with only a mere discernible hint of the occasional movement of shadows scuttling by outside.

I stopped and looked about the Grand Dining Room. Then I saw Jack sitting at the far end of the room.

"Good morning Jack, did you sleep well?" I asked, on gaining his table.

"Not really. I woke up early and so had some American newspapers brought up to my room and just sat on the bed reading various reports, trying to catch up with the news back home in the States. Nothing much seems to have happened in our absence other than the fact they have indicted the murderous Doctor Howard Holmes in Chicago," replied Jack, handing me the *Chicago Tribune*, "I have brought them down for you to read."

Though this newspaper was obviously a few days old, it did have as its banner headline the report that Doctor Holmes had indeed been indicted on numerous counts of first-degree murder.

"Jeez, Theo," said Jack, interrupting my reading, "what is it about us? We find ourselves in the Castle Hotel on West 63rd. Street in the Englewood neighborhood of Chicago, whilst playing the Majestic Theater to eager crowds attending the World's Columbian Exposition in that city. We then discover that the hotel in which we had been staying for several weeks was run by a proprietor who was also a doctor, by the name of Holmes. And, that he was systematically murdering his hotel guests, possibly in excess of two hundred!

"Having survived his attempts on our lives; only then we found ourselves staying as guests in Hilldrop House, next to Hampstead Heath, a house run by another good doctor. Only he was called Crippen and he murdered, in Hilldrop House, Bella Elmore, his wife, Music Hall artistes and one of Loge's *Three Graces!* And, furthermore, Theo, both good doctors attended the University of Michigan Medical School in the county capital city of Ann Harbor. And, I will bet they must both have been contemporaries of each other, whilst reading medicine at that University.

"I will bet they concocted their dastardly plan whilst

reading for their medical degrees. You can imagine the scenario Theo; Crippen to Holmes; 'you go to Chicago and bump off a few hotel guests including Vaudeville artistes and I will go to London and knock off Music Hall artistes there!'" said Jack.

"There is an even more disturbing link," I replied, "than that of both doctors attending the University of Michigan Medical School. And, it is the fact that you and I are the causational link, a common link, as it were, between the two, in that we both were potential victims of either doctor. After all we stayed in Holmes's Castle Hotel in Chicago and at Crippen's house at Hampstead!"

I then just realized the enormity of what I had just said. I did not feel too good. Jack was engrossed with his Brätwürst on rye bread, so I reverted to the *Chicago Tribune* and continued reading the report in the paper. Our experiences in that Castle Hotel, whilst attending the Chicago Columbian Exposition, still brought shivers down my spine just thinking about it. The report was pretty clear and unambiguous in describing just what

World's Columbian Exposition – Ticket

this hotel proprietor had gotten up to whilst running his hotel.

He was arraigned, not as Doctor Henry Howard Holmes, but under his real name of Herman Webster Mudgett, a bigamist no less, out of Philadelphia. The fact that he was a doctor out of Michigan University Medical School was irrelevant. The report went on to inform readers that apparently the police had come across a villain who had tipped them off about the murderous activities of a hotel proprietor, called Mudgett, in the Englewood district of the Chicago.

According to this report I was reading, both Jack and I were certainly in constant danger of being done away with, by any number of means at Mudgett's disposal. His Castle Hotel on W. 63rd. Street was situated less than two miles away from the site of the World's Columbian Exposition, which is due east and was convenient to many visitors to Chicago. Therefore, he may have taken in an unknown number of victims, most of whom were women.

Incredibly, some of his victims were gassed whilst locked in soundproof chambers. Other victims were instead left to suffocate in a huge soundproof bank vault located in the basement, conveniently adjacent to a crematorium he had especially constructed. Nor was he above cremating his victims in two giant gas furnaces he had built in an outhouse next to the basement of the main hotel building.

We later learned that the heat from these crematorium ovens was used to provide central heat throughout the hotel! Nor indeed, was he hesitant in placing their corpses in lime pits in addition to acid baths. It was later discovered that he had a fully operational stretching rack! Poisons were a favorite of the good doctor, and often administered to recalcitrant hotel guests, irrespective of resistance, age or gender.

That the good Doctor Holmes built the hotel specifically with the intention of committing multiple murders in mind could never be doubted! He used several constructors, all at different times, and working on just a part of the building. So no one person, except him, had any idea of the overall plan or layout of the Castle Hotel, or indeed its intended murderous purpose.

The most unnerving aspect of what Holmes had gotten up to was the actual construction of the hotel. In particular, its peculiar layout produced, as it were, the architecture of death. The building had over one hundred rooms, with most of them being without windows! Some of the hotel rooms were fitted with doors that only opened on to brick walls. Other doors could only be opened from the outside the room and not from within! Hallways were built at an odd angle and stairways leading to nowhere.

And the general peculiar construction together with a labyrinthine maze of corridors and hallways was inordinately complicated for no apparent reason. The building did not appear to me to be constructed in the usual and normal way one would expect a large house or hotel to be built.

I remember our good Doctor Holmes was always quick to point out to curious guests that the eccentric nature of the building added a kind of Victorian charm to the place.

There was a strong pervasive musty odor that occasionally drifted down hallways. In retrospect I realized that it was the smell of death creeping down the corridors. At the time on discovering exactly what was happening in that hotel of death, I was unable to conceal the sheer horror and revulsion which I felt. Especially when I realized that I had been surrounded by corpses on the other side of the walls of my hotel room or indeed on the floor above my ceiling and in the room below mine.

"My God Jack, we could have been nothing more than toast or ashes at the time," I said, unable to contain the enormity of my abject horror at what I had just re-read about our murderous hotel proprietor.

I remembered the *New York Times* reported at the time that Holmes had confessed to at least twenty-seven other murders in the hotel though the police believed the figure could be in excess of two hundred!

I handed the newspaper back to Jack and looked at the white linen tablecloth and decided that I did not now much feel like taking break-fast, so restricted myself to black Santiago coffee. For some reason reading about serial murders and the distinct possibility of my being one of the victims, did not, ironically, stimulate my appetite. All this, I thought, because of the World's Columbian Exposition being held in Chicago.

"Theo, since we are scheduled to perform at the Empress Music Hall later today and meet with Loge there, do try and eat something now whilst it is in front of you. We neither of us got murdered, either at the Castle Hotel in Chicago or Crippen's house here in London. If there is a place where we might possibly meet a violent end, I would suggest that place to be Loge's house in the Bergen Avenue, either because of our having eaten rotted food there or at the murderous hands of the demented, if loquacious Aloysius, Loge's man-servant," said Jack.

"Just where is this Empress Music Hall Jack?" I inquired, with a smile playing on my lips.

"It is at a place called Earl's Court, a mile or so from

the Royal Aquarium & Winter Garden in Victoria," Jack informed me.

I looked at the menu.

"And, Loge did mention last night," continued Jack, "that the best way to get there would be to ride the metropolitan urban rail road to it."

"If Lodge has suggested it; that is good enough for me," I replied, whilst ordering from the menu.

Jack looking at me in response, merely shrugged his shoulders and returned to his break-fast of Brätwürst on rye.

"Jack, that urban rail road Lodge suggested we take to Earl's Court, from my recollection of Bäedeker's Guide to London I think, goes to a station opposite the Metropolitan Music Hall. Remember the place with the bar overlooking the auditorium protected by a glazed screen?" I said.

"I do indeed Theo," replied Jack, "and also the manager, a fellow called Goss, who suggested we look him up with a view to performing there."

"Do you think it would be a good idea to pay Goss a visit en-route to Earl's Court?" I inquired of Jack.

"Absolutely Theo," came his reply.

After we had completed our break-fast and changed, Jack and I met later in the foyer. We did so to hand in our keys to the still truculent and over confident concièrge wearing his black morning-coat and black top hat with blue rosette affixed to the side.

In response to a polite inquiry from Jack, the concièrge, an arrogant and sarcastic individual at the best of times, merely reached below his desk and produced a battered copy of Bäedeker's Guide to London.

"To Earl's Court you wish to go? My advice is to ride the urban rail road to it," and then promptly marched off to another part of the reception abandoning us!

Under the circumstances, that encounter with the rather over confident, black morning-coated concièrge, within the confines of his undoubted domain, the reception area in the foyer of the St. Pancras Hotel, was not too bad an experience, I concluded.

"Jack, as it happens, the advice offered by the concièrge was not entirely erroneous. And from what I could make out of this urban rail road map it seems the quickest way to the Edgware Road Station and on to Earl's Court is to take a train of the Metropolitan Circle urban rail road. We can avail ourselves of it from below this very hotel," I said with a flourish.

Minutes later, we had left the comfortable and opulent surroundings of our hotel and were enveloped in swirls of the acrid fog that showed no signs of dissipating. Eventually we managed to locate the entrance to what was, I believed, the rail road station from which a train of the Metropolitan Circle urban rail road departed to the Edgware Road and on to Earl's Court stations. After some uncalled for discourtesy whilst purchasing our tickets, we made our way down to two parallel rail road platforms.

A signboard indicated upon which platform we should wait for a train of the Metropolitan Circle urban rail road. It was whilst we were waiting upon the platform I noticed that not one square inch had escaped the attention of the advertiser. Advertisement posters of every description were plastered on any available surface, including those of rail road equipment and buildings. This plethora of gaudy advertisements made it difficult to search for useful rail road information, and indeed, almost impossible to achieve.

Irrespective of this vexation, Jack and I had our attention arrested by a series of the most blatant and preposterous advertisements, affixed to the wall opposite the platform. The kind of which one could never be allowed to displayed in New York, for fear of being indicted. One in particular was difficult to accept as being serious in its claims!

Presently, the noise of a locomotive hauling the carriages of the Metropolitan Circle urban rail road was heard and people looked up the platform in anticipation. Moments later, it came thundering down the side of the platform causing a rush of wind which blasted the fog in front of the engine out of the way. As the locomotive, in its purple livery colors, rushed by us, it created an instant sensation of heat upon our faces, and from its smoke stack discharged a cloud of black smuts, notably onto our top-coats.

Finally as the train screeched to a stop, carriage doors were flung open in a reckless way, allowing passengers to alight on to the platform that suddenly seethed with humanity moving in different directions. We attempted to make our way to an open carriage door and after some undignified pushing and determined behavior, by others, succeeded in boarding the train.

We looked about for a seat but found none and were thus compelled to stand. Neither Jack nor I normally use the public urban rail road, but we have found travelling around London by horse drawn carriage an inefficient and slow method especially in dense fog. In this respect the urban rail road is quicker, if nothing else.

With a lurch our train progressed down the side of the platform and then plunged into a tunnel. The noise of the aëther travelling past the outside of the carriage was tremendous and a sense of exhilaration attended my sensibilities. Presently Jack spoke to me over the noise.

POTTS'S
IMPROVED ARTIFICIAL LEGS,
WITH
GRAY'S IMPROVEMENT

PATRONISED BY
PRINCE ERNEST OF HESSE PHILLIPSTHAL
THE MARQUESS OF ANGLESEY
THE FIRST NOBILITY AND GENTRY AND THE
MOST EMINENT SURGEONS
THROUGHOUT EUROPE, AND ALLOWED BY ALL
TO BE THE PERFECT DESCRIPTION OF
ARTIFICIAL LEG HITHERTO PRODUCED.

THEY ARE MADE SOLELY BY WILLIAM GRAY, OF
10 CHARLES STREET, GROSVENOR SQUARE, LONDON,
APPRENTICE, MANY YEARS MECHANICAL ASSISTANT,
AND NOW SUCCESSOR TO THE INVENTOR, THE LATE
CELEBRATED MR. POTTS, OF CHELSEA.

ALL PERSONS WANTING ARTIFICIAL LEGS
SHOULD COMPARE THEIR MERITS WITH ANY
OTHERS AT PRESENT MADE.

EVERY INFORMATION MAY BE OBTAINED BY APPLYING
AS ABOVE.

AN EXPERIENCED FEMALE PROVIDED
TO ATTEND LADIES

ALL LETTERS MUST BE POST PAID.

"It is as well we are visiting Goss at the Metropolitan Music Hall without the intervention of Loge, especially after that fiasco of an audition at the Oxford Music Hall."

"Possibly; but Jack, more importantly, after we had taken luncheon with Mabel and Lodge at the Criterion, you suggested abandoning them or their Choral Anthem Symphony. Why did you do so?" I inquired.

"Well, I guess to an extent, as we still need Loge to act as impresario for us. But heed my advice Theo, as I remarked at the time; we are Vaudeville, not extras in a Choral Anthem Symphony or what other musical extravaganza Loge has in mind for us, in which to make clowns of ourselves. No Theo, we have to concentrate on our stage careers now that we are playing the Music Halls in London. Hence the reason we are high-tailing it to the Metropolitan Music Hall without the intervention of Loge."

We both fell into silence to marshal our thoughts and think about the implications of what Jack had just said. Jack knew in his heart that I agreed with him. I looked away from him, rather than stare.

Moments later our carriage blasted into Gower Street Metropolitan Station [1] and continued down the side of the platform. The usual chaos attended our arrival. Passengers jostled on to the train and one particular woman pushed by me in order to secure a spare place on the timber crossbench. The peculiar sight of this woman arrested my attention, more so because of the distinctive tawdry manner in which she was dressed.

She wore a purple colored velveteen jerkin with red sleeves, slim blue cross-gartered hose and a large brown falcon's feather in her broad brimmed hat, worn tilted to one side over her ear. Below her head she wore a large fur boa around her neck, clasped with an imitation jewel of olive green chrysoberyl, which I knew turns red when illuminated by artificial lamplight.

Her short hair was auburn and matched the color of her eyes, which were set in a round face of overwhelming anonymity and a vague searching expression. A blank face, ready to be filled with experience, as it were. She looked nervous and agitated as the fingers of one hand caressed the tips of the dove colored carriage glove she wore, whilst her other hand held a 'Penny Dreadful', which seem inordinately popular with those who are compelled to travel around the metropolis by urban rail road.

Her jacket complemented her deep blue dress, underneath which she wore a pair of brown, dulled and scuffed leather high-heeled boots, tied up tightly with black cotton laces. My attention was focused on her hands, which she continuously twitched, as though afflicted with St. Vitus's Dance, rather like Lodge's man-servant Aloysius. However, upon closer examination, I noticed her gloves were made of fine linen, the fingertips of which appeared stained with blue ink.

I reasoned that she was probably in regular contact with one of those new-fangled finger operated mechanical contraptions one reads about, called the 'Improved Patented Typewriting Apparatus', an invention by an American from New York City, named Charles Babbage.[2] I therefore concluded with a betting certainty and confidence that she was, manners apart, one of those women who were prepared to operate such a type-writing device used in the rapid production of documents containing the written word without recourse to the fountainpen.

At length upon arriving at Portland Road Metropolitan Station, [3] she gathered her chattels, got up from the crossbench and left the carriage. She then pushed her way along the platform to her destiny with the Improved Patented Typewriting Apparatus. After an interminable wait at the station, our carriage began to glide effortlessly along the side of the platform and continued on into the tunnel.

I mentioned to Jack the following fact.

"According to the Bäedeker's Guide to London, we should change trains at the next station which I believed to be called Baker Street."

"Baker Street, now, that rings a bell," said Jack, "though for what reason, I cannot immediately recall. But I do associate the street having some importance attached to it, which I was aware of when here in London some years ago during the Fall of 1898."

"Is there a Music Hall located in that street or some other Vaudeville establishment?" I inquired, becoming rather inquisitive myself as to the significance of the street.

Jack knitted his eyebrows and lowered his head as though in deep thought. I looked around the train carriage. Suddenly he lifted his head up.

"I remember now!" said Jack, shouting in my ear; "I

Portland Road Metropolitan Station

recall the reason why Baker Street stuck in my mind. It was the home of a famous person, whose name eludes me."

Jack looked into the middle distance, in order to avoid distraction and search his memory. Moments later he resumed his gaze at me.

"I have it!" he announced with a flourish.

"Well who was the famous resident of Baker Street?" I inquired out of curiosity based on Jack's initial comment.

"It was Theo, a famous person and linked forever in the annals of crime for in the collection, are displayed some of the most notorious villains who ever walked abroad this metropolis. That person continues to exhibit those grotesque wax mannequins in rooms, located in a bazaar at number 55 Baker Street!" stated Jack.

"That person, who is that person?" I asked.

"Tussauds," answered Jack, "that person is Madame Tussaud and her chamber of wax mannequins which can be viewed, for a fee, by the public, should one really feel compelled to do so!"

"Oh, I thought you were alluding to the famous Pinkerton detective who resided at number 221 Baker Street, or at least according to Lodge he did."

I continued looking around the carriage, but it was whilst I was concluding my observation brought on by abject boredom riding the train, that Jack nudged me and nodded to the window of the carriage

Suddenly the carriage began slowing down and the syncopated clicking of the steel wheels pounding the iron track below decreased in rapidity. Presently, from our carriage windows, we saw two platforms in the station we were approaching. However, our carriage did not proceed to those platforms, but instead veered off to the right as we steamed towards another set of platforms.

221. Baker Street

Moments later we stopped with a screeching sound alongside one of the platforms.

All of a sudden passengers in the carriage, in which we were standing, as if by a hidden signal, rose from their benches and made towards the doors, through which to alight from the carriage. Within moments they were flung open in an abandoned manner and a mass evacuation of the carriage commenced. Jack and I found ourselves in a surge of humanity making its way down the platform.

"Come on Jack, according to the concièrge's copy of Bäedeker's Guide to London, we need to change for a train of the Circle District urban rail road which I believe departs from platform No.1 in this station.

Presently we found ourselves at a loss in Baker Street Station, apparently abandoned by the surging crowd. Again the plethora of gaudy advertisement posters affixed to every available wall surface, made searching for relevant rail road information as to our destination, difficult to find.

"We need to change to a train operating along the Circle District urban rail road and headed for a destination called Wimbledon, a place where I believe the peculiar English sport of cricket is played, but, en-route, the train should call at the Edgware Road Station as well as Earl's Court Station," I said to Jack as we made our way through the various corridors of Baker Street Station in search of the correct platform.

"I think you will find it is the game of rugby that is played at Wimbledon, not cricket," Jack corrected me.

Whatever the sport, eventually we located an obscured notice indicating that it was from platform No.1, the trains of the Circle District urban rail road departed for Wimbledon. Accordingly, we made our way through this main hall of Baker Street Station and over the bridge to

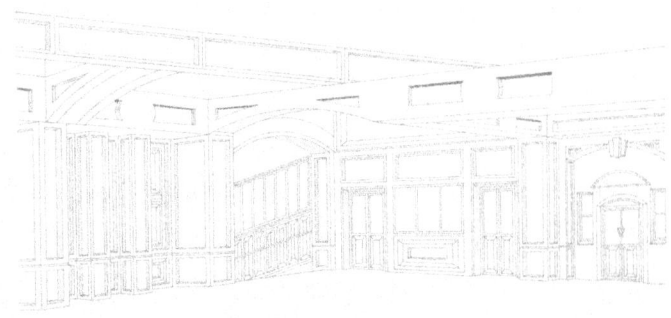

Baker Street Station Main Hall

the platform to await our urban rail road train to Edgware Road Station.

An age went by before a train, in its green livery color, of the Circle District urban rail road came thundering down the permanent way of the rail road tracks alongside the platform, now filled with impatient people. Again, doors were flung open in a careless fashion as a prelude to yet another surge of humanity attempting to invade the train carriages.

Eventually we too clambered into a carriage of the Circle District urban rail road in the full confidence that we had boarded the correct train and headed in the right direction in order to gain our destination at Edgware Road Station.

"In order to increase the seating capacity of the Metropolitan Music Hall to about two thousand, according to the infallible Loge," said Jack, "this Metropolitan Music Hall was rebuilt again 1897 to designs, by the eminent and prolific theater architect Frank Matcham, re-opening its doors on the 22 December."

"Unusually, this Music Hall is actually owned by the impresario Henri Goss, who struck me as being a rather decent and considerate gentlemen," I responded.

Within a minute or so we arrived at the Edgware Road Station, which in comparison to the stations we had traversed through appeared almost deserted, as though a ghost station. We made our way up from the platform and into the Edgware Road. This road was yet another busy thoroughfare of the metropolis, along which seethed almost every type of vehicular conveyance contrived by the ingenuity of man.

However, negotiating our way across this highway was, I remembered from our previous visit, potentially hazardous, especially in the fog, due simply to the sheer amount of traffic lumbering on its way to respective destinations. I noticed too, that the commerce and trade being conducted in this road was not in any way diminished by the presence of the damp and acrid fog swirling about the place in vortexes.

Coal tar gas flames blazed out from large brass lanterns hanging in front of the shops and other street establishments together with coal-burning braziers lining the sidewalk. Eventually we managed to cross this busy carriageway and found ourselves outside the imposing Neo-Classical façade of the Metropolitan Music Hall, which resembled more a dignified classical Greek structure, than a place of lush entertainment.

We made our way in from the road and entered the main foyer, whereupon we were approached by an usher wearing a powder blue tail-coat. Having explained the purpose of our visit, we were escorted up a grand staircase to the *piano-nobile* and asked to wait for Mr. Henri Goss on the landing next to the well-appointed Crush Bar.

Whilst doing so, Jack opened a highly varnished mahogany double-leaf door leading into the ostentatious, but ornate appointment of the auditorium. Inside was

Metropolitan Music Hall

the usual extravagant Victorian scarlet plush one has come to expect in such establishments, and this Metropolitan Music Hall was no exception.

Except here, the designs were based on a late Flemish Renaissance style complete with a magnificent highly decorated ceiling. The interior designs reflected those decorative features we had noticed on the Edgware Road façade of the Music Hall. Apart from the gallery, there was a stage box, one at either side of the proscenium arch, each seating at least fourteen persons.

These boxes were supported by columns in the form a decorative female figurines. James Bookbinder, we were told during our previous visit, created the designs for the lavish and opulent interior. In addition, he may have been responsible for the murals set into the plasterwork of the ceiling alcoves, in which each depicts a scene of jollity; English Merry Making, French Carnival, Spanish Revelry and an exotic Indian Festival.

It was during our first visit here with Lodge, not long before, that I remembered the nearby Crush Bar, which was at least thirty feet in length, and in particular, a timber structure positioned in between the Crush Bar proper and an opening giving out into the auditorium, was a polished elm framed glazed screen.

The purpose of such a structure, I recalled, was to allow patrons at the bar, having vacated the auditorium, in favor of refreshment, to continue to watch or hear the acts on the stage whilst drinking. An innovative and civilized structural contrivance, I thought then and continue to do so now.

At that moment the proprietor and manager of the Metropolitan Music Hall, Mr. Henri Goss came marching up to us with his hand outstretched.

Goss must have read the expression upon my face looking at the elm screen, as he had done during our last visit here.

"As you can imagine gentlemen," reminded Goss, looking at me, "our Crush Bar rarely become very busy, or *crushed*. It was for that underlying reason to avoid the *crush,* as it were, that we decided to build this elm framed glazed partition screen. And in so doing, encourage our guests to drink steadily, but responsibly, throughout the various performances on the stage over a period of time.

By this innovation, our patrons may still see their favorite acts, without the stampede creating a *crush* during intervals. And as you can see, due to our innovative approach, our guests are relaxed and there is no rush imposed upon them! Theo and Jack, as usual, I am pleased to see you both again; and thank you for dropping by."

He then motioned us to follow him to place at the bar and upon gaining it, ordered drinks for us all. Having acquired our drinks, we launched into a discussion about what had become of us since Jack and I last met with Henri Goss and our aspirations for the future, including joining up with Cinderella.

"Where is that impresario to end all impresarios?" inquired Goss.

"Busy coaching his new soprano, Mabel Green, in order that she may be inducted into the Pantheon of his precious *Three Graces,*" Jack replied.

"Mabel Green a soprano, interesting" Goss said this, whilst raising his eyebrows and with a pronounced wry smile on his lips. "So I take it Lodge is still trying to promote that Cholera Anthem Symphony of his?"

We continued to talk further with Henri Goss but at length he concluded with a remark.

"The last time we met," said Goss, "I recall that I made an offer to you both. That if you decided to get involved in the London Music Hall circuit, then I would be happy to book you in to performing here at the Metropolitan Music Hall. When you have sorted out your new stage act with Cinderella, let me have a description of your turn, its length in terms of stage time and any props you would require."

We all shook hands and Goss finished his drink and turned to leave.

"Oh by the way, your joining up with that Cinderella is an excellent move. I looked forward to witnessing your new act with her here whenever you are ready!"

And with that welcome Parthian shot, promptly marched out of his Crush Bar back to his office to run his Metropolitan Music Hall.

Naturally enough we stayed at the bar for a welcomed celebratory drink on hearing our good news from Goss.

"It is a pity that we are performing at the Empress Music Hall later this evening because I really would prefer to stay here and experience the ambience of this Crush Bar as well as view the stage acts through that glazed screen," I informed Jack.

However, as we made our way out of the building, I mentioned to Jack that everybody we spoke to expressed surprise at Lodge's offering Mabel Green the rôle of soprano in his precious *Three Graces*.

Jack did not reply but just looked about him whilst surveying our immediate locality as we crossed the busy, if treacherous, Edgware Road.

Presently we found ourselves back on the platform the Circle District urban rail road awaiting our train to Earl's Court. As usual there was the plethora of advertisements plastered on every available wall space. One outrageous

poster which caught my attention to the extent I motioned Jack to read it. Such were the exaggerated claims contained in its reckless boasts.

I was grateful that a train did eventually arrive and allowed us to continue our journey, which we did through a series of intervening stations as, Praed Street Station,[4] Queens Road Station, [5] Notting Hill Gate Station and then Kensington Station [6] in rapid succession.

"Good," I said to Jack, "we are making good progress; next stop Earl's Court Station.

Our train then steamed into the next station and we prepared to alight from our carriage.

"Theo, what is this?" asked Jack, pointing with his cane to the station nameplate on the platform.

I looked through the carriage window and saw in distinctive lettering the name of the station emblazoned on the platform wall as being Brompton! [7]

In a blind panic we alighted from our carriage and immediately confronted a rail road servant upon the platform. Jack almost demanded of him why it was that this station was called Brompton and not Earl's Court.

The rail road servant dressed in his black velveteen uniform with blue piping viewed Jack with an experienced eye.

"Possibly sir because you are in fact at Brompton Station," he advised," if Earl's Court is where you intend to go then the next train on that platform over the bridge will take you there."

I thanked the servant for his help and followed Jack up the steps and over the bridge, cursing Bäedeker's Guide to London under my breath.

Needless to say a train did arrive and delivered us to Earl's Court Station where we alighted on to a particularly busy platform and made our way at an agonizingly slow

Hall of Machines

pace through a labyrinth of corridors packed with people. At length we gained the steps leading to the upper section of the station and made our way up them into a busy road, albeit a fog-bound roadway.

On the other side of the road was a large Victorian structure constructed of brickwork, iron columns, girders and glazed panels of which the walls and roof were comprised. We walked up a wide and steep flight of steps towards the massive structure, a veritable cathedral of iron columns all stretching up to a steel framed, glazed apex roof.

"This magnificent building, very much resembles the impresasive Hall of Machines in Paris constructed by Gustav Eiffel, which I had visited some years back," I remarked to Jack.

"Surely Theo this cannot be the Empress Music Hall; it looks for too grand for that purpose?" asked Jack.

The building Jack and I continued to approach, was illuminated with large coal gas-fuelled lamps, in the form of clusters of white opaque globes, pouring out their powerful light onto the steps below up which we were climbing.

It was Jack who asked the inevitable question.

"No sir, this is not the Empress Music Hall; this alas is the Earl's Court Exhibition Hall," said a liveried usher in a lugubrious voice reminiscent of our surly concièrge at the St. Pancras Hotel, in answer to Jack's polite inquiry. "The Empress Music Hall, that dubious establishment is farther down this road and on the left hand side."

1. Now Euston Sqaure Metropolitan Station
2. It was Philo Remington
3. Now Great Portland Street Metropolitan Station
4. Now Paddington Underground Station
5. Now Bayswater Underground Station
6. Now Kensington High Street Underground Station
7. Now Gloucester Road Underground Station

Chapter 10

The Empress Music Hall

We did in fact struggle in the all-embracing dense acrid fog to locate the Empress Music Hall, and on two occasions had to defer to complete strangers for directions. Both gave conflicting advice. And, I am certain, that we had walked past one particular building twice. It was almost a case of the blind drunk leading the blind. But at length we found the Empress Music Hall shrouded in the fog.

As we stepped up to the foyer a faded poster arrested our attention, the print on which was smudged due to the dampness of the all-pervasive fog. Both Jack and I stopped as we could just make out the information contained on the poster displayed on the wall next to the main doors of the Empress Music Hall.

Both Jack and I were acquaintances of Fred Roberts, living in Brooklyn, as he does, though originally from London, England. We were a bit dismayed at realizing that he had performed here only five nights ago. We would certainly have attended his performance, since we were resting that particular evening. Roberts is one of the truly clever comedians whom we have the pleasure of knowing. If you tell a humorous anecdote to Roberts. Before you have even completed it. He will take it from you and improve upon it!

EMPRESS MUSIC HALL

LILLIE ROAD, EARL'S COURT, LONDON, SW

PROPRIETOR & MANAGER – MR. IMRE KIRALFY,

'SHE BOLTED WITH

THE BOARDER

TO

CHICAGO'

COMIC SONG & REFRAIN

Written, composed & sung

by the

Lion Comique

Fred^k. Roberts

from

New York

PUBLISHED BY M. WITMARK & SONS, 51 WEST 28TH. STREET

Still despite that disappointment, we were none the less grateful having gained the foyer and to be out of that accursed acrid fog which seems all pervasive; causing as it does irritation to one's eyes, breathing and facial skin.

When our irritated eyes had adjusted to the light in the foyer, we focused on Lodge, resplendent in his mid-night blue colored sheen suit and black silk top hat, in deep conversation with Mabel, his new soprano protégée. Eventually upon seeing us, he immediately disengaged himself from Mabel and looked at his gold Hunter and then at us again.

Lodge was clearly put out by our late arrival and made that clear in his facial expression.

"Blame the rail road, Loge," was Jack's response to Lodge's facial admonishment.

"Here at last! Mabel and I thought that perhaps you might have forgotten our rendezvous. Anyway, the manager is waiting on us. Shall we attend him?" said a phlegmatic Lodge, unabashed by Jack's remark.

He then pointed with his gold-capped ebony cane to a grand brass-railed and red carpeted staircase leading up to the *piano-nobile*. We all of us ascended the stairs and followed Lodge down an ornately decorated corridor, complete with a deep pile red carpeted illuminated by crystal chandeliers suspended from a stucco ceiling impressed with embedded raised gilded filigree designs. As Lodge escorted us along this lush corridor, he pointed out to us some salient facts, no doubt, for our interest, but more for our instruction.

"This Empress Music Hall," said Lodge, "here at Earl's Court, was built for my good friend and fellow impresario Imre Kiralfy, to the designs of the acclaimed architect Allan Collard in 1890. The Music Hall is unique, in that the seating is all on one level, the floor of the hall. The auditorium measuring three hundred seventy feet in width and two hundred twenty feet in length, makes it the largest theater in the metropolis, therefore the Empire and perforce the world.

The auditorium can seat comfortably about five thousand persons, anyone of whom, from any position, will have an uninterrupted view of the stage. The stage, the width of which is a prodigious three hundred seventy feet is easily six times wider than the biggest theaters currently in use in London, and therefore, England. Even the orchestra is hidden out of sight and located behind the proscenium arch fronting the stage.

The Music Hall benefits immensely by the crowds which attend the nearby Earl's Court Exhibition Halls. Often it is de-rigueur to make a visit to some exhibition and then finish the day off by perhaps attending a performance on the stage here.

Another aspect of the place is that the Empress Music Hall is renowned for staging spectacular extravaganzas, such as the immensely successful show, which 1888 started out in New York with Barnum and Bailey, and was called, '*Nero and the Destruction of Rome.*' You might remember it Jack, being from Jersey City," said Lodge.

"I do not," was Jack's considered response.

A moment or two later we arrived at a highly polished elm door with the name Manager, in large brass letters affixed to the raised cruciform creating four distinct recessed door panels.

Lodge tapped quietly and stood back. Immediately a response was heard.

"Come in!"

Lodge gripped the highly polished, fluted brass door handle and turned it. We all followed through after him. All four of us stood before a person who appeared as though he were about to tread the floorboards upon his own stage, for such was his garish and flamboyant attire. He stood at least six feet tall, excluding the black silk top hat on his head. In addition, he wore a black cape with an extravagant silk lining, resembling a blazing wall of fire as it shimmered, very similar to the ostentatious cape that Lodge has a penchant to wear, when he dares to.

"Imre Kiralfy; my good friend," said Lodge, "let me introduce you to my new two protégés in the persons of Vaudeville artistes, Jack Mitchell and Theo Houston, both from New York. Mabel you already know of course, from our earlier meeting, whilst waiting on Jack and Theo to arrive here on time."

These words had a singular effect on the tall person standing up behind his desk. He placed his large Havana cigar in a nearby faceted glass ashtray, and, with great agility for one so tall, moved from behind the desk, and marched up to where Jack and I were standing. With a single action he lifted both his arms into the aether and brought his hands down on to Jack's shoulder and then on to mine, with such force as to nearly knock us both off our balance.

He then looked at us straight in the eyes and said;

"Mitchell, Houston? How are you doing? What the hell are you doing in London? And, do tell me, did that Tony Pastor,[1] the 'Father of Vaudeville,' finally get rid of you? I did warn him years ago, that you two were a couple of wasters, and that you would never amount to anything, but together almost certainly bankrupt his precious Fourteenth Street Theater. Full as it is, with almost every jingoistic brand of American patriotism!

"Hey tell me Jack, something must have put the fear of God into you, to make you quit Jersey City? Jeez, Jack, it was always a major performance to get you to cross the

Hudson River from Jersey City into Manhattan. So what made you desert Jersey? And you Theo; I always credited you with more brains than Jack. But, I see you are here too. So tell me, my friends, what are you doing here and, do you still drink neat whisky?"

"Well if you give us a minute, you failed robber-baron, we can tell you," said Jack, "and, we are actually performing on your stage tonight and, yeah we still drink neat whisky at every opportunity, including now."

"You are performing here on my stage? That is news to me, but then I have not a clue about what happens on my stage. I am here to run a Music Hall, not to manage the stage acts. I pay stage managers to do that," said Kiralfy, as he poured large amounts of whisky into five glasses, which he then proceeded to hand out.

During this brief encounter Lodge looked stupefied at Jack and me. Perhaps it could never have crossed his mind that Jack or I might actually know impresarios and persons engaged in Vaudeville. As it happens we have known Imre for most of our working lives doing Vaudeville in New York. In fact it was Imre, who had gotten us our first engagement at Tony Pastor's Fourteenth Street Theater in Manhattan, all those years ago.

Pastor was pivotal in the development of Vaudeville in New York, of course, of which we are a part. His influence cannot be understated and accordingly he is known with sincere reverence as the, '*Father of Vaudeville.*'

In the early 1880s Pastor, became an impresario, where his skill was to put on polite and sensitive variety programs in several of his Music Halls in New York, principally in order to attract the expanding middle classes with their undoubted spending power. Pastor is credited with introducing Vaudeville, in the style that attracted females and families, on 24th October, 1881 at the Fourteenth Street Theater in New York.

This new genre of acceptable Vaudeville, with its absence of feisty or suggestive lyrics, typical of Marie Lloyd, soon attracted those patrons who ensured healthy box office receipts for Pastor, something Lodge would no doubt appreciate, if not envy. In addition, Tony Pastor banned the sale of alcohol in his Music Halls. This move did in fact mean that audiences were invariably less volatile and more attentive to the various acts or turns being performed on the stage. However, I remain unconvinced with regard to that particular draconian policy regarding the absence of alcohol.

Though often we Music Hall artistes refer to Vaudeville as a general term, expecting the person to whom we are addressing to hold the same definition, in practice understanding the term changes from person to person, be they impresario, artiste or member of the audience. I know that when Jack and I came to London to tread the Music Hall floor boards we both had difficulty understanding the differences amongst the terms, Vaudeville, Music Hall, Burlesque or Variety.

I recall with horror our inability to do so, believing erroneously that Music Hall in England is the same as Vaudeville in America. What Jack and I did not understand was that Vaudeville in America is not the same as Music Hall in England. In addition, what in England might be considered Burlesque would, in America, be certainly be termed Vaudeville!

However, Lodge did take great care to explain to us a simple fact that might help us gauge our Music Hall patrons in future and accordingly change our stage act to suit a particular audience assembled in the auditorium. What Lodge advised us two Vaudeville artistes out of

New York, was simply the fact that Music Halls in London originated from the saloon bars in *Public Houses*. These emerging *Quality Wets* replaced the London *Pleasure Gardens* such as those at Vauxhall, Ranelagh, Marylebone or Cremorne, where debauchery was practiced on an inconceivable level and licentiousness on an even more unimaginable grand scale. Both vices were rife and usually encouraged by the operators of such gardens.

Vestiges of that *Unbecoming Behavior,* as it was termed, could occasionally manifest themselves at awkward moments on the stage, even in the well-appointed red plush Music Halls. Such was our débâcle at that infamous Imperial Music Hall embedded in the depths of the Royal Aquarium & Winter Garden in Victoria. A Music Hall where we totally misjudged a staid and sober audience at our dear cost when we made imbeciles of ourselves during our début there.

But none the less the meaning of the term for the Vaudeville is obscure and despite the occasional talks on the subject with Jack, we neither of us had come up with a convincing definition of it. Jack was of the opinion that the word Vaudeville derives, or at least can be attributed to, the French expression, *voix de ville*, which I take to mean *City Voice*, however nonsensical that may sound to us Americans.

I have always held the belief that the term comes from a roving fifteenth-century minstrel Olivier Basselin and his famous, if satirical, song, '*Vaux de Vire.*' Though admittedly, one can see the word *Vaudeville* emerging from both definitions.

However, I am inclined to accept the definition propounded by Tony Pastor, the *Father of Vaudeville* – at least on the eastern seaboard in America. He was of the opinion that both definitions are not incorrect; but that they evolved simultaneously and claimed that the term is a corruption of the French *Vau de Vire,* meaning *Vire River Valley*, in the English language, an area in which Basselin was reputed to have lived, or roamed. Despite this learned description attributed to Pastor, I liked his usual and long-lasting definition of the term *Vaudeville* as being nothing more than a, 'sissy and Frenchified successor to Gentrified Variety!'

Despite its uncertain beginnings in the fifteenth century Vaudeville reached an apotheosis of a kind in the recent construction of the Palace Theater [2] located at 1564 Broadway and West 47th. Street, New York. Though a new theater, it was gaining rapidly a legendary reputation among us Vaudeville artistes as the theater to perform in.

Indeed some Music Hall artistes are prepared to take a pay cut for the privilege of playing the Palace, as an indication that a Vaudeville performer had informally reached the pinnacle of their career. One erudite performer was moved to confirm his thoughts in writing in attempting to make sense of this phenomenon.

'Only a vaudevillian who has trod its stage can really tell you about it... only a performer can describe the anxieties, the joys, the anticipation, and the exultation of a week's engagement at the Palace. The walk through the iron gate on 47th. Street through the courtyard to the stage door, was the cum laude walk to a show business diploma. A feeling of ecstasy came with the knowledge that this was the Palace, the epitome of the more than 15,000 Vaudeville theaters in America, and the realization that you have been selected to play it. Of all the thousands upon thousands of Vaudeville performers in the business, you are there. This was a dream fulfilled; this was the pinnacle of variety success.' 3

Jack and I had performed there, on full fees of course, under the auspices of Albee. We did so just before our departure for the Majestic Theater in Chicago in order to entertain the vast crowds attending the World's Columbian Exposition being held in that beautiful, if windy city.

Although the Palace Theater on Broadway was designed by theater architects Kirchoff & Rose, from Milwaukee, the theater, which seats twenty-seven hundred plus, was in fact paid for by the renowned San Francisco based Vaudeville entrepreneur, Martin Beck. He built the theater in a serious attempt to challenge the Keith-Albee eastern seaboard, including New York, monopoly. An agreement was reached. Or, as Lodge would no doubt say, for mutual benefits of box office receipts. This deal ensured that artistes performing on the Keith-Albee circuit of theaters, would get to perform at the new Palace Theater.

I remember when the Palace Theater opened with Ed Wynn, but it was not a success and for many months afterwards, it lost money. This was partly due to the internal design of the auditorium, especially the layout of the second tier Dress Circle on which virtually every seat had its view of the stage and the acts there on, obstructed. After some corrections had been made the Palace Theater now is breaking all box office receipts relentlessly. This of course would greatly please our impresario in the person of Michael Lodge who lives only for such returns.

In so thinking I turned to look at Lodge, who, I

noticed, appeared uncomfortable in this situation where he was not master of events or the conduit between Jack or me to a third person. His inner turmoil was reflected in his resorting to his monomaniacal nervous affliction of looking over both his shoulders at too regular an interval. Even Mabel was moved to stare with her blank expression upon her face at this abnormal activity. Imre was oblivious to Lodge's peculiar condition.

When Jack mentioned to Imre, that we were hoping to hook up with a certain Cinderella to form a new act, Lodge looked aghast at Jack, as though we too, had become a traitor to the cause of Music Hall.[4]

"We remain optimistic about our new show with Cinderella, where I accompany her on the pianoforte," said Jack, to Imre.

To which the Empress Music Hall manager responded, "I have the greatest contempt for optimism!"

None the less, I believe Imre thought the idea to be excellent and would naturally wish us both good fortunes in our exciting venture with Cinderella.

"I have seen that Cinderella here on my stage, and I have to admit, she has a unique style born of innovation which is a rare ability in Music Hall artistes. Some possess it; most do not, including you two!" remarked Kiralfy.

At this juncture, Lodge could not contain himself any longer and stood up.

"Come, Mabel and gentlemen," he said, "we have an audience to entertain and they shall not be kept waiting, not even for Jack or Theo."

"Oh very well," said Imre, "though why do you need to perform on the stage of this Music Hall, when the prospects of causing unadulterated humor and laughter are right here in front of your very eyes in this very room?" said Kiralfy, looking at Mabel.

None the less, we did as Lodge suggested and bade our farewells to our friend, with the overt threat of meeting up with him in the very near future. He gladly consented to our explicit promise.

"I did not know that you knew the man," said Lodge, as we made our way back down the ornate red-carpeted corridor.

"You did not ask us," said Jack, as we descended down a flight of stone steps into a more utilitarian corridor leading to our changing rooms in the basement.

Presently, having changed into our stage clothes, we emerged from our changing room and made our way up to the stage wings inn order to be able view the various acts and turns as they came on and get a feeling for the mood of the audience. It did not take long to gauge it; the audience was feisty. Also, Lodge was not exaggerating; the width of the stage was impressive. Even at three hundred and fifteen feet in width, the other wing of the stage seemed an eternity away. The costermongers, I noticed, were in evidence occupying the cheap seats immediately in front of this wide stage platform.

The compère, sporting a large handle bar moustache and wearing a red tail-coat strode past me, reeking of alcohol and on to the stage, standing there for a few moments until everybody in the audience had noticed his presence. He then lifted his arms into the aëther and made the following announcement.

"A big welcome to everybody, welcome to the largest Music Hall in England and therefore, by implication, our glorious empire. Tonight for your delectation we have the incomparable Flora Miller and a special treat in the form of two Vaudeville artistes from the New World. It is their début here at the Empress! Tonight, ladies and gentlemen, promises to be a spectacular, no, no, not failure, but experience, as we make our way through a range of truly breath taking acts. And, fact-defeating turns uniquely for your unbridled jollification, that or possibly even enjoyment!" said the compère, wiping his sweating brow with an ostentatious red paisley patterned handkerchief.

Listening to this generous compère, introducing Jack and me as a special treat from the New World, made me feel nervous. Experience tells me that the more the build-up, the less I feel inclined to live up to that praise, however well intentioned. Such performances usually end up as a débâcle, witness our disastrous début a few weeks previously, at the Imperial Music Hall, located in the depth of the Royal Aquarium & Winter Garden in Victoria.

The compère retreated to his box and with his gavel announced the opening stage act. The gas lights of the auditorium, as if by magic, simultaneously dimmed, whilst the illumination afforded by the footlight increased their intensity.

In an instance, the *Cremorne Belles* had tip-toed on their arches on to the stage as though ghosts, whereupon they performed a slow formation dance with neither musical accompaniment nor song. They danced, in fact in silence, as though they were but fleeting shadows at the close of the day. Of course, Mabel Green, Lodge's new protégée, used to perform with this troupe before her elevation to the Pantheon of the *Three Graces*.

The *Cremorne Belles* were clearly a favorite with the Music Hall-going public in London and even I had seen them first at Wilton's Music Hall and again at the Alhambra Music Hall. On both occasions, they had been a delight to watch. Their choreography remained a fine example of coördinated precision, and was matchless as it was faultless. They continued for some minutes dancing in silence, with fleeting shadows playing on the scenery behind them, caused by the stage foot lights.

But now a low murmuring from the *Cremorne Belles* could be detected. Gradually, this sound was converted into a low E flat minor chord by the orchestra, hidden from view, but present behind the proscenium arch. Then, all of a sudden, as if obeying a hidden signal, all the *Belles,* forty odd of them, lined up in front of the footlights. Just as well that the stage was 315 feet wide, I thought. And, curtseying in sequence individually from stage right to left, they all burst in unison into song. They did so whilst pointing at the costermongers assembled in the front row cheap seats which comprised the stalls.

The song they sang was, I remembered, called, *'Orpheus in the Underground,'* after Jacques Offenbach's opera. 5 After ten minutes of rousing songspiel involving the costermongers en-masse, the *Cremorne Belles* reverted to their silent, complex choreography with coördinated precision, as they in turn gave way to the next act. This was not before the costermongers had settled down again in their cheap seats having been roused by the *Cremorne Belles,* who had now yielded the stage.

The next act, introduced by the compère, involved that perverse Flora Miller and her Aëolian Pianola. On this occasion she was dressed in a flowing, iridescent, pink satin gown and positioned herself in the soft limelight so as to engender a look of angelic innocence about her person. That contrived look of innocence evaporated almost the moment Miller opened her mouth and began singing for her supper, to the accompaniment of the Aëolian Pianola.

Of course Jack and I had seen her before. She sang verses of such a blatant nature, about being in the garden shed looking out amongst the carrot and peas, which made me feel weak at the knees listening to them. They had done this when first I heard her singing in the Hungerford Music Hall at Charing Cross a few weeks earlier. She continued singing to the accompaniment of the sublime tinkling of arpeggios and triple A's emanating from the Aëolian Pianola that struggled to keep up with her frenzied attack on musical harmony and verse.

A feeling of deep vulnerability attended me whilst enduring her lascivious act, involving as it did the Aëolian Pianola, which she stroked suggestively during her recital of verses, some of which were so lewd to a degree that I did not know could be permitted to be sung on a London stage, even though Jack and I had in fact witnessed her performance again in the recent past at the Oxford Music Hall.

Despite the fact her verses and suggestive manner caused acute embarrassment to me and, I suspect, others of refined sensibility. They did not, it appeared, to upset the occupiers of the seats which made up the stalls and were filled with costermongers. Most of whom were eager to chant out their equally vulgar responses to Miller's overt suggestions. In fact, they seemed thoroughly entertained by her lyrical renditions and obvious invitations to respond to her lyrical encouragement.

Consistent with her singing and dancing was her cavorting at the Aëolian Pianola, which she still continued to stoke tenderly in a highly provocative, totally unabashed and suggestive manner. Rather as Rachel D'Arcy did with her ukulele we saw at Daly's Music Hall recently. Miller continued to sing verse after verse, including one particular song which I did recognize and cordially invited the audience to join in the chorus.

"Altogether now," she exhorted the audience.

Thereupon, she sang verses laced with covert vulgarity and lascivious innuendo, quite clearly audible over the audiences' singing the normal accepted verse! The costermongers could barely contain themselves as they sang loudly and enthusiastically, in duly obliging Miller who encouraged them further with her hands.

"She is an absolute gem of the first water," other artistes in the wings kept saying during Miller's performance as she worked her audience into a frenzy of immoral singing. At one stage, Miller whilst approaching the finale to her rendition and questionable behavior, actually managed to get most of the costermongers in the cheap stall seats, to stagger up on to their feet, and, in so doing chant out, with unbridled enthusiasm, their coarse responses the end of which attracted thunderous applause and great verbal acclaim.

Other acts or turns, before ours, were performed on the stage for public's delectation, but which involved the audience in an informal way. It was against a background of disruption, such as Miller's, that other artistes on stage had to contend and which made them resort to being even more outrageous and impudent in order to gain the attention of a distracted audience, including the massed ranks of the costermongers occupying the stalls, now especially worked up by Flora Miller.

My heart sank at the prospect of marching on to the stage with Jack trying to out-perform Miller's questionable and disgraceful spectacle. However, a reprieve was at hand, as it was now time for the interval. The lowering of the curtain signalled what can only be described as, a panic-driven mass stampede of biblical proportions by the costermongers, to the numerous and crucial Crush Bars ranged strategically about the Empress Music Hall.

After a lengthy time the audience resumed their seats

in the auditorium. Jack and I stood with other artistes at the side of the stage. When the heavy purple velvet safety curtain, bearing a coat of arms of dubious authenticity, eventually ascended into the attic, it revealed on stage for the audience, what I took to be the next act on the bill, the monologist.

He stood there motionless, wearing a pair of voluminous yellow and brown checked trousers. Then in an instant, he strode from the back of the stage confidently and with purpose, positioning himself directly in front of the footlights to achieve maximum illumination of his person and loud attire. Before he had even opened his mouth he attracted a standing ovation, especially from the costermongers only feet away from him down in the cheap seats.

What then transpired could only be described as a recitation of interminable nonsense, that only the costermongers, sitting attentively in the front rows of the stalls, understood, and showed this by nodding their heads at regular intervals and murmuring intermittent approving sounds of encouragement.

Nonetheless, when the monologist wearing his voluminous checked trousers vacated the stage the compère exhorted the audience to show no restraint in welcoming from the New World and Vaudeville, à la New York, Messrs. Theo Mitchell and Jack Houston. As Jack and I strolled onto the stage from either wing meeting in the middle, a peculiar thing occurred, besides the fact that the compère had gotten our names wrong.

As my eyes became accustomed to the glare of the footlights, I noticed, without any signal being given or heard, that about half the costermongers in the stalls simply got up and walked out of the auditorium! Irrespective of this discourtesy, Jack and I went through our routine. I wearing my sennet straw hat and holding a cane, whilst singing to Jack's pianoforte accompaniment. The desultory applause we received at the end of our act was such that I hoped to God Imre Kiralfy was not looking down on to the stage at us, from some vantage point or window hidden amongst the gilded opulent décor of the upper walls of his auditorium.

1. Tony Pastor was a leading impresario behind American Vaudeveille, but died in 1908
2. The Palace Theater opened in 1913
3. Jack Haley, quoted in, *No Applause, Just Throw Money*, by Travis Stewart
4. Lodge thinks Cinderella a traitor because of her duplicitous rôles onstage to avoid the *Exclusivity Clause* Based on an opéra bouffon by Offenbach but properly called, '*Orpheus in the Underworld*.'

Chapter 11

The Odyssey to Oblivion

We had débuted here at the Empress Music Hall, but, given the level of licentiousness in the audience, we had not fared too badly. It was almost as though we were back in the glorious days of the *Pleasure Gardens*, such as those at Ranelagh, Marylebone, Cremorne or Vauxhall. The trick was obviously to get on the stage first or early and not have to worry about following other perhaps more superior acts or turns. Clearly, Flora Miller's Aëolian Pianola turn was not an act to follow.

After our performance on stage, we naturally repaired to the extravagant appointments of the Crush Bar at the Empress Music Hall. Eventually, however on deciding to leave, it was as much as I could do to get Jack to quit the sumptuous and inviting bar. He then suddenly announced that he was not leaving Earl's Court until he had been up to the Exhibition Hall and to have a quick look around the exhibits that were on display.

I elected not to go as they were of little interest to me. Anyway, I had witnessed enough entertainment for one evening, and instead, I decided to make my way back from Earl's Court to our hotel above King's Cross Metropolitan Station.

Lodge then suggested nonchalantly, as he slipped his dazzling red silk lined cape over his shoulders, which he closed with an ornate and ostentatious brass buckle. That I might wish to ride the Great Northern, Piccadilly & Brompton Underground Rail Road, as being by far the easier way to get back to the St. Pancras Hotel.

"I did not know such a rail road existed here in London," I responded, "and I have consulted Bradshaw's Rail Road Guide on numerous occasions and even checked with Bäedeker's Guide to London."

"Oh yes, it is a deep level, subterranean rail road completed in 1906 and runs through central London from here to King's Cross and beyond. Come," insisted Lodge, "we can walk up with Jack on his way to the Earl's Court Exhibition Hall which is next to the station leading down to the to the Great Northern, Piccadilly & Brompton Underground Rail Road."

Presently we found ourselves walking back up the Warwick Road, I think, in the direction of the Exhibition Hall and Earl's Court Underground Rail Road Station. En-route, we walked past a peculiar looking monolithic structure more reminiscent of an Aztec styled building with its various terraces. The presence of this Aztec styled building constructed of massive limestone blocks in the midst of Earl's Court seemed incongruous, I thought but there it is.

Eventually we gained the entrance to the Exhibition Hall whereupon Jack, Lodge and Mabel climbed the steps up into its spacious halls. This was the place, of course, that Jack and I had mistaken for the Empress Music Hall when we arrived earlier in the evening. However, I continued on my way to the Earl's Court Underground Rail Road Station located on the other side of the road. A few moments later I reached the entrance and walked in to the station to begin my odyssey on this subterranean rail road.

Aztec Building, London

Of course both Jack and I had ridden surface trains in America, including, of course, the Elevated Rail Road in Chicago, the *Loop* and trains coming in to Pennsylvania Rail Road Station in New York through the tunnels beneath the Hudson and East Rivers. But never had I travelled along a continuous underground rail road embedded in a tunnel in the midst of a huge city. I was looking forward to experiencing this mode of rail road transport, where the engine hauling the carriages of which the train is comprised, is powered by electricity according to Lodge

I entered the station and went to purchase a ticket. I did so at the remarkably low price of two pennies. I then made my way to the subterranean platform, where I joined other persons in a tide of humanity, as we descended into the depths of the station down what looked like a steep flight of stone steps. These were the kind on which one would certainly not wish to fall, as there were no intervening landings to prevent one from tumbling all the way down to the foot of the steps.

At length, I gained the eastbound platform, I think, and waited for my train to arrive. In the meantime a glaring advertisement poster fixed to the curved wall of the tunnel facing the platform upon which I was standing caught my attention. Its claims were in keeping with the majority of advertisements plastered on to rail road property that I had witnessed frequently in urban rail road stations throughout London.

Then, suddenly there was a barely perceivable movement of the aëther accompanied by a rushing noise. Most people looked up the platform to the mouth of the tunnel. Within seconds, a train came blasting out of it and progressed down the side of the platform. As it went past me, a heat wave from the electrically powered locomotive assailed my face, creating an instant sensation of burning heat. I staggered back thinking the engine was on fire. No other passengers on the platform appeared concerned, so I pretended nonchalance at my re-action. Again, after some pushing and general *determined behavior*

'WHY BE RUPTURED ?'

GET CURED AND
THROW YOUR TRUSS AWAY

A Great Chance
TO GET CURED FOR – FIVE GUINEAS!
Are you ruptured? Then go at once to Dr Flint at
35 Oxford Circus Avenue (3rd Floor)
London, W
The great Rupture Specialist.

He cures without cutting, without chloroform
and without laying off from work.
This is a fine chance for farmers and working people
to get cured.

Come at once!

Many cases can be cured in one visit. Dr Flint's
regular price for curing ordinary ruptures is **Eight Guineas**
but for this month he will cure many of these cases for as
low as only **Five Guineas.**

FARMERS & NAVIGATORS
So many ruptured people are farmers & navigators
that Dr Flint wishes to call the attention of, and all active
hard-working people that now, while the weather is cool, is the
best and most convenient time to cure ruptures.

Furthermore, you can get cured very cheaply now
"Cured My Rupture Without Cutting"
So Say These Hundred Men

by some passengers, we all managed to reach the interior of the train's elongated tubular carriage.

Was it normal in London, one wondered, where, every time a train stops at a platform to let some passengers alight and others to get on, that it is accompanied by a general commotion. There was nowhere to sit in the rather cramped and crowded carriage. Then with a severe jolt that nearly knocked my top hat off my head, the train glided down the side of the platform and then, in an instant, plunged into the tunnel. Looking vaguely self-conscious in my stage outfit with grease paint on my face, I tried to appear nonchalant and unconcerned.

Immediately, we were all then subjected to a very loud whistling noise as the aëther rushed past the carriage as it blasted its way through the tunnel. The brick walls illuminated by the occasional flickers of light from electric lamps fixed to the brickwork tunnel lining, raced by me. Whilst the ride was in some ways exhilarating, it was also slightly frightening and certainly able to resurrect dormant feelings of latent claustrophobia, accompanied by my ears popping. Despite being thrown around like rag dolls, we emerged at the station for Brompton Road intact and still en-route, I think, to King's Cross.

Again, there was the attendant commotion as people made their way through the open doors to gain the platform. I remained standing, as I knew my destination was not far off from this station. Again, the doors of the carriage having been closed, the train lurched off in the direction of the King's Cross Station, my destination.

We traversed through a series of intervening stations along this underground rail road, including Brompton Oratory,[1] Knightsbridge, Down Street, [2] Dover Street [3] and Leicester Square. Consulting my steel case pocket watch, I worked out that we had traversed from Earl's

Court to Leicester Square in less than nine minutes; simply incredible! However the claustrophobia, still attending me, was increased as I realized that we were now not far from the river Thames!

What if the waters of the Thames were to come flooding through the brickwork of the tunnel? Would we all perish in a watery grave? I looked about the carriage expecting to discern from other passengers the same concern I felt for our predicament, but detected none. Did I have a heightened sense of catastrophe? Was I alone in recognizing our danger? Then it happened. I felt my body move forward unbidden as the train's carriage began to ease in its velocity and eventually came to a juddering stop at a station named for Covent Garden.

Eventually, when we reached King's Cross, I was, for all my experience, grateful to abandon the carriage and make my way up to the surface, albeit at a crowded King's Cross Rail Road Station. I arrived in the semi-circular glazed rail road station structure that is the terminus there, teeming as it was with the travelling public of all classes and complete with seasoned pick-pockets, the activities of whom were evident to those with keen eyesight, such as I have in these matters, coming as I do from New York.

However, not being a regular user of this rail road terminal, and therefore uncertain as to the exits which led to the St. Pancras Hotel nearby, in the Euston Road, I approached a rail road servant upon the platform. He was, naturally, dressed in his velveteen uniform, and listened politely and attentively to my inquiry.

He then promptly informed me, in a condescending manner, that he was a rail road servant of the Great Northern Rail Road, and not a bureau for the dissemination of geographical information. He smiled, and then turned on his heels and walked off smartly through the station and down to toward the platforms.

I was astounded at this truculent person's attitude to me, but took solace in the fact that this kind of confident behavior appeared to be quite normal, if not expected, within the precincts of rail road stations in London.

I now found myself abandoned, as it were, beneath a quite spectacular, if vast, iron and glass roof covering the station, under which the noise emanating from several locomotives in red livery colors, was tremendous. Beneath this extensive iron and glass canopy of the station roof were suspended enormous town gas light globes. Though not of the chandelier type, they did illuminate the scene of chaos beneath, as various trade wagons, pantechnicons, vanguards and other delivery vehicles competed for precedence amongst the piles of luggage.

I stood there transfixed by the concentrated commotion coming from the platforms, which were teeming with people in search of their trains or those departing from them. The scene was one of utter chaos, as one train after another clanked noisily into King's Cross Rail Road Station, disgorging their passengers; whilst other trains departed along platforms with a great show of steam and even more noise. Amongst the chaos were flitting shunting engines, hissing steam fiercely, while marshalling carriages to larger locomotives, painted in deep red livery and eager to depart hauling their passengers and not inconsiderable luggage or freight.

Amongst this vicissitude of transportation and commerce, children played with their dogs dodging, miraculously, cumbersome wagons and pantechnicons which went lumbering by, paying them no heed. Some children were of the street urchin type, whilst others, wearing varnished boots, were clearly passing through the station or waiting for a train. The expression upon their faces proclaimed as much, as they stood there, wrapped up tightly in their high quality travelling coats.

Some of them gazed, awestruck amid these new experiences. Within this concentration of the travelling public were other persons, some of whom, conducting the business of commerce, pointed accusingly to delivery orders or shipping manifests, then in the direction of where none existent goods ought to have been. Some people were appealing, in the last resort, to unconvinced servants of the rail road, whilst others merely watched, including nurses pushing their perambulators, oblivious as to which direction they did, among the general chaos prevailing upon the various platforms.

The smell of choking smoke from the engines was appalling; and I understood why some people were walking rather quickly along the platform in their bid to leave the confines of the station. In so doing one person was unfortunate to be passing a locomotive engine at the very instance it evacuated its surplus steam straight into his pathway. In an instant, a steam fog had enveloped this hapless person, making him momentarily vanish! When he did reappear, he was wiping frantically the sticky residue from his face, with an ostentatious paisley patterned handkerchief.

Then I saw something, which left me quite aghast. It was an experienced pick-pocket, in full action, but oblivious of an observant rail road servant upon the platform who too was watching him perform his delicate action. Suddenly the observant rail road employé shouted at the pick-pocket, and then gave chase.

Immediately upon the station platform, it seemed that pandäemonium was let loose. A sheaf of papers and a bowler hat erupted into the smoke filled aether and from beneath this plume of papers and headdress, I noticed that the pick-pocket had crouched down and was removing himself quickly from the mêlée. However, in his haste he collided with a pantechnicon with London & North Eastern Rail Road Co. Ltd. emblazoned on its highly polished side panelling.

This however, did not impede his egress from what was I think, a concerted attempt to apprehend his person. By now of course the view-halloa was in full cry, as both uniformed representatives of the law and the observant rail road employé dressed in his velveteen uniform, if hatless, gave chase in the hue and cry. Surprisingly enough, a woman of quite stout demeanor, wearing a frilly bonnet, and several billowing and voluminous mauve and purple silk skirts, intercepted the fleeing pickpocket and quite literally fell upon him and very nearly succeeded in frustrating his escape.

However, at the last moment, she missed her footing and hit the ground, bonnet and all, with pronounced force as the fleeing pick-pocket made good his escape out of the station precinct and into the fog and liberty. I also observed from the corner of my eye, that another seasoned pick-pocket, a true cannon, was clearly taking advantage of a particular victim distracted by the commotion caused by his brother pick-pocket!

I had not yet even left the precincts of the King's Cross Rail Road Station before I was compelled to witness behavior that would be quite simply unacceptable at Chicago La Salle Rail Road Depôt, or indeed in New York City's Pennsylvania Rail Road Station.

However, whilst I was contemplating this extraordinary scene on the station platforms, another servant of the rail road approached me. The insignia on his pristine

Pennsylvania Rail Road Station

velveteen uniform, with red piping, informed me that he was an employee, not of the London Midland & Scottish Rail Road, nor indeed the Great Northern Rail Road, but of the London & North Eastern Rail Road. He asked if he could be of assistance.

I asked him out politeness if was he a bureau for the dissemination of geographical information. He just smiled. I therefore continued and advised him of my predicament and the search for the exit from this station that would lead me up to the St. Pancras Hotel.

He looked at me somewhat askance and thought for a moment.

I braced myself mentally for an onslaught of facetious comments and inordinate confidence from this servant upon the platform.

"Ah, but you can only mean the Grand Midland

Hotel," [4] he said quite clearly as he corrected me, "you need only go through that red brick arched portal the steps from which will lead you up to your hotel. Do have a good evening sir."

I shall, I thought to myself, I most certainly shall in that well appointed bar for which my hotel is justly renowned. I had arranged to meet Jack there later to discuss our visiting the Queen's Concert Hall in Langham Place, to support Lodge in his attempt to get his Choral Anthem Symphony performed there. Or as Jack has taken to calling it, the *Cholera* Anthem Symphony; since the work rather does bring out similar symptoms in one, upon hearing it.

1. Brompton Oratory Station now closed
2. Down Street Station now closed
3. Dover Street Station now Green Park Station
4. This, in fact, is the correct name for the St. Pancras Hotel

Chapter 12

The Encounter at Lusby Music Hall

The previous day had been fortunate, in that we had been given an offer by Henri Goss, the manager to perform at his esteemed Metropolitan Music Hall at our convenience, and with Cinderella. We had also met with an old friend of ours in the ebullient and gregarious personality of Imre Kiralfy, proprietor, no less, of the Empress Music Hall located at Earl's Court.

Our day had begun with our having cause to visit the American Embassy opposite Lees Place in Mayfair. Having sorted out our domicile documentation, eventually, we headed off into the fog, still swirling about the London streets, to a particular restaurant to take a late luncheon, which, Lodge had recommended. it was situated on the fourth floor of a building in Oxford Street near Marble Arch. The views from our windows in the restaurant, or at least from the bar, overlooked the roof of the Cumberland Hotel next door and nothing much else due to the fog.

"We need sustenance now, if we are to cope with the trauma that is to be unleashed on the floorboards at Lusby's Music Hall later this evening," Jack said, in jest to me.

Having being shown to a table, we sat down and perused the menu. We had some time before we were

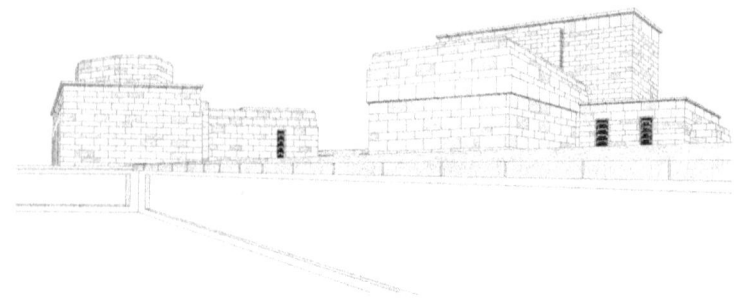

Cumberland Hotel Roof, Marble Arch

due on stage to perform our new act with Cinderella in her guise as Marmaduke. Cinderella was also performing there in another of her different rôles; that of Little Bo Peep.

Presently a different waiter appeared at the table to take our orders. I instructed him accordingly.

"Roast sirloin beef olives in mushroom sauce and the baked custard tart with stewed fruits and a bottle of chilled Chablis," I ordered.

Jack followed in with the stuffed roast veal with anchovy sauce and for dessert he chose the Boodle's Orange Fool trifle. He also ordered a bottle of Bordeaux. Later when we were enjoying our brandy and a selection of cigars from the proprietor's collection, I reëxamined the menu. I had not noticed the Boodle's Orange Fool trifle was laced with an alcoholic drink; for if I had it would have been my preference too. Instead I had been stuck with alcohol free baked custard and stewed fruits! No wonder Jack was in an expansive mood.

"Do you think that members of the audience actually realize that Cinderella, Little Bo Peep or Marmaduke are one and the same person?" I inquired of Jack.

"Beats me Theo, but I suspect not. Cinderella is far too smart for that!"

We both of us fell into a silence brought on by our substantial meal, that or the alcohol. Looking around the restaurant I came to realize that the establishment was quite remarkable for its interior décor. Gentlemen patronized it, the majority of whom wore black morning-coat and pinstripe trousers, of the type which are usually worn by men from the higher professions.

The restaurant itself was quite long but not necessarily narrow. The bar was about thirty feet in length, the front of which was fabricated with highly varnished carved mahogany panels. The surface of the bar was completed in a lavish style, with slabs of marble; deep yellow in color, but warm in appearance that only *Giallo Siena* exudes. Placed on this impressive bar were various gasogenes, bronze candelabras and carafes filled with various colored liquors.

Despite its plush opulence and general appointment of ostentatious extravagance, I was amused to see, when glancing down at the floor against the front of the bar, several strategically placed spittoons! I had only ever seen those in bars west of Virginia.

Behind the bar, contained in bottles on shelves fixed to the wall, was a wide range of spirits and wines from around the world. The restaurant was also bathed in diffused daylight, due to the fog that was able to penetrate its deepest recesses. This daylight was afforded by the fact that the ceiling of the restaurant comprised a glazed apex roof, running the full length of the room.

We had no sooner finished our brandy and cigars than it was time for us to leave in order to make our way to Lusby's Music Hall in the Mile End Road in east London. Accordingly, we abandoned the restaurant and eventually stepped out smartly into Oxford Street and the attendant all pervasive fog. Upon doing so, we immediately approached a highly varnished Barouche carriage pulled by a couple of chestnut colored horses, waiting by the edge of the sidewalk.

"Lusby's Music Hall in the Mile End Road," instructed Jack, to the liveried carriage driver, as we both climbed in and sat down on the buttoned down green leather upholstered seat.

"This carriage is taken sir," said the coachman, "I am waiting for my fare, who is inside that milliner's shop."

"Alright, ten guineas right now for you, if you take us to the Mile End Road," offered Jack, "I am pretty sure the gentleman in the shop will not object."

"My fare is a lady," replied the liveried carriage driver.

"The offer still stands," negotiated Jack!

"Jack, hey Jack," I intervened.

After some oaths had been exchanged freely, most of which were muffled by the dense fog, we were still compelled to alight from the carriage. We began walking east along Oxford Street, but still found ourselves without a carriage and standing on the junction of Baker and Oxford. More accurately, I noticed that we were in fact outside the newly constructed notions store built in Baker Street, by Mr. Harry Gordon Selfridge and opened recently in 1909.

I remembered reading about this store in the *New York Times*. At the time it described this new building, designed by Chicago based architect Daniel Burnham, as an excellent exponent of the architectural style sweeping America called Beaux-Arts. With its distinctive use of massive polished limestone or sandstone blocks fixed to a steel frame style of construction very similar to buildings we have back home in America. Such buildings,

I recall as the Union Station in Chicago, in addition to Grand Central Terminal or Metropolitan Museum of Art, both of which are back home in New York.

At length we intercepted a Hackney carriage travelling east along Oxford Street. Making our way along this thoroughfare was painfully slow, but did afford us an opportunity to take in the general aspect of this major road of the West End. Our reduced progress, provided Jack with the opportunity to offer up s few observations based on his previous visit to London some years ago. In particular he mentioned, the Argyll Arms Public House, situated on the junction of Argyll Street and Oxford Street near the northern end of Oxford Circus Avenue.

"I remembered that public house," said Jack, pointing with his cane to the bar in question just visible from our Hackney carriage. "It remains one of the finer examples of opulently appointed interiors typical of public houses known as, Quality Wets. And usually comprise, an innovative and interesting combination of etched glass, mirrors, highly polished brass ornate fixtures and carved varnished mahogany timber finishes. I have fond memories of that place, especially the interiors, all which create a series of magnificent Victorian red plush salons of the vernacular type so beloved of our Victorian forbears, including those back home in America.

"I also remembered that the pianist and composer, Franz Liszt, the works of whom I studied whilst at the Julliard School of Music, lived at the end of Argyll Street in 1841, in a building located just around the corner, I think at 16 Great Marlborough Street. Hence my knowing about the Argyll Public House; gleaned when on my first pilgrimage to Liszt's residence there!

"Speaking of which, Liszt represented that progressive

movement in the music of the middle nineteenth century termed the, 'Music of the Future,' and was later to be given powerful expression in the works of its great exponent, Rickard Wagner, in developing the *leitmotiv* and who became Liszt's son-in-law. Wagner was himself, no stranger to the area, having lived in 1839 at 23-25 Old Compton Street, in nearby Soho."

Minutes went by before we were on the move again, driving past several horse-drawn omnibuses forming a continuous traffic block. Despite the weather, Oxford Street was a hive of activity with various street traders, costermongers and other sundry vendors selling their wares to anybody who would stoop down to such misplaced trust.

Suddenly our Hackney carriage came to an abrupt halt again, as some altercation and commotion erupted in front of us. This involved a pantechnicon with the 'Fortnum & Mason' cipher emblazoned on its side, and a wagonette carriage under the control of a loquacious individual.

To avoid this unpleasantness, I looked to my right and could just make out a fine looking building called, I think, the Pantheon, or at least so a sign proclaimed. The building looked somewhat out of place in Oxford Street, especially with its massive elegant masonry dome sheltering those in need of entertainment.

A few moments later we went clattering by the Royal Princess's Theater looking forlorn but promising, so a prominent advertisement poster declared, an entertaining evening of Bellini's operetta, *'The Sonnambulist,'*[1] followed by a Burlesque called, *'The Yellow Dwarf.'* Entertaining, I thought, if one is amused by what promises to be an experience involving the grotesque.

We continued our progress as the Hackney carriage

negotiated its way through the street with the Regent's Circus behind us. Here I remarked to Jack how Oxford Street deteriorates as one travels east along it. His response was that the street reflected every aspect of life from the rich and fortunate to the desperate or poor. I dwelt on his word poor as we rattled down what was becoming a seedier and grubbier street almost by the yard.

At one stage we drove past a substantial building in Holborn, which I remembered Lodge pointing out to us once as being a mausoleum to a great Victorian worthy, the name of whom he failed to inform us. However, it was now Jack who pointed out to me this impressive building, complete with a mysterious and minatory look about it seemingly abandoned in its own grounds and splendid isolation, but surrounded by tall iron railings.

I noticed that our coach driver was taking our carriage along a road that was a continuation of the Oxford Street into Holborn. Again Jack pointed out with his cane, the Holborn Empire Music Hall, in which, of course, our fervent hope to be able to perform in one evening. We continued to make our way east along a series of twisting

Mausoleum Building, London

cobbled streets. To our left, but only just visible, was St. Paul's Cathedral, I think, looking itself like a domed mausoleum looming up into the shrouds of fog.

Eventually we pulled in to the Whitechapel Road and progressed along it until we reached the Mile End Road. Whilst traversing it I observed the crowds of people hurrying along the sidewalk. Some of whom were engaged in commercial activity, which prevailed along this mighty thoroughfare of Empire that links the City to the mercantile areas and docks, and in to which the wealth and produce of the British Empire are delivered.

Children were very much in evidence everywhere, including some who had that look of being undernourished and in a perpetual state of inanition.[2] However, they did look contented and cheerful. Especially the little girls, in their white cotton dresses and tiny black boots, as they played and danced amongst the horses pulling dray carts and other lumbering wagons transporting goods of every description from the nearby docks on the river Thames.

Costermongers abounded, and pestered every passing pedestrian with their wares. Suddenly, as if by magic they melted back into the fog, as did the children. The reason was the arrival of two police constables on horseback, trotting down the middle of the Mile End Road. Their appearance caused pantechnicons and other carriages to slow down and swerve to avoid them. Some drivers actually turned the horses completely around and clattered off quickly in the opposite direction.

An age seemed to go by before the carriage driver eventually pulled up outside Lusby's Music Hall.

"Here we are Guv," announced the driver, holding out a grubby hand for his fare.

We entered the Music Hall through its main entrance

Lusby's Music Hall

and were immediately impressed with the splendid and opulent interiors, together with the grand size and the generous proportions of the foyer in which we found ourselves. It was easy to understand why the word *palace* was reflected in the original name of the place, being that of Lusby's Summer & Winter Palace. On an adjacent wall was a poster advertising tonight's acts and turns including Little Bo Peep's and ours.

"Lusby's Music Hall started out in the Mile End Road, London, as a Public House called The Eagle, under a the landlord by the name of Wilton Friend. In 1868 William Lusby who renamed it Lusby's Music Hall bought it later in 1877. The hall was reconstructed and called Lusby's Summer & Winter Palace.

"In 1878 Lusby's Music Hall was sold to theater operators Crowder and Payne, but January 1884 the building caught fire which resulted in major areas of the Music Hall being destroyed. However, the new owners Crowder and Payne commissioned Frank Matcham, the renowned theater architect, to design a new building. Completed in 1886 the theater was called the Paragon Music Hall. Despite this name, the theater is still referred to as Lusby's Music Hall for the sake of continuity.

"This later magnificent Music Hall was erected 1886 to meet the needs of the Music Hall going public, located in the East End of London in particular, and the Mile End Road was as good a place as any in which to do so," Jack informed me.

We made ourselves known to one of the ushers who escorted us to the general manager's office to meet with Cinderella and Lodge. On the way we had an opportunity to view the interior of the auditorium, which was about sixty feet wide, a hundred feet in length and thirty-eight feet in height. An impressive horseshoe shaped balcony was fixed to the side and back walls of the auditorium and housing four private boxes, and below which were two large stage boxes.

The floor containing the stall seats rose by a shallow angle from the orchestra pit to the entrances to the hall,

Lusby's Music Hall

PROGRAMME

AËRIAL GYMNASTIC PERFORMANCE OF MADAME
SANYEAH USING HER JAW

THE 'JAP OF JAPS' DEXTEROUS CONJUROR D'
ALVINI

LITTLE BO PEEP

MARTINETTI'S TROUPE PERFORMING THE COMIC
BALLET- MAGIC FLUTE

MURRAY AND THE WHITE MINSTRELS

THE MUSICAL MISS KATIE BELE

MR. ALEXANDER LUMSDEN

THE TALENTED MISS EMILY ADAMS –
JUVENILE BURLESQUE ACTRESS & SINGER

HOUSTON, MITCHELL & MARMEDUKE

THE NIMBLE-FOOTED MR. E. MOSEDALE

THE SISTERS MELITA & HARRY FISHER
DISPLAYING VOCAL & TERPSICHOREAN SKILL

THE YOUTHFUL MASTER SIDNEY, THE
SENTIMENTAL SINGER OF GOOD ABILITY

**AN EFFICIENT ORCHESTRA
CONDUCTED BY MR. THOMAS CARTER**

CHAIRED IN A BECOMING MANNER BY FRANK
ESTCOURT WHO ALSO SINGS MOTTO & OTHER
SONGS,

at the back of the auditorium. This enabled persons sitting at the back of the auditorium to have an uninterrupted and clear view of the stage. I also noticed numerous well-appointed large Crush Bars placed conveniently next to the entrances.

The stage looked pretty impressive too, and in reflecting the large scale proportions of the place had a proscenium arch of at least thirty-five feet in width and thirty feet in height with a depth of about forty-five feet fitted with star traps and other appropriate mechanical contraptions to aid the performers on stage. I was looking forward to marching on to this generously proportioned stage later in the evening

The general decoration of the auditorium comprised a frieze, adorned with classical fresco paintings surrounding the auditorium. Complemented with raised papier mâche mouldings finished in gold and silver colors together, created a restrained, if opulent effect without degenerating into the garish or over extravagant. Moments later we were walking down a highly varnished oak panelled corridor and presently ushered into the office of the general manager, Mr. Wilton Friend, who had remained with the theater over the years.

During our stay in London playing the Music Halls we had the pleasure of being introduced to several Music Hall and theater managers. The majority of whom were generally sharp, resourceful and somewhat lean, if not gaunt, in appearance. Most, if not all, resorted to alcohol as an almost necessary adjunct in their lives, possibly to compensate or assist them in having to deal with temperamental or highly emotional Music Hall artistes, the public at large or simply just the stress running a Music Hall. These challenges, or having to contend with the Metropolitan Board of Works or the venal Salvation

Army. Both of which together, with moral crusaders such as, Ormiston Chant or Lily Langtree, wish to despatch forthwith Music Halls into oblivion.

The manager of Lusby's Music Hall, to whom we were now being introduced did not conform to this notion of a Music Hall manager. He was sitting behind a large, ornately carved, mahogany desk finished with inlaid tooled red leather to its writing surface. On each of the front two corners of the desk was a bronze lamp radiating a soft light through an opaque and patterned glass globe. In between these lamps was an elaborate and ostentatiously decorated red *Rosso Verona* marble ink well and combined quill stand.

Wilton Friend's office comprised nothing more than a well-appointed and comfortable chamber. It was filled with expensive items of furniture, ranged around a large airy room with a high ceiling, from which was suspended an intricate brass and crystal chandelier. The walls of the room were covered in red flock silk wallpaper with raised velvet decoration.

Hanging on these walls was an extensive array of silver-nitrate daguerreotype likenesses of famous Music Hall artistes, in impossible poses and with banal expressions upon their faces. Other images depicted musicians, some of whom were clutching their fragile instruments. Complementing these photographs were three large gilt-framed paintings of theatrical stage scenes, placed there, as it were, in an attempt to lend further verisimilitude to the room, I thought.

Set into one wall were three large windows which looked out on to the Mile End Road. Framing these, but pulled back and secured with a gold colored twisted cord terminating with large tassels, were deep red brocade curtains, indicating further opulence. Built on to the opposite wall was an extensive library, the shelves of which were filled with thespian journals or theatrical reference books.

Ranged around the room were ubiquitous palm trees in highly polished green glazed urns placed on top of polished mahogany jardinières. The floor of Friend's office was surprisingly uncarpeted revealing bare elm floorboards, which created a soft warm appearance. Clearly this was more of an office of a dilettante than a hard headed Music Hall manager.

The reason I was able to indulge in my visual peregrinations of this well-appointed office was simply because the manager, Wilton Friend, was still in the process of trying to get up from his chair to welcome us. Eventually he succeeded, but only after thirty seconds or so had elapsed.

The person who we had witnessed struggling to get out of his Chippendale chair was probably six feet in height and at least three across and weighed about two hundred seventy pounds. After a few more seconds he had negotiated his portly bulk to the side of his desk and held out a plump hand. I was the first to accept his offer of welcome.

In so doing I noticed he was dressed in a powder blue morning-coat with red piping, striped trousers and spats covering a pair of highly polished patent leather brown boots. His shiny silk shirt was of blue tint and completed with a necktie of deep red satin, fastened with a pin finished with a stone of sparkling red beryl, his only concession to fashion. Despite his evident gravitas born of embonpoint,[3] he was dressed very elegantly.

After mutual salutation had been exchanged, he motioned us sit to down and make ourselves comfortable in various Chippendale chairs, the seats of which were covered in a pink moiré silk. We did so as he retreated to behind the ornately carved mahogany desk, whereupon he collapsed back into his Chippendale chair. As he did so I felt certain I heard a cracking sound coming from it.

Though not an authority on eighteenth century furniture, and certainly not those made by Chippendale. I was always under the impression that Chippendale chairs, in particular, represented the last word in refined beauty and elegance, the slender features of which were incorporated in to the furniture as standard. Without doubt the Chippendale chair in to which our portly manager had just collapsed in to, must have, at some stage in its existence, been seriously modified and strengthened structurally to withstand Friend's regular use of it.

Being of large proportions, I had expected Friend to have a deep resonant voice. He did not; rather he spoke in a high pitched almost squeaky voice that somehow complemented his flamboyant attire.

"I am pleased to welcome you all to Lusby's Music Hall," he squeaked out, "and trust that you will find the arrangements for your convenience and benefit, to your satisfaction."

"I feel confident that they will be perfect in every detail," said Lodge, whilst manœuvring his chair to the front of the manager's ornately carved mahogany desk.

He did so, I think, in order to gain center stage during our meeting with Friend.

"I have been introduced to Little Bo Peep and to Houston and Mitchell but not to this Marmaduke fellow. Might he be joining us later in order to complete your act on stage this evening?" inquired Wilton Friend, pointing to this evening's hand bill listing the various turns and acts to be performed.

"Possibly, Wilton but you…" answered Lodge.

"Sorry, I meant to say earlier," interrupted Jack, "Marmaduke, I have been reliably informed, races in a carriage to your Music Hall, Wilton, even as we speak and…"

"He will be joining us shortly," I interrupted Jack.

I did so deliberately in order to lend further credence to Jack's interruption of Lodge's developing faux pas, which we both recognized immediately.

"Oh very well, "continued Friend, "perhaps I shall have an opportunity of meeting with him when he does arrive. But, that will have to be in the dressing room or back of stage, for now I have to prepare tonight's performances. As you know, an audience will not tolerate a late commencement of the entertainment for which they have purchased tokens for."

"As you wish," said Jack, rising from his chair and stretching over Wilton Friend's ornately carved mahogany desk to shake his hand.

Wilton did not bother to rise from his Chippendale chair again, but merely looked at Jack and then shook his hand. Moments later I followed with mine, as did Little Bo Peep with hers. Lodge, looking somewhat put out, did the same.

Within a few moments we found ourselves again outside the manager's office and making our way back along the highly varnished oak panelled corridor and to our respective dressing rooms located in the basement. At length we arrived, and immediately helped ourselves to bottled beer and whelks, thoughtfully provided by the management. We had some time to ourselves before Little Bo Peep's act, or ours with Marmaduke, were scheduled to take place. So we sat down and relaxed whilst drinking the beer and eating the whelks.

Lodge, who had conspicuously refused a bottle of beer or a plate of whelks, left us in order to take his place in the Dress Circle. We continued to help ourselves to the bottles of beer and whelks, during the course of which we began laughing and talking noisily with each other.

"I would know that laughter anywhere," came a voice through the open door of our dressing room.

We all instinctively looked at the open door leading into the subterranean corridor in which there were several artistes' dressing rooms.

A person appeared in the timber-framed doorway, dressed in a billowing electric blue ball gown with sequins sewn into the various layers of silk and velvet.

"I immediately recognized your laughter Theo," said Queenie Leighton, as she progressed to where I was sitting!

We all got up to greet her.

"This is an unexpected surprise Queenie. What brings you here tonight; are you attending as a guest; since your name is not on this hand bill?" I asked gushingly, pointing to the handbill.

"I attend tonight in order to sing for my supper! As it happens, I am filling in for a friend of mine Katie Bele, who is indisposed this evening. I only agreed to step in at this late moment because I was given to believe that there is a new act in town which I am anxious to see," replied Queenie.

"Which act would that be?" inquired Jack.

"Why of course yours, that new turn called, *Houston, Mitchell and Marmaduke*! Hello Cinderella, how are you? I simply cannot wait to see you do your Marmaduke act!" said Queenie, whilst accepting a plate of whelks and a bottle of beer from Cinderella.

1. The Sleepwalker
2. Exhaustion from lack of nourishment
3. Plumpness

Chapter 13

The Reckless Generosity

The evening spent at Lusby's Music Hall performing our new act with Cinderella in the guise of Marmaduke, had been an outstanding success to the extent that even the manager, Wilton Friend, had come down to our dressing room to tell us so. He particularly congratulated Marmaduke, still wearing his stage clothes, on his masculine portrayal of a tortured soul given cogent expression in a ventriloquist's dummy. Cinderella, Jack and I now believed that we had a successful formula for our new act. Queenie Leighton had also sung for her supper, and to great acclaim. After our respective acts we had all managed to slip away from the Music Hall and find a local restaurant, in which we regaled ourselves with drink, stories and laughter well into the small hours.

The next morning, still feeling euphoric, whilst taking our break-fast Jack and I were joined unexpectedly by Lodge with Mabel on his arm. Having seated themselves at our table, Lodge remarked that he had some astounding information of the upmost import which he wished to relate to us. Before doing so he looked sneeringly at Jack's plate upon which were slices of Brätwürst and rye bread, a New York styled break-fast that Jack had reverted to.

It seemed that under great conditions of sworn secrecy

for some days past, Lodge had been using his undoubted connections and contacts with important people with whom he had some *sway*, as he called it. It is his intention to organize a spectacular extravaganza concert, a Titanic Benefit Concert, as it were, worthy of his talents as an impresario and reputation within the realm of Music Hall. Together with his legendary *reckless generosity*, in order that he might raise monies for the benefit of those dependent widows and children of the drowned victims of the recent ill-fated *Titanic* tragedy.

Lodge went on to outline his carefully thought out stratagem which, he claimed, would ensure more than acceptable, all important box office receipts and still enable him to make a *recklessly generous* donation for the benefit of the *Titanic* victims' dependents. This spectacular extravaganza is to be based on a so called White Star Line Songbook which comprises various songs, for different classes of passengers, of course. Ranging from first class to second class descending to third class. It was doubtful whether songs imported from the third class repertoire would have any real significance for the high class audience he envisaged and intended to attract.

"If this does not earn me a knighthood; then nothing will and I may have to make do with Companion of Honor being bestowed upon my person instead," Lodge remarked, jestingly. "After all, if that Enrico Caruso could sing at a benefit concert for families of victims of the ill-fated *Titanic* at the Metropolitan Opera House in New York, within two weeks following the disaster. Then it is surely incumbent upon me to organize a benefit concert here in London."

This remarkable development came as a total surprise to both Jack and me since neither of us knew that there was in existence such a thing as a White Star Line Songbook. Especially since Jack and I had steamed across the Atlantic recently from New York on the *Olympic*, a ship of the White Star Line and sister ship to the stricken *Titanic*, and no songbook was in evidence anywhere. Neither did we hear the crew, passengers or even stowaways singing a selection of uplifting songs from it.

Despite this, Lodge had somehow managed to avail himself of a copy of the White Star Line Songbook as the basis of his extravaganza. Knowing him we suspect him to be motivated by his all-consuming and abiding interest in his precious box office receipts rather than by altruism towards the victims of the doomed *Titanic*. Irrespective of this plausible suspicion, he produced a small hand bill of the event which he handed to us to admire.

Looking through the list of songs and singers reflecting First and Second Class. I could well appreciate for once, Lodge's rational in this respect, in not including into his dignified extravaganza, songs from the songbook for the delectation and amusement of third class passengers. Indeed this would appear to make sense; especially with such title as, *'My Old Dutch,' 'Two Lovely Black Eyes,' 'The Man on the Flying Trapeze,' 'I Live In Trafalgar Square,'* or the resounding song, *'I Do Like To Be Beside The Seaside.'* Songs I thought hardly appropriate when there had just been a major disaster at sea with a loss of over 1,500 souls.

None the less we remained cautiously optimistic about Lodge's new venture. An stratagem, which he assured us, would sweep all before it in creating an all time high in box office receipts. And, further augment his standing as an established impresario, not only in London but America too. Since the dreadful sinking of the ill-fated *Titanic* affected both our nations.

"This is all very well Loge," said Jack, "but will there be a rôle for Queenie?"

"Who?" replied Lodge.

"Since I recall," continued a phlegmatic Jack, undaunted, "she is more than capable of moving an audience in a controlled and emotional way and in a manner you are proposing with regard to your *Titanic* tragedy extravaganza. You were there Loge, when Queenie appeared on the stage at the New Bedford Music Hall unannounced. Yet within minutes of her appearance on the stage, she had the audience in tears. Such was the depth of emotion she was able create with members of the audience about the tragic loss of life on the stricken ill-fated *Titanic*. And Loge, during our thirty years each playing Vaudeville both in America and now in London, neither Theo nor I have ever witnessed such a natural depth of talent and..."

"Jack is absolutely right," I interjected, "we all of us witnessed an amazing ability that evening. I certainly recall her gliding on to the stage to tumultuous applause from all the sections in the New Bedford Music Hall. Rich or poor, crude or refined, drunk or sober; all were united in according her great acclaim, and justifiably so. The spontaneous applause which erupted simultaneously across the auditorium, lasted for quite some seven minutes, during which Queenie neither said, sang or did anything, save to stand there in her ethereal elegance.

"Presently she then raised her arms, and, with the palm of her hands facing down towards the stage floor lowered them slowly and in so doing silenced the audience. A hush descended over the stalls, dress circle and balconies making for an atmospheric tension throughout the auditorium. I remembered that action and hope to use it one day in my attempt to control an audience. But then she spoke and asked of the attentive and hushed audience how many had lost dear ones, friends or sweethearts when that ill-fated *Titanic* went down. In so doing, the doomed *Titanic* took with it their souls and dreams as it plummeted to the depths of the Atlantic Ocean.

"The responses from the individual members of the audience seated in either the dress circle or the stalls were astonishing as Queenie unleashed a tidal wave of emotion. People spoke of personal losses in loved ones, husbands, sons or daughters in a totally unabashed manner, crying freely in front of strangers with whom they felt no embarrassment.

"Some were moved to share their losses with statements such as, '...a very dear and loving husband of forty-five years married life, who was besotted of me.' Or, '...a loss, in the person of my husband, who was the epitome of faithfulness and selfless devotion, with a burning love the likes of which I shall not ever experience again.'

"But it was the words Queenie said which got members of the audience to respond, as total strangers started to hug each other affectionately and with a shared sympathy at their mutual loss. She stated with a measured dignity of delivery that the ill-fated *Titanic* had now become an 'Iron Mausoleum.'[1] Forever marooned on the seabed at the bottom of the Atlantic Ocean with all those souls trapped inside her iron hull, consigned to oblivion for eternity.

"It was then that Queenie began to sing from the your Choral Anthem Symphony in the particular rôle that addresses *Hope*! But before doing so, she told an attentive audience that it dealt with those deep feelings of sadness which have pierced our hearts, causing our love to leak away though the wound.

"The rhythmic development of the main melody

caused some members of the audience to move in unanimous synchrony from side to side in sympathetic response to Queenie as the music became more intense, during which the meaning of *Hope* was given powerful lyrical expression. This was so, for all to appreciate throughout the various sections of the auditorium of the New Bedford Music Hall. Queenie had delivered such a powerful and resounding tour de force in her rôle, that was fully appreciated by an audience who would not let her leave the stage at the end of her recital. They demanded more of her." I concluded.

Typically Lodge's response was predictable.

"This rôle cannot be for Queenie, Marie Lloyd, Dot Hetherington or indeed Katie Lawrence," was the only response we could elicit from Lodge, who still refused to acknowledge Queenie for her undoubted talent. What in the distant past had he done to her to cause this alienation, I wondered? I have often asked myself that burning question.

"Well, do tell us Loge, who will sing that precious and demanding leading rôle in your Titanic Benefit Concert?" asked Jack.

"I should have thought the answer to your inquiry was obvious," replied Lodge with clear asperity in his voice.

"I would not ask such a question if I already knew the answer. Surely that must be obvious," informed Jack.

"There is only one person Jack, only one soprano with the requisite wide tessitura and the ability to moderate her vibrato and who could be capable of doing justice to that demanding rôle to which you have just alluded," responded Lodge.

"Who is that person, Lodge," I asked.

"Why Mabel here of course," responded Lodge, "who else could I possible engage to do it?"

Having known Jack for over thirty years, I have seen a range of expressions upon his face. But never before such as the one which I was seeing at that very moment.

1. The Iron Mausoleum - A case of Sherlock Holmes and the Titanic. ISBN Number 978-0-9571629-0-7

Chapter 14

The Middlesex Music Hall

Our esteemed impresario in the person of Michael W. Lodge had shared his secret intention with us, to organize a spectacular extravaganza concert, a Titanic Benefit Concert, to raise funds for the benefit of the dependent widows and children of the victims of the ill-fated *Titanic* tragedy. Surprisingly the rôle of the lead singer in the concert would be none other than Mabel Green, much to Jack's amazement, if not astonishment.

Irrespective of this thespian largesse, Jack and I had considerations on our mind other than Lodge's apparent generosity. However overtly reckless, and no doubt designed to initiate box office receipts, an all too important aspect in Lodge's life.

We were discussing this and other issues over a late luncheon in the Grand Dining Room of the St. Pancras Hotel.

"I see that the repercussions from the sinking of the ill-fated *Titanic* continue to affect us even now. Not only was there a very great loss of life, but also a considerable loss of artwork too. In *The Chronicle,* there is a report in the Stop Press section, of an insurance company announcing the loss of a consignment of valuable art destined for an exhibition in America.

"The artwork, so the report states, is literally

irreplaceable and contains original works including Danby's *Wood Nymph,* and Scott's *The Enchanted Island.* Several paintings by Atkinson Grimshaw were in the hold of the stricken liner, including *The Deserted House,* which I have seen and liked immensely. There were paintings too, by European artists including Böcklin's *The Isle of the Dead,* Casper Friedrich's *The Ship Among the Icebergs* and huge paintings of classical architectural scenes by Moreau and Claude Lorrain. The sinking of that *Titanic* really is now assuming cataclysmic proportions as the repercussions are realized.

"Given Lodge's propensity for reckless generosity, he might wish to organize yet another benefit concert, only this time for distressed artists!" I said, handing *The Chronicle* newspaper to Jack.

"Do not forget, Theo," responded Jack, "later today we are scheduled to attend the Middlesex Music Hall in Drury Lane, Covent Garden to see our old friend from New York, Heywood Broun, who is booked in this afternoon's matinée to perform there."

"It is an undiluted pleasure to listen to Heywood Broun. He is, by far, the most accomplished of monologists performing in any of the Vaudeville theaters, including the Palace Theater on Broadway and 47th. Street. Not only is he an acclaimed exponent in his chosen field, but also remains an expert dialectician on a par with Professor Higgins who is a leading character in that play, *'Pygmalion,'*" I replied.

"But the astonishing aspect of Heyward Broun's character," continued Jack, "is the fact that he can talk at length on just about any current topic with such concentrated sarcasm or wit, as to defy belief. That is unless you actually go and listen to him. I remember when we went back stage at the Palace Theater in New

York to present our compliments to him after a sparkling performance. He spoke to us in exactly the same way as though he were still addressing the audience from the stage!"

"Still, an even more amazing fact about Broun," I said, "is the fact that he is also the drama critic working for the *New York Tribune*. 1 Can you believe that?"

Presently our waiter offered us Trichinopoly cigars, from a red velvet covered cigar box, to enjoy with our fine whiskies.

"So tell me Jack, you know about the Middlesex Music Hall, or the Mogul as you call it, what are the goods on the place?" I inquired.

"The Middlesex Music Hall in Drury Lane," Jack replied, "as with most impressive Music Halls in London, has a long and varied history, and has been called different names at different times during its existence. It started out originally as the Mogul Tavern, named for the Mogul of Hindustan.

"From 1828, the famous impresario Henry Cook ran, what cautiously might be described as a Glee Club, a hall in which meetings were held and songs sung. In 1847, the hall was rebuilt and renamed the Mogul Saloon. Performances, turns or acts, took place there on an elevated platform - the stage. In typical fashion, the place was renamed again, in 1851, this time to the more dignified sounding Middlesex Music Hall in honor of the county in which it was built.2

"Believe it or not, yet again in 1868 a fellow by the name of H. G. Lake took over the Middlesex Music Hall and instituted new building works that were completed by 1875. In 1878 control of the hall went to the landlord of the adjacent Mogul Tavern, a Mr. J. L. Graydon, who in 1891 rebuilt it yet again. Though now officially called the Middlesex Music Hall, just to confuse people, it is also sometimes called *The Old Mo,* and was immortalized by Walter Sickert in 1906 in a painting by him, of the balconies entitled, *'Noctes Ambrosianae.'*

"Then the Middlesex Music Hall was renamed the Middlesex Theater of Varieties, and then later in 1911 called the Winter Garden Theater. The theater has been incorporated into the rebuilt Music Hall, as the stalls bar and subsequently renamed for Nell Gwynn, who frequented the Mogul Tavern in her day. Do you follow me here Theo?" asked Jack.

"No," I replied, looking pensively into my whisky.

Later, having retired to our rooms to dress for our excursion to the Middlesex Music Hall, we reconvened in the foyer of the hotel. I was all for staying in the hotel and repairing to the well-appointed bar, rather than battling through the acrid fog that waited menacingly for us outside. When we did eventually step out into the porte cochère, the yellow fog immediately assailed my eyes causing irritation them. Thankfully we were able to step into a waiting covered Brougham carriage that provided some protection from the blinding fog that was now impressed with an unpleasant odor.

After some time clattering through the fog-bound metropolis, we arrived at the Middlesex Music Hall in Drury Lane. I looked up at it from the glistening sidewalk. Without doubt the building was impressive being constructed of red brick and dressed with Portland stone and polished granite complete with a corner topped with a tower addressing the roofline level. According to Jack, Oswald Stoll erected this building to the designs of the famous theater architect, Frank Matcham.

It was through the Shelton Street entrance that we entered the building. As we did so, Jack handed the stage doorman a note for the attention of Heywood Broun; which I knew was a note inviting him for a drink at the Crush Bar during the interval.

We then made our way through the building into the foyer, the décor of which was in a restrained Renaissance style. The large auditorium, into which we then proceeded, was more than capable of holding up to three thousand persons and decorated lavishly in the contrasting arabesque style . Presumably this was intentional and done to reflect the Music Hall's earlier association with the Mogul of Hindustan. Though personally, I could not see the stylistic connection.

We took our allotted seats in the Dress Circle and awaited the curtain rise. Despite the auditorium being capable of holding three thousand people; it was only half full. Probably the fog, which this evening was more dank and acrid and not at all pleasant to be in, was almost certainly responsible for this cataclysmic assail on box office receipts. As Lodge would no doubt interpret this detrimental situation.

Gus Elen was first to hit the limelight. According to the hand bill he is from Pimlico, near the Imperial Music Hall embedded in the Royal Aquarium and is a comedian and singer. On cue with the orchestra in the pit, he sang several cockney songs. Including, *'If It Wasn't for the 'Ouses in Between,' 'Down the Road,' 'Arf a Pint of Ale'* or *'It's a Great Big Shame.'* All of which he performed whilst acting about on stage in style imitating costermongers. Or at least so I believed.

His métier was as a *Coster Comedian*, through a stage character he had invented called Elen. Accordingly, whilst singing for his supper down there in the limelight he would strut about the stage, decked out in his costermonger's outfit, which comprised striped jersey, a neckerchief around his neck and a peaked cap worn at a slant. When he was not singing or talking, he would insert a short clay pipe into the side of his mouth and display for all to see his costermonger argumentative attitude together with his bad tempered personality. He was funny, but also courageous; for I certainly would not wish to impersonate a stall full of costermongers, for reasons which came flooding towards me, rather like a deluge of biblical proportions!

The comedian, Harry Tate the originator of the phrase, '*How's your father*,' so we were informed by a barely audible weak-voiced compère, was indisposed, but a certain Russell Alexander, the euphonium virtuoso and musician would be stepping in to fill this slot. He did so, with feats of magic whilst playing his silver plated instrument covered with engraved designs and from which he would occasionally extract pieces of vibrant red silk material from the horn, or at one stage, from his ear. Both Jack and I applauded enthusiastically for him.

One person who was not deterred by the fog and who would not ever be put off, no matter what the perceived danger, was the irrepressible Ella Shields, of Baltimore. We, of course, knew her from our early days of Vaudeville and she was always good fun to be with, especially back stage after an evening's performance. She was an acclaimed Music Hall singer, but specialized in impersonating male impersonators!

I recalled the time when I saw Vesta Tilley being impersonated by Ella in a song, written by Shields' husband and manager, William Hargreaves called, '*Burlington Bertie from Bow.*' This song became an immensely popular adaptation and parody of the song, '*Burlington Bertie,*' which was performed by Vesta Tilley. One can imagine what Vesta now thinks of Ella Shields.

"It is obviously the night of the impersonator," said Jack, during a lull in the proceedings, "because I see that Bessie Bonehill [3] is on next! You and I remember her Theo, as a Vaudeville singer, comic entertainer and male impersonator. Though I believe in fact she is English, we do remember seeing her in various theaters in the mid-west and on the eastern seaboard during the 1890s. And, did she not appear at Joplin, Missouri?"

"I believe you are right Jack. We met with Bessie when she was touring America with her own company. In particular, I remember the time when she arrived at Joplin Rail Road Station [4] to a tumultuous and considerable waiting crowd of well-wishers and supporters. We thought at the time the well-wishers had gathered for our benefit! Not at all, we were ignominiously leaving the station, having had a disastrous run performing at the Crescent Hotel in Eureka Springs in the Ozark Mountains. Rumor has it that she is one of the wealthiest Vaudeville artistes on the circuit," I said.

"Well Theo, facts have it that Bessie Bonehill, as the

Joplin Rail Road Station

progenitor of the male impersonator, is the inspiration for later artistes including, Vesta Tilley and Hetty King, to name but two. I recall her male impersonation acts were cheerful and contained no vulgarity, which at the time was a new departure in this kind of stage turn," said Jack.

"Indeed I recall an article in the *New York Times* describing her as, '...lithe and frisky, strident as to voice and nimble as to feet... and much at home in masculine garb as if to the manor born...' Her rise to fame started when our old friend Tony Pastor persuaded Bessie to perform her act at his Theater on 14th. Street back home in New York. I remember distinctly at the time that she was considered a valuable asset in Vaudeville and often appeared on the bill as, 'England's Gem.' [5] Or as, 'England's Favorite Comedy Cantatrice.' [6] It is probable that they were correct," I said.

"Well, let us see if she justifies such wealth; for here she comes," replied Jack, as we too applauded her entrance on to the stage.

As usual, she was a joy to hear and witness her impersonations of a couple of characters, which she accomplished accurately and with unabashed fun. After much bowing and repeated calls to return to the stage, Bessie finally made her exit.

The next act was by a certain Joe Jackson and listed as the Incredible Bi-cyclist and Comedian.

"I do not know this artiste from anyone, do you?" I whispered to Jack.

"Vaguely, I think he was born Josef Francis Jiranek in Vienna, Austria, where he began competing in bi-cycling races and finishing up in circuses roving the country, clowning around with his bi-cycle. He appeared last year on the stage in the United States for the first time. From memory, his act involves entering the stage dressed as a clown attempting to ride a bi-cycle that is slowly disintegrating, with bits falling off it including invariably the handle bars with which to steer the new fangled contraption.

Though do not be fooled. The man is a very talented and intrepid bi-cyclist and will often, as you will no doubt see, end his turn on stage with a series of astonishing tricks performed on his virtually dismantled bi-cycle," advised Jack.

"Why am I confusing him with another bi-cyclist called Barbette?" I asked Jack, who invariably is often quite knowledgeable in these matters.

"Barbette, or Mr. Vander Clyde Broadway, as he was called when he was born in Texas. After witnessing trapeze artistes and aërialists in action in the aëther inside a large circus tent, he desired to become one. Eventually an opportunity arose to which he responded. The Alfaretta Sisters, an aërial act, were seeking a replacement member for their troupe. He was successful in gaining the position; but alas in order to fit in sartorially with the rest of the troupe began dressing as a female with their enthusiastic encouragement.

"Such was his impersonation fame, that he continues this act today, though he left the Alfaretta Sisters some time ago and is now travelling around Europe, including London," said Jack, pointing to an agile individual progressing through the aëther above the stalls, much to the consternation or delight of the costermongers occupying the seats below the intrepid aërialist.

He did not so much as yield the stage to the next act, but rather flew off into the upper wings. Then all of a sudden the footlights were lowered and the stage plunged into darkness. Presently a solitary beam of soft yellow limelight punctuated the darkness and into this beam of light stepped an individual. He turned around to face his audience and in so doing the beam of soft yellow limelight illuminated the face of our accomplished monologist and expert dialectician in the person of Heywood Broun.

He started off in typical form.

"Tell me, anybody out there in the audience, how to make a small fortune being a Music Hall impresario," he demanded of us.

After a suitable pause, he furnished an answer.

"Easy, you start off with a large fortune!"

"I do not drink anymore; but then I do not drink any less!"

And so he went on in such vein, but he in turn gave way and abandoned the stage to Blanche Bates, from Portland, Oregon, who Jack remembers from her early days as being a serious actress when she appeared at the Palace Theater on Broadway and 47th. in New York.

She now clearly prefers playing Vaudeville for higher fees and more entertainment following her Vaudeville début playing Mirtza in the, 'Great Ruby,' in 1899 at Augustin Daly's Music Hall in New York having joined his company in 1898. She is of course famous for her rôles in, 'The Darling of the Gods' and 'The Girl of the Golden West.'

At length we too decided to abandon our seats and head backstage to meet with our old friend Heywood Broun, dialectician, monologist and esteemed drama critic of the *New York Tribune*.

"I think from memory Theo, Broun owes us a drink," advised Jack.

Accordingly, we increased our walking pace considerably to a well-appointed Crush Bar.

1. Later he was to become the drama editor for Vanity Fair
2. Historically that part of London was in the County of Middlesex
3. Bessie Bonehill died in 1902
4. Joplin Rail Road Station was built in 1911
5. Publicity for R Bonehill: England's Gem: The Story of Betsey Bonehill
6. Stevens Point Journal December 1894

Chapter 15

The Gaiety Theater

It was our intention to take the evening off, having met with our old friend, Heyward Broun from New York, performing during a matinée at the Middlesex Music Hall. But Lodge's invitation to accompany him, with Mabel on his arm, to the Gaiety Theater, as his guests was far too tempting an offer to refuse. Aside of which, Lodge is of the opinion that we need to experience the performances in that Music Hall. Accordingly, we had arranged to meet with him outside the Middlesex Music Hall at seven o'clock and on the dot.

Having said our farewells to Heyward Broun and threatened him openly with another session at a Crush Bar in the near future, we staggered out into the inclemency of the fog-laden weather. To the minute, Lodge's Barouche driven by Aloysius came looming out of the fog and towards us.

"His timing is too good to be this punctual," said Jack, "he has obviously been sitting, out of our sight, in his open Barouche carriage in imperial splendor, for the benefit of people passing by."

Irrespective of this, Jack and I clambered into his highly varnished Barouche carriage and sat on the green buttoned down leather upholstered bench opposite Mabel and Lodge, both of whom were illuminated by the bright carriage lamps on either side of them. Sitting behind them, on the bracket bench, driving the carriage was Lodge's man-servant, the inscrutable, but rude, Aloysius. He was decked out, as usual, in his ostentatious livery, comprising powder blue uniform impressed with gold braid and epaulettes complete with black top hat beneath which he sported a powdered gray horsehair wig.

Besides Lodge's suggestion, Jack and I had heard about the Gaiety Theater and were intrigued by it, so here was an opportunity to see for ourselves exactly what the place was all about. Rather that heading south down Drury Lane to where the Gaiety Theater was located, , at the eastern end of the Strand, according to Jack. Lodge had instructed Aloysius to take a detour through Covent Garden and approach the Gaiety Theater from the Strand.

"As an impresario," Lodge announced, looking at Mabel, "I have to be seen to be omnipotent. It is not enough that I am here; rather I have to be *seen* to be here!"

Lodge propensity for catachreses [1] was still very much in evidence. I think the word he intended to use was omnipresent, unless of course he meant something totally different, which, again, knowing Lodge may well have been the case.

"So, Mabel how are you doing?" asked Jack.

"Oh, I am fine. And, thank you sir for inquiring," replied Mabel, before emitting a repressed giggle to herself.

Our tour of Covent Garden progressed down one fog-bound street after another with Lodge looking out anxiously from his seat in the vain hope of being recognized. At length we pulled off a lane called Long Acre and made a left into a street in which there seemed to be a commotion ahead of us, as shadows danced in the opaque fog.

As our Barouche came upon the scene, I noticed we were outside a building, attached to the front of which were several intensely bright gas lamps in the form of globes. These lamps illuminated the commotion on the glistening sidewalk, which involved various people arguing with uniformed constables. I also noticed that Mabel astutely turn her head and looked the other way as we passed by. I assumed the scene of this unpleasant disturbance would upset her refined feminine sensibilities.

Presently we made a right into Tavistock Street, so the road plate informed me and then progressed on Lodge's frolic into Southampton Street, at the end of which was a building even I could recognize.

It was Jack who said it, pointing with his cane at the structure.

"That is where it all happened, in that very building there, the Vaudeville Music Hall."

"What did," asked Mabel, looking at Lodge appealingly with her large round eyes set in a face of overwhelming anonymity, "what terrible, what horrible tragedy or unmentionable thing happened in that, that Vaudeville Music Hall?"

"A wake Mabel.., said Lodge.

"Pardon! But I am awake," interrupted Mabel.

"No, no Mabel, a *wake*, we all of us here attended a Wake of Remembrance for a departed friend, whom we all loved dearly and continue to miss her sparkling personality," replied Lodge, lifting his eyes up and looking into the aëther above us, or at least into what the fog would allow him to look at.

"Oh you mean that Bella, what was her name, Bella, Bella Elmore, the comedienne; was she not done in by her husband the good doctor Crippen some weeks past?"

Vaudeville Music Hall

asked Mabel, marshalling her profound skills at ad hoc inventive diplomacy.

"No, no, no, Mabel, Bella has passed on…" replied Lodge

"Well I realized that Michael. Otherwise you would not have held a wake for her if she had been alive now would you?" interrupted Mabel. "And, I was making a polite inquiry as to how she died at the hands of her loving husband Crippen and not the fact of her being dead or passed on, that is all. Rather reminds me of that other Music Hall artiste Gerda Krum, who nearly, as you say, passed on, in 1907 when she survived a murder attempt on her life by her doting and loving husband, name of Ludvig Nathansen. Apparently he did so because he had ceased being besotted with her and, was jealous of Gerda's more successful career! After his failed attempt, he then committed suicide. Well, so much for being besotted with someone, that is all I can say."

"Tell us about the Gaiety Theater;" I said, endeavoring to change the subject, "what are the goods on it?"

"The Gaiety Theater is managed by the legendary George Dance. It is a relatively new theater, by the standards of existing theaters in London, including that Vaudeville Music Hall past which we have just driven. The Gaiety Theater opened in October 1903 and is irrevocably associated with Augustin Daly's Music Hall, the one in Leicester Square, not the one in New York on Broadway and 30th. Street.

"Like all Music Halls in London, this one is no exception in having a convoluted history. It started out, like me, with noble intentions, as the Strand Music Hall, built on the former site of the Lyceum Theater, not surprisingly, in the Strand located between Catherine Street and Wellington Street. It was then reconstructed in 1868 and renamed the Gaiety Theatre, but was in essence a Music Hall influencing the evolution of accepted musical comedies, including, *'Faust up to Date,'* *'Carmen up to Date'* and *'Cinder Ellen up too Late.'*

"That original theater was demolished in 1903 and a new theater built on the corner of the Strand and the Aldwych, that building over there, to which we are now headed," said Mabel, pointing with her white cotton lace parasol in the direction of the Gaiety Theater.

After some uncalled for discourtesy in the lobby, aimed at Lodge whilst he was queuing up to purchase tickets, we eventually took our seats in the Dress Circle. Jack and I flanked Lodge and Mabel, who sat to my immediate right.

We had only just time to do so, as the auditorium lights were dimmed signaling the commencement. Furthermore, as a direct result of Lodge instructing his liveried coach driver, Aloysius, to swan around Covent Garden, in order that the people might be afforded an opportunity to see him amongst them. We had not an opportunity to avail ourselves of refreshment at the tantalizingly well-appointed Crush Bar we had observed fleetingly on our way up to the Dress Circle.

This major calamity in no way impeded Mabel, who having made herself comfortable in her spacious, scarlet velvet upholstered seat, promptly whipped out a large, ornately engraved silver, hip flask from which she drank liberally. Having done so, she breathed out noisily. I could smell the whisky quite distinctly; and envied her. Nor did she offer her flask to me but instead rested it on top of the balcony wall immediately in front of us.

A hush descended on to the auditorium, but the purple velvet safety curtain had barely risen by a foot or two, before the compère banged his gavel on the block. From experience, I knew this to be always a bad sign at this initial point in the proceedings.

"Ladies and gentlemen, attend me please. Due to the pea-souper we are enduring outside, I am afraid to say that the valiant and victorious Vesta Victoria cannot be with us this evening. Nor can the incorruptible Lily Langtry and her leading man, Lionel Atwill, to quote excerpts from their new play, '*Ashes*,' which goes on tour at the end of the month," said the compère.

"Thank God for that mercy; the one thing I cannot bear is that dreadful woman, that Lily Langtry. Having to listen to her attempt to sing is bad enough, but having to endure her incessant ranting about the Blue Ribbon Brigade is even more than my tortured soul can bear. That woman, that accursed Valkürian woman Langtry is the one real threat to our cherished Music Halls, simply because she can never tire of promoting the strictures of her loathsome society, the Blue Ribbon Brigade, an abominable organization, which is committed to the ridiculous notion of banning alcohol in drink," said Lodge.

By now he was working himself up into such a state as to attract Mabel's attention, who in the meantime had stopped lifting her hip flask to her lips. Instead she replaced it on to the top of the balcony wall, with a look of surprise upon her normally vacant facial features.

"Accursed Valkürian woman indeed," were the only words Mabel could utter in response to Lodge's anguished description.

"Ladies and gentlemen," the compère continued, "all is not lost! We have for your amusement and delectation the flamboyant, if flaming, florid Florrie Forde!"

A rather plump looking woman marched on to the stage and immediately positioned herself virtually on top of the footlights. She did not wait for the orchestra to begin the introductory bars but simply looked out over the audience'

"This pea-souper irritates the eyes and makes seeing things ever so difficult. I cannot even see my old man, where ever he is and I do not mean in the *Battlecruiser* [2] either. Aside which, would you not rather be beside yourself with me beside the seaside?" She shouted out in to the auditorium. And then immediately burst into the song, '*I Do Like to Be Beside the Seaside,*' whilst exhorting the audience to join with her in singing this rousing rendition, in an attempt to banish the effects of the fog on the auditorium and box office receipts.

That song out of the way and the costermongers in the stalls suitably excited, she launched into another popular favorite called, '*Has Anybody Here Seen Kelly?*' which she sang out of tune with the orchestra, but with gusto. Without doubt, Florrie Forde has a powerful charismatic presence, when appearing on stage singing songs.

She also had an unerring ability to inveigle an audience into joining her in singing, especially the choruses, the words to which were memorable and easily repeated. Her last song was, '*Down at the Old Bull and Bush,*' during which most of those sitting in the stalls got up onto their feet and started swaying in unison with the rhythm of the song. Much, I noticed, to Lodge's disgust.

"She is scheduled to appear at the Royal Command Performance this season alongside Sam Torr and Marie Kendall," Mabel informed us, whilst taking another mouthful of whisky from her ornately engraved silver flask.

Moments later the second turn came on, in the person of Bothwell Browne, a female impersonator of such accomplishment that even Mabel screwed the cap of her hip flask back on. She then secreted it back into her sequined covered leather handbag and sat up to give her undivided attention to the performer. Bothwell started her turn, impersonating a woman, by strutting around the stage with a rolled up white cotton parasol and ranting on, in verse and lyrics, about the joys of being a woman.

I mentioned to Mabel that most of the acts we had seen thus far that day, including those at the Middlesex Music Hall, involved impersonators, especially men impersonating women. Mabel gave me a searching glance and then reached into her handbag to retrieve her hip flask, from which again she drank deeply.

Lodge's reaction to an inquiry by Jack about Bothwell, was to describe her as being;

"...a veritable peach!"

The singer and comedienne Helen Broderick was next on the boards, with a series of none stop wise-cracking comments and caustic observations. I remember Broderick, from Philadelphia, when she started out on as a chorus girl in Florenz Ziegfeld's famous, '*Follies of 1907*,' the first of many successful annual revues.

She in turn yielded to Ina Claire, from Washington DC. She made her impressive theater début in 1907 impersonating Harry Lauder during a Vaudeville act called the, '*Dainty Mimic*.' She achieved such great critical acclaim, that a booking agent I knew was moved to described hers as being one of the best single acts that he had seen during that season. And that she possesses a great deal of magnetism and was in short, a great hit with audiences. [3]

Since then Ina Claire had performed in two Broadway musicals which I went to see, such were the glowing reviews; '*Jumping Jupiter*' and '*The Quaker Girl*.' I knew she went on to tour Vaudeville on the Orpheum, Keith and

Proctor circuits. I was pleased that we had accepted Lodge's offer to join him here at the Gaiety and have that opportunity to see Ina performing again.

I was glad about being there, because it was apparent to Jack and me that most of the artistes performing on the boards that evening, were out of the United States. No doubt Lodge knew this and had therefore been motivated to invite us. Sometimes he moved in mysterious ways and could be influenced by the noblest of ideals and sentiments, other than box office receipts.

The safety curtain had not dropped but a few inches before an invisible signal triggered off what could only be described as a mass evacuation of the auditorium in preference for the Crush Bars. We followed suit.

It was whilst we were in the Crush Bar that I had an opportunity to speak with Jack. Mabel was standing with us waiting for our drinks from the bar.

"That woman, Bothwell Browne we saw earlier Jack, did not she just finish a Broadway production called, '*Miss Jack*,' which opened to great reviews at the Herald Square Theater last September? And, did she not perform with a Vaudeville artiste called Kathleen Clifford in a double-act of sorts?" I asked.

Jack looked at Mabel. A moment later Mabel, thinking she had recognized someone in the crowded Crush Bar, curtsied and left us.

"Theo, Bothwell Browne was born Walter Bothwell Bruhn in Copenhagen and is an acclaimed female impersonator," said Jack

"What he is, Danish?" I inquired.

"Well, Theo yeah, but he grew up in San Francisco and went into, where else, Vaudeville. You mentioned Kathleen Clifford in a double-act they performed together, she impersonating men and…" replied Jack.

"Here we are gentlemen," said Lodge, handing us a glass each and pouring champagne into them. "Where is Mabel?"

"Oh she recognized someone in the crowd over there and went off to say hello," offered Jack.

"That girl, that wretched girl, is never where she ought to be; I swear to God she will be the undoing of me yet!" replied Lodge.

Jack placed his fluted glass of champagne to his lips and then proceeded to pour the entire contents down his throat in one go, during what sounded like a stifled giggle.

1. Incorrect use of words
2. Public House
3. Quoted from Ohio State University - Theater Research Institute.

Chapter 16

The Quen's Hall

Yesterday, whilst taking break-fast at the St. Pancras Hotel, Lodge had informed Jack and me of his intention to put on a dignified musical extravaganza, an oratorio, including a performance of his precious Choral Anthem Symphony. The benefit concert shall comprise anthems and songs in an attempt to raise badly needed funds for widows, children and other dependents of the victims who had perished in the recent sinking of the ill-fated Titanic ocean liner. A laudable intention, no doubt, but with attendant suspicion as to the altruistic aspect of the venture, which Jack sees as nothing short of yet another exercise in a desperate attempt to increase box office receipts. More for Lodge's benefit not the intended beneficiaries. The extravaganza is to be held at the Queen's Hall in Langham Place, just north of Oxford Street. Having completed our break-fast; it is to that august establishment that we are now headed, in a Landau carriage, with Mabel and Lodge.

"What is it that makes you think of putting on such a noble and dignified concert? What is it that propels you to such extravagance of virtue by which you magnanimously intend that others might benefit from your selfless and undoubted and reckless generosity? What motivates that inner nobility of character, that will out, without any regard or consideration for that certain drain upon your time, munificence or resources, Michael?" asked Mabel.

She did so from the buttoned down red leather upholstered seat of our Landau, as we made our way along the fog-bound streets of the metropolis en-route for the Queen's Hall.

"Alas Mabel, I am cursed with a reckless generosity; I am irredeemably propelled by it, as all who know me will testify readily without hesitation or doubt. I simply cannot help myself at times; would that I could, more so especially when I see the plight of others much less fortunate than myself," replied Lodge, with an angelic look about his face, but still looking into the middle distance.

On reaching the Queen's Hall, Jack and I offered to help Lodge down from the Landau, much to his irritation and chagrin at being treated as though he were a confirmed, chronic valetudinarian in constant need of medical care and attention.

"Unhand me," he would utter, "unhand me I say, I am more than capable and I have not, as yet, been consigned to helplessness. Unhand my person this instant!"

Whilst Lodge fiddled about opening his purse, clearly unused to frequent bouts of reckless generosity nor extravagance of virtue, I looked at the front of the Queen's Hall. Even in the all-embracing fog it was evident to see that the building was indeed handsome, being clad in Portland stone creating a façade comprising rich carved details, including busts of famous composers and Greek gods and goddesses represented as pier torsos. All this was set beneath an overhanging, limestone framed, triangular pediment supported by fluted columns capped with Corinthian capitals, which added an ethereal majesty to the building.

We then all walked in to the hall, past two stone statues of Olympian gods in the guise of Atlas and Hercules who appeared to be bearing the entire colossal weight of the building upon their broad shoulders. Having gained the foyer, Lodge approached an usher resplendent in his black morning-coat with red piping, and informed him that we had come to see Robert Newman, the general manager.

The usher offered to escort us to Newman's office. Having ascended a broad, red-carpeted staircase to a landing on the piano-nobile, we continued down a corridor the walls of which were adorned with photographic images of famous composers and conductors. Upon reaching the office of the general manager, we were shown in to it and asked to make ourselves comfortable whilst waiting for Robert Newman. Indeed we did make ourselves comfortable on Chippendale chairs, the seats of which were covered in a pink and yellow striped moiré silk.

In front of us was a large elm desk with a bronze lamp stand in the style of a fluted Corinthian column supporting a green lamp shade radiating a soft light down on to the a pile of documents and scores which littered the desk. Newman's office was a well-appointed and comfortable chamber, hanging on the walls of which were an extensive array of images of conductors and musicians, clutching their fragile instruments. On the wall, above a well-stocked drinks cabinet, was an image of Gustav Mahler, whom Jack and I had met when he was in charge of the Metropolitan Opera and the New York Philharmonic Orchestra back home.

Complementing these photographs, were framed likenesses of artistes in impossible poses and with banal expressions upon their faces. On the walls, covered in

Gustav Mahler 1860-1911

red flock silk wallpaper with raised velvet decoration, were large gilt-framed paintings of sylvan scenes, including a Claude Loraine that I recognized.

Set into one wall, were three elongated, ceiling high, French windows leading out onto a balcony fenced with iron railings. Framing these windows, and pulled back and secured with gold colored twisted cords terminating with large tassels, were deep red and gold brocade curtains. Ranged around the room, were the ubiquitous attendant palm trees in highly polished green glazed urns placed on top of mahogany panelled jardinières.

Suddenly we heard voices, becoming louder as they approached the closed door. In an instant it burst open, and in stepped Newman, wearing a black frock-coat, striped trousers and spats covering a pair of highly polished patent leather black boots. His shirt was of white cotton and the outfit completed with a necktie of deep red silk fastened with a pin finished with a stone of sparkling yellow chrysoberyl, his only concession to fashion. As he approached Lodge, he threw down on to the red velvet covered chaise-longue, his shiny black silk coat, with a generous collar of luxuriant Astrakhan fur, rather like Lodge's own bulky coat.

"Lodge," said Newman, "good to see you again, after quite some time now, I think! Got your cable-gram, and of course, would be delighted to help in any way that I am able to in putting on your, is it the Cholera Symphony, to raise money for recent cholera victims?"

"No Robert it is not," corrected Lodge, "it is called Choral Anthem Symphony. No, the innovation I am about to unleash on an unsuspecting public is to be known as the Titanic Extravaganza Concert in order to raise funds for the victims' families."

Newman then approached Mabel and held out his hand. He repeated this gesture to Jack and then to me.

"Theo, of course, it is good to see you too!"

We shook hands, after which Newman bid us to resume our seats.

"First things first; what can I fix you all?

Mabel may I persuade you to take some Veuve Clicquot champagne?" inquired Newman.

"You most certainly can," responded Mabel, without any hesitation and whilst curtseying before resuming her seat.

"Lodge, your preference, from memory," said Newman, "is for the Coca~Cola with your whisky?"

"If it is that dark, aërated beverage made with cocaine and sugar, and has more punch to it than your ordinary Schweppes aërated water, then I should say so!" replied Lodge, rubbing his hands together.

"Oh, could I have some of the Coca~Cola in my champagne too," asked Mabel.

Jack and I contented ourselves with straight whisky, as being the only way to drink the stuff. Newman then opened his red velvet covered Trichinopoly cigar box and offered it to each of us, including Mabel, who took two cigars from it. After we had settled down with our drinks and cigars, Lodge started in.

"It is my intention Robert, to organize a memorial benefit concert in order to raise funds for those victims who are now suffering as a result of the dreadful sinking of the ill-fated Titanic boat, just these few weeks past. The concert will be attended with all the dignity and noble cause that such a virtuous and solemn occasion demands. My magnanimous gesture must be reflected in only the best of decoration and finest décor when we deck out the Queen's Hall. There will be laurel leaves abounding, red and purple pennants and flowers of course; lilies of the valley and red roses. As for the stage, that too will be decked out majestically with palm leaves, wreathes and black ostrich plumes…"

"Are we having a funeral service or a musical concert and which ever, do you propose to hold it in Hyde Park?" interrupted Newman.

"It is a memorial concert for those who perished Robert; we could hardly turn it into a festive light-hearted occasion. No, it must be a dignified and a solemn time of reflection and expression in anthems and lyrics to ease those hearts wrenched with emotions," delivered Lodge.

Mabel then got up and helped herself to more champagne and the Coca~Cola.

"There will be no compromises and no half measures. Only the best will do. And by that I mean, only those with money will be invited. After all, we do not want the

Undeserving Poor turning up en-masse and cluttering up the stalls demanding their share of the benefit fund there and then.

Extravagant gestures and money are no object; indeed it is my intention," continued Lodge, with a sweep of his arm backwards to indicate possession, "to spare no expense, for one needs to speculate in order to generate - box office receipts of course. There must be a pervasive aura of dignity throughout the concert expressing solemnity and a gravitas worthy of my reputation as an impresario. Therefore there cannot be a Music Hall feel to this occasion, even a vestige, hence Robert, the reason we wish to hold it in your august and eminently respectable Queen's Hall."

"Quite possibly," answered Newman, pouring out more whisky into our glasses, "although it really depends on how one might define, what exactly constitutes being effectively a Music Hall or not. Certainly, the Palace of Westminster boasts a variety of regular acts and turns almost on a daily basis, together with the fact, that it remains the only establishment I know of, which functions on mass absenteeism…"

"Is the Palace of Westminster a Palace of Variety or a Music Hall?" inquired Jack.

"A Palace of Variety Jack," answered Newman, "though if one were to describe that place as an Emporium of Taste, as Lodge defines the Royal Aquarium & Winter Garden, then one would do the latter an injustice! But I take your point Michael, the Queen's Hall is far removed from Music Halls such as the Royal Aquarium & Winter Garden and is an appropriate destination for your Titanic disaster, sorry, Extravaganza!"

"Just what will this dignified Titanic Extravaganza comprise?" asked Jack.

"Well apart from the hymns and anthems you saw printed on the hand bill, there will be a performance of the Choral Anthem Symphony, with Mabel here leading the singing in the rôle of *Courage,* supported by Katie Lawrence and Dot Hetherington espousing the rôles of *Aspiration* and *Hope* respectively," answered Lodge.

"Is that all?" asked Newman.

"No," replied Lodge, hesitantly, "I of course shall open the extravaganza and deliver a solemn, if dignified address, explaining precisely why we are all gathered at the Queen's Hall. At the end of the evening I will deliver a concluding speech with some well chosen sentiments to bring to a close the august proceedings. Believe me Mabel, Robert, Theo and Jack, that day will go down in history, you have my word on it!"

"What will Jack and Theo be doing, Michael?" inquired Mabel.

"Sitting in the very back of the stalls," answered Jack.

Chapter 17

The Visitation to the Madame

Our meeting with Robert Newman, the manager of the Queen's Hall had gone as well as one could reasonably expect. As for whether he was convinced about the efficacy of putting on a performance of the so-called Titanic Extravaganza was another matter. More of a concern for Lodge to worry about rather than or Jack or I. Naturally, being Vaudeville artistes, we were excluded from appearing in it, a prospect which did not particularly concern me; though I confess Jack and I remained curious about the outcome of the venture. For the time being however, we have an appointment later that day with the Madame.

We stood in the foyer waiting on Lodge whilst he finalized some detail regarding gas lighting in the auditorium. Mabel made her excuses as she felt some concerted effort was needed on her behalf rehearsing, if she was to do justice to her rôle and acquit herself with distinction. When Lodge finally deigned to join us, having completed his discussions with Newman, he had at least the decency to suggest that we take some much needed refreshment, perhaps in Soho, before we met with the Madame. It was however, whilst we were stepping out of the Queen's Hall and in to Langham Place that Lodge stopped us in our tracks and made a profound announcement.

"Rather than going into Soho, I will show you two something of interest," declared Lodge, "that will make your eyes boggle! There is a rather remarkable bar located in the basement of that Langham Hotel, that you see on the other side of the road, which is dedicated to the provision of every type of vodka distilled by the ingenuity of man!"

Indeed, only just visible in the fog was a large building with soft red lights radiating from the various levels of windows punctuating the façade of the building.

"It is perforce our noble duty to explore with relish every facet of life in metropolitan England.[1] Lead on Loge," said Jack.

Lodge merely looked at Jack as though the reason had been stricken clean out of his mind.

"I feel we may well need some fortification," continued Lodge, ignoring Jack's vacant expression, "if we are to acquit ourselves effectively with the extravagant Madame Duse, for she can be, as most accomplished thespians are, overpowering, even at the best of times. But irrespective of her forceful character, her acquaintance is worth making."

Lodge uttered these words with pronounced trepidation in his voice, which I notice had risen by at least an octave. For such was his nervous demeanor at the prospect of the meeting with her, the Grand Dame of the Theater. Clearly, I concluded, he must have had a frank exchange of views, to say the least, when last he spoke with her.

Moments later, we all three of us walked under the magnificent and elaborately sculptured stone vestibule, gathered our wits, and stepped up smartly into the Langham Hotel.

"It is to be remembered gentlemen," Lodge said, still with a squeaky voice, "that inside this hotel, within the chambers of his own state apartment, is the exiled French Emperor, Napoleon III, chafing at his confinement."

"Really?" inquired Jack.

Lodge then propelled Jack and me towards the grand staircase. Upon reaching it, rather than ascend the stairs, we followed Lodge and descended into the depths of the building and onwards to the subterranean vodka bar. Clearly Lodge knew his way around the basement of the place and made us follow him along a rather less grand corridor. At length, we walked up to a buttoned-down red leather covered door. Lodge then tapped on the wooden door frame with his ebony gold capped stick. A few moments later the door flew open, and standing there in the doorway was a person attired in what I took to be the red silk garb of a Cossack.

"Impresario, always a pleasant surprise to see you!" the Cossack said, whilst pulling at Lodge and me in his eagerness to usher us both into a large chamber, the type of appointment and décor of which I had never experienced before. Jack followed in after us. The general effect of the room was crimson and gaudy with gold relief impressed upon various raised decorative details reminiscent of Tsarist Russia. We walked upon a deep red silk carpet among items of furniture ranging from red damask covered chaises-longue to burgundy colored buttoned-down leather upholstered Chesterfields. Tall, gilt-framed mirrors hung upon the walls and some were affixed to the ceiling, rather precariously, so I thought.

We were not the only patrons present, for throughout the large, dimly lit room I could make out other persons sitting at tables deep in conversation with each other. No one looked at Lodge, Jack or me as we made our way to the bar. Our presence had no appreciable effect of the proceedings taking place prior to our arrival.

"Gentlemen, this will make your eyes bulge," said Lodge, as he indicated, with a sweep of his hand the back wall of the well appointed bar. There before our very eyes, in full sight of God, was the largest collection of bottles containing various kinds of vodka known to man which either Jack or I had ever seen. The wall of glass bottles, in which the spirits were imprisoned, must have measured at least twenty feet in length by eight feet in height. Indeed, our impresario had in no manner exaggerated his claim, as I now realized through my ranine eyes!

I was then introduced to Alexis, the proprietor of the bar, dressed in his extravagant Cossack garb. The style of outfit would make the ostentatious and flamboyant liveried uniform worn by Lodge's man-servant, Aloysius, look positively plain by comparison, I thought. Alexis began immediately to ply us with a range of exotic vodkas, made from, so it seemed, every vegetable or fruit, and some even containing gold leaf floating in the elixir.

For over an hour or so, I think, the drinks went down well enough, in conjunction with freely exchanged experiences and anecdotes. It was, therefore, with great reluctance that we eventually agreed to leave, and with even more difficulty in getting off our bar stools, and attempting to make our way into the fog-bound world upstairs,

"Carriage sir?" asked a liveried doorman, on our eventually reaching the ornate stone porch beneath the porte cochère in the front of the Langham Hotel.

At our instruction, the doorman stepped out in front of the hotel, and with a short shrill whistle, summoned a Landau four-wheeler carriage, that presently materialized from out of the still pervasive acrid yellow fog.

"To the Villa Duse at St. John's Wood in the Avenue Road, the Regent's Park end," instructed Lodge. With that injunction, our Landau carriage driver shook his reins, flicked his whip and turned the horses' heads north and clattered up into Portland Place. Presently we pulled into a colonnaded crescent, at the end of which I knew, was the very busy thoroughfare called the Marylebone Road. On this corner, Lodge had previously informed Jack and me, was a classical styled pavilion building through which one could gain access into a private garden, and from this garden, by way of a hidden tunnel, a so called Nursemaids' Tunnel, step in to a secret gentlemen's club called the Iron Vault.[2]

"That Nursemaids' Tunnel of course," Lodge went on to say, "you may recall my mentioning it sometime ago, also leads to that most remarkable establishment, a gentlemen's club called the Iron Vault.

Lodge then went on to remind us about that subterranean paradise. Indeed, I recall the last time Lodge

Nursemaids' Tunnel

spoke about this club, I resolved there and then to seek membership of it.

"The club to which I have alluded in the past is primarily made up of professional gentlemen who reject the more formal type of club, such as the Athenaeum, Reform or Carlton. In the main those members who comprise the club tend to have a more radical and tolerant attitude and include bishops, artists, University dons, Barristers, explorers and physicians. The prevalent atmosphere in the place is one of understated gentility and courtesy, in which members are unabashed and have a relaxing manner, quite the epitome of a gentleman's club, albeit in a series of Iron Vaults.

"Indeed, the club is made up of a series of rusting cast iron walls supporting cast iron vaults, forming arches upon which the Marylebone Road above is constructed. Adorning the rusting cast iron walls of the establishment, which gives off a reddish hue, are large pictures, in gilt frames, of ethereal or classical scenes forming an extensive private collection of rare masterpieces by artists such as Claude Lorrain, Atkinson Grimshaw, Böcklin or Thomas Cole.

"Large button-down red leather Chesterfield sofas and arm chairs are numerous as they are comfortable. Various polished brass objects are ranged around the large vaults, reflecting the light radiating from several crystal chandeliers suspended from the curved cast-iron vaulted roofs. Upon the floor is a luxuriously thick almost iridescent deep red silk carpet punctuated with gold fleurs de lys in the pattern, which certainly adds to the prevalent and opulent ambience of the place. The all important zinc plated bar is extensive and extremely well appointed," completed Lodge.

"How does one become a member?" I inquired.

"One has to be proposed by three existing members," replied Lodge.

"That might prove problematic, since I do not know anyone there, apart from your good self of course," I said.

"I have my connections," intimated Lodge, tapping the side of his nose with his index finger, "I have my *sway* with some members who may be persuaded to nominate you."

"That is gratifying to know," I responded, "I certainly did not realize it would be that simple to gain membership of such a prestigious establishment as that Iron Vault Gentlemen's Club."

"Nonsense," replied Lodge, "some members would be delighted to nominate you. They would do so for the simple pleasure of being able, at a later stage, to blackball you!"

Lodge looked ruefully at the innocuous looking pavilion as we drove past it and then over the Marylebone Road and through a set of ornate park gates. We then found ourselves in the Regent's Park, the fog in which was made denser by the all-pervasive dampness in the stilled aether.

"Come on Loge," said Jack, impatiently, "what are the goods on this dame; is she some kind of femme fatale or what?"

Lodge thought for a moment. To him, *she* would always be *the* Madame.

He then pulled his Astrakhan collar up, and as someone who had determined a course of action, commenced a description of the Grand Dame, more, I thought, to ameliorate his own obvious apprehension.

"Eleonora Duse was born in Vigevano, Lombardy in 1858 into an Italian acting family. Earlier in her life she commanded recognition by her acting rôles, made famous later by the indispensible Sarah Bernhardt, or rather Rosine Bernardt, as is her real name.

As Duse toured Europe, the United States, and even Tsarist Russia, she left in those countries a reputation bordering on genius as an actress of great repute, even if I say so myself. That reputation was to a great extent based on her interpretations of plays written by such august persons as Henrik Ibsen or Gabriele D'Annunzio, especially his play based on the *Francesca da Rimini* tragedy written in 1901.

Duse came to prominence when she joined Cesare Rossi's theater company in 1885 and travelled on tour to South America. Returning a year to Italy, she formed her own theatrical company, assuming the rôles of manager and director. Later she came to London and it was then that I first encountered her, which itself was an event of monumental proportion," Lodge informed us.

He looked for a moment into the middle distance, or at least as much as the fog would allow him to do so. At the same time, I distinctly saw him brush away a tear drop from his eye! Lodge, on noticing my observation of his momentary lapse of toughness of character, immediately qualified his act with a statement.

"Damned fog, got a smut in my eye, shall we be ever rid of this appalling irritating condition?"

He then applied his ostentatiously patterned paisley handkerchief to his eye with an inordinate conspicuous fuss, but then continued his narrative.

"Always one for having torrid affairs with the literati, between 1887 and 1894, Duse embarked on a liaison with the Italian poet Arrigo Boito, who you will recall was Verdi's librettist for his operas. In fact he was responsible for writing the libretto for the opera, '*La Traviata*,'[3] set to music composed by Verdi and based on the, '*La Dame aux Camélias*,' a rôle in which Duse made her own.

Later in 1895 she met the writer and dramatist Gabriele D'Annunzio. The two collaborated professionally with D'Annunzio writing numerous plays for her including, '*Francesca da Rimini.*' However, the affair came to a bitter end with a furious fight, when D'Annunzio gave the leading rôle for the première of his play, '*La Città Morta,*' to Sarah Bernhardt instead of to Duse," said Lodge ruefully.

"La Citta what?" inquired Jack.

"The *Dead City,* Jack, the Dead City," answered Lodge.

"I thought that opera was composed by Erich Korngold," Jack responded.

"It is probable that you are thinking about Korngold's opera, '*Die Tote Stadt*', which means the same but was composed later," said Lodge.

"Remarkably," Lodge continued, "whilst Sarah Bernhardt's personality could be described as being gregarious and extroverted and thrived on publicity. Duse's in comparison was introverted and contemplative, but given to wild outbursts based on her Italian ancestry. Notwithstanding this inflammable characteristic in her personality, she was sought out by numerous public and famous people. During a tour of the United States in 1896, she was invited to take tea, in her honor, at the White House with your President Cleveland and his wife, both of whom were followers of hers and indeed attended every stage performance whilst she was in Washington.

She has now of course retired from the stage, though there are repeated calls from her admirers and followers to return to the theater. But she is resolute in her refusal to do so."

"Why is that?" Jack asked.

"Ah, alas my lips are sealed and Valkürian horses, pulling on adamantine chains, could not drag the secret from the depths of my soul," replied Lodge, looking away from us.

I found myself becoming fascinated by Lodge's description of this Madame Duse.

"It was noted," Lodge continued, "that whilst on the stage, Duse wore very little facial make-up, preferring instead to present herself naturally and realistically in order to allow the inner compulsions representing grief or joys of the characters she portrayed to use her body as their medium for expression.

"It was this technique that defined Duse's genius in setting a new precedent which she described as, *elimination of one's self,* to internally connect with the character being portrayed and allow expression to occur naturally. Previously, of course, actors would use artificial or fixed expressions to convey emotions," said Lodge, whilst specifically looking at Jack, who responded accordingly.

"This dame, Eleonora Duse, was not she the one who had her American début in the New Fifth Avenue Theater on Broadway, managed by Augustin Daly, when she reprised her acclaimed rôle of, *'La Dame aux Camélias,'* in 1893?" asked Jack of no one in particular.

"You are correct Jack," I replied, "in fact we both of us went to see her in that New Fifth Avenue Theater. The reason we went, if you remember, was not so much to see her, but rather to experience the new sensation of being in the first theater to be fully air-conditioned!"

We all of us lapsed into silence to absorb what I had just said; that or what Lodge had imparted about the Grand Dame of the Theater, Eleonora Duse.

In the meantime, the hooves of the horses hauling

our Landau carriage clattered in time on the cobbled stone road which appeared to be a perimeter carriageway of the park, We progressed past ornate stucco clad classical buildings and terraces painted in a dull cream color as we negotiated our way through the fog. Eventually, we left the confines of the park and pulled into the Avenue Road, so our liveried coachman informed us.

"What number Avenue Road Guv?" the driver inquired of Lodge.

Minutes later we arrived at the Villa Duse and Jack and I were the first to step down from our carriage. Lodge, wearing his outsized overcoat with luxuriant collar of Astrakhan fur, still rejected Jack's offer to assist him down from the Landau to the York flgstoned paved sidewalk.

"Let me alone! Let me alone I tell you. I am in no need of your unwarranted help; for I am not quite valetudinarian, I will have you know," Lodge reminded us.

Clearly Jack was not convinced and continued to support Lodge's elbow.

We looked at the white painted Villa Duse, just discernable in the swirling fog. Lodge looked even more apprehensive and there was indeed a feeling of trepidation as we made our way along the pathway leading through the garden. The pathway led up to the villa's front door, which was frame in a concrete pilaster-styled structure. As we approached the building its architectural details came into sharper focus.

Essentially the building was, if anything, cubic in design with only a coffered cornice projecting out from above a series of unarticulated windows reveals punctuating a flat regular façade. The mannerism of the villa clearly

The Villa Duse

reflected early traces of a new style of design I think they call *Jugendstil*.[4] The Grand Dame's house of imposing dimensions had only been constructed recently; for there was evidence of building works still being carried out on the structure.

To the side of the house barely discernable in the fog was a vestibule, the flat roof of which was supported by square columns with intricate fluted groves etched into the flat surfaces.

It was Jack who reached the front first and accordingly knocked upon it, much to Lodge's chagrin. We waited for a while. After a few minutes Jack knocked upon the door again, but louder this time. Eventually we did elicit a response but alas, not from where it was expected.

Instead of the front door being opened, a diminutive servant dressed as though he were an undertaker in a black tail-coat appeared at our side.

"May I be of assistance?" came a lugubrious voice that sounded as though it emanated from a marble lined tomb.

"We have an appointment with your mistress," said Lodge.

"If you mean Madame Eleonora Duse, she is hardly

my mistress, for I am an employé in her service," replied the servant.

"Possibly," responded Lodge, somewhat put out, "and impertinence noted. However, we have, in fact come to talk with her and not you."

"Perhaps," said the man-servant, "but I understood that an impresario of sorts had an appointment with Madame Eleonora Duse. She is not expecting this group of persons, whom I am reluctant to allow admittance into this house. Madame Eleonora Duse, follows an inflexible routine, allowing no uninvited persons to disturb her."

"I beg your pardon!" exploded Lodge, enraged by this man-servant's confident attitude and impertinence in front of us. "Does the name Lodge, Michael W – impresario mean anything to you?"

"I cannot say it does, but then I do not attend the theater nor Music Hall to watch a person doing impressions of other people, for that is what I assume an impresario does on stage," replied the man-servant.

I noticed, as indeed Jack did too, that Lodge's monomanic affliction, that of looking over both shoulders had returned, due to the stress he was now enduring.

Lodge was beside himself with controlled anger at having to endure this truculent flunkey behaving in such a confident manner at his expense in front of us all and, I might add, with no shame. Whilst I could not believe this situation in which we found ourselves, I do believe that Jack found it amusing.

"Do you propose to leave us standing outside this front door and is this the normal way you greet guests of Eleonora Duse in such a belligerent manner?" demanded Lodge.

"I will confer with Madame Eleonora Duse" he said,

stifling our protest at the ill-treatment meted out to us, and promptly walked back along the pathway to the side door entrance beneath the vestibule.

"This is intolerable," said Lodge, "never in my life have I been so shamefully treated by a man-servant.

"Is he, I wonder, in any way related to the obstreperous Aloysius, your man-servant?" inquired Jack of Lodge

A full twenty minutes elapsed before we heard a shuffling noise from behind us. It was the man-servant and he had returned, but had clearly taken his time in coming back to us.

"I have conferred with Madame Eleonora Duse and as a direct result of my interceding on your behalf, she will grant you an audience, during which Madame is prepared to tolerate members of the public, such as yourselves!" the man-servant had the audacity to announce.

We followed this individual along the pathway to the side door entrance into the villa. The indignity of using the tradesmen's entrance to the villa only added to Lodge's seething annoyance at being so insulted at the hands of a flunky, no less!

"I can well understand Lodge's trepidation at visiting this woman," I whispered in Jack's ear.

At length the man-servant abandoned us in what I took to be the main hall of the villa. A peripheral balcony set on the *piano-nobile* surrounded the hall. I looked up expecting to see Madame Eleonora Duse peering down, over this parapet wall, at us. Instead my eyes caught a most peculiarly decorated ceiling. It reflected the coffered cornice projecting out on the outside of the building we had seen whilst waiting for the surly man-servant.

The ceiling comprised an elongated panel with a recessed deep blue glazed inset. This panel in turn was surrounded by a series of smaller square coffered panels, again with a recessed deep blue inset. The ceiling though ostentatious was also very elegant.

My attention was taken away from this ornate ceiling by the re-appearance of the impertinent man-servant who merely looked at us.

"Walk this way and follow me," he then instructed.

"Why, what is wrong with the way we walk already?" asked Jack.

The man-servant chose not to respond to Jack's facetiousness and instead led us through one dimly lit salon after another. Eventually he tapped gently on one of two large, double-leaf, mahogany doors and then opened them both fully.

"Madame," he began, "the impressionist is here accompanied by two other characters. He then bowed and retreated, closing the mahogany double-leaf doors behind him.

The drawing room in which we found ourselves was large and the walls were covered in a heavy, dark purple, flocked silk wallpaper. The only illumination in the room came from four wall-mounted brass candelabras, but the light from them was weak and served only to add to the subdued feeling in the drawing room and further augment the heavy stillness of the aëther within the chamber .

There were three sets of ceiling high French windows punctuating one of the walls of the drawing room, but the heavy green velvet drapes in front of them were drawn excluding all light from the outside. Around the room were various palm trees embedded in large red glazed urns placed on top of limestone jardinières. A highly varnished Aëolian Pianola occupied one corner of the room.

In the background a phonograph could be heard softly echoing, through its large engraved brass horn, elegiac arias which I recognized were from Verdi's opera, '*La Traviata*,' adding to the strange surreal atmosphere in the darkened room. The feeling was as if one were standing in the presence of a goddess, about to offer up adoration.

We all of us looked around the dimly lit chamber expecting to be greeted by Eleonora Duse at any moment. Then, imperceptibly at first, I detected a sound, above that made by the phonograph, followed by a movement behind a palm tree at the far end of the drawing room. We all began to walk in the dim light toward the movement. As our eyes became used to the dimness we could now make out what had caused the noise accompanied by the movement. It was she; the Grand Dame of the Theater, Madame Eleonora Duse, lying outstretched on red velveteen covered chaise longue and looking for all to see very much like the *La Dame aux Camélias*, racked with consumption.

Lodge re-acted instantly, abandoning himself to an extravagance in manner by blowing exaggerated kisses with his fingers into the stale aëther inside the drawing room.

"Cara Mia! Cara Mia! My precious! My Eleonora!

To which she responded by rising imperiously, if serenely, from her reclined position upon the chaise-longue.

"Michaeli, Michaeli?" she responded questioningly, "What a pleasant surprise, my butler has only informed me that you have just this instant arrived!"

Jack and I just stood there.

"How charming!" she continued, with a benign dignity exuding from her statuesque presence.

She was dressed in a mid-night blue silk gown

complemented with a red scarf partially covering her head in a style beloved of Pre-Raphaelite artists when endeavoring to depict the Greek goddess Athena. Beneath her radiant face, and secured around her neck, was a magnificent brilliant faceted ruby stone that complemented her red velvet elbow length gloves.

After Lodge and Eleonora had exchanged a few pleasantries with each other, Lodge turned around to Jack and me, and bade us to come forward to be introduced to the great Eleonora Duse.

"Eleonora," he started in, "may I introduce Jack Mitchell and Theo Houston, Vaudeville artistes from New York. They are in England, as my guests, in order that they might experience and perform in various London Music Halls."

On approaching us, she held out her hand. It was Jack who accepted it gratefully, holding it up to just near his lips in a very chivalrous manner.

I followed in a few moments later as she then turned to me and offered her hand with such dignity that I felt obliged actually to kiss it with a bow, if not a flourish.

She really was quite a striking looking woman, not beautiful, more handsome, but of course her character and presence were the result of her many accomplishments. I knew from reading several articles about her in the *Variety* journal over the years, that she had many admirers too. Standing before her it was easy to see just why that was the case. Even in the dimly lit drawing room, she would have been quite attractive in an earlier life.

"American you say? I took tea, you know, with your President, Grover Cleveland actually in the White House when last I performed on the stage in Washington DC. So, we will have tea now," she announced, and promptly struck a nearby bronze gong with a wooden mallet.

Within moments the surly man-servant re-appeared, bowing in an ingratiating manner to the Madame Eleonora Duse.

"Carlo, bring tea and, bring a cake too?" she instructed, with a wave of her hand. "And Carlo, push the plug back into the wall socket; otherwise the electricity will leak out on to the floor."

"Eleonora's admirers and followers, and they are legion, continue to try and tempt our precious Eleonora into returning to the stage. But alas my Cara Mia, my Eleonora will not hear of it. Could I, Eleonora, beg you to return to your devoted audience, who want you amongst them again," pleaded Lodge, crossing his chest with his arms in mock supplication.

Eleonora merely looked at him with a questioning, almost disdainful, look upon her face.

"Michaeli, you know that I have no wish to return to the stage," she at length responded.

"But, Cara Mia..!" pleaded Lodge.

"If I had my will," continued Duse, "I would live in a ship on the sea and never come nearer to humanity than that!" [5]

"Fair enough," said Jack.

"Think about those glorious reviews about your brilliant portrayal of the heroine in, '*The Second Mrs. Tanqueray*,' at the Lyceum Theater in London during the 1900 season. Even *The Echo* newspaper was moved to declare your interpretation as being a resounding tour de force for all who follow you to learn from. And your spell-binding rendition of '*La Dame aux Camélias*,' at Daly's Music Hall in Leicester Square," begged Lodge, "your audience awaits you!"

"Why do you ask such a meaningless question," said Eleonora, "you know that I have decided to retire from

Rowenlea Mansion, Pittsburgh

the stage, therefore what reason could possibly enter my mind to make me contradict myself?"

I noticed Jack's eyes looking upward to the ornate plaster ceiling of the drawing room and Lodge looking slightly uncomfortable.

"But think of your devoted and faithful audience Cara Mia. Surely the pleasure you give them might, just might, be enough to soften your heart and relent and return to us," said Lodge, in a sycophantic way, whilst rubbing his hands together.

Eleonora's response to Lodge's pleadings was unexpected as it was decisive.

"It is my intention," advised Eleonora, turning to face Jack, "to travel to Pittsburgh in the state of Pennsylvania soon and there stay with a very good friend of mine, Alexander Peacock. He lives in a wonderful house he has named Rowenlea. A beautiful place that I have always enjoyed being in. Do you know Pittsburgh in Pennsylvania Jack?"

"We both of us do Eleonora. My partner here, Theo,

and I were there not long ago performing actually at Rowenlea Mansion for Alexander Peacock, the steel magnate," replied Jack.

This fact alone endeared Jack and me to Eleonora almost immediately. She could hardly contain herself in having in front of her two people who had not only been to Pittsburgh, but, actually knew Rowenlea House and Alexander Peacock in particular. She was delighted and her soft brown eyes indicated so.

"Tell me about your experience there, I beg you. Come Jack please, Theo you too, come sit and tell me all about Rowenlea," said Eleonora clutching Jack's arm. Jack relished in this overt show of affection and showed his delight, much to Lodge's chagrin, if not annoyance.

We duly sat on either side of Eleonora on a large green damask upholstered sofa, leaving Lodge to find a seat some distance away on a blue satin covered foot stool.

Consequently, we all of us noticed that Lodge's affliction, his monomania for looking over both shoulders, having started as a re-action to the man-servant's confident attitude to him at the front door, was now increasing with a vengeance. Such was his nervous state which could bring on his monomania when subjected to stress as he was now enduring at the hands of Madame Duse.

Not for the first time had Jack supplanted the affections of a woman for Lodge by his arrival. I remember when we were in the Alhambra Music Hall in the Leicester Square recently, when Marie Lloyd turned up at the Crush Bar. Within minutes she was arguing with Lodge over the famous *Exclusivity Clause*, [6] whilst obviously smitten with Jack's showering her with glowing compliments, including calling her a Greek goddess in human form.

"Yes, Eleonora, we were there only recently," Jack continued, "as a rsult of Theo and me being booked to perform our stage act at the famous Duquesne Club in Pittsburgh, during a high society wedding reception organized by the millionaire in question, the steel baron Alexander Peacock. Afterwards he personally invited us to join in the celebrations which were now being moved to his newly built residence called, Rowenlea. As far as I am concerned, and I know Theo agrees with me, I guess Alexander Peacock remains one of the most remarkable persons we have ever had the pleasure of meeting with. Up until then Theo and I really had no idea who Peacock was."

"As you know Eleonora," I said, "Peacock has constructed his large mansion house on Jackson and Wellesley in the very wealthy district of Highland Park in Pittsburgh. Our being there turned out to be one of the most amazing experiences Jack and I have ever

Duquesne Club, Pittsburgh

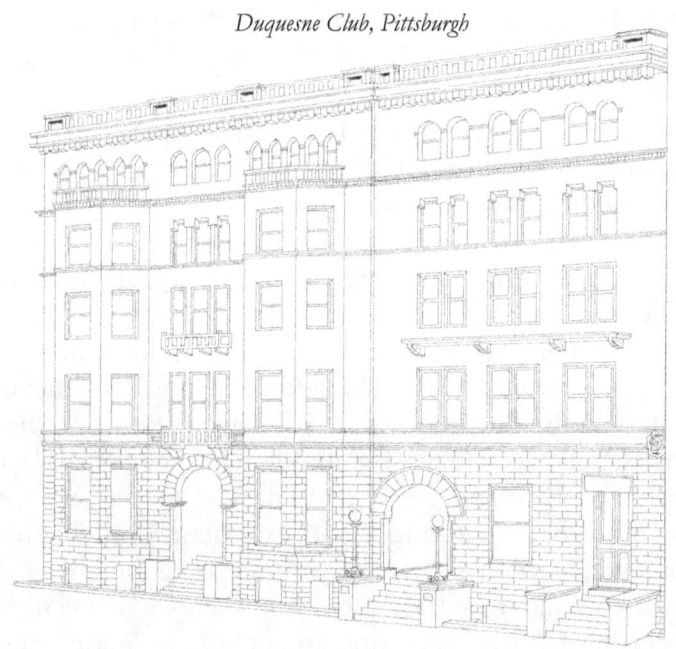

experienced in the whole of our stage careers. Whilst at Rowenlea we witnessed a variety of experiences, including listening to the music being created by six gold-plated Aëolian Pianolas simultaneously throughout the house and all playing different musical pieces!"

"He certainly is a fascinating person and so is his residence," said Eleonora, wistfully, "when last I visited there, it was a time a great happiness for me."

"Will that happiness attend your person when you return there soon, Eleonora?" inquired Jack.

She smiled at him with a deep affection in her soft brown eyes.

"Jack, the weaker partner in a marriage, is the one who loves the most as much as sorrow is the real cost of love," [7] she responded, before turning away momentarily, "Una Sospiri."

"Madame Duse, where will you go?" asked Jack.

"Evidently to where destiny leads my weary soul," she replied.

"Can this be the brave Eleonora I know of, who dispatches fear to oblivion and courage to the frightened?" inquired Jack.

"Fear is my nearest relation; with courage being but a distant cousin and curiosity a recent in-law," she replied, smiling.

Jack thought for a few moments, but continued.

"That Rowenlea was a handsome building could never be in doubt in my mind Eleonora. Peacock has constructed his Valhalla, but in doing has made it a place in which to live and create happiness. This was not the first time that Theo and I had experienced enchanted moments, particularly in our appreciating buildings. I know you did too Eleonora. But there at Rowenlea, especially to the accompaniment of the sonorous arpeggios emanating from the several Aëolian Pianolas resounding throughout the mansion and into the garden, even more so. The whole experience of being there was magical, in every sense of the word." said Jack.

"What made me, particularly, enjoy immensely being at Rowenlea, and I feel certain you will agree Eleonora," I suggested, "was the fusion of masonry and foliage which complemented each other. In so doing, they created a mysterious and delightful place where something new or unexpected would stimulate one's senses at every turn, providing a series of pleasant surprises. Experiencing the house, in conjunction with the gardens released in me at the time, reservoirs of imagination to which I could readily apply to inspired uses."

"We can only envy, Eleonora, your being invited back to Rowenlea and the possibilities of experiencing again the magic atmosphere of the mansion and gardens," concluded Jack.

"This Rowenlea mansion seems like an interesting place," said Lodge, to which nobody responded.

At that juncture, the drawing room double-leaf doors opened and in walked the man-sevant, name of Carlo, pushing a trolley with a variety of comestibles on it, including fairy cakes with cream, surrounding a large tea pot.

"Ah, tea," announced Madame Eleonora Duse, "you will all please take tea with me and fairy cake too?"

1. The capital city, London.
2. For a fascinating account of this place refer to novel The Iron Soul - A case of Sherlock Holmes and the Napoleon of Crime, Chapter 3
3. The Fallen Woman
4. Art Nouveau
5. Quoted by Eleonora Duse
6. Prevents artistes from appearing in different Music Halls in the same neighborhood
7. Quoted by Eleonora Duse

Chapter 18

The Flame of Life

Having been introduced to Eleonora Duse, the Grand dame of the Theater. She had taken an immediate liking to Jack and me. Perhaps on account of our knowing of Rowenlea Mansion. A fabulous residence built in the wealthy district of Pittsburgh and owned by a steel baron, name of Alexander Peacock, and for whom Eleonora has a profound and fond affection. That she was imperious in her manner could not be in any way doubted; for within minutes of our being introduced to her, she had relegated Lodge in favor of giving her undivided attention to Jack and me. In the meantime, her surly man-servant, Carlo, was busy preparing tea on the trolley he had just wheeled in to the drawing room.

"Jack, how do you take your tea, a concoction or infusion?" she asked, nonchalantly.

"Oh, a concoction every time for me, Eleonora," replied Jack.

"And Theo?" she inquired of me.

"An infusion, please Eleonora," I replied confidently, knowing precisely which I was choosing.

Lodge, she did not bother to ask, but merely nodded at her man-servant to ascertain his preference. Moments later we were handed gold rimmed white china cups on saucers containing our tea.

"Might I persuade you Jack, to indulge yourself in these delicious *Bloaté Delights*.[1] These small sandwiches made from bloater pâté are simply divine and a favorite specialty in Lombardy. Theo, I insist you too try some," said Eleonora.

I complied with her imperious demand and helped myself to three of the small triangular shaped sandwiches bulging with Bloaté pâté. The moment I took a bite of one, I knew that I had made a mistake of monumental proportions. The smell that came off the sandwich was disgusting as was the taste, both of which combined to induce faint nausea in me almost immediately.

I think the fish may have been semi rotted. Or was this pâté supposed to be rotted as a particularly Italian specialty. Either way I was now left with two on my plate and desperately trying to think of a method of surreptitiously disposing of them. Especially under the eagle eye of Eleonora and the ever watchful Carlo, her facetious man-servant. He, needless to say, had noticed my predicament.

"Please Theo, please, you must eat your *Bloaté Delights*, whilst they are fresh. And Carlo, give fairy cake with cream to Theo too" insisted the Grand Dame of the Theater.

"We were discussing, on our way here, your meteoric rise to fame," I offered, whilst accepting innocently a fairy cake from the man-servant Carlo, "especially your American début in the New Fifth Avenue Theater on Broadway in 1893. Together with your notoriety generated as a result of your acclaimed rôle of, '*La Dame aux Camélia,*' in that play written by the French novelist, Alexandre Dumas. I remembered your powerful interpretation and remain, even today, very moved and impressed by it.

"How did you feel about your début performance Eleonora? I ask this because Jack and I, and indeed the whole of the theater attending public then were fully aware of how you applied your unique ability. A gift which allowed the character you were portraying to emerge from your personality in a very natural way, free of artificiality."

"Theo," she responded, with a slight blush to her pale face, "you are too kind. I have always sought to be a real interpreter of character on the stage, and it is for that reason I will only portray those characters whose personalities are such that they possess depth, which I am able to express, as you say Theo, without recourse to emotional sentimentality or artificiality."

"Does that preclude your inventing the character on stage beyond that envisage by the playwright?" asked Lodge, interjecting to make his remote presence known.

"It is not for the playwright, dramatist or the creator of a character to instruct us, the actresses, in how we represent their characters on stage. For what do they know? They remain pre-eminent in their field of writing. It is for us to express their thoughts in the reality of the theater; be it on stage or in the arena, for the audience to experience, and might I ply you with more cake Jack?" asked Eleonora, handing him a plate upon which was a generous portion of cake with cream.

"But surely the playwright or dramatist must retain some idea of how they wish their literary creations to be expressed, rather than being interpreted..." replied Lodge, despite Jack's glaring at him.

"No, no, never" interrupted Eleonora, "it is the province of the actress, not the creator, to interpret the rôle of the character. A writer confined to his garret in the attic producing one work after another is not in a position to understand how that work will translate on stage in front of an audience. We the actresses do understand; it is what acting is all about. We portray the character.

"Take for example the rôle I played in Alexandre Dumas's play, '*La Dame aux Camélias.*' Had I interpreted that character according to the ideas he formed for his heroine, the play would have been an unmitigated disaster for all concerned. I gave his thoughts life by my acting in a real and natural way for the audience to enjoy and more importantly, appreciate and for…" said Eleonora.

"But, Eleonora…" Lodge butted in.

"I have not finished yet!" interrupted Eleonora, glaring at him with her dark smouldering Latin eyes, but nonetheless continued.

"…the playwright creates in his mind a scenario, but it is the actress who converts that dream into a reality using the theater as the medium to give meaning and life. But, that concept of today's theater is now passé."

Jack looked intently at Eleonora.

"To save the theater," Eleonora Duse said, "the theater itself must be destroyed; the actors and actresses must all die of the plague. They poison the aëther, they make art impossible. It is not drama that they play, but pieces for the theater. We should return to the Greek way and play theater in the open; the drama dies of stalls and boxes and evening dress, and people who come to digest dinner." [2]

"Well, I would not go quite that far, Eleonora," said Lodge, whilst accepting another *Bloaté Delight*.

I think he did so only to please Eleonora. For they were decidedly, revolting and comprised, without doubt, rotted bloater fish, the type we would immediately throw back into the Hudson River back home in New York.

"What do you mean, you would not go that far?" retorted Eleonora, looking at him with her blazing Latin eyes.

"We can hardly destroy all the theaters in London, Paris or New York now can we? Were we to do so, where would the audience go to listen to your powerful renditions? London, I am afraid to say, as with New York, is not quite Athens, where there they are able put on a Greek play, or melodrama, outside in the open in an amphitheater.

"In this respect, the Mediterranean climate is more conducive to this facility than the weather in fog-bound London. Imagine it Eleonora, were you to perform on stage outside in Trafalgar Square especially in the fog; we would neither be able to see nor hear you," said Lodge.

The Madame refused to even acknowledge this faux pas by Lodge. Jack, however was about to respond to Lodge, but Duse simply looked directly at him.

"It is like this room where we are sitting," she said, "with all the tables and chairs. Do I care whether others have possessions as twenty or twenty-five links on their necklaces? Other actresses and the rest of them; it is not that I want! I want Rome and the Coliseum, the Acropolis in Athens; I want beauty. I want the flame of life!" [3]

Lodge drank deeply from his glass then breathed out noisily. He looked at the Madame with a studied expression upon his facial features. Both Jack and I, and one would suspect Eleonora too, could determine by Lodge's manner that he was going into his Theseus mode. Whereby, according to Cinderella, he was a dab hand at extricating himself from awkward situations. Mentally I braced myself accordingly for a master class by Lodge.

"It is a well known axiom Eleonora," said Lodge, slowly and with great deliberation, "that erudite statements and altruistic intentions are all very well and they have their rôle in some circumstances and may even be applicable in the course of a philosophical treatise or proposition. However, the rationale of theater be it Music Hall, Vaudeville or even that Shakespeare fellow, is that of entertainment, not of instruction.

"Jack and Theo here will testify to you, if pressed, that recently I had an opportunity to admonish successfully, the Metropolitan Board of Works, here in London, because of their endeavor to proscribe or at least define what the great British public want in terms of entertainment. This wish can be readily translated into box office receipts. We none of us will make a living on the stage if what we propose to offer is simply rejected by the public, who are able to vote with their feet as to what they find acceptable, or not. And..." continued Lodge.

"The Metropolitan Board of what?" interrupted Eleonora Duse.

Lodge was now fuelled with that burning passion that Jack and I had in the past witnessed, especially on the occasion which Jack and I attended and saw him take on the Metropolitan Board of Works, who at the time did in fact wish to revenge themselves upon his person.

"The Metropolitan Board of Works," continued Lodge, "is a public body here in London charged with the task of building deep level sewers, an unenviable work for which they are without rival and eminently suited."

"They build deep level sewers; this Metropolitan Board of Works? They are in charge of opera in London?" asked Madame. "I am talking about the flame of life; not deep level sewers."

Lodge looked up to the heavens ,or at least to the ornate stucco ceiling of the drawing room.

"Not really. The Metropolitan Board of Works attempted to impose their regime of what they consider to be acceptable in our London Music Halls, but I was having none of their artistic belligerence..." explained Lodge

"I think that I understand," interrupted Eleonora, "but the fact is still there that the glorification of the person often is emphasized at the expense of the art. This of course is a trait of the bourgeoisie, which will always defeat their endeavors to rise in social standing, because of this endorsement of the cult of the personality, which is destructive to art and artistic creation.

"Endeavoring to gain access into the class immediately above them is perforce their undoing. The bourgeoisie can never change to become that which is beyond them. What they do instead is to infiltrate aspects of the upper classes' domain, especially in England; Goodwood Races, Henley Regatta, Wimbledon, hunting or even the opera. Rather than adapting, which they cannot, they try to impose their values, including the cult of the personality. In so doing they destroy the very thing they desire!

"The only thing they achieve is to shunt upwards that class above them, who of course, will find refuge in alternative interests and pastimes. The bourgeois class will, yet again find themselves with only a Pyrrhic victory resounding in hollowness as they survey the deserted rationale of their endeavors. And yet the reason is simply; rather than dwell on the importance of music – its structure, its sublime beauty, its ability to inflame our passions, release our soul or ignite our imagination; they concentrate on the performing musician to the exclusion of the music.

"And, rather than consider the depths of the painting, its composition, its fine representational detailing, its ability to excite our imagination or confirm our thoughts, the bourgeois class will applaud the painter only and relegate the artwork to irrelevance. This is how their minds work, in their consuming inordinate adoration of the cult of the personality. Irrespective of profound talent and ability, because of that adulation of the *persona*, cult of the personality at the expense of the art form often accompanied by a manifestation of being ego-centric and sybarite.

"How many of us here sitting here in my drawing room have seen where culture has been acquired by the yard, especially in the homes of the newly enfranchised bourgeoisie? Libraries filled with shelves of un-cut books written by famous writers. Bronze or porcelain figurines by famous sculptures positioned badly in a room, or oil paintings by well-known artists exposed to direct sun-light and other wonderful creations by acclaimed designers?

"No? It is because wealth allows the bourgeoisie the ability to acquire instantly the accoutrements of success without any concept of appreciation of the works by those creators. It is similar to demanding that a Haydn string quartet be played merely to fill a vacuüm of silence and in so doing so they reveal their real philistine distain and real contempt for the arts of which they know nothing.

"Were this villa to be engulfed in flame, I would reach for nothing more, except that bronze representation of an outstretched hand that you see on the table over there. It was fashioned by the acclaimed master, Auguste Rodin. I know Auguste and we have spent many occasions with each other over the decades discussing art. He admired my acting technique; I his art. He wanted to capture that quintessence of me. Not in the form of a bust of what my head and face might look like were they cast in bronze. No, he chose to represent me, but only in the expression of that hand.

"He felt that I interpreted very effectively physically aspects of character portrayal with my hands. After all our hands, after our mouths, are the second expressive means we have at our disposal to apply. In this respect, I can read Rodin's mind whenever I gaze upon that sculpture. And, I would never be without it; not because it represents my hand, but rather it interprets my thoughts," concluded Eleonora Duse.

"Fair enough Eleonore, but we cannot all come from privilege where meeting the famous and revered comes naturally as drinking tea. Some of us exist to provide for others. And here I am speaking Music Hall and yes, acting too. Since we four sitting around your drawing room are involved in theater, even if I mention so myself putting my hands up, or should I say hand?" asked Lodge, in a failed attempt to mitigate himself.

Whether Lodge was being facetious or indelicate I could not determine, but I suspect Jack had no such difficulty in deciding which. However it was Duse who replied.

"Ever since I have known you Michaeli, you have reflected this thinking, that is to debase art for financial reward only. To you the performing artiste is all important; irrespective of the interminable nonsense they act or sing. And I include in this class that Marie Lloyd, whom I know you venerate!"

That last remark by Eleonore Duse, was calculated for even me to appreciate. She had, without doubt, insulted Lodge by attacking his precious sacrosanct beliefs in box office receipts and his being a sybarite. Whilst in the same breath, dismissed Marie Lloyd as being a good an example of nonsense. That would please Lodge, but at what cost, one wondered. Certainly a protracted discourse at best or a polemic at worst was in the making as both verbally squared up to each in what could only be described as engaged in a Titanic battle of wits. And for the present, so it appeared to me that Madame had the upper hand against Lodge during this encounter.

"I was at the esteemed Royal Aquarium & Winter Garden, you know the temple to the arts and instruction in Victoria, when..." said Lodge.

"Can it be that you are trying to improve your mind Michaeli; for there is much that could be done?" inquired Duse.

This witticism elicited an unexpected response from Lodge, in the form of a restrained high pitched giggle combined with rubbing both hands together, another idiosyncratic trait of his.

"Not at all Eleonora, but I was speaking with George Leybourne the manager there, about you in fact. We both of us concluded that yours was a voice, an interpretation to witness, simply because people go in their droves to hear you because..." said Lodge, ingratiatingly to entrap.

"No, no," interrupted Duse, "still you do not understand Michaeli what it is I am saying; you never do. Try to stop thinking in your bourgeois manner. I once dispatched a reporter in New York who thought he was complimenting me on my vocal *interpretation* of Verdi's, '*La Traviata*,' by saying that I gave it life by acting out the various roles rôles in that dramatic expression.

I did no such thing. A literary work called, '*La Dame aux Camélias*,' was born of the mind of its creator, the French novelist, Alexandre Dumas. That work in turn became the basis of a libretto written by Francesco Maria Piave, which was set to music composed by Verdi and now known as the opera, '*La Traviata*.' [4] The life of the opera stems from its origin in, '*La Dame aux Camélias*,' and it was this salient fact that the reporter in New York failed to grasp. As indeed you are doing Michaeli because..."

"Then do tell me!" interrupted Lodge, in exasperation, born more of the primary stages of alcohol intake than considered diplomacy. One presumably attends the theater, Music Hall or Vaudeville to experience accomplished artistes acting and regaling an audience, and not to inveigle then into something approaching amaranthine introspection, no?"

For myself I was unable to differentiate between Lodge's bellicose stages of inebriation with which he was now becoming clearly affected, including his resorting to the use of catachresis.[5] We all know from bitter experience that it is a cardinal mistake to drink vast amounts of alcohol if one is feeling particularly anxious! It is likely I thought to myself that Lodge on this occasion will not merit the distinction of being called Theseus. Nor indeed be able to extricate himself from his dilemma.

"I could," continued Duse, "recite the meaningless alphabet set to music and go up and down the scales if it is just my voice you want to hear. But as I have said before; it is not about the performer and this obsession with the cult of the personality, often to the detriment of the art form. It is about the *elimination of one's self*, to act as conduit for the original thought," so said the Madame, baring her soul on the matter, but clearly exasperated with this conversation and indicated so with her demeanor.

I was about to get up and applaud these sentiments, expressed by the Madame Eleonora Duse, but, the nauseating effects of eating those putrid *Bloaté Delights* together with suspect fairy cakes in which the cream was rancid, washed down with sweet anæmic tea, prevented my doing so. In fact it was too much for me to bear and so I resumed my seat on the sofa next to Eleonora.

Then both Jack and I witnessed a scene from the front row seats, as it were.

Lodge must have been distracted by the vile *Bloaté Delights*, he was attempting to deal with; that or his attention to detail had momentarily deserted him. Eleonora, had on two occasions, desisted from admonishing him, deservedly, over his inordinate and confident replies to her. Erroneously, Lodge evidently though therefore he was gaining the ascendency in this discussion. Both Jack and I knew this to be not the case. Her intense personality wound up by her Italian emotional temperament, and evident for even the blind to see, finally broke and erupted as Mount Vesuvius might.

"Michaeli, you make light of what I say," she said, whilst rising from the sofa. "Do you think I merely talk without giving any thought to what I am saying as though I were an automaton?

"Do you think that because you are impresario, feeding off other artistes' talents with your abominable *Exclusivity Clause* [6] that you really understand the theater and those of us who work in it?

"In the time I have known you, the only abiding love you have ever shown is to your precious box office receipts and to nothing or anybody else," said Elenora, in a way that was not offensive, but rather endearing.

"Somebody has to look after the underside of theater and Music Hall. We cannot all be thespians quoting interminable nonsense. Someone has to look after the Music Halls; because at the moment, they do not look after themselves, as if by magic. They have to be funded by impresarios, such as me. And were this not to be the case, no artistes, famous or unknown, would have the ability to perform let alone sing for their supper.

"Even with the greatest of intention, highfaluting concepts which abound, do not make box office receipts. That is to say money, yes money with which we pay fees and wages and provide work for countless persons we engage and employ..." said Lodge

"What do you mean?" interrupted Eleonora, "Do you have the temerity to even suggest that we, we artistes, rely upon you for engagement in your theaters or Music Halls? It is you who rely upon us!"

"We both of us need each other," replied Lodge, in a conciliatorily manner, though without conviction, "it is our contacts, our knowledge which enable you to perform in theaters and Music Halls throughout America, England or Europe. Alas, we too have our rôles to play on the world stage of life."

"To help, to continually help and share, that is the sum of all knowledge; that is the meaning of art," [7] were the only words with which Eleonora replied.

She then relit her Trichinopoly cigar whilst looking at Lodge and with a sigh pronounced the following words carefully and slowly.

"If the sight of the blue skies fills you with joy, if a blade of grass springing up in the fields has power to move you, if the simple things of nature have a message that you understand, rejoice, for your soul is alive..." [8]

After she had uttered these words she looked at Lodge. Then, with a wave of her arm, Eleonora retreated into a far corner of the drawing room.

Two aspects of Eleonora's character came into sharp focus and became abundantly apparent to Jack and I to appreciate; her intense real personality, together with her stage persona portraying characters, both of which were lethal.

I now understood why Lodge was filled with trepidation during our carriage ride here. He knew Eleonora sufficiently well enough to realize fully the type of character which he would be engaging with on our arrival here at her home. But as with all people who endeavor to impress others; they risk annihilation, as it were, at the very hands of the person whom they seek to control for their own purpose in order to impress others. This afternoon's engagement between Eleonora and Lodge did, if nothing else, demonstrated this fact.

We were all for leaving if only to acquire some alcohol, for it was to be remembered we had only been offered tea, weak anæmic sweet tea and sandwiches of rotted *Bloaté Delights* made from bloater fish turned into a pâté and cream cake. We had not been offered any alcohol, even low grade alcohol and were not surprisingly, aching to leave and get some real refreshment.

It was Jack who walked over to the corner to be with Eleonora. I decided to stay where I was as a result of my being incapacitated due to a rapidly increasing upset stomach brought on by the *Bloaté Delights,* one had been compelled to eat, more out of politeness rather than hunger. Lodge, in comparison, looked even more uncomfortable at the juncture upon the realization of the delicacy of the situation. However, he had but little time to consider it, because at that very moment, the man-servant Carlo, reappeared with Lodge's shiny silk top hat in one arm and his oversize overcoat with collar of luxuriant Astrakhan fur on the other.

Lodge merely accepted the garb from the insolent man-servant, almost as though it were a coup de grâce.

Lodge looked at Eleonora and bowed in taking his leave of her.

She acknowledged his farewell stiffly, with a wave of her arm cover in her red velvet glove.

"Arrivederci Michaeli, arrivederci." 9

After Lodge's departure, we all three of us resumed our seats on the sofa, but it was clear that Eleonora Duse had been slightly put out by Michael Lodge's, or Michaeli's, insensitivity. It must be obvious when dealing with such an august person as the Madame Duse, that tact and decorum were essential in any liaison, if only because the occasion demands it. This oversight was not a Lodge trait. Quite the reverse; normally Lodge is impeccable when dealing with recalcitrant persons, except that is, that woman, Marie Lloyd, for whom he has no forgiveness!

I would be disappointed to believe that Jack derived some pleasure or indeed Schadenfreude 10 from this latest episode with the Madame and Lodge; but I suspect that he did!

We did speak with Eleonora for quite some time and it was only when the man-servant came into the drawing room to advise Madame of the time, that we all realized that night had descended up us. Of course we had been oblivious to the diffused fog-laden daylight outside, as the window curtains had been drawn during our visit.

Never the less the Grand Dame of the Theater invited us to stay over night as her guests. We both of us fell in eagerly with her suggestion, for such an opportunity as this could never be turned down. Accordingly, she instructed the man-servant to prepare two bed chambers for us. She herself looked somewhat exhausted, and got up from the sofa to retire to her own chambers. Before leaving she expressed the sentiment that she had thoroughly enjoyed our company and fervently hoped she could do so again in the near future!

And with that, bid us a peaceful sleep as Jack and I, in turn, took her glove covered hand. She then withdrew through the large double-leaf mahogany doors leading out of the drawing room and into the adjacent salon, leaving Jack and I somewhat perplexed by our experiences during the evening.

1. Smoked bloater fish turned into pâté
2. Quoted by Duse
3. Quoted by Duse
4. 'The Fallen Woman'
5. Incorrect use of words
6. Prevents artistes from appearing in different Music Halls in the same neighborhood
7. Quoted by Duse
8. Quoted by Duse
9. Until we see each other again
10. Delight at somebody's else's misfortune

Chapter 19

The Music in the Night

We had been invited by the Grand Dame of the Theater to stay overnight at her new villa in St. John's Wood, a wealthy neighbourhood north of the Regent's Park. During the course of our visit which lasted into the late evening, Lodge had met his Nemesis, in the person of Eleonora Duse. She had dispatched him off forthwith to oblivion for daring to express ideas or opinions clearly at variance with hers. I put this down to Lodge not giving due consideration to his replies to Eleonora. And in this respect totally underestimating her innate Latin temperament or re-action to those responces. In comparison, I too had not taken into account the debilitating effects of the vile *Bloaté Delights,* made with rotted bloater fish, a delicacy in Italy, and stale fairy cakes with rancid cream. I was compelled to consume these comestibles, more out of courtesy than appetite. For now I was paying for my misplaced courtesy to please Eleonora, as a dull ache worsened in my stomach.

Having been shown to my bed chamber by Carlo the man-servant, I simply collapsed upon the bed fully clothed. I stared at the ornate ceiling, punctuated with small domed lamps, which radiated a soft light throughout the chamber.

I drifted off into a half sleep as I tried to reëxamine

some of the profound remarks which we all of us had heard earlier emanating from Eleonora. Including such deep and penetrating remarks as,

'...the theater itself must be destroyed; the actors and actresses must all die of the plague.'

Or,

'...if I had my will, I would live in a ship on the sea and never come nearer to humanity than that.'

A touch draconian, I thought, but guess there it is!

In my half sleep, I also came to realize that hers was a personality founded on high intelligence blessed with a natural compassion for those concepts which comprise her surroundings. Her character was complex, because she addressed those profound and intricate ideas which punctuate our lives. Hence her natural expression of reality, through, as she calls it, *the elimination of one's self,* and its attendant ego-centric cult of the *persona* in order to achieve that ethereal state of mind.

It was this technique, of course that defined Duse's genius in representing the grief or joy of the characters she portrayed to use her body as their medium for expression. A genius I had come to appreciate, having been offered the privilege of making her acquaintance earlier. Or perhaps I had simply come to understand her abilities and personality in not using contrived expressions to convey emotions on stage or, deploying inane artificiality off stage.

I came out of my reverie motivated by the light coming down from the ceiling mounted lamps and by my raging thirst caused by the stomach discomfort I was enduring. I therefore rose from my bed, looking at my steel case pocket watch as I did so and discovered the time was twenty five minutes past the mid hour at night.

I opened the door of my bed chamber and stepped out

into the landing, partially illuminated by wall mounted appliqués, in the form of angels holding forth in their hands firebrand-shaped torches at the end of which were opaque lantern globes radiating a weak light. It was however, sufficient for me to be able to see where I was walking in my search for water.

I made my way down stairs, not certain where I was headed or indeed from what room I would find a source of water. Then I recalled seeing a carafe of water upon the sideboard in the drawing room. I knew where the drawing room was from the staircase down which I was now descending. Accordingly I quickened my pace, in order to alleviate my thirst with water from that carafe.

I had only walked for a few moments or so in the direction of the drawing room when my attention was arrested by the faint sound of muffled singing and tinkling from the Aëolian Pianola I had seen earlier. Nothing unusual in that, given we were in the house of a renowned thespian. I progressed toward the double-leaf mahogany doors which I knew, with confidence, would lead into the drawing room and as I did so the music became louder.

Urged on more by my thirst than curiosity, I opened one of the double-leaf doors quietly. I peered inside expecting to see Eleonora singing accompanied by a soloist, possibly her supercilious man-servant Carlo, playing the Aëolian Pianola. I did not. Instead I moved cautiously farther into the drawing room, still shrouded in semi darkness, as we had left it earlier with the heavy velvet drapes still drawn against the ceiling high French windows.

Not wishing to disturb the musician, but only to avail myself of the carafe of water, I continued. It was where I remembered it being, there on the sideboard in front of me. I moved towards it. And in so doing became aware of several silver-nitrate images, of the daguerreotype method encased in tooled red leather surrounds, which I had failed to notice before. Though I was certain they had not been present when we were in the drawing room during the course of the evening.

I picked one up. It was a sepia tinted likeness of Eleonora Duse looking resplendent in her black silk stage robes. I studied the image. It was taken perhaps some years ago when her beauty was all too evident to appreciate fully with her imperious, though dignified, appearance radiating from the tarnished photographic image.

I picked up other leather framed silver-nitrate images and as I did so my attention was then caught by a strange light at the far end of the room that emanated from beneath a door leading into an adjacent salon. I stopped and squinted at this light coming from the room next to the drawing room and tried to make sense of it.

As I moved towards the open double-leaf salon doorway from which the light came. I realized that the music being performed was that of the Abbé Liszt's original transcription for pianoforte called, 'Années de Pèlerinage,' [1] in particular, the, 'Troisième année,' [2] leading into the harmonious, 'Les jeux d'eauà la Villa d'Este.' [3] I knew instinctively that the music was being created by the Aëolian Pianola rather than by a pianist. I elected to sit on a nearby chintz upholstered Chippendale chair and drink the water from the fluted glass that I was holding, which I had filled with warm water from the carafe. The feeling was surreal, if ethereal, as the sonorous arpeggios and triple A's assailed my ears.

Accompanying the Aëolian Pianola paraphrasing, was an accomplished soprano singing softly with a coördinated precision and synchronised to a perfection with the music emanating from the mechanically operated pianola. It was divine and made up for my stomachache. Eventually, the sublime arpeggios ceased as the triumphant finale faded away into silence.

I sat there for a few moments savoring the exquisite sensation my senses had just been subjected to. I got up quietly to leave and return to my bedchamber having quenched my thirst, when all of a sudden another noise assailed my ears. It was a phonograph recording of an aria which I too remembered as being the haunting one from Verdi's opera, '*La Traviata*.'

I decided not to resume my seat but rather to explore the origin of this music. On reaching the open double-leaf salon door I hesitated for a moment, but curiosity as to why this divine music was being played at night, drove me on. Possessing my soul I walked into the room only to be confronted by a sight that took my breath away and creating a vacuüm in my chest.

The chamber was empty save for a huge white *Carrara* marble fire place set into one wall and a chandelier tinkling with cut glass. All the walls in the room were lined with shimmering black silk. Cut into one wall were three full height French windows, in front of which were white fine lace curtains flapping in a light breeze as though they were ghosts chained to the floor.

It was not the Spartan décor of the room that had surprised me; rather it was a vision, an ethereal vision of Eleanora. She was dressed from head to foot in a black silk robe leaning against the white *Carrara* marble chimney piece with one arm hanging loosely at her side, and the other covering the top of her head, as though in deep contemplation of memories past.

The elegiac music emanating from the phonograph

was that for which she became famous in her accalaimed interpretation of, '*La Dame aux Camélias*,' and immortalized in the opera, '*La Traviata*.' I also came to realize that her poise and demeanor represented those of regret, as if the flame in her life had been extinguished.

Suddenly an overwhelming feeling of profound sadness enveloped me, made more acute by the pervasive feeling of stillness of the aëther in the room. At the same time, the words she had imparted to Jack earlier in the drawing room came flooding back to me. I came to realize the full implication of those words she had said; and now they have more meaning for me.

'When we grow old, there can only be one regret; not to have given enough of ourselves.' [4]

Not wishing to intrude or be discovered, I withdrew from the salon and left the Grand Dame of the Theater to her solitude and recollections of a rich life of experiences.

1.   Years of Wandering
2.   Third year
3.   Fountains of the Villa d'Este, Rome
4.   Quoted by Eleonora Duse

Chapter 20

The Reëncounter at Kettner's

The next day Jack and I, having slipped away from the Villa Duse in the early hours, were taking break-fast in the Grand Dining Room of our hotel during the course of which we talked about our meeting the previous day with the august Eleonora Duse. We both agreed that hers was a formidable character shaped by a life filled with variety and experiences, including those of sadness and happiness. I was pleased to have made her acquaintance and hoped to do so again. Lodge cabled us earlier to say that he would be picking us up in his Barouche carriage at noon. He had specifically requested we join him in a meeting, at Kettner's Restaurant, that had been arranged between him and Marie Lloyd, at her insistence.

"I wonder just what it was that alienated Eleonora from Loge." Jack had posed this challenge whilst reclining on a blue satin upholstered chaise-longue in the Grand Salon of our St. Pancras Hotel to where we had repaired to, having taken break-fast, whilst waiting on Lodge to collect us.

"Beats me Jack," I replied, "but I imagine Lodge's consuming adoration, to all exclusion, of box office receipts and Eleonora Duse's profound love of life, could cause anguish or at least conflicting priorities between them. And I suppose over the years they kind of drifted apart from each other."

"It is nearly noon Theo. and I suppose we had better brace ourselves mentally for Lodge's encounter with Lloyd, which could turn ugly!" said Jack ruefully.

At that moment Lodge appeared in the large ornate double-leaf open doorway of the salon. He paused before entering the spacious room, in a gesture designed to allow people time to notice his presence. Eventually he made his way to where we were sitting. Negotiating his way around various items of furniture, palm trees and sofas as he did so with a seasoned skill.

"Good day gentlemen, are we rested after that gruelling day at Eleonora Duse's yesterday? She can, as I feel certain you noticed then, be rather trying and prone to be melodramatic! But then I did intimate this characteristic trait of her's to you."

Jack did not even look up at Lodge but continued to read *The Daily Telegraph*. I knew he was not the mood to tolerate Lodge's veiled attack on the woman whom Jack admired.

"Why do you want that we should accompany you to Kettner's for your meeting with Lloyd?" I said, in an effort to restore some semblance of respect and courtesy amongst us.

"Because I believe your presence will be of great value and have a calming effect on that Lloyd woman, who can become emotional and dogmatic, especially when forced to have to hold a reasoned discussion. And also, I remember that woman, that dreadful woman Lloyd, who has taken against me, is prone to hysterics. As you well know, the last time I had the misfortune of encountering her was at my poor Bella's Wake of Remembrance at the back of the Vaudeville Music Hall in the Strand.

"There Lloyd acquitted herself in a thoroughly disgraceful manner with behavior not only unbecoming, but typical of her roughened character. And I might add, she was drunk as well as being intolerably rude to all and sundry. But that she was certainly out of control could never be in doubt, falling in and out of your arms Jack; well rather like Jack in the Box, as it were," said Lodge, with asperity.

To Lodge, Lloyd will always be that woman, that infernal woman.

"I seem to recall Loge, that Marie Lloyd spent a lot of time in deep intelligent conversation with the impresario, Sir Augustus Harris, the manager of the Theater Royal at Drury Lane. It was only later that Marie drew herself away from Sir Augustus and came up to Theo and me to offer her condolence over Bella's untimely murder at the hands of her doting husband, Doctor Crippen," said Jack.

"Really Jack, you surprise me. I recall that woman Lloyd on first meeting you in the Alhambra Music Hall and your response to her. Calling Lloyd, quote, 'my precious Greek Goddess in human form.' Could you have really meant those words or were you quoting some Music Hall rhyme?" inquired Lodge

"Of course I did Loge; good manners are my forte," replied Jack.

"Her response was, if I remember correctly, less than dignified and certainly did not involve good manners. What was her ostentatious response to your calling her Grecian goddess in human form?" asked Lodge.

'Cor you're a one! I told you there and then, London born and bred I am, Hoxton in fact, in the East End, nothing Greek about me,' she had replied.

"And," informed Lodge, "you may recall when we were in that Crush Bar in the Alhambra Music Hall..,"

"The place where Marie Lloyd *crushed* you!" interrupted Jack, with a smile.

"You may recall," a phlegmatic Lodge continued, "where that Lloyd tried unsuccessfully to traduce me because of her treacherous rôle in the Music Hall Wars, which she has organized because of the continued fair imposition of the *Exclusivity Clause.*"

Jack had not quite forgiven Lodge over his attitude and treatment of Marie Lloyd, a woman with whom Jack immediately had affinity, telling her on their first meeting, that she was indeed, a Greek goddess in human form. But now Jack was paying the price to Lodge for his flattery of both Marie Lloyd and Eleonora Duse.

On both occasions, Jack had come out as the chivalrous gentlemen. Whilst Lodge had been relegated, as witnessed falling out for good with Marie Lloyd and his friendship with Eleonora Duse, now somewhat remote. Jack was letting Loge, as he calls Lodge, vent his frustration. However, we were now about to embark on an encounter with Marie Lloyd, and whatever that might involve, at a meeting of her calling.

We left the comfortable confines of the salon and made our way to Lodge's highly varnished Barouche carriage with his inordinately over confident man-servant Aloysius acting as liveried coachman. Having climbed up into it we headed out from the beneath the stone porte cochère and into the yellow, swirling fog which still held the metropolis in its acrid grip.

I am fond of Marie Lloyd. To me she represents the essence of English Music Hall with all its vulgarity and sentimentalism, but together with a deep affection for, as it were, genuine public feeling and responses. The re-action of the dreadful sinking of the doomed *Titanic* got more real attention in Music Halls, both in America and in England, than in any of the so called learned journals on maritime matters.

As I also remembered the, Woman in Red, now known to me as Queenie, and especially her performance in the New Bedford Music Hall in Camden Town. There she invited the whole audience to join her in consolation over the ill-fated *Titanic*. The response moved me profoundly and I could never forget the impact it had on the audience who simply could hardly contain themselves in their overt emotianal reponses.

Though Marie was in February 1870 born in the London neighborhood of Hoxton and was christened Matilda Alice Victoria Wood. In 1884, she made her professional début under the name of Bella Delmere. She later changed her stage name the following year to Marie Lloyd for publicity convenience, even though ironically, her nick name remains Tilly, as in Matilda, not to be confused with her compatriot, Vesta Tilley.

Lloyd, with her special brand of lascivious innuendo and double entendre during her stage performances, often gets her into trouble, both with the New York Police Department and the Lord Chamberlain's office here in London as a result of the risqué contents regarding some of her songs.

The songs which she sings tirelessly including, '*Oh Mr. Porter What Shall I Do?*' '*My Old Man (Said Follow the Van')* or '*The Boy I Love Is Up in the Gallery.*' are still popular with the Music Hall going public. Even today the public continue to adore and shower praise upon her and she is affectionately known as the, 'Queen of the Music Hall.'

Lloyd enjoys an enviable successful reputation where ever she performs and frequently tops the bill at prestigious Music Halls ranged across London and in the West End. She continues to be recruited by such influential impresarios as Sir Augustus Harris for appearances at his spectacular pantomime extravaganzas staged at the Theatre Royal, Drury Lane at Covent Garden.

I remembered seeing Lloyd during her international tour between 1894 and 1900 when she played to audiences in New York and then in Australia, France and Belgium with her unique Music Hall performance that was easily expressed in different audiences in countries around the world.

I then found myself oblivious to the argument between Jack and Lodge and instead dwelt upon our meeting with Eleonora Duse. I came to realize that Jack and I were indeed very fortunate to have had an intimate audience with her.

Eventually, our Barouche carriage turned off Oxford Street along which we had been travelling and into a square with large trees in it. I instantly recognized it as being Soho Square. This was the same square in which we had been trying to catch up, in the fog, with Queenie Leighton, the Woman in Red, as I called Queenie, before I knew her.

I also recalled a building in the square with an impressive overhanging door canopy under which Queenie waited for a few moments whilst in the fog.

At length we clattered down Greek Street en-route and on time for our rendezvous at Kettner's Restaurant, I was also reminded of our previous visit to this place, in particular the surly concièrge behind his reception desk, aided and abetted by his two giggling acne faced assistants. On that occasion Jack and I had told the concièrge that a certain Mr. Michael Lodge expected us as his luncheon guests.

The concièrge had then turned on his heels and disappeared into the recesses of his domain, abandoning

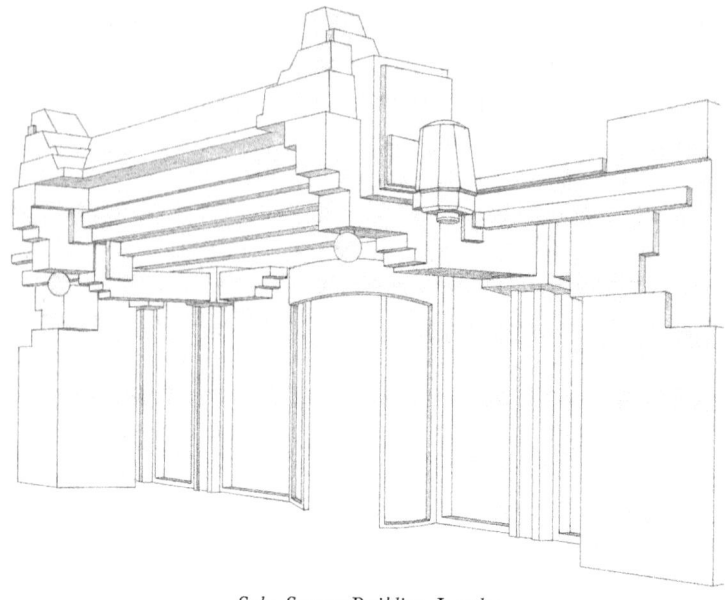

Soho Square Building, London

us in the process. A few minutes later he re-appeared, and asked with whom did we expect to meet for luncheon.

I had fielded the question.

"We are expected by an impresario, name of Lodge, Michael W. Lodge," I said, informing the surly concièrge, "and is this encounter going to turn into matinée performance?"

The concièrge deliberately chose to misconstrue my remark and inquired was it that we wished to see a matinée performance in which a certain Mr. Michael Lodge did a turn on the stage? In which case, he added, we might like to try the Palace Theater next door along Romilly Street, since Kettner's was a restaurant and not a Music Hall. He could not, of course, say for certain whether this Lodge artiste fellow would be doing his turn on the stage or not.

The concièrge said this with such a look of seriousness upon his face as to make it difficult to determine whether he was being facetious or not.

It was only when Jack in sheer exasperation asked, if Loge could ever be trusted to deal with simple luncheon arrangements? At that point the concièrge interrupting Jack stating that they had a certain Loge here who had booked luncheon for three. After which he escorted us to a well appointed and comfortable bar but not before the concièrge's assistants burst out into uncontrollable giggling, with barely concealed joy.

We made our way down Greek Street in Lodge's Barouche carriage driven by Aloysius who was also the man-servant at Lodge's house in the Bergen Avenue, but in this respect, he was certainly no coachman. On at least three occasions we were nearly involved in collisions with other carriages including a pantechnicon, with a Harrods cipher emblazoned on its highly varnished side. A Brougham four wheeler and a military wagon lumbering along in the fog. On each near collision pandäemonium was let loose, with attendant oaths being freely exchanged between Aloysius and the other drivers.

However, at length and intact, we pulled up outside Kettner's Restaurant. Having stepped down from our Barouche carriage onto the glistening sidewalk, made wet by the condensation of the fog on the York flagstones, we followed Lodge into the red carpeted foyer. We then marched up to the concièrge's desk as we had done before. Sure enough the same concièrge and his idiot acne faced assistants were there ready, as it were, to dispense facetiousness and unbridled sarcasm.

Lodge approached the concièrge and at the same time produced a gold sovereign coin from his waist-coat pocket, In full sight of the concièrge, Lodge twirled this

Palace Theater, London

coin in his fingers. Immediately the concièrge became amenable and even smiled at Lodge. His two assistants were also moved to adopt a more respectful expression upon their usually insolent faces.

"I am meeting with a lady, a certain Marie Lloyd at one o'clock," said Lodge.

"Would she be the acclaimed Music Hall artiste of the same name sir,?" inquired the concièrge.

"I do not know about the acclaimed aspect, but yes, she has been known to occasionally sing for her supper."

To this reply the concièrge raised his eyebrows, but still focused on Lodge's gold sovereign. He then asked Lodge if there was anything else that he could do for us.

"Yes you can," replied Lodge, still twirling his gold sovereign, "you may escort us to the Grecian Bar and inform Lloyd when she arrives that we are there waiting on her."

The concièrge duly obliged and escorted us through the various salons of which Kettner's is comprised including its famous restaurant, beloved of Oscar Wilde. The general décor of Kettner's was based on simplicity of design and restrained elegance which favors understatement, rather than ostentatious embellishment to lend opulence to the place.

This was in marked contrast to the exuberant decorative style prevalent at the more ornate and lush Criterion Bar facing the Regent's Circus.[1] Accordingly, I instinctively found it pleasing to be here and felt at ease with the place. At length we were shown in to the well-appointed and comfortable Grecian Bar and immediately made for the *Carrara* marble clad counter to order our drinks.

Lodge, I noticed, replaced his sovereign into his silver waist-coat pocket next to his gold Hunter, much to the chagrin of the expectant concièrge.

Having gotten our drinks at the bar, we were discussing Marie Lloyd, and in particular, her critical rôle in the current Music Hall dispute and Lloyd's active condemnation of the unfair *Exclusivity Clause*, whilst waiting on her arrival to meet with Lodge. We did not have long to wait. For almost to the minute of the agreed time, there was a commotion in the adjacent salon. Sure enough Lloyd appeared in the doorway wearing an inordinately large hat with feathers and a billowing dress that only just allowed her to get through the generous door opening.

"Lodge, Michael Lodge the impresario to end all impresarios! How are we my little cherub, still searching for your elusive mausoleum or have you found it yet?" Lloyd screeched out whilst approaching us, and looking directly at Jack.

"There is one born everyday! I have heard of people being taken in over a horse race or buying a house or even a public house that did not belong to the person offering it for sale. But to buy a mausoleum, a limestone one at that, which you had not even seen but paid ready cash for, in Highgate and in the fog too, really does take the biscuit!" guffawed Marie Lloyd.

She evidently still found the situation a cause for great hilarity.

"Jack and Theo, how are you both?" she continued, whilst shaking our outstretched hands. "And Jack, I hope you do not still think of me as Greek goddess in human form? Cos I am not see; London born and bred in Hoxton and am a good East End girl, that is all, but thank you for the compliment Jack, always welcome."

Lodge, I noticed, did not offer his hand, but manœuvred himself slightly behind Jack.

"Now down to business," continued Lloyd, "word has

it on the street you have engaged that voiceless creature, Mabel Green, ex *Cremorne Belle* to fill the vacancy with the *Three Graces* left by Bella Elmore's untimely murder? Oh well good luck. But seriously, I also understand too, that you have rescinded the abominable *Exclusivity Clause*? Am I to believe this; is it true or just a rumor?" she asked.

"You may take that as being very much the case," responded Lodge.

"What, that it is just a rumor?" inquired Lloyd.

Lodge gave Lloyd a withering look.

"Good, "continued Lloyd, "because I represent the cream of London's Music Hall artistes, including Emma Eames, Jean de Reszke, Emma Calvé, Dan Leno, Harry Nicholls Herbert Campbell, Eva Carrington, Katie Meyrick, Ellen Terry and Nellie Melba..." said Lloyd.

"Do you mean the Nellie Melba my, *'Little Peach'?*" interrupted Lodge.

"Do I?" continued Lloyd, "never the less, I take it the removal of the *Exclusivity Clause* applies to each and every one of them?" insisted Lloyd in a show of real business efficiency I did not think a woman of her jocular demeanor or disposition could ever have possessed.

"It does," answered Lodge, "and to everybody. The clause is no more!"

"In that case we will call our strike off at the Holborn Empire Music Hall and elsewhere forthwith," responded Lloyd.

"This is excellent news," enthused Lodge, "and calls for a celebratory drink; bar-tender!"

"About time," said Lloyd, "I have been standing here at the bar for more than six minutes and you gents have not offered me a drink yet!"

Later whilst Lloyd was engaged in a heated argument with another Music Hall artiste, who happen to be drinking at the bar, Lodge confided to Jack and me that he had great plans for us at the Holborn Empire Music Hall, and then abandoned us in order to speak with the bar-tender.

"Did Marie Lloyd say earlier that she represented the cream of London Music Hall artistes including Eva Carrington, Ellen Terry and Katie Meyrick?" I asked.

"Yes she did. Why do you ask?" inquired Jack.

"Well Jack, I recall vividly an incident at Bella's Wake of Remembrance not these few days past where all those women were present, albeit in various states of inebriation that would land them in jail in New York City!"

"Remind me Theo, you have an excellent memory," invited Jack, with a grin.

"You were talking with Marie Lloyd about the possibility of her returning to Lodge's *Three Graces*, which she had left recently. She replied that she would not return or sing for Lodge for all the, 'tea in Cheng.' It was at that precise moment, Eva Carrington, overcome with either grief or alcohol, fell into a table fully laden with bottles of drink, knocking a few of the bottles to the floor which smashed causing the wooden floor board to become wet and slippery.

"Another artiste, who went to help Eva to her feet, slipped on the wet floor boards and promptly joined her in a heap of black crêpe and veils on the floor. At the same time a very audible argument could be heard between Ellen Terry and the even more loquacious Katie Meyrick about the altruistic rôle of Music Hall artistes.

"'I am an *actress* capable of rendering Shakespearean verse, not some *performing artiste* fit only for the Music Hall!' Ellen Terry was heard to screech out, before she too collapsed to the floor in a stupor and joining the others.

"'You could not render a wall with plaster,' came the

considered repost from Meyrick, who then in turn fell against a nearby convenient wall and slipped down to where the other three inert women now lay."

"So that heap comprised the cream of English Music Hall artistes?" inquired Jack, in response.

"Absolutely Jack, absolutely," I replied.

"Ah, Loge," said Jack, as Lodge rejoined us, "what was it you were saying earlier about the Holborn Empire and the great plans which you have for us?"

"Quite right Jack," replied Lodge, "I do indeed have plans for you. I have communicated with the manager of the Holborn Empire and he has booked you in for the evening after tomorrow. You will appear after Dan Leno but before Marie Lloyd, now she has come to her senses and released the Holborn Empire Music Hall back to its operators."

"Really," said Jack.

"Incidentally, I always knew I could bend that woman, that Marie Lloyd, to my will," boasted Lodge.

"But it was you who dispensed with the hated *Exclusivity Clause*, by your own volition, and not her choice," said Jack.

"A strategic re-adjustment, Jack," replied Lodge, "just a re-adjustment."

"Well if you insist Loge," responded Jack.

"In the meantime, gentlemen, I have acquired tickets for you at great expense to my impoverished purse to attend the London Pavilion Music Hall this evening as I feel it will be of great instruction to you," announced Lodge, with a flourish.

1. Incorrectly known as Piccadilly Circus

Chapter 21

The London Pavilion

Lodge, in his capacity as an acclaimed impresario, has met with Marie Lloyd at Kettner's Restaurant, or rather to be more precise, in the Grecian Bar. They have done and resolved their differences over the *Exclusivity Clause* currently in operation which prevented artistes from performing in different neighboring Music Halls on the same night. This has ended the strike affecting certain Music Halls. This agreement was reached despite Lloyd's insulting comments about Lodge having engaged that voiceless creature, name of Mabel Green, an ex *Cremorne Belle*, to fill the vacancy with the *Three Graces* left by Bella Elmore's untimely murder. As a consequence of the strike ending; we are now to appear at the renowned Holborn Empire Music Hall. This is excellent news for both Jack and me, and we look forward to performing there.

"Now that Lloyd has staggered out and gone on her merry way, may I offer you two gentlemen luncheon?" said Lodge, in a gesture of inordinate magnanimity.

Jack accepted Lodge's offer instantly on our behalf.

"In order to celebrate my irrefutable victory over the woman Lloyd," Lodge insisted, repeatedly.

After a few more drinks, we escorted him into the restaurant.

"As I pointed out earlier, my friends," remarked Lodge, "I have, at great expense to my impoverished purse, purchased tickets for us to attend the London Pavilion this evening; tickets for a private box no less."

"You mentioned at the time that our attending the London Pavilion would be of great instruction to us. Why should this be so?" asked Jack.

"Quite simply," responded Lodge, "do you remember when you played the Imperial Music Hall in the Royal Aquarium & Winter Garden? Just before you went up, my friend George Leybourne the manager turned up to wish you both all the best. He also had something else to say. 'Gentlemen,' he said to you both, 'please allow me to offer you some advice. Not that you need it, but none the less, it may prove to be useful to you. Firstly, Music Hall in England is not the same as Vaudeville is in America. Secondly, what you term as Vaudeville in America is not the same as Variety Theater in England. And thirdly, what in England might be considered Burlesque would be termed Vaudeville in America.'"

"Yeah, and we know what the result was of not heeding that profound piece of advice," said Jack, "our so-called début there rather than being even marginally successful, instead deteriorated, with minutes of our marching on to the stage, into organized concentrated idiocy worthy of a pantomime of the lowest order and performed by imbeciles."

"As usual Jack," said Lodge, "I cannot argue against your choice of words here, concentrated idiocy, lowest order or imbeciles! But I would ask you to think back to Leybourn's use of words and in particular a descriptive term; notably, *Theater of Variety* in England."

"What exactly do you mean?" I inquired.

"Let me ask you to cast your minds back to my spirited

and valiant defense of our precious Music Halls when I addressed the Fourth Estate at the Charing Cross Hotel recently. There I argued persuasively and, as you probably remembered, with conviction, about a concerted onslaught upon our Music Halls in general from various quarters. Including the ubiquitous Metropolitan Board of Works and in particular the great loss of our famous Music Halls, in the continuing campaign the Salvation Army is waging against impresarios, such as me and Music Hall operators.

"This action clearly indicates, if nothing else, the depth of their resolve to eradicate this necessary social establishment. I also referred to the London Pavilion as a case in point, and of its being pivotal in the demise of the Music Hall and its gradual replacement by the so called Theaters of Variety.

"The evolution of our Music Hall is not complete, As a result of the activities of the Metropolitan Board of Works and that, that Lily Langtry, there is now what they call the emerging Theaters of Variety, complete with the application of red plush and brass division rails, on a pervasive and almost monumental scale. This is so in order to give the impression of the utmost respectability and lend verisimilitude to those new establishments.

"This type of Theater of Variety was promoted and accepted when they decided to rebuild the old London Pavilion at the Regent's Circus end of the Shaftesbury Avenue during 1885. And, I might add, to the deliberately extravagant and opulent designs of James Ebenezer Saunders, an employé, no less, of the Metropolitan Board of Works.

"The London Pavilion was constructed by the Peto Brothers Building Company to the interior designs by James Ebenezer Saunders, from the Metropolitan Board of Works with the classical façade and elevations designed by R. J. Worley. When the London Pavilion Music Hall was completed in November 1885 it was considered to be the most lavishly appointed Music Hall in London. This was intentional; the idea being that the London Pavilion would function as a high class theater, devoid of turns or acts, typical of Marie Lloyd's, normally seen at other Music Halls. Smugness and decorum were to be the by words used when one described the place.

"In this respect this was to be not so much a Music Hall but rather a Theater of Variety, complete with a great palm court built of *Norwegian Rose* granite at the back of the auditorium, able to seat comfortably over a thousand persons who could be served with tea whilst enjoying music from an orchestra playing daily, very much in the dainty, almost bourgeois manner, as one might experience in a konditorie in Vienna or a brasserie in Paris.

"In this case a concerted attempt was made to sever, in one fell swoop, all connections with the Pavilion's, so-called, gaudy if tawdry origins, in the roofed over stable yard of the Black Horse Inn, which previously occupied the site. Typically, in this Music Hall, exotic and other strange acts and demonstrations were performed. From then on, the new Theaters of Variety, their promoters declared, would conform to abstemious decency. They should be places of opulence, respectability in every aspect of their design and appointment and, more alarmingly, operate in the absence of alcohol. Imagine!

"The Theaters of Variety achieved their recognition and progress to smug respectability, especially in the auditorium where drink is not permitted under any circumstances. The apotheosis of the evolution of the

Theaters of Variety was when the first Royal Variety Performance, commanded by King George V[th.] took place during the 1912 season at the London Pavilion. This one fact confirmed overnight the notion that Theaters of Variety were now acknowledged as respectable places of entertainment.

"During another Command of Royal Variety Performance, this time at the London Pavilion, it was instructive to note that the popular Marie Lloyd, though at the height of her career on the Music Hall stage, is considered to represent the old Music Hall style, based on the *Pleasure Garden*s type of entertainment. Especially, with her lasciviousness and avalanche of innuendos and double entendre, to the extent that she is thought to be too risqué to perform in front of a reigning monarch. Why, one wonders. Nevertheless, Lloyd was then, consequently excluded from appearing. This is the legacy we have received from the advent of the London Pavilion.

"However, gentlemen, much as I loathe their existence and smugness, I have to acknowledge that they are a reality and must be dealt with accordingly," Lodge said these words with a sadness in his eyes, which looked blankly into the middle distance in front of him. Presently he pulled himself together and continued.

"Theo, Jack you need to experience this type of Theater of Variety, for no other reason than that they exist and that is why, as I say at great expense to my purse, because these theaters are not cheap, I have bought tickets for tonight's performance. You shall, no doubt, judge for yourself the efficacy of this type of theatrical entertainment!" said Lodge.

Our luncheon had in fact continued until the early evening. I was particularly interested, curious even to witness this new kind of Music Hall entertainment in the

London Pavilion, Piccadilly

guise of respectability. Jack too was eager to attend the London Pavilion and see if our act could be applicable there, and at other Theaters of Variety.

We left Kettner's Restaurant in Romilly Street in the fog-bound depths of Soho and decided to walk to the London Pavilion at the western end of Shaftesbury Avenue. We elected to do so as a means of taking our constitution before sitting down for the evening in the auditorium. Or, as Madame Duse would accuse, 'digest our dinner.'

Some considerable time later, we arrived at the London Pavilion in Shaftesbury Avenue, or *Avenue of the Theaters,* as it is sometimes referred to, and made our way into the plush foyer. Lodge's description of London Pavilion as being the apogee of opulence, only there to lend, as it were, smug respectability, was justified. Without doubt the fine marble panels affixed to various walls were worthy of the Forum in ancient Rome during the apotheosis of Roman imperial ambition. Brass and crystal chandeliers were numerous, pouring out their glittering iridescent light illuminating the foyer below.

However, the first thing one noticed about the place was the lack of large Crush Bars. This disappointment however, in no way impeded the general feeling of excitement in the foyer. The Crush Bar we did see was of such a small size, it really made one consider seriously the possibility that going there and waiting to get served might in all probability, turn out to be a futile exercise. And in all probability, not worthy of the time or indeed raising one's hopes or expectations, only to be finally dashed, I thought. In the meantime, Lodge escorted us into our private box with red plush and brass ornamental fixtures.

The interior décor in the auditorium was similarly impressive, with a continuation of the opulent style we had witnessed in the foyer. The seating in the stalls and various tiers of Dress Circles was covered in deep red plush velvet adding to a sense of opulence and luxury carried throughout the theater. Certain stalls were divided by glittering brass rails and lamp stands.

We had barely taken to our plush red seats when the purple safety curtain began its ascent in to the attic above the proscenium arch framing the stage.

The first act commenced and was performed by Emma Carus. I knew Emma when she used to work Proctor's Theater on 23rd. Street in New York doing Vaudeville comedienne turns and singing for her supper.

She was followed by a peculiar act called the Regurgitator, who was billed as the, '*Egyptian Enigma.*' His act involved swallowing gasoline followed by water. After regurgitating the gasoline and igniting it, the '*Egyptian*

Enigma' would put out the blaze with the regurgitated water. During his act, he would also swallow, and then regurgitate, nuts or even live goldfish.

Again, it never ceases to amaze me the attendant fires risks allowed on the stage in London. Even during our stay, there had been a fire at the Oxford Music Hall in Oxford Street. These fires are not isolated cases, but rather a regular and somewhat expected consequence of providing the audience with exciting, if potentially combustible acts or turns on the stage irrespective of the very real and inherent dangers of a major conflagration.

When the, *'Egyptian Enigma,'* had finished threatening the London Pavilion Theater of Variety with being engulfed in an instantaneous conflagration, he reluctantly left the stage, coughing quite badly. A few minutes later, a commotion from the back of the stage was heard. Presently two jugglers appeared on stage throwing objects at each other quite forcibly, including knives, which they caught and then threw back in return. These were of course the Cook Brothers, billed as *'The Juggling Kids.'* I seemed to recall seeing Joe Cook making a solo appearance, again at Proctor's 23rd. Street Theater in New York about six years previously. At the time he was known for adding monologues and comedy to his act.

The claim that the London Pavilion was supposed to represent the respectability of the emerging Theaters of Variety, seemed to be at variance with the acts we had thus far seen. Irrespective of the notion, according to Lodge, that such places were of conceited and smug aspect and there only to lend verisimilitude to the idea of respectability, the acts listed on the hand bill did not promise otherwise.

On the completion of their knife-throwing act, the safety curtain came thundering down with an indecent haste. We all, by consensus, elected to stay in our seats, as going to the too few in number so-called small Crush Bars would not justify the effort or exercise. Whilst Lodge engaged Jack in a pointless discussion about the diminishing rôle of the Music Hall in ecclesiastical matters, I took the opportunity to observe from our private box, the interior décor of the auditorium illuminated brilliantly by several acetylene gas fuelled glass chandeliers

Suddenly the heavy red velvet curtain covering the entrance to our private box swished back. We all instinctively turned to see who had dared invade our privileged privacy. There, standing in the doorway holding back the red velvet portière, was a tall gentleman immaculately dressed in a black tail-coat, varnished boots and wearing a top hat at a slight angle. Assuming him to be the manager come to pay his compliments to Lodge, Jack and I looked back towards the auditorium.

"Thought it was you Lodge, saw you during the first half from our seats in the Upper Grand Circle and wondered what the deuce you were doing at a place like the London Pavilion. But, do tell me, how the devil have you been?" inquired the gentleman.

"Busy, oh so busy George, never ending commitments, always innovating, when will it cease I ask myself constantly, when will it cease? But George, please allow me to introduce you to my guests; Jack Mitchell and Theodore Houston, Vaudeville artistes out of New York. Jack, Theo, this is George Grossmith.[1] George is very much Renaissance *polysmith*, as it were; an actor, theater producer, manager, director, playwright and songwriter! He is also a dab hand in creating successful musical comedies.

We shook hands and Jack invited Grossmith to sit

down and join us. I also noticed that Lodge's catachreses had returned which it does when he is trying to impress or ingratiate himself to someone he reveres. When he just described Grossmith as being a Renaissance *polysmith*, I think the word he intended to use was *polymath*. Or at least one would suppose; but as usual with Lodge, that might prove to be a massive and incorrect assumption!

"Are you two out of Tony Pastor's 14th. Street Theater?" ask Grossmith.

"We are indeed," replied Jack.

"Thought so," continued Grossmith, "I have heard of you and in fact saw you perform at Pastor's 14th. Street Theater some years ago. A very polished act, I thought."

"And did we not see you recently at Daly's Music Hall during your recital of anecdotes and witty remarks, whilst playing a pianoforte?" Jack inquired, "Because Theo and I were very impressed with your playing, especially your fine interpretation of the Liszt's *'B minor Sonata,'* together with Robert Schumann's *'Faschingsschwank aus Vien.'* We both of us at the time agreed that perhaps you should be performing at the Bechstein Hall in Wigmore Street; such was your evident talent at the keyboard."

"Indeed you are correct Sir, I did perform there. And thank you for your kind compliments," answered Grossmith, who seemed genuinely moved by Jack's remarks.

"George is endeavoring to introduce to London audiences," announced Lodge, in an attempt to gain center attention, "what we impresarios have termed 'cabaret' or 'revues' on stage, which will comprise a series of sketches reflecting topical subjects. George is remembered for the magnificent first rôle he played on the age of eighteen in a performance of the stage musical, *'Haste to the Wedding.'* That was created as a result of the highly successful collaboration between George's famous father, also a talented actor-songwriter, and the operetta promoter Richard D'Oyly Carte's librettist, William Schwenck Gilbert," [2]

"Pray do tell me, what brings you to the London Pavilion George?" Jack asked.

"Escape the wife and to lend moral support, as it were, to my sometime stage partner Edmund Payne, who is performing here this evening with Gertie Millar. They are doing a scene from their double act called, '*Spring Chicken*,' which continues to attract good reviews," answered Grossmith.

"I have not seen Payne on the stage in quite some time," offered Lodge, in his continuing endeavors to regain Grossmith's attention from Jack.

"Edmund Payne, or 'Teddy' as I call him, has for the last few years formed a successful partnership on stage creating comic rôles in a series of musical comedies. But he is now hoping to strike out and develop in other directions. He is currently appearing with Gertie Millar in several shows including, '*In Town*,' '*The Shop Girl*,' '*The Circus Girl*,' '*The Girls of Gottenberg*,' '*Our Miss Gibbs*,' '*The Sunshine Girl*' and of course the ever popular, '*Spring Chicken*.' I see a great future for him," said Grossmith.

"What is this innovative idea of yours about introducing cabaret and revues," I inquired, "it sounds quite interesting?"

Alas, that question was to remain unanswered, as the lights in the auditorium began to dim. Grossmith got up shook our hands again, wished us all the best and retreated from our private box and back to his superior seating in the Upper Dress Circle.

After the all too short interval, clearly designed so patrons would not be able to drink very much, Gertie

Millar came prancing on to the stage singing very enthusiastically, and with great agility and vigor, a song about being a shop girl. After that, she launched herself, with equal energy, into a song reflecting her love for a *Messenger Boy*, taken from one of her shows. Surprisingly, after further bouts of singing she left the stage shouting that she would, 'be back!'

The footlights dimmed and only a solitary shaft of limelight illuminated the center stage. It was into this single beam of yellow light that Daisy Dormer stepped. Both Jack and I looked at each other. We had good reason to, for we knew Daisy quite well. Jack in fact, had been helpful in establishing Daisy on the New York Vaudeville circuit. Though born Kezia Beatrice Stockwell, in Portsmouth, England, she changed her name to Daisy Dormer and became famous for her song, '*After the Ball is Over*,' composed by Charles Harris.

That song alone, the sheet music to which sold over five million copies, was instrumental in forming in the 1890s, what we in New York City call, 'Tin Pan Alley,' which is a loose collection of songwriters and sheet music publishers. They tend to be located in Manhattan around West 28th Street between Fifth Avenue and Broadway. True to form, she sang, '*After the Ball is Over*,' to great acclaim by the audience. Even Lodge was moved to stand up, during his sustained applause for her.

During the lull before the next act, Jack leaned over to me and pointed to the hand bill and in particular Gertie Millar's listing with Edmund Payne in their scene from, '*Spring Chicken.*'

"You know Theo, that Gertie Millar is quite an accomplished performer in every respect. When I knew her, back in New York, she would often talk to me about her early days playing provincial Music Halls in England, such as the St. James Theater in Manchester, especially playing pantomimes, rôles including, '*Babes in the Wood,*' at the tender age of thirteen years and as a singer and dancer in the various Music Halls around Yorkshire in England.

She then moved to London later, appearing as Dandini in, '*Cinderella*' at the Grand Theater in Fulham, I guess near the Empress Music Hall at Earl's Court that we visited recently. Her break came when she played in a series of musical comedies produced by George Edwardes, including the, '*Messenger, Boy*' and '*The Toreador,*' performed at the Gaiety Theater in London. Her rise to fame now is phenomenal and attracted the attention of composer Lionel Monckton who signed her up playing the rôle of the bridesmaid Cora in the musical, '*Keep Off The Grass.*'

That success led to Moncton, whom she later married in 1902, to compose other songs for her, including, '*Captivating Cora*' and '*I'm Not a Simple Little Girl.*' Millar is now one of the most photographed women as a result of her successes on stage, playing Rosalie in the, '*Spring Chicken.*' And later playing Mitzi in, '*The Girls of Gottenberg,*' in the Broadway production in New York and her rôle in the Wagnerian parody called, '*Rhinegold,*'" concluded Jack.

"A Wagnerian parody called '*Rhinegold,*' you said? I should very much like to witness that. Could such a thing be created given the fact that Wagner's grand opera, '*Das Rheingold,*' would seem to have very little in it that could be parodied in a meaningful way?" I said.

"Well, Theo if you look at the hand bill closely," said Jack, pointing to an item in the schedule, "you will see that they will be singing a selection of songs from their parody called, '*The Rhinegold.*' the reason being, I believe, that pantomime, is currently being performed at the New National Standard Theater in a place called Shoreditch, where ever that is. So you are in luck Theo; for you shall go to the ball!"

A hush descended over the audience as the footlights increased in intensity. The empty stage was now bathed in a soft yellow light. Presently Millar and Edmund Payne came marching on to it from each wing and meeting in the middle of the stage, whilst singing the duet, *'Two Little Sausages,'* to great applause. Later we heard selections from their successful collaboration in the, *'Spring Chicken.'* Eventually, after much bowing and waving to the audience, albeit in an abandoned style, the duo left the stage to the sound of thunderous applause much of it generated by Jack's loud clapping.

Maud Allan came on next. She was, of course, infamous for her creation of that exotic, if overtly risqué, *'Salomé Dance,'* which I actually saw at the Palace Theater on Broadway, in New York in 1910. On that occasion there, the auditorium was filled to the rafters with admirers. During that particular performance, I remembered Allan being very energetic as she propelled herself across the stage. She did so whilst astutely avoiding a replication of a decapitated head, placed on the deck of the stage, as launched herself, in a series of gravity-defying dance routines of her own creation.

Looking at my handbill, I read that the final act was to be performed by the talented Hetty King, as usual, in men's clothes, always a favorite with an audience. I could not wait to see her, as she did make Jack and me laugh. Aside of that, she remained quite the protégée, and appeared aged six years with her father at the Shoreditch Theater in 1889 and then in 1904 at the Empire - Hippodrome in Ashton-under-Lyne, as *'The Society Gem,'* working the Broadhead Circuit of Music Halls. She later refined her act by 1905 by adding the impersonation of males and in particular *Swells or Toffs*.

All of a sudden brightness from the footlights illuminated the stage, as Hetty King marched on to it in as confident a manner as any. Dressed as a *Swell*, she wore a black tail-coat with a white carnation, black trousers and silver colored waist-coat on top of a white starched shirt and finished off with a shiny black silk top hat.

I confess, she did look very elegant and dapper in her male clothes. However, without any introduction, she burst into song that the pit orchestra was obliged somehow to try and catch up with her. On this occasion she sang the song for which she is famous called, '*I'm Afraid to Come Home in the Dark.*' Harry Williams wrote it to music composed by Egbert Van Alstyne. I also noticed on the handbill that the copyright to the song is retained by the music publisher, Francis, Day & Hunter, at 138-142 Charing Cross Road, Oxford Street End, West Central.

At the end of her recital to great applause, we made our way out of the London Pavilion into the Shaftesbury Avenue at an agonizingly slow pace. I was all for heading for the nearest bar to quench a long standing thirst. Jack, I knew, would concur enthusiastically with me. Lodge, I was not certain about.

1. George Grossmith died in March 1912.
2. WS Gilbert was the librettist in the Gilbert & Sullivan partnership

Chapter 22

The Rhinegold Pantomime

We had been to the London Pavilion Theater of Variety and found the various acts or turns on the stage quite not what we were expecting. Clearly, Lodge's description of that type of Theater of Variety, as being essentially places of tame, conceited or even smug entertainment fit only for the bourgeoisie did not appear to me to be the case. In this respect neither Jack nor I could discern any appreciable differences, apart from the obvious lack of Crush Bars, between the acts on the stage at the London Pavilion and those extant on the stages of other Music Halls.

However, what remained of vital importance to me was the fact that Jack had mentioned the day before that there was in existence a parody, bordering on pantomime called, '*The Rhinegold*,' based on Rickard Wagner's grand opera called, '*Das Rheingold*.' I thought Jack was joking. Apparently not; for such a work is in existence! And by good fortune, there is to be a performance of this rarely-heard pantomime at the New National Standard Theater in a place called Shoreditch.

As to how one could have possibly conceived of a pantomime based on a grand opera by Wagner, which itself is based upon two distinct Teutonic mythologies was beyond my comprehension. One such myth, called the *Völsunga Saga*, is a series of Scandinavian legends of monumental complexity. And the other; the *Nibelungenlied*, or Song of the Nibelungs, based on a twelfth century High German poem is of equal labyrinthine involvement.

Rickard Wagner had incorporated ideas and concepts taken from these two epic legends. He had then combined them together in order to create the, *'Der Ring des Nibelungen,'* comprising four linked operas each one leading into the next. These series of operas begins with, *'Das Rheingold',* then *'Die Valküre'* followed by, *'Siegfried'* and culminating in, *'Götterdämmerung.'* [1]

All four operas contained in the *Ring Cycle* had been received positively in when first premièred here in London and remain a favorite in the operatic repertoire. They were introduced to the London audience in 1882 by the impresario Alfred Schulz-Curtius, a person whom Lodge claimed a close friendship with at the time. The first organized staging of, *'Der Ring des Nibelungen,'* was under the acclaimed director Angelo Neumann and the orchestra conducted by Anton Seidl.

Given the rationale of the, *'Der Ring des Nibelungen,'* it is all the more remarkable when one considers that, *'Das Rheingold,'* upon which the pantomime is based, is the first in that series of four linked operas of which, *'Der Ring des Nibelungen,'* is comprised. And although, *'Das Rheingold,'* comes first in the four operas, it was, in fact, the last to be written. This was because this series of operas evolved backwards from a saga about the death of a hero-type, name of Siegfried and the intervention of a Valküre,[2] name of Brünnhilde.

The scale of this operatic work is truly of epic proportions; typically it is over sixteen hour long in its performance. It is grand opera in its fullest majestic sense and during its composition; Wagner introduced new musical concepts to assist the listener in understanding the complex scenarios being played out.

Typically, the parameters and proportion of, *'Der Ring des Nibelungen,'* are established at the beginning of the work. The introductory vorspiel, or prelude, is itself over an unprecedented 140 bars in length starting with a low E flat chord. This then evolves into an elaborate variation of the E flat major chord representing the turbulent river Rhein. During this vorspiel is contained perhaps the most famous drone piece [3] to be found in the concert repertory, lasting approximately four minutes. Other innovations include the musical concept of the leitmotiv.[4]

I could barely contain myself during the day, such was my impatience to experience this parody or pantomime based upon Wagner's opera. Nor could I bend my mind to anything else. Thankfully, we were not scheduled to be performing that night, since we were booked in to the Holborn Empire Music Hall the following evening. However, we were scheduled to meet with Lodge imminently to discuss a couple of his ideas regarding our presentation on stage.

I was in the process of asking Jack, whilst we were sitting at the bar in the St. Pancras Hotel waiting on Lodge, why we should need his advice on our stage presentation. When true to form, Lodge turned up with Mabel on his arm, just as I was ordering another round of drinks.

"Mabel, Lodge, what can I fix you," I felt obligated to ask.

"Oh, the usual please," replied Mabel.

"The usual what?" I asked, with defined asperity in my voice.

"Why, champagne and the Coca~Cola of course; whatever else could it be?" she retorted.

I deigned not to answer that question.

Lodge made do with a *Sweet Sherry*, whatever kind of cocktail drink that is.

Having made ourselves comfortable on two red silk covered sofas placed on either side of a low *Rosso Antico D'Italia* marble table, we started to discuss some suggestions tendered by Lodge. I let Jack do the talking as my mind was elsewhere and not really in the mood to discuss our presentation on stage. I fell into a kind of revelry thinking about, *'Das Rheingold,* complete with gold, giants, river maidens, gods, demi gods, dwarfs...

"Theo, Theo, you seem to be miles away. What do you think of my suggestion?" asked Lodge.

"I do not know, ask Jack," I replied, "and, where is Shoreditch?"

"Why, why do you need to know?" asked Lodge.

"Because I need to get there this evening, to the New National Standard Theater in Shoreditch in fact," I replied.

"Theo, I know where it is," intervened Mabel, "and the best way to get there is to ride the urban rail road out of St. Pancras Station to Shoreditch Rail Road Station. Then it is just a short walk to Shoreditch High Street in which the New National Standard Theater is located."

"What is the attraction for you there Theo?" asked Lodge, looking perplexed.

"According to Jack, they are performing, *'The Rhinegold,'* pantomime at the New National Standard Theater this evening and I am anxious to see it. For the simple reason that I cannot possibly imagine a pantomime based on a Wagnerian grand opera, especially, *'Das Rheingold,'* which itself reflects profound Teutonic mythological concepts," I replied.

"Oh, not at all," said Lodge, "I kid you not; Wagner's operas have been the inspiration for several interpretations evolving into pantomime. I remember in my younger days attending the pantomime based on Wagner's, *'Die Valküre,'* with Sarah Fairbrother performing at the Theater Royal in Drury Lane. And only four years ago, I myself produced a pantomime at the Coliseum Theater of Variety, in St. Martin's Lane, Charing Cross, based on Wagner's epic opera or music drama if you will called, *'Parsifal.'* The audience loved Parsifal clowning around with Amfortas in their buffoon-like attempts to steal the Holy Grail!"

"Why at the London Coliseum?" I asked of no one in particular.

"The reason being Theo, both artistes and the public were talking about the theater at the time, because it was the topic of conversation, primarily because the London Coliseum Theater of Variety, or the, 'People's Palace of Entertainment,' in St. Martin's Lane, Charing Cross, was built to the designs of the foremost theater architect Frank Matcham for my friend, the impresario Oswald Stoll. It has a distinctive ornate classical campanile surrounded by an Ionic colonnade supporting an embellished tholos punctuated with decorated lucarne window reveals and strengthened with dressed flying buttresses, guarded by four stone lions.

The whole limestone structure rises up and culminates in a lead-covered cupola on top of which are placed eight sylvan figures supporting on their backs an open-framed representation of the globe. Opened in 1904 on 22 December, it is one of largest and, as it exterior designs suggest, most luxuriously appointed Theaters of Variety in London. It is also remarkable for its hydraulically powered Ascending Rooms in which patrons are propelled to the Upper Dress Circles of which there are three."

"Well I hope the both of you enjoy your expedition to Shoreditch and no doubt we shall meet up tomorrow evening at the Holborn Empire Music Hall," said Lodge rising from the sofa.

"Alas, Theo, I will not be accompanying you tonight, I have had enough of Wagnerian operas for the time being!" said Jack.

Later that afternoon, I changed into my evening dress, comprising black tail-coat, silver colored waist-coat, white carnation and polished black boots. Having done so, I found myself looking out through the stone framed quatre-foil window of my hotel room as I wound up my steel case watch. The fog looked particularly thick and menacing as it swirled in vortexes in the aëther outside.

Still, my mind was on *'The Rhinegold,'* and the unbearable anticipation building up inside me. I kept reminding myself that it was but a pantomime; and nor was it a serious interpretation of the acclaimed epics which the *Völsunga Saga* or *Nibelungenlied* are renowned to be. At length I abandoned my hotel room and stepping into the hydraulically operated Ascending Room, made my way down to the foyer.

Upon reaching it I handed in my key to the concièrge dressed, as usual in his black morning-coat and black top hat with a blue rosette affixed to the side. On this occasion I had no need to consult his Bradshaw's Railway Guide or Bäedeker's Guide to London, as Mabel had informed me earlier that the best way to Shoreditch was to ride the urban rail road to it from St. Pancras Station, which of course was behind this hotel.

Accordingly, I buttoned up my coat and headed out through the back of the hotel and into the station precincts and continued on into a nearby ticket office. After queuing up for what seemed an inordinate length of time, I managed eventually to gain the ticket office window. Behind this acid-etched window sat a solitary rail road employé looking as if he held the universal copyright on ennui.

After some unnecessary and frank exchange of views, I was able to purchase a ticket to Shoreditch. Not being familiar with the St. Pancras Station. I approached a rail road servant upon the platform for directions.

"I am looking for a train that will take me to Shoreditch my good man," I said.

The rail road servant, dressed in his black velveteen uniform with red piping merely looked at me and then promptly marched off quickly to the far end of the platform. Ironically I was not offended, merely because I have gotten used to this discourtesy when travelling by urban rail road in this city.

Instead, I consulted the board indicating the times of trains leaving, their destination and from which platform. I figured that the train I should need to ride would leave in fourteen minutes and from platform 4. In the meantime I did what everybody was doing whilst waiting for a train in a London urban rail road station.

I allowed my attention to be distracted by the boastful claims contained in several advertisement posters strategically placed on wall surfaces around the platform. The advertisements contained information I should not under any other circumstances find remotely relevant. Aside of this, it helped me think away the time whilst waiting for my train.

Presently a train did come bursting in from the fog and thundered down the side of the platform, belching out black smoke and smuts which deposited themselves on to my over-coat and top hat. I braced myself for an expected tide of humanity alighting from the train and

𝕳𝖎𝖌𝖍𝖊𝖘𝖙 𝕬𝖜𝖆𝖗𝖉
for
TAXIDERMY
Established 1845

~ o ~

Gold Medal and Diploma, Great Exhibition, York, 1889.

~ E. ALLEN ~
35 Albany Street, Camden Town,
London, NW

𝕹𝖆𝖙𝖚𝖗𝖆𝖑𝖎𝖘𝖙 𝖆𝖓𝖉 𝕿𝖆𝖝𝖎𝖉𝖊𝖗𝖒𝖎𝖘𝖙.

𝕽𝖊𝖋𝖊𝖗𝖊𝖓𝖈𝖊 𝖙𝖔 𝕹𝖔𝖇𝖎𝖑𝖎𝖙𝖞, 𝕮𝖑𝖊𝖗𝖌𝖞 𝖆𝖓𝖉 𝕲𝖊𝖓𝖙𝖗𝖞.

British and Foreign Animals Heads mounted on an Improved System.

ENGLISH & FOREIGN SKINS DRESSED & MOUNTED FOR RUGS

All work executed by Skilled Assistants under
Professional Supervision

~ o ~

sweeping down the platform upon which I was standing, ready to engulf me. To my surprise nobody got off. So I stepped into a single compartment room and made myself comfortable on the bench seat upholstered in a blue brocade material.

An age seemed to go by but eventually a whistle was heard and our train, after a jolt, began to glide down the side of the platform, still pouring out even more smoke as the locomotive labored to gain speed. As soon as we cleared the glazed station roof, we plunged into dense fog to the extent that the windows in my carriage became almost opaque. Minutes later we went steaming passed the lunatic asylum, located in the St Pancras Hospital, made more evident by the muffled screams I heard drifting through the fog-laden aëther and into the open window of the train carriage.

In no time at all we were clanking into an elevated station by the name of Camden Road. The lunatic asylum, Camden Road, I thought? We must be in the vicinity of Camden High Street in which is located the New Bedford Music Hall and the plush Camden Theater I had attended with Jack. After a couple of minutes the train was on the move again and steamed through the clouds punctuated by roof tops and buildings seemingly built precariously close to the rail road track.

One felt that if the train stopped, one could without any difficulty converse, through their open windows, with the occupants of the buildings adjacent to the elevated permanent way; for such was their proximity to the train carriage. At length we screeched into Maiden Lane Station, then several minutes later into Barnsbury Station. The names of these stations of course meant zilch to me, not being familiar with metropolitan London. The train was travelling quickly and I felt that I was making good

Camden Theater, London

time. We continued along the track rattling over viaducts and bridges and onward through to the next station, the name of which I failed to register, such was our speed steaming through it.

We then drew in to a station called Mildmay Park and stopped. I looked out of my carriage window and observed that the station platform was deserted. In fact I got the distinct and eerie impression that I was the only person riding this train! This induced in me momentary anxiety. Was I on a train that was hurtling through the fog and in to oblivion? Then with a jolt, that caused my head to hit the side of the door window frame, the train was on the move again. I continued looking out of the window over the roofs of buildings and occasionally glimpsing people in their homes adjacent to the elevated rail road tracks.

The next station the train entered was Dalston Junction after which the train veered sharply to the right and continued down into the next station which on arrival, I found was named for a place called Haggerston. A few minutes later we steamed into a station with the name Shoreditch indented on the platform pressed metal nameplate. No one got on and no one alighted from the train except me, and I did so on to a ghostly quiet fog-bound platform. I made my way down a steep flight of slippery steps leading from the deserted platform to the street level and the entrance to the station.

On arriving I discovered that the booking hall, from which several doors led out of the station, was empty. I opened one door and stepped out into a street filled with the blinding fog. I could barely see in front of me. The road in which I had stepped into was not very busy and in fact seemed more deserted than active.

Mabel had told me earlier that I had to get to Shoreditch Station and from there it was but a short walk. I knew that I must be in Brick Lane and that I needed to get on to Sclater Street. At the moment a solitary Hansom carriage came clattering by. As he did I hailed him and asked in which direction was the New National Standard

Theater. I then realized immediately the faux pas I had made in asking a cab driver for directions!

"The National Standard Theater is in the Shoreditch High Street which is through that alley, toward Sclator Street," he said, pointing with is whip.

I started to walk in the direction he had suggested and on turning back, I noticed that the driver had not whipped up his horse to leave. But rather sat there motionless with hunched shoulders, watching me disappear down into the fog bound alley, only dimly lit with coal tar gas globe lamps.

I found myself walking along side a large brick building I took to be a brewery of sorts judging by the strong smell of fermenting hops or barley. The lane I walked down in was in fact a miserable place with the dregs of society clinging to gas lamp posts or huddled in doorways. Mingling with the dense fog, was the odor of putrid vegetation, lying on the sidewalk, that assailed my nostrils. This induced a faint sensation of nausea, made all the more unbearable by the stench of the swirling fog-laden aëther.

The lane comprised the usual gin shops and dens where all kinds of abuses took place. Just in front of me, though invisible at present, I could hear a commotion of some kind. I slowed my pace and proceeded cautiously. Sure enough a woman and a man were screaming at each other and waving their arms about. I noticed too that they were immediately outside a public house and had obviously been drinking heavily; especially so the woman.

I continued to walk and then tried to negotiate my way past both of them. But the woman, on seeing me, purposefully propelled her rickety perambulator, containing an infant of vile and repellent aspect, into my path. Her action caused me to collide with perambulator.

Whereupon she grabbed the grubby child, yelling that I had hurt her baby. This incident was staged deliberately in the hope that I might be persuaded, no doubt by her shouting rough male companion, to make compensation to her with money for the supposed harm I had caused to her baby.

I looked at the woman. Being from New York's Lower East Side, I am not all that easily intimidated. However, I did not know the area or where I could have gotten too as a resort. The woman in the mean time, had ceased squawking but now looked intently at me in turn. She was dressed in cheap, tawdry clothes, ill fitting and dirty. Her hair was short and greasy and she wore what looked like the remains of a bonnet that had clearly seen better times. Indeed it was difficult to determine whether it was the lining of a hat, or a hat in its own right.

On her thin neck were quite easily observable, bruises she attempted to cover with the aid of a greyish neckerchief. Her dress may have been linen at one stage in its life but was now covered by a matted woollen shawl that she draped upon her shoulders. The scuffed boots she wore on her feet were neither of the same style or color.

I then averted my gaze to the rough man. He wore a long cord waist-coat with numerous pockets and brass buttons and a pair of baggy, faded velveteen trousers, the kind one throws away after a couple of uses. On his feet were dirty heavy pit boots, but in his case they were matching. I noticed too, that he wore a silver colored ring in his ear lobe that looked infected.

"You want that I should give money huh? Yeah well, being out of New York, I do not carry money about me alright," I said, in my thickest New York - Lower East Side accent.

He considered me, and, with his mind made up, immediately grabbed the woman and her rickety perambulator containing that infant of vile and repellent aspect and barged back inside the public house from whence they had come, to continue, no doubt, their reckless drinking.

As I made my way down the lane, I did so with a mixture of feelings. Those attending me in the main, were very similar to those which I experienced, when I found myself, some weeks ago, lost in that fog-bound slum district near the Charing Cross Road called the Rookery. I remembered, with dread, that mausoleum which seemed to defy the very presence of the swirling fog extant within the Rookery.

I did not care to linger in this vicinity of Shoreditch, so continued on through the dense acrid fog. And, then ironically I began to feel grateful that for once the dense fog made me invisible, especially to that rough who might, being drunk, change his mind an endeavor to incommode me.

Presently I came to a rail road bridge under which the

Mausoleum in the Rookery

lane continued. As I walked towards it I noticed that there were several people seeking shelter under the bridge and gathered around a blazing brazier, belching out thick acrid smoke. Though not afraid, I did become anxious as there were enough persons present to seriously inconvenience me. None the less I continued walking under the bridge. And as I did, it became apparent to me that I was essentially walking through a group of people who were smoking every type of impregnated combustible leaf and alkaloid substance.

I recognized immediately the distinctive aroma of paregoric, a tincture of opium, often used in the relief of pain, or abuse. Through the smoky haze and dimness, a vision of bodies presented themselves to me. Some were reclining in a strange and unnatural manner. Others were almost interlocked in a mass of humanity huddled together for mutual support or comfort.

The damp, fog-bound aëther beneath the bridge was punctuated with dark lackluster eyes that were trying to focus on me, as an interloper, in their domain. From these dark shadows glimmered little red circles of flame as laudanum addicts coughed and inhaled their burning, insidiously additive poison. Some addicts muttered to themselves, but most were silent. A few attempted to communicate with each other, in monotonous and strange low voices.

Sometimes their conversation was vivid and nervous, as each addict mumbled out thoughts of his own, but with little attention to the words mumbled by his neighbor. Then, silence reigned as they descended again into melancholic stupor. As I walked under the viaduct bridge, people looked up and stared at me.

I felt as if I were walking in a Gustav Doré ink illustration.

However, as I approached the stone abutments of the rail road bridge, through which I needed to walk, and passed those seeking shelter. I concentrated on an advertisement fixed to the bridge rampart and pretended, in an overt nonchalant manner, to be inordinately more interested in the poster's uplifting claims, than in the condition of those persons around me on the side walk.

By dexterous foot work in stepping over various inert bodies on the footpath and dodging a ceaseless onslaught of drunks, I made my way through the lane and emerged into what I assumed was the Sclator Street. This street turned out to be not dissimilar to the vile lane I had just walked down. In fact it was only marginally brighter, for the dense fog had the effect of absorbing the weak light emanating from the all too few gas lamps supposedly illuminating the sidewalk.

As I walked along the road, hopefully in the right direction to the New National Standard Theater, my attention was arrested by a peculiar sight that induced feelings of mortality in me almost instantly. Next to the carriageway kerb, were standing two black horses with black plumes on their heads, stamping their hooves on the roadway and snorting, as though impatient. Immediately behind them and to which they were hitched was a gleaming black varnished hearse with floral decoration and ornate features and details. Including acid etched glazed side panels through which I could see an empty space normally reserved for a coffin.

Behind the hearse and through the fog, I could just make out a person, a peculiar individual, who had positioned himself at the foot of a considerable flight of stone steps leading up to the front door of a sizeable, but forlorn and run-down Gothic mansion.

The Gothic mansion, though large was dominated by

Every Man and Women in Britain & the Empire
should Use

DR SCOTT'S ELECTRIC
'FLESH' BRUSH

WHY ?

Because it quickens the circulation,
opens the pores,
&
enables the system to throw off those impurities
which cause disease.
It instantly acts upon the blood,
nerves, and tissues.
Imparting

A Beautiful Clear Skin
New Energy and New Life,
TO ALL WHO DAILY USE IT
AND IS WARRENTED TO CURE
Rheumatism and Diseases of the Blood,
Nervous Complaints, Neuralgia, Toothache,
Malaria, Lameness, Palpitations, Paralysis
&
All pains caused by impaired circulation.
It promptly alleviates Indigestion, Liver
and Kidney Troubles,
Quickly removes those "Back Aches"
peculiar to Ladies,
&
Imparts wonderful vigor to the whole body.

ALL DEALERS WILL REFUND PRICE
IF NOT AS REPRESENTED.

*All Checks, Drafts or Post Office Orders made payable
to Dr. Geo. A. Scott, 842 Broadway, London SW*

Abandoned Gothic Mansion

a substantial tower, which the fog seemed powerless to obscure. For some reason I had a notion that the mansion was in fact, abandoned the house had, in the past, evidently been the residence of a wealthy person, but presumably now had fallen on hard times as reflected in the general state of decay and dilapidation affecting the building, evident, even to me, standing in the roadway.

However, not immediately obvious to me, is what precisely this character was doing on the steps leading up to the front door of the abandoned mansion. Though still uncertain of what he was doing. He himself was fairly certain in his actions and indeed quite conspicuous. In fact it would have been difficult not to notice him. He was dressed in an ill-fitting black frock-coat made of robust broadcloth that matched his tight fitting black trousers that were made of a similar material. His boots, though originally black, were scuffed in several places, which indicated to me a lack of care or of self-esteem.

I noticed too, that the socks he wore comprised bands of color, forming garish ring patterns. His shirt had clearly started life possibly white, but had become grey, as the years had taken their toll upon its fabric. Nonetheless, the frayed collar was closed with a rather flamboyant black silk necktie secured with a stud in which was set a polished purple stone. Capping this sartorial assemblage was a rather absurd tall top hat of the stove-pipe variety, slightly crumpled but in keeping with the rest of his tired attire.

Upon closer examination, I noticed that the top hat was not so much crumpled, but rather had wrapped around it, a kind of black crêpe material, giving the impression of a ribbed textured fabric to the hat. Two black ribbons hung from the back, completing the arrangement. His face was pock marked and of a blank pallor, as though he had applied a white powder to it, or had been rendered in plaster. However, his facial complexion did complement the white gloves he wore on his hands, which twitched as though he were in a state of extreme agitation. That, or he was afflicted severely by St. Vitus' Dance.

Indeed his whole manner appeared to be one of concern and his black eyes rolled aimlessly around in their sockets set in his white powdered face. It then occurred to me as I realized with confidence, precisely why the individual was dressed in this peculiar manner.

He was, of course, clearly a Dumb Mute! I had heard about these persons and remembered seeing one such person or actor, perform on the stage at Wilton's Music Hall in Whitechapel.

These characters are, I believe, an optional funereal feature and very popular in the East End of London. His sole function, on occasions such as this, I recalled, is to re-live the agonies of dying for the benefit of those members of the family or friends who were unfortunate enough to miss the actual recent death of the master of the household!

I simply could not imagine for a moment this kind of practice taking place in New York or any other large city in America.

I was pondering this singular state of affairs when suddenly, a Rudge-Whitworth two-wheel velocipede came upon me out of the blinding fog like a ghostly apparition. It did so at such a velocity that it gave me a start as it glided past my face. The shock was made all the more intense by the fact that the two wheeler's appearance was silent due to the new improved Dunlop pneumatic, rubber tires fitted to its metal wheel rims.

The rider was sitting upright and high on his saddle as he pedalled his bi-cycle furiously. Indeed his eyes set in his glistening face appeared to be in some sort of manic trance and he was totally oblivious to the fact he had just driven his dangerous contraption into my person.

By the time I had gathered my wits and recovered to re-act, he had disappeared back into the opaque folds of fog and was literally out of sight. Outrageous, I thought. Outrageous, that a person, by using a mechanical device such as that velocipede, was able to propel himself in such a reckless manner, abandoning all sense of propriety and public regard. And, more alarmingly, that the driver of such a dangerous locomotion contraption, was often able to achieve a velocity of more than six statute miles within a continuous period of one hour, which is allowed on the roads in the midst of this metropolis.

Notwithstanding this incident, I continued along Sclator Street, for I had more pressing matters to attend to, not least getting to the New National Standard Theater to witness a performance of, *'The Rhinegold,'* pantomime based on Wagner's epic grand opera called, *'Das Rheingold.'* Though, as it happens, I was experiencing pantomime in the street, whilst on my way to the theater.

At length this street continued into a wider roadway called the Bethnal Green Road. According to Mabel, this street, will lead me into Shoreditch High Street in which the New National Standard Theater is located. I hoped against hope she was correct in her directions. It then struck me; when I leave the theater later this evening. I would have to get myself home. But I sure as hell will not be retracing my footsteps back along the way I had come.

At length I managed to make my way into Shoreditch High Street and found the theater. The front of which was illuminated by several large opaque glass globes pouring out a powerful light, in their rôle of being, quite literally, beacons in the dense fog.

The façade of the New National Standard Theater, or at least from what I could discern in the fog, appeared to be a most peculiar assemblage of buildings, given the fact it is a fully functioning Music Hall. And, according to Lodge, this theater contains the largest auditorium in Europe, even though the front of the building or indeed its location in an outer district of metropolitan London would not immediately suggest these facts.

The front elevation of the Music Hall addressing Shoreditch High Street was dominated by a four storey high tower complete with elaborate design details in the masonry. The structure was crowned at the upper level with a substantial over-hanging decorated architrave. Comprising ornate recessed alternate deep consoles used for corbelling, supporting a lesser detailed stepped

New National Standard Theater

cornice, typical of a Renaissance style of classical architecture. This ornate building seemed somewhat out of place, and almost at variance with the area of London in which I had found myself wandering through to get here.

Indeed the building I was about to enter comprised the tower, the base of which was an archway leading into the main foyer of the Music Hall. Almost buttressing that tower structure, as it were, was a rather plain-looking building with very little ornamentation to its plain façade. That building too contained two archways leading to where; I could not, from my location on the sidewalk and also due to the fog, determine with any degree of confidence. But presumably, they too must lead into the Music Hall, I conjectured.

I made my way through the archway at the base of the tower and up some steps into the brightly illuminated foyer of the New National Standard Music Hall. I was grateful to be out of that acrid and odorous fog which had irritated my eyes whilst walking here. As my eyes adjusted to the fogless brightness of the foyer, I noticed something whilst looking down at my boots.

That Rudge-Whitworth two-wheel velocipede, which had been driven over my right foot by that reckless bi-cyclist, had in fact, deposited a vulcanized tire imprint on to my highly varnished boot. I tried there and then to rub away the blemish, but found that I could not. Some what slightly annoyed by this revelation I continued on in to the foyer.

More importantly, I thought. I had gotten here in time to buy a ticket and program brochure and hit the Crush Bar for twenty minutes before curtain up. I did precisely that and having availed myself of a ticket to the Grand Dress Circle no less, made my way up to the Crush Bar.

Whilst standing there with a large whisky in one hand and the program brochure in the other. I read some interesting facts about the New National Standard Theater in the introductory notes in the front of the brochure.

The Music Hall, it read, was built originally in 1837 as the Royal Standard Theater, It was named after a Public House, which had previously occupied the site, bearing the same name. The horse shoe configured auditorium could seat about three thousand four hundred persons. In 1866 the theater caught fire and was raised to the ground. No surprise there, I thought, London theaters are for ever going up in flame.This almost predictable fact of theaters burning down, appears to be very much an accepted and integral part of Music Hall existence in London.

Aside of this fact, what I found even more astonishing, as I read through my brochure, was that within a year, the Music Hall had risen from the ashes, almost like a re-incarnated Phoenix, and re-opened a year later in 1867. It was now called the New Standard Theater. The new theater was built on a much larger scale, but with a reduced, albeit more comfortable and opulent auditorium, able to seat about three thousand persons.

As it would seem to be the practice in London; the New Standard Theater was rebuilt for a third time to the designs of the acclaimed theater architect, Bertie Crewe. Though now the auditorium could only seat about two thousand five hundred persons; it still claimed the accolade of being the largest theater in Europe. Though from memory, I seem to recall Lodge informing me that the auditorium at the Empress Music Hall at Earl's Court, was capable of seating comfortably about five thousand persons, anyone of whom, from any position, would have an uninterrupted view of the stage. And that the stage at the Empress Music Hall, the width of which being a prodigious three hundred seventy feet wide, was per force the largest theater currently in use in London.

Irrespective of this assertion, the program brochure continued to inform me that the New Standard Theater pit in which the orchestra is contained, was larger than that of Sir Agustus Harris's Drury Lane Theater. Indeed there was, in the past quite an intense and acrimonious rivalry between the New Standard Theater and the Drury Lane Theater, especially in the area of the production of pantomime. In 1845 the theater was sold, so I read, to an impresario, name of Douglass, John Douglass, who promoted and staged pantomimes, very similar to those at Harris's Drury Lane Theater. However, which of the two impresarios could claim to be the originator of expanding the rôle of the pantomime remains debatable.

On numerous occasions, so the brochure informed me, Douglass claimed that Harris copied his theatrical innovations produced at the New Standard Music Hall in Shoreditch. And because of these innovations, Douglass was able to attract all the best west end actors to appear on his stage. These sensational stage events introduced at the New Standard Music Hall, could include live horses on stage, real rain creating a deluge or flood and all with the confines of the auditorium.

Interesting, I thought, as I drained my glass. Not for the first time have I concluded that there is more Music Hall drama off stage than upon it. I then made my way to the Grand Dress Circle to experience an even greater pantomime called 'The Rhinegold' and given expression based upon Wagner's opera of the same name.

To my utter amazement the auditorium was filled to the rafters. I considered myself extremely fortunate in being able to get a ticket just minutes before the commencement of the pantomime. Suddenly the gas fueled chandeliers, illuminating the mauve plush auditorium, the biggest in Europe, so a prominent poster informed me, were dimmed, plunging the theater into darkness.

Whilst sitting in the darkened, hushed auditorium it occurred to me that of course, it was from the opera, '*Das Rheingold,*' Lodge had derived his sobriquet name of *Loge*. Irrespective of Loge's somewhat venal character in the opera, I wondered who actually thought up the idea of giving Lodge this name. And, more interestingly, why did they do so?

I stared ahead of me into the darkness, full of expectation. Then, imperceptibly at first, but becoming louder was an orchestral prelude starting with a low E flat chord which gradually changed into an elaborate variation of the E flat major chord lasting just over four minutes. The curtain had been raised during the orchestral prelude revealing a darkened stage, but gradually, a dull light began to illuminate a backdrop scene.

So far the pit orchestra was doing justice to Wagner's music, as witnessed by their controlled development of the prelude. This prelude, in effect an orchestral drone piece, extends for over one hundred forty bars, and represents the turbulent waters of the river Rhein.

Act I

Over a period of minute or so, the light became brighter gradually revealing an enchanted scene of the river Rhein flowing through a forest. In the foreground we were presented with the river bank in a forest clearing at dawn. As dawn was breaking we could see through the

THE
NEW NATIONAL STANDARD
THEATER
SHOREDITCH

LARGEST & MOST ELEGANT THEATER IN EUROPE
OPEN EVERY EVENING
SOLE PROPRIETOR   MR. JOHN DOUGLASS

A PERFORMANCE OF THE WIDELY ACCLAIMED

THE RHINEGOLD
A PANTOMIME

BASED ON THE OPERA

DAS RHEINGOLD
BY WILHELM RICKARD WAGNER

CAST

WOTAN - DAN LENO
FRICKA - MARIE LLOYD
FREIA – CINDERELLA
ERDA – GERTIE MILLAR
LOGE - GUS ELEN
ALBERICH - LITTLE TICH
FASOLT - VULCANA
DONNER – GEORGE ROBEY
FAFNER - MADAME HECULINE
FLOSSHILDE - MADEMOISELLE ARIEL,
WOGLINDE - MADEMOISELLE ADA
WELLGUNDE - MADEMOISELLE GILLERT
FROH - WINIFRED BARNES

harmonies of color and delicate interplay of light, three Rhein-maidens, Flosshilde, Woglinde and Wellgunde, splashing each other and playing around on the shore of the river. They were played by three the taffeta-wearing masculine danseuses in the persons of Mademoiselle Ariel, Mademoiselle Ada, and Mademoiselle Gillert respectively.

Woglinde, played by Mademoiselle Ariel was the first to haul herself out of the river and began singing a song in the key of A flat, the melody of which would become the leitmotiv representing the Rhein-maidens throughout the pantomime. So I read in my program. She was joined by her sisters, Flosshilde and Wellgunde who, whilst strutting around the stage, sang in unison, of their boundless happiness of living in the river Rhein.

The music changed to a feeling of foreboding as Alberich, an ugly and venal Nibelung night-dwarf, played by Little Tich, appeared from behind one of the trees next to the river bank. Immediately the Rhein-maidens changed the song about their happiness to one about Alberich's patently conspicuous ugliness which was calculated deliberately to annoy him. Little Tich burst in to a song about his being a decent chap really and was simply looking for a lady friend. The Rhein-maidens refute this claim by Alberich and continue to mock him.

He retaliates by throwing a rock at Woglinda. Within seconds of doing so the Rhein-maidens descend upon him with a fury equal to that of incensed Walküre.

Within a short period of time, the Rhein-maidens wrestle Alberich to the ground and then attempt to drag him into their river where they fully intend to drown him. They very nearly succeed, but at that moment dawn breaks fully, revealing the sun. The Rhein-maidens abandon the half drowned Alberich in order to offer praise to a golden glow coming from a rocky island in the river. Other dwellers of the forest, including the fairies, which made up the corps de ballet, now awakened, come into view. They began mingling around the stage singing of their love for the river and of the sun the light from which still continues to glint off the rock.

Then, if by a hidden signal, the corps de ballet reassembles itself into formation. And then with a coördinated precision, execute some complex manœuvres with an occasional pas de deux, much to the delight of the audience. Little Tich as Alberich, now somewhat recovered from his watery ordeal has the audacity to ask Flosshilde what is that golden glow coming from the rock. But the taffeta wearing corps de ballet of fairies, remind Flosshilde, the Rhein-maiden, that she and her sisters are sworn under oath to their father to guard the gold and not divulge its magic powers to anyone.

In response, Flosshilde walks over to where the fairies are assembled and then burst into song. She is later joined by her two sisters. They all sing of the gold on the rock and the fact that it can be fashioned into a ring with magical powers. Including letting the wearer of the ring become the undisputed master of the world, but only if that person has renounced love. The Rhein-maidens sing of Alberich's immediately obvious and conspicuous ugliness and his revolting lustful ways. They then conclude, in a rousing finale to their song, that they have very little to fear from such a loathsome and visually repulsive night-dwarf such as he, and then they return to the river.

"Did not we say, do not divulge the secret of the gold on the rock?" asked the fairies, in unison.

The Rhein-maidens ignore this question and instead splash each other and then some of the fairies too.

The fairies re-act to this splashing and begin to swoop down on the Rhein-maidens. Whilst the Rhein-maidens are pre-occupied with the angry fairies, the embittered Alberich seizes the opportunity and swims out to the rock and to source of the golden glow coming off the rock. Having gotten to the rock, Alberich grabs the lump of gold and holds it aloft in his hand as he curses love. He then returns to the river bank and into the depths of the forest leaving the Rhein-maidens screaming vengeance at Alberich and at the fairies for distracting them from their duty of guarding the gold.

However, it becomes apparent to all but the blind, the drunk or indeed blind drunk, that the stage was now set clearly for what looked like a limbering up for a battle of Titanic proportions between the fairies and the Rhein-maidens in the form of the taffeta-wearing danseuses. I was uncertain as to which would prevail in this monumental struggle. Then it happened as each of the fairies leapt into the waters of the Rhein in order to deal effectively with the Rhein-maidens. I counted at least thirty fairies which comprised the corps de ballet. The frenzy in the water was particularly vicious, as bits of taffeta erupted into the aëther, despite the intimidating presence of the three Rhein-maidens.

Eventually the Rhein-maidens managed to extricate themselves from the mêlée and climb up the river bank to comparative safety. Alas, this was not to be so for still on land were those ballerinas who had not leapt into the river. Accordingly, they marched determinedly across the stage sweeping all before them, including the Rhein-maidens trying to dry their sodden hair. Unfortunately they were unable to escape in time to avoid receiving some well placed kicks from the massed ranks of the taffeta-wearing corp de ballet, now in a frightful temper.

Again, the discerning audience erupted into ecstatic applause for the fairies, which still had not quite finished with the Rhein-maidens. For at that very moment of apotheosis of the clapping one of the more masculine of the taffeta-wearing Rhein-maidens, Mademoiselle Gillert, leapt up gracefully in to the aëther. She did so on what we all assumed to be the beginning of an elegant pas de deux.

It was not to be, because at the height of her graceful arched leap into the aëther, three of the fairies from the corps de ballet grab the swooning Rhein-maiden and pull her down to the stage with an audible crash. Again, the action, vicious as it is instant, was hidden by a flurry of taffeta, Rhein-maiden sodden hair and the occasional fairies' wings. It was during this thunderous applause that the safety curtain descended, and in so doing, triggering off a blind stampede to the various Crush Bars ranged around the Music Hall.

Act II

After a suitable interval in which one was able to come down to earth at a well appointed Crush Bar, I returned to my purple plush seat in the Grand Dress Circle. Just looking around the brightly illuminated, vast swathes of mauve colored velvet seats, it was easy to appreciate that this auditorium was the largest, most elegant in Europe. The stalls were extensive and the Grand Dress Circles numbered four with private boxes on each level overlooking the stage. Perhaps, after all, I should at some stage give Lodge's regards to the sole proprietor and manager, John Douglass, and compliment him on his lush Music Hall.

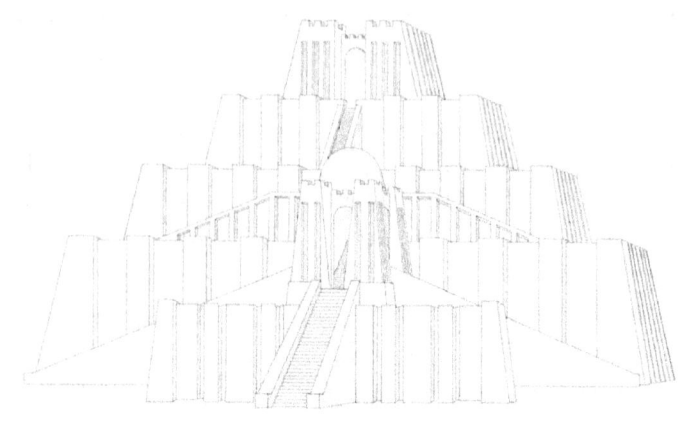

Valhalla

However, that thought paled into insignificance as the second act opened with the safety curtain rising into the attic. The scene presented to us was one of a mountain set in the distance. Upon this mountain was built a large magnificent structure, called Valhalla, the new abode of the gods. Complete with a majestic and extensive flight of red *Nembro Rosato* marble steps leading up to a dome and into a series of blue *Azul Macaubas* marble terraces and walls which formed a large imposing apex structure which rose into the sky.

Indeed the Valhalla exuded all that ethereal and nobility one would expect to radiate from the house of the gods. The music, coming from the orchestra in the pit, was subdued, as the ruler of the gods, Wotan, played by Dan Leno, came strutting on to the stage followed by his wife Fricka, played by Marie Lloyd and who was clearly besotted with her husband, Wotan.

Lloyd turns to the audiences and, pointing with her wand at the castle on the back drop, begins singing about their new home Valhalla, which has just been built for them. Her husband eventually joins her and together they break into a duet, *'If it wasn't for the Houses in Between,'* which the audience join in without being invited to do so.

In another duet, Wotan and Fricka sing of their suspect pact with the two Titans Fasolt and Fafner, who together had constructed the castle, Valhalla. They did so under the delusion that Wotan would give them, as payment for their labors, Fricka's sister Freia, the goddess of beauty, youth and feminine love.

At this stage the corps de ballet re-appeared and trailing silver ribbons in their hands, commence, with coördinated precision, a complex dance routine and singing praises for Wotan, their lord and master. They in turn are joined by some aërial fairies swooning around in the aëther above them. Some even swoop out over the costermongers sitting in the front rows of the stalls. And on each occasion, the costermongers duck in their seats in a perforce and exaggerated manner.

However, whilst this activity was going on, Fricka began to sing in the plaintiff chant of D flat minor, of her deep worry for her sister Freia. She tells the audience, in song, of Wotan's real intention which is not to give Freia away, but instead to buy the Titans off with an alternative gift. Lloyd sings of her uncertainty about this. And remarks on the fact that even Wotan has sent Loge, his duplicitous and scheming vassal, to find an alternative gift to satisfy the Titans.

However, before Lloyd is able to finish her lament. Freia, her sister, in a graceful pas de deux, lept on to the stage in a blind panic closely pursued by the Titans Fasolt and Fafner. I could not believe my eyes nor in fact could the audience who stood up, without bidding. Simultaneously they commenced a thunderous applause for the three characters which had just entered the stage. One of whom was Freia, being played by Cinderella!

The two Titans were being played by Vulcana,[5] the strong woman dressed in her male clothes in the rôle of Fasolt. And Fafner was portrayed effortlessly by another strong woman in the person of Madame Heculine, again suitably attired in masculine garb. She is also affectionately known as Lady Samson, and evidently fresh from her tour de force appearance at Humber's Waxworks in Aberdeen in Scotland, so I read in the brochure.

After a few minutes of running around in front of the scenery, the Titans stopped and approached the front of the stage. There they appealed to the audience, singing that they merely want payment for constructing on time and on budget the Valhalla castle for Wotan and his family of gods. What could be fairer than that, they sing, Fafner and Fasolt and pointing with their clubs down to the costermongers in the stalls who were attentively looking up at them. Moments later a unanimous shout erupted from the costers.

"Pay the Titans, pay them what they deserve and pay them now," they responded, in perfect unison.

It was Vulcana, in her rôle of Fasolt, who then approached Wotan and demanded fair payment for having constructed Valhalla, the new home of the gods. Fasolt was then joined by Madame Heculine playing Fafner and together they sang about the sanctity of a written contract and the inequity of the evil *Exclusivity Clause* [6] which afflicts many of their friends who work hard for their supper.

Vulcana then informs Wotan that he has signed a contractual agreement with the Titans, the terms and consideration of which were carved into his spear. Madame Heculine, playing Fafner, also tells Wotan that he cannot break this agreement. At this stage the fairies, at Wotan's bidding, began surrounding the Titans and poking at them and generally behaving in a confident manner. The predictable happened and with seconds another fight breaks out with a least thirty fairies pulling and pushing the Titans about.

The Titans respond by throwing some of the fairies into the aëther. They in turn are caught by their sisters, the aërial fairies swooping above the mêlée. This pandäemonium is brought to an abrupt halt by the arrival on stage of Donner, the god of thunder, played by George Robey, accompanied by Froh, the goddess of spring, Winifred Barnes, who swears fealty in songspiel with the fairies in order to defend their sister goddess, Freia, from the advances of the Titans, Fafner and Fasolt. This of course was the same Winifred Barnes who auditioned, unsuccessfully for the vacant rôle of soprano with the *Three Graces* in the Oxford Music Hall recently.

However, at that juncture Wotan faces the audience and sings about the contract, and that it is his divine right and intention to use force to break the sanctity of a contact, any contract, even those containing the reviled *Exclusivity Clause*. Cinderella then joined Wotan in her rôle of Freia, much to the applause of the audience. She then sang of her fervent wish that the venal, if mercurial vassal Loge, will be able to find a suitable alternative gift acceptable as payment to Vulcana and Madame Heculine, the Titans, who were still fighting off the fairies.

Then, as if by a hidden signal, everybody on stage faced the audience and burst into song about their faith in Loge's nefarious resourcefulness in solving this problem with the Titans. The stage then clears, leaving only Wotan, Fricka and Freia, Dan Leno, Marie Lloyd and Cinderella respectively.

A deep sound of a low E flat melody which twists and turns in variation as it changes continually, as Proteus would change shape, heralded the arrival on stage of the mischievous Loge played by Gus Elen. Immediately the fairies dispersed, averting their eyes from him. Loge, smiling and rubbing his hands then turned to the audience, especially the costermongers, with whom he evidently has some *sway* and a symbiotic relationship. He then tells them in songspiel, of his trials and tribulations in trying to reach a settlement with the Titans.

"Can I try hard enough already, I ask you? These Titans, they will have their way, I tell you," Loge bemoaned lyrically, holding his hands out with palms facing upwards.

As Loge bursts in to yet another song, he addresses Wotan and tells him that the Titans will accept nothing in exchange for Freia. At this point Cinderella in the rôle of Freia, collapses to the floor seemingly lifeless. Loge goes on to murmur in Wotan's ear that he has found someone. Alberich, the night-dwarf, who has more than willingly renounced love for something infinitely more tangible and desirable, in the form of the Rhine gold. The very same gold he has stolen recently from the Rhein-maidens and from which he has now fashioned a powerful and magic ring.

The Titans, Fafner and Fasolt then re-appear on stage and sing a duet together, during the course of which they tell Wotan that they will accept in payment, as an alternative to Freia, the Nibelung Alberich's stolen golden treasure formed into a magical ring.

Wotan responds by striking the ground with his spear and refuses to agree. Loge tries to intercede, but to no avail. Wotan is adamant. The Titans depart, and as they do, snatch the goddess Freia, taking her hostage.

Later we see a mournful looking Cinderella, in playing Freia, the goddess of beauty, youth and feminine love and pivotal in the lives of the gods. Freia then begins to sing that it is she, and only she, who as the goddess of youth, with her golden apples, was able to keep the gods eternally young. Now in her misery as a captive of the Titans Vulcana and Madame Heculine Cinderella, as Freia, tells of her fears that, in the absence of her golden apples, the gods will begin to age and that their power over the Titans will become weaker.

The lights illuminate another part of this large stage and we are presented with a scene of Dan Leno, in the rôle of Wotan, singing to his wife Fricka, Marie Lloyd. He breaks into song about his resolve to retrieve the golden band, even if that should involve him, Wotan, going to the very depths of hell to do so, in order to secure Freia's freedom.

Fricka remains unconvinced and lowers her head in despair. She then looks at Wotan and addresses him.

"We are doomed," she sings in a controlled recitative, "we all of us are doomed! We have placed ourselves in the hands of that mercurial Loge, and in so doing, we are treaty to a Faustian contract from which there will be no escape. This calamity will consume us all, including our new glittering home, Valhalla, there on the top of that mountain, and into which we have not yet even moved. What have we done Wotan, more importantly, what have you done?"

Fricka then turns away from Wotan in despair and looks out over the audience. She then begins a slow plaintiff chant in E flat minor leading into a song of lament. She does so to an attentive and hushed audience from a darkened stage with only a blood red sky surrounding Valhalla castle painted on the backdrop scene. The song she begins to sing is instantly recognized by all in the auditorium, including me.

It is the famous *Abendlich*, which within a chord or two, has the audiences, in their mauve plush velvet seats, swaying from side to side in harmonic sympathy, at the end of which the heavy velvet safety curtain descended in an ominous manner with portents of even more doom to come on stage.

The stampede to the various Crush Bars during the interval was, on this occasion, even more manic.

Act III

Act three opened with the corps de ballet, which comprises the fairies, dressed not in their usual taffeta and lace but now covered in silver armor and carrying clubs. They are, of course, resolved to follow Loge and Wotan, their lord and master and ruler of the gods, down into the depths of the earth to Nibelheim, in pursuit of the stolen gold. This is the place where Alberich, with his new power of the ring, has managed to enslave the race of Nibelung dwarves.

The crusade goes marching off, with coördinated precision on its noble quest singing cheerfully, '*We are off on a Day's Excursion*,' led by Loge, as they descend to the gloomy depths to Nibelheim, the acrid, smoked filled domain of the Nibelung. Moments later we began to hear the faint sound of anvils being struck with force, indicating the toiling of the enslaved dwarves there.

When at length Wotan, Loge and the armed fairies arrive, they come across Alberich's brother and a skillful forge smith, name of Mime, played by Bessie Bonehill. Mime tells Wotan of Alberich's treachery and the forging of the golden magic ring, together with the unceasing misery he has wrought upon the Nibelung dwarves he has enslaved under his rule. More frighteningly, Mime relates the fact that his brother, Alberich has forced him to fashion, from the stolen gold, a magic helmet, a Tarnhelm, which makes the wearer, notably Alberich, invisible or able to change shape, as Proteus could, for advantage!

Alberich returns, singing out more audacious orders to the enslaved Nibelung dwarves. When he has finished his song, he addresses Wotan and Loge. He tells them about his plans to become master of the world, and, as he has done to the dwarves; enslave the fairies too. And he can achieve this easily by using his magic Tarnhelm, which makes him invisible.

"I find that difficult to accept," Loge declares in songspiel.

The chorus of armored fairies clusters around Alberich and repeat the question.

"For how could you," Loge continues, in recitative, "protect yourself against a thief whilst you are asleep?"

Again the chorus of fairies repeats this inquiry, to which Alberich responds, to a deflated Loge.

"A magic helmet, a Tarnhelm, that Mime has fashioned for me, will hide my person or change my form during the time in which I slumber!"

"We do not believe such boasts!" sing the fairies, in unison.

"Neither do I; it is just too fanciful to believe that you can change shape, even with Proteus for advantage," comments Loge in songspiel.

"We do not believe you," cry the armored fairies.

"Yes", replies Loge, "If what you say is true, then prove it. Prove to us that you have mastered this magical power; or is it all talk just to appear to be impressive?"

The fairies now begin to openly mock and shout at Alberich.

"You will not be as fortunate as you were with the Rhein-maidens Alberich, when they attempted to drown you, for we shall finish our work on you!" they jeer, whilst still mocking him.

"The fairies are correct Alberich; yours is only an empty boast, because neither Wotan, myself or the fairies believe in your wild and fanciful assertions. And even now you are unable to demonstrate your claims," sings Loge, whilst motioning Wotan to leave the subterranean realm of Nibeheim.

Incensed by this treatment Alberich brings down his hammer on to a rock and shattered it with one blow. He then turns to Loge.

"Watch me if I cannot change shape. Watch me,"instructs Alberich.

Alberich dons the golden Tarnhelm. Moments later a myriad of light dances around Alberich's body and he seemed to glow. Then, imperceptibly at first, but gradually parts of his body were becoming transparent. Eventually other parts of his body appeared to change and disappear until there was nothing left for us to look at.

Presently, Alberich re-appeared and smiled at the suitably impressed Wotan and Loge. He did not bother to acknowledge the now quiet fairies.

"Very impressive, but one more demonstration Alberich, so all in future shall know of your undoubted magical powers. Can you reduce your size in order to conceal yourself anywhere at any time?" asked Loge, deferentially and with a subservient bow.

"Of course I can," "announced Alberich, "watch me."

Again he put on the Tarnhelm, accompanied by the display of different colored lights dancing around his body, parts of which started to turn green and shrink. Within a minute hopping about on the floor was Alberich. He had turned himself into a toad!

The audience, amazed at the magical feat, rose from their seats to gain a better view of the stage. However, Loge the seized the toad and locked it an iron box. Triumphantly, Loge takes the iron box containing Alberich and marches out of the depths of Nibelheim followed by Wotan and the clamoring fairies singing, *'We Have Him Now.'*

They then all make their way to the top of a mountain from which they will be able to view the magnificent Valhalla, the new abode of the gods.

I was beginning to understand more fully Loge's pivotal rôle in this pantomime, *'The Rhinegold,'* based as it was on Wagner's grand opera, *'Das Rheingold.'* And why Lodge continues to bask in the nick name he had been given, that of *Loge,* presumably because he could, with his nefarious skills, fix things or was able to achieve results. Impresario, indeed, I thought to myself!

Moments later I saw the safety curtain plummet to the stage deck. That triggered off another mindless and frenetic stampede to the numerous Crush Bars ranged around the New National Standard Theater.

Act IV

When the audience eventually returned from the Crush Bars to the auditorium, which had been deserted for the better part of an hour, a hushed silence descended upon it.

We all of us were truly enthralled and in the grip of this Teutonic saga involving greed, grand theft, kidnapping, organized lying, enslavement, fraud, extortion and assault, by several individuals, too numerous to mention, let alone indict.

The curtain was raised on a scene depicting the top of

a craggy mountain. In the background was the new Valhalla, resplendent in its ethereal majestic splendor shimmering in the brilliant sun light. From Valhalla light emanated through window openings in its complex of walls, turrets and towers. It was an impressive sight to behold.

In the meantime, standing at the front of the stage was Wotan and Loge. Both were trying to force Alberich to agree to hand over his wealth in return for his freedom. Eventually he agrees to do so and Loge therefore unbinds his tethered hands. Alberich, unwillingly and hesitantly summons the enslaved Nibelung dwarves from Nibelheim, deep in the earth, to bring to Wotan the stolen hoard of gold.

After he has the gold delivered to Wotan, Alberich then demands the return of the Tarnhelm. However, Loge refuses to do so and sings that it must remain part of the ransom. In return, Wotan demands the ring from Alberich who declines to give it, singing about Loge's refusal in turn, to hand back the magical Tarnhelm. Wotan, in a rage seizes the gold band from Alberich hand and puts it on his own finger.

Alberich, in disgust at this trickery perpetrated by the gods, leaves the stage. He does so swearing revenge, and places a Death-Curse upon all those who would wear the ring upon their finger, to the haunting sound of a powerful, dread-filled, melodic leitmotiv in E flat major,

"Until the ring is returned to me," sings Alberich, "whoever does not possess it will desire it and whoever possesses it will live with the imminent threat of death by those who seek to possess it!"

"Fair enough," replies Loge, in controlled recitative.

Eventually, Fasolt and Fafner in the guise of Vulcana and Madame Heculine return, strutting on the stage, carrying between them the goddess Freia. They sing in perfect unison of their fervent wish to exact payment from the gods and will only release Freia when she could be totally hidden from view by gold piled high enough.

As the Titans, helped by the fairies, pile up the treasure into a mound, they come to realize that there is insufficient gold to hide Freia completely. Fasolt demands the final chink, through which Freia's eye can be seen, be filled in with the ring on Wotan's finger, or the deal is off.

It is the mercurial Loge, who now breaks out into songspiel, and reminds Wotan, the Titans and the fairies that in law, the ring belongs to the Rhein-maidens, whose sworn duty is to guard it for eternity. Wotan, unmoved refuses to part with the ring. He sings that the ring is his, as of divine right, being the ruler of the gods. Loge looks at Wotan shaking his head as the Titans seize Freia again and forcibly march off with her through the massed ranks of fairies, pushing them out of their path. Wotan motions the fairies not to retaliate, but to bide their time.

Next to enter the stage is the acclaimed Music Hall artiste, Gertie Millar, in the rôle, of Erda, the primeval earth goddess who exceeds in age all the gods including Wotan. She progresses up to the footlights and looks out over the audience and then bursts into song, during which, in an impassioned plea, she urges Wotan to surrender the cursed ring. Or, she foretells, be prepared for an impending doom and indeed bring about that which the very gods most dread, *'Götterdämmerung.'* [7]

Wotan, after considering Erda's pleas, recalls the Titans. They return, and Wotan hands over to them the golden band. They in turn release Freia, who immediately falls into the arms of Fricka.

The treasure is now offered over into the possession

of the Titans. However, Alberich's curse begins to reveal itself mercilessly and brutally as the Titans start to argue as to which of them should wear the magical ring. Suddenly, Fafner attacks Fasolt, with what looked like great enthusiasm, beating him to death to the sound of Alberich's predictable Death-Curse leitmotiv; already claiming its first victim!

Wotan recoils back in horror at what he had just witnessed. He realizes that the Death-Curse invoked by Alberich on those who would possess the gold ring was now not only a certainty, but with it came a terrible power. He summoned his wife Fricka, played by Marie Lloyd, to his side. She looked dotingly at him and sings a lament, '*Take me home I'm tired and want to go to Bed.*'

Again without any encouragement from Wotan, Fricka, the other gods or Loge, the costermongers join in singing this lament, adding their peculiar variations to the verses accordingly.

Wotan complies with Fricka's wish and commands the gods to attend him. He then orders Donner, the god of thunder, played by George Robey, to summon a thunderstorm during which the gods will take possession of the new home, Valhalla. The gods assemble in a line at the front of the stage and looked down at the costermongers. They, in mutual respect, stagger up from their seats and stand there with their heads bowed in deference to the gods above them.

When the storm had subsided, Froh, the goddess of spring, played by Winifred Barnes, creates a bridge from the mist laden aether, a rainbow bridge which glistened in the sun light as it arches over the abyss and up to the imposing entrance to Valhalla.

Wotan summons the assembled gods to follow him. They do so; and with their heads bowed, as though in deep contemplation, they walk in a solemn and measured tread over the rainbow bridge into Valhalla. This final scene showing the majestic entry of the gods into Valhalla, is accompanied by the closing bars of a mighty extended crescendo created by considerable orchestral forces augmenting the thunderous applause from an appreciative audience and standing costermongers. At the end of which the usual panic driven stampede to the Crush Bars was all together quite as frantic as it was remorseless.

1. Twilight of the Gods
2. Warrior daughters of the Teutonic god, Wotan
3. A drone is a harmonic accompaniment where a note or chord is continuously created during a piece of music
4. A reference expressed in music of a recurring reoccurring idea or character
5. Katherine Williams was a friend of the murdered Bella Elmore
6. The *Exclusivity Clause* prevented artistes working in nearby Music Halls on the same night
7. The End of the Gods

Chapter 23

The Holborn Empire
Music Hall

In my stay in London thus far, the previous night was by far the most revealing. Not only had I witnessed '*The Rhinegold*,' pantomime based upon Rickard Wagner's grand opera, '*Das Rheingold*,' but was invited to the backstage party afterwards. This fortuitous situation came about as a result of my going back stage to compliment Cinderella in her rôle as Freia. There I met with the sole proprietor and manager of the New National Standard Theater, John Douglass, and indeed, did pass on Lodge's regards to him. I also met with some of the more accomplished Music Hall artistes. But what intrigued me then and continue to do so, is the extraordinary ability the English have to diminish seriousness; and to parody the profound. The pantomime of the night before showed me this ability was in equal measure. However, for the time being, I now needed to concentrate on my appearance that evening, not as a Teutonic god in a Wagnerian opera or pantomime, but rather as a Vaudeville artiste on the stage at the Holborn Empire Music Hall with my stage partner Jack Mitchell.

"The original Holborn Empire Music Hall," so Lodge informed Jack and me whilst we were travelling in his open Barouche carriage to the Holborn Empire Music Hall, "was built on the site of an existing public house

Holborn Empire Music Hall

called the *Six Cans and Punch Bowl*, the landlord of which was one Henry Weston. He built the then Weston's Music Hall in 1857 as a deliberate response to the successes enjoyed at Charles Morton's Canterbury Music Hall at Waterloo.

"At Henry Weston's establishment the entrance fee for an evening's entertainment was a mere six pennies, including a, 'refreshment' ticket which entitled the holder to see the turns and acts on the stage. In 1861, Morton re-acted to Weston by constructing the Oxford Music Hall in Oxford Street, less than a half mile away and in the same road. You may remember, at the time Weston objected to the Oxford Music Hall, being built at all, claiming there were too many Music Halls already in the same road [1] and immediate vicinity.

"It must be said though, that never has a Music Hall as Weston's changed its name as many times. Weston's Music Hall in High Holborn, a continuation of Oxford Street, was opened in 1857 by Henry Weston. In 1866 John Samuel Sweasey acquired it from Henry Weston's son Edward and renamed it The Royal Music Hall and then sold it to W. T. Perkiss. In 1887 the Royal Music Hall closed and was completely rebuilt to the designs of Lander and Bedells. The Music Hall then changed its name yet again in 1892, becoming the Royal Holborn Theater of Varieties.

"Recently, in fact, in 1906, it changed its name even again to the Holborn Empire after the building was re-modeled by the esteemed theater architect, Frank Matcham. A notable feature about the Holborn Empire is its wide stage and ability, with ease, to produce major spectacles including ballet or opera. The Holborn Empire became so successful that it was considered a serious rival to Charles Morton's Canterbury Music Hall, which at the

Canterbury Music Hall

time was the most popular and therefore profitable theater in London.

"The Canterbury Music Hall, of course, is the favorite haunt of their graces, the Dukes of Cambridge and of Teck," concluded Lodge.

"Yes, I remember your remarking sometime back that their graces enjoyed attending Music Halls," said Jack.

"The Holborn Empire Music Hall," continued Lodge,

"should not to be confused with the Holborn Theater. For never was a theater blessed with so many names. The Music Hall was designed by Thomas Smith and built by Thomas Ennor and was named the New Royal Amphitheatre. Even whilst being constructed in 1867 the theater was renamed the Royal Amphitheatre and Circus. Six years later its name was changed again to the Grand Cirque & Amphitheatre. Only a few months later, another change occurred to that of the National Amphitheatre," said Lodge.

"The following year" Lodge continued, "witnessed yet another change to the Holborn Amphitheatre. In 1878, the theater was renamed Hamilton's Royal Amphitheatre, but within a year that name was changed to the Royal Connaught Theater. True to form in 1882 it changed its name again to the Alcazar Theater, however within a few months another change occurred to that of the International Theater, and in 1884, it was renamed the Holborn Theater. In the period of seventeen years the theater had changed its name no less than ten times.

"Whilst my good friend Charles Gulliver manages the Holborn Empire Music Hall, the turns and acts on stage are presided over by the compère, an ebullient character called William B. Fair. You will not know this but years ago he was very famous for his song, '*Tommy, Make Room for Your Uncle.*' That song was, in succession, sung by the likes of TS Lonsdale, Tony Pastor probably in his 14th. Street Theater, New York and that Marie Lloyd woman.

"William B. Fair's job, as compère chairing the proceedings on stage, was to choose the turns for the evening. In some respects, he was credited with introducing some famous Music Hall acts to the Holborn Empire, such as JH Stead and Bessie Bellwood. In addition William B. Fair was always known to be fair in his dealings with artistes and also being a dab hand at getting his audience excited for the succeeding acts throughout the evening. He was well known for encouraging the audience to participate with the performers. In this respect, at least, the costermongers needed no such encouragement.

"Of course it was at the Holborn Empire, where artistes, musicians and stage hands went on strike, organized by that Marie Lloyd and the Variety Artistes' Federation. Subsequently, the strike spread to other Music Halls ranged across the metropolis and came to be known as the, 'Music Hall Wars.' But now of course that foolishness is behind us and a glorious future of untrammeled box office receipts awaits those who would seek them.

"In the meantime though we must renew our efforts and never be distracted from making up those precious lost box office receipts," said Lodge, with equanimity and a glint in his eyes but with a smile upon his lips, as we pulled up outside the classical styled façade of the Holborn Empire Music Hall.

Upon entering the foyer we immediately saw, affixed to a wall, this evening's schedule of acts and turns to be performed. We were gratified to recognize our names

Looking around the auditorium to get a feel of the place, I noticed that the designs of the classical façade of the exterior of the building had been continued into the auditorium lending it a dignified presence. The walls of the auditorium were lined with highly polished panels of green *Verde Patrizia* marble. The auditorium was of fine proportions and constructed in such a manner as to enable each member of the audience to be able with ease to both see and hear the various acts on the stage.

Surrounding the auditorium was a wide and spacious

HOLBORN EMPIRE MUSIC HALL

RUN IN CONJUNCTION WITH PALLADIUM

MANAGING DIRECTOR: CHARLES GULLIVER

MANAGER: BERT ADAMS

OVERTURE: MARCH ROYAL

MUSICAL DIRECTOR: S. CLARKE-RICHARDSON

THE DORTMONDES - TRICK & COMEDY CYCLISTS

DUSTY RHODES - THE SINGING COMEDIAN

SIE TAHAR TROUPE - PRESENTING A NOVEL ACT

DAISY TAYLOR - SCOTLAND'S FOREMOST COMEDIAN

MISS JANE CROFT - POPULAR SOPRANO
AT THE PIANO-FORTE MISS ERICA PIERPOINT

MR. MORDECAI JAMES - PSYCHOLOGIC EXPERT

DAN LENO - COMEDIAN & SINGER

MITCHELL & HOUSTON - VAUDEVILLE SINGERS

MARIE LLOYD 'THE BOY I LOVE IS UP THERE
IN THE GALLERY'

INTERMISSION

'HOLBORN POT-POURRI'- SELECTED BY S. CLARKE-
RICHARDSON

FOUR SEGMANS - BONELESS WONDERS

KING & BENSON - 'BACK FROM THE HUNT'

ROB WILTON - COMEDIAN
ASSISTED BY MISS FLORENCE PALMER

JOHN HUMPHRIES - COMEDIAN

balcony, supported by fluted cast iron columns, which overhung part of the stalls and pit below it. Rather than large expanses of the usual crimson covered seats there in the stalls, the seating was elegantly upholstered in blue velvet material. Here, unlike the Oxford Music Hall, this Music Hall was constructed of fireproof material, where possible.

The spacious seats in the balcony comprised a covering of Angora goat-hair satin within polished elm wood armchairs. A grand staircase on each side of the stalls led up to the Grand Circle and into well-appointed Crush Bars, from where patrons could continue to watch turns on the stage without foregoing the pleasures of drinking. Very civilized, I thought.

"Speaking earlier about their graces the Dukes of Cambridge and of Teck, you may be performing in front of them this evening, as I understand they may be making an appearance in the royal box," said Lodge, as we entered our dressing room in the basement.

"I recall you mentioning their graces enjoy attending Music Halls," said Jack.

"They most certainly do," replied Lodge, "and they remain enthusiastic supporters of Music Halls and the itinerant artistes that work them. Indeed his grace the Duke of Cambridge, took the stage actress Sarah Fairbrother as his wife, a commoner, who worked the Lyceum Theater and Theater Royal in Drury Lane. You may remember that you performed in front of their graces only a short while ago at the Criterion Theater."

"I remember both of them," I said, "when we were performing at the Criterion, and I also recall their graces looking very imperious and thoroughly bored with our act involving Judd the ventriloquist's dummy, down on the stage below them. That occasion was also memorable too, because of the anguish that followed on that fateful evening. It had started out innocuously enough. The *Three Graces*, sopranos, Jack and I were back stage at the Criterion waiting to go out and perform. Lodge, you were dressed in your dapper outfit comprising your favorite mid-night blue silk suit, ebony cane and top hat and had come up to us and made a heart-warming little homily about us giving our all for the benefit of mankind.

"But more importantly, you had gone on to emphasize, in your moving little speech, the incalculable benefits of box office receipts, and asked us all to bear that little thought in mind during these next few trying hours. It was then that you had advised us that we would be performing in front of royalty, as their graces Frank and George, were sitting in the Royal Box," I completed.

"You are correct Theo," responded Lodge to my observations, "but gentlemen, best behavior and no lascivious innuendo in front of their graces this evening, or you may put my knighthood in jeopardy!"

He then tapped his shiny silk top hat and disappeared to take his seat in the Dress Circle. A few minutes later we heard one of the stage hands shout down to us.

"Curtain up now, please standby."

We all of us artistes ascended the steps from the basement dressing rooms and then tiptoed to the side wings of the stage in order to watch the various acts to be performed. We could hear William B. Fair the compère who was chairing the proceedings on stage, talking to the audience and introducing the first act which involved the Dortmondes, a troupe of trick and comedy bi-cyclists. Given their energetic racing about on the stage, it was just as well that they were performing here at the Holborn Empire with its particularly wide platform.

They completed their act to moderate applause and were succeeded by Dusty Rhodes, a singing comedienne. Not from what I could hear, standing at the side of the stage. Other acts and turns followed on in rapid succession as they were introduced by the compère. These included the Sie Tahar Troupe presenting their novel act, and Daisy Taylor, apparently one of Scotland's foremost comediennes, who sang eloquently for her supper. She was actually quite funny and very direct in her expressive powers of description, which gave force to her anecdotes.

At this stage in the proceedings however, things became a little confused. Certainly the order of appearance was out of tilter with the person who in fact was now standing on the stage. According to my hand bill, the next act should be a Miss Jane Croft, the popular soprano, ably assisted by Miss Erica Pierpoint at the pianoforte, performing a series of uplifting arias.

The character on the stage, albeit illuminated by a brilliant shaft of limelight, did not in any way conform to my idea of what a soprano is, or indeed ought to be. In this respect, the individual on the stage, neither resembled a soprano, nor indeed was dressed as one might expect. In fact, the person occupying the stage wore a black, somewhat tawdry frock-coat. In addition, his black hair was long, lank and greasy and thinning in places. But clearly evident, from where Jack and I were standing in the wings, was the fact that the individual on the stage had a severely pockmarked face. His singing ability, of course, we could not attest to.

Eventually, the compère banged his gavel and announced the act now in progress to be no less than Mr Mordecai James, the acclaimed Psychologic Expert.

Mordecai seemed affable enough and even managed

to engage some of the costers occupying the front rows in ribald backchat. Two distinct facts however struck me about this odd gentleman. One, he had an appalling stammer and the other that he was simply incapable of constructing a sentence without relapsing into slang or cockney talk, complete with covert innuendo. This kind of esoteric language, was of course, beloved by the assembled costermongers; and there were enough of them in sitting in the stalls this evening.

At length he dispensed with his limbering up talk and informed the audience about just what he intended to do on the stage for their delectation.

"Ladies and gentlemen," he stammered out, "I will invite, from the audience, a couple who have been together for at least fifteen years. Then I will demonstrate, by my psychologic probing, their extensive knowledge of each other's habits and foibles, or indeed, not!"

James then looked out into the auditorium moving his head in a sweeping arc from left to right wearing a broad smile on his pockmarked face.

"May I have the first couple up here on the stage please," he asked.

To this polite inquiry expressed by Mordecai James for the first couple to accept the challenge; two costermongers immediately arose from their cheap seats and staggered up to the stage. They did so to thunderous clapping from their brother costers seated around them.

Some even felt moved to offer out advice; freely.

"Go to it my tulips; and remember, do not let that psychologic fellow panic you into answering questions about which you are not confident; nor indeed know the answers to," said one particularly conspicuous, if loquacious individual.

A feeling of intense anticipation spread throughout the auditorium, or at least in the cheap seats which comprised the stalls, occupied by the costermongers.

Gradually the couple clambered up to the stage platform and upon doing so immediately began waving to their costermonger friends and engaging some in confident exchanges of opinion, the likes of which I have never experienced in a Music Hall or even Vaudeville before. It took all the diplomatic skills of both the compère and Mordecai to regain control of the stage. At length with the aid of a couple of stage hands they succeeded in establishing a tenuous control sufficient for Mordecai to stammer out his next promise to the audience.

"Ladies and gentlemen, I will explain the nature of my acclaimed experiment applying psychologic powers, by blindfolding one of the couple and secreting that person in that small sound-proofed wooden sealed chamber you see there on the stage. Thus the person in that sealed chamber will not be able to see or hear the questions put to their partner. But ladies and gentlemen I, with my psychologic powers, will reveal the truth in the answers given by that person when released from the confines of the sound-proofed wooden chamber!" he declared, confidently.

He did so whilst indulging in a deep bow to the audience. Both Jack and I looked at each other and shrugged our shoulders.

"What are your names?" he inquired of the costermonger couple.

It was the male who replied.

"She answers to the name of Ade as in Adelaide; named after that city in Australia to which her father was sent just before she was born. And I am called Sidney for similar reasons. And we have known each other for more than fifteen years since we settled our arrangement when I handed her my silk neckerchief, I am proud to say…"

"Which you demanded back forthwith a few days later," interrupted Ade, to the general laughter of the audience.

Both of them looked a sight, but obviously were enjoying every moment of their ephemeral, if short lived, fame on the stage. He was dressed in baggy corduroy trousers a long cord waist-coat with several voluminous pockets and brass buttons. On his feet he wore a pair of yellow pointed boots. Around his neck was a large silk neckerchief, known, so I believe, as a King's Man and a flat worsted cloth cap worn on one side of his head. It was also evident to see, that this coster also sported a silver colored ear-ring from one ear, the lobe of which, looked to be mildly infected.

She wore a dress of indeterminate material and a bright green shirt partly covered with a gaudy shawl and numerous tawdry ostrich feathers fastened together and with which she fanned herself nervously. The boots, from what I could see, appeared not to match; being neither of the same style or color.

"Who will elect to go into the chamber first?" asked Mordecai James of Sidney.

"She will," replied Sid, "best place for Ade and keep an eye on her; for we do not want her blabbing away with all the careless freedom of a magpie now do we!"

And with that injunction Ade staggered over to the wooden sealed chamber and clambered in, whereupon Mordecai James slammed the wooden door closed upon her.

He then approached Sidney and viewed him with deep suspicion, born, no doubt, of experience.

"Sidney," started in Mordecai James, the Psychologic

Expert, "you say that you have been with Adelaide for over fifteen years. In that time what would you say your favorite dish was. And ladies and gentlemen of the audience, I invite you to take note of the answers furnished by Sidney here."

"My favorite dish is of shrimps from the river followed by Bubble and Squeak and finished off with Lord Mayor's Trifle. And we all like Bubble and Squeak do we not?" Sid asked the audience which responded with a deafening affirmative.

Sid then on his own initiative and without any encouragement from Mordecai James or the compère went on to recite a touching little verse about Bubble and Squeak, which earned him another extended ovation.

When 'midst the frying pan, in accents savage,
The beef so surly, quarrels with the cabbage,
Whereas the onions and potatoes hold their tongue,
And converse gently with the chopped liver and lung.'

"Fair enough," responded Mordeci James, who then beamed a broad smile out to the audience," and at what time of the day do you take your favorite dish?"

"Five o'clock sharp, neither a minute before nor after," answered Sidney, to the verbal approval of the now seated costermongers.

"Absolutely!" one of whom was heard to enunciate clearly and loudly.

"What is your favorite pastime, I mean legally that is?" stammered Mordecai.

"Of a Sunday afternoon, we like to stroll down, with the whippets, to the Postman's' Park and view the gravestones marking deceased relatives. We then to the

Columbia Market for whelks, sprats and mackerel or anything else they have on offer. All rinsed down with porter whilst Ade will treat herself to a sweet sherry. We then make our way along the Mile End Road and turn down to Limehouse.

"Or, occasionally if the fancy takes us, we get on the tramcar down to the Borough High Street in Southwark to visit on blood relatives to make sure they have not died or cheated us out of our inheritance. If they have not; we then will indulge in a bit of dancing. Usually the "Two-penny hops or jumping at Clog-hornpipes followed by a visit to the theater to listen to Reynolds's 'Mysteries of the Court.'"

"What is the one thing that irritates you?" inquired Mordecai.

"The interfering Metropolitan Board of Works," replied Sidney, resoundingly whilst beckoning at the costermongers embedded in the audience. They in turn responded with a standing ovation.

Eventually, the costers settled down and a hush descended over the stalls in anticipation of the next question.

"Think carefully now," said Mordecai James, "what is Ade's favorite pastime of an evening?"

"She likes to meet up with the other gals, and enjoy a game of cards, especially *Cribbage, All Fives* or *Put,* any of which she is a dab hand at," replied Sidney, "especially where money is involved."

During the course of the next few minutes Mordecai James, the Psychologic Expert continued to ask searching questions about Sid and Ade. And in so doing gained the full attention of the costers who during the proceedings nodded their approval with the odd murmur of agreement to Sidney's considered replies.

"One final question," stammered James, "what is Ade's favorite hat?"

This seemingly innocuous question somewhat threw Sidney. Because even from where Jack and I were standing in the wings at the side of the stage, one could see that Sidney's eyebrows were knitted. Reflecting the inner turmoil and concentration he was experiencing in formulating his profound and considered reply. At length he did so.

"She wears a lilac green felt hat that she has a fancy to when the occasion takes her; usually at funerals and the like kind," said Sidney.

Whilst Sidney answered this last question, a stage hand was busy trying to open the door to the sealed chamber, albeit with some difficulty. And only with the intervention of both Mordecai and the compère did they eventually manage to do so, releasing Ade in the process. When Ade finally stepped out of the sealed box and back to the front of the stage she looked unsteady. One immediately got the distinct impression that Ade had occupied herself drinking whilst locked in that sealed wooden chamber.

A straight backed cathedral chair was brought on to the stage for Ade to collapse on to. In the mean time Sidney entered the sealed chamber, looking back furtively towards Ade as he did so.

"All will now be revealed," I heard Mordecai James announce to the audience, as I looked at Jack in disbelief.

"What is Sidney's favorite dish" James asked of Ade.

"Angels on Horseback [2] or their less holy cousins, Devils on Horseback," [3] responded Ade confidently. She even managed to stagger up from her cathedral chair and present a shallow curtsey to the audience.

Even the costermongers were moved in to a stunned silence as Mordecai quoted Sid's reply of his liking shrimps followed by Bubble and Squeak and Lord Mayor's Trifle.

"Bubble and Squeak; I will not have such botched up rubbish in the house, I will have you know. I cannot for the life of me imagine where he might get such an unspeakable idea from."

"At what time of the day does Sid take this favorite dish?" asked the Psychologic Expert.

"When he gets back from the, *Battlecruiser* 4 at anytime between eight and ten of an evening depending if he has had any luck pawning items he has acquired during the day; that or winning at cards," replied Adelaide.

"Not Five o'clock sharp?" inquired Mordecai.

"You may well be an expert in the psychologic; but I am telling you right here and know that I have never, ever seen our Sid in doors at five o'clock of an evening. Am I not right gals," asked Ade of the female costers embedded in the stalls. To which they responded unanimously in the positive.

"What is Sid's favorite legal pastime?" inquired Mordecai of Ade, hesitantly.

I did not think that he had one," replied Ade, in all sincerity.

Undaunted by Ade's reply Mordecai continued.

"Sidney told us, the audience, whilst you were in the sealed chamber," Stammered Mordecai, "that your favorite pastime of a Sunday afternoon, was strolling down to the Postman's' Park with your whippets and look at the gravestones marking your deceased relatives. And then making your way to the Columbia Market for whelks, sprats and mackerel or anything else that there was on offer. All rinsed down with porter that Sid enjoys whilst you made do with a sweet sherry to which you are extremely partial.

"You then make your way along the Mile End Road and on in to Limehouse. Or occasionally down the Borough High Street in Southwark to visit on blood relatives to make sure they have not died or indeed cheated you and Sid out of your inheritance. After which you were partial to a bit of dancing the "Two-penny hops or jumping at Clog-hornpipes before a visit to the theater to listen to a recitation Reynolds's 'Mysteries of the Court.'

"A stroll down with the whippets to the Postman's Park," answered Ade, "where is that place, I ask you?" For we do not keep whippets and, I cannot abide sherry, filthy stuff, fit only for the *Undeserving Poor*. And as for the so called relatives in the Borough High Street at Southwark, I was under the impression they had all died of the cholera but these ten years past. And for Reynolds's so called 'Mysteries of the Court;' the only mystery that I know of, is where the money for the rent is coming from or we will finish up in the court."

"What is the one thing that irritates your partner Sidney?" asked Mordecai, in his attempt to gain control of the stage.

"Everything," came Ade's resounding reply.

"Not the Metropolitan Board of Works," responded Mordecai, with an unconfident flourish.

"The Metropolitan Board of What?" inquired Ade, "Sidney is always, *bored* of work.

This witty repost at least earned Ade a sustained applause form the costermongers, if not from the Dress Circle too.

"What is your favorite pastime Ade of an evening?" asked Mordecai.

"Nothing, for I am too tired having been charring all day. By nine o'clock of an evening, I can hear my bed calling to me," replied Ade.

"Sidney in fact replied that you like to meet up with the other gals and enjoy a game of cards, especially *Cribbage, All Fives* or *Put* any of which you excelled at," stammered James.

"I am a Chartist, I will have you know; and do not believe in gambling in any shape or form. And certainly I do not hold with cards, where the odds on those games are stacked against you from the origin," answered Ade.

"Adelaide, do tell the audience, what is your favorite hat?"

"The one that I am wearing now," said Ade, "this blue silk hat, well not really a hat; more the silk lining of a hat, the outside of which deteriorated years ago!"

"Not a lilac green felt hat when the fancy takes you, especially at funerals and the like?" asked Mordecai.

"We never ever get invited to funerals. People are too scared that we will drink all the porter at the Wake of Remembrance, as if we would, and certainly not wearing a what; a lilac green felt hat?" stated Ade, with a questioning tone in her voice.

Upon receiving this reply, Mordecai James, the renowned Psychologic Expert, seem to give up with a look of exasperation and helplessness on his pockmarked face. He then motioned to one of the stage hands to release Sid from the sealed chamber.

"Ladies and gentlemen," said Mordecai, with clear trepidation in his stammer, "we shall put Sid and Ade together and explore their responses to my questions. I feel confident that we shall all find it amusing!"

He was in this assumption probably correct, as a silence descended over the audience accompanied by a very real feeling of anticipation. Even the costers ceased their murmurings, adding to an air of expectation extant throughout the auditorium.

Presently, Sidney came over to Mordecai and Adelaide, who was now standing. Even from where I was standing at the side of the stage. I could see Sid giving Ade a searching look with his eyes the eyebrows above which were furrowed in a questioning expression.

"Sidney you said your favorite dish was shrimps followed by Bubble and Squeak and Lord Mayor's Trifle," asked Mordecai.

"Correct," answered Sidney emphatically

"No it is not; you like Angels on Horseback and sometimes Devils on Horseback," responded Ade, "I have never cooked no bubble and squeak concoction for you."

"Sidney when asked what time of day do you take your favorite dish, whatever it is, you replied at five o'clock sharp. Was that correct?" asked the Psychologic Expert.

"Absolutely," came Sid's reply.

"No you do not. It depends when you get ejected out of that, *Battlecruiser* you live in and that can range between eight and ten o'clock of an evening," stated Ade.

"Do not be silly gal, I takes my repast at five o'clock after a hard day's grafting to support the family," countered Sid.

Ade just turned to the audience and raised her hands with the palms facing upwards in exasperation whilst nodding her head.

Mordecai James the Psychologic Expert intervened.

"Sidney you stated that a favorite pastime on Sunday was to stroll down with your whippets to the Postman's Park or visit relatives in the Borough High Street at Southwark…" said Mordecai.

"Yes what is it with the whippets?" interrupted Ade, "for we keep no whippets, not at least in my house. And as for visiting relatives in the Borough High Street, well they are dead, died of the cholera years ago. If you have relatives down there I do not know of them. And, if so, who in fact are they?" demanded Ade.

"You know full well who they are you have shared a drink with them often enough. And as for the whippets, I keep them in the outhouse," answered Sid hesitantly.

"And what is this about my taking sherry. I cannot abide the stuff; fit only for the *Undeserving Poor* of which I am not a member, well a least not yet" said Ade fanning herself ostentatiously with her ostrich feathers. "And come to think of it, what is this about meeting up with some of the gals to play cards, including *Cribbage, All Fives* or *Put* at which I am supposed to be a dab hand and enjoy gambling."

"Yes you do and you are good at it," replied Sid.

"How dare you! I am a Chartist, and do not believe gambling, well not with cards," shouted Ade as she waved her index finger at Sid. To which the costers spontaneously got up from their cheap seats in the stalls in anticipation of what was obviously going to be a final reckoning between Sid and Ade.

"Sidney," intervened the Mordecai James, "when you came on to the stage you stated in full sight of Christ, the audience, the compère and me that you have known each other for more than fifteen years…"

"Well not as such," interrupted a nervous Sidney, "for we have an understanding…"

"We have a what?" demanded Ade, whilst prodding Sidney in the chest with her closed fan.

"Do you two in fact actually know each other? I ask this basic inquiry because the replies from both of you to the questions which should show an intimate knowledge of each other's habits do not bare this out," stammered Mordecai of Sid and Ade.

That remark by Mordecai triggered a response from

the costers standing up and banging their hob nailed boots on the floor of the stalls. Some were even moved to shout out advice to Ade or Sid. According to where their loyalties perforce lay, in which of the two deserved their complete sympathy.

Jack turned to me.

"It is almost a betting certainty that Sid and Ade have not been together for over fifteen years; more like fifteen minutes. They probable met in the foyer whilst making their way into this auditorium!" said Jack, with a grin on his face.

"Hang on a minute," Adelaide was heard to scream at Sid, "what is all this about me wearing a lilac green felt hat when the fancy takes me? I do not have a green felt hat, only the one that I am wearing now, this blue silk hat, which is the silk lining of an old hat I used to have. So who is this woman that wears a green felt hat? Answer me now this instance."

"It was now becoming apparently obvious to all, but the deaf and blind, that these two costers were accomplished and inveterate liars. For never in my life have I ever witnessed such organized lying and on such a grand scale and on the public stage too. However, Jack found it highly humorous and entertaining.

Alas, poor Sidney must not have thought so; for at that very moment Ade was berating him about the fact that he must be keeping another woman who has a fancy for green felt hats, keeps whippets, has blood relative in the Borough High Street and partial to whelks out of Columbia Market on a Sundays. And what was her name and place of abode.

At one stage Ade actually attempted to pick up the wooden cathedral chair. One can only imagine that she intended to use it in order to emphasize her questioning demands, but was prevented from carrying out her intention by the arrival of the compère, who immediately began to introduce the next act.

The costers could hardly contain themselves; and expressed this emotion overtly with an eruption of thunderous applause. The pockmarked and stammering Psychologic Expert, Mr. Mordecai James, to me looked somewhat redundant. In this respect, I could not determine whether in fact his act had been a success or an utter débâcle. One simply was not certain. Sid's future however, looked very much uncertain.

Eventually, when the auditorium had regained its collective attentiveness, the compère introduced Miss Jane Croft, a soprano, assisted at the piano-forte by a Miss Erica Pierpoint, gave a series of morally uplifting and rousing songs which even I could see were inducing chronic ennui in Jack and, I suspect, the audience. At the end of her recital the applause was, predictably desultory. However, it was this act that I was particularly interested in watch. It was our friend Dan Leno, the accomplished singer-comedian. Not to mention the fact he had played Wotan, last night, in the pantomime, *'The Rhinegold,'* at the New National Standard Theater in Shoreditch.

Also, Jack and I had met with Leno [5] at Highgate Cemetery not so long before. On that occasion he offered Jack and me a lift back to London and to Bella Elmore's Wake of Remembrance backstage at the Vaudeville Music Hall. I did not realize, until Lodge mentioned it in passing, that Dan Leno was born George Wild Galvin, in the neighborhood of St. Pancras behind the hotel in which Jack and I continued to reside.

He was particularly known for his outrageous rôles, especially those of pantomime dames often performed at the Theater Royal in Drury Lane in Covent Garden under the auspices of Sir Augustus Harris. When on stage his specialty turn was to comment on current news, chores and everyday banal subjects laced with humorous songs, together with accurate and acute, observations on life in general.

On stage he often portrayed a series of working class types to emphasize his remarks or observations including his performance of the, *'Huntsman,'* which he performed in 1901 for King Edward VII[th.] in private, at Sandringham which resulted in his becoming known as the, *King's Jester.*

True to form he performed a series of sketches which went down well with the audience that spent more time applauding. Not a good sign for Jack or me who were to follow on immediately after Leno.

Our allotted time arrived and accordingly Jack and I strode on to the stage from either wing and met in the middle and shook hands, as was our routine. Jack then repaired to the stage pianoforte and I, wearing my good luck Sennit straw hat walked up to the footlights and began our first song, *'Alabama in the Morning.'*

Predictably, after we had performed this opening song, we were met with blank indifference, with some members of the audience not even bothering to clap, and some even getting up and leaving the auditorium, for numerous the Crush Bars, one suspected.

I had just cause in the past to rue having to follow on from an accomplished Music Hall artiste whose reputation preceded them in a positive way. Having watched Leno in the past, I knew he was clearly a dab hand at getting the audience to respond to him. In this respect he could probably get an auditorium full of blind and deaf persons to respond to him somehow.

Eventually our act settled down and grudgingly the applause for each song increased if only marginally. Jack and I did not even consider doing an encore, even if one had been demanded. Instead we abandoned the stage to Marie Lloyd, who, within seconds of our doing so, had the audience clapping and laughing raucously, even before she commenced singing, *'The boy I love is up in the gallery.'* We headed off to the nearest Crush Bar for a well-earned dose of solace.

1. Effectively Oxford Street
2. Oysters wrapped in rashers of bacon and cooked under a grill
3. Prunes stuffed with chutney wrapped in bacon sprickled with grated cheese and cooked
4. A Public House
5. Dan Leno died in 1904

Chapter 24

The Royal Princess's Theater

Our turn at the Holborn Empire Music Hall had been marginally successful, but did indicate problems involving the position one's name or act appeared on the program. I knew back in New York managers would often put little known artistes in between well-known acts by popular performers. This happened to us that night. Whilst we are known on the Vaudeville circuit in New York, Mitchell and Houston is not a well known act in London. This is not to infer that our act is unappealing. Rather it was our being position on the bill appearing between two undeniably accomplished artistes as Dan Leno and Marie Lloyd. In this respect, I knew of one manager in New York, who claimed maybe three acts were worth the audience's attention and the price of an entrance ticket. The other acts were there just to fill in the evening!

For the time being however we were assembled in the Crush Bar at the Royal Princess's Theater, in Oxford Street, to have, as it were, a full dress rehearsal of the Choral Anthem Symphony with Mabel singing the lead rôle of *Courage* in front of an audience. Katie Lawrence will sing of *Aspiration* followed up with Dot Hetherington lyrically espousing those sentiments devoted to *Hope*.

The Royal Princess's Theater is located on the north side of Oxford Street and built on the site formally known as the Queen's Bazaar. So Lodge informed us previously. The original theater was, in 1829, destroyed by a fire, a re-occurring hazard in Oxford Street, so it would seem. The present Music Hall was rebuilt to the designs of Mr. C. J. Phipps in 1880 with an impressive façade of Portland stone.

Addressing this façade on the *piano-nobile* was an open loggia, eight feet in depth, forming a balustraded balcony over looking Oxford Street. The balcony forms an added feature for those patrons from the Dress Circle or adjacent Smoking Room and Crush Bar to allow them access to the aether during intervals.

The ever present threat of fire does seem to be a very real and frequent danger in London. Given the fact the Oxford Music Hall went up in flames only these few weeks past as a result of a danseuse performing her bawdy rendition of scenes, albeit with coördinated precision, from Stravinsky's new ballet *The Fire Bird*. The hapless ballerina got carried away in a reckless trance brought on by the ecstatic and rapturous applause she had generated from an appreciative audience.

But, as often can be the case, in her dancing delirium, she bowed too near to the blazing footlights and in so doing her protruding, starched, taffeta costume made contact with the gas flames causing it to catch fire! The applause increased as she ran about the stage in a blind panic, which the audience mistook as being part of her original *Fire Bird* act. It was not so much as what happened to the hapless blazing taffeta-wearing danseuse, as to what her flaming taffeta costume did to the stage scenery, which too went up in a conflagration of flames.

"We do not talk about such calamities as those. Imagine if you dare, the appalling and devastating impact on box office receipts!" said Lodge, looking more concerned than I had ever seen him before.

Accordingly, I felt compelled to offer him a drink at the Crush Bar in the Royal Princess's Theater where we were discussing this evening's program before taking our seats. In response he muttered something about a large whisky to calm his shredded nerves, born of constant anxieties about Music Hall fires and their devastating effects on box office receipts and resultant financial calamity.

"Make those three large ones please, bar-tender," I said, in response to Lodge's moist eyes looking at me.

Despite such occasional catastrophes, Lodge informed us, the Royal Princess's Theater was rebuilt in 1833 and exhibited the *Physiorama*, gallery two hundred feet in length as a feature to attract the public. However, the venture was not a financial success and in fact nearly bankrupted a silversmith from Leicester Square, name of Hamlet. Subsequently, the theater was totally rebuilt to the designs of the architect Nelson in 1841 with interior decorations by Mr. Crace. Together both designers have created an elegant intimate theater with three tiers of boxes and comfortable red plush seating. In its first year of operation, the Royal Princess's Theater, 1 featured a series of promenade concerts.

Eventually, Lodge staggered out of the Crush Bar, stating he was needed by his protégées back stage.

Jack and I stayed in the comfortable well-appointed surroundings of the Crush Bar.

"Looking at this evening's program Jack," I said, "it would appear that the Choral Anthem Symphony is to take precedence in occupying the first half. And then after the interval the stage will be given over to a succession of acts and turns including those by Nellie Wallace, Hetty King and Belle Baker."

Royal Princess's Theater

Eventually after the last bell we took our seats in the Dress Circle to witness yet again the Choral Anthem Symphony, or *Cholera* Anthem Symphony, as Jack has taken to calling it, since that term is more symptomatic of what it really is.

The symphony was a resounding success and in no small part due to Mabel who carried all before her. We immediately vacated our seats in the Dress Circle and headed forthwith back to the Crush Bar; for we knew that is where she would be. We were correct. By the time we had gotten there, Mabel was well into her second glass of champagne with the Coca~Cola.

Lodge was beside himself with pride at the performance of his new protégée Mabel, the new soprano in his *Three Graces* and especially in her lead rôle of *Courage.* He continued to blow kisses into the aëther with his fingers in an extravagant, if reckless manner; such was his delirium of pleasure.

We all gathered around Mabel and offered her our congratulations. Even some of the Music Hall artistes, drinking at the Crush Bar before their act after the interval, were moved to applaud her. Eventually, we heard the sound of the bell announcing curtain up in five minutes.

On this occasion Lodge made his excuses saying that as a result of Mabel's sensational success on the stage, he would now have to meet with another theater owner to capitalize on this sensational triumph, but would see us the next day. He then marched off almost with a skip in his stride.

Reluctantly, we abandoned the bar yet again, in order to take our places back in the Dress Circle. Mabel announced she was going elsewhere to celebrate her resounding success. Having managed to stagger back to the auditorium, Jack and I regained our seats. Just in time; for moments later the curtain was raised revealing a backdrop scene of ornate park gates.

George Robey, born George Edward Wade and nicknamed the *Prime Minister of Mirth* was first on with his characteristic unique brand of comic sketches and pathetic singing. Randolph Sutton, singing for his supper and then by Hetty King doing what she does extremely well, impersonating males, followed him in quick succession. At one point I swear she attempted to impersonate George Robey. Next to tread the floorboards was Nellie Wallace, sometimes known as '*The Essence of Eccentricity.*' She was succeeded by Belle Baker. Both Jack and I knew of her from earlier days.

"I remember Bella," said Jack, "when she first ventured on to the stage encouraged by the actor, Jacob Adler and Lew Leslie, the well known theater producer. I was there when she had her début in Vaudeville at Scranton, in eastern Pennsylvania. More recently, in fact last year in 1911, you and I were appearing on the same bill at Hammerstein's Theater in New York. She is a fine singer and became famous with her song, '*Cohen Owes Me Ninety-Seven Dollars,*' being one of the public's favorite, especially in New York,"

"She remains a competent actress too," I replied, "and I believe she appears on a regular basis at the Palace Theater on Broadway and 47th. Street."

After Bella had quit the stage, the compère got up and banged his gavel on the block.

"Ladies and gentlemen, we have received some late news. Due to unforeseen circumstances Ella Shields cannot be with us tonight. But all is not lost; we have a woman who is an accomplished impersonator of men. Please welcome Mr. Franklyn Smith."

The artiste who had strutted on to the stage elicited an immediate response from us. I looked at Jack and he returned my gaze! The individual who had just marched confidently on to the stage was dressed in white trousers, white shoes and a red and blue striped blazer and wore a Sennit straw hat, with a Sarapis ribbon around the crown, on his head at a tilt, similar to the hat that I wear on stage. The artiste carried a cane in one hand and a lit Trichinopoly cigar in the other, which the performer occasionally drew upon and within moments had burst into song about the joys of playing cricket and other manly pursuits, such as fencing. The artiste on stage swaggered about in a very naturally masculine manner, which I thought must have taken some considerable practice and told Jack so. He just looked at me.

The songs that the artiste sang too were sung in a very realistic way, as a man might sing them, with a deep natural masculine resonance. Then the performer, still strutting around the stage, burst into a final song about wishing to join the navy; '*To do for my country what my country has done for me!*' He sang this song to great acclaim and drew sustained applause from everybody in the auditorium including, I noticed, some of the players in the pit orchestra.

Whatever the turn, something stuck in my mind and I noticed Jack still looking at me with a bemused expression upon his face.

1. The Royal Princess's Theater closed in 1902 due to difficulties with the lease.

Chapter 25

The Titanic Benefit Concert

The performance at the Royal Princess's Theater in Oxford Street was quite revealing in many ways and one was compelled to wonder whether Lodge was as observant as he might have been. However, the day, a day that will go down in history, or at least so Lodge claims, has at last dawned. For today is the day on which he will have performed his wildly ambitious Titanic Benefit Concert in the Queen's Hall. Ostensibly this memorial concert has been arranged in order to raise funds for the now impoverished families of those victims who perished when the ill-fated *Titanic* ocean liner collided with an iceberg in mid Ocean. And subsequently sank with a loss of over fifteen hundred souls but a few weeks past.

The day went by in an agony of trepidation, suspense and self doubt, at least for me. Jack appeared impervious to what the evening with its Titanic Benefit Concert might bring. To him, the concert or whatever it was supposed to be or achieve, was a matter of insuperable indifference.

Presently, Cinderella joined us, I suppose, in a kind of mutual support or sympathetic capacity. It was her remark that got us thinking about the impending event.

"Theseus," as Cinderella refers to Lodge as, "reckons

that this day will go down in history; I do not doubt it! But for what reason, at this stage, I think that I could still probably guess!"

After a late luncheon Cinderella, Jack and I stepped into a Victoria carriage driven by a liveried coach man and headed off to the Queen's Hall. Cinderella looked resplendent in her white evening gown with a silver fox fur stole around her neck and intricately fashioned silver tiara on her head.

She never ceases to amaze me with her dress sense. Given that one minute she can be strutting around a Music Hall stage in pit boots executing with coördinated precision delicate balletic pas de deux with an elegance and ability born of talent and resolve. Or her falling over during her pathetic Little Bo Peep routine together with her Marmeduke act. Then next seated on the bench upholstered in buttoned down red leather of our Victoria carriage, looking very much the regal lady she really was, smothered in elegance and grace.

I remarked upon this to her, and she returned the compliment.

"Oh sir you are too kind," responded Cinderella in a mock drawl of a southern belle, "but I simply had to wear something to keep up with you two fine gentlemen, looking very elegant in your evening dress of black tail-coats, red carnations and shiny silk top hats. But to be honest I was considering attending tonight's concert dressed as Marmeduke, the ventriloquist's dummy, as being by far the more appropriate dress given the occasion!"

That remark made us all burst out into laughter.

"I suspect before this day, this historic day is over, we will have further cause to laugh again," continued Cinderella. We were now just passing Portland Road

Metropolitan Station and past the bronze bust of a dead president shaded by an apple tree. At length we turned into Park Crescent and then Portland Place and clattered down in the direction of the Queen's Hall.

We continued then into Langham Place, at the end of which is located All Souls Church that was designed by John Nash. Famous for its colonnaded rotunda of columns capped with Ionic capitals, supporting a plinth with a parapet wall surrounding it and rising from it was its distinctive tapered stone spire, now piercing the fog-laden aëther.

"Cinderella, how long have you known Loge?" asked Jack.

"Too long!" replied Cinderella.

"I know you have previously explained to Theo here why you refer to Lodge as Theseus. But as a matter of curiosity, why do you?" inquired Jack.

"For the same reason you refer to him as Loge and Theo refers to him as Lodge. I call him Theseus because he is known for thinking up the most outré of ideas, or stratagems, as he calls them. Usually to get him out of an awkward situation or to enhance box office receipts, for which he has a universal reputation. Hence we three are travelling in the fog to meet with destiny at the Queen's Hall this evening over his Titanic venture.

"And as with the mythical Theseus from ancient Greece, Lodge too is sure to find his way out of the Minotaur-infested labyrinth of tunnels, bearing problems, as it were, but do not be fooled. I have known of him on and off for about twelve years and he is a committed person...no, no Jack not in that respect, I mean in terms of dedication," Cinderella informed us.

Despite our drive being slow, due to the fog, we arrived at the august Queen's Hall, actually earlier than we had anticipated. Outside the hall there were several carriages of every type; polished Broughams, Clarences, Landaus, highly varnished Barouches and Phäetons. All delivering guests dressed elegantly and clearly reflecting wealth which Lodge had devised in his stratagem. I noticed some carriages bore coats of arms on their doors. Having alighted from our humble Victoria carriage, we immediately joined this large gathering making its way into the foyer.

"The Queen's Hall is not so much a concert hall," Cinderella said, as we all stood on the sidewalk waiting in line to gain access into the hall, "but rather a 'Temple to Music' and this fact is reflected in its grandiose classical designs shown in the façade. Though the hall looks as though it was constructed some decades ago, it was in fact built recently in 1893 to the designs by Thomas Knightley.

"See the rich ornate detailing and the myriad of busts of composers as Mozart, Gluck or Handel! And the exposed balcony on the *piano-nobile*, festooned with various statues in the form of torsos of Greek gods fixed to the front in between several French windows which allow access to several balconies and to the aether during a concert interval."

"I agree with you Cinderella," responded Jack, "Theo and I were remarking on the grand architectural design of the Queen's Hall when we accompanied Loge here the other day."

Eventually we managed to get into the foyer and make our way up to the first tier level of the Dress Circle, where at length we took our seats in a red plush private box, Lodge had in fact reserved for us. We all settled down in our comfortable seats covered in scarlet velvet for whatever the evening would bring. I could see Cinderella and Jack both straining to take in the beautiful appointment of this highly decorated auditorium with its ornate plaster work panels on the walls complete with gold filigree raised detailing.

The ceiling was a feast of art too, depicting classical cherubs cavorting in a sylvan landscape where ribbons were very much in evidence. In the middle of the ceiling was a series of ornate raised circular patterns culminating in a massive chandelier tinkling with cut glass.

This sumptuous assembly of light globes looked as though in the act of defying gravity in all its arrogance. A massive organ encased in gilt covering with side balconies facing the audience completed the pervasive opulence evident throughout the large auditorium.

Irrespective of the impending Titanic Benefit Concert, the stage was a sight to behold, for it represented nothing short of a floral extravaganza in its own right. Such was the extent of floral decoration positioned on the stage that it was difficult to see where the performers might place themselves. It had been decked out as Lodge had wished in a mass of green fawns, palm leaves, black feathers and festooned with large ostrich plumes. Hanging from the back of the stage were deep red and purple silk pennants shimmering as though in a breeze.

The front of the stage was dressed in ruched purple material creating an effect of waves with intermittent suggestions of the Stars & Stripes and Union Jack, signifying the two nations which suffered the most from the ill-fated *Titanic* tragedy. Not one square inch of surface had escaped the designer's attempt to create an atmosphere of reverence and solemnity. One could only hope that the performance of the Titanic Memorial Benefit Concert would also be equal to the task.

I consulted the program, which had been placed on

each seat. It was quite an impressive line up of artistes all brought together under Lodge's aegis as impresario to do justice to his Titanic Extravaganza.

Lodge's Choral Anthem Symphony was there at the end, presumably to extract what little emotion there was left within the souls and hearts of members of the audience. Including their graces the Dukes of Cambridge and of Teck, both of whom were ardent supporters of Music Hall and attended regularly. During a performance of the Choral Anthem Symphony, it is always interesting to witness how the so-called *Three Graces* would re-act with each other.

Invariably whilst singing their respective rôles of *Hope*, *Courage* or *Aspiration*, these three divas vied with one another for the position of prima donna, as it were, to such an extent as to turn the *Three Graces* into the *Three Disgraces*.

Then, at that very moment, sporadic clapping could be heard, which spread rapidly throughout the auditorium. This heralded the arrival of a person, wearing a black silk top hat and who manœuvred himself amongst the plants and decoration festooning the stage with skill and agility, as though a seasoned waiter moving in between dining tables.

He then marched up smartly to the podium enclosed by a gleaming brass railing. A few moments later, having assumed the podium, he beamed out a wide smile at the assembled audience in the Queen's Hall. The manner of the person on the podium was such, that even from our position in the auditorium; he exuded an inordinate amount of confidence.

He was wearing a mid-night blue colored tail-coat with matching trousers and a silver-toned finely woven silk waist-coat and a large gold Albert chain connected to

Titanic Benefit Concert

IN THE PRESENCE OF THEIR GRACES THE DUKE OF CAMBRIDGE
AND THE DUKE OF TECK

UNDER THE AUSPICES OF IMPRESARIO, MR. MICHAEL W. LODGE,
TO RAISE CHARITABLE FUNDS FOR THE BENEFIT OF THE
DEPENDENTS OF THE VICTIMS OF THE SINKING OF THE ILL-
FATED

Titanic

ORCHESTRA CONDUCTED BY MR. DAVID MOODY

*

THERE IS, A GREEN AND PLEASANT PLACE – SUNG BY
DOT HETHERINGTON

SONGE D' AUTOMME – SUNG BY KATIE LAWRENCE

ABIDE WITH ME – MABEL GREEN & AUDIENCE

SOMEWHERE A VOICE IS CALLING – SUNG BY DOT
HETHERINGTON

BY THE SAD SEA WAVES – VESTA TILLEY

ABOVE US THE WAVES – VESTA TILLEY

INTERMISSION

ABENDLICHT – SUNG BY EMMA CARUS

FOR THOSE IN PERIL ON THE SEA – SUNG BY MABEL
GREEN   WHITE WINGS – ELLA SHIELDS & AUDIENCE

NEARER MY GOD TO THEE – SUNG BY FLORRIE FORDE
TANTUM ERGO – SUNG BY KATIE LAWRENCE

CULMINATING IN A PERFORMANCE OF THE WIDELY
ACCLAIMED ELEGIAC

CHORAL - ANTHEM – SYMPHONY

each pocket. His white shirt was fronted by material creating a ruched, ripple effect, finished with a collar secured by an ostentatious purple stone of amethyst. His shoes were black and covered in a highly varnished finish, which gleamed beneath the lights illuminating the stage.

At length the person removed his shiny silk top hat and then placed a monocle carefully in front of one eye and looked out again into the audience. Only this time he moved his face in a sweeping arc from left to right in order to make certain no one, but no one sitting in the audience, should fail to see it.

It was Lodge and clearly in his element.

Since the clapping showed no sign of diminishing, Lodge simply stood there bathed in a single shaft of pale yellow limelight from an arc lamp trained on his person, the effect of which was to make him look benign and imparting a vision of ethereal nobility of purpose. The sustained clapping was such as to immediately suggest that Lodge had obviously planted persons in the audience, and whose only rôles were to applaud enthusiastically and thus instigate others to clap too, whether deserved or not. Clearly Lodge had not omitted to attend to this important aspect in any public assembly where adoration is required or indeed obligatory.

However, as though impatient to begin the proceedings, Lodge raised his hands with the palms facing upward and then turning them downward, brought his arms down slowly. This had the desired effect, and the applause subsided, but only gradually. His lackies which he had planted in the audience made certain of that. I also remembered that Queenie Leighton had used this gesture recently to bring her ecstatic audience to silence at the New Bedford Music Hall in Camden Town. Clearly Lodge learned quickly and was copying her technique.

He commenced his address to the audience.

"Your graces, lords, ladies and gentlemen, distinguished and honored guests welcome to the Queen's Hall. We are gathered here this evening to experience the Titanic Benefit Concert in order to commemorate the recent sinking of the ill-fated White Star Liner, *Titanic*, with anthems, hymns and songs taken from the hymnal on board that stricken ship."

He paused, and again swept his face in an arc around the auditorium for all to see and admire his conspicuous altruistic intention. He then continued.

"How many of us here have lost sweethearts, friends or dear ones as a result of the ill-fated *Titanic* sinking in the dark waters of the Atlantic? And when it foundered robbed those victims of their dreams, hopes, aspirations and ultimately, their lives. We grieve for our loss of their companionship as the *Titanic* plummeted to the depths of the ocean, and in so doing, consigned their bodies to the permanent iron mausoleum, which the *Titanic* has now become, forever marooned in oblivion.

"My friends, I and the artistes gathered for this momentous occasion, would like to remember all those who perished during that fateful night, by sharing with you, the great British audience, sentiments expressed in a range of anthems, hymns and songs. All for your delectation and consideration in the newly acclaimed and sacred work called the Choral Anthem Symphony which will be performed as the climax, no apotheosis, to our evening.

"But suffice for me to say that in our glorious Choral Anthem Symphony there are sentiments to help release those deep feelings of sadness which continue to pierce our hearts, causing our love to leak away though the wound," said Lodge, quoting freely from Queenie's address to the audience at the New Bedford Music Hall.

Clearly, Lodge really does learn quickly, I thought. Though his quotes were not quite verbatim, but more indicative of what he thinks about the acclaimed Music Hall artiste, Queenie Leighton; not very much. But do they not say that imitation is the highest form of praise, I wondered

Jack and I have, occasionally postulated on Lodge's background, and concluded that he must have treaded the stage in Music Halls at one point in his life. Jack and I have come to this conclusion, simply because his timing not only remains impeccable, but also he possesses an unerring ability to memorize. Or in this case, his ability to plagiarize was beyond doubt and in fact, pretty impressive. We had witnessed these abilities recently at the Charing Cross Hotel when Lodge addressed members of the Fourth Estate in defense of Music Hall against censorship.

However, in his present rôle as compère, Lodge continued to persuade a hushed audience to share with him their experiences or losses and perhaps hopefully, a part of their wealth too.

"There are times," Lodge continued, "in our all too brief lives when we need to find strength to continue, and the knowledge to understand those tribulations which affect us. We none of us expected a great ship of the line to founder at sea; but alas it did, taking with it over fifteen hundred precious souls. But there is light and relief from our suffering, as we together embrace our fears, emotions and sadness in song and recitation of anthems so fashioned to bring perhaps a suggestion, just a suggestion of a smile to our faces.

"Your graces, lords, ladies and gentlemen, please welcome Dot Hetherington who will sing for us the hymn, '*There is a Green and Pleasant Place*,' from the Hymn Book of the First Class section, of course, on the doomed *Titanic*."

Thereupon, Hetherington dressed in a billowing yellow silk gown made her way from the back of the stage, through the decorations and foliage, to the front of the concert platform. She stood there motionless bathed in that single shaft of pale yellow limelight, from the arc lamp, which had been previously trained on Lodge. The conductor, David Moody, with a downward stroke of his baton, launched the orchestra into a resonating E flat minor chord which was picked up by Hetherington who took it up to C minor and breathed life into the lyrics of her song. Looking about me I could see that the audience, by its attentiveness, was impressed. So was I.

At length she completed her fine recital to sustained applause, bowed and withdrew out of the limelight to stage left. In so doing she nearly disappeared amongst the prevalent palm leaves rising out of large green glazed urns placed on top of limestone jardinières, wrapped in purple crêpe.

Lodge manœuvered himself again back into the limelight, which then illuminated his mid-night blue colored suit and suave personality. Without hesitation or resorting to catachresis, he introduced, for our delectation, Katie Lawrence to sing, '*Songe D'Automne*.'

Of course the sopranos Hetherington and Lawrence together with Mabel Green comprise the *Three Graces*, beloved of Lodge. One is under the impression that Lodge believed this was his especial gift to humanity; or at least that part of humanity which regularly occupy Music Halls and can generate readily box office receipts. All *Three Grace* were, in fact, very accomplished sopranos, though I think Mabel's voice was the huskier of the three.

Upon completing her recital, Lawrence yielded the stage to Lodge, but was accorded suitable recognition for her excellent singing, with which no doubt, she would be pleased. All seemed to be going according to Lodge's stratagem and the evening of songs and anthems had gotten off to a dignified and optimistic start.

Lodge, again in his element, continued to wring emotion after emotion from the hearts of a willing audience. He invoked all manner of threats, promises or reprisals for those who felt they could not give their all in the, 'name of humanity.' Eventually, he himself looked depleted and emotionally drained, as though he had ingested a little rat poison to create this desired greying effect, according to Cinerella.

He at length finished his address as the introduction bars to hymnal *'Sweet Sacrament Divine'* [1] were being played by the orchestra, under the direction of Mr. David Moody. At the same time as Lodge eased himself down from the podium, Mabel Green stepped in to the single shaft of pale yellow limelight. She then invited the audience to lift up their hearts, and join with her, in singing this beautiful melodic hymn to those who were adrift upon the sea. Several members of the audience duly coughed and cleared their throats in order to be able to do so.

> *Sweet Sacrament of rest,*
> *Ark from the ocean's roar,*
> *Within thy shelter blest*
> *Soon may we reach the shore;*
> *Save us for still the tempest raves*
> *Save, lest we sink beneath the waves:*
> *Sweet Sacrament of rest,*
> *Sweet Sacrament of rest.*

Mabel's rendition of the hymn was quite spectacular and she showed her tessitura off quite effectively as she entered the last stanza assisted by her enthusiastic audience;

> *Sweet Sacrament divine,*
> *Earth's light and jubilee,*
> *In thy far depths doth shine*
> *Thy Godhead's majesty,*
> *Sweet light, so shine on us we pray,*
> *That earthly joys may fade away,*
> *Sweet Sacrament divine,*
> *Sweet Sacrament divine.*

On completion of the hymn, the applause understandably was tremendous and well deserved. Not an inconsiderable number of eyes were moist. Mabel bowed repeatedly to her sister *graces*, Hetherington and Lawrence and at the audience, who were by now on their feet.

Eventually, after a period of sustained clapping, Mabel then lifted her hands with the palms facing upward and then turning them downward, brought them down slowly and in so doing the applause gradually subsided. Rather as Lodge had done earlier.

"Your graces, lords, ladies and gentlemen, distinguished and honored guests, it is my privilege," said Mabel, to an auditorium filled to the rafters, "to be with you during this momentous evening and share with you our thoughts, feelings and memories of loved ones taken from us recently with the dreadful sinking of that ill-fated *Titanic* boat.

"Help me, I implore you! Help me by affirming the hymn, '*Abide with Me*,' in order to banish from our wounded hearts, those vestiges of sadness which still linger there and allow us to perhaps live again in hope and in peace with our cherished memories."

The audience duly obliged, and, remaining on their feet, joined in as the introductory bars drifted up from the orchestra pit. We had only gotten in to the first stanza, when a sound was heard, a very audible sound in the auditorium.

1.   Composed by F. Stanfield. 1835-1914

Chapter 26

The Night of the Nihilists

Cinderella, Jack and I were attending, in the august Queen's Hall, the Titanic Benefit Concert extravaganza put on by the impresario Lodge for the benefit of the victims resulting from the *Titanic* boat catastrophe. The concert had commenced in a dignified manner with Lodge clearly relishing his rôle not only of impresario, but that of compère too. Especially wearing his mid-night blue colored tail-coat suit with matching silver toned waist-coat and looking quite resplendent bathed in the single shaft of pale yellow limelight shining down from an arc lamp. However, all of us sitting in the auditorium had heard a sound, an ominous loud sound and naturally assumed that it had come from the concert platform. However a few moments later it had become apparent to us, from exactly where that ominous noise had originated. It was as a result of a large, fake limestone jardinière, supporting a green glazed urn containing a decorative arrangement of flowers and palm leaves of intricate design, which had fallen over.

Surrounding the toppled jardinière was a commotion, which seemed to involve individuals who were waving their arms about in an agitated manner. We all of us then realized the awful truth, that the jardinière had not fallen over, but rather it had been pushed over deliberately. My heart sank at the implications of this. Sure enough several Nihilists embedded in the audience, concentrated mainly in the cheap seats within the stalls, were now standing up and disrupting the concert.

Mabel still stood at the front of the concert platform ready to continue singing the sublime hymnal, '*Abide with Me*," along with members of the audience whom she had invited to join in. The orchestra continued playing apparently oblivious, as indeed their conductor was, to the commotion both on the stage and in the auditorium, very much as it might have been on the *Titanic* as the band played on during the actual sinking.

As the orchestra here played on with the music, Mabel, looking undaunted at the prospect of organized disruption, looked at the Nihilists with a concentrated malevolence in her eyes. A couple of the Nihilists even backed away from her. The orchestra, under their conductor David Moody, were fully aware of the fact that Mabel and indeed any members of the audience were singing along to their playing, but knew nothing of the commotion surrounding them, for such was their concentration on the score.

It was only when the dreaded chant by the Nihilists went up; '*be it now or never,*' that members of the orchestra, and Moody looked around themselves with expressions of total bewilderment on their faces. But now the low murmuring by the hecklers and Nihilists had developed into a mighty crescendo of chants and slogans with the odd threat thrown in such as, '*incommode the rich now; our failing to do so shall be at our utter peril.*'

The scene in the stalls below our private box was one of utter pandäemonium

Some were enunciating quite clearly their avowed intention to, '*Correct, with vigor and determination, the inequalities of a society, which is terrorized by the over indulgent upper classes augmented by the even less practical bourgeoisie.'* The Nihilists had clearly bought tickets, albeit for the cheap seats, in order that they might gain entry into the auditorium and the Titanic Benefit Concert. Obviously, so it seemed, to ensure that they would not miss out on such an opportunity to literally inconvenience the rich and on such an occasion as this.

Their chorus was unceasing…*'annihilate all extravagances, which are practiced by the profligate and carefree privileged upper classes.'* Their sole aim was to dispatch forthwith the upper classes into oblivion. And, *'…wage ceaseless agitation against the mindless privileged few,'* as they saw us. In their all-embracing quest, to remove all privations from society, the Nihilists would agitate anywhere and at anytime. We sat there aghast at what was unfolding before our very eyes.

Memories of the débâcle we endured on stage at the Majestic Theater in Chicago engulfed me like a cataclysmic flood of almost biblical proportions, as did those experiences and resulting mêlée, of the hecklers and Nihilists when they descended upon the Criterion Theater some weeks past, when Jack and I were on stage with Judd, our ventriloquist's dummy.

One particular vociferous Nihilist looked up towards us as we stared down from our privileged red plush private box and waved his clenched fist at us shouting, *'Dispatch forthwith those privileged classes up there in their red plush private boxes to oblivion this instant; our failure to act now shall be to our utter detriment!'*

Eventually, after a lot of shouting and confident behavior by the hecklers and Nihilists, Newman, the Queen's Hall manager and several tough-looking ushers resplendent in their black morning-coats with red piping, entered the stalls in a well rehearsed phalanx. They eventually succeeded in removing those who would seek to disrupt this solemn and dignified occasion, organized by Lodge. I looked at Jack. I think he was enjoying the débâcle erupting below him in the stalls.

"I somewhat knew it was splendid idea to agree to accept Loge's offer to attend this concert," was all Jack said in response to my looking at him.

After some hesitant starts by the orchestra and some re-arranging of the decorations and the upturned jardinière with glazed urn, the concert got underway again. Mabel led the audience in a heart-wrenching rendition of, '*Abide with Me*,' during which she had the audience swaying in unison with her waving her head from side to side. Occasionally Mabel would point her finger at recalcitrant members of the audience not singing and physically exhort that person, by pulling the fingers of her hand towards her, to join in and sing along with the audience.

We had only gotten in to the third refrain when another, concealed set of Nihilists got up and started another commotion. Obviously, their plan was to sabotage the concert throughout. It became clear to me now; that each time one set of disruptors was ejected, then another would emerge later in the concert to take their place and carry on the disruption. Clearly they had been well drilled and were working to a well-prepared plan indicating prior concerted effort.

This time they were more confident in their disruptive behavior. One such Nihilist actually clambered up onto the stage and began to deliver his radical speech to the audience! Mr. David Moody, conducting the orchestra seemed more interested in keeping time and did not regard the commotion taking place all about him as anything other than a slight mishap in the seating arrangements.

Yet again a body of black morning-coated ushers controlled the situation by removing those causing the disruption. But by now, the concert was fatally compromised by the actions of the Nihilists and hecklers and accordingly, some members of the audience were seen to be abandoning their seats and leaving the hall and the commotion.

Undaunted throughout and ably aided by Mr. David Moody conducting the orchestra. Mabel continued with her song, and went on to complete it with the help of some stalwart members of the audience who accompanied her, despite the commotion, and proceeded to the finale with thunderous applause.

When the applause for Mabel had subsided, Dot Hetherington appeared front of stage center to do justice to her song called, '*Somewhere a Voice is Calling*,' which she did, much to the acclaim of an appreciative audience.

Despite the hecklers and Nihilists making a disruptive appearance, Lodge's Titanic Benefit Concert appeared to be marginally successful. We all sat back in our comfortable red plush seats to await the appearance of Vesta Tilley, booked next in the program, to render the song written by Leslie Stuart called, '*By The Sad Sea Waves*,' and billed in order to lend some relief to what might otherwise turn into a dour concert of amaranthine proportions.

"Will she appear on stage, dressed as a man, a judge, a soldier or even a toff?" I asked Cinderella.

"There is no telling with our Vesta," replied Cinderella, with an unusual look of concern upon her face.

Moments later, having been introduced by a visibly nervous Lodge, Vesta stepped into the pale yellow lime light that expanded instantly to illuminating the whole of the concert platform, including the lush floral and plume decorations. Vesta stood there motionless. She was dressed in a long, fitted, fawn colored coat beneath which she wore striped trousers.

Her shirt was white and with a high stiff collar fasted with a stone of some indeterminate origin. Her slender pointed boots were black and highly varnished. Upon her head was a black silk top hat and in her right hand she carried what looked like a riding crop. She was, dressed as a West End *toff* or s*well* as we call them, back home in America.

Having welcomed her audience and engaged a few in banter and chitchat, she flew into her first song. It was from a selection written by a Mr. Albert Hall set to music by Abraham Walter de Frece from the, *'German Prince,'* which Moody with his orchestra were at pains to keep up with. She accelerated through the verses deliberately to get as many sung as was humanly possible, given the restraints on her time on the stage.

She then launched herself into a favorite song called, *'Burlington Bertie,'* which totally caught Moody by surprise, as she was billed to sing the anthem at this stage called, *'Above Us the Waves.'* None the less, Vesta discarded the anthem and instead sang her song out without the orchestra. Vesta had barely got to the last line off the third verse from, *'Burlington Bertie,'* *'He's wealthy and foolish, but if you want pluck,'* when at a hidden signal the depressing Nihilists were at it again. A general groan from the audience went up to equal the loud murmuring and chanting by the hecklers and Nihilists.

On this occasion, the hecklers and Nihilists were not just sporadic groups, intent on disruption, but rather a concentration of them with concerted intentions in mind.

At one stage it appeared half those persons sitting in the stalls had risen from their seats and were engaged in confrontation with anyone and anything. Newman reëntered the auditorium and as usual, was leading his ushers, resplendent in their black morning-coats, into the thick of the mêlée in his endeavors to reëstablish some semblance of order in his Queen's Hall.

Well dressed people, some in velvet gowns and tiaras and others in evening dress were leaving in their droves, unwilling to be subject to such disruption or determined behavior by ill mannered revolutionaries. I noticed Cinderella got up without saying a word and disappeared though the portière curtain shielding the door of our private box. I could not blame her, for the last thing Jack and I wanted was a repeat performance from these individuals who wished to forcibly impose their views on society, and I informed Jack as to my annoyance and views on these trouble makers.

"Fine Theo," replied Jack, "but we have been in this situation before when we were attending that concert, where was it? Ah yes, in the St. James's Hall in the Portland Road near Oxford Street. I said then, and I meant it then as I do now; this type of disruption kind of makes sense. Think about it Theo, if the Nihilists or Futurists or any revolutionary group wish to bring to the public's attention their thoughts and ideas, especially about the evolution of society in whatever respect, then one has to choose carefully just how to achieve that."

"How would one achieve it then?" I inquired.

"Notice their method," continued Jack, "in so doing and getting the public's attention. They do not agitate in the streets or at rail road stations; which must contain a greater number of persons at any one given time than a concert hall or theater ever could. No, they focus on the concert hall or theater, deliberately, because it is within such places that precisely those important persons whom they are trying to affect or even influence are to be found.

That is to say, wealthy people with influence who are moved to attend Lodge's Titanic Benefit Concert or enjoy classical music as they do here in the Queen's Hall. It is precisely those people who the Nihilists have in their sights; and not persons who attend Music Hall or Vaudeville. On that basis the Nihilists would never invade a Music Hall, simply because the audience in such a place would not even know what Nihilism was about, let alone be influenced by their beliefs!" said Jack.

"But they invaded the Criterion Theater where we performed only recently," I reminded Jack.

"Ah but Theo, the Nihilists were outside agitating for a showdown with those undoubtedly privileged diners enjoying themselves in the Criterion Restaurant next door to the theater we were performing in," replied Jack.

"That may well be the case Jack, but it does not make me feel any better, nor am I willing to sit here being incommoded by a bunch of attention seeking clowns. It is a ridiculous situation that we find ourselves in and we are only adding credibility to the Nihilists' and hecklers' cause in condoning their actions and tolerating them by staying here.

"Rather than endure this impromptu disruptive coup de théâtre, I suggest we follow Cinderella and abandon the Queen's Hall since our presence here is becoming untenable and our staying cannot help Lodge or his predicament. Those Nihilists down there in the stalls, Jack, are here for the evening and will not quit until the hall is emptied of patrons of the Titanic Benefit Concert. Very unfortunate Jack, but believe it," I said, baring my soul on the matter.

"I agree with you Theo," replied Jack, "but that is what is happening to concert halls, in that they all seemed to be filled with hecklers, revolutionaries or Nihilists. But, one wonders will there be any room for the ordinary members of the audience who attend such places for entertainment and not to be exposed to radical ideas or witness people registering dissatisfaction with the status quo."

There had, of course, originally been a commotion at the side of the concert platform resulting in a large fake limestone jardinière, supporting a green glazed urn containing floral and palm leaves being knocked over by a diminutive person. That had been the signal to start off a series of disruptive acts of sabotage.

Suddenly, as if responding to a hidden signal, the manic commotion in the stalls abruptly ceased. I peered cautiously over the brass railing in front of our red plush private box into the stalls below. People were resuming their seats, in an orderly manner, as though returning from the interval. I looked at Jack and we both shrugged our shoulders. Then we both of us saw the reason why.

My heart nearly skipped a beat when we recognized her. Making her way cautiously through the singers assembled on the concert platform and dense green foliage adorning the stage and looking bewildered, was Little Bo Peep, followed by her lamb! In her hand was her shepherdess's crook, which she held in order to support herself.

On approaching the front of the stage and manœuvering herself squarely into the single shaft of pale yellow limelight shining down from an arc lamp, she then stood there bathed in its translucent light trained only on her person. Lifting her other hand up to shield her eyes from the glare of the limelight trained upon her face, she looked about her in an uncertain manner unsure of what to do next. So did the lamb that continued bleating for all its worth whilst following Bo Peep around. The audience too responded to her unannounced presence on the stage with a hushed attentiveness that most Music Hall artistes could only dream of.

"Little Bo Peep," I whispered to Jack, "is the only person I know of, who is able to hold an audience enthralled by simply just walking on to the stage and doing very little else. I now appreciate why she is called *Little* Bo Peep!"

At length she turned to withdraw from the stage. But due to the intense limelight in her eyes, she failed to notice a large laurel leaf lying on the timber floor of the stage. In the next instant she had stepped on it causing her to slip and fall to the concert platform with such a pronounced thud that was audible throughout the auditorium. People gasped in horror at witnessing this unfortunate accident on stage. Instantly Little Bo Peep grabbed her knee that by now appeared to have a red patch on it, as though she had cut herself.

Within a moment or two she was crying her eyes out with such a sustained intensity and more noisily and with increased passion than I had ever previously heard from her. I feared she may really have seriously hurt herself, such was the force of her fall to the floor. I also noticed that she resorted to my red paisley patterned handkerchief in an attempt to stem her tears. This distressing scene went on for quite some time and I became concerned that no one was going to her assistance either from the audience or indeed from those persons assembled on the stage witnessing her predicament. It all seemed rather a bit callous, I thought.

My fears alas, were groundless, as it became apparent

to all, including eventually me, that this was of course her speciality act. She was, it must be said, very effective. At length she hauled herself up from her ground, recovered her shepherdess crook and burst into song about losing one of her lambs to a crafty local fox. When she had completed her song, to the accompaniment of a weak smile and gushing tears, worthy of Niagara Falls in late spring, she bowed to the audience and limped across stage to her exit, followed by her bleating lamb.

She did so to tumultuous applause from an ecstatic audience, including the hecklers and Nihilists, one of whom, was even moved to throw a rolled up bank note at her, which she caught with one hand, as was her custom!

After a few minutes of applause and calls for her return, the audience had settled down again and regained some semblance of being attentive to a very different artiste who appeared center stage. She was Emma Carus and was down on the program to sing, '*Abendlich*,' by Rickard Wagner from the closing section of doom laden Act II, scene 3 from his acclaimed grand opera, '*Götterdämmerung*.' [1]

She did so in front of an attentive audience who swayed in their red plush velvet seats in sympathetic response to her powerful operatic scales, which, with majesty and dignity, reverberated throughout the auditorium of the Queen's Hall. Her's was an act which seemed to restore a degree of verisimilitude to the proceedings.

The intermission had been dispensed with because of the earlier disruptions and it was with indecent haste that we accelerated through the remaining songs such as, '*For those in Peril on the Sea*,' performed by Mabel Green. Ella Shields remained with us and went on to sing the sentiments expressed in the song, '*White Wings*,' with an enthusiastic audience participating. Florrie Forde, who never ceases to amaze me came up to the footlights and commenced with her offering, '*Nearer My God to Thee*,' with such nobility and affection that I swear I have never heard that anthem sung with such feeling or depth of sincerity.

However, there was one hymn I was waiting to hear. That Eucharistic hymn was the beautiful *Tantum Ergo Sacramentum*, from the Corpus Christi hymnal. The sentiments contained in this affirmation are expressed by the most sublime and sonorous of chords and melodic transfer, which have never failed to move me and induce contemplation. The words instil an inner feeling of contentment and of renewed resolved to overcome adversity and dispatch forthwith all doubt and anxiety to where they ought to reside, far removed from one's heart.

It remains a powerful and sonorous vocal expression, especially if sung by someone such as Katie Lawrence, who retains a powerful voice together with an ease of achieving vocal range. And who can not only sing beautifully, but her timing is impeccable too.

On this occasion, Katie Lawrence started off in the melancholy key of E minor, but gradually progressed in to D minor. She did so with David Moody controlling, remarkably expertly, the huge orchestral forces needed to express the sentiments in this hymn in a powerful, but meaningful way.

Tantum Ergo Sacramentum [2]
Veneremur cernui
Et antiquum documentum
Novo cedat ritui
Præstet fides supplementum
Sensuum defectui.

Genitori, Genitoque
Laus et jubilatio
Salus, honor, virtu quoque
Sit et benedictio
Procedenti ab utroque
Compar sit laudatio. [3]

Both Lawrence's singing and the orchestra, conducted by David Moody, did not disappoint. On this occasion, I was certainly impressed by both and appreciated their skills in delivering this beautiful affirmation and witnessing the spontaneous response expressed in sustained and loud applause for Katie Lawrence.

There are times when Lodge did surprise me, in that he was able to rise up in what he endeavored to achieve. His incorporating the *Tantum Ergo Sacramentum*, was indicative of his skills in the juxtaposition of this hymn with other hymns and songs being sung that evening. Though I confess, I did not think Lodge even knew about the existence of the, *Tantum Ergo Sacramentum,* let alone its application to the human condition.

In this respect, one could also see glimpses of the way Lodge's mind worked, in his application of the concept; such as that of the ridiculous to the sublime. His incorporating the *Tantum Ergo Sacramentum* into the Titanic Benefit Concert, was indicative of his way of thinking and accordingly impressed the concert with a nobility of purpose and a profound, almost sacred dignity. This was not Music Hall; this was an ecclesiastical expression of a faith in humanity. Let us hope this profound understanding of faith was duly rewarded somewhere and was reflected then, in more than acceptable box office receipts.

At last we came to the part of the Titanic Benefit

Concert devoted to a performance of the acclaimed Choral Anthem Symphony. Both Jack and I agreed never could so much be expected from this symphony in trying to salvage what had been a débâcle of the first order and reëstablishing a degree of nobility of purpose to the proceedings.

Apart from the *Tantum Ergo Sacramentum*, other hymns or songs had been disrupted. But, even the Nihilists were moved to remain quiet during its performance; on the basis perhaps that it engendered respect across the revolutionary divide.

However, the *Three Graces* were now assembled on stage and waited for a now visibly disturbed Lodge to introduce them. Some aspects of the evening were still however functioning, including the all-important single shaft of pale yellow limelight trained on Lodge. Again, an aura of ethereal grace and restrained dignity seemed to intensify about his person, illuminating into a dazzling sheen his mid-night blue tail-coat and matching trousers.

It remained to be seen whether such nobility of purpose could be reëstablished, let alone maintained. Such action would, I thought, confirm or dispel the worst suspicions which Jack and I continued to harbor about that evening's proceedings. We both of us remained grateful that we were in a private box and our stage names not linked with the performance on the concert platform in front of us.

Whilst the stage was illuminated brilliantly with incandescent footlights, the auditorium remained in subdued lighting. In the silence of the theater a lone voice was heard.

"Ladies and gentlemen, imagine for a moment, those noble ideals, for which we all of us continue to strive," the voice invoked, "I refer to such ideals as *Hope,*

Aspiration or *Courage;* especially when one has to deal with them in the face of continuing adversity in our short but tragic lives. Imagine if you will, a symphony, a symphony in which those noble ideals are encapsulated and given laudable expression. The sentiments, behind the acclaimed elegiac Choral Anthem Symphony, are there to establish those affirmations which we know to be imperishable. And, in doing so, lend dignity, address fortitude, and imbue the soul with a nobility of purpose in addition to conveying such ideals as perfection in harmony and song for the benefit of all mankind in its various guises.

"Your graces, lords, ladies and gentlemen, the Queen's Hall is pleased to present, for your delectation, the *Three Graces*, who shall sing the rôles, especially composed for soprano, in espousing those noble ideals and promulgated in this magnificent and sublime Choral Anthem Symphony.

"Please welcome the unforgettable Mabel Green who will be singing the rôle of *Courage*. Our renowned and delectable Katie Lawrence will sing those sections devoted to *Aspiration*, and will be followed by the incomparable and indomitable Dot Hetherington who will bring up the rear and sing those sentiments devoted to *Hope!*"

As each of the sopranos was called one by one, especially in their combined rôles as the *Three Graces* the intensity of the applause increased accordingly, culminating into a tremendous crescendo, where everybody in the auditorium rose from their seats. Some did so whilst clapping, thus demonstrating unequivocally their unadulterated approbation for their favorite sopranos. Also during this ecstatic welcome for the *Three Graces* some members of the audience erupted with unbridled enthusiasm, whilst others induced themselves into an uncontrolled delirium at the prospect of hearing their acclaimed sopranos sing in this choral symphonic extravaganza.

"It is possible he may actually pull the evening off," Jack said to me.

At that moment, Mabel Green, in the rôle of *Courage,* stepped forward up to the footlights. She did so in order to achieve the greatest illumination of her presence on stage. In response to the introduction by the string section symphony orchestra under the competent direction of the conductor, Mr. David Moody, she commenced her lyrical expression of harmonic structure in the key of C # minor. The powerful brass section thundered out those chords, which together represent *Courage,* further augmented her singing and presentation on the stage. Green was able to hold her own against such thematic forces generated by the orchestra and her singing, on this occasion, took us all up to the heights of sublime ecstasy.

After fifteen or so minutes of this musical expression by Mabel Green, her individual recital in this Titanic Benefit Concert concluded with a sustained crescendo, which then only gradually descended into silence. After much bowing and raising her hands, she finally withdrew to the rear of the concert stage among the floral decorations. I also noticed the look of utter contempt on the faces of the other two sopranos who viewed her with distain and a smouldering antagonism in their eyes. Such behavior, as trading visual insults amongst sopranos is normal, I thought.

At length Katie Lawrence glided to the very front of the stage as near to the incandescent footlights as possible, in order that she too might be illuminated to the fullest intensity. She then launched into her singing very audibly those words devoted to the noble ideal of *Aspiration*. During her recital, it became evident that her singing, though good, was nothing more than a thinly veiled attempt simply to out-sing her rival in Mabel Green.

And, that the dignified noble ideals and considerations expressed in the Choral Anthem Symphony were of little relevance or of real significance in her vocal attempt to out-perform Mabel Green's effort. But despite the apparent sublime lyrical intensity of her singing, Katie Lawrence was still able to project rôle of *Aspiration* in a very convincing and affectionate way. Even though her words were sometimes expressed in a manner approaching that of falsetto, but irrespective of this weakness, her rendition was well received.

Having sung her rôle in espousing the cause of *Aspiration*, at length, Lawrence too began her slow and gradual withdrawal from the front of the stage. She yielded the position, albeit reluctantly, and only eventually after the introduction chords for the rôle of the next soprano, Dot Hetherington, were being played by the orchestra.

Lawrence's progress to the back of the stage was indeed slow, as it was ponderous, with the occasional steps forward in order to respond to her clamoring admirers. When she did retreat it was not quite to the back of the stage. Rather she positioned herself deliberately occupying a place in front of Mabel Green and only just behind Hetherington, but certainly not out of the glare of the footlights.

The third soprano, in the person of Dot Hetherington, came to the fore in her rôle to espouse the noble cause of *Hope*. She began her recital slowly and with deliberation whilst moderating her vibrato in conjunction with intermittent orchestral refrains with which she managed, amazingly, to keep in synchronization.

Quite then what Dot Hetherington did remains a mystery to me, even though I witnessed it with my very own eyes. All of a sudden she had the audience swaying from side to side in their seats, in response to her waving her head from side to side. Here was an accomplished mistress giving a master class, primarily for the instruction of the other two sopranos, Mabel Green and Katie Lawrence whom together comprise the *Three Graces*.

Hetherington's achievement in getting the audience going and to re-act in sympathetic harmony was to the very obvious annoyance of the other two sopranos, especially, given the fact that both had somehow failed to move the public in the auditorium in quite such an enthusiastic way. After twenty minutes of ecstatic re-action from the audience and calls for encore and bravo, Hetherington finally conceded the front of the stage.

At this point, I recall, the Choral Anthem Symphony follows a programmatic development involving set integrated and precisely coördinated singing and actions by all three sopranos.

However, irrespective of this, Hetherington then had the temerity to actually summon the two other sopranos to join with her in holding hands! Neither Mabel Green nor Katie Lawrence could scarcely reject this overtly magnanimous and apparently noble gesture by Hetherington and were somewhat compelled to comply with her invitation. Hetherington, standing in the middle of the sopranos holding hands, had without doubt, executed her very effective coup de grâce, upon her co-sopranos in establishing just who was the *prima inter pares*. [4]

At one stage in performing the so called Choral

Anthem Symphony, all three sopranos were required to sing in unison as their respective noble ideals came together, as it were, in the face of adversity.

Though as to which adversity, the Choral Anthem Symphony simply failed to define. The three sopranos did not so much sing together in unison. But rather looked, with almost concentrated hostility and envy, at one another in vying as to who could basically out sing the others whilst putting them into the shade. The performance was clearly turning into a singing match between the *Three Graces* worthy of Wagner's opera *'Tannhäuser und der Sängekrieg auf Wartburg.'* [5]

It was amusing to experience this rivalry, just in order to hear which of the sopranos could sing the loudest. And do so with sheer fortissimo, accompanied by the inevitable falsetto to dismiss audibly the other singers into oblivion.

The resultant cacophony was powerful, as it was ear shattering. There was a sence of relief when at last we reached the finale in one explosive crescendo involving the combined thematic forces of the orchestra in the pit and the three screeching sopranos. The finale was barely concluded when there was a resounding call for bravo, encore and more. The *Three Graces* duly obliged, in a final bid to out-sing or out-perform each other.

Then it happened. It was during this final vocal display that the Nihilists and hecklers erupted again. Whether this was so because of the singing, one did not know, but clearly Newman and his body of ushers wearing black morning-coats had not entirely got rid of them and some had remained quiet, deliberately to avoid recognition, and subsequently from being ejected from the auditorium earlier. Now they were set on causing more disruption and annoyance.

This second set appeared to be more vociferous and determined in their avowed intention and stated so verbally for all to hear.

"*Inconvenience the rich now; our failing to do so shall be at our peril,*" some were heard to chant.

Others preferred the more blood curdling slogans as "*Dispatch forthwith the upper classes and bring about an end to their tyranny of we, the lower orders,*" or, even more alarmingly, "*Condemn their profligate use of our national wealth; our failure to do so will be our utter destitution and penury!*"

During this mêlée another consignment of tough-looking ushers appeared and removed forcefully those who were intent on causing further disruption. However, two Nihilists actually gained the concert platform and after deliberately knocking over decorative palm trees, urns and jardinières, proceeded to scatter their pamphlets in an abandoned way and showering those in the stall with their revolutionary ideals and commitments. Even Mabel was seen to be struggling with one of the more determined Nihilists and at one point appeared to have the upper hand in subjugating him.

People began to make their way out of the stalls and Dress Circle, as they feared for the safety of their persons and even their graces, the Dukes of Cambridge and of Teck had abandoned their red plush royal box for the infinite safety of the fog-bound streets of London.

Lodge was beside himself with rage and succeeded in clearing the concert platform of artistes and his sopranos before physically turning to face a number of Nihilists who had also climbed up on to the stage to confront him. It was only with the intervention of Newman at the head of a body of determined ushers in their black morning-coats that prevented what could have been incommoding for Lodge, brave as he was in his endeavors.

The concert came to an undignified close as people simply got up and made their way out of the auditorium. Eentually, Jack and I left and made our way out of the Queen's Hall and into the street to wait for Cinderella, Lodge and Newman. Whilst waiting for them outside in Langham Place, my attention was caught by an advertisement poster plastered, without permission, on the Portland stone wall of the building. Its claims struck me as being too preposterous, but somehow more relevant than the extravagant débâcle or fiasco we had witnessed earlier inside the august confines of the Queen's Hall.

Mabel was the first to join us. After some time, Lodge

appeared too, being supported on each arm by Cinderella and Newman. Lodge looked like a man possessed, with his erratic mannerisms. The top hat he wore was placed on his head at an angle, and his eyes were glazed and had a distant, almost vacant look about them as though he were staring into oblivion.

When Newman beckoned Lodge to climb into the Landau carriage, which Mabel had somehow acquired for him, he was most adamant in his refusal to do so, insisting he would not be moved from where he stood. Though at the same time, Lodge offered no reasonable explanation for this irrational decision. To support his contention Lodge, with the strength of a committed demoniac, gripped, with both his hands, the long brass fluted bracket of the Landau carriage door. He did so with such continuing adamantine strength that we none of us could release his hold upon it.

At the same time his penchant, or monomania affliction, for looking over his shoulders increased to such an extent that Mabel was compelled to secure his head in her hands, lest he cause himself irreversible injury. At one stage, Lodge kept repeating that he would not budge and, that he was done for, such was the unmitigated disaster which had unfolded during the evening.

Eventually, it was a much as Jack, Newman even Cinderella and myself could do to get Lodge in to the Landau carriage. And this was only achieved when Mabel took Lodge firmly in her hand and forced him to comply with her requirement and to pull himself together.

"Otherwise one will be left open to public comment and ridicule. Or at worst become an object of derision, because of your remarkable behavior," insisted Mabel, firmly.

Eventually, the Landau carriage, containing Lodge in the adamantine grip of Mabel clattered off into the fog as Jack hailed a passing Brougham carriage into which Cinderella, Newman, Jack and myself climbed.

"Café Royal," instructed Cinerella, "and step on it."

If he had wanted to avoid the stigma of Music Hall at least on this one occasion," said Jack, "Loge was going to be profoundly disappointed. In actual fact it has turned out to be one of the best impromptu entertaining evenings I have ever experienced. If Cinderella here, had gone on to the stage dressed as Marmeduke and performed her ventriloquist's act, it could have only been an improvement. What their graces, both the Duke of Cambridge and the Duke of Teck thought of the spectacle, a Titanic spectacle at that, this evening from the safety of their royal private box, was, in my opinion, anybody's guess!"

Having secured a *Travertino Oniciato Scuro Venato* marble topped table in the salon together with chilled champagne, Cinderella later confided in us that that with Newman's collusion and permission, she had organized the delivery of her Little Bo Peep costume and bleating lamb to the Queen's Hall. Since both she and Newman suspected that a turn on the stage by her may well be needed in order to quell a not totally unexpected unruly consignment of Nihilists or others intent on causing a commotion. For such persons, they knew, were ranging abroad the metropolis that evening!

Not for the first time have we, especially Lodge, been indebted to Cinderella and the beneficiaries of her clear thinking.

1. Twilight of the Gods
2. Therefore we before the Sacrament.

3. Therefore we Before thee bending
   This great Sacrament revere
   Types and shadows
   Have their ending
   For the newer Rite is here
   To the everlasting Father,
   And the Son Who reigns on high
   With the Holy Spirit proceeding
   Forth from each eternally,
   Be salvation, honor, blessing,
   Might and endless majesty.
4. First amongst equals
5. *Tannhäuser and the Singers' Contest at Wartburg Castle* - opera

Chapter 27

The Anguish and Despair

We had attended the Titanic Benefit Concert at the Queen's Hall. Unfortunately, the concert had deteriorated into a disaster that people were saying was equal in magnitude to that of the actual sinking of the stricken *Titanic*, for which the benefit concert had been organized by Lodge in a desperate and speculative attempt to increase box office receipts. The reason for this catastrophe was the appearance of the Nihilists, who are by way of being revolutionaries and others, including Hecklers intent on disrupting the concert and creating pandaëmonium at every opportunity. In this respect, at least, they had succeeded beyond their wildest expectation, leaving the promoter of the concert, Lodge, devastated mentally, but more importantly, perhaps even financially. Eventually with the help of Cinderella we physically manhandled Lodge into the Landau carriage and dispatched him with Mabel forthwith off to his town house in the Bergen Avenue.

The next morning Jack and I were taking break-fast and having a fascinating conversation about just what we had experienced at the Queen's Hall the previous evening.

"I do not have access, of course, to Loge's box office receipts from last night, but chances are there will few of them," offered Jack, whilst munching on his rye bread and Brätwürst.

"It is possible that Lodge will have made a loss and be in no position to be offering charitable funds to the dependents of victims who drowned when the *Titanic* sank. Indeed I would hazard a guess that it will be he who is in need of charitable donations," I responded.

"I reckon that by the time we had gotten to the beginning of the second part of the concert, where there should have been the intermission, half of the audience had abandoned their seats and left. Who could blame them?" asked Jack.

"Well Lodge could," I replied, "especially the disrupting Nihilists who must have worked out that at this benefit concert, a product of Lodge's stratagem, those attending, for a laudable cause would have only paid a small amount of money for their tickets. The expectation is that one donates at the concert, which provides the opportunity to be ostentatious by letting all and sundry know just how conspicuously generous one can be. The Nihilists ensured no such opportunity would take place; least not in the Queen's Hall last night, under Lodge's auspices."

"Being an impresario, with his monocled eye constantly on box office receipts and forever inventing strategies for increasing them will perforce have its reward but also attendant risks. Whilst the concert was in itself a laudable intention, the mere fact of advertising it would have alerted the Nihilists to the types of guests more than likely to attend. In this respect, the concert was an opportunity to demonstrate and promote their revolutionary ideals, as the concert was doomed from its inception, and not only…" said Jack.

Jack had not completed his sentence when Lodge,

supported by Mabel, almost staggered into the Grand Dining Room. He shuffled over to where we were sitting and collapsed on to a nearby Chippendale chair, the seat of which was upholstered in yellow and white striped moiré silk. He looked drawn and agitated and his hands twitched constantly to the point of exceeding that of his man-servant Aloysius's affliction with the St. Vitus's Dance disease.

Mabel reached over to an adjacent table for a cup and from our pot poured black coffee in order to revive Lodge. He grabbed the cup with both hands and attempted to drink the coffee. But such was his nervous condition; he succeeded only in spilling the contents on to the Grand Dining Room green silk broadloom carpet with integral gold-colored fleur de lys designs woven into the pattern.

Presently, he laid his cup down and looked at me then at Jack then around the Grand Dining Room at others taking break-fast, as though galvanizing an impromptu audience to bear testimony to his plight.

"I shall be ruined! I shall be ruined I tell you, I shall be destitute, I shall become one of those who are of the twilight, the *Undeserving Poor!*" He said this repeatedly, whilst wringing his hands in despair. "Those Nihilists have done for me. They have buried me in financial ruin and disgrace. I should never have embarked on such a risk-embedded venture, but my generosity, my conspicuous generosity, my inherent generosity; oh my innate generosity for my fellow man will always out.

"But, a pestilence upon the fool who uttered that reckless intention, '…if I can help someone as I go along; then my living shall not be in vain.' Never again will I succumb to such rash abandonment of financial sense.

"And now, now I am to be possibly ruined I tell you.

Last night was a tragedy on a scale equal to the sinking of that damned *Titanic*, an unmitigated disaster and now I too am sinking with not a trace of my altruism or reckless generosity left behind. Only the wreckage of my generosity drifting on a sea, a sea of indifferences as to my plight and now open to scorn and ridicule and possibly becoming an object of derision too. This alas is the reward for putting others less fortunate before me. What am I to do; you see, they shall have their way with me?"

Lodge repeated this plea a few times before the words trailed off into a series of incoherent mumbling sounds coming through his purple lips.

We were all watching Lodge aghast at his behavior, and in public too. His eyes took on a vacant look as they rolled around aimlessly in their deep sockets. For a fleeting moment he had assumed the mannerism and character of a dumb mute, the type of which we had experienced on the stage at Wilton's Music Hall some time ago, and I had witnessed in a street in Shoreditch on my way the New National Standard Theater.

His emotional mannerism was interesting here, because it reminded me of something he said in confidence when answering a question Jack had asked him about his rôle in Music Halls and Soho in particular. Lodge's reply was instructive as it was revealing.

'For what is Soho but one large stage; upon which we are all invited to do our turns or acts?'

He had replied, spontaneously and, in an overtly thespian manner. Somehow, I felt that I had heard that remark before, but could not quite recall where or from whom.[1]

However, his reply at the time sounded innocuous and somewhat exaggerated. But now the implications of what he had said and how he had delivered the words, came rushing back at me. Indeed I was now more convinced that possibly Lodge had started out as a Music Hall artiste, and, that he had personally, to great acclaim, evolved and perfected the rôle of the dumb mute, making it his own, as it were. [2]

For the present however, he was beside himself with anguish laced with despair, indeed worthy of a dumb mute's performance.

"There is talk amongst my creditors," he continued, speaking with an even squeakier voice, an audible octave higher than usual, "who even now, as we talk, are stalking me, as hyenas would their prey. And now rumors abound of having to sell my beloved town house in the Bergen Avenue that..."

Again his words trailed off into incoherent mutterings and then silence. However, his inherent nervous affliction of looking over both his shoulders for no discernable or apparent reason had increased to such a chronic level, that we feared he might well, literally lose his head.

I did not now feel like completing my break-fast, especially with Lodge's misery imposed upon me, taking away my appetite, but instead viewed Lodge. He was not quite the gibbering wreck as he now stared obliviously into the middle distance, but still looking distraught as a man in his situation might. He clearly had not slept well. The red circles around his eyes bore testimony to this fact. Nor had he attended to his ablutions this morning either. He looked quite disheveled; to the extent I was surprised that he was permitted access into the hotel, let alone to this Grand Dining Room.

Presently, after some gentle encouragement from Mabel, Lodge pulled himself together, cleared his throat, and made the following announcement.

"Gentlemen, gentlemen," he said, "attend me. As Mabel will confirm, I have decided that it is my intention to abandon London!"

Both Jack and I exchanged looks of concern on hearing this news of great moment.

At the same time Lodge looked at me. He then looked at Jack. Then around the Grand Dining Room, to see if any other interested persons taking break-fast had heard and appreciated this news of great import. Together with the realization of the inevitable consequences and devastating implications as yet to be realized for the future, the very future of Music Halls as we knew them.

He then returned his attention to Jack who responded accordingly.

"I must confess Loge, to being somewhat surprised by your response to last night's calamity. But to abandon the metropolis; is that not over re-acting?"

"Well only for a few days," he replied, "in order that I might be afforded an opportunity of recovering my dignity and self esteem. And, to put yesterday evening's dreadful affair which attended our venture behind us."

Both Jack and I seized immediately on the fact of Lodge's use of the plural *our* and *us* to imply that we were all part of his tragedy and that it was not his alone to bear. The mere fact that Jack and I were sitting in the Dress Circle in a private box during the débâcle and played no part in the concert, other than that of spectator, appeared to have entirely escaped Lodge's attention.

"I have communicated with an old colleague of mine," he continued, "who resides in a country mansion in Buckinghamshire, twenty or so miles out of town. I suggest we all repair there and rejuvenate our depleted souls to enable us to take on with confidence those challenges that life invariably throws at the deserving and heroic. I still have my Barouche carriage, at least for the moment, driven by my faithful retainer Aloysius who could never abandon me, to take us all to Marylebone Rail Road Station. And from there avail ourselves of a steam train of the Great Central Rail Road to convey us to Beaconsfield Station and thence on by carriage to the Abbey Grange at Chalfont St. Giles."

Mabel looked hard at Lodge.

"Oh yes, and at Mabel's suggestion only," continued Lodge, "we have invited that Cinderella woman. She may yet prove to be useful as a housemaid or in some other servile capacity to wait upon us and attend to our every whim or fad, during our prolonged sojourn at the Abbey Grange."

Both Jack and I exchanged glances and I knew Jack was not happy at the prospect of being holed up in some house out of town. In addition though, both of us were aware of one salient fact that we have recognized before.

Lodge, thus far, had been a reliable source of inspiration for us. He had at unflinching cost to his now depleted purse, contacts and good will, assisted Jack and me in our endeavors to establish ourselves in various and prestigious Music Halls ranged across London. It was this fact that I reiterated in my attempt to inveigle Jack into agreeing to accompany Lodge to the Abbey Grange.

"This news is indeed of momentous report and we shall certainly accompany you to your friend's residence in Buckinghamshire. We will be there for you," I responded.

Jack and I thus nodded our consent at falling in with Lodge's suggestion. Aside of which we neither of us have been outside of London, nor escaped the acrid fog's grip on the place since we first arrived some weeks past.

"I shall not be joining you, as I have chores to do, not

least in rehearsing other stage rôles, for alas the show must go on" said Mabel, rising from her chair and curtseying to us.

We all of us in turn got up to shake her hand.

"I trust things will work out and settle down again," she said, taking our hands in turn, and with that dropped a shallow courtesy and marched out of the Grand Dining Room – an integral part of the pervasive opulence of the St. Pancras Hotel, whistling gently to herself.

Presently Jack and I left the Grand Dining Room too and having collected some necessaries from our bedrooms made our way down to the foyer to join Lodge. He then led the way out to the ornate stone porte cochère under which Aloysius, true to form, was waiting impatiently sitting on the bench of the Barouche carriage. We all climbed in and instantly our horses pulled our carriage into the blinding fog. I could only hope that the Abbey Grange was not in the grip of such an acrid fog as this one, that we are compelled to endure.

Whether it was because Lodge had kept Aloysius waiting beneath the stone porte cochère at the St. Pancras Hotel, we could not be certain. But Aloysius whipped up his two chestnut horses drawing our Barouche, to such an extent, as to make them bound down the Euston Road. However, it became apparent to us as we progressed slowly past both Portland Road Metropolitan Station and then the bronze bust of a dead president, shaded by an apple tree that the traffic was increasing. Aloysius looked at his pocket watch anxiously and then at the road ahead crowded with every kind of conveyance progressing along this very busy thoroughfare.

We had no sooner passed this memorial bronze sculpture, than suddenly our Barouche carriage slowed down due to the vicissitude of traffic. Because of this,

Park Crescent Pavilion

we were able to view a peculiar looking structure, in fact a stone built small pavilion building set in what looked like quite substantial and extensive private grounds, which had been cultivated into gardens, containing large laurel bushes and forest trees.

On our numerous peregrinations abroad in the metropolis, we have driven by this classical styled pavilion, which forms the entrance into a large fog-bound mysterious garden. The structure has never ceased to intrigue me. Of course we have never seen the garden in sunlight, due to the pervasive acrid yellow fog that has London in its grip. And this has been the case since we arrived from New York some weeks earlier. However, the garden, especially shrouded in fog always appeared hauntingly enigmatic, as though hiding a secret in the depths of its grounds.

Certainly, the fog in the garden appeared to be stilled and not swirling in vortexes as one might experience on the Marylebone Road. Some time ago, whilst passing this very place. I had questioned Lodge as to the ownership of the garden. Was it private, part of someone's residence, or open to the public to enjoy? His reply, succinct of course, was that the garden was owned by the Crown, the English Crown. Indeed the Crown Estate & Paving Commissioners, were charged with maintaining the garden, in addition to looking after the vast expanse of neighboring Regent's Park, on the other side of the adjacent Marylebone Road.

And no, the garden was not open to the public. It might be enjoyed, for a fee, by the residents of the town houses in the neighborhood, especially maids, in the employ of wealthy families. They might use what they called the Nursemaids' Tunnel beneath the Marylebone Road which linked the garden to Regent's Park proper without the need to cross over that busy road with their young charges.

"Does not the Nursemaids' Tunnel allow access to that subterranean gentlemen's club, the Iron Vault, or whatever, you have previously described to us?" I asked Lodge, in an attempt to inveigle him into conversation.

"I believe the tunnel does allow one access to such a place; but it may as well lead to oblivion, for such is my misfortune," replied Lodge, as he dismissed my inquiry with a wave of his hand.

I decided not to pursue the matter with him, as clearly his mind was on other things. However, it is my intention to pursue possibly obtaining membership of that fascinating club.

In the meantime we were still progressing slowly down the Marylebone Road, in our Barouche carriage driven by an irate Aloysius. At length, he decided to turn off the busy Marylebone Road and instead negotiate his Barouche carriage down a less busier Harley Street. As we did so, the particular and mysterious house which dominates this junction came into view.

I remembered Lodge telling Jack and me about this house too, when we first came to London, especially its secrets and mysterious past. [3] He informed us that a careful study of the substantial four-storey town house, built of Portland stone, would reveal a peculiarity in its construction.

Immediately above the ground floor window frame arches, where the keystones were fitted, was a protuberance of stone resembling a balcony three feet in height and jutting out by about twenty inches. This regular undecorated projection girdled the building, creating an overhanging plinth upon which, so it appeared, the rest of the upper section of the building had been constructed. This protuberance, according to Lodge, contained a secret floor!

The building itself was a substantial four-storey town house built of Portland stone and occupied a site on the junction of Harley Street and the Marylebone Road and set in a clump of large forest trees partially concealing it. Running the length of the front and side façades of the building, were pilasters capped with flattened Ionic capitals that divided the deep set window reveals of stone into which glazed panels had been inserted.

Stone panelled spandrels, rich in Roman foliage relief decoration, were set in between the windows on the *piano-nobile* and on the second floor. The façades to the building were dominated by a substantial and richly decorated over-hanging deep architrave, supported by a series of pronounced and ornate recessed alternate deep

The House in Harley Street

consoles. Here they were used for corbelling which supported a detailed stepped cornice, above which was a stone balustrade fronting the attic at the top of the building.

The ground floor had two door entrances, and each comprised tall oak double doors, set in frames of stone, with intricately decorated corbels, supporting the entablatures, of ancient Greek design, above both sets of doors. The door frames built of stone, displayed peculiar design details upon them; especially on their upper sections above each door. The relief panels were of a later

417

fashion and not consistent with the overall design of the structure. At least from what I could determine from our Barouche carriage and in the fog.

We continued down Harley Street and eventually turned right into Devonshire Street. We had only driven down this street for a few minutes when a vision of a structure one would not expect to see in the center of the metropolis. The building in question was constructed on the junction of Devonshire Street and Devonshire Close and was built out of brick and three stories in height. We sat in our Barouche carriage transfixed at the sight of this building that the fog was powerless to shroud fully.

It was clearly a residential building, but rising up from the third floor, and forming the attic, was a tiled clad structure in the distinct shape of a pyramid with the fog swirling around it. The pyramid seemed totally out of place and menacing and yet strangely hypnotic, almost as if one were being drawn to its magnificence, making it difficult to ignore or disregard.

Two ornate Victorian cast iron fluted gas lamp posts, rising up from the street next to it, illuminated this pyramid and the fog in a pale yellow light. In so doing these Victorian gas lamp posts, gave an added credence to this eerie spectacle in the form of a pyramid structure, which dominated the house. And, as it were, conferred upon this peculiar building, as it were, acceptance of the pyramid's presence in a fog-bound Victorian street in the middle of London. Having recovered my wits from this unexpected vision, I spoke with Jack and Lodge as we continued along this deathly quiet canyon of a street lined, as it was, with ornate and elegant Victorian and Georgian town houses dressed in pale Portland stone.

I have noticed during our peregrinations abroad the

Devonshire Street Pyramid, London

metropolis, the English penchant for pyramids. The town house we had just driven passed here in Devonshire Street was a good example of this preference. I also remembered, the time when Jack and I were guests in the home of the murderous Doctor Crippen and his wife, Bella Elmore, who he subsequently done in. They lived in a large rambling house, near Hampstead Heath, the top of which was dominated by a pyramid forming the central roof structure.

In New York, I know of only two structures which

reflect pyramids in their design. One is the recently built Banker's Trust Company building on Wall Street, with its distinctive stepped pyramid crowning the tower. The other, is the Metropolitan Life Assurance Building on East 23rd. Street. A tower I have a fondness of since it is dressed in warm limestone which reflects the various hues of sun light throughout the seasons and weather conditions.

At length we crossed over the Marylebone High Street and turned into a street the nameplate of which was obscured due to the fog. As we travelled along, Lodge then pointed with his gold-capped ebony cane at another railed garden, in the center of which was a limestone mausoleum just visible in the swirling fog.

Our journey was slow, even with the impatient Aloysius at the reins of our Barouche carriage. Furthermore, I was beginning to feel the suffocating and claustrophobic aspects of this stultifying acrid fog. Looking at the mausoleum in the depths of the Marylebone Gardens did not inspire me to rise above my situation. Accordingly, I made my feelings known to Lodge.

"Why could we not have availed ourselves of an urban rail road train to this Marylebone Rail Road Station? After all, our hotel is located above the rail road tracks which lead to that station. At least according to Bradshaw's Railway Guide, or even our surly hotel concièrge's copy of Bäedeker's Guide to London. Why must we subject ourselves to this unpleasant and irritable accursed fog, when there is an easier means to gain our destination?" I said with asperity in my voice.

"Because, I do not travel by public conveyance; I am, after all, an impresario and not quite a fully paid up member of the *Undeserving Poor,*" replied Lodge.

Marylebone Gardens Mausoleum

In self-imposed silence, we continued over Baker Street and clattered along Crawford Street until we came to the junction of Gloucester Place over which we continued carefully. For it is to be remembered that the fog can very effectively mask the onward approach of a carriage or wagon. We had already nearly collided on two occasions with other carriages. Tentatively we crossed over Gloucester Place and continued making our way along Crawford Street.

I then became aware of the noise caused by the clattering hooves of several horses pulling a heavy lumbering pantechnicon coming up behind us. It caught my attention because the speed at which the horses seemed to be moving was odd given the area and the dense fog we were in. Aloysius reined his horses into Wyndham Place and just avoided being hit by the pantechnicon being driven recklessly.

Having pulled off this street, we found ourselves approaching quite an impressive classical building. Even with the fog swirling about we could make out the tall sandstone campanile of the bell tower, on top of which was a thoros completing the structure.

"That is the famous Church of St. Mary directly in front of us, Theo," Lodge offered, noticing my interest in the structure, "and it marks an exercise in Robert Smirke's successful attempt to create Neo-Classical architecture, albeit based on Bramante's colonnaded rotunda in Rome, not dissimilar to the rotunda of the church next to the Queen's Hall, that place of my undoing. However, having designed this church Smirke then went on to build an even bigger monumental Neo-Classical structure in Holborn." [4]

We passed along the roadway leading through the churchyard and emerged into York Street, over which we crossed and continued by the Royal Oak Public House, as we progressed into Circus Road.[5] Given our mission to the Abbey Grange and this claustrophobic fog unsettling me, I was all for abandoning our journey and instead repairing to this perfectly inviting bar with its whisky, rather than proceed in this fog or indeed to the Abbey Grange.

However, by the time I had formulated this alternative plan in my mind, Aloysius had driven our horses half way up the street. At length we came to the busy Marylebone Road again, even more lethal to cross, especially in the fog. Somehow, by sheer luck rather than judgment,

Aloysius negotiated our Barouche carriage across the road dodging a series of other carriages progressing along this busy thoroughfare. We gained the other side of the Marylebone Road and having travelled for a few moments along it, turned left into a roadway with a nameplate proclaiming it to be Great Central Street in which the Hotel Great Central was constructed.

We continued up this street and entered Melcombe Place, making our way to the ferro-vitreous ornate metal structure in the form of a port cochère under which, we entered Marylebone Rail Road Station. Given its name of Great Central Rail Road I expected a rather grand looking edifice to house the station. Instead the station appeared to be rather small and in no way reflective of its name, unlike say Grand Central Terminus in New York City. That Beaux-Art designed rail road building *is* very grand in every way.

In fact, the entrance to Marylebone Rail Road Station resembled very much, the arched portal to the Necropolis Rail Road Building in Waterloo we had, under Lodge insistence, walked through some weeks ago, to inspect no less, what was in effect, a functioning morgue!

Eventually we made the confines of the Marylebone Rail Road Station. Lodge immediately went off into an oak panelled booking office to obtain tickets for our journey. Jack and I fell into a discussion about just what we were going to do, locked down in the English countryside with Loge, who was passing in and out of lucidity at an all too frequent and alarming rate.

"Do we Theo, really want to be holed up with Loge in some secret house in the depths of the English countryside? What if he should turn on us in his mental state of anguish? Jeez, Theo, our being marooned in that place at the Abbott's range or whatever, could turn out

Necropolis Rail Road Building

to be another life threatening experience. It might well be similar to our being hotel guests of the murderous hotelier who ran the Castle Hotel on W. 63rd. Street in the Englewood neighborhood of Chicago. Eventually we learned that the proprietor had systematically murdered possibly more than two hundred of his hotel guests. And, did so whilst we were staying there!

"Having survived that ordeal we then we find ourselves staying overnight as guests at Hilldrop House, next to Hampstead Heath, a house run by another uncaring murderer, called Crippen. There in Hilldrop House he murdered, Bella Elmore, his wife, Music Hall artiste and one of Loge's *Three Graces!*

"Are we, I have to ask myself Theo, making the right decision in agreeing to accompany Loge in his mental state of mind to his destination at the Abbott's range or what, in the middle of nowhere, wherever that is? What if Theo, what if Loge were to lose that weak grip he has on reality and then go for us determinedly with some of the blunt medieval weapons which no doubt adorn such walls in those old houses? What if Loge, in defending his murderous intentions against us invokes divine inspiration in carrying out commands, in which he, and he alone, could hear voices in his head? Tell me Theo, tell me?" implored Jack.

That question was to remain unanswered, for at that very moment, Cinderella, armed with a white cotton lace parasol, came marching, in a determined manner, through the station hall, to where we were standing. Presently, Lodge rejoined us clutching three 1st. Class tickets, two of which he handed out to Jack and me, and a 3rd. Class ticket to Cinderella.

"Oh you are too kind sir," responded Cinderella, whilst dropping a shallow courtesy.

Lodge chose to ignore Cinderella's action; either that,

or he was oblivious to it. But moments later did venture an inquiry.

"I assumed you travelled here by carriage?" Lodge remarked vituperatively whilst looking at his gold Hunter,

"No," replied Cinderella, referring to her half-Hunter and tapping the glazed screen, "I travelled by the Metropolitan Rail Road to Baker Street then availed myself of the Baker Street & Waterloo Rail Road train en-route to the Edgware Road deep level station alighting at this Great Central Station en-route. And, I might add. I was able to do so, with ease, by consulting my updated Bradshaw's Railway Guide, without which one invites the usual pandaëmonium associated with travelling by a rail road train, that I know with certainty, you Theseus, have had much experience of."

Having gotten our tickets we made our way down to Platform 3 from which our train was scheduled to depart. When we arrived there, no train was waiting for us. I looked at Lodge for an explanation. He did not notice my staring at him because he was pre-occupied looking obliviously into the fog-laden aëther swirling above the platforms within the precinct of the station.

It was Cinderella who prodded me with her rolled up white cotton lace parasol, and then looked at Lodge.

"Who precisely is your friend upon whom we are going to imposed ourselves?" inquired Cinderella of Lodge.

"Sir Augustus Harris, replied Lodge.

"Who is he?" Jack asked facetiously.

"Sir Augustus is an impresario and manager of the Theater Royal in Drury Lane, in Covent Garden and has remained a dear and valued friend for many years. One might go as far as to say he was a mentor to me. I have received a lot of useful advice from him including…" answered Lodge.

"Such as what," interrupted Jack, "increasing box office receipts?"

Lodge refused to respond, but instead leaned on his gold capped ebony cane, and feigned some interest in a nearby poster extolling the virtues of patented rubber contraptions or some other such devices, rather than deal with Jack's indelicate inquiry.

Whilst we were still waiting on the platform for our train to Beaconsfield, I looked up the track and could just discern, though the fog, a green tender lamp heralding the approach of a train. A minute or so later, a locomotive pulling a train came into the station and made its way down the side of our platform hissing steam fiercely but eventually came to a juddering stop.

Suddenly the platform, upon which we were standing, was engulfed in a tide of passengers making their way down and who, judging by their attire, were rather well to do. Certainly they did not come from the realms of the *Undeserving Poor*, as Lodge may soon be doing. It was of course, Cinderella who informed us that the Great Central Rail Road, at least at its southern end, served the wealthier districts of Buckinghamshire, the county in which the Abbey Grange was located.

As the tide of passengers alighting from the train subsided, we in turn made our way in the other direction along the platform in search of a 1st. Class carriage. We found one, and made ourselves comfortable on the blue brocade covered seats, complemented by intricately designed, white cotton, antimacassar headrest coverings. Cinderella, disregarding her 3rd. Class ticket, joined us.

"Lodge will just have to pay the difference, despite his near penury status, if challenged by a guard," said Cinderella, smiling.

Our train was made up of carriages of the compartmentalized room type, which are not served by a corridor, making it unlikely that we would be disturbed or possibly incommoded by a guard, on our journey to Beaconsfield. For it had, of course, occurred to me, that every time we boarded a train of the urban rail road, we ended up enduring some sort of performance, not published in Bradshaw's Railway Guide usually involving rudeness or *determined behavior,* by others, including rail road staff upon the platform.

Minutes later our carriage received a severe jolt. But then, imperceptibly at first, our train began to glide down the side of the platform and into a brick canyon in which the permanent way is constrained as it made its way out of Marylebone Station and along the tracks of the Great Central Rail Road.

As the engine took on more steam, we could feel the train's increase in velocity, as it raced up the rail road track toward the Finchley Road Metropolitan Station, through which it blasted its way. The usual sideways rolling and rocking motion of the carriage attended our progress up the permanent way towards the next station, Harrow-on the-Hill.

It was Cinderella who pointed with her white cotton lace parasol at a partially assembled structure of steel girders rising above the misty fields to our left. It looked to me to be the beginning of a tower. Cinderella must have read my thoughts.

"That collection of steel girders rising into the aëther," she said, "is the beginning of a tower,[6] to rival in size and height that of the Eiffel Tower in Paris, France. It is the dream of Sir Edward Watkins, the Chairman of this Great Central Rail Road, along the tracks of which we are travelling."

"Why, why does this chairman of a rail road company wish to construct a metal tower to rival that of Eiffel's in Paris, France?" inquired Jack, looking at Lodge.

"Because Watkins thinks it will become a place of interest and attract the teeming masses that will have to use his Metropolitan Rail Road out of Baker Street Metropolitan Station to get there. One can only envy his ultimate success in generating profits, which would appear easier to achieve with rail road passengers than with the occasional visitor to a Music Hall.

"Hence the reason he wants to supersede the existing size and height of the Eiffel Tower, for who could blame him. They say that with this daring innovative venture he may well corner the international tourist market and encroach on Thomas Cook's monopoly. Well at least he does not have Nihilists, hecklers, revolutionaries or ungrateful audiences to contend with and who are set on my financial and moral destruction…" answered Lodge, looking with concentrated envy from his red rimmed and swollen eyes at the partially built tower rising from the mist covered fields.

He continued to look vacantly at the structure for some moments.

"Would that I ran a rail road;" he suddenly declared, "then truly I should indeed become master of the world!"

Jack looked at me with concentrated horror in his eyes. I too was beginning to harbor thoughts that Jack may well be correct in his assumption of Lodge's fragile state of mind and his tenuous grip on reality. Especially with the imminent prospect of our being locked up or isolated in a secluded mansion at the mercy of a deranged Lodge roaming around the place with selection of blunt medieval weapons at his disposal.

Our train continued past the steel structure that Lodge seemed unable to let go from his vision. Eventually we steamed into Harrow on the Hill. As the name suggests, Harrow is on a hill and consequently the fog had not quite gripped this outer metropolitan district. Visibility was therefore less impaired, though to view quite what, was debatable.

Having stopped for a few minutes, our train continued into the Chiltern Hills, which dominate this part of Buckinghamshire, bathed as it was in a subdued sun light, as we sped by in the comfort of our rail road carriage.

Lodge, I noticed, maintained a distracted look throughout the journey as though in deep thought. Our journey from Marylebone Rail Road Station to

Beaconsfield and onward to Chalfont St. Giles, situated as it is in the depths of the countryside, was thus far uneventful.

"Here we are Jack and Theo, England is not always in the grip of pervasive fog!" Cinderella said whilst gesticulating through the carriage window with her folded white cotton lace parasol at the fields and hedges clearly visible to us. We continued to steam through the Chiltern Hills and various towns. Eventually, the speed of the train began to lessen, as did the sound of the syncopation of the iron wheel clicking the steel rails below our carriage as we approached Beaconsfield.

Our journey had lasted just under an hour and it was exhilarating to be out of a fog-bound metropolis if only for a short while. A few minutes later we had alighted and were standing outside the rail road station looking around expectantly. There was no horse drawn carriage of any description to be seen. I turned around to light up a Trichinopoly cigar and found myself looking at yet another ubiquitous advertisement affixed to the station building.

Eventually a small wagonette came cantering along the lane towards the station. Considering Lodge was supposed to be in the depths of despair, he was remarkably agile in leaping out in to the carriageway to intercept this lone one horse drawn vehicle. Could it accommodate all five of us including the carriage driver, I wondered.

Presently, as a direct result of Lodge's robust intervention, the carriage stopped just along the way from where we were standing. We all of us walked over to it and joined Lodge. To my astonishment he had already spoken with the driver and bade us to get into the carriage. The carriage was of a type, I believe, they called

CURE OF DISEASE
WITHOUT DRUGS OR MEDICINE

With the patented Airtight Dry Cell Pocket Battery, which furnishes 4000 Electro-Magnetic Vibrations Per Minute. ARE you afflicted with either Partial or Total Deafness?

Or

Catarrh, or Catarrhal Deafness, Rheumatism, Neuralgia, Lumbago, Gout, Nervous Debility,

Or

Any other Disease, from any cause or of any Length of Standing!

Then apply

DR HUBER'S ELECTRO-MAGNETIC DRY CELL POCKET MEDICAL BATTERY SUPPLIED WITH CONDUCTING CABLES, ARMATURES TO FIT ANY PART OF THE BODY OR LIMBS AND ADJUSTABLE EAR & NASAL ELECTRODES

The Battery and different Appliances can be used by all the members of an entire family for various ailments.

Trial of Batteries and Appliances and Electrodes **FREE** at our office at THE DR. HUBER'S DRY CELL POCKET MEDICAL BATTERY CO.

35 Tottenham Court Road,
(3rd Floor above Windmill Street entrance)
London, W

in this country, a Horse and Trap, a kind of dog cart, or carriage of sorts drawn by a single horse.

"The Abbey Grange at Chalfont," Lodge repeated his instruction to the driver. Then with a look of total despair upon his face he turned to Jack and continued.

"What with me having to make do with this dog cart, I already feel impoverished and inescapably becoming transmogrified bit by bit into a dysfunctioning member of the *Undeserving Poor.*"

Needless to say, it was all we could do to help Lodge in to the dog cart. Feeling rather cramped we made our way along a short country road on the outskirts of the town and eventually came to a set of gates at the foot of a drive. The gates were slightly ajar, but incapable of being opened further due an encumbrance occasioned by neglect and rust.

Consequently, we dismissed our wagonette or dog cart, and walked up the stone strewn driveway, punctuated with pot holes, leading to the house. On either side of the drive was wild scrubland land shrouded in a light mist that created a subdued light that pervaded the grounds with dullness. The fog hovering above the gardens was, if anything worse and probably due to the pervasive dampness of the ground surrounding the mansion.

As usual, there was the attendant dankness that always seems to be present where a garden is unkempt and allowed revert to its natural wildness. We continued to make our way up the stony drive that itself was in a state of disrepair and flanked with high evergreen shrubs and trees, some of which looked withered, a few leafless and others looked sick and in need of pruning or severe curtailment.

We proceeded slowly up the drive and then we saw it. We could now see a large ranging building in the middle distance with its size and presence outlined in the fog

The Abbey Grange

that was attempting to shroud it. The mansion was a large, rambling, somewhat forlorn-looking building that had more of a sinister aspect to it than a welcoming one, especially given the minatory look about it.

The drive abruptly curved left, on to a flight of four steps, and then to the right and over a small arched bridge, built of brick, that spanned a dark stagnant brook. The drive continued until it terminated abruptly in front of the house immediately opposite a flight of steps leading up to the front door of the mansion.

"This is place looks not only deserted, but abandoned," said Jack to Cinderella.

"And that is not the only odd thing. Look at the drive. It is not a carriageway built for carriages! It was built for walking upon and walking only. That in itself would prevent any carriage approaching this house; or should I say fortress?" replied Cinderella.

"The Abbey Grange, looks to me as though it had been designed to deter visitors or the inquisitive, from what I can see," said Jack, looking up at the substantial mansion house.

"Well, we are the only visitors to this house of late," said Cinderella, pointing to the ground with her white cotton lace parasol, "because there are no foot prints on the wet gravel surface!"

Apart from the features of a carriage-less carriageway and a presentiment of the place being abandoned, the rest of the mansion displayed clearly symptoms of neglect. The red brick, of which the building was constructed, showed signs of profound damp penetration causing areas of the brickwork to become green. This had in turn caused purple fungi to colonize and present a growth that was creeping around the building. Also, the façade of the building appeared to be crumbling away in places.

The mansion was of indeterminate architecture, but reflected a Neo-Gothic style reminiscent of the mid Victorian era, with Jacobean rectilinear windows, most of which were dark, grimy and framed in a timber reveal that also was splintering and deteriorating with evident dry rot.

Continuing in the Neo-Gothic vane, the house comprised three storeys and was, at an earlier stage of its existence, quite a handsome building, reflecting Jacobean influences. It was four square and the façades were built of soft red brickwork with sandstone corner dressing and horizontal banding. The building was buttressed by two towers at either side of the front of the house. One tower, was tall and slender with four crenellated gable ends forming the upper section rising up to a open belfry canopy. The other tower, though only three storeys in height, was more substantial in structure with a flat roof surrounded by a balustraded stone fence forming an ornate parapet wall.

As we approached the steps leading up to the front door of the house it was Cinderella who summed up the prevalent feeling coursing through my mind; and knowing Jack's, his too.

"We none of us have gotten into the house yet," said Cinderella, "and already, I guess, we all feel a presentiment of foreboding. I know I certainly do!"

It was Lodge who led us up the flight of steps to the front door of the Abbey Grange. It was Jack though who knocked loudly on the oak door leading into the mansion. An age seemed to go by waiting for our summons to be answered. This reminded me of waiting outside Lodge's house in the Bergen Avenue, and also outside Madame Duse's villa in St. John's Wood. On both occasions we were kept waiting for some considerable time. I suppose one could expect the same here.

My expectation proved to be correct; for it was only after a full eight minutes that at last our knocking on the door was finally answered! It was a further three more minutes, after listening to the noises of several latches being released and bolts drawn back, that eventually the oak door finally creaked open, but only partially. We all of us peered into the darkened recess from which a face of gaunt magnitude returned our inquisitive searching.

"Ah Christie," said Lodge, addressing the man-servant, "we have arrived."

The man-servant looked bewildered and surprised at seeing the four of us standing on the door threshold.

"Mr. Loge is it sir?" he asked, looking intently at Lodge, as if he were uncertain as to who Lodge was.

"Yes, it is me - Lodge," replied Lodge, correcting the man-servant's mispronunciation of his surname and with evident asperity in his voice.

"Oh very well," the man-servant responded, giving us all a searching glance, "I supposed you had all best come in then."

We stepped through the door opening and into the hallway. The man-servant, probably a near relative of Aloysius, Lodge's surly man-servant at Bergen Avenue, beckoned us to follow him down a dark, musty smelling corridor leading into the main domain of the house. Indeed, the aëther in the mansion was dank and stale with odors laced with the smell of decay.

We followed Christie the man-servant, down a corridor with bare timber floorboards with neither paintings nor mirrors to adorn the walls. The presence of several doors cut into the corridor walls, indicated the existence of chambers or rooms behind them.

Following Christie, we continued to walk down the corridor and on reaching one such door, he turned the brass fluted handle and opened it. He then motioned us to enter the room, which we did.

"I will go and fetch the master and he will join you shortly," the man-servant advised us, before closing the door and abandoning us in the room. Lodge appeared more distracted than he had previously been and simply stood there, leaning on his gold capped black ebony cane. We found ourselves in a large chamber with a wide bay window, to which I instinctively walked and looked out from it into the garden below, still shrouded in clammy fog which swirled around in vortices.

"Is this it; have we left the stifling acrid London fog to find ourselves here in this Gothic wreck? Are we going to be actually holed up here Loge, in this decaying pile, this decrepit mansion house, a building which is crumbling apart in slow motion, in order to enable you to recover your dignity and self esteem?" asked Jack, whilst sitting down on a battered Chippendale chair that creaked the moment he did so.

"I think so," answered Lodge, "for I simply cannot think of a better place in which to recover than here at the Abbey Grange, far away from the turbulent world of Music Hall derision and gossip about our concert last night. Together with cynical aspersions being made by my enemies about our sincere endeavors to release my generosity unreservedly for a worthy and noble cause, would you not agree Jack?"

Jack was not having it, and tried to persuade Cinderella to support him in informing Lodge of his dissatisfaction of finding himself holed up in a damp Gothic hovel in the middle of nowhere with a strange, suspect butler roaming about the place.

Jack was not at all happy with our predicament. I contented myself with taking in the appointments of the room in which we were waiting, in an attempt to find some saving grace at our being here.

The room itself was shabby and comprised various pieces of furniture which had seen better days. On one wall of the room, separating long windows were full-length green velvet curtains, which had frayed and were faded on the folds. That the room had once been a library was evident by the empty shelves built into a wall, in order to bear a considerable weight of knowledge. The walls of the room were greyish, probably with age rather than by decorative choice. Strangely enough they showed no signs of ever having been adorned with paintings.

No carpet lay on the floor revealing badly set elm floorboards which had warped due to the pervasive dampness in the building. The fireplace surround had been ripped out, but probably would have been an ornate marble structure in keeping with mid Victorian mansion houses, of which the Abbey Grange had once been a good example.

The plaster ceiling was plain and undecorated and supported only one glass chandelier, from which dust sprinkled down rather than glittering illumination. Placed in the middle of the room, was a red damask covered sofa with an evident layer of dust that had congealed on the cloth, due the dampness in the upholstery, creating a scaled patina effect. In fact, the smell of decay, prevalent outside in the damp grounds, had now penetrated the interior of the house.

In one corner of the room, I noticed a large polished elm bureau, an escritoire, in the style of Salon Francais and decorated with gilded fluted Corinthian columns to each corner. This was the only concession to opulence in an otherwise austere room. On approaching the escritoire, I observed that it had numerous miniature brass handles, indicating it contained several drawers filled with curiosities. I wondered what casquets of visual gems might be found within them. I was sorely tempted to open one, but at the very moment of doing so, voices could be heard outside in the hallway, loud voices. I desisted from my investigation and instead looked expectantly at the library door.

The voices became louder and presently the door of the library swung open and in stepped Christie who held it open. Moments later he was followed by a tall distinguished looking gentleman who beamed out a wide smile from his ruddy face.

It was Cinderella who re-acted to the invasion of our library by this person.

"You incorrigible sybarite," she screamed, whilst rushing up to embrace him, "so this is where you secret yourself for days at a time leaving the rest of us in the metropolis in despair at your absence!"

"And how is our incomparable Cinderella?" he inquired.

After the two had exchange pleasantries, the sybarite turned to Lodge.

"Marie Lloyd not with you?" he asked, "I naturally assumed you would be bringing her with you. Still it is always a delight to see Cindy here"

"Marie Lloyd is otherwise engaged," answered Lodge.

Jack and I needed no introduction to this gentleman, but Lodge formally made one.

"May I introduce Jack Mitchell and Theodore Houston, both Vaudeville artistes out of New York? Gentlemen, this is Sir Augustus Harris, the esteemed general manager of the Theater Royal in Drury Lane at Covent Garden," said Lodge, rubbing his hands in a sycophantic fashion.

We both of us shook hands with the eminent impresario.

"I recall seeing you at Bella Elmore's Wake of Remembrance back stage at the Vaudeville Music Hall some weeks back, Sir Augustus," said Jack.

"Jack, Theo and you too Lodge, you are my guests," responded Sir Augustus, "please do not call me Sir Augustus; my name is Gus and that will do very well. Now, why the deuce did Christie ask you to wait in this miserable room, since we are about to have it and this part of the mansion comprehensively redecorated? No matter, but please, follow me."

We did so and abandoned the musty library and its mysterious escritoire.

Cinderella and Gus led the way laughing loudly, with

Jack and I following with Christie and Lodge brought up the rear. We proceeded down one corridor and along another.

"A more jovial a character would be hard to imagine," I said to Jack, as we turned into a gallery of such monumental proportions, as to come as a total surprise.

Walking through this gallery, I was struck immediately by a fact born of experience of other large houses. Most of those mansions had several things in common; art was dripping off the walls and uncut books were bought and displayed by the yard in libraries, together with paintings, purchased as if to hide stains upon the silk-flocked wall paper which adorned the walls.

Such places were full of symbolism and allegorical meaning, which were reënforced in the fact of art being displayed, to the point of defeating, obviously, the original concept. This one fact showed me that many successful people have but little sense of art for its own sake. As indeed Eleonora Duse had remarked when we visited her recently. Rather, it is apparent that they have been advised on how to convert success into a tangible acquisition of beauty, usually as a mark of their having arrived. The question is, arrived from what, poverty or a life without privilege?

Not so with Gus here in the Abbey Grange; he knew his art. Within his collection alone we had walked past works by Atkinson Grimshaw, Thomas Cole, Sir John Millais and Sickert. However, one drawing alone caught my attention. It was a fine ink drawing of a vision of a group of classical structures called *Classical Perspective*.

As we progressed through another gallery, we came across something I wished were in my possession. It was a bronze figurine of an angel about eighteen inches in height and set on a carved circular plinth made from a

Classical Perspective

442

peculiarly deep red *Rosso Laguna* marble. The wings, though metallic, looked as if they were made of the finest iridescent wings of a butterfly. A plaque attached to the marble base proclaimed the sculpture to be the '*Love of the Angel,*' but in fact made no reference to its creator, who possibly may have been Auguste Rodin.

At length we followed Gus and Cinderella into a ferro-vitreous [7] constructed conservatory. We all of us, including Lodge, looked about us in awe as though lost children entering paradise. But the immediate effect of entering the place was a choking re-action to the dense and very humid aëther, laden with a bewildering variety of scent and pollen. For housed within this complex metal and glass structure was one of the finest collections of orchids of every type and color, and certainly made for a spectacular display amid the multitude of plants, foliage and flowers in this man-made Eden on earth.

On leaving the conservatory, our nostrils were assailed by yet another all-pervasive ubiquitous and distinctive smell; that of beeswax, impressed into every item of furniture and into the timber floorboards of the gallery we had just walked in to. Making our way along this elegant gallery, we were treated to a further ostentatious display of wealth, in the form of even larger works of art, adorning the walls.

"It must be fascinating to own all this art and to be able to appreciate its beauty as one sees it on an almost daily basis," confided Jack, pointing with his cane to one painting in particular on the wall.

Needless to say the oil painting on the wall that we were looking at was without doubt, an authentic Staunton '*Special.*' [8]

"I know of several metropolitan art galleries, which would part with a substantial sum of money to acquire even half of what Gus has ranged around his mansion here," continued Jack.

"They probably could, and with a substantially lesser sum of money," I replied, "were they to resort to Kleinmann's Picture Emporium in 35th. Street near the Waldorf-Astoria Hotel back home in New York!"

Whilst discussing our visual experiences, we were walking down a particular ornately decorated corridor. At the end of this opulent gallery was a huge oriel stained-glass window that trained a myriad of subdued colors onto the highly beeswaxed polished floorboards. Presently we turned from the gallery that led into a hallway, from which a grand staircase ascended up from the *piano-nobile* and into the upper floors of the mansion.

Dominating this staircase was a large oil painting of a society beauty, in mediaeval garment. Inscribed on the brass plate on the ornate gilt frame were the words, '*Astarte Syriaca.*' [9] On the flank wall of the staircase was an even larger painting by Claude Lorrain entitled, '*Landscape with Psyche and the Palace of Amor.*'

Eventually, Gus led us down another corridor decorated in pink and cream Regency striped wallpaper, at the end of which was a highly varnished mahogany door with brass fittings. Christie opened the door and Gus ushered us into the room. As I entered I immediately took an intake of breath. I could not believe my eyes. Ranged above this huge, spacious room was a highly decorated white plaster ceiling with patterns in the form of raised filigree relief. The ceiling continued down to the walls to form an extensive highly decorated architrave with overhanging ledges.

Proceeding to floor level were four walls forming the room, all of which were lined with red velvet, silk flocked wallpaper, with a matching full-size broadloom scarlet silk carpet. Against the walls were fitted dado high glass-fronted bookcases, upon which were placed white *Carrara* marble figurines from classical antiquity. The whole effect was to create in this, what we though to be moribund dormant mansion on first arriving, a drawing room of resplendent and lush exquisiteness, together with flamboyant décor and design extravagance at every turn.

However, it was not the appointments of the room's plush and voluptuous interior design that arrested my attention, nor the fact of its unbridled opulent luxury or even the refined beauty of the proportional elegance of the room. What focused my gaze were several paintings hanging on the silk-flocked wallpaper covered walls! I do not claim to be an art aficionado, but my dealings with art galleries, both legitimate and those not so, had given me an insight that certainly assisted me in my immediate appreciation of works of art.

I recognized instantly several paintings by Atkinson Grimshaw ranged around the huge drawing room in which they were hanging. There was the melancholy glory that is called, *'Autumnal Regrets'* reflecting in red and gold colors the sadness that can be present in an autumnal scene during the Fall. Grimshaw's exploration of sadness in color as represented in pale yellow and gold interspersed with pink due to a light fog, was captured to great effect in his painting of, *'Knostrop Hall, Early Morning.'*

In addition there were his characteristic paintings of huge stone built mansion houses with distinct gable ends and bay windows, from which lights blazed out, onto a darkened or autumnal landscape.

Usually these mansion houses, like the one typical in his painting, *'Golden Light'*, were set behind stone walls, adding more speculation to their mystery and melancholic romanticism, as expressed in another painting called, *'Sixty Years Ago.'* But, set in its isolated splendor was the one painting that I had taken a fancy to, whilst visiting Kleinmann's Picture Emporium in 35th. Street in New York some months ago.

He then offered to *'procure'* one for me. I declined, but later regretted not taking him up on his blatant offer. Admiring this one, original or a copy, only reinforced very much that regrettable decision I made. The painting in question of was course the, *'The Deserted House,'* and made even more famous by the lines in Alfred Lord Tennyson's lamented ode.

> *All within is dark as night:*
> *In the windows is no light;*
> *And no murmur at the door,*
> *So frequent on its hinge before.*

Atkinson Grimshaw captured very effectively the aspect of the house being deserted, not by the absence of people in the painting, but rather by the building's presentation. It looked forlorn, and being set in dank and overgrown autumnal grounds augmented very persuasively the look of dilapidation and neglect. It was these aspects, which suggested that the house *was,* in fact deserted.

So at least, I remember Kleinmann telling me! Looking more closely at the painting it was easy to imagine Atkinson Grimshaw using this Abbey Grange as the inspiration for his *'Deserted House'*, given that the similarities were evident in both. My respect for Augustus's taste in art was increasing almost by the minute.

It then occurred to me that Gus owned this mansion,

The Acropolis

the Abbey Grange, which was of the very same kind as those atmospheric, melancholic and brooding houses depicted in the paintings by Atkinson Grimshaw, including the one we were then in. I could well understand Gus. Did he, I wondered, choose Atkinson's style of painting because of the style of mansion house he inhabited, or choose his house because of Atkinson's paintings, of which he remained clearly an admirer?

Another gilt frame displayed a very beautiful and detailed drawing entitled, *'The Acropolis.'* The drawing combined images of the ethereal elegance and glory of the re-constructed temples, which comprised the Acropolis in Athens, into one perspective vision. This masterpiece alas, was unsigned by its skilful creator, making me even more curious.

As we all looked about the drawing room my eyes rested on two paintings almost hidden in an alcove. Again, both were recognizable as works from the Hudson River School,[10] of which Jack and I are familiar; being New Yorkers, and interpreted by a fellow called

Thomas Cole, so his signature on the canvasses informed me.

In one painting he called '*The Architect's Dream,*' Cole painted an array of classical structures all ranged together in an impossible, but ethereal scene. The painting depicted a scene of classical temples, such as the Parthenon and part of the Erechtheion, constructed at the Acropolis. As were columns, arches, colonnades, porticoes, viaduct, architrave, ancient Egyptian entrance pylons, hypostyle halls, sphinxes and obelisks all subject to the dominating splendor of a huge pyramid in the background. His other masterpiece is in fact a series of paintings called '*The Course of Empire*' of which the, '*Consummation of Empire*' is the penultimate.

In this painting, Thomas Cole depicted an ethereal scene of classical structures in which people are seen enjoying prosperity and contentment. It was however, Cole's skill in drawing people in the background, which was so endearing and attractive. They appeared minuscule in comparison to the buildings they inhabited. They were shown generally enjoying themselves on and around the buildings, including those lying down on the various roofs of temples disporting themselves in the sun light! I was fascinated to note the date of this canvass as being 1844.

"Sir Augustus is quite the connoisseur of art," I remarked to Lodge, who made no reply, but instead wore a vacant expression upon his tired face.

"Excuse me Cinderella, gentleman," said Gus, "I just need to attend to something. Please do help yourselves to drinks from the cabinet over there."

Moments later he left the room. Jack in the meantime had moved quickly to the drinks cabinet, generously laden with bottle of every type of elixir and proceeded to take orders from us.

Fonthill Abbey

"This place reminds me of Fonthill Abbey," said Cinderella, "another rambling Gothic mansion house, where a few of us performed in a Christmas pantomime, based on Wagner's opera, *'Die Feen'*, for some deranged, but wealthy, megalomaniac. This mansion, the Abbey Grange, from what we have seen, is nowhere near the pure fantastic almost stupefying proportions of Fonthill Abbey.

"My first experience of Fonthill Abbey, and its imposing presence, was on a tempestuous and windy late November evening with clouds racing by in the sky. On approaching that huge structure, one instinctively felt a menacing aspect, almost a presentiment; and yet at the same time, an exhilaration. The place looked more like a foreboding scene out of Wagner's grand opera, '*Götterdämmerung,*' than a country mansion.

"That aspect in itself was ironic, because I distinctly remember my initial feelings about the place in regard to my particular rôle in the pantomime we were to perform at Fonthill that evening. I was to play one of the fairies; and my pivotal song in the pantomime was called, '*Abendlich,*' which of course means, evening light. However the lyrics of, '*Abendlich,*' in my mind, together with the visual spectre of Fonthill Abbey, looming up in the twilight of the evening, made for very surreal experience.

> *'Abendlich dämmern deckt den Himmel*
> *Heller leuchter die hütende Lohe herauf*
> *Was lecht so wund*
> *Die lodernde Welle zum Wall*
> *Zur Felsenspitze waltz der feurige Schwall,'* 11

"Apart from the pantomime, the massive building was a fusion of architectural motifs; complete with crocketted pinnacles, crenellated gable ends, steeply pitched roofs, and raised detailed tracery designs on exterior wall surfaces. Dominating the Abbey below and at least three hundred feet in height, was a huge octagonal Gothic tower reaching up into the reddening evening sky. I for one was moved by this experience of the pure exhuberance of wild Romanticism.

"The description I had been furnished with previously, before arriving there, certainly did not do justice to the place. In fact, it had wildly understated the spectacle of this building and its vicinity, including the fact that a twelve-foot high perimeter stone wall eight miles in length enclosed the Abbey! Everything about Fonthill Abbey was built on a monumental scale.

"Including the fact that the whole building was constructed to the size and dimensions of a full-sized Cathedral, stretched to terrifying proportions, in order to achieve the creator's unbriddled Gothic fantasy. Ironically, its creator was another megalomaniac, in the person of William Beckford, who in his day was probably the richest man in the known world!" said Cinderella, accepting a large glass of whisky from Jack and responding by offering her red tooled leather cigar case to us.

"And so it was," continued Cinderella, "that we performed our pantomime based on Wagner's opera, *'Die Feen,'* on a dark tempestuous November evening in that rambling Gothic structure filled with shadows. But, if you think that being at Fonthill 12 was a surreal experience in itself; you should have witnessed what we did to Wagner's melodramatic opera, *'Die Feen!'*"

"Do tell us about it Cinderella," invited Jack, "I could do with some unadulterated humor now that we are holed up in this Gothic pile."

"'Die Feen - eine Grosse Romantische Oper,' 13 to call it by its proper name, is grand opera in the romantic idiom and an early opera by Wagner. The first act revolves around a group of fairies, notably Zemina and Farzana, who with other fairies, are amusing themselves in a fairy garden. They do so, whilst at the same time, are discussing their mistress Ada. She is only a half-fairy, but in order to spend the rest of her life with Arindal, a mortal, whom she loves, has irrevocably renounced her immortality.

"One can already hear echoes of doom-laden and

forsaken love in Wagner's later operas as yet unwritten, especially, 'Götterdämmerung and Tristan und Isolde or even Parsifal! So far so good, but the plot becomes convoluted when the Fairy King sets a stringent condition on Ada, which Farzana and Arindal know cannot be fulfilled, even with the help of Groma, a magician. Never the less, the other fairies and spirits all pledge to try and separate Ada, the half-fairy, from Arindal.

"Which is just as well, because in the second act we find ourselves in the Fairy King's palace; out in the fairy garden with Ada singing. She sings of her love and of the fact that she is prepared to renounce her immortality as the price to win Arindal. Moments later Arindal arrives and he too declares his love for Ada again. Ada then changes her mind, for some inexplicable reason, and declares, in an extended songspiel, that Arindal will abandon her on the following day!

"One can imagine readily the potential for misunderstanding degenerating in to farce, was too much. So we decided to re-write Wagner's libretto and incorporate some dignity and seriousness when putting together the pantomime.

"Now you can see why, with a plot like that, we decided to turn it into a pantomime. Otherwise it simply would have become something approaching a series of doom-laden unrequited love scenarios and prolonged agonizing regret of amaranthine proportion!" concluded Cinderella.

"I can appreciate fully what you are saying Cinderella," responded Jack, "because when I attended the Julliard School of Music back in Morningside, New York City, we had lessons in counterpoint and Wagner. Especially in exploring Wagner's use of counterpoint – in emphasizing by contrast a music or tonal idea played against another, as we might find often in his early operas.

We were also fully aware of Wagner's ability to place himself on top of a pedestal from which, of course, it is easy to fall off.

"I am minded of his first opera, with the grandiose title of *'Das Liebesverbot' - eine große komische Oper*,' [14] that we analysed. What I did not know, reading the program notes, was the amusing history behind this seemingly innocuous opera, an early one, by Wagner. Why he had chosen to construct this particular libretto for the basis of his opera must remain an enigma.

"That Wagner conducted the première in 1836 is not in doubt, what was in doubt was the lead singer's ability to remember her lines, which she forgot, and had to improvise – in front of Wagner! The opera, not surprisingly, was a resounding failure. Its second performance fared no better, and had to be cancelled even before the purple velvet safety curtain went up, as a result of a major brawl backstage between the lead tenor Ignaz Freimüller and the prima donna, Karoline Pollert's husband, clearly besotted with her.

"When the opera eventually began, only three people made up the entire audience! Needless to say, the creator of such later powerful works as, *'Der Ring des Nibelungen,'* and the sacred music dramas of, *'Parsifal'* or *'Lohengrin,'* never witnessed that opera in his lifetime again— presumably thankfully, since it's potential for failure may be found in its very pretentious title, *'Das Liebesverbot' - eine große komische Oper*'!" completed Jack.

Having gotten our drinks we made ourselves comfortable on various moiré silk upholstered sofas ranged around the room. We drew contentedly on our Trichinopoly cigars. At length it was Jack who broached the subject whilst looking at Lodge.

"What are the goods on this Gus, our host?" Jack asked.

"Good question," answered Cinderella, who fielded the inquiry. "Sir Augustus Harris,[15] the impresario to end all impresarios, was born in Paris, but spent his childhood in London. He first came to prominence with his farcical play called, *'The Pink Dominos,'* performed at the Criterion Theater in Piccadilly with Charles Wyndham and Fanny Josephs playing leading rôles. This was the same Wyndham who set up Wyndham's Theater in the Charing Cross Road, near Leicester Square opposite the Alhambra Music Hall.

"From 1879 he became the manager at the Theater Royal in Drury Lane at Covent Garden. There he promoted the rise of pantomime remorselessly; indeed he remains a very enthusiastic supporter. His Christmas specials became legendary involving a cast of famous Music Hall artistes, such as Marie Lloyd, Herbert Campbell, Dan Leno, Jean de Reszke, Nellie Melba, Harry Nicholls and the two Emmas – Calvé and Eames. As a result Gus is often referred to as the, *'Father of Modern Pantomime,'* or simply, *'Augustus Druriolanus!'* Indeed the rise of the pantomime has reached its apotheosis in him," finished Cinderella.

"What, they gave him a knighthood for putting on a few farcical shows or pantomimes, as you call them here?" said Jack.

"No," replied Cinderella, "they gave him a knighthood because of his involvement in practical metropolitan politics; [16] that, or because of his being the chairman of the renowned Eccentric Club. A gentlemen's' club, no less, in May's Building in the St. Martin's Lane which leads into Charing Cross and is able to counts amongst its membership such august persons as, the actor-manager Sir George Alexander, theater impresario Sir Walter de Frece and Sir Gerald De Maurier, another actor-manager.

"In addition there are Sir Edward Seymour Hicks the famed Music Hall performer, George Robey, the *Prime Minister of Mirth*, Lord Birkenhead the hard drinking statesmen, Sir Herbert Tree, manager of the Haymarket Theater who founded, eight years ago our Royal Academy of Dramatic Art. And of course Dan Leno is a prominent member. But interestingly, Sir Henry Wood, the conductor, who was engaged by our good friend Robert Newman, the manager of the Queen's Hall, to introduce an innovative event they cautiously term the *Promenade Concerts,* is an esteemed member," advised Cinderella.

"Is that the same Henry Wood who declined the offer of chief conductor for both the New York Philharmonic and Boston Symphony orchestras?" inquired Jack.

"It most certainly is Jack," replied Cinderella.

"This club, this gentlemen's club, the Eccentric sounds as though it might be worthwhile visiting," I said, "because it conjures up aspects of that club [17] we visited contained within one of the iron vaults, upon which the Marylebone Road is constructed."

"Previously," continued Cinderella, "from 1781 until 1846 the number of members reached upwards of four thousand including Richard Brinsley Sheridan the manager of the Theater Royal in Drury Lane, Gus' predecessor, Charles James Fox, the politician and Lord Brougham, famous for something you ought to be familiar with."

Jack and I looked at each other and shrugged our shoulders.

"Brougham holds the record for speaking non-stop for over six hours in parliament!" said Cinderella.

"Really Cinderella," said Jack, "you will be telling us next that this earl, this Lord Brougham invented the Brougham carriage or at least gave his name to it," said Jack.

"Well actually Jack, he did!" replied Cinderella.

1. Marmeduke the ventriloquist's dummy had uttered these words to Cinderella and Theo at Bella's Wake of Remembrance.
2. For a fascinating account of the Dumb Mute refer to novel, Royal Aq – Queen of Music Halls Chapter 21
3. For a fascinating account of this house refer to novel The Iron Mausoleum - A case of Sherlock Holmes and the Titanic, chap 19
4. Sir Robert Smirke went on to create the British Museum as the apotheosis of neo Classical architecture in London.
5. Now Enford Street.
6. The equivalent of the Eiffel Tower in London was started in 1907 on what is now Wembley Stadium
7. Iron and glass structure
8. A particularly outstanding fake
9. Phoenician goddess of love
10. Art movement in America.
11. Evening twilight veils the sky
    Brighter blazes the guardian fire
    Why does the blazing wall of flame
    Flare up with such fury
    As seething fire surges to the summit
12. For a fascinating account of Fonthill Abbey refer to novel, The Iron Vault Chapter 6
13. The Fairies – A Great Romantic Opera
14. The Ban on Love - A Great Comic Opera.
15. 1852 - 1896
16. He was Sheriff of London
17. For a fascinating account of this club refer to novel, The Iron Soul - A case of Sherlock Holmes and the Napoleon of Crime, Chapter 3

Chapter 28

The Polemical Discourse

Following Lodge' catastrophic failure of his speculative Titanic Benefit Concert; some people were soon saying it was a disaster equal in magnitude to the actual sinking of the ill-fated *Titanic* itself. However described, the débâcle, for that is what it was, from all accounts, has severely shaken Lodge to the core. In an attempt to recover his self-esteem and dignity, we are staying, as guests of Sir Augustus Harris, at the Abbey Grange, his rambling Gothic mansion in the depths of the English countryside.

The drawing room door opened and in stepped Gus.

"My friends, luncheon is served," he said.

We all of us drained our glasses, which we had just refilled and then followed Gus through another series of corridors which penetrated farther into the mansion. The dining room, when we eventually reached it, was well appointed and decorated in the Regency style. This was at variance with the mansion's general Neo-Gothic mode of architecture, including quatre-foil stone window reveals and crennelated arched timber door frames and decorated in the Victorian style. But this room was decorated in typical Regency pink and cream colored striped wallpaper, which made for a refreshing change from the Victorian purple, red or green heavy flocked silk wallpaper that was pervasive elsewhere.

On the walls were gilt frames bearing drawing of buildings. Some were of theaters, in particular the Schauspielhaus in Berlin and also one of the Theater Royal in Drury Lane, of which, as we were told by Cinderella earlier, Gus is the esteemed general manager.

Though the Schauspielhaus Theater in Berlin, with clear geometric lines, represents the apotheosis of classical buildings constructed in the early part of the nineteenth century, it reminded me of the other architectural line drawings we had seen earlier whilst taking our drinks in the drawing room. In particular, I think, the Parthenon temple at the Acropolis on which the Schauspielhaus Theater, is evidently based.

Another very beautiful and detailed drawing caught my attention, because I had seen it in Lodge's town house in the Bergen Avenue. Lodge too was studying the drawing, which from memory was called '*Visions of Architecture.*'

As the name suggested, the drawing comprised a representation of exquisitely drawn elegant classical buildings and other structures from antiquity and was clearly created with affection and skill. And as with the drawing at Lodge's house it was unsigned, which imbued it with an aura of mystery to the talented creator of the image. It occurred to me that possibly, both Lodge and Gus were the proud possessors of prints of the original drawing.

Looking for the second time at this drawing called "*Visions of Architecture,*' adorning the dining room wall in Gus's mansion, it seemed to radiate a remarkable beauty which emanated from its creator's patience and detailed execution of perspective vision. The drawing combined an ethereal elegance with serenity interpreted as a perspective of an idealized vision of several classical buildings from antiquity.

Visions of Architecture

"It is the eclectic perspective of the various buildings represented by the complex lines which together create such an ethereal beauty in the detail that no other medium is able to express quite so succinctly. Would you not agree?" I asked Cinderella, who too was entranced by the image, set in its gilt frame.

"The fascination is in the sharp details which together comprise this drawing of classical buildings, represented in this ostensible vision of architecture. The overall effect, of this panoramic view of several monumental classical structures, is one of intense concentration. That, and the ability to create an image, composed of several buildings, with evident affection, together with a deep love for the construction of beauty expressed in masonry," responded Cinderella.

"Do you mind my asking," said Lodge, turning away from the drawing and addressing Gus, "what did you pay for this drawing?"

"No, I do not mind you asking," replied Gus.

"Well, what did you pay for your drawing?" continued Lodge.

"Nothing," said Gus, "it was a present."

We all of us sat down on Chippendale chairs, the seats of which were upholstered in red and cream striped moiré silk. We pulled them up to the large oval dining table made of walnut with a highly polished surface, upon which the highly polished silverware had been laid out.

We helped ourselves to wine, several bottles of which were placed strategically in the middle of the table and, within easy reach of everyone. In the meantime, Christie, the man-servant, was limbering up with the soup tureen. At length he plunged a ladle into it. He then looked over his shoulder furtively at the assembled diners seated around the dining room table.

"You have a very interesting house in the Abbey Grange Gus, complete with an enviable art collection. Have you lived here long?" inquired Jack.

"I bought the place about six years ago," replied Gus, "and have been gradually restoring the building to its former glory. You probably did not see much when you arrived, due to the mist. But on a sunny day the Abbey Grange takes on a beautiful soft reddish hue, as a result of the building being constructed in red brickwork.

"The Abbey Grange has a fascinating history and was designed by a famous architect, name of Sir George Gilbert Scott

"You probably know that from 1840 onwards, when it came to building in London, Neo-Gothic architecture was the preferred style of commerce and of the Establishment, including churches, Universities and other public institutions. Ironically, and to my knowledge, the Neo-Gothic style was never taken up in theater architecture; at least not in London, almost probably because the Gothic designs are somewhat at variance with the essential frivolous nature of theater.

"Though, I believe the Gothic idiom, became the dominant style of the Victorian era after Sir Charles Barry's successful application of Neo-Gothic designs at the new Palace of Westminster which was finally completed by 1870. This was a natural progression following the lead set at the Palace of Westminster which was an exercise in Neo-Gothic architecture on what can only be described as, on a grand and pervasive scale," said Gus.

"Where does the Abbey Grange fit in the scheme of things Gus?" asked Jack.

"There has always been an Abbey Grange house on the land here going back over the centuries. The last but one burned down in 1857 and the present building we are sitting in was completed during the year 1863. Rather like our theaters in town eh Lodge; forever burning down and having to be rebuilt! However, just after Sir George Gilbert Scott, built the Abbey Grange, he submitted in 1865, his basic design for the Abbey Grange in a public competition held to build a new Foreign Office in Whitehall for the British Government.

"At the time headed by Lord Palmerston, as First Lord of the Treasury,[1] who ironically rejected Scott's Abbey Grange styled Neo-Gothic designs of 1860 for the new Foreign Office as being unsuitable and insisting instead on a style based upon Italian Renaissance. Ironically, Italian Renaissance is the most preferred style of architecture applied to the designs of our Music Hall and theaters.

"Despite this apparent setback the Gothic style expressed as Neo-Gothic, or the Gothic Revival, was established from 1840, and later deployed at the St. Pancras Hotel in London to great success in 1867. The very same hotel I believe both you and Theo are staying in. I cannot fault your choice of residence. However, the original architectural concept for the St. Pancras Hotel, by Sir George Gilbert Scott first appeared in his design for the Abbey Grange country mansion.[2]

"This Italianate Neo-Gothic house is effectively a scaled down proto-type version of the more famous St. Pancras Hotel in London, where George Gilbert Scott, used many of the design details extant here at the Abbey Grange's on the new hotel. Indeed it becomes easier to recognise this fact when one views the front of the St. Pancras Hotel in comparison with the southern façade of the Abbey Grange. One is looking at a smaller version of the St. Pancras Hotel building.

"This fact came about because, as I pointed out, the actual Neo-Gothic designs, developed from the Abbey Grange, as submitted by Scott for the competition to construct the government's new Foreign Office in Whitehall, were rejected in favor of a building in the more Classical style. Subsequently, the London Midland & Scottish Rail Road commissioned Scott to build their new hotel, properly called the Midland Grand Hotel, together with their rail road terminus in the parish of St. Pancras in London. Scott duly obliged and did so in 1867, applying successfully those rejected Gothic designs and stylistic embellishment which were modelled on the Abbey Grange," completed Sir Augustus Harris.

We all sat around the dining table in awe of Gus' historical description of the very mansion we were staying in, and its influence on the nation's architecture. Lodge appeared to be unmoved by Gus' narrative and was drinking heavily, having already consumed a glass of wine whilst waiting for the soup. Though, who could blame him? At length Christie went up to Lodge's side and served him with the soup first.

Christie himself was not beyond the peculiar. Apart from his gait, he had a pronounced defect in one eye that kept twitching, almost in keeping with the constant tick tock of the Ellis & Lloyd brass carriage clock on the mantelpiece. As to his physical demeanor, his resemblance in several ways to Lodge's man-servant Aloysius was alarmingly similar and disconcerting. Even then, looking at Christie, the similarities between him and Aloysius, were such as to make it difficult to differentiate between the two of them. Christie, as with Aloysius, appeared to be suffering from Parkinson's disease, or he was in the final stages of a severe affliction of St. Vitus' Dance.

"What the deuce happened last night at the esteemed Queen's Hall, Lodge? I understand that there was a major disaster in the making, which would easily relegate the dreadful sinking of the ill-fated *Titanic*, into the shade as a minor mishap on a boating lake. What were you thinking of? Did you not know that the Nihilists and Futurists were in town spoiling for an opportunity, to gain last night, precisely what they had been hoping for, at your expense? We Music Hall managers knew they were in town and accordingly, exercised our right to refuse admission to those we suspected for whatever reason we deemed fit."

The person who said this was none other than Augustus Harris, Gus, to his friends.

His remarks caught Lodge off balance and he sat there transfixed by the words with his soup spoon half way to his mouth, frozen in action.

"Even Cindy here had the good sense to have a plan

ready to deploy, in attempting to restore some semblance of order in the auditorium, which she did as Little Bo Peep. Well done Cindy! You owe her a debt of gratitude, Lodge," continued Gus.

Lodge put his spoon down, drained the contents of his wine glass and then breathed out noisily. Focusing on Gus, he cleared his throat.

"Gus, I have always maintained that one has to speculate in order to accumulate; be it good will or box office receipts, preferably the latter. To achieve this eminent state of affairs, either one must be seen to be doing good deeds for the benefit of others, as in the Titanic Benefit Concert, or, applying in a clever way a well-thought out stratagem.

"The stratagem I constructed for our Titanic Benefit Concert was perfect in every detail. And, had it not being for the intervention of the Nihilists would have produced the expected level of returns…" said Lodge.

"Well it could hardly have been perfect in every detail, Loge," interrupted Jack, "because the Nihilists did turn up and certainly sabotaged your concert!"

"Nihilist, Futurists or hecklers are quite simply trouble makers," said Gus, "we have our ways of dealing with them. These people will not compromise my box office receipts on any account. From my experiences, most people attending concerts and the theater are not interested in the Nihilists or the demented and nonsensical Futurists. What with their ridiculous notions on how music should or ought not to evolve, but rather be forced into reality of the day – even the future. They may be dab hands at causing trouble, riots even, but we will be ready for them and by the time we have finished with the Futurists, their own *future* may not be that certain!"

"That may well be the case at the Theater Royal in Drury Lane, Gus where you only put on pantomime or farcical shows where the Nihilist or Futurist could hardly turn up and disrupt people who would attend such entertainment. In this respect, the Nihilists or the Futurists would gain nothing by such disruption except the enmity of the audience and all that suggests. Conversely, I could hardly put on a pantomime as a dignified memorial concert for the victims of the ill-fated *Titanic* where over fifteen hundred souls perished in one night.

"If one is going to organize concerts where serous music is performed, then one can reasonably expect a certain type of audience to attend such a concert. In the main they will comprise intelligent well to do persons from the middle or upper classes, aristocracy even. Usually such people want to attend concerts where they can listen to the music in peace and quiet.

"These self same people are the decision makers whom the Nihilists and Futurists together wish to influence. My Titanic Benefit Concert was designed to inveigle that class of people; the intelligentsia, if you will. It follows therefore that in so inviting those influential persons to attend, I am perforce attracting trouble makers and invoking their wrath at worse, disruption at best," said Lodge.

Lodge was now marshalling his thoughts, and becoming animated in the process, as the alcoholic drinks he had been consuming were beginning to take effect on him.

"Yes I like to get out and about and be seen in the right places," he continued, "that is how I make my contacts, rather as you do Gus, and gauge what my audiences want. On that occasion they wanted something to reflect their emotional involvement with the loss of life on that stricken, ill-fated *Titanic*. As we all of us sitting around this table know, one has to be seen to be everywhere almost at once. In this respect, you know, I have to be omnipotent."

Lodge said this last word slowly; as though not quite convinced it was the correct word to use.

I think the word he was looking for was omnipresent, but as usual with Lodge, one could never be certain about just what he intended. Unless of course he was referring to something entirely different; which, knowing him, might well have been the case. Still unabated or challenged, he continued regardless.

"As I have said before, when I addressed the Fourth Estate at the Charing Cross Hotel recently, in defense of our Music Halls, being an impresario has it responsibilities. I have to take risks, which of us impresario does not? Were we to pander to the lowest form of entertainment, we would be on the same level as the *Pleasure Gardens*, such as those located at Marylebone, Vauxhall, Ranelagh or even Cremorne.

"Because I put on innovative and daring spectacles and commission new serious music, I become that pioneer constantly forging ahead in to new territories seeking only the best. There will be disappointments, of course, they are to be expected, but they are worth it in the long run for the greater glory. In this respect, pioneering is not for the faint hearted. I can bear these setbacks because I know ultimately my public will stand by me. I expect good things to accrue!" Lodge concluded.

"Pioneering is not for the faint hearted," quoted Jack, "then what are we doing here at Gus's Gothic retreat twenty or so miles out of London?"

"In fairness, I suppose," said Cinderella, deflecting that

question, "one could hardly expect Michael to lock down a concert hall just because trouble makers might turn up. How would one possibly recognize any of them as they queued up to gain access to the auditorium?"

"The trick is to deal with the root causes of the trouble," said Gus, refilling his wine glass.

Looking at Lodge, he was clearly in his element. From being morose and introspective a couple of hours ago, he was now, due to his prodigious intake of alcohol, his old suave and amenable self once more. His reversion to his chronic catachresis showed me this was very much the case. Lodge was now rubbing his hands, in a disquieting manner, as though a presentiment of a surprise were imminent.

Neither Jack nor I had seen Lodge experience quite such a devastating scenario as the failure of the Titanic Benefit Concert, although largely due to the organized sabotage of the Nihilists or Futurists. However, what was of interest to Jack and me was Lodge's ability to recover, almost magically, as it were. One fully appreciated then just what alcohol could do to a person's confidence.

Nevertheless, a return of confidence, even induced by alcohol, could restore that optimism when one sobered up later. I mentioned this to Cinderella, who agreed with me, whilst replenishing my wine glass. I continued studying Lodge, or Loge, as Jack called him. Cinderella, of course, refers to him as Theseus. By what other names, I wondered, was he known.

Lodge continued his polemic with us, whilst Christie struggled to put the food from the trolley on to the dining table.

Though Lodge might be considered a pleasant enough fellow; there was something not quite right about him. But as usual with Lodge, it was difficult to quite put one's finger on that aspect of his character. He had the most disconcerting habit, a monomanic condition, which manifested itself in his constantly looking over both his shoulders. He did so for no discernable reason, as though he were about to react to a premonition or expectation of a presence to materialize behind him.

Indeed, everything about this Lodge fellow was odd, what he thought and said, what he did, his man-servants, what he ate and his gastronomic preferences. The music he listened to and from what questionable origins he derived his singular pleasures.

Lodge continued to espouse his opinions and thoughts on a range of matters in answer to questions put to him by the others seated around the walnut dining table. Whether the alcohol had really taken hold of him, I could not be certain, but time and time again, I would witness a basic flaw or misunderstanding that indicated to me a mistake not of comprehension or commission, but rather a fundamental mistake of principle.

Jack put a polite inquiry to Lodge, about what his thoughts were on our American English, in particular using a verb as a noun, as we are inclined to do, and how this might affect Music Hall grammatical expression on the stage. A relevant example was typically; *The American drinks*. This remark could either mean; pointing to a stash of American liquor - a noun and phrase. Or, actually an American in the act of drinking- a verb and a sentence.

Lodge thought for moment and then enunciated his considered reply.

"The American drinks - drinks what?" he asked, in all honesty, whilst slurring his words slightly.

He uttered these words whilst at the same time dealing with Christie, who was now attempting to serve slices of roast beef to him. Despite Lodge helping himself freely with wine, he still indulged in his habit of looking over his shoulder, which I found unnerving. I kept expecting to see or hear someone standing behind him. Jack once said that such a habit could be contagious and that we might find ourselves doing it. In that case, only God could help us!

What I found even more disconcerting was the certain probability that Lodge was living proof that a little knowledge could be dangerous, especially in his present state. I have in the past, had good reason to make this comment on Lodge's behavior. Somehow, he managed, to inveigle Augustus Harris, the impresario, into a discussion about the essential altruistic rôle of the Music Hall in society, including his Theater Royal in Drury Lane.

"In particular," Lodge argued, "there were educative aspects of the Music Hall, which I promote tirelessly and its ability to lend dignity or imbue the soul with nobility of purpose. For example, emanating from these eminent establishments, oh and your Theater Royal in Drury Lane too with its pantomimes, could be such noble ideals as hope, aspiration, courage or even fortitude in the face of profound absurdity.[3]

"Such a case was when I tried to encapsulate in my elegiac Choral Anthem Symphony, for my three sopranos - the *Three Graces*, which I knocked off with Gustav Mahler the other week. Indeed, such magnanimous intent should be conveyed in the idiom of music and song for the whole of humanity, in its diverse forms, to endure, and not just for clever people like us sitting around this walnut table."

"But surely the whole concept of Music Hall is essentially relief from pre-determined drudgery and ..?" asked Cinderella.

"No, no, no," interrupted Lodge, with a dismissive wave of his arm. "What is but Music Hall? It stems from the puritan regime, when church organs were ripped out of their sanctified places and finished up with tavern keepers offering the *'Free and Easy'* to their customers. Those taverns in turn became known as harmonic clubs because of the musical connotation.

"Theaters were prevented from developing in the formal sense unless they had a royal warrant, typically Gus's Theater Royal in the Covent Garden. The alternative to these officially recognized, if highly regulated places, by an officer of the king, usually in the person of the Lord Chamberlain, were the *Pleasure Gardens*, such as the Cremorne, Ranelagh, Marylebone or Vauxhall. They in turn evolved into the Penny Gaffes 4 and then later into the Saloon Theaters, leaving these precursors of the Music Hall to develop popular concepts and entertainment, but under the guidance and enlightenment of people as Gus here and myself," informed Lodge.

"Please go on," said Cinderella.

"I am acutely aware that what I am saying is profound and often difficult to understand," Lodge said pretentiously, as he moved in arm in a backward arch to reëmphasise his point. "Music Hall must evolve! And believe you me such is my resolve in this respect that I continue to live to help it evolve or I will die trying. As I have expressed in my favorite axiom innumerable times: the public be damned, box office receipts come first. In this respect, might not the Music Hall be used to convey such ideals as perfection in harmony, and indeed thought, not just humorous anecdotes or turns, but convey serious music as part of the evening's entertainment?

"I am thinking now of that Mozart fellow and the

aria from his ballet, *'Dan Giovanni,'* very tuneful and promising. If it got the audiences going in arrogant Vienna it is sure to go down well in our London Music Halls, I am seriously thinking of contacting Mozart's agent and having a word. People want something new and lively full of hope and memorable tunes. In days gone by, composers wrote songs for people, not purely for entertainment you understand, but to educate. Now take that Frenchman, Ravel, and his *'Pavane pour une infant défunte'* [5] and that dreary song about a dead child. We none of us want any songs about dead children now do we, including, *'Kindertotenlieder'* [6] by Gustav Mahler.

"Nor do we want death-laden symbolism creeping into music, like that Roman composer Delius and his so-called *'Mass of Life.'* Sounds more like a *Requiem* if you ask me. Even though it is based on that God-less fellow Nietzsche, who was inspired by ideas in his work he calls, *'Also Sprach Zarathustra.'* Songs are supposed to cheer us up, and get the audience going, not consign us to misery or into Freud-induced manic depression and prolonged introspection of amaranthine proportions!"

Lodge continued his extravagant descriptions about the defining rôle of Music Hall. Invoking all manner of uncorroborated testimonials to support his exaggerated and pretentious claims about what he could, given enough notice, lay his hands on to improve the rationale of Music Hall in general.

At one stage Lodge engaged us all in a deep consideration on the ethics of art, especially the rôle of the clown in opera. He then went on to claim that it was an anachronistic oddity carried throughout opera and in need of revision. He then sat back in his Chippendale chair and with a smile of expectancy upon his face, looked around the table for a response. His impatience however, compelled him to pre-empt this.

"I know, I know, words fail you!" he said, before lapsing back into his Chippendale chair with a manic grin on his face worthy of Judd, the ventriloquist's dummy at the height of its expressive powers.

He was right; we all of us were frozen in a paroxysm of disbelief, simply unable to speak!

1. The Prime Minister
2. The designs of the St. Pancras Hotel are based on a Kelham House in Nottinghamshire by George Gilbert Scott
3. An example of Lodge's affliction with catachresis. The word, I think, he meant was, adversity
4. A Penny Gaffe was a popular form of entertainment for the lower orders
5. A death-dance for a noble child
6. Songs on the Death of Children

Chapter 29

The Recumbent and Ethereal

Following a disastrous Titanic Benefit Concert we had repaired to Sir Augustus Harris's country mansion in order that Lodge might recover his dignity and self-esteem. Given his present state, it would appear that he had failed to recover either. For it was only a matter of time before Lodge's alcohol fuelled exuberance would desert him, leaving his slumped person in a Chippendale chair at the luncheon table complete with his near *rigor mortis* fixed grin on his face.

"At least he has broken the agony," said Sir Augustus Harris, or Gus as he prefers to be called, pointing with his fork at a recumbent figure oblivious to our remarks. "It is a risk to put anything on, including benefit concerts irrespective of disruptors turning up unannounced."

"I am not so certain, Gus," said Jack, "Theo and I had a dose of Nihilists disrupting our act when we played the Majestic Theater in Chicago a few weeks back. Their disruptive tactics confused us and other artistes on the stage. We could not understand why there was such a consistent rejection of our act. It was not as though they did not appreciate a particular act or turn; it was indiscriminate condemnation as a principle.

"We hooked up with comatose Loge there, slumbering away, and he did suggest a course of action. That in itself has worked out positively, but almost only by chance and not as a result of Loge's stratagem. What in effect the disruptors indicated to us was that our act was tired, perhaps even dead. It was only when we came to London and toured the Music Halls that we realized that the Nihilists were right. Our act was out of date, not contemporaneous and failed to address those pressing issues which an audience might be concerned about.

"I realized our weakness when I saw Queenie Leighton address the audience at the New Bedford Music Hall in Camden Town. What she did to the audience amazed me. And yet, Gus, at the same time, it frightened me. I guess because it showed Theo and me there and then just how far we have yet to go. Theo and I have not even started our journey yet. However, with Cinderella here, with us on the stage, I believe we can make up for lost time," concluded Jack, whilst toasting Cinderella with his wine glass to which we all responded by raising our wine glasses too. Lodge desisted.

"Cinderella has, of course," said Gus, "appeared at my theater and I hope will do so again for one of my pantomime specials this coming Christmas. Needless to say gentlemen, my offer to appear at the Theater Royal in Drury Lane is open to you both."

We sat in gratitude of Gus's offer and did so in silence for a few moments, rather as Loge was doing.

"What is the theme of your proposed pantomime for this Christmas Gus?" asked Cinderella.

"It is a secret," replied Gus, "but I am happy to confide in you all. This year's pantomime is as daring, as it will be recklessly abandoned and hopefully, will bring the house down. It will be based on one of two operas by Rickard Wagner. We have not, as yet, decided upon which opera will form the basis of our pantomime."

"Where did you get the inspiration to base a pantomime on a musical work by Wagner?" inquired Jack.

"We were inspired by the potential for a combination of the absurdity with the sublime, which are always present when watching any of Wagner's early operas. We have not, as yet, decided upon which of two to base our pantomime, but it will be either from his libretto for his very first opera called, *'Die Laune des Verliebten.'*[1] or alternatively, *'Das Liebesverbot,'* [2] answered Gus, smiling. "And, let me assure you all, it will be a sensation, as anything to do with Wagner usually is. We might even import a couple of the Valküre [3] for more dramatic effect!"

"I shall be honored to play the leading rôle," replied Cinderella, blushing slightly, "and if I know my Wagner, it sounds as if it has potential and certainly beyond such immortal lines as, *'And you shall go to the ball!'*"

"More likely, 'you shall be dispatched forthwith to Valhalla than to the ball I think!" added Jack.

"Cinderella, gentlemen, let us abandon Lodge to the arms of Morpheus with whom he appears content and instead make our way to the parlor and see if we can compete vocally with my new imported American Aëolian Pianola," suggested Gus.

We all immediately fell in with his idea and left Lodge to his slumbers.

We made our way down yet another ornate Gothic corridor, the ceilings of which were fan vaulted and intricately detailed with raised filigree designs. Moments later we found ourselves standing in front of a highly polished mahogany door set in to a timber framed pointed archway cut in to the wall. Gus turned a fluted brass door handle and pushed the door open without a sound being made.

We all stepped into the parlor and were immediately

struck by the lush furnishings and appointments of the room, the center of which was indeed dominated by a large Aëolian Pianola, a self playing piano. This was no ordinary instrument and in fact I recognized it as being a Steinway Welte-Mignon built under license by the Weber Aëolian Pianola Company, located in the Aëolian Hall on Fifth Avenue and 35th. Street in New York.

This particular player piano, I knew, had two options; the Metrostyle or the Thermodist, both of which were demonstrated during a performance I attended, of the fourth movement, taken from Saint-Saëns's Third Symphony in C minor, with four hand piano accompaniment. [4] I remembered well the recording made for Duo Art piano rolls, in the Weber Aëolian Pianola Company's own recital and recording auditorium, which could seat comfortably one hundred fifty persons.

This particular Steinway Welte-Mignon player piano was an improved self-playing piano and could be driven either pneumatically or mechanically. Each method was able to literally operate the action of the keys by way of programmed instructions recorded on to metallic rolls or perforated paper.

This instrument itself, a large upright player piano, was made of dark highly varnished ebony wooden panels and brass edge trims and was truly a sight to behold. The four corners of the box frame were decorated with gilded fluted Corinthian columns the two fronts ones of which supported the overhanging keyboard. The silver colored keys were made of prestine ivory.

Below the keyboard were three foot pedals shaped as lion's feet. Above the keyboard was a varnished soundboard, a panel complete with intricate inlaid rosewood patterns surrounded by shallow beading creating a decorated raised rectilinear frame. In the center of which resting against this panel was an ornately wrought and intricately designed sheet music rest made of polished brass. Flanking the music rest on either side were two large bronze candelabras bearing several candles from which a myriad of iridescent light illuminated the keyboard and other brass fittings decorating the instrument.

We all four of us looked in anticipation at each other aching to run our fingers along the keyboard and in so doing create heavenly arpeggios and sublime triple fifths and A's. Jack of course, attended the forerunner to the Julliard School of Music [5] in New York and was trained to play classical music and in fact is very much an accomplished and versatile pianist. The Julliard, I remember started out in 1905 as the Institute of Musical Art on Fifth Avenue and 12th. Street, based on the fact that we did not have, in the United States, a credible premier music academy.

Jack tells a humorous story about the Institute. When it moved, in 1910 from Fifth Avenue to Claremont Avenue, located in Morningside Heights, a prosperous neighborhood in Manhattan, it did so into premises which were formerly the Bloomingdale Insane Asylum! The story went that it was difficult to tell the former inpatients from the undergraduates, attending musical studies, who were then matriculated under the aegis of Columbia University, as Jack did.

Irrespective of how beautiful these player pianos looked, they had an unenviable reputation of being the main instigation or cause of copyright infringement. I remembered not so long ago at a concert in the Carnegie Hall on Seventh and 57th. in mid town Manhattan. There, in the Crush Bar I met with John Sousa, the famed composer of typically patriotic and military marches. Our

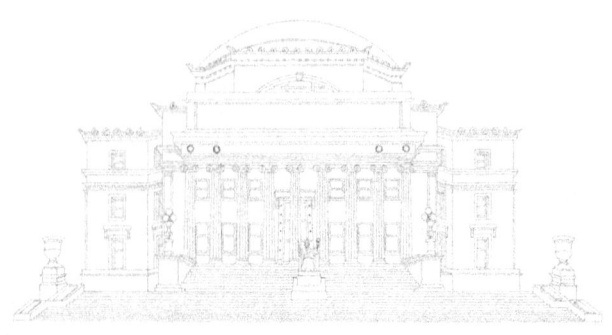

Columbia University

conversation centered on copyrights and how we both agreed, that keeping people from borrowing freely from our works without permission, was of paramount importance.

He was particularly concerned, that the advent of the player piano was, effectively, reducing demand for sheet music, together with the resultant reduction on copyright royalties he used to receive, which those sales of sheet music generated. To add to this iniquity, Sousa went on to say, the player piano companies refused to pay composers those royalties for music they had impressed on to those piano scrolls of perforated paper, the type of which controlled the player mechanism in the self-playing piano in performing a particular piece of music, albeit mechanically.

In response to criticism by composers, the player piano companies contended that the rolls did not repeat the music composed by any individual and that they were within the law. The music was being performed, they contended, not by an individual, but rather by an automaton, and played mechanically! And, Sousa had asked at the time, could I believe such idiocy!

Sousa went on to quote from a recent legal case [6] which he found to be absurd in its entirety. There the Supreme Court in Washington held that the player piano companies had not infringed copyrights simply because humans could not read player piano perforated rolls and were not in fact copies of the musical compositions they encoded. This absurdity was corrected a year later by an unusually vigilant Congress. They legislated [7] that all compositions, music or otherwise which were repeatable, would be subject to a compulsory license fee to be paid, irrespective of whether permission was obtained or not.

However, standing before this beautiful Steinway Welte-Mignon player piano, such considerations evaporated, as a sublime tinkling and arpeggios emanated from deep within the instrument. Cinderella had gotten to the keyboard first and was caressing the ivory keys with the tenderness and affection that only a girl could. We made ourselves comfortable on red velvet upholstered seats ranged around the parlor and witnessed her playing the Abbé Liszt's transcription for piano called, *'Réminiscences de Norma,'* based on elegiac melodies from an opera by Bellini.

We had no sooner gotten through this beautiful evocative work by Liszt, when Cinderella launched herself into an even more sublime and serene work for piano. I instantly recognized it as being originally a paraphrase for pianoforte of the, *'Liebestod,'* [8] from Rickard Wagner's opera, *'Tristan und Isolde.'* Her playing was magical as it was ethereal. I sat back in my chair, mesmerized by her delicate finger work manipulating the keys with a smooth action as her hands glided along the keyboard.

Cinderella then lifted her head back. Her face, illuminated by the soft lights radiating out from the candelabras, looking as though in a trance induced by the music, but in total absorption with the arpeggios, triple fifths and triple A's she was creating on the player piano. Her playing was such as to leave a sensation almost like that of a vacuüm in one's chest brought on by an emotional response to this ethereal combination of sensual musical ability and tonal dexterity. Our Cinderella was clearly a person of unfathomable talents and demonstrated them with an unassuming ability bordering almost on nonchalance.

Upon completing her recital, Cinderella got up and curtsied. Jack took her place and without hesitation depressed the base foot pedal and commenced playing another operatic transcription for pianoforte by Liszt; that from Verdi's opera called, *'Ernani.'* If Jack was playing that particular work, I knew he would almost certainly play the closing section and finale from Schonberg's, *'Gurrelieder,'* [9] a favorite of his. He would do so with that brilliant coördinated precision he has when playing the pianoforte, which I have experienced over the many years of knowing him.

Whilst I can play the pianoforte, such was my reservation I had no wish to play this beautiful Steinway Welte-Mignon player piano, especially having witnessed two very accomplished pianists in Cinderella and Jack. No such reservation attended Gus, who sidled up to the instrument and opened the lid of the four-legged stool upon which Jack and Cinderella had sat whilst at the keyboard. He then reached in and produced a sheaf of sheet music, which he placed on the brass music stand.

Having sat down on the stool he peered at the sheet music, coughed and began to play with a labored intensity scales resembling robarto, as opposed to arpeggio. None-the-less we all joined in enthusiastically in singing a hearty rendition of, *'Come Where the Booze is Cheaper.'*

Gus was in fine fettle as he extolled the lyrics and even tried to attempt the harmonies; but in doing so, only succeeded in sounding as if he were singing out of tune. This did not in any way deter him from his intended purpose, to render a good song. Seamlessly, as Cinderella turned the sheet music over, Gus continued his playing and continued with, *'Boiled Beef and Carrots,'* composed by Fred Murray and Charles Collins and originally sung by Harry Champion about a favorite English dish and loved even more by Cockneys.

> *Boiled beef and carrots,*
> *Boiled beef and carrots,*
> *That's the stuff for your Derby Kell,*
> *Makes you fit and keeps you well.*
> *Don't live like vegetarians,*
> *On food they give to parrots,*
> *Blow out your kite, from morn 'til night,*
> *On boiled beef and carrots.*

It was becoming self evident that Sir Augustus Harris' choice of Music Hall song was of a lower echelon of taste, which probably accounted for his being known as the *Father of Modern Pantomime.* His preferences in songs were similar to those beloved of Marie Lloyd; lewd, brimming with lascivious innuendo and double entendre flaunting decency. As well as singing the indescribable for the benefit of costermongers.

It was Cinderella who explained to me, during a lull in the singing, that typically; *That's the stuff for your Derby Kell* – Derby Kell' is Cockney rhyming slang for belly as in

Derby Kelly. And that *Blow out your kite, from morn 'til night,* 'Blow out your kite' being slang for 'fill your stomach.'

Without any preamble or fuss Gus launched straight into the next song called, *'Daisy Bell - Bi-cycle Built for Two,'* [8] and led by Cinderella.

This song has significance for Jack and me because we actually met the composer of the song, Harry Dacre, in New York, during his first visit to America in 1890. On that occasion he brought with him from England a new improved patented bi-cycle but had to pay import duty on it. This ridiculous situation went around Vaudeville in a flash and even the songwriter William Jerome was reported to have said, '..it is lucky you did not bring a bi-cycle built for two, otherwise you would have to pay double duty!'

This of course provided the inspiration for the song which was performed in London by Katie Lawrence, one of Lodge's *Three Graces.* Later, in New York, I remembered watching Tony Pastor sing it in his famous Fourteenth Street Theater. Though it was only when Jennie Lindsay sang it at the Atlantic Gardens Music Hall on Elizabeth Street in the Bowery district of Manhattan in the Lower East Side that the song really became a favorite with audiences both in America and England.

When I spoke with Pastor after he had sung it, he informed me that one of the reasons he felt audiences liked the song was because it contained several parodies. Typically, he said, the word, *tandem* could be taken to indeed describe bi-cycle or matrimony; *Bell* as in ringing or *Belle* as in beauty. These double meanings left the verses open to parody or satire with some verses actually of an risqué nature being added later, such as this particular chorus containing an *answer;*

There is a flower within my heart,
Daisy, Daisy,
Planted one day by a glancing dart,
Planted by Daisy Bell.
Whether she loves me or loves me not
Sometimes it's hard to tell;
And yet I am longing to share the lot
Of beautiful Daisy Bell.
Chorus &c.
Daisy, Daisy, give me your answer, do,
I'm half crazy all for the love of you.
It won't be a stylish marriage,
I can't afford a carriage,
But you'd look sweet upon the seat
Of a bi-cycle made for two.
We will go tandem as man and wife,
Daisy, Daisy,
Peddling away down the road of life,
I and my Daisy Bell.
When the road's dark, we can both despise
Policemen and lamps as well.
There are bright lights in the dazzling eyes
Of beautiful Daisy Bell.

Chorus &c.
I will stand by you in weal or woe
Daisy, Daisy,
You'll be the bell which I'll ring, you know,
Sweet little Daisy Bell.
You'll take the lead on each trip we take.
Then if I don't do well
I will permit you to use the brake,
beautiful Daisy Bell
Chorus &c.

Michael, Michael, here is my answer true
You're half crazy if you think that that will do
If you can't afford a carriage
There won't be any marriage
Cause I'll be switched - if I'll get hitched
On a bi-cycle built for two!

It becomes easier to understand why artistes, such as Marie Lloyd, can capitalize on an audience's instinctive disrespect for the pompous, together with a voracious appetite for parody, albeit expressed apparently innocently in double meaning or innuendo.

At one stage Jack attempted to play the Steinway Welte-Mignon player piano, in the style of Mozart. That is, with his back to the keyboard and playing the keys in reverse. But, Jack only succeeded only in bringing the Aëolian Pianola's lid down on to his fingers. With the resultant sound of several keys being depressed simultaneously and creating in the process, an impressive lengthy crescendo which reverberated around the parlor, almost as a sustained drone, for quite a remarkable length of time.

Despite Jack's injuries, the four of us continued singing, drinking and eventually dancing well past the mid hour at night. Our impromptu, if sustained merriment, was brought to an abrupt halt by the appearance of Lodge, standing in the doorway of the parlor, looking rather bemused at our antics.

1. *The Mood of the One in Love*
2. *The Ban on Love - A Great Comic Opera.*
3. Warrior daughters of the Teutonic god Wotan who ride winged horses
4. This movement is remarkable for its complex four hand piano arpeggio accompaniment
5. The Juilliard Foundation was named for Augustus D. Juilliard

6. White-Smith Music Publishing Company v. Apollo Company, 1908
7. U S Copyright Act of 1909
8. Love scene
9. *Songs of Gurre*

Chapter 30

The Empire Music Hall

Somewhat exhausted from our extended visit to the Abbey Grange and our tiresome train journey back into London, we decided to stay inside the hotel, preferring to play the rôles of exhausted thespians, lounging around in a perfected and listless manner, worthy of *La Dame aux Camélias*. No amount of luxury or pampering could be too much. It was thus how we spent the morning, away from the cares of the world. But upon Cinderella's arrival in the middle of the afternoon, we decided to practice a few of the intricacies of our new routine with her. Later on, of course, we were scheduled to try it out in front of an audience at the Empire Music Hall in the desperate hope that it would sweep all before it. That, or banish us back permanently in to obscurity, abject ridicule, oblivion, or worse; objects of derision.

Later our Phäeton carriage pulled up outside the Empire Music Hall located on the northern aspect of Leicester Square in the heart of London's West End. Cinderella was the first to leap down to the sidewalk followed by Jack and then me. We made our way in to the foyer and eventually an usher, resplendent in his powder blue colored morning-coat escorted us to the manager's office.

"Ah Jack, Theo and Cinderella," said Lodge, as we

were shown in, "please do come in. This, of course, is Mr. George Edwardes, the esteemed manager of the Empire Music Hall."

"Cinderella, I believe you may already know," said Lodge.

Edwardes did not respond but gave Cinderella a searching glance, as though something had stirred in the back of his mind. Possibly, I conjectured that she had performed reviously at Empire Music Hall in breach of the *Exclusivity Clause*.

Cinderella responded to Edwardes' stare with a shallow curtsey.

"Jack and Theo you have met with in the past, on our previous visit here. My protégés, in Theo and Jack, intend to introduce a new double act involving a living ventriloquist as a '*Spesh*,'[1] said Lodge, looking at Edwardes.

We all of us shook hands and discussed pleasantries with each other, whilst Edwardes poured out five decent measures of scotch.

It soon became apparent that our performing there at the Empire Music Hall was as a direct result of Lodge knowing George Edwardes with whom he had some *sway*, as he called it.

"Jack and Theo are unanimous in believing their new double act, with a chap called Marmeduke, to be innovative and daring in its presentation to an unsuspecting audience. We all of us remain quite, quite optimistic about their sweeping all before them in consolidating their inevitable success," declared Lodge.

"I have the greatest contempt for optimism," responded George Edwardes, before drinking deeply from his glass.

We had of course, through Lodge, heard of this manager when we first arrived in London from New

York. In fact I remembered Lodge being quite emphatic and animated when talking about Edwardes and his Empire Music Hall. Though, in fact, this was not our first visit to the establishment. We previously attended as guests of Lodge, and saw Little Bo Peep perform, but the reputation of the Empire Music Hall had more than preceded it. Rather it had defined the place.

In fact, Lodge had gone on to say, the main rival to the Alhambra Music Hall, on the eastern aspect of the Leicester Square was the Empire Music Hall. The Empire, under Edwardes' management, had acquired a well deserved, though some would say, contrived, reputation.

The infamy of the Empire Music Hall was made all the more complete and widespread by the fact that it unashamedly, and with inordinate enthusiasm, continued to promote its main attraction. This was usually in the form of displaying alluring ballet dancers who featured on a regular basis, for the sole delectation of its patrons attending the Music Hall. This activity also attracted the attention of Laura Ormiston Chant and her loathsome Social Purity Alliance, hell bent on closing down the Empire and indeed the nearby Alhambra Music Halls.

In addition, the Empire Music Hall also maintained a notorious promenade along which both courtesans and those in search of pleasure were encouraged to traverse and disport themselves. One could not talk about either the Alhambra or the Empire Music Halls without referring to both. For they remained alas, mutually exclusive, constantly locked in a deathly embrace for popular supremacy with a floating audience of pleasure seekers. The Music Hall-going public flocked to Leicester Square to see which of the two Music Halls would have the most alluring entertainment on offer, for their delectation, during the course of a particular evening, so I remember Lodge informing Jack and me at the time.

Lodge, in a very animated way, discussed various issues regarding the Empire Music Hall with Edwardes. In the meantime, I occupied myself watching this manager, Mr. George Edwardes. He seemed more interested in his whisky glass than in listening to Lodge, and occasionally held the glass up to the light, as though suspicious of what it might contain. It then occurred to me that it was highly likely that he could be drunk. After all he had clearly been drinking with Lodge whilst waiting on Cinderella, Jack and I to arrive.

Irrespective of his having been drinking, the manager appeared to be an amiable fellow, if absent minded. For it cannot have been but a few minutes since we were introduced to him, and he could not recollect who we were or what we were doing in his Music Hall, nor that we were to perform on his stage later that evening. The mere fact we were also down on the billboard as performing that night seemed to be of complete indifference to him. Cinderella, is of course is performing her rôle of Cinderella; and then, unbeknown to Lodge, join us in our new act as Marmeduke, the living ventriloquist.

Presently, Edwardes did us the courtesy of offering to escort us to our dressing rooms in the basement of the Music Hall; still uncertain as to whom we were exactly. Lodge decided to join us on our descent into the depths of the building.

Once inside our dressing room it was Cinderella who made straight for the whisky and poured out four decent measures which she then handed out to us. Lodge, for no particular reason, felt obliged to give us a little run down on the Empire Music Hall, since this was to be our début here performing with Cinderella.

EMPIRE MUSIC HALL

LEICESTER SQUARE, WC

Programme

Miss FANNIE LESLIE

ARA, ZEBRA & VORA

Miss LUCY CLARKE

THE CELEBRATED HARRISON TROUPE

Lew Bloom - Comic Monologist

MARIE LLOYD – 'A COSTER GIRL IN PARIS'

Miss CHRISSIE ANGUS

CINDERELLA

Intermission

HOUSTON, MITCHELL & MARMEDUKE

THE GREAT BOISSET TROUPE – An Evening Party

MR CHARLES BIGNELL

MR TED MORRIS

Little Tich

PROFESSOR THORNBURY

MR CHARLES DEANE

Miss DAISY WOOD

The SISTERS BELFRY

EDWIN BOYDE

Empire Music Hall

"The Empire Theater of Varieties, to call it by its proper name, with its distinctive classical architecture complete with a richly decorated façade and ornamentation was designed by Thomas Verity and opened in 1884. Later in 1887, the Empire Theater was redesigned by Frank Verity into a Music Hall called the Empire Theater of Varieties with a new vestibule added in 1893 reflecting a greater ostentatious flamboyancy in its architecture.

"The film pioneers Auguste and Louis Lumière in March 1896 projected the first film on to a screen for the public to see at the Empire Theatre of Varieties. These short films continued to be a regular feature for eighteen months and were shown in between live acts on stage. Though having said that, I have my reservations about the advent of this so-called Kinetoscopic creation of two-dimensional movement superimposed on a white cloth screen," Lodge admitted to us.

"We assume you are referring to film," said Jack.

"As I have explained before," [2] continued Lodge, with a degree of authoritative gravitas in his voice, "it was not so much the fact of Auguste and Louis Lumière putting on novel film shows that the Empire Music Hall acquired a sullied reputation. Rather, it was more because of the existence of its alluring corps de ballet, which naturally enough attracted pleasure seekers roaming around the theater district and especially Leicester Square, now considered the center of the West End. The Empire had acquired its well-deserved, though some would say, contrived, reputation. The infamy of the Empire Music Hall is made all the more complete and widespread by the fact that it unashamedly, and with inordinate enthusiasm, continues to promote its main attraction, the corps de ballet.

"Some of their acts could include scantily clad women, who comprise the corps de ballet, and still continues to attract controversy, in particular, the keen attention of moral crusaders, especially from such persons as the interfering Mrs. Ormiston Chant or indeed the chairman of the Metropolitan Board of Works, both of whom wish to close the Empire Music Hall down.

"However, from 1887 up until the present time, the art designer, name of C. Wilhelm created both the scenery and costumes for several of the questionable ballets performed albeit with coördinated precision, at the Empire Music Hall. His stage designs were legendary and admired and subsequently copied in other Music Halls.

"Despite of the attitude of the Ormiston Chant or the Metropolitan Board of Works, the ballets proved highly popular with the paying public because of the display of alluring ballet dancers which feature on a regular basis, for the sole delectation of its patrons. In addition, it also maintains a notorious promenade along which both courtesans and those in search of pleasure are encouraged to traverse and disport themselves.

"Not unreasonably, this leads both establishments, which glare across at each other, during the absence of fog, from either side of the Leicester Square, to resort to even more draconian measures. This can be in the form of outré act and turns, or just pure sensationalism involving the so called, '*Specialité*' acts in order to try and attract the floating audience frequenting Leicester Square.

"Both the Empire and the Alhambra, as Palaces of Pleasure, appeal in the main, to the undiscerning or to the man of leisure, including aristocratic young men, some of whom, it has been known, have actually married a number of working class Music Hall artistes performing in either Music Hall in Leicester Square. Other patrons comprised members of the lower orders, in search of immediate gratification, for which both Music Halls cater. They do so by featuring the same alluring ballet dancers engaged in provocative or risqué dance routines.

"You can imagine gentlemen, the Metropolitan Board of Works have had both Music Halls in their sights for quite some time now, but to date have failed to curtail their invaluable and necessary sociable operations. It is probably true, that the reputation for unruly audiences and reckless abandoned behavior stem from those two Music Halls alone. No doubt this is based to an extent on the intense, often bitter, competition which exists between the two, located but yards from each other in the same square.

"The middle classes, of course, continue to avoid the Empire and Alhambra Music Halls. They treat both places as though they were harbingers of cholera, or some other rampant contagion. But what do they know? As I have always maintained in my axiom of life, the public be damned; box office receipts come first! I shall not be deflected from that noble aspiration. In addition, the middle classes also consider those establishments to be teeming with disease, degradation or immorality on a vast scale, invariably complete with mindless, vulgar and risqué entertainment, fit only for the *Undeserving Poor*," concluded Lodge.

He then bowed before leaving the dressing room in order to claim his place of honor in the plush surrounds of the Dress Circle.

"I think we are all set to take the audience by storm, do you not agree?" asked Jack of Cinderella, dressed as a southern belle, in her billowing white satin dress.

"We can only but do our best Jack!" responded Cinderella, to Jack's polite inquiry.

"That is precisely what bothers me!" I offered.

I then donned my straw Sennit hat and polished my gold-capped ebony cane ready for our début upstairs on the stage of the Empire Music Hall. All three of us made our way through a labyrinth of white painted brick lined corridors up a flight of stone steps leading to the back of the stage. We stood there with other artistes waiting our turn whilst the first act was in progress out front on the stage.

I was all for going up to the Crush Bar and spending our waiting time more constructively there. However, looking around me I noticed on the faces of several artistes a look of concern and on others a distinct look of abject terror. Jack led the way to the front of the side wings of the stage to have a peep through the heavy velvet curtain at the audience, which had instilled such fear in the performers assembled backstage.

He was the first to look through the gap in the curtain and immediately drew a sharp intake of breath between his teeth and looked visible shaken. Rubbing my chest I too looked through the gap and immediately understood why. There, in the audience, in full sight of God and man was the greatest concentration of the costermongers disporting themselves not only in the front row of the stalls, their favourite place, but now were occupying the whole of the stalls with the *Undeserving Poor* occupying the seats at the back of the auditorium!

A quick mental calculation of the seating capacity of the auditorium of the Empire Music Hall left me with the frighteningly inescapable probability that there must be a least six to seven hundred of them assembled there in their speckled costumes and belligerent attitudes. Clearly, from what I could see, the Empire Music Hall was without doubt the unchallenged domain of the costermongers, or dog stealers, as Jack sometimes calls them, when they were assembled en-masse for a good time. My heart sank but, at that very moment, Cinderella wearing her billowing white satin ball-gown, brushed by me and opened the gap in the safety curtain.

"Do not be in the slightest bit perturbed," offered Cinderella, "they love a big meet now and then, but I shall keep them in check."

"With what?" was all Jack could ask of Cinderella.

I withdrew from the opening in the curtain, aghast at what I had just seen. Jack still looked horrified at what he too had witnessed occupying most of the stalls. We had of course seen these individuals before at the Hungerford Music Hall beneath the Charing Cross Rail Road Station, but never a bevy in such numbers as they now comprised.

Elements of the grotesque were already in evidence, even after the curtain had gone up. This large contingent of costermongers, a rough and vital set, was picking arguments with total strangers even as they entered the auditorium. Those who were not arguing were gambling with each other. All were talking in an esoteric language, using a cryptic vocabulary, incomprehensible to all but them. They spoke in this manner, in order to keep the meaning of their talk with each other secret, and could involve speaking words backwards.

The costermongers were in their element shouting at each other, and offering abuse to all and sundry, including the artistes performing, who were not immune to threats of their being thrown off stage. Encouragement, advice or demands to leave the stage were freely bandied around, as were nuts and orange peel. Most were eating something and wiping their sweaty faces with playbills, acquired from somewhere or someone. Regardless of the general commotion all round in the stalls, some were playing cards to gamble in a forlorn bid to enrich their purses.

Their women sitting in the stalls, if anything, were worse and even bolder in their opinions. Freely offering advice or insult to the players on stage, it seemed perfectly reasonable to them to argue with total strangers in the audience. Whilst indulging in this *behavior* some would wave and fan themselves with their shabby feathers in an exaggerated and perforce suggestive manner.

It was against such a background of disruption with which the artistes currently performing on the stage, the so-called celebrated Harrison Troupe, had to contend. This of course made them resort to being even more outrageous and impudent in order to gain the attention of a distracted audience of costermongers. In addition they spent most of the allotted time of their engagement, returning to the costermongers a continuous volley of abuse with equal impromptu wit.

I was all for abandoning this evening's début as I did not feel equal to the task of dealing with the massed ranks of the costermongers who clearly were out for the blood of any performer who, in their opinion, did not match their paid for expectation of raucous entertainment.

Cinderella pulled both Jack and me away from the curtain and sat us down on a large wicker basket.

"Do not fret, their disruptive noise is worse than the fear they instil which is only imaginary. They remain generally harmless and only want to enjoy themselves!" advised Cinderella.

"That is precisely what bothers Theo and me," responded Jack.

"Just what are costermongers?" I inquired.

"Costermongers are a vital set of charming, if belligerent London street people and vendors usually of vegetables, nuts or fruit. They also supply other materials or goods from stationary stalls, such as iron, hence ironmonger or indeed fish, as in fishmonger. They have a reputation for singing loudly or chanting their wares in order to attract the attention of buyers. They sell their wares from carts which are either stationary as in a market stall or horse-drawn as they make their way round the streets in a certain area.

"Costermongers are recognized usually by their wearing a King's Man, a large silk neckerchief tied round their necks. Hawkers, on the other hand carry their wares in baskets. The so called *Coster style*, has been described by a seasoned observer of costermongers:

> 'I am a true coster in my flamboyance and my love of color in, my violence of feeling and its immediate response in speech and action. Even now I am often caught with a sudden longing regret for the streets of Limehouse as I knew them, for the girls with their gaudy shawls and heads of ostrich feathers, like wind, and the men in their caps, silk neckerchiefs and bright yellow pointed boots in which they took such pride. I adored the swagger and the showiness of it all.' [3]

"Both costermonger and hawker are renowned for their dislike of authority, especially of the police. Accordingly they speak amongst each other in an esoteric language indecipherable to all but them. Most live in slums, such as the Rookery in St. Giles' just off the Charing Cross Road, which is legendary. And of course, Theo and Jack, you both experienced that place not these few weeks past, so you related to me.

"Whatever else they may be, costermongers have been around certainly in London since the 16th century, and were described by luminaries such as Marlowe or Shakespeare. They have however, gained a repugnant reputation for their 'low habits, general improvidence, love of gambling, total want of education, disregard for lawful marriage ceremonies, and their use of a peculiar slang language [4]

"Being essentially a competitive and vital set of persons, they do have an inexplicable and inordinate respect for elder costermongers in their community whom they elect to the status of pearly kings or queens. They, attired in their coats adorned with silver colored sequins, were there to keep the peace and arbitrate between rivals. This innate respect appears to be at variance with their general disregard for authority in any shape or form.

"However, theft and other crimes, though perpetrated enthusiastically on unsuspecting members of the public, are in fact actually rare among costermongers themselves. This is not to impute inherent honesty, but rather a recognition, as it were, of looking out for one another for mutual benefit and protection especially from others, such as navvies [5] or the police, towards whom their animosity is extreme.

"This is so because of the Metropolitan Streets Act 1867, the provisions of which seek to curb their less than legal street activities and are enforced by the Commissioner of the Metropolitan Police. As a result a constant state of warfare exists with civil authorities, such as the Metropolitan Board of Works, which also on numerous occasions, endeavors to control the costermongers street vending activities," concluded Cinderella.

Cinderella's description did little to alleviate the concern I had in performing in front of the massed ranks of costermongers, clearly out for a good time at the expense of us artistes performing on the stage. Still we could only possess our souls in patience and hope for the best. At that moment sporadic applause could be heard coming from the auditorium signaling that the act involving the Harrison Troupe had come to an end, in all probability, before the allotted time.

The next act involved Lew Bloom, an experienced comic monologist and a so-called society tramp. I decided to stay put and watch him to see how he might deal with the costermongers. I may actually learn something from his endeavors.

At that very moment, he stepped smartly in to the limelight wearing a ridiculously tall stove-pipe top hat, voluminous blue and yellow striped trousers and a countenance of such repellent and conspicuous ugliness as to defy description. His condition however did not in any way impede the confidence with which he applied his skills, as an artiste in reciting a series of verses back to front and backwards as well as talking interminable nonsense!

The audience, in the cheap seats, predictably erupted into ecstatic applause, for what sounded to me, at least, to be a rather interminable and nonsensical dialogue. That the words were impressed with innuendo, could never be in doubt, and were intelligible only to the costermongers who accorded him their undeviating attention and silence in which to perform his monological discourse.

Miss Chrissie Angus was on next, followed by Cinderella, the respite of the intermission, and then us. My heart sank.

1. Special act or turn
2. Royal Aq. Chapter 33
3. Quoted by Betty May in *Tiger Woman: My Story*.
4. Quoted from John Camden Hotten.
5. Navvies or navigators are road makers

Chapter 31

The St. Vitus Dancer

We were about to go on stage at the infamous Empire
Music Hall in Leicester Square. Nothing unusual in that,
since both Jack and I are Vaudeville artistes out of New
York with over sixty two years' combined experience
performing on stage in front of a variety of audiences;
some hostile, but most forgiving. What was of concern
to Jack and me on this occasion was the massed ranks of
what they call in London, costermongers, and a vast
contingent of them were assembled in the cheap seats
comprising the stalls. They are known to be a vital set
of belligerent persons with a well-deserved reputation for
disruption which would put the professional heckler or
Nihilists to shame.

"I hope this in not going to be a repeat of the
performance we were compelled to endure at the
Criterion Theater the other week or indeed the one also
at the Majestic Theater in Chicago," I said to Jack, as we
watched Chrissie Angus sing for her supper in front of
the costermongers who appeared indifferent to her
efforts. Eventually, having concluded her recital she
promptly walked off, stage right.

The costermongers were oblivious to her leaving the
stage since most of them were pre-occupied gambling or
shouting abuse at each other, as is their custom in public,

to give the false impression of disunity amongst their fraternity.

"We have learned a lot about disruptive hecklers and the like whilst we have been in London, Theo. Let us not lose sight of that fact," said Jack, trying to appear nonchalant at the prospect of performing out there in front of the costermongers.

Before the next act commenced the gaslights in the auditorium had been turned up. I suspected to observe closely and monitor the nefarious activities of the costermongers. However, it did afford me an opportunity to observe the audience throughout the auditorium, which in fact was filled to the rafters.

It did not take long to locate Lodge sitting in the Dress Circle, especially since he was wearing his rather ostentatious mid-night blue colored suit, beneath an equally if flamboyant black cape with an outrageous flaming red silk lining.

However, he did not appear happy at his situation. I could, even from my position in the wings of the stage, see why. Some of the costermongers had gravitated up to the Dress Circle and were sitting in seats which surrounded Lodge. Indeed on either side of Lodge's seat were costermongers jumping up and down and waving their arms about in an exaggerated manner.

This action could only have been exceedingly annoying for him, especially with his delicate sensitivity. And he expressed his visible discomfort and showed his disgust by continually looking at them acting like clowns on either side of him. Jack too, with a grin on his face, had noticed Lodge's predicament and disdainful attitude to his neighbors.

The auditorium lights were dimmed as the footlights increased in their intensity. All of a sudden Cinderella, in her satin ball-gown, burst on to the stage and immediately insulted the costermongers!

"And how are we this evening, you fine examples of the *Undeserving Poor*?" she demanded to know.

This surprising if inordinately confident behavior did in fact have the desired effect in concentrating the costermongers' attention on to her as well as eliciting a response. They did so unanimously and spontaneously in one remarkable accord with a deafening and decisive reply.

"We are too rich by half but not poor enough to get back into home sweet home, the poor house!"

"Oh you are all too kind," replied Cinderella, whilst dropping a shallow curtsey," we will see about that."

She then strutted around the stage humming the melody of a song for the orchestra to take up. Presently they did so, and Cinderella broke into a particular song accompanied enthusiastically by those costermongers sitting in the front row seats of the stalls. They all evidently knew the words by heart and chanted out their vulgar responses led by the octave higher voices of the female costermongers. I could only pity Lodge having to endure this ordeal in the midst of the now excitable costermongers up in the Dress Circle.

It became apparent to me that Cinderella was acting in the rôle of what I believe they call here in London a *Lion Comique,* a type of popular entertainer who excels in imitating the style of upper-class *toffs* or *swells,* as we call them in America, but made popular by Vaudeville artistes. Performers such as G. H. MacDermott or Alfred Vance and all are usually immaculately, if conspicuously dressed, rather like Lodge in his deliberately sybaritic and ostentatious mid-night blue suit and flame colored silk lined cape. Sickert immortalized the *Lions Comiques* in

New Bedford Music Hall

various oil paintings, especially when they were performing at the infamous New Bedford Music Hall in Camden Town.

Lion Comique, such as George Leybourne, or his greatest rival Arthur Lloyd, sometimes known as '*swells*' are a very popular type of character singers of songs about drinking champagne and the high life and are usually well dressed in the latest fashion, rather as Lodge often is.

One commentator described recently these *Lions Comiques,* as individuals who set women just a little higher than their bottle of champagne, witness George Leybourne's famous song, '*Champagne Charlie,*' as indicative of this attitude and approach.

Another famous *Lion Comique,* is the Great Vance. He is noted for singing songs about fashionable places in which to be seen; typically in the Zoological Gardens in the Regent's Park immortalized in his song, '*Walking in the Zoo.*' This song has done more to make the Zoological Gardens a preferred place of destination than the Royal Aquarium in Victoria, a song about which Leybourne composed called, '*Lounging in the Aq.*'

The *Lions Comique* specialize in singing songs, which extol the joys of drinking, extravagance at every turn, idleness or philandering.

"Well, is that not what life is all about?" I once heard Lodge say in reply to this description.

However, such an extravagant style of living was characterized in George Leybourne's [1] song entitled, '*Champagne Charlie*' or '*Lounging at the Royal Aq.*' [2] Leybourne was one of the first *Lions Comique,* and indeed we had the pleasure of meeting him in his Imperial Theater within the Royal Aquarium & Winter Gardens, of which, of course, he is the manager.

That occasion was marked by a singular event involving Lodge. Jack and I were waiting on Lodge whilst standing at the Crush Bar when our attention was arrested by a vision of an image. Affixed to a nearby wall was a large, glazed, timber frame, containing a poster advertising the performance of a symphony, a choral anthem symphony or some such musical extravaganza. However, printed upon the poster and contained within a circle was a silver nitrate daguerreotype image, an unmistakable likeness of the promoter of this musical concert.

The image depicted a well to do person, looking quite dapper, in his black shiny silk top hat worn at an angle and white gloves with a large cigar in his mouth and monocle in his eye. The promoter of the concert, that Jack and I both instantly recognized, was none other than Lodge!

I distinctly remembered that we both of us were aghast at seeing such a display of reckless confidence, which was further compounded by the fact, that Lodge wore upon his face, as he stared out from the poster, such a conceited fixed grin as to indicate clearly a sustained contempt for all and sundry. Moments later he re-appeared arm in arm with a fellow, who he promptly introduced to us as Mr. George Leybourne, actor manager of the Imperial Theater. Every time I think of Leybourne, I recall that preposterous poster with a likeness of Lodge's face upon it, complete with cigar and monocle looking out contemptuously.

Another reason for remembering George Leybourne, was because of some sound advice he imparted to us just before we went on stage for our début at the Imperial Music Hall. I wished to God then, that I had heeded it.

'Gentlemen,' Leybourne had said to us, 'please allow

me to offer you some advice. Not that you need it, but none the less, it may prove useful to you. Firstly, Music Hall in England is not the same as Vaudeville is in America. Secondly, what you term as Vaudeville in America is not the same as Variety Theater in England. And thirdly, what in England might be considered Burlesque would be termed Vaudeville in America. But then gentlemen I feel certain that you know this. Good luck!'

And with that Parthian shot Leybourne abandoned both Jack and me to our fates.

Jack and I did not really understand these critical differences, much to our subsequent resulting embarrassment on stage.

Continuing the idea of the *Lions Comique*, it occurred to me that Cinderella, looking like a wealthy well-dressed girl of the ingénue type, fitted well into thus genre as a visible comparison between her refinement and the uncouth behavior of the assembled costermongers. As usual her act was a resounding tour de force, but did little to increase my confidence in going out in front of the costermongers. The presence of who filled me with a nameless foreboding and a dread, equal only to that found in the finale to the second act of Wagner's opera, *'Götterdämmerung.'* [3]

However, that time had arrived now the intermission was over and we awaited our introduction by the compère; it was soon enough in coming.

Jack was attired in his outfit of white flannel trousers and striped blazer and waited opposite in the wing of the stage. I in my white moygashell white linen suit complete with straw Sennit with purple and blue band around the crown, waited in the other wing. We both put our thumbs up and through closed teeth, grinned at each other across the stage behind the drawn heavy purple velvet safety curtain, as was our habit before hitting the boards.

"Ladies and gentlemen," shouted the compère, "pray silence for a new innovative act, involving our friends from the New World with their new mystery partner, who wish to bring, for your delectation and unadulterated delight, an act so amazing and daring in its creation and execution, that it will leave you dazzled and your senses in a state of total disarray. My friends please welcome Houston, Mitchell and Marmeduke!"

In an instant the safety curtain rose up into the attic above the stage, exposing both Jack and me in the wings. Immediately I marched out to center stage with my hand outstretched to shake Jack's on meeting him. Whilst doing so, a dull feeling in the pit of my stomach welled up as a total reaction to the compère's over-generous introduction to our act. It never pays, in my experience, to over rate an act before it is completed. An audience will naturally denigrate the act before it has even stated.

"What have we this evening my good friend, to regale our worthy audience with?" I asked Jack, as he made his way to the pianoforte and I approached the footlights at the front of the stage.

"Our new song of course, *'Moonlight on the Strand,'* 4 especially written for our début here in this fine Music Hall in the heart of the West End," replied Jack, as he began to move his hands over the ivory keyboard. In so doing produced such a beautiful elegiac sonority of harmony that a hushed silence descended immediately upon the audience.

I started to twirl my gold capped ebony cane in my right hand whilst waving my straw Sennit in my left. The introduction bars completed, I enjoined and in a low E flat key began my song, *'Moonlight on the Strand.'*

Walking down a moonlit Strand,
On an evening bitter with cold,
I chanced upon a flower girl,
A life away from old.

Refrain:
Oh Sir, please buy my flower,
It is the last I have to sell,
It will reflect the silver moon light,
And look good upon your lapel.

I look upon this pavement primrose,
With a sweetness in her eyes...

I had not gotten into my stride for the second verse, when it happened. All of a sudden and unbidden, the costermongers rose up from their plush red seats and were swaying in anticipation of the melodic intensity of the next verse. Jack accordingly, led with chords from the pianoforte and I followed with the lyrics. I had not reached the end of the second line of the second verse when instinctively the costermongers joined in perfect pitch and sang the words along with me.

I could not figure out how they were able to predict with such accuracy and melodic development the song, but somehow they were able to do so. Needless to say upon completion of our song, the costermongers applauded themselves generously. Some, I noticed, attempted to ascend into an induced state of delirium; such was their delight at our successful joint effort.

I continued with another favorite song, *'Alabama in the Morning.'*

At the end of which and after much foot stamping and general commotion in the stalls, the audience again settled down in anticipation of more of this innovative act of ours. Lodge, I noticed, had in the meantime, abandoned his seat in the Dress Circle. And was nowhere to be seen in the auditorium; even wearing his flamboyant, if overtly ostentatious mid-night blue colored suit. It is possible he felt a little uncomfortable being in the midst of the costers, who had migrated from the stalls to the Dress Circle, normally his undoubted domain.

Suddenly the lights in the auditorium were dimmed, as were those illuminating the stage. I could just see Jack sitting at the pianoforte playing softly, almost inaudibly, François Couperin's haunting '*La Barricade Mysterious,*' an introduction for the next turn which involved Cinderella in the guise of Marmeduke, the living ventriloquist's dummy in her new rôle of a ventriloquist's dummy. Apart from Jack's sublime arpeggios cascading out from his pianoforte, the auditorium was filled with a deafening silence; such was everybody's expectation. I was standing stage right in the wings experiencing first hand this feeling of anticipation.

Gradually a shaft of weak, flickering, pale yellow limelight created by an arc lamp was trained on a section of the stage scenery. The flickering limelight looked as if it might be extinguished at any moment, for such was its anæmic weakness and fragility. Moments went by but then the limelight appeared to increase in its intensity sufficient to illuminate further areas of the stage backdrop including a large wicker basket, which appeared to move or have within its confines something which was alive or struggling.

Jack increased the amplitude of the triple fifths coming from the pianoforte creating a distinctive tinkling sound, as though a cascade of diamonds were ricocheting off slabs of marble. This ethereal music evolved into a complex variation on Couperin's serene, 'La Barricade Mysterious.' It was to this sublime, but haunting sound, that we witnessed, in the subdued light of the stage, the lid of the wicker basket open gradually.

Rising from the wicker basket was a hand followed by an arm. Presently the back of a head appeared and eventually we could just make out a body rising up as if being hauled out of the box by unseen wires. Without turning around the body threw one leg over the side of the basket and then paused. It did so, as though gathering its strength to continue attempting to climb out of the wicker basket. At length the body just succeeded, and lifted its other leg over the side of the box. It stood there still with its back to the audience.

The lighting on the stage continued to be subdued, adding to the sense of uncertainty; but from what movement I could make out, the form appeared to be swaying, as though caught in a breeze.

Jack persisted in racing through his scales made on the pianoforte, the arpeggios from which based on, 'La Barricade Mysterious,' now created a sinister impression as though indication a presentiment about to manifest itself on the gloomy stage still bathed a subdued light.

Then it happened, the body turned around to face the audience. At the same time the intensity of the footlights increased to the general simultaneous and spontaneous gasp of horror from the audience, including the costermongers and Undeserving Poor. I too felt a vacuüm in my chest, as the full impact of the vision of this spectacle before me, assailed my sensibilities.

From where I was standing in the side wings of the stage, I was witnessing something, which instilled a peculiar sensation within my soul. The figure was dressed in immaculate clothes, but assembled on its body in a slovenly, almost dishevelled manner. Still shuffling slowly to the front of the stage, the body wore a tall top hat, of the stove-pipe variety; beloved of the early Victorians, except this hat was covered in dull black velvet in place of the usual silk material. In addition two long black satin ribbons, reflecting the light from the footlights, were trailing from the back.

As the body shuffled towards the footlights, I could see that it was wearing a full-length black frock-coat buttoned up tightly, as if to bind its swaying body together. Below the frock-coat, it wore light grey shirt with frayed wing collars fastened with a dark purple neck-tie secured with a stone of pure black jet. Its trousers were tight-fitting and made of black herringbone patterned broadcloth. The boots on its feet were black and heavily varnished to the extent they reflected the footlights to which they were gradually moving towards. On its hands it wore dove grey kid gloves.

It then stopped its shuffling gait and stood still swaying from side to side. Several moments went by before I could discern any other movement. But then, I did. Gradually the figure lifted its head up into the faint shaft of weak, flickering, pale yellow limelight that had followed it whilst moving from the back of the stage to the footlights. Its face was of such repellent aspect as it became visible for the first time, that another general gasp of horror rose from all in the audience, which reverberated around the auditorium as an echo might in a cave.

The face staring up into the yellow limelight was severely pockmarked; indicating that the sufferer had fought desperately with disease in earlier days and had only just survived the contagion afflicting it. However, the weak yellow limelight was sufficient to reveal two jet black eyes, which were sunk deeply into, their sockets set in its scared face. But, those eyes reflected sadness, as though they had, in the past witnessed much unhappiness, as they stared out into the darkness of the auditorium. From where I was standing I could discern no hair protruding from beneath its top hat and so concluded the creature to be bald.

Then for no discernable reason that I could determine, the figure began to shake, as though it were in the middle of having a violent convulsive fit or was seriously afflicted with rampant St. Vitus' Dance. Both its gloved hands were shaking at the side of its body as it looked up into the pale limelight. Its legs also shook in synchronized sympathy both with the St. Vitus' Dance and Jack's manic creation of arpeggios racing out from the pianoforte still accompanying the stricken form.

It then turned its face to the right of the stage. Moments later it parted its purple colored lips, and in so doing, revealed to a stunned audience, a set of rotted yellow teeth, some of which were missing, creating black gaps in the array, together with a glaring manic expression. It then moved its face from right to left in a sweeping arc across the auditorium. The figure returned its attention to the front of the auditorium looking out blankly at the audience assembled in front of it.

By now it had shuffled its way to the very front of the stage immediately above the gas fired footlights, the light from which then created long dark shadows coming up from its chin. These shadows had the effect of turning its manic expression into one of an exaggerated grotesque image. The audience remained silent throughout and even the costermongers were moved to remain respectfully quiet whilst they witnessed this, this thing in front of their very eyes.

The thing stood at the very precipice of the stage, still shaking for some considerable time. Eventually, in desperation, it folded its arms on to its chest. It did so, I could detect, in a vain effort to control its evident affliction. At the same time it moved its head assumed a circular motion with the occasional baring of its rotted yellow teeth, reënforcing that unnerving manic facial expression.

At one stage, the severity of its affliction was such that it was then compelled to kneel down on one knee, as though in genuflection, begging for relief or merciful release from its appalling torment. Then, with its head bowed low, we could detect a low murmur coming from the recumbent figure illuminated by the footlights. These low sounds soon developed into a plainchant accompanied by Jack still playing elegiac, if mournful, arpeggios from the pianoforte.

At first I had difficulty understanding what the creature was trying to chant. Eventually it began to enunciate clearly and I started to appreciate what it was attempting to utter. It described having cholera, then typhoid, quickly followed by scarlet fever before it was but four years of age and told how its mother, to avoid contagion, put it into a basket and shoved it out in to the out-going tide at Wapping Reach on the Thames.

It related this story, whilst pointing, with a shaking arm, to the basket from which it had just emerged. How that basket, began to leak, when out on the river and in which he began to drown, but for the swift selfless action of a kindly nearby costermonger who, at the time, was wading through the shore tide.

The figure then chanted with an intense sadness of missing its home, and told that it had spent its life searching the Reaches of Wapping for its mother and still continues to do so to this day. How it was put into living bondage, because of its scarred face, and forced to work as a grave digger. And it was only fed just enough whelks from the river to enable it to labor continuously. But, when it asked for a pay rise of only a farthing each year, so it could continue to search for its mother, the employer tried to bury it alive, in the very grave it was digging for another corpse.

Then for a few moments, the figure paused and fell silent. It then gradually raised its head again up into the shaft of weak yellow limelight. Again, the shaft of light illuminated the manic expression on its face, caused by the baring of its rotted teeth and his coal black eyes still rolling around aimlessly in their deep dark sockets. Despite the grotesque features upon its face, it turned its head in a wide sweeping arc for all in the auditorium to witness.

Gradually and with great difficulty, it got up from its recumbent genuflection, and shuffled about the stage, still shaking from the St. Vitus' Dance, which now had noticeably increased in its intensity. Facing the audience it proceeded to sing slowly of its affliction and deep loss. It did so, with such emotion and depth of feeling together with a sad lyrical intensity as to induce visible tears in the eyes of some of the costermongers. It continued to chant about a deep fervent hope of one day, of being released from its torment and loneliness from being torn away from its mother.

Watching this from the stage wing, I could feel over whelming depths of emotions welling up inside me. This was such as to induce profound feelings of sadness and helplessness inside my heart. The form continued to address the attentive audience.

Now standing above the footlights at the very precipice of the stage, the specter continued to relate its story about its unbearable and continuous longing. And, being condemned to search perpetually for its mother, from whom it remembered only the experience of love and tender affection during its illness and despair, with death constantly hovering above the cot.

And, had anybody here in the audience seen her?

That was it. To this pleading sentiment the costermongers and, indeed some in the Dress Circle, finally failed to control themselves. They erupted into unbridled applause with some even induced a mild form of delirium into their re-action to what they were witnessing on the stage.

There were even audible offers to the creature from some of the costermongers and even some in the Dress Circle of an immediate home and family, starting this very evening. More of the costermongers, I noticed, were now moved to tears and were clutching at each other for emotional support.

The applause showed no sign of diminishing and indeed it was a tremendous response to the figure. Removing its black velvet covered stove-pipe top hat it bowed to an appreciative audience and then clambered back into its wicker basket.

The applause from the audience by now had reached a deafening crescendo, in expressing their appreciation for the afflicted St. Vitus' Dancer.

I could not believe just what I had experienced. But I knew one thing. That I was standing in the presence of a genius; in my witnessing Cinderella's innovative act. From whence did she get these moments of pure inspiration? I continue to ask myself this very question.

1. Manager of the Imperial Music Hall
2. Royal Aquarium & Winter Garden
3. Twilight of the Gods – opera
4. Lyrics by Edward Plesse

Chapter 32

The Brave and the Damned

Jack and I were in the Grand Dining Room at the St. Pancras Hotel, enjoying a celebratory champagne breakfast with Cinderella following our début at the Empire Music Hall the previous evening. Cinderella's portrayal of Marmeduke, the real ventriloquist's dummy, had been an outstanding success and her performance a resounding tour de force. I had harbored feelings and doubts at one stage fearing it might degenerate into a complete fiasco, a débâcle even. It had not, thanks to Cinderella's interpretation and our new song, *'Moonlight on the Strand,'* which seemed to go down well with the audience. We were now searching eagerly through the morning newspapers, most of which had reviewed our performance and were unanimous in their praise, confirming us as being innovative and polished to a shine.

"Another bottle of chilled Veuve Clicquot champagne, my good man," instructed Cinderella, to a passing waiter.

"Certainly ma'am," came his welcome response.

Champagne or no champagne, Jack would insist on having his Brätwürst and rye bread for break-fast. Cinderella and I were just happy just to drink the champagne and smoke our Trichinopoly cigars.

"For the first time since we arrived from New York," said Jack, "I actually feel as though we achieved something last night, with no small help from you Cinderella!"

"Oh sir you are too kind sir," replied Cinderella, in a mock southern belle drawl, "but read what the *London Post* has printed about us."

> 'A veritable coup de théâtre was performed at the Empire Music Hall yesterday evening by a triple act called Houston, Mitchell & Marmeduke. To sublime arpeggios emanating from a stage pianoforte played competently by Mitchell, the other performed a surreal dance ritual revolving around a specter come back to life seeking its mother who abandoned it at an early age due to it having contagious diseases. The acting and presentation held the audience enthralled for good reason, as indeed it did to the writer of this review.'

"Here is a good one," said Jack, handing over the copy of the *Daily News* to Cinderella.

> 'A new *Vent* [1] act is playing in the West End, brought to us by an enterprising trio named Houston, Mitchell & Marmeduke. After a successful début at the Empire Music Hall, the audience was treated to a truly ghostly apparition of a specter seeking its mother who abandoned it in childhood. The rôle of Marmeduke, the specter, was performed with an intensity worthy of Garrick.'

"There is an article by the eminent theater critic William Archer, writing in *The Times,*" I offered.

'The combination of sublime and ethereal pianoforte playing and the apparition of a top hat-wearing specter in search of its mother, must rank as one of the most innovative Music Hall turns I have witnessed in a long time. Houston, Mitchell & Marmeduke are to be commended for this interesting innovation, polished to a shine.'

"Here is one about you Theo," said Cinderella, and began reading a review from *The Daily Telegraph*.

'Mr Theodore Houston from the new triple act called, Houston, Mitchell and Marmeduke regaled audiences yesterday evening at the Empire Music Hall in Leicester Square with several new songs, including, *'Moonlight on the Strand,'* written especially for their début at the Empire Music Hall. It remains a joy to be able to hear fresh new songs that the audience clearly responded to warmly as they sang along last night accompanying the singer. Those songs were vastly different to a later turn by the same the triple act, which evolved into something totally unexpected and well worth the experience.'

"Read this one," suggested Jack, "from *The Globe,* newspaper.

'Not every portrayal of a specter need fill us with a Gothick dread. Sometimes an apparition may invoke deep feelings of sadness or sympathy for the human condition compelled to endure the almost unendurable. Those of us who were present at the Empire Music Hall last night, could not fail to have been moved by a sterling performance of a specter from a new act called Houston, Mitchell & Marmeduke. The intensity of the acting was augmented and made all the more poignant by the atmospheric music emanating from the stage piano which was played to a remarkably accomplished level.'

"Well done Jack," congratulated Cinderella.

"What surprised me at the time Cinderella," I said, "was the fact that the audience in the stalls made up in the main by our friends the costermongers, or costers, as we have learned to call them, sang along as *The Daily Telegraph* has reported. We only received the song a day or two before our début there."

"Oh," replied Cinderella, "I had arranged to have the song printed in the handbill for our evening performance for the costermonger's benefit so they could sing along. They could not remember one song, let alone predict the lyrics of a newly unheard song, with its melodic intonation, especially since most of them are tone deaf!"

At that moment Lodge appeared in the doorway of the Grand Dining Room. As usual he stopped in his progress, so that others, taking break-fast, might be afforded an opportunity to notice him. He looked about the place, and then came over to us swerving around the various break-fast tables as a seasoned waiter might. As he did so, he blew kisses into the air in an exaggerated and ostentatious manner.

"I knew we could do it", he said, whilst helping

himself to our champagne and Trichinopoly cigars, I knew we could do it, did I not say so and...?"

"Hold on Lodge," I interrupted, "what is it with the *we*; so far as I could make out it was Marmeduke and Jack here who made it happen, so where were you? As far as we could see, during our act you had abandoned your comfortable plush red velvet covered seat in the Dress Circle amongst the costers."

Lodge, phlegmatic as usual, did not appear to be put out in the slightest by my incisive remark, but merely tapped the side of his nose with his index finger.

"A favor here, a favor there; a word here and a word there, including speaking with the manager of the very place of your resounding success, the Empire Music Hall. And, by the way, where is the elusive Marmeduke?" asked Lodge, pouring the contents of his fluted glass down his throat and then, breathing out noisily

"I believe he is resting," said Jack, looking at Cinderella.

"However, another reason I have come by, is to say that we will be performing the acclaimed, if sacred Cholera,[2] sorry I mean Choral, Anthem Symphony at the Royal Albert Hall within the next few days! Mabel, of course, will be in the title rôle supported by Dot Hetherington and Katie Lawrence.

"The Royal Albert Hall is not strictly a Music Hall, you understand, but there it is. None the less though, it is the place where many Music Hall artistes have perfected their acts. More importantly, it remains the largest concert hall in Europe, or at least so the newspapers would have one believe. I do need a large auditorium; for such as the large numbers of persons we anticipate witnessing our divine choral oratorio," said Lodge as he rose to leave, "au revoir, my protégés; until this evening when we rendezvous at the Theater Royal in Drury Lane!"

I had noticed that over the period of time that we have been aware of his Choral Anthem Symphony, Lodge has been gradually investing the work with an ethereal almost ecclesiastical and revered significance. One could only conclude that this was in order to impress upon the work an inordinate importance in his endeavors to elevate the Choral Symphony above the mundane and lend it an air of verisimilitude. Presumably, this is in order to gain yet unheard of record box office receipts.

"Cinderella, Theo," said Jack, after he had finished the last of his Brätwürst and rye bread and raising his glass of champagne, "to our new successful act! Let us continue to be creative and innovative."

1. Ventriloquists were known as *Vent* acts
2. Since the Alhambra Music Hall manager, ET Smith, mistakenly called the Choral Symphony, the *Cholera*, the name has stuck in Lodge's mind.

Chapter 33

The Theater Royal, Drury Lane

Our new *Vent* act with Cinderella seemed to be a success and showed if nothing else that we were doing something correctly. Equally of import was the news that Lodge had imparted to us, in a nonchalant manner, of his hiring of the Royal Albert Hall. I must confess, his achievments as an impresario never ceased to amaze both Jack and me. By general consensus, the Titanic Benefit Concert, during which, of course, the august Choral Anthem Symphony was performed, had, in retrospect, turned out to be an unmitigated disaster. But Lodge is now revising his assessment of the results and has actually intimated to us that the concert may not have been quite the calamity or débâcle we had all supposed it to have been. For seated in the audience that evening was the general manager, over whom, based on his alleged cult personality, Lodge, has some *sway*. This same manager has now invited Lodge to organize a performance of the venerable Choral Anthem Symphony at the Royal Albert Hall at his earliest convenience. In the meantime we were en-route to the Theater Royal in Drury Lane, Covent Garden.

There was a chill in the evening air, impressed with the acrid fog which still showed no sign of abating, as our Clarence carriage, driven by our liveried coach man, pulled up outside the Theater Royal in Drury Lane in Covent Garden, to witness the latest pantomime there. Jack and I were suitably attired in our evening dress of black tail-coats and trousers, white carnations, silver colored waist-coats, and highly varnished boots. Beneath our tail-coats we wore white silk shirts with starched wing collars secured by restrained mauve bow ties, all completed by our shiny black silk top hats and gold capped black ebony canes.

Lodge, for some reason looked gloomy; possibly pantomime was not his forte, or he disliked being associated with it. For whatever reason, I simply could not imagine. This fact was not helped by his choice of garb, in that he resembled more a funeral undertaker than one dressed to attend the theater. He was dressed in a black herringbone patterned broadcloth frock-coat and trousers and wearing a pair of dull, and in places scuffed, black boots.

On this occasion he had dispensed with his usual flamboyant black cape with its blazing red silk lining despite the chill. The shirt he wore was equally uninspiring, in that it was off white, almost a light grey in color and the collars of which were tied with a neckerchief of purple silk secured with a pin of amethyst, his only concession to ostentatious or conspicuous fashion.

His top hat was patched and in need of brushing in order to restore the sheen in the silk. In effect, despite the occasion, his somber frock coat, combined with the solemn facial expression he wore, made him appear as though he were on his way to a funeral. Possibly leading the *cortège in person*, I thought, *whilst carrying the black pennant, rather* than a carefree thespian en-route to the theater to witness serious pantomime.

Disregarding Lodge's subdued demeanor, we stepped down from the Clarence on to a wet Drury Lane, the sidewalk of which was glistening from the effect of the fog condensing upon the York flagstones. They in turn reflected a myriad of garish lights created by various gas lamps fixed to the front of the Theater Royal. It made for a kind of magical experience, especially given the occasion we were attending.

We took our places in the queue to gain access into the foyer, which was busy with people searching for Crush Bars, tickets or each other. Jack then tapped me on the arm and nodded to a bill posted in a glazed timber frame fixed to the foyer wall next to the doorway through which we were about to enter.

"I cannot wait to see how Cinderella will perform in this acclaimed pantomime given her experiences and innovative skills. For never have I known a person who is able to assume the rôles of such a wide variety of characters with so much ease as our Cinderella does!" said Jack, affectionately.

Jack's remarks did not entirely surprise me; for I too had concluded the same and looked forward to seeing Cinderella execute her rôle. Quite how she would express it and acquit herself only added to the excitement and anticipation.

"And," continued Jack, "I shall be more than interested to see how Mabel Green acquits herself in whatever rôle she has been assigned!"

What concerned me, however, was my ability to understand the proceedings on the stage, since the plot of any pantomime becomes somewhat irrelevant to the antics or events on stage.

Jack then pointed with his cane in the direction of the general mêlée in the auditorium. I looked over

The
THEATER ROYAL
DRURY LANE
General Manager: Sir Augustus Harris

PROUDLY PRESENTS

THE
GOLDILOCKS
PANTOMIME

BASED ON
RICKARD WAGNER'S

'Männerlist größer als Frauenlist
oder
Die Glückliche Bärenfamilie'

STARRING

THE INCORRIGIBLE   CINDERELLA
KING'S JESTER   DAN LENO
EVERLASTING   VESTA TILLEY

WITH

LITTLE TICH
NELLIE POWER
ELLA SHIELDS
MABEL GREEN
MALCOLM SCOTT
MADAME HECULINE
VULCANA

expectantly. So did Lodge who also had noticed Jack's gesture. Within moments Sir Augustus Harris came into view and passed through the crowds in the foyer, to where we were standing.

"Jack, Theo good to see you again, though I certainly did not expect you, Lodge to attend such a lavish pantomime occasion as this and grace us with your presence, but welcome to the Theater Royal. I feel confident we can just about squeeze you into the red plush private box I have secured for us. Gentlemen, time is on our side, so please do follow me," said Sir Augustus Harris, referring at his gold Hunter.

We felt more delighted than obliged to fall in with his idea, since we all knew exactly where we were headed. Even Lodge cheered up at this prospect. Sure enough having ascended the wide sweeping red-carpeted stairs up to the *piano-nobile,* we were then escorted down a corridor finished in opulent décor. We then entered an even more extravagantly appointed room containing a circular Crush Bar, the counter of which was capped in *Breccia Pernice Rossa* marble. It was up to this marble topped bar that we repaired, as Sir Augustus Harris ordered Perrier-Jouët Blason Rosé champagne.

At few moments later, when we had secured our champagne, Lodge raised his fluted glass and offered a toast.

"To Sir Augustus Harris and his new pantomime and the inevitable successes this venture will bring him."

We all clinked our glasses together and drank liberally from them.

"As I have said before; to my friends I am Gus and not Sir Augustus Harris," he said looking specifically at Lodge.

"Gus, as we entered the foyer down stairs," said Jack,

"we noticed that the story upon which the pantomime is based has somewhat changed. When we spoke at the Abbey Grange some time ago, you invited Cinderella to perform in a pantomime based on Rickard Wagner's first opera, *'Die Laune des Verliebten.'* [1] This intrigued me and I am sure Jack and Loge here, and..."

"Yes I noticed that glaring omission as we entered your esteemed Theater Royal Gus," interrupted Lodge.

"The answer is quite simple Jack," replied Gus, "when we began rehearsals, it was Cinderella who suggested that the plot, or rather libretto forming the plot for Wagner's opera, *'Die Laune des Verliebten,'* was simply just too convoluted, even by his standard. It did not lend itself to immediate suggestion or indeed anecdotal jocularity, which of course, both form the basic rationale of any pantomime.

"So we decided to abandon that opera, and instead base our pantomime on another early Wagnerian opera written in 1837; that of *'Männerlist größer als Frauenlist oder Die glückliche Bärenfamilie.'* [2] This opera too is still based on a rather convoluted story, typical of Wagner. But it is more susceptible and amenable for adaptation into continuous form of reckless and abandoned hilarity that will amuse our discerning audience!

"The plot, if there is one, is based on Julius, a silversmith, who claims to be of aristocratic lineage. He is persuaded by Leontine to arrange to marry her cousin Aurora, the conspicuously unattractive daughter of von Abendthau, a pretentious baron. Having realized his action was rash, he looks for a way out from his promise to marry Aurora. At that moment Julius recognizes, in the street, a passing bear-keeper as being really his father, and that the dancing bear is his long lost brother in costume! When Julius' real parents are known, he is denounced by the baron leaving Julius free to marry Leontine! As you will no doubt have determined; the plot is clever, convoluted and innovative," said Gus.

On learning of the plot on which the night's pantomime was based, an expression of abject horror crossed Lodge's face, as the full implication of what he was now going to have to endure; possibly the unendurable, became all too apparent to him. His monomanic affliction increased noticeably to such an alarming extent that we feared the worst. However, he leaned for support against a nearby limestone jardinière, in an attempt to steady himself.

Eventually, Lodge recovered his composure, after some light cajoling by Jack and persuasion of a more intimidating kind from Gus. At length he relinquished his grip of the jardinière and consented reluctantly, if hesitantly, to accompany us to our reserved private box. We made our way through a labyrinth of corridors and galleries before being admitted into our box, the door of which was held open by a most peculiar looking individual.

He was clearly a liveried flunky in full regalia wearing blue velvet knickerbockers and white silk stockings and buckled shoes, together with a pink tail-coat elaborately decorated with gold braid on his chest and epaulettes on his shoulders. Had it not been for the white powdered grey horsehair wig adorning his head; I could have mistaken him for Lodge's man-servant Aloysius and his odd penchant for fancy, if servile, uniform.

After much bowing by our door flunky, we made our way into the box. But, before taking our seats, we all instinctively looked around the full auditorium. This was more to enable the audience to see us in our red plush private box, than our appreciation of the all too important box office receipts, expressed in the full house below us, the kind of which Lodge could only dream of.

We took our seats, with Lodge electing to sit at the back of the box, out of sight, and precariously seated next to a table laden with chilled Pierre Darcy Brut NV Champagne, to which he helped liberally himself without hesitation, or indeed I noticed, reserve.

"What are the goods on this Theater Royal Gus, does it have a royal warrant?" inquired Jack, as we made ourselves comfortable in spacious scarlet velvet upholstered seats.

"As near as damn it," replied Gus, pointing to the royal coat of arms emblazoned on the purple colored safety curtain." This Theater Royal, the fourth such one to be built on this site, has a most illustrious history and remains the oldest functioning theater in London.

"Previously English theater was subject to repressive laws because the Church considered theater plays or acts to be thinly disguised pagan rituals and accordingly outlawed their performance. Gradually over the centuries *Miracle Plays* were allowed, primarily as a means of instruction or explanation of biblical stories to the illiterate masses, most notably the *Undeserving Poor*. Inflexible censorship has always plagued English theater and this was always the case up until the restoration of King Charles II [nd.]

"Theaters in England however, continued to be highly regulated by the Crown, which might grant permission, over the Church, to run a theater in the form of letters patent, in particular to Sir William Davenant, and also to Sir Thomas Killigrew, who built the first theater on this site in 1666 and engaged the famous actress Nell Gwyn and Charles Hart. These letters patent allowed only the Theater Royal in Drury Lane, or the Theater Royal at

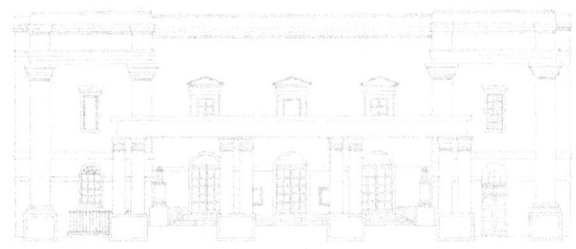

Theater Royal, Drury Lane

Covent Garden,[3] to stage *straight* drama involving spoken dialogue. Note the designation *royal* in the theater's name. Other none royal theaters, without the grant of letters patent, were required to express their acting sentiment not in words, but in mime! You can now perhaps appreciate from where *pantomime* originated.

"In 1660 an senior officer of the Crown called the Lord Chamberlain, was charged with enforcing the provisions within these letters patent in order to make sure that the law was neither being broken or abused. His powers were later redefined in the Theatrical Regulations Act, 1843. [4] Thereafter the Lord Chamberlain could only intervene and order a play to be stopped, where he felt that, '...*it is fitting for the preservation of good manners, decorum or of the public peace so to do.*' [5]

"The 1843 Act also empowered local justices of the peace to license theaters, and helped remove the monopoly of theaters operating on the letters patent to the disadvantage of non patent theaters. This one piece of legislation in the 1843 Act, effectively facilitated the unhindered spread of popular saloon theaters in public houses or supper rooms, as in Late Evans Supper Room, up the road from here, leading on to the inevitable inescapable development of our beloved Music Hall.

"Irrespective of the powers exercised by the Lord Chamberlains, many plays were performed in public as a result of innovative and resourceful playwrights. Often, they could write lines which appeared innocuous, according as to how they were spoken, with the ingenious use of lascivious innuendo, double entendre or simple inflective of which the noted exponent of this practice today is our Marie Lloyd or Vesta Victoria. This clever use of words, grammatical resort or sound can still defeat the Lord Chamberlain or various Vigilance Committees' examination and continues to thrive in our Music Halls today," concluded Gus.

"You say this Theater Royal is the fourth such one to be built on this site?" asked Jack.

"That is very much the case Jack," replied Gus, "for alas, as was common in those days, in 1672 the first Theater Royal caught fire. Undaunted Sir Thomas Kelligrew built another theater to the designs of the architect Sir Christopher Wren, shortly after completing his Cathedral named for St. Paul. That theater building was called by its current name, the Theater Royal in Drury Lane and opened two years later in 1674. The Theater Royal was managed by my predecessors, including such esteemed thespians as Colley Cibber or David Garrick. It was Garrick, who in 1775 commissioned the famed architect Robert Adam to redesign the interior of the auditorium. Fifteen or so years later, it was demolished in 1791!

"This was ostensibly to make way for a larger theater which opened in 1794 to the designs of Henry Holland with Richard Brinsley Sheridan in the rôle of actor-manager. Alas that fine theater too caught fire and burned down in 1809. The theater, the fourth built theater, we are sitting in at this present moment, was constructed in 1812 by Benjamin Wyatt. The architect and father of James Wyatt, the creator of that phäntasmagoric structure called, Fonthill Abbey, that Cinderella referred to when you were guests of mine at the Abbey Grange. As I stated earlier, this Theater Royal is the oldest theater in London,," said Gus, pointing vaguely to the full house in front of us, resembling a sea of red plush illuminated by several acetylene gas-fuelled glass chandeliers.

I looked around the spacious well-appointed auditorium dripping with history.

"Despite its impeccable antecedents and history," continued Gus, "the Theater Royal continues to draw the crowds into its auditorium which can seat over two thousand persons. Only recently, two years ago in fact, we staged very successfully extravagant play called, 'The Whip,' That play included an excursion train crash and a horse race from the legendary 'Two-Thousand Guineas Stakes' involving twelve horses running on a specially constructed on-stage treadmill!

"Our pantomimes, such as the one we are about to enjoy, are now a yearly tradition; in that our public expect, no indeed demand, a pantomime extravaganza. It was when I was dining at Romano's restaurant, not far from here, that I first engaged the rising Marie Lloyd as the principal girl, especially for one of my, 'Lane' [6] pantomimes. At the time she amazed me when having advised her where the pantomime would be staged; here at the Theater Royal in Drury Lane, she responded by saying that she had always thought this building was a garrison!" said Gus.

"How could she conclude so? Your building looks exactly as a theater ought to look," I replied.

"Quite simply Theo, Lloyd assumed this indeed was a garrison on account of the number of soldiers to be seen in the vicinity of the theater. In days gone by, the Theater Royal, because of its royal connection had, similarly to the Bank of England, its own military guard. Now we keep a guard of sorts, dressed in blue velvet knickerbockers and white silk stockings and pink tailcoats to maintain order and keep the Nihilists or hecklers in check!

"Rather like your débâcle which attended your ill-fated Titanic Benefit Concert, eh Lodge? You should have held it here, at the undoubted home of extravaganzas or pantomime, secular or profane," commented Sir Augustus Harris, manager of the Theater Royal at Drury Lane.

"Really?" muttered Lodge, under his breath, "the public be damned; box office receipts come first."

I looked around to view Lodge as he made this remark. It became apparent to me that the monomania, which periodically afflicted him, especially when stressed or annoyed, his habit of looking over his shoulders for no discernable reason, had increased markedly. I also remain certain that I heard him, under his breath, denounced Sir Augustus Harris!

In addition to that revelation, I observed, in the corner of my eye, Jack turn to Sir Augustus.

"Lodge will be more his amenable self when he has drunk a bottle or two of champagne; please exercise patience and give him a few minutes in which to do so," advised Jack.

However, no sooner had Jack uttered these words, than the lights in the auditorium were dimmed. Gradually a solitary beam of silver limelight illuminated the golden royal cipher supported by the lion and the unicorn emblazoned on to a dark purple velvet safety curtain suspended within the proscenium arch.

1. The Mood of the One in Love
2. Men Are More Cunning Than Women, or The Happy Bear Family.
3. Covent Garden Opera House
4. Also known as the Theaters Act, 1843
5. Theatrical Regulations Act 1843, Section 12 - running an unruly house.
6. Nickname for the Theater Royal in Drury Lane

Chapter 34

The Pantomime of Elegance

Seated in our red plush private box in the Theater Royal, Drury Lane were Sir Augustus Harris at the front flanked by Jack on his left and me to his right. Lodge was sitting behind us in the corner of the small room, precariously next to the table laden with chilled Pierre Darcy Brut NV champagne. Being New Yorkers, though Jack is from Jersey City, we were not really into pantomime, which we both considered to be a very English trait, and an acquired taste. What was of abiding interest to Jack and me, I guess, is how Cinderella and Mabel Green will acquit themselves; and in what rôles will they play within the confines of the proscenium arch defining the stage down there below us. The anticipation was unrelenting.

We did not have long to wait, because the very next moment the orchestra, situated in the pit, began playing. It was directed by an overtly energetic and constantly smiling conductor, wearing a flamboyant white tail-coat, white trousers and more alarmingly, white shoes. At length he plunged the orchestra into a prelude of sorts, which comprised, presumably the pantomime's thematic musical narrative, expressed through a series of leitmotivs. [1]

At the end of this extended prelude, the purple safety curtain ascended into the attic space above the stage revealing a backdrop depicting a forest scene, the center piece of which was a rustic ginger-bread cottage with a yellow thatched roof. For some inexplicable reason, a series of extended chords of Wagnerian music went racing across my mind in a re-action to this rustic stage set.

The large backdrop then wobbled as a preliminary to imminent activity. The darkened windows of the gingerbread cottage suddenly were illuminated from within with soft yellow lights. The front door of the cottage then opened, creating a shaft of light, and out stepped a girl dressed in matching rustic attire including a white cotton smock the front of which was tied up with yellow laces.

One can only assume she was in fact Goldilocks. On her long legs she wore thin white stockings and wooden clogs upon her feet, in which she proceeded to strut about the stage in a peculiarly masculine manner. Upon her head, from which locks of golden curly hair cascaded, she had donned a large straw hat with trailing blue ribbons. But below that was a face, a face which exuded such a smouldering indifference and arrogance as to relegate its owner to the status of that approaching a femme fatale.

I could not determine whether this femme fatale was Cinderella, Mabel Green, Vesta Tilley or indeed Dan Leno; for he was listed in the cast and, I felt certain, was sure to be ambling about somewhere. Then all of a sudden Goldilocks stopped strutting about in her clogs and approached the front of the stage above the footlights. This had the effect of making her loom up, casting a shadow back over the stage. She leaned forward and placed the edge of her hand above her eyes and peered out into the middle distance over the audience.

She looked disappointed and turned around as if to make to reënter the gingerbread cottage. As she did so several ballerinas, dressed as bears, came scampering down the four aisles, which divided the seating in the stalls. Several actually leapt from the floor of the stalls straight up onto the stage in graceful arcs. Others battled their way through the orchestra pit oblivious as to what instruments they commandeered or used, in to order to assist their efforts in getting on to the stage.

Within a short period of time, the stage was teeming with at least forty ballerinas, all dressed in the costumes of bears, milling around and generally getting in each other's way. Not for long; because at that precise moment Goldilocks, who had by now acquired a cane, and had resumed strutting around the stage, started to bellow out orders to the bears to line up. This the bears felt obligated to do so, given the intimidating way Goldilocks addressed them.

Within moments they had formed two ranks of twenty facing the audience. It was at this point I realized just how wide the stage was at the Theater Royal. Notwithstanding this observation, Goldilocks was busy marching up and down the rank and file of bears, and berating them for the flimsiest of reasons. Then instantaneously, the two ranks of bears split in the middle allowing Goldilocks to proceed to the front of the stage, whereupon they all burst into song about the lack of honey bees in the forest, at least I think so, from what we could hear.

Then, the first verse out of the way, the bears danced in complex formation executing a series of delicate, if intricate manœuvres combined with an impressive coördinated precision amongst themselves. This culminated in a few of the larger ballerinas, in bear costumes, carrying out graceful pas de deux, much to the evident delight of some members of the audience, who by now were standing and applauding wildly. Then, as quickly as the bears appeared, they scuttled off, stage right and left. Some even leapt down back into the stalls and raced up the aisles to the rear of the auditorium, from whence they had originally come.

Goldilocks, finding she was alone on the stage, broke into a lullaby about being abandoned in the woods and forced to live in that hovel, whilst pointing with her cane to the gingerbread cottage. She yearned about her fervent wish to be able to join the happy band of forest tree cutters and clear the land of horrible trees. Whilst she expressed this sentiment, there was some evidence of activity in the wings of the stage.

The lights on the stage dimmed, but only marginally and moments later a stout red faced woman with even redder cheeks, clearly no ingénue, [2] and who was in all probability a man, stepped smartly into the limelight. This might well be Dan Leno, I thought. Though in the back of my mind, it occurred to me, for a fleeting moment, the impossibility that it could also be Mabel Green. Apart from that, I could not possibly think of what rôle Wagner had in mind for Dan Leno, wearing women's clothing several sizes too big for him, but there it is I suppose. However, the probability remained that she was in fact actually Aurora, the ugly daughter of the Baron von Abendthau, if the plot of the pantomime was anything to go by.

Within seconds of arriving on to the stage, Aurora was engaged in a heated argument with Goldilocks. I did not think such language was permitted on stage and in public too. This encounter went on for several minutes whilst the two contestants expressed in recitative their utter contempt for each other. The audience could barely contain themselves at witnessing this wanton and outrageous lyrical behavior by Goldilocks and the ugly Aurora.

Now of course, the whole idea and basis of this pantomime, I had to remind myself, was based on Rickard Wagner's opera which essentially is about the profound concept of the fact that, *'Men Are More Cunning Than Women; The Happy Bear Family,'* so the title of the opera printed on my hand bill informed me.

The plot concerns Julius a silversmith, who claims to be an aristocrat. He was persuaded by Leontine to arrange to marry her cousin Aurora, the unattractive daughter of von Abendthau, a pretentious baron. Unfortunately, Julius now wants to escape from his promise of marriage the ugly Aurora.

In the mean time, a few of the bears had poked their noses from behind the side screen of the stage, for so great was the commotion on center stage. Indeed some of the bears actually came on to the stage and took sides with the adversaries including sparring amongst themselves, which was expressed in a series of graceful intricate dance pieces. Goldilocks, in her endeavour to reëstablish her position over the stout woman Aurora, executed a very effective pas de deux around her, causing Aurora to lose her footing and fall to the stage floor with a pronounced thud that reverberated around the hushed auditorium.

Eventually Goldilocks and Aurora joined in a duet, aided by those bears on stage, asking whether beauty, or the lack of it, was more important than being sensible. Thus all the contestants on the stage expressed in the songspiel the lyrical climaxes to their various rôles leading to a thunderous crescendo. But, at that very moment an event occurred that no one could have predicted.

To stage right a solitary shaft of limelight focused on the far right-hand corner of the stage backdrop of the forest scene. Imperceptibly at first due to the dim light but becoming visible slowly, a singular movement became discernable. It was a lamb, bleating as it made its way to the center of the stage, unsure as to what to do or what it might find there. The contestant continued singing, whilst looking, with visible disgust, at the lamb's loud bleating fortissimo interruption and intrusion into their performance.

It was predictable and the audience knew this even if the contestants singing on stage did not. From stage left, Little Bo Peep entered, to tumultuous applause from the costermongers, as she limped onto the stage with her shepherdess' crook. She then stood directly in front of Goldilocks, Aurora and the bears, all of whom were still singing. Little Bo Peep looked about the auditorium with swollen red eyes and a sad bewildered expression upon her face.

Lowering her head in shame, she then made to collect her lost lamb, which she attempted to gather up in her arms. She stumbled on account of her limp and fell down heavily on to the hard timber floorboards of the stage, dropping her shepherdess's crook whilst doing so. The lamb on cue then started to bleat even more loudly disrupting further Goldilocks and Aurora's singing. That was it; within moments of her fall she was rolling around the stage clutching her visibly damaged knee that was now bleeding profusely.

The sound of her crying combined with the lamb's bleating was considerable. Then it happened. During one particular loud episode of her distressed crying, she hauled herself up from the stage floor. But because she could not quite reach her shepherdess' crook, she was unable to support herself and collapsed again back down to the stage deck with a look of helplessness upon her face, wet with tears which glistened in the soft limelight for all to see. Even the lamb started to lick away the tears from her face.

The utter contempt upon the faces of the femme fatale Goldilocks and the ugly Aurora, unable to do anything about Bo Peep's unscheduled appearance at the expense of their glory, was something indescribable. However, Bo Peep was not quite finished yet. Unable to stand up, she dragged herself along the boards, to the accompaniment of desperate crying, to where her shepherdess'crook lay, some several feet away.

On approaching it, she reached out feebly with her thin arm and tried to pull it towards her. After an agonizingly long time she succeeded in retrieving it. Then the audience was subjected to another outburst of tears and crying to the accompaniment of the lamb's even louder bleating, as Little Bo Peep pushed her wet face up into a shaft of golden limelight.

And moving it in a sweeping arc for all in the audience to witness or that no one should fail to see her sad tearful face full of pathos and reflecting the miserable predicament she and her lamb found themselves in. The audience could not believe their good fortune and showed their appreciation by thunderous applause and stamping their feet on the decks of the stalls, balconies and especially in the Dress Circle.

Goldilocks, Aurora and the ballerinas standing around aimlessly in bear costumes, in comparison could barely conceal their overt, unadulterated contempt and seething repulsion, at being out-staged, out-performed and out-applauded by this pathetic bonnet-wearing, frilly dressed with ribbons, concentrated cuteness, who, was able, within seconds of arriving unannounced on stage and with ease, relegate them into total oblivion whilst they sang their parts on stage.

Little Bo Peep ended her impromptu appearance in the pantomime with the lamb bleating for all its worth as it led a limping Bo Peep off the stage to deafening and sustained applause from a delighted audience.

Regardless of the unscheduled arrival of Little Bo Peep and of her bringing the house down, I still tried to remind myself of the plot, if indeed they were vaguely sticking to it, whilst performing this pantomime, ostensibly called, *'Goldilocks,'* but based on a Wagnerian opera with the name of, *Männerlist größer als Frauenlist oder Die glückliche Bärenfamilie.*

Still progressing through the first part of the pantomime, the stage by now was deserted. Again the backdrop wobbled indicating more imminent activity. It came through the gingerbread cottage door with the arrival on to the stage of a woman with pronounced bovine features, dressed in men's clothes. It was of particular note that she was wearing a leather apron, as a silversmith might. This was Julius the silversmith who had rashly promised to marry the ugly Aurora in order that he might become a real aristocrat. It was also very obviously, Ella Shields.

Before the limelight had actually focused on Julius, he burst into song about his rashness in offering to marry the conspicuously ugly Aurora, saying he had made the offer only for her title as an aristocrat but really wanted to marry her cousin, the delectable Leontine!

He would like to woo her with his mandolin, but had given it to Aurora as a pledge of his marriage troth. Having completed his song, he lamented to the audience as to his predicament, the lost mandolin and the troth he had made. Then our energetic and constantly smiling conductor, wearing his flamboyant white tail-coat, white trousers and white shoes, plunged the pit orchestra into an orchestral interlude.

I looked at Jack who also had turned to observe my re-action to the music now coming up from the pit orchestra. We had just heard it play an extended prelude involving a compilation of sonorous musical leitmotivs from the pantomime. The music we were experiencing now was nothing more than that taken from Rickard Strauss's orchestral work called, '*Aus Italien.*' [3] In particular the exhilarating and sublime opening section of the third movement. Followed by the commencement of the first phrase of the fourth movement, which we were now listening to, resembled a comical interlude more fitting for an extended, '*March of the Clowns.*'

Within moments of our realizing the music and its origin, the stage again was inundated with the ballerinas dressed as bears tramping about in an abandoned way with no coördinated precision.

I was beginning to understand pantomime as being an exercise from the ridiculous to the sublime, the preposterous attended by the profound, as we had just heard in Rickard Strauss's music!

This notion of the incongruous was immediately unleashed upon us, based on the notion of the lost mandolin, in a rendering by Julius and the bears of the serenity of chord and elegance surrounding *the* Lost Chord! [4]

I remembered Clara Butt performing this song with a sonority few have matched since. Many singers have tried with the Lost Chord, including Enrico Caruso, whom I had heard sing it previously at the Carnegie Hall and again at the Metropolitan Opera House both in New York. I believe he may have sang it recently at a benefit

The Lost Chord

Seated one day at the organ
I was weary and ill at ease
And my fingers wandered idly
Over the noisy keys

I knew not what I was playing
Or what I was dreaming then
But I struck one chord of music
Like the sound of a great Amen;

It flooded the crimson twilight,
Like the close of an Angel's Psalm
And it lay on my fevered spirit
With a touch of infinite calm

It quieted pain and sorrow,
Like love overcoming strife
It seemed the harmonious echo
From our discordant life

It linked all perplexed meanings
In to one perfect peace
And trebled away into silence
As if it were loath to cease

I have sought, but I seek it vainly,
That one lost chord divine
Which came from the soul of the organ
And entered into mine.

It may be that death's bright Angel
Will speak in that chord again
It may be that only in Heaven
I shall hear that grand Amen

concert organized, within thirteen days of the sinking of the ill-fated *Titanic*, for the families of the victims affected by that dreadful disaster.

I was trying to fugure out the relevance of the Lost Chord being sung on the stage. When someone, dressed in the costume of a large bear, came bounding on to center stage in a heavy manner. The fact that the bear was wielding a barbell, as though it were a baton, made me suspect it to be the indelicate Vulcana, the famed strong woman.[5]

After a few moments of staggering around the stage in her rôle as Father Bear, this bear was joined by a troupe of smaller bears, comprising the corps de ballet. Without any warning they all erupted into a song about the dreadful loss of some of the forest to an axe-wielding girl, notably that Goldilocks, to which the audience responded by swaying their heads from side to side in sympathetic response to the bears on stage inviting them to sing along.

Father Bear and the ballerinas wearing bear costumes were, in turn, joined by an odd looking character in the costume of another bear. This creature wore a white cotton bonnet, signifying it was the mother bear and she was carrying a large saucepan, presumably full of porridge. The bear, I recognized as being Dan Leno. He waved to the audience, some members of which, notably the costermongers in the cheap seats, waved back at him.

The débâcle on the stage gathered apace. Vulcana attempted to re-organise the smaller bears, of which there were upwards of forty milling around on stage, into some semblance of cohesion in readiness for another outburst of song, based on a different theme. After some pushing and general *confident behavior* by some of the ballerinas wearing bear costumes, she succeeded.

Somehow, given her build, one could never have ever doubted that. At one stage Vulcana, the strong woman, as Father Bear, picked up one of the recalcitrant ballerinas, wearing a bear costume and hurled her into the aëther above the stage. This ballerina, flying through the aëther, immediately executed a rather tasteful pas de deux in mid flight. And at the end of it, she landed on the stage with a delicacy and grace, which elicited a thunderous applause from an appreciative audience.

During the applause, the lights in the gingerbread cottage came back on again. Slowly the backdrop scene wobbled and the front door of the cottage opened slowly. At the same time all the bears scattered to stage right and left. Some were even moved again to leap off the stage and run up the aisles, in between the stalls, to the back of the auditorium.

During this lull in the proceedings on stage, there appeared to be some discernable commotion in the Dress Circle, which caught Gus's attention, as indeed it did mine, and others too.

"I do not like the look of this," said Gus, in a concerned way and showed his agitation by rubbing the palms of his hands on the top of his thighs.

Presently, he got up and promptly left the comfortable confines of our red plush private box.

My first thoughts were that some Nihilists had commenced some kind of disruption, but I could detect no visible signs of such activity.

Eventually, my attention was diverted to the activity in between the proscenium arches; on the stage, which had not diminished despite the apparent commotion in the Dress Circle.

Assessing the action on the stage thus far, I recognized some frantic activity going on but tried to determine why this was so. I then realized it was Goldilocks, and she had come out to investigate the commotion outside her rustic gingerbread cottage with a yellow thatched roof, and sang a song to this effect. She had not gotten into the third stanza of her songspiel, before the small bears started to poke their muzzles through gaps in the scenery flanking the side of the stage.

Without any predetermine signal or cue, the bears simultaneously leapt back onto the stage from the side wings. At the same time those which had run up the aisles to the back of the theater, now came racing back down the aisles with a vengeance, screaming dire warnings whilst leaping on to the stage in graceful arcs.

Within a minute of leaving the sanctuary of her gingerbread house, Goldilocks was surrounded by at least forty angry bears, all ambling about her person. Her being a femme fatale was no match for the bears, who invited her to re-act to them as they homed in on her weakness. Subsequently, Goldilocks disappeared rapidly under a pile of paw punching bears, fur and taffeta. Those few bears unable to actually get at Goldilocks, entertained the audience with a series of well choreographed dance manœuvres and balletic feats executed with impressive coördinated precision, much to the increasing delight of an audience, especially the costermongers, who clearly relished such activity on the stage.

At one stage Goldilocks appeared to be successfully affecting an escape from this mêlée, but alas was dragged back into the degenerating cauldron of bear fur. When eventually Goldilocks was able to escape, she did so, but walked straight into the waiting arms of Vulcana, in her rôle as Father Bear. Vulcana promptly held high above her head for all to see, a dishevelled and distraught looking Goldilocks.

When, at length, the applause died down, the pile of bears began to disintegrate as each bear disentangled itself from the others. In the midst of what was a pile of bears, shone a single shaft of limelight on the back of a person.

Gradually the person turned around to reveal their face. It was Cinderella, and she had come to save the bears from Goldilocks. Then on cue, Cinderella and the small bears burst into song and danced vigorously about the stage in pure delight at the arrival of Cinderella. But then they suddenly stopped in their tracks and gathered around Mother Bear and Father Bear, still holding Goldilocks above his head.

It was Cinderella who asked a question of the audience.

"What shall we do with the horrible tree-cutting Goldolocks?"

The reply from the audience was spontaneous as it was unanimous.

In response to the demands drom the audience, Father Bear dropped Goldilocks down on to the stage. Mother Bear then handed her large saucepan to a smiling Cinderella, who accepted it gracefully, curtseying at the same time.

"Ooh you are too kind!" Cinderella was heard to say to an expectant and hushed audience sitting attentively in the vast swathes of scarlet seating throughout the opulent interior of auditorium of the Theater Royal, Drury Lane during this farcical pantomime based on Wagner.

Cinderella then, whilst holding the saucepan high above her head, carried out a flawlessly executed graceful pas de deux, landing immediately in front of the hapless Goldilocks. It was then that Cinderella, in an elegant turn on her arched toes, emptied the entire contents of the full saucepan of porridge on to Goldilocks' head of blonde curly hair, which instantly assumed the color of grey.

With this pronounced coup de grâce delivered brilliantly on the poor unsuspecting hapless Goldilocks, the applause from an ecstatic audience erupted as a disturbed Vesuvius might.

Still dripping with porridge from her head, Goldilocks went screaming back into her gingerbread cottage slamming the front door behind her.

With Goldilocks vanquished and back inside the gingerbread cottage with a yellow thatched roof, all gathered on the stage burst into song about prevailing, at long last, over the nasty femme fatale Goldilocks, whilst parading around the stage.

Eventually, all the bears, led by Cinderella, abandoned the scene exiting into the right and left wings of the stage. They did so, not only in a display of impressive and coördinated choreography, but also in perfectly harmony with the music comprising thunderous crescendos pounded out by the orchestra. The closing bars of the music, powerful as they were, were instantly interpreted as a cue for what can then only be described as a panic driven, mass stampede out of the auditorium and into the various well-appointed Crush Bars strategically located throughout the Theater Royal in Drury Lane.

1. A reference expressed in music of a recurring idea or character
2. The ingénue is young woman, endearingly innocent, virtuous and candid, but lacks sophistication or cunning.
3. Aus Italien, Symphonic Tone Poem Op. 16. (1887)
4. Written and composed by Adelaide Procter and Arthur L Sullivan
5. Vulcana, the strong woman, was a friend and confident of the late Bella Elmore. See Music Hall –the Saga Goes On. Chapter 29

Chapter 35

The Absurdly Profound

The pantomime we were watching had already turned into a performance complete with the extraordinary and the absurd. Although Vesta Tilley and Mabel Green were listed on the playbill as artistes performing in the show, I had failed, thus far to identify either. It could be that this was part of the integral practice and mystery of the pantomime; trying to recognize certain artistes dressed peculiarly or wearing inappropriate costume, however ridiculous. Notwithstanding this minor encumbrance, during one performance on stage, our host, the manager of the Theater Royal, Sir Augustus Harris had observed a commotion in the auditorium. Having made his apologies, he had abandoned us in order that he might investigate. That was before the interval which brought the first act to an indefinite conclusion.

"Well Loge, is it all making sense to you? Are you able to predict what will happen in act two?" inquired Jack, as we made our way down the red carpeted stairs to one of the numerous, if essential, and all too well appointed Crush Bars.

Lodge, deigned not to reply but feigned to be pre-occupied in searching out, with the movement of his head, a worthwhile route to an increasingly busy Crush Bar. Somehow he managed to gain the *Rosa Atlantide* marble covered counter in a remarkably short period of time. Jack and I stood away from the crowded Crush Bar and waited for our drinks.

Whilst doing so waiting on Lodge to acquire the drinks, using his effective method, based on his, *'with whom I have some sway,'* approach, I remarked to Jack about the incongruity or the implausible aspect of pantomime. In particular, the rapid unrelenting series of absurd or profound incidences assailing the audience's sensibilities, almost on a monumental scale, especially in terms of the expression of the music being played during the course of the pantomime.

Jack looked at me in a way that told me that similar thoughts had also gone through his mind too. It is to be remembered that Jack had attended, in the early days, the precursor to the Julliard School of Music in New York [1] and was a more than an accomplished classically trained pianist and musician.

'It would be easier to give up playing classical music as a performer and go into Vaudeville,' he had once confided me, 'than cease playing Vaudeville. And instead try to become a performer playing classical music, in the event of compelling economic circumstances!'

"I do agree with you Theo. You and I are New Yorkers, so this type of entertainment is not really us. But, I am able to fully appreciate the complex ideas on stage and rhythms present in the music being played. I noticed, for example, our orchestra conductor, in his dapper white tail-coat and matching shoes, was quite at ease, when he conducted a complex musical quotation from Rickard Strauss's Symphonic Tone Poem, *'Aus Italien.'* And, in my opinion, he did so in a very accomplished manner in expressing serene profundity.

"And then within several bars of orchestral music, had

us in full anticipation of something comical, clownish even, a *March of the Clowns*, as it were, about to erupt on to the stage. The incongruity of this juxtaposition is the fact that both pieces of music originate from the same symphonic work. The trick here is how they are used as a *leitmotiv* - a signal of something to come!

"They have, in effect, selected pieces of music to express an idea that the composer, when drafting the original music, may not have had in mind! Almost, as it were, as though an artist had painted the face of a beautiful woman and then found the image being used in an advertisement to sell boot polish! No? Read this example in terms of the music being played out there by the orchestra. You understand basic musical theory Theo, since we have discussed music ever since we hooked up together thirty years ago doing our Vaudeville act.

"Take the basic chord you and I are familiar with, in music, as being effectively any harmonic set of simultaneously heard three or more notes, but not necessarily played together creating arpeggios. A sequence of chords may frequently be used in creating triads, or three distinct notes or combination forming tetrads, of four typically such as seventh chords. Variations or multiples of this basic form produces tone clusters or added tone chords, including extended chords. In the early days of what became the Julliard School of Music, in particular, we were taught in the main, that triads form the basis of the classical music tradition and are expressed as major keys, minor keys, augmented chords, or those chords which diminish.

"Though not to be confused with the sub-mediant, being of course, the sixth degree of a minor or major scale, to denote a lesser importance. Here the mediant occupies a position between the tonic and dominant, whereas the sub-mediant exists in equidistance from both the sub-dominant and tonic. The one dominant is five degrees above the tonic whilst the other is five degrees below.

"This of course remains a cardinal tenet of serious music and is abused typically in pantomime or other disrespectful interpretation, such as parodies.

"It is this interplay between the accepted evolvement of music which leaves the listener, not so much confused, as stretched either way between the profound and absurd, the profane and the sacred or the sublime and the ridiculous. Take for example the development of a symphonic idea. Consider the case of an intensely serious composer, such as Gustav Mahler. You and I have heard Gustav Mahler conduct his *Titan* Symphony with the New York Philharmonic at the Carnegie Hall in New York. There we listened to a symphony in the general

Gustav Mahler

key of D major, that is, the triad forming the basis of that major key.

"The Symphony No. 1 in D major, known as *Der Titan,* 2 originally had five movements; the *andante* was in between the first and third movements, but was removed upon a subsequent revision. The symphony is now set in the usual four movements; *allegro comodo, scherzo, lento moderato* and *finale* being in the form of an *allegro furioso.* The program structure for the symphony is based freely on that of the literature of Jean Paul Richter. Especially Richter's novel called, *'The Titan,'* a book which influenced Mahler profoundly when he was drafting the symphonic structure in 1888 and from whence the symphony gets its name.

"*'The Titan,'* as a sobriquet for the symphony is, I think, interesting Theo, because as you probably know, the Titans were a race of demi-gods who were defeated by Zeus, and this new order of gods based in Olympia, introduced a new régime. The Titans, Rhea and Cronos, were descended from Uranus, Gaia and Chaos. The Titans' sons in turn were, Zeus, Poseidon and Pluto. These three children, in effect, ended the long reign of their parents, the Titans, Rhea and Cronos.

"It was Zeus, who persuaded his brother Pluto, to create a living entity, in avarice, to be so powerful that it could defeat their parents, Rhea and Cronos. It did, and subsequently, Zeus became ruler of the heavens, Poseidon, of the oceans and, Pluto that of the underworld of Hades. Zeus created man, in order that humans might feast upon the adoration of the gods, and in so doing, the Olympian divinities might derive perpetual life. Are you still with me here Theo?" asked Jack, smiling, whilst moving his head around in his visual search for Lodge with the drinks.

"I did not realize pantomime had such an illustrious pedigree of gods and Titans!" I remarked, to Jack.

"It does not," replied Jack, "but can you see the makings of a pantomime here Theo?"

"I can only detect the creation of an implausible farce Jack," I replied.

"The term *Titan*," Jack continued, in the absence of Lodge with the drinks, "has come to mean powerful and gigantic. We have heard recently of the dreadful sinking of the ill-fated *Titanic* ocean liner, named so because of her gigantic size and powerful turn of speed. But also, in terms of philosophy the term *Titan* has been applied in the sense of unassailable fact, in establishing an inflexible *à priori* in order to conclude a propositional truth; as in a *Titan of intellectual prowess* or an, *unassailable truth*, as in the existence of the Christ.

"In this respect, Mahler's first symphony, *Der Titan*, is unusual in that the beginning of the first movement is one of the most beautiful openings in the symphonic repertoire. The sustained high octave A-major chord gradually unfolds a sequence of descending fourths. The First Symphony, because of its integral sonority remains without doubt a major contribution to the symphonic repertoire.

"The symphony is divided into two distinct symphonic sections; Part I, *Days of Youth,* concerns itself with concepts from nature as, *Frühlings,* [3] dawn of nature, flowers and a positive progression. Part II, *Commedia umana,* reflects on disaster, resulting in a funeral march, in the manner after a woodcut image by the mediæval Weimar printer, Jacques Callot. In that woodcut image, used by Mahler for inspiration, Callot's depiction of a cortège forms the basis of the symphony's third movement, which is essentially a funeral march, devoted to a dead hunter.

"The hunter's cortège is made up of creatures of the forest, which include hares carrying pennons in front of the hearse, followed by deer, cats, foxes, bears and other animals, all of whom are playing musical instruments! The originally inspired music of the funeral march, contains within it, sounds of stepping *Fourths*, as the rhythm for the *trauer marsch* proper.[4] Albeit this is conveyed as a cynical parody of the music, which is given further expression in the then popular song, '*Frère Jacques*,' creating a form of *pantomimic* mannerism.

"These sub titles in the symphony were an afterthought, reflecting a motif symbolism of Heaven and Hell and earlier expressed by Wagner as redemption in his sacred music drama, '*Parsifal,*' and by the Abbé Liszt in his Dante Symphony - in defining the Cross of the Crucifixion. In the finale to the First Symphony, Mahler begins this fourth movement addressing '*Inferno et Paradiso*,' from the Dante Symphony, with a piercing dissonance, as *allegro furioso* depicting a shrieking hell.

"This opening section further addresses the concept of a living hell conveyed as a, '*wound to the heart,*' and attendant reaction after emotional crisis. In this respect Theo, the emotions are being bombarded, or tormented, with concepts of heavy profundity or banal absurdity.

"Here Mahler's First Symphony, *The Titan*, reflects ideas first explored in his song cycle, '*Lieder eines fahrenden Gesellen,*' [5] aspects of which are re-incorporated in the final movement, but given eventual triumphant interpretation. The concept of forest animals, all of which are playing musical instruments, may appear rather incongruous; but it is based obviously on symbolism and not realism.

"The mere fact that the dead hunter has spent his working life hunting down these forest animals seems to have entirely eluded Callot in his wood cut depiction of the funeral cortège; the idea from which Mahler has incorporated into his Titan Symphony.

"It is certainly not about whether one believes in such nonsense involving instrument playing animals! It is about the juxtaposition of the absurd to emphasize a reality. Typically; bitter against sweet, heavy against lightness, or tall against short, you see the point I am making here? These perceived concepts, as it were, exaggerate the properties of the characteristics of the opposite by the fact of their being adjacent to each other.

"A further example is to be found in another symphony by Mahler, his fifth.[6] This particular work commences with yet another funeral march, the effects of which pervade the symphonic structure throughout. However, it is in his *rondo finale* movement to the symphony where Mahler's imagination exceeds that of even the lunatic Dante Rossetti. In the orchestral score, horn calls, receive a reply from the bassoons, which themselves quote from, *'Lob des hohen Verstandes,'*[7] which is taken from, *'Des Knaben Wunderhorn.'*[8] A series of songs set within the symphony, where it becomes abundantly clear that reference is made to a competition between the animals of the forest!

"Consider the possibility of hares carrying pennants. It could be that one might possibly be able to train a hare to do so. But, what certainly cannot be achieved, even with a rampant imagination found in a pantomime, is the ridiculous notion expressed in Mahler's Fifth Symphony in which an animal, an ass no less, is judging a singing contest, presumably to the standards set in the grand opera, *'Die Meistersingers von Nürnburg,'*[9] by Wagner!

"This complete idiocy, absolutely worthy of a pantomime, continues as the ass is chosen to judge the singing ability between a cuckoo and a nightingale on the basis it should be able to hear well because it has big ears! The fact he chose the staccato-sounding cuckoo over the sonorous nightingale is neither here or there," concluded Jack, in all sincerity.

"Jack, with respect, it all appears rather ridiculous to me. Are you not reading too much into what the French simply call *farce*?" I asked.

"No Theo, the point that I am trying to establish, is simply that pantomime is not a recent invention or development by John Douglass from the New Standard Theater or Augustus Harris, even as the, *Father of the Pantomime*. No it is an evolvement typically in the English idiom of disrespect for the pompous, the highfalutin or the snobbish. Pantomime in one form or another has existed from the times of stupid mindless plots or idiotic libretti expressed in recitative, from early seventeenth century Italian and French operetta or *opéra bouffe*. English pantomime is simply a continuation of this coded disrespect.

"Take for example the *Lost Chord* we heard earlier in the first half of the pantomime, albeit about Goldilocks and the bears no less. Ostensibly the Lost Chord is a sanctimonious anthem; an affirmation of the hereinafter where that elusive chord, will be repeated for the faithful, especially those who have spent their lives seeking its wondrous and sonorous sound, and by implication, when they arrive in Heaven, they shall be rewarded for their diligent and chaste life, by an angel finally playing that Lost Chord for them.

> *It may be that death's bright Angel*
> *Will speak in that chord again*
> *It may be that only in Heaven*
> *shall I hear that grand Amen*

"Yet the person who composed the music to those illustrious and dignified lyrics, based on a poem written a sanctimonious and devote Christain called Adelaide Anne Procter, was none other than Sir Arthur Sullivan. Probably the foremost of English operetta composers and whose operettas in their day,[10] explored the furthest unknown regions of moral absurdity and aspirations!

"It is this juxtaposition Theo, which one has to keep in mind when considering the pantomime. One has to read it in terms of symbolism, not realism, as we have seen in Mahler's symphonies, otherwise the ideal would appear to be absolutely ridiculous – which is what pantomime is, but is not the only domain for this idiocy.

"Mahler's symphonies, beautiful and sonorous as they are, do convey the notion of this absurdity even in the classical repertoire - cats playing fiddles being an example in Mahler's *Der Titan* symphony. Or asses judging a singing contest between birds as expressed in *Des Knaben Wunderhorn* invoked in his Fifth Symphony!

"Typically this Titan Symphony was constructed over four distinct sections each dominated by a prevalent key. The music develops themes or melodic intensity as it progresses in normally a sequential basis. One movement flows, as it were into the next forming a cohesive body of work, which is recognizable in the main as being *symphonic* in structure to the listener.

"In comparison, pantomime dispenses with such excessive structural formality and instead it conjoins, butts together, concepts as disparate as they could ever be. This is easy to see in terms of visual affect, odd clothes, ridiculous outsized costumes, big hats, stout red-faced people and general idiocy played out on the stage. It is slightly more difficult to hear this in music, unless you have been to the Julliard School of Music!

"But, the audience are in fact able to detect it in the music; and without their knowing why.

"In this respect take our conductor of the orchestra. He is a very accomplished conductor, of great orchestral forces, which he controls with a seasoned sense of timing and practical experience. Yet he has set himself up to look as though he were a dilettante, clownish even.

"His white tail-coat, white trousers and more alarmingly, as Loge pointed out earlier, his white shoes, of which he is extremely proud, are testament to the required image of a clown, which he seeks from the audience. They in turn, will dismiss him accordingly as purely auxiliary to the evening's clownish entertainment from the stage. Yet, his involvement is not only pivotal, it is crucial to the whole success of the pantomime or whatever is erupting on stage!"

"Theo we are in the middle of experiencing Wagner's opera, '*Männerlist größer als Frauenlist oder Die glückliche Bärenfamilie*,' reëxpressed as a pantomime. Rickard Wagner, as we know, was instrumental in the expression of extended melodic chords witnessed in his later operas such as, '*Parsifal*,' '*Lohengrin*' or '*Der Ring des Nibelungen*.'

"However, take one of the successors to Rickard Wagner in the person of Franz Schreker; especially in terms of his very expressive musical compositions based upon lush romantic melodies and tonal textures. Schreker is from Vienna and is the creator of the recently acclaimed opera, '*Der Ferne Klang*.' [11] He is therefore evidently a composer who takes music very seriously.

"Though he is influenced by Wagner and Rickard Strauss; typically, his music reflects a harmonic language that is clearly tonal but inflected with polytonal or chromatic sections. In 1895 he founded the Verein der Musikfreunde Döbling [12] and twelve years later the

Vienna Philharmonic Chorus. Later he became a Professor at the prestigious Vienna Academy of Music.

"More importantly, Schreker is noted for his enthusiastic promotion of Schönberg's atonal music. Including Schönberg, '*Gurrelieder*,' [13] which is a monumental and progressive musical work for solo voices, orchestra and chorus and is ranked in importance, in terms of musical innovation and development, as Wagner's '*Der Ring des Nibelungen*.'

"There is here Theo, a tenuous link with pantomime. '*Gurrelieder* is a heavily chromatic work and reflects the late Romantic style of Wagner. Subsequently, no devoté of Wagner could remain unmoved by Schönberg's '*Gurrelieder.*' It remains a giant in the post Wagnerian orchestral repertoire, comprising broad melodies and ponderous chords creating sustained rhythmic vortices.

"In '*Gurrelieder*,' the woodwind section alone comprises a profusion of instruments in order to enable it, to create the required chord within each tonal group. Schönberg's '*Gurrelieder*' is contemporaneous with Mahler's Fourth Symphony, the one in G major and written in 1900. However, Schönberg did not actually complete *Gurrelieder* until recently in 1911.

"The text of the work, Wagnerian in its Labyrinthine plot and density, is based upon a work by Jens Jacobsen after Kierkegaard and Andersen and brings together the concepts embraced by the European vogues of Impressionism and Symbolism. The story, follows Wagner in its corollary, and is narrated, in verse and prose. The similarities from the Wagner's, '*Der Ring des Nibelungen*,' are evidently present. Essentially, '*Gurrelieder,*' is about the heroic and anti-heroic exploits of various characters assembled in the mediæval castle of *Gurre*.

"These include King Waldemar, (Wotan in Wagner's

opera, *Das Rheingold*) his jealous queen (Brünhilde from Wagner's opera *Die Valküre*). Followed by the court jester called Klaus (*Parsifal*), the death of a heroine as related by a talking wood dove (from Wagner's *Siegfried*), The Wild Hunt (Wagner's *Götterdämmerung*), the Ride of Waldemar's Dead Warriors (*Die Valküre*), Revenge (*Das Rheingold*), ghostly apparitions, a funeral cortège, (Siegfried's trauermarsch in *Götterdämmerung*), finishing with feelings of resurrection emulating Mahler's Second Symphony in C minor, (*Die Auferstehung)* and redemption echoed the finale to Wagner's Act II or Act III of *Götterdämmerung,'* the final opera in the '*Der Ring des Nibelungen,'* cycle of four inter-linked operas by Wagner.

"The compositional aspects of the melodic music, complete with huge extended chords and expansive rhythms, which make up, '*Gerrelieder,'* are punctuated throughout by typical Wagnerian tonal mechanisms. Such as E major chords and post Wagnerian added sixths in augmenting a harmony chromatically enhanced producing a tendency to a polyphonic structure.

"Throughout the work the chorus, augmented by the massive brass section, give expression to the apotheosis of the complex score and equal in power to the Vassals' choral scene in Wagner's '*Götterdämmerung.'* In the closing choral section of, '*Gurrelieder,'* Schönberg expresses the concept, via Waldemar, of the appreciation of natural form, of life echoing Mahler's interpretation of polyphony and a reconciliation of the ego with the real world.

"In addition to an understanding of a final redemption through the dead heroine's love (Brünhilde in *Götterdämmerung*) culminating in a massive orchestral crescendo. This then leads into the final theme of a variation on the C major chord developing into A major, based on the opening thematic motif. The first performance of this highly complex tonal composition, reflecting Wagnerian motifs, was only recently in Vienna.

"Schönberg's *'Gurrelieder'* is without doubt, a grandiose orchestral work with voices and chorus, and goes beyond the accepted oratorio form. Indeed Theo, it may have been influenced by Mahler's *'Das Klagende Lied'* or even Sibelius's choral Symphonic Tone Poem, *'The Kullervo.'* In composing *'Gurrelieder,'* Schönberg calls for huge orchestral forces, in order to perform the work. Far more than those required in Mahler's mighty Eighth Symphony, the so-called, *'Die Symphonie der Tausend.'* [14]

Schönberg himself was hailed as a great exponent of music by both Rickard Strauss and Gustav Mahler and later, by Franz Schreker, a conspicuous champion in continuing the post Wagnerian Romantic idiom in music.

However despite, or in spite, of his austere musical background; Franz Schreker felt the need, compulsion almost, to write in 1908 a pantomime called, *'Der Geburtstag der Infantin.'* [15]

"Think about it Theo. Of the five important composers we have just mentioned; Wagner, Strauss, Mahler, Schönberg or Schreker all composed in the style reflecting a serious late Romantic idiom. Yet within that group of five influential composers; Schreker certainly composed pantomimes including, *'Der Geburtstag der Infantin,'* *'Der Wind,'* [16] *'Valse Lente'* [17] and *'Ein Tanzspiel.'* [18]

"Closely followed by Rickard Strauss's cross-dressing based operetta called, *'Der Rosenkavalier,'* [19] and his later opera, *'Ariadne auf Naxos,'* based on a libretto by Hugo von Hoffmannsthal. Consider Rickard Strauss - not the *Waltz King,* but the serious composer of such intense works as, *'Tod und Verklärung,'* and *'Ein Heldenleben,'* [20] Yet that opera called, *'Ariadne auf Naxos,'* Strauss combines slapstick comedy, worthy of pantomime, with indescribably beautiful and sublime music.

"Wagner, of course, produced several, one of which; *'Männerlist größer als Frauenlist oder Die glückliche Bärenfamilie,'* we are at the moment enduring, together with other works including, *'Die Feen,'* [21] *'Die Laune des Verliebten'* [22] and *'Das Liebesvebot,'"* [23] said Jack, with a grin upon his face.

"It all sounds rather convoluted Jack," I replied," can you be certain that one is not reading too much into those composers' musical works? I ask this because next you will be suggesting that pantomime stems from a profound, if not noble, involvement in the evolution of operatic works of the stage."

"Not at all Theo; quite the reverse; it is about the expression of Impressionism and Symbolism, including outsized hats, and its evolving form!" said Jack, pointing with his cane to an irate looking person making his way towards us.

At last Lodge re-appeared with a large bottle of Bollinger Special Cuvée champagne and three fluted glasses. He had obviously acquired the champagne, though without his legendary *sway*, as he calls it, since he had been absent for at least fifteen minutes, during the entire time of Jack's profound discourse on the pantomime.

"How are you enduring the pantomime Loge?" Jack responded, as he took the glass of champagne offered to him by an irritable Lodge.

"Pantomime; do you not mean pandäemonium? Never in my life have I witnessed such travesty on stage," replied Lodge, who then poured the entire contents of his glass of champagne down his throat. Thought for a moment and then breathed out noisily.

"In my day," he continued, "a pantomime was a solemn, if dignified occasion, where one took one's grandmother, but certainly not mother. That very fact indicated it was a place of decorum and dignity and not an excuse to let loose of an evening, the inmates holed up in the local asylum for the criminally insane."

"It is an opportunity to relax and enjoy some well-rehearsed fun, I mean after all..." said Jack.

"In my book," interrupted Lodge, "it can never be an excuse to abandon one's self to idiocy. Or indeed, dispense with self esteem or self respect in how one conducts one's self in public on or off the stage and ..."

"You talk about dignity, self esteem, respect or grandmothers," interrupted Jack, "yet neither Theo nor I witnessed any of those ideals present at your much vaunted débâcle. The one you called the Titanic Benefit Concert, which we were compelled to endure the other day at the Queen's Hall. Nor did the notion of your slinking off to the Abbey Grange in order to, and I quote you Loge, '...to leave London only for a few days in order to recover your dignity and self esteem...' whilst being a guest of Sir Augustus; the very person who is, as you say, in charge of this mad house, the Theater Royal."

"I am an impresario and do not run theaters or mad houses where the inmates are clearly in charge. In this respect this Theater Royal will always have a full house, since clearly there are sufficient numbers of lunatics abroad the metropolis that walk about seeking instant gratification in what they call pantomime entertainment. But, what I term as being pandäemonium.

"And speaking of a person running a mad house, such as this one, is that not our esteemed general manager of the Theater Royal, Sir Augustus Harris, over there? Endeavouring to hold, what looks like a particularly animated conversation with an inmate from the local asylum, who I noticed left his seat in the Dress Circle just before Gus left us in our private box?" inquired Lodge, of no one in particular, whilst pointing with his empty champagne glass in the general direction of Sir Augustus Harris.

I turned my head around slowly, as invited to do so by Lodge. Upon doing so, I was aghast to see Sir Augustus locked in what indeed appeared to be dysfunctional behavior, with another top-hat wearing individual. Both, it must be admitted, looked a peculiar sight.

They were sitting on a large red velvet upholstered sofa, set in between two large limestone jardinières placed at either end. Each jardinière supported a red glazed urn. Rising from each urn was a large palm tree. The branches of both palm trees met above the center of the sofa, framing as it were, the two top hat wearing individuals.

They seemed to be deep in conversation and oblivious to their surroundings. They clinked their fluted champagne glasses repeatedly and exuded all the joys of the occasion,including laughing loudly, singing, shouting and behaving in a manner that indicated clearly to all who would look at them, that without, doubt, their senses had been stricken clean out of their minds!

1. The Julliard School of Music was established in 1905
2. The Titan
3. Spring-time
4. Funeral march
5. Songs of the Wayfarer
6. Symphony No 5 in C # minor
7. In Praise of High Intellect
8. Youth's Magic Horn, based upon rustic folk poetry
9. The Mastersingers of Nuremburg
10. Commonly known as Gilbert & Sullivan operas
11. The Distant Sound

12. Döbling Music Association
13. Songs of Gurre
14. Symphony of a Thousand – performers
15. The Birthday of the Infanta
16. The Wind
17. Slow Waltz
18. A Dance Piece
19. The Cavalier of the Rose opera
20. A Hero's Life
21. The Fairies opera
22. The Mood of the One in Love opera
23. The Ban on Love opera

Chapter 36

The Wagnerian Pantomime

It was self evident to all and sundry that Sir Augustus Harris would not be joining us for the second half of the pantomime, the story line of which continues to elude me; but not the audience seated below us in the stalls. Still assuming that the pantomime was following some predetermined and coherent order, we expected to be apprised of the development thus far, in what Richard Wagner had deliberately intended to be performed on stage in terms of his serious grand opera, *'Die Glückliche Bärenfamilie.'*[1] It would be of interest to see how the pantomime develops in giving expressive form to Wagner's intention that, *'Die Glückliche Bärenfamilie,'* be taken for a serious, if solemn, *Music Drama,* equal in stature to those of, *'Parsifal,'* or indeed, *'Lohengrin.'*

As the audience settled down, the lights too were dimmed in anticipation of further antics. Moments later the heavy dark purple safety curtain, bearing the royal crest, again ascended into the attic above the stage floor. In so doing, it revealed a backdrop of a scene borrowed, purloined or taken straight out of Wagner's opera, *'Tannhäuser und der Sängekrieg auf Wartburg.'*[2] complete with mediæval half-timbered houses which lined a cobbled street.

"Well here at least is a recognizable Wagnerian idiom,"

I said to Jack, next to whom I was sitting in the absence of our guest in the person of Sir Augustus Harris, "having experienced an adaptation of Wagner's, *'Das Rheingold,'* into a pantomimic parody called, *'The Rhinegold,'* recently, a pantomime that even Sir Augustus Harris called a, 'damned pantomime.' It will be interesting to discover how this pantomime develops in terms of reflecting Wagner's very precise and meticulous directions as to performing the work!"

Lodge had resumed his seat, in the corner behind us, but next to the table still bearing unopened bottles of Pierre Darcy Brut NV champagne to which he was helping himself in a liberal, if abandoned, manner.

The contestants had re-assembled on stage, except this time the corps de ballet were dressed in costumes reminiscent of the mediæval, *Undeserving Poor.* As the plot evolved into Labyrinthine complexity, I assumed that the individual wearing a leather apron, standing in the soft limelight and singing his heart out about his unrequited love for Leontine, to be Julius, the silversmith. Leontine, it will be remembered, was the cousin of Aurora, the ugly daughter of the pretentious Baron von Abendthau.

Or at least, so I thought. For at that moment, Julius, the silversmith ceased singing, and looked instead with visible horror on his facial features upon a fellow who was leading a large bear through the crowded street scene. According to the original opera synopsis, the passing bear-keeper should be Julius' father and the large dancing bear, no doubt was in fact his long lost brother, played by another strong woman, Madame Herculine.

Needless to say, Julius recognized, rather ashamedly, his father and his brother too, albeit in the disguise of the large bear led by his father. In the meantime the *Undeserving Poor* made a clearing to allow all three, Julius, his father and the bear to meet center stage. With an audible leitmotiv from the orchestra, Julius and his father burst into a complex duet about being reunited, albeit in a public street.

The father, in unison with Julius' lyrical refrains, sang about the importance of wealth, then family. The father was in fact none other than Vesta Tilley, dressed as a prosperous mediæval merchant, making her first appearance in this pantomime. Upon completion of her heart-rending song, Julius, whom I now suspected to be Mabel Green, retorted by still declaring her unrequited love for Leontine. The exchange of duets continued in recitative, that is, until the bear, Julius's brother, rose up on its hind legs with its paws covering its ears. Such was the cacophony which was clearly tormenting the bear.

Presently, the bear then commenced a deeply resonant solo piece over the songs still being sung by Julius and his father, the bear-keeper being not a particularly large person. The bear continued to sing about being oppressed and made to act as a juggler and only being fed enough food to enable him to perform for his captor. The small bears, comprising the belligerent corps de ballet, listened attentively to the pleadings of the enslaved bear and gathered around it.

Vesta Tilley was having none of it. She burst to the front of the stage precariously above the gas fuelled footlights, and with her hands on her hips commenced singing a medley of songs, which the audience felt obliged to join in with her.

The silversmith, Julius, also attempted to steal the limelight, from Vesta and accordingly some unseemly and unpleasant *determined behavior* broke out between them. That was the cue for the audience, led by the costermongers, to get up out of their seats and begin chanting all manner of advice and suggestions to the participants strutting around the stage.

It was also a signal for the enslaved bear to physically pick up his cruel small bear-keeper, and holding him high above its head, tramp around the stage followed by the small bears. The bears, through their song, encouraged the enslaved bear to emancipate himself from this cruel master. What the enslaved bear did next brought an audible gasp of horror from the entire audience, including both Jack and myself, but not, I noticed, Lodge, who was by now oblivious to any of the Wagnerian *Bärenfamilie*, proceedings on the stage, or arena, below us.

With one mighty show of strength, the bear threw the bear-keeper into a knot of small bears, who upon having caught him, miraculously promptly engulfed the hapless keeper in a flurry of bear fur and set about his destruction, to the sustained applause of the audience! After a few minute of unbridled savagery, the mêlée was brought to order by the appearance of the pretentious baron in the person of Ella Shields, who, dressed as a prince of the realm, in a long red velvet robe complete with ermine, burst into song about the sanctity of money, then that of forgiveness.

This forbearance did not in any way prevent the baron from denouncing Julius, having recognized him as a humble silversmith unworthy of his daughter Aurora's hand, and thus leaving him free to marry Leontine.

I tried to assimilate the action in the pantomime with that which Wagner had intended to be staged in his opera; but found that I simply could not. Nor could I determine, with even a vague degree of confidence, as to whether this pantomime was actually based more on Wagner's, *'Die Glückliche Bärenfamilie,'* or that of Robert Southey's Goldilocks storey of 1837. I also suspected too that the audience were equally lost as to the plot, but given their enthusiastic support and sustained applause to the performers on stage, that minor detail was clearly of insuperable indifference to them.

I turned to Jack for some kind of re-action, if not explanation, given what he had previously espoused in the Crush Bar. His talking about the interplay between the accepted evolvement of music or action, had left the listener, not so much as confused, as stretched either way between the profound and absurd, the profane and the sacred or indeed the sublime and the ridiculous.

At that juncture, the safety curtain descended with indecent haste, bringing the action on the stage and in the stalls to a temporary close.

Having refilled our glasses with Pierre Darcy Brut NV Champagne, I looked down into the stalls at the audience now seated and settled in anticipation of the next installment of this balletic pantomime. They comprised an eclectic mob. It was not so much the antics and cavorting on the stage that Jack and I had witnessed previously, but rather what the audience consisted of.

They did not so much as make up the decent general public, but rather were the massed ranks of the London fraternity of costermongers, a rough and vital set of persons and conspicuous by their clothing. Or they were a loose confederation of rivals, intent on entertaining themselves at each other's expense.

We had already witnessed, when we first took our seats in the safety of our private box, elements of the unpleasant or grotesque already in evidence before the curtain had even been raised. I also noticed in attendance was a not insubstantial number of the *Undeserving Poor*. All of whom looked as if they were in the later stages of inanition, with greasy unkempt hair and their clothes a stage above the level of being relegated to the status of rag.

Having experienced the costermongers in every Music Hall we had visited or performed in thus far, they seemed to be a prevalent and permanent feature in the audience. Here they were in their element shouting at each other, and offering abuse to all and sundry, including to the artistes who had performed on stage earlier. Encouragement, advice or demands to leave the stage or auditorium were freely bandied around, as were nuts, apple cores or indeed, pigs' trotters.

Most were eating something and wiping their sweaty faces with playbills, acquired from somewhere or someone. Irrespective of the general commotion all round, there was an aura of expectancy and anticipation, of something untoward about to erupt on the stage, or more likely, in the stalls.

Others, in order to entertain themselves at the beginning before the pantomime proper began, and now during this interval, were picking arguments with persons unknown to them, even as they entered the auditorium to take their allotted seats. Those who were not arguing with total strangers, were, as usual, gambling blatantly with each other in a contemptuous manner in order to enrich their grubby purses.

Some were talking in an esoteric language, using a cryptic vocabulary, and sign language, incomprehensible to all, but themselves, and the initiated. They spoke in this manner in order to keep the meaning of their seditious talk with each other secret. This behavior could involve speaking words backwards, so Lodge had informed us during previous encounters with them.

Their women, if anything, were worse and even bolder in their opinion on anything, offering freely, advice or insult to the players on stage, members of the orchestra in the pit who were tuning their instruments, or indeed, to other members of the audience with whom an argument with total strangers seemed to them, quite, quite normal. Whilst indulging in the, *behavior* some would wave or fan themselves with their shabby colored ostrich feathers in an exaggerated, suggestive manner. The ushers, in their pink tail-coats, I noticed did very little to quell the costermonger's boisterous behavior throughout the evening.

The heavy purple velvet safety curtain did indeed rise again into the attic and in so doing revealed a gloomy stage scene, during twilight, of what looked like a clearing in a forest illuminated by a greyish waning moon. It was difficult to determine much more, since the stage backdrop lighting was at such low level. I turned and looked at Jack, sitting next to me in the gloom of the auditorium and could just discern him shrugging his shoulders. All was quiet both on the stage and in the auditorium and even the costermongers and *Undeserving Poor,* were moved to remain silent in anticipation of more unbridled pandäemonium, both on and off the stage.

Imperceptibly at first, but becoming gradually clearer, as the lighting on the stage and the backdrop increased, I could just about to begin to make out that indeed the scene was in fact a field. Then suddenly I could see movement on the stage. The stage lighting increased, as indeed so did what sounded like a prelude, or introductory music from the orchestra in the pit. The music was obviously energetic, as though it were scored deliberately for the ballet.

I then realized that the music being performed was indeed for the ballet, and that the fleeting shadows and figures moving around in the subdued lighting on the stage, were in fact members of the corps de ballet. I also remembered that it was not unusual for Wagner to provide for some lighter divertissement, a balletic diversion, an *entr'acte* as it were, from the main drama being performed during his operas.

This was very much the case in his grand operas such as, *'Die Meistersinger von Nürnberg,'* or *'Tannhäuser und der Sängekrieg auf Wartburg,'* in which the famous Venusberg Music in the form of a bacchanalia is expressed as an extended ballet.

It would appear to me that this pantomime, albeit based, loosely, on a Wagnerian opera, was in fact following a custom in the style of Wagner in having a balletic interlude during which the corps de ballet was able to demonstrate its choreographic skills in precisely coördinated balletic manœuvres on the stage.

This in itself was an interesting development in the progression of the pantomime and I looked forward to experiencing just how this would manifest itself. I did not have long to wait. For in the next instant, the illumination from the lights on the stage was increased, but only slightly and in synchronization with the level of the sound coming from the orchestra pit in the form of an orchestral prelude, in anticipation of the action on stage which was about to commence.

As the stage scene became visible we were confronted with a vision of a graveyard! Dancing around the cemetery were several ballerinas dressed in black, flowing, silk robes creating an effect of ghouls or such similar apparitions. Some of these apparent ghouls leapt into graves, whilst others seemingly rose from their earthly confinement having been resurrected.

I looked at Jack. Between us we were unable to figure out the link, which could involve Goldilocks, the bears or a graveyard, even in this loose pantomimic interpretation.

Then the music from the orchestra changed abruptly from previously being that of sustained gaiety or abandoned harmonic progression to one of somber chords and foreboding. I recognized immediately the change from the frivolous expression in the music to the formal dirge sounding stepping *Fourths,* as though in a march, a distinct march more resembling a marching rhythm for a cortège creating almost a funeral march. Indeed the music was appropriate; for at that moment, coming into view from both wings of the stage, were marching columns of grave diggers in pit boots, carrying shovels on their shoulders with hooded heads bowed!

As they marched across the stage, all sang about the joys of burying anything. Indeed some of them broke off from what was, effectively their, '*March of the Grave Diggers,*' and, from what I could ascertain in the gloom, attempted to grab some of the fleeting ghouls, who danced in and out of their marching ranks. Some of the ballerinas, from the corps de ballet, in the rôles of ghouls, were caught by the grave diggers and thrown into open graves. Others attempted to escape from their graves; but their efforts were only thwarted by the relentless grave diggers' avowed intention on burying anything, as they had chanted when marching in to the grave yard.

At one point in the ballet, the stage was teeming with grave diggers and ghouls. All were dancing in what was clearly a complex and carefully choreographed and precisely coördinated routine. This balletic dance involved bodies popping up out of graves, whilst others disappeared into them. It was very effective and the variegated stage lighting made for an interesting interplay of shadows both on the side screens and backdrop.

Some of the ghouls, supported by wires, were flying through the aëther above the stage. A few of these aërial ghouls occasionally would soar out over the heads of the costermongers seated in the front rows. Each time they did so, the costermongers would conspicuously duck to avoid contact with these dreaded aërial ghouls.

Other stage-bound ghouls executed graceful pas de deux in their in their attempt to evade capture by the grave diggers. They in response continued their remorseless march across the stage in their pit boots. Eventually, this march developed into a precisely coördinated and intricate, *Grave Diggers' Dance,* involving the ghouls who flitted in and out of their measured steps. They did so whilst avoiding the shovel-wielding grave diggers.

Then, as quickly as the drama erupted it began to dissipate as the ghouls who comprised members of the corps de ballet dispersed. The fleeing ghouls returned to their graves whilst the grave diggers resumed their relentless march, off the stage, to the sound of a solemn dirge pounded out by the orchestra.

The costermongers and others ranged around the auditorium erupted from the red upholstered velvet seats in their spontaneous delivery of applause. Both Jack and I too were impressed by what we had experienced from the stage and registered this fact by our enthusiastic clapping. We did so as the purple safety curtain descended whilst the audience still showed its enthusiastic appreciation for the corps de ballet's magnificent performance.

A few minutes later the curtain rose again. On this occasion, we found ourselves looking down on to a stage illuminated by a solitary shaft of yellow limelight. It was into this light that an energetic individual strutted. Jack and I recognized her immediately as being Mabel Green. She was dressed as a princess and suitably attired wearing a purple colored silken jerkin and a white flowing cotton dress complete with velvet slippers and a resplendent, finely wrought, silver tiara resting on her head.

She sang in a restrained and unemotional manner of her unrequited love for Julius, the silversmith, but with the reality of the futility of it all, due to his humble status. She seemed to be making sense of the situation and in fact adding what might, cautiously be termed, dignity to the action on stage so far.

Suddenly, a person, three feet away from me, in the adjacent private box started talking loudly and pointing with his gold capped cane at Mabel on the stage below, singing purposefully and intently in her pantomime rôle. It would seem that this person in the box next to us, probably knew Mabel, though in what capacity, I could not venture to suggest. I peered over the wall of our private box and looked down at Mabel, on the stage now singing for all her worth.

The person in the box next to me was intent on having his say and spoke loudly about Mabel, clearly enough for me to continue to overhear.

"I find what that person down on the stage, dressed as a princess, is singing about, rather incongruous; for is that not our friend from Camden Town, the one who purports to be of the *drag*,[3] but on the stage only?" he said to the person sitting next to him in his private box.

I turned my head around gradually and surreptitiously to the right to see just who had uttered these remarks and found myself observing, albeit fleetingly, an individual dressed soberly and with restrained elegance. His hair was silver in color and he sported a shallow well-trimmed beard. In one eye he wore a monocle. His dress was immaculate, complete with tail-coat with white carnation and cream-colored waist-coat. The gloves he wore were dove colored and made from the finest silk. He exuded all the confidence of a successful and very distinguished looking professional, clearly at ease at the theater and in a private box.

Jack was unaware of my neighbour's talk. He was too engrossed watching the action on the stage, which was now teeming with the corps de ballet, dressed as little bears and dancing around Mabel. Presently all the bears lined up at the front of the stage above the footlights and holding paws with each other, with Mabel in the middle, burst in to a raucous song. Immediately the Costers rose up spontaneously from their scarlet velvet covered seats and joined in the songspiel, albeit uninvited.

After repeated calls for encore and, '*go to it my sweetness,*' the bears, in a well executed and flawless choreographic manœuvre, involving coördinated precision, split into two ranks leaving Mabel in the middle of the stage lamenting her woes. Not for long, because in the next instant on came Vesta Tilley wearing the uniform of the Captain of the Guard from the town barracks. Within seconds of her arriving on stage, she broke out into a song about the harsh life of the army; but that it was the only way to live. Another song followed on qickly.

Tilley had soon finished her second song, which involved her donning the robes of a mediaeval toff, or some such person, whom she was imitating. According to my program, this was not part of the rehearsed pantomime and it was possible that Tilley had gotten above herself and departed from the script. Unfortunately at that very moment, Ella Shields strode on to the stage dressed as the toff, Tilley had just been impersonating.

On recognizing that she had been parodied, Ella

looked hard at Tilley. Spontaneously the two squared up to each other. Both looked severe, intolerant and implacable. And, certainly they had the physical attributes to prevail successfully in any physical encounter, intentionally or otherwise, with any person of either gender on the stage, or indeed, off it. The anticipation throughout the auditorium was as real as it was unbearable.

Jack and I may have been innocent about the real personalities of these two cross-dressers, but the audience clearly knew something of them that we certainly did not. I noticed that some of the costermongers turned their heads away and shielded their eyes in anticipation of the imminent action about to erupt on the stage.

Possibly something ugly was about to unfold before their shielded eyes, since Tilley and Shields very appearance on the stage had ushered in a deathly silence. Even the ballerinas from the corps de ballet, in their bear costumes performing on stage, tip-toed out of the way from the approaching cross-dressers who were now completing their manœuvres with a coördinated routine towards each other.

Despite the intimidating presence of Tilley and Shields standing against the gloomy backdrop of a rustic scene in a forest clearing, the harmonies of dull colors continued to be very effective and yet foreboding. It became apparent to all but the blind that the stage was set clearly for what looked like a limbering up for a battle of titanic proportions between Tilley and Shields.

I was uncertain as to which of them would prevail in this monumental struggle, and intimated so to Jack.

At this point the action became confused, primarily due to the number of bears crammed on to the stage, some of whom appeared to know what they were supposed to be doing. Others clearly did not seem to appreciate quite what their rôles were, or indeed where they should be. It looked innocent enough from the security of our privileged red plush private box, but what was happening onstage had gotten the audience in the stalls into quite a frantic and highly emotional state in anticipation of the encounter between the titan cross-dressers.

Most, if not all, were clapping unrestrainedly and, I might add, with reckless abandon, whilst other members of the audience were deliberately inducing themselves into an unbridled delirium. The two cross-dressers continued to square up to each other in a series of prim and tasteful manœuvres, clearly not exactly their début in this respect.

Then as if by a hidden signal, the most appalling behavior erupted between Tilley and Shields, such that I did not think would be permitted on the London stage. There was evidently a catastrophic failure of tolerance as the two came into close contact. Within seconds the bears had surrounded both Tilley and Shields and again bits of taffeta and bear fur erupted into a plume above the pandäemonium.

Unfortunately, we could not quite see the impromptu re-action by Shields or Tilley on account of the fact that the corps de ballet immediately enveloped the resultant mêlée which perforce inhibited our viewing the scene. This inability did not in any way diminish the audience's response and pure delight in what was happening on stage and in fact increased their remorselessly baiting the contestants.

At that moment the safety curtain came hurtling down bringing the action to an abrupt halt. The costers knew what was happening, as they made no sound and remained standing in front of their seats ready for the continuation of the action on stage. When the curtain rose again, for the fourth and final part of the pantomime, it revealed a scene of tranquillity set in a forest clearing beneath a bright silver moon. The costers in the stalls resumed their seats, with a sigh of disappointment.

No sooner had the curtain gone up than the audience broke out into applause. It was for Dan Leno who had walked on to the set now dressed as a prosperous burgher in his fine and fur trimmed garment. Within minutes he was singing and holding a dialogue with the costermongers, most of whom clearly relished his being there to regale them. He then broke into an unscheduled song about walking down the Mile End Road. That to me seemed incongruous, given that the pantomime by Wagner was supposed to be set in mediæval Germany and ostensibly about Goldilocks' virulent encounter with a bunch of vigilante bears in the forest.

No sooner had Leno finished one particular song, than Little Tich made an appearance, almost as a cameo rôle, wearing his inordinately long boots. Only this time he wore iron spurs on the heels. Together they sang a duet extolling the virtues of wine, women and song, à la, *Lion Comique*, to which the costers readily agreed verbally and some in song.

Then in an instant the stage was filled with small bears rushing around in every direction, singing songs about their love of honey. The stage was also filling up with other characters, including one wearing a billowing cotton gown, whom even I knew to be Malcolm Scott, famous for his impersonations dressed as a woman. He was followed in quick succession by Mabel dressed in her princess robes strutting around the stage in a masculine manner and Vesta Tilley in the costume of a prince. All were adding to the chaos on the stage, the arrival of

Cinderella in her rôle of the heroine. Nellie Power, dressed as a soldier was seen flitting in and out of the side scenery and large groups of bears sang resonantly.

Within a few moments, Cinderella had brought order to those assembled on the stage. We were then in the final scene as we approached the apotheosis of the pantomime. All the performers took up their various positions on the stage as Cinderella commenced the closing song. She was joined eventually by the massive chorus of bears and other singers assembled on the stage, as we headed to the finale of the pantomime. Then, the huge orchestral forces began their relentless development of a thunderous crescendo involving all the performers on stage and creating a choral climax, which was deafening as it was exhilarating.

Moments later the curtain descended but this did not diminish the sustained applause. As the curtain rose revealing all the artistes lined up on the stage the intensity of the applause increased. Eventually on the last descent of the purple velvet safety curtain, the auditorium began to empty as an insane stampede gathered apace, to the various Crush Bars located throughout the Music Hall.

1. The Happy Bear Family - opera
2. Tannhäuser and the Singers' Contest at Wartburg Castle - opera
3. The acronym drag, 'Dresses Resembling A Girl,' is a theatrical term from 1870s, describing a male posing as a woman.

Chapter 37

The Invitation to Attend

Whilst the pantomime we had witnessed the previous night at The Theater Royal was instructive; it was also good fun. We had all enjoyed the various characters on and off stage. Clearly it was a form of entertainment Jack and I could never perform in. Nor indeed would it interest Lodge, who now had other concerns at an altogether higher level to occupy his mind. In this respect, Lodge has been invited to have his Choral Anthem Symphony performed at the prestigious Royal Albert Hall, near Hyde Park in central London. To celebrate his good fortune and the undreamed of potential for his precious box office receipts, he had invited a very select few to a drinks reception at his town house in the Bergen Avenue. Both Jack and I had been advised to attend the party on what promised to be a glittering occasion worthy of his public image and stature. That day had now arrived.

"Well, today is the day; it has now arrived and I must be seen to be the conduit through which great things are possible. In addition, I must also be seen to share my unusual philoprogenition [1] and successes with those who seek to be guided by my wisdom," said Lodge, pensively whilst looking into his empty glass. He did so whilst we were all sitting at the well-appointed bar at the St. Pancras Hotel.

"Just who is this Royal Albert Hall, Loge, "is he a royal person, a prince or something or what?" inquired Jack.

"Could it be that he is a manager or an impresario perhaps," I joined in, ribbing Lodge.

"None of those things," replied Lodge, in all seriousness, "the Royal Albert Hall remains a concert hall. Not a Music Hall, but a philharmonic concert hall where only great works from the classical repertoire are performed. We are walking with destiny here and with the great and immortal who have had their works performed there.

I am talking Handel's *Messiah*, Wagner's opera, '*Das Liebesmahl der Apostel*,' [2] Haydn's, *The Creation*,' Mendelssohn's, '*Elijah*,' or even Elgar's, '*The Kingdom*,' and other great composers of oratorio. More importantly Jack, the Royal Albert Hall is built similarly in shape to the Coliseum at Rome and accordingly can seat comfortably over five thousand persons. But just think of the box office receipts which could be generated by such prodigious a number, reflecting as it does my undisputed resounding tour de force for my solemn Choral Anthem Symphony. As I say, on that day I shall walk with destiny!"

"Well of course Lodge, both Jack and I are delighted by your good fortune and hope to be able to attend the Royal Albert Hall to witness this resounding tour de force and ultimate success," I said.

"Ah, here to attend me is my faithful Aloysius," said Lodge, pointing with his empty glass to a shuffling uniformed individual making his way to us.

Indeed Lodge's man-servant, the peculiar and insolent Aloysius had just walked into the salon and moments later he was at Lodge's side.

"Ah, here comes my faithful retainer, Aloysius. Tell

me, do you bring with you my highly varnished chariot of the gods, to be hauled by wild Valkürian steeds, ready to convey my person back to my Valhalla in the Bergen Avenue?" asked Lodge, in an expansive and conspicuous show of thespian exaggeration.

Aloysius studied Lodge, as though he were formulating a response to an imbecile.

"Well, if you will be meaning, do I have the usual two chestnuts horses and slightly tarnished rickety Barouche out there beneath the porte cochère in front of the ridiculously phäntasmagoric façade of this St. Pancras Hotel; then yes sir, I do," replied Aloysius.

Insolence noted, I thought to myself.

"Well Jack, Theodor, I must away and prepare for this evening's festivities. Do not forget; we expect you at the hour of seven o'clock," said Lodge extravagantly, as he followed Aloysius out of the bar, like a man- of- war in full sail during a gale.

It was Jack who broached the subject.

"The day has now arrived. For that matter so did *that* day on which the Titanic Benefit Concert was held, attended by the same feeling of misplaced euphoric confidence, I seem to recall," said Jack, with a rueful smile on his face.

"One can only hope there will be no similarities between the event taking place today and those that erupted on that day. A fateful day, on which that ill-fated concert took place, ostensibly to raise funds for the benefit of those dependent widows and children of the victims of the *Titanic* tragedy," I responded.

"I see similarities here Theo; inordinate importance attached to the essentially mundane," said Jack.

"Same again gentlemen?" inquired a very attentive and understanding bar-tender.

St. Pancras Hotel

The rest of the day went by in an agony of suspense and doubts made bearable only by our being at the well appointed bar at the St. Pancras Hotel. At length the fateful hour descended upon us and it was with reluctance that we made our way down to the ornately decorated stone dressed porte cochère of the hotel. On our way we handed in our keys at the reception desk in the foyer, and in particular to the perpetually obstreperous concièrge, wearing as usual his black morning-coat and top hat with a blue rosette affixed to one side.

I had often wondered what would be the outcome of an encounter between this surly top hat wearing concièrge and the insolent Aloysius, Lodge's inordinately over confident man-servant. A battle of wits would ensue, without doubt; a conflict of Titanic proportions an absolute certainty. Though I would have no wish to be exposed to the consequences, nor I should think, would Jack.

On reaching the porte cochère we stepped up into a waiting Phäeton carriage and promptly clattered off into the acrid fog and up to the Euston Road. Upon reaching it, we waited to cross, and whilst doing so witnessed the dull light of dancing green lanterns radiating out from the various tender lamps of carriages, including those of pantechnicon, dray or military, making their way towards us.

In silence, they went lumbering by, leaving their receding red lamps bringing up their rear, but suspended eerily in the fog. Eventually our two grey horses plunged across the carriageway of the Euston Road and were reined to our right by our liveried coachman. We clattered along for some minutes past a building, looming out of the fog, which I knew to be an accurate replica of the Caryatid Porch, formed by six female draped statues, attached to the main Temple of Erechtheion, at the Acropolis in Athens.

Temple of Erechtheion

It was ironic, because I had seen the original temple. One of course associates that fine structure bathed in warm sunlight beneath a clear blue Aegean sky. Located on the Acropolis in Greece, this temple, constructed by Erechteus, King of Athens, is built of white *Pentelic* marble with a black *Eleusinian* limestone frieze to the entablature at this temple complex.

The temple was built to an irregular design, due to its having to accommodate an existing sacred burial site and was therefore constructed on two distinct levels, both of which incorporated three porches and an attached colonnade. This distortion in design however, did not detract, in any way, from the fact that the temple retained an elegance and beauty, culminating in the statue group in the Caryatid Porch comprising six female draped figures eight feet in height and supporting the entablature above.

It was a copy of this porch that I was now looking at. It seemed incongruous to be driving by this structure, in an open Phäeton carriage and witnessing the remarkable similarity of construction with the original temple in at the Acropolis. Especially since the building we were now passing was erected at the center of the largest metropolis on earth and for the time being, shrouded in fog.

It was all the more remarkable, since this Caryatid Porch adorned, not the Acropolis nor did it overlook the straits of Salamis, but rather graced the fog-bound Euston Road. But even the acrid yellow fog which swirled around in the aëther was powerless to obscure totally the porch's elegant and beautiful classical proportions and symetry.

Whilst I was pondering the incongruity of the positioning of this classical styled building, Jack pointed with his cane to another classical structure to our right and just visible in the yellow fog-laden aëther. As we drove towards it, a monumental archway structure appeared. Its sheer size was apparent to us, even though it was partially shrouded in the fog's embrace.

As our Phäeton carriage continued along the road towards the arch, it became clear to us that it was equal in size to the Washington Arch on Fifth Avenue in New York. I have been to the Acropolis and remember seeing the Propylaea. The design of this huge classical structure was based clearly on the Propylaea, the formal entrance to the Acropolis and the collection of temples within that sacred precinct.

As my eyes became accustomed to the fog swirling around the structure it caused vortices. This had the effect of making the fog thin out in places, and in so doing created a brief vision of the gigantic size of this

Propylaeum Arch, Euston

arch. It must have been at least one hundred fifty feet in height. Certainly the proportion of this megalithic classical structure as it occasionally presented itself, became obvious to me.

The Propylaeum Arch was essentially constructed of two elongated recessed granite piers with cornicing, each rising from the ground based crepidomas. Those piers, in turn, supported a granite architrave, the upper section of which comprised a substantial masonry beam. In turn this elongated stone block was decorated with a series of carved triglyphs and guttae. But with unadorned metope panels forming the entablature upon which was supported a stone framed triangular architrave pediment confining an undecorated tympanum.

In between these elongated masonry piers were two intervening massive fluted columns rising up to annulet collars set immediately below the echinus which carried the abacus informing the Doric capital. These columns added further support to the architrave spanning the piers. The details to the front façade, I imagined, were repeated on the rear of the arch structure.

Living in an eastern seaboard city, such as New York, I am familiar with fog. I have always found it to be mysterious and welcome its all-embracing presence, if only for short periods at a time; not continuously as we are enduring in London. But I confessed to being slightly disappointed at the fog at this precise moment because of its ability to partially shroud a building or structure. I should very much have liked to have seen the magnificent Propylaeum Arch, in all its glory illuminated by a blazing sun. Alas, the persistent London fog to date had prevented my seeing this, and other structures too.

One wondered whether the fog would ever lift and disperse. Not only was the London fog oily and acrid, it also smelled. I remarked upon this to Jack, but he was too busy wiping his face with his ornately paisley patterned handkerchief, in an attempt to rid himself of the clammy feeling caused by the acrid fog.

"Apparently Loge has invited quite a number of Music Hall artistes to his party this evening," offered Jack eventually, as we continued down the Euston Road, "but I wonder if he has consulted Aloysius. I ask this only because if Loge has not obtained his consent, then the consequences could be dire!"

We continued in silence for some time, each of us concerned with our own thoughts.

This would be our third excursion to Lodge's imposing town house in Bergen Avenue, yet neither Jack nor I had any idea just where the house was. On our previous journeys there had, of course, always been made in the blinding fog. Having given our instruction to the liveried coach men in the past, we retained no control on just how we got there, or by what route.

There were, of course, some landmark buildings which we had seen on those previous occasions to Lodge's town house. One such landmark I recognized, as being the Exhibition Building, according to Lodge, loomed up out of the fog as we clattered by it.

I have always admired this building, or rather, what one was able to see of it surrounded, invariably so it seemed, by the acrid and swirling fog. One day I should very much like to visit the place and explore its mysterious interior.

I remembered Lodge on the former occasion had informed us that the building was in fact constructed as a museum, but he failed to mention of which type. I began to dwell on what kind of artifacts could make up a scientific collection housed in that fine Exhibition

Exhibition Building

Building, when Jack interrupted my thoughts.

"Theo, you are a hero type; what did you think about the pantomime we witnessed yesterday evening? I ask only because I remain uncertain about a couple of things that we saw on the stage."

"About which things in particular are you unsure?" I inquired.

"The penchant, especially in London, for Music Hall artistes to climb into clothes usually worn by the opposite gender, is pervasive as it is expected. During the pantomime we witnessed this strange behavior throughout the performance. Why is this so Theo?" Jack asked of me with a contemplative look upon his face.

"It is odd that you ask this question Jack, because when we were at Bella Elmore's Wake of Remembrance back stage at the Vaudeville Music Hall this was a question that I asked Dan Leno. You were busy talking with Marie Lloyd at the time. Leno answered my polite inquiry with some long winded reply, but then launched into an historical perspective of why some artistes actually wear such clothes, whether on the stage or not!

"Apparently, in seventeenth century England it was strictly against the law for women to perform on the stage in theaters. Accordingly where the rôle of a female was required it was played by cross-dressing men or boys. As this solution was translated to Music Hall performances, singers or comedians such as Marie Lloyd, Gus Elen, George Robey or Dan Leno, migrated to pantomime and became famous in their cross-dressing rôles there. Such pantomimes were especially organized under the auspices of Sir Augustus Harris, as he related to us when we spoke with him recently in his mansion house, the Abbey Grange.

"And Jack, cross dressing is not restricted to the pantomime in England; the practice is prevalent in Europe. Think about it. You and I went to see the première, at the Metropolitan Opera House back home in New York, of Rickard Strauss's opera, 'Der Rosenkavalier,' conducted by Gustav Mahler. That bourgeois opera opens in ther first scene with a girl dressed as a boy, Octavian, and the predictable misunderstandings, which follow as a result! This situation or behavior is not only tolerated, but now an accepted form of expression, even in such vaunted and illustrious grand operas as Rickard Strauss's. Neither are Wagnerian opera characters exempt; as we seen in the recent past!" I commented.

"Well Theo, what about the woman Leonora dressed as a man in Verdi's blood thirsty opera, 'The Force of Destiny?'" asked Jack.

"Even reserved Nordic composers," I continued, "such as, Jean Sibelius, feel compelled to portray certain characters dressed in inappropriate clothing. Typically a recent theater play called, *'Ödlan,'* 3 inspired the Finish composer Sibelius to compose incidental music of an atmospheric and ethereal quality. Yet the play is about the questionable behavior of a ménage a trois, one of whom is a temptress, a femme fatale, if you will, who has a penchant for dressing up as a lizard!

"During the course of the play, set to that dark music by Sibelius, Ölmer the male member of the ménage, sees Ödlan, the temptress, in the act of easing herself in to the lizard skin. Beside himself with angst and feelings of betrayal, he promptly throws her off a balcony to her death. He then obligingly goes mad!"

"Jeez Theo, and we thought that Siegfried, the hero type in Wagner's doom-laden opera, *'Götterdämmerung,'* was hard done by. At least Hagen, the slayer, had the decency to stab Siegfried in the back when the hero was in male clothing!" said Jack.

"Even more remarkable," I said, "was the fact that some Music Hall artistes began to specialize in doing impersonations of well known characters only. Typically, your woman Nellie Power started out impersonating the manager of the Imperial Music Hall, our friend George Leybourne. Conversely, men, including Dan Leno, would impersonate females and thus become celebrities virtually overnight. And as women began to feature in Music Hall programs, impersonation of males by women increased in demand and popularity and became an established turn or act on stage by the late 1890s.

"Music Hall artistes such as Vesta Tilley, Ella Shields or Hetty King played, with relish, the rôle of men to such a degree that their impersonations created a rumor which suggested that each one of them may have, in reality, been male. All three typically specialized in a range of types including sailors, policemen, navvies, soldiers, working class men or even priests. Needless to say all were dressed immaculately in properly tailored outfits worthy of tailors out of Fifth Avenue or even Savile Row, here in London, England.

"Vesta Tilley, in particular, is one of the highest paid Music Hall artistes of all time, simply by her wearing trousers on stage and singing popular songs, such as, *'I'm the Idol of the Girls,'* with attendant swagger, which she has perfected. Conversely, Malcolm Scott became famous with his acclaimed impersonation dressed as a woman. Born in 1886, he started out as a serious actor performing at the Theater Royal at Margate, on the southern seaboard in Kent. But eventually took on the rôle of impersonating females, which led him invariably to playing, in pantomime, the part of a dame. Including, playing successfully the rôles of Nell Gwyn, Queen Boadicea and even Oscar Wilde's, *'Salome,'* to great critical and public acclaim," I concluded.

"Jeez Theo, it would appear that the golden rule is wear the clothes appertaining to the opposite gender and one cannot go wrong," said Jack.

At that moment our Phäeton carriage clattered by a tower building I recognized. I never did ask Lodge what the building was used for, but I knew then that we could not be far from our destination at Bergen Avenue.

Our peregrinations in the fog had caused us to arrive at the drinks party considerably later than seven o'clock as requested. Irrespective, we had arrived and our Phäeton carriage pulled up outside Lodge's town house located at 536 Bergen Avenue. As we did so both Jack and I looked up at the austere looking town house, from which we could quite audibly hear the sound of laughter and shrieking voices.

Tower Building, London

Jack and I exchanged glances with each other.

"Clearly the events happening inside are not what one might describe as being conducted with dignity and restraint," I offered.

"Good!" was Jack's considered reply.

Other guests had already arrived; as was evident by a traffic block that comprised several char à bancs and carriages lined up against the sidewalk.

We had been here before. Lodge's town house was one of those four storey buildings, the red terra-cotta façades of which were without doubt quite imposing as yhey were clearly designed to be, in reflecting the general august style of Italianate Renaissance. The house we were about to enter comprised three bay windows, each containing three window reveals, which addressed the front of each of the floors, from the basement up to the *piano-nobile*. The three-sided bay window structure was crowned with a substantial overhanging decorated architrave, comprising ornate recessed alternate deep consoles used for corbelling; supporting a lesser detailed stepped cornice, typical of the Renaissance style.

We ascended the steps leading from the pavement to the front door threshold. What I do remember about this front door entrance to the town house was its peculiarity. The two over-ornate double-leaf doors, I noticed, neither of which had any brass decoration nor paraphernalia, in the form of door handles, letterbox, knocker or nameplate one would expect to see on front door of town house. Even more disturbing, I thought, was the conspicuous absence of a kick-plate to each of the doors. It was, as if one were entering a home of the impoverished or destitute. Or even, God forbid, the, *Undeserving Poor.*

In his impatience to get in to the party, Jack immediately pulled vigorously at the rusting iron bell rod. We stood there for quite some time, waiting for the door to open. Jack again pulled repeatedly at the bell rod to alert Lodge, Aloysius or any of the guests as to our presence at the front door. Eventually some one

The House in Bergen Avenue

answered our summons. I braced myself for an encounter with Lodge's insolent man-servant, Aloysius.

I figured that Aloysius would, almost certainly be annoyed with having his quiet and peaceful inflexible routine disturbed by the arrival of numerous guests in his house attending Lodge's reception. And in particular, Jack and I on his door step, demanding entry.

However, the door did begin to open very slowly and to our astonishment it was opened not by Aloysius, but by Hetty King who pulled us over the threshold and into the spartanly decorated hall way.

"Jack Mitchell and Theo Houston, we are guests of Mr. Michael William Lodge," I said to King, who simply closed the front door and walked off abandoning us in the bare uncarpeted hallway, devoid of any decoration or fittings to the grey-tinted walls.

"Come on Theo, from memory the action in this house takes place on the *piano-nobile*," said Jack, pulling at my coat sleeve, "if nothing else we need only follow the sound of revelry!"

We ascended the uncarpeted timber staircase past the gaudily and over ostentatiously gilded plump faced cherub positioned on a timber column from which the stair banister commenced.

A minute or two later we walked into the uncarpeted room, the walls of which were covered in a dull greenish yellow paint, complemented by a white oiled based finish applied to all the timber surfaces, including skirting, window and door frames. Two sets of arched double-leaf doors, both of which had half acid-etched glazing and a timber chimney piece set into the wall, were also finished in white and reflected an evident interior décor design that was Romanesque in style.

The white décor continued on the ceiling, where it was

applied over raised beading details, which formed square patterns, and to a stepped cornice, connecting the ceiling to the walls. Suspended by string from the ceiling were two elaborate brass chandeliers, tinkling with cut glass, giving out a surprisingly weak light, including one illuminating an alcove formed by the bay window. The windows were undressed in terms of the usual velvet drapes, of which there were none. Nor, I noticed, were there any paintings or fixtures adorning the walls.

These observations did not make the room in itself peculiar; but rather the furniture of which it was comprised. What furniture there was resembled an eclectic combination assembled without any systematic coördination or aforethought. It was as though Lodge had acquired the furniture, as a job lot, from possibly a forced sale of various items at an auction.

Typical of this collection was an oversized Salon Français styled red velveteen covered chaise-longue that had possibly once graced a large salon in France, but remained totally unsuited for the room because of its huge size. Other items of furniture were of a gaudy aspect and most were finished with a gold colored paint.

There were two Biedermeier styled sideboards, which had seen better days. Upon one of the sideboards was another gold painted cherub that in one hand was holding forth a lantern in the shape of a firebrand. And in the other a bunch of grapes, some of which were missing. Indeed several fingers from the cherub's hands were also missing, possibly from a fall the statue had clearly experienced at some early stage in its existence.

Most of the furniture was in the late Victorian style, and had been heavily varnished by an inexpert hand. Before moving on through this room in search of the party, I pulled back several folds of a dusty, purple, heavy velvet material that clearly had once been drapes to a window, and in doing so, knew what to expect. The last time we were in this room we discovered a drawing of indescribable beauty underneath this curtain. Sure enough we revealed the same large ornately decorated gilt frame that contained an incredible drawing, of such exquisite beauty as to defy description entitled, '*Visions of Architecture.*'

We had, of course, seen a reproduction of this drawing at Sir Agustus Harris' mansion, the Abbey Grange when we were guests there recently. The drawing quite simply never failed to move me. It combined a surreal elegance with serenity interpreted as a perspective of an ethereal vision of buildings from antiquity.

Jack and I admired the drawing and discussed quickly its finer points and then decided, motivated by thirst, to move on through to the next room which we knew would lead us to the drawing room. Or at least should do.

It did not take us long to locate this parlor and when we flung open the door, we did so on a bacchanalian scene of excess and abandonment, worthy even of Belshazzar's Feast.

1. It is probable Lodge means philanthropy
2. Te Love Feast of the Apostles
3. The Lizard

Chapter 38

The Reception at Bergen Avenue

Having staggered in to Lodge's peculiarly appointed drawing room, we saw a scene that did not resemble a dignified gathering of thespians discussing crucial issues affecting Music Halls or even theater. Rather it was more reminiscent of debauchery and a prevalent devil may care attitude with regard to drink. Despite this, we looked about for Lodge in order that we might pay our regards and thank him for his generous invitation to his drinks reception, of which we intend to take full advantage.

We could not locate Lodge, but did find Aloysius, his surly man-servant. In fact it would be difficult not to notice him dressed in his outré attire to match his evident annoyance at having to endure this episode, in his master's house, of reckless abandon and *Unbecoming Behavior* being indulged in on a grand scale.

I have had good reasons in the past to make comment on this individual and his peculiar personality. His character is one of bluntness and exuding a total disrespect for his lord and master, the impresario Michael Lodge. The flamboyant uniform he wears with a misplaced pride comprises a powder blue tail-coat complete with gold braid emblazoned on to the front and gold tasselled epaulettes on the shoulders to match. To complete this absurd if over ostentatious uniform the man-servant wore a powdered grey horsehair wig. Despite his rather over ornate and extravagant uniform he was attired in. His black trousers were baggy and the boots he wore were brown and scuffed in places.

Not only did he seem decidedly uncomfortable, he appeared vaguely ridiculous wearing this rather over ornate and preposterously designed tunic, the uniform of which was of indeterminate rank. In fact he looked vaguely ridiculous attired as he was and as though if he had just returned from a Louis XIV[th.] pageant held at the Palace of Versailles in Paris, France. None the less we approached him with our polite inquiry as to where his master was.

"What do you want?" he asked, with characteristic bluntness, whilst smoking a cigarette and still uttering oaths under his breath.

"We are seeking your lord and master, the impresario, Michael Lodge," said Jack, with equal disdain in his voice.

"I would not know about that, since I am occupied keeping a watchful eye on these clowns you see around you which he has seen fit to invite into our home," replied Aloysius, still shaking with his St. Vitus' Dance, of which he is afflicted.

He then promptly marched off in the direction of a Music Hall artiste, a woman who was clearly drunk. We recognized her as being Bessie Bonehill, the acclaimed male impersonator. However, upon reaching Bessie, Aloysius began remonstrating with her over an Ellis & Lloyd carriage clock she had taken down from the intricately carved ochre colored *Rosso Collemandina* marble chimney piece.

It appeared that she was about to immerse the carriage clock into a nearby bowl of ice water in order to stop its infernal ticking. Aloysius eventually manage to retrieve the clock and place it back on top of the ornate marble fireplace mantlepiece from whence it came. This, of course, was the same Bessie Bonehill we had met when she was arriving as we were leaving Joplin Rail Road Station in Missouri during the 1895 season.

Eleonora Duse was present, stretched out on the red velvet covered chaise-longue looking very much like, '*La Dame aux Camèlias,*' in full distress, racked with consumption, and all the more valetudinarian. She was acting as if she were about to endure her supreme moment, there and then, or at any rate pass out. I must speak with her, I determined.

Having acquired our drinks at the makeshift bar in the corner of the large, spacious drawing room, Jack and I gravitated to a group arguing in full swing in the middle of the room, presumably there for all to enjoy, if not contribute to. Before we had even gotten there, I heard some finely chosen words being expressed by those contributing to the polemic.

"Well, well, well if it is not our Rosine Bernardt," said Phyllis Broughton distinctly, after which she poured the contents of her champagne glass down her throat.

"No, no, no I am afraid you are addressing the wrong person. For my name is Sarah Bernhardt. You almost certainly would have heard of me; Bernhardt, Sarah, the divine Sarah Bernhardt?"

"Do not be silly Rosine, it is me, Phyllis, Phyllis Broughton and I have known you for over twenty years. Your name is Rosine; what is this Sarah nonsense?" asked Broughton, slightly slurring her words.

"Presumably Phyllis you will have no need of work anymore, now that you have extracted a large sum of money in an out of court settlement for a breach of promise to marry you, by the Viscount Dangan. I am led to believe, by my reliable sources, that the viscount felt the settlement of £2,500 was well worth it and only a fraction of what he would have been willing to pay to be released from his grim entanglement with you! But the settlement does have the advantage of now leaving the stage free for real thespians and actresses, such as I, upon which to interpret our demanding rôles," said Sarah Bernhardt, with a fixed grin on her lips.

"Sarah what? Thespian and actress; to me, Rosine Bernardt, you are neither. You simply remain an impoverished artiste with inordinate aspirations embarrassingly beyond your reach. As reflected in the little confidence you have, even in your own surname," retorted a phlegmatic Phyllis Broughton, totally unperturbed, but flush with her winnings from her court settlement.

"How dare you! How dare you express yourself with such confidence and, more astonishingly, in front to me, me the divine Sarah Bernhardt!" retorted Bernhardt, whilst steadying herself against a particularly ornate fluted green *Verde Vecchia Chiesa* marble jardinière supporting a gilded cherub with an enigmatic smile carved into its chubby facial features.

At that moment Vesta Tilley, dressed in a thorn proof rustic Harris Tweed suit and armed with a bottle of Veuve Clicquot champagne staggered past us whilst trying to reach Ella Shields, who was unaware of her approach. Ella, I noticed, was wearing a smart military uniform, more I suspect to irritate Vesta who preferred to be seen in men's clothes.

"Well Shields, do tell me, have you thought up any original songs yet to augment your pathos on stage, or will you continue to borrow mine?" inquired Tilley of Shields.

"Why, Tilley I did not realize it was you standing there trying to catch my attention with your naturally squeaky voice! I thought for a moment you were the waiter come to attend us. But really dear, do you not think a thorn proof rustic Harris Tweed suit is rather masculine, even for you, at a reception in a town house in London? We are, after all, we are not in the middle of Hyde Park now, are we?" replied Ella.

Jack and I knew Ella Shields from her early days, when she first came out of Baltimore, to play New York. She began her career in Vaudeville doing song-and-dance acts. In 1904 Shields was invited to London where she became known as the, '*Southern Nightingale.*' Her success grew on appearing at the opening night of the London Palladium in 1910. Her induction into cross-dressing as a male impersonator, came about as a result of filling in as a male in a two-man musical act, where one of the males was off sick.

Whilst Ella is an acclaimed Music Hall singer, she now specializes in impersonating male-impersonators, including the time when I saw her impersonating Tilley. She did so in a famous song called, '*Burlington Bertie from Bow,*' written by her manager, now besotted husband, name of William Hargreaves. This song became an immensely popular adaptation and parody of the song, '*Burlington Bertie'* which continues to be performed by Tilley.

It then struck me. Jack's remark made earlier on our way here kind of rings true; in that it would indeed appear that the golden rule is wear the clothes appertaining to the opposite gender and one cannot go wrong. I think that he is correct.

Shields, as I remembered, was though always good fun to be with, especially back stage after an evening's

London Palladium

performance and she appeared to be fun as we watched her dealing with Tilley. One can only speculate as to what Tilley thought of Ella Shields.

"I cannot for the life of me think why you should wish to adapt my song, which my adoring public knows was written in 1900 by Harry Norris especially for me to sing, given my unique voice and remarkably wide vocal range augmented by my acting ability," offered Tilley.

"Your words, "responded Shields, "set to that lyrical

nonsense you call, *'Burlington Bertie,'* displays, especially when sung by you, all that is vulgar about persons who impersonate the opposite gender. For you, impersonation is a matter of assuming a character and exaggerating the personality traits of that gender. So for as you are concerned, dressing up in the uniform of a sergeant major, gives you carte blanche to behave in a thoroughly despicable and appalling manner. Vesta Tilley; *'an angel without wings,'* as it were, I think not. Whoever thought that phrase up, must now have cause to regret it, and a headache the following morning.

"In this respect you denigrate the whole concept of the noble practice of impersonation. Can you not see that if one impersonates the other gender; it must be to explore or express concepts that originate from the former gender? A woman's view in a man's world; or even vice versa. For example, take that Bessie Bonehill, and for whom I have the highest respect; as the progenitor of the male impersonator.

"Her male impersonation acts are of a cheerful disposition and contain no vulgarity, unlike yours. In this respect they remain a pleasure to witness and are thoroughly enjoyable. It follows therefore, that it cannot just be about strutting around on the stage acting like a buffoon in a stylistic manner dressed in appropriate clothes," completed Shields.

"So my songs, including, *'Burlington Bertie,'* inspire you. After all, do they not say that imitation is the highest form of praise?" inquired Tilley.

"Do they? I would not know about such faint praise, since I am rarely the recipient of it. But I do know that whilst Harry Norris composed the song, *'Burlington Bertie.'* The copyright resides with Frank Dean and Company of 31 Castle Street behind the Royal Princess's Theater in

Oxford Street. And that the song, ridiculous as it is, may be sung in public without fee or license except in theaters or Music Halls. That in itself must tell you something," retorted Shields.

"Praise is praise from whatever quarter. After all you do imitate me; therefore my songs perforce must inspire you," reposted Tilley.

"No they do not. *'Burlington Bertie,'* is a preposterous song and merely describes a toff about whom nobody is really interested. That is to say, except you. The reason I sing on the stage my song called, *'Burlington Bertie from Bow,* is to demonstrate the idiocy in your song. I took your song and gave it life and meaning to an audience that wants to be entertained not subject to a person unsure as to what or indeed who they are. Incidentally, earlier I saw that intense ballerina, Anna Pavlova. Perhaps you ought to discuss with her your identity crises about your name and seek a resolution from her. After all we know she is extremely sensitive to such matters appertaining to the intensity of the soul and what we are and what we are not!" advised Shields.

"Let me remind you Shields…" started Tilley.

I left Tilley and Ella to explore their differences and went to the bar in search of more drink. Having gotten a refill I approached two well dressed gentlemen. I assumed them to be Music Hall owners or at least, managers.

"How do you do, my name is Houston, Theo Houston, out of New York. I guess you both must be involved in Music Hall here in London?" I offered in according them every courtesy and civility, during my attempt to engage with them in conversation. "And what awful weather we are enduring with this accursed acrid fog."

Both looked at me askance in their response to my

particular, if relevant polite inquiry. Thinking they were close acquaintances of Lodge, and might prefer that I were formally introduced to them. I made my excuses and left them with their perplexed facial looks following my departure.

Having finished my whisky I made to go to the bar again but was, however, intercepted by Lodge who suddenly appeared from nowhere. He insisted that I should meet with an old and dear acquaintance of his, a certain Sir Charles Wyndham or something or other. Accordingly, he made the introductions, but then abandoned me, still without my drink. The person with whom I found myself was of the most peculiar aspect, if not laconic, again confirming my suspicions about Lodge's questionable choice in friends, or close acquaintances, as he calls them.

He wore, despite being inside the drawing room, a very luxuriant coat of dense wool with a collar of Astrakhan fur. He wore it more, I think, for protection from people at the party, rather than the weather. His face was ordinary, if aquiline, but upon his nose he wore a gold *pince-nez*, through which he viewed Lodges' collection of friends, including me, in a perturbed and agitated manner.

He displayed all the symptoms of being ill at ease, being in such close proximity to Lodges' close Music Hall acquaintances. My experience as a Vaudeville artiste had taught me to recognize this condition, if nothing else. Nevertheless, we both hesitantly chatted about the fog-laced weather and other sundry topics, in which, I realized eventually, that we neither of us had the slightest interest.

When I had finally managed to extricate myself from that living and breathing example of structural ennui,[1] I found myself wondering over to the pianoforte where Gus Elen was just preparing to play.

Then to my horror a perverse woman, a danseuse,[2] name of Flora Miller, came marching towards me. But suddenly, at that very moment, Aloysius came by with a full tray of drinks. Predictably, grasping hands seeking filled glasses immediately engulfed him. Within an astonishing five or so seconds, Aloysius was still standing there with a tray devoid of glasses. Miller, along with the glasses, had also disappeared.

As to that perverse Flora Miller; I simply cannot bring myself to speak with such a woman. I remember seeing her on at least on three occasions in the recent past, and all to my utter disgust. The first time I saw was when she attempted to sing, to the accompaniment of a wind-up Aëolian Pianola, at the Hungerford Music Hall beneath Charing Cross Rail Road Station.

I remember that occasion well because in anticipation of the next act I was straining out of my seat to view the stage. Then, to my surprise a rather diminutive and plump looking woman came on to the stage from the right. Assuming the turns on the stage were in some kind of order, my handbill informed me that she was a 'Flora Millar, Danseuse performing with her ornately engraved brass plated Aëolian Pianola.'

Indeed, following behind her, were two stage hands. They in turn wheeled on to the stage an impressive brass-plated Aëolian Pianola on to which ornate intricate raised designs had been etched in to its metallic surface. She looked about her and then produced from her billowing dress, a not inconsiderably sized brass handle which she inserted into the side panel of the Aëolian Pianola. Miller then proceeded to wind up the ornate Aëolian Pianola in a very lewd and very suggestive manner. An aura of calm expectation descended over the audience.

Having wound up her brass-plated Aëolian Pianola apparatus to its limit, she turned and faced the audience. Then with a flourish and a bow, she immediately launched off into bouts of singing in the irritating key of C # minor. She sang in the most appalling voice, whilst waving her head from side to side, which I remembered, got the audience going in sympathetic response. She spent her entire act singing verses of such a blatant nature exhorting the audience, especially the costermongers, very evident in the stalls, to join in with her, which they did, enthusiastically chanting out their repulsive and indecent responses.

Another time I heard her was at the Oxford Music Hall, in Oxford Street and that was a disturbing experience. However, the last time I saw her was at the Empress Music Hall at Earl's Court during which I had to endure her appalling act yet again, On that occasion however, in an attempt to lend, as it were some dignity if not respectability, she was dressed in a flowing iridescent pink satin gown. There she positioned herself in the soft limelight so as to engender a look of angelic innocence about her person. That contrived innocence evaporated almost the moment Miller opened her mouth and began singing. And for good reason too.

Her lascivious lyrics were laced with such barely concealed obscenity to the point of being blatant. Her act, of course, involved the sublime tinkling of arpeggios and triple A's emanating from her highly polished brass plated Aëolian Pianola which she stroked tenderly during her recital of questionable verses. On numerous occasions, she inveigled the costermongers, as usual, to join in with her lewd verses.

'Altogether now,' she exhorted the audience, on each occasion, while she sang verses laced with overt vulgarity and lascivious innuendo. Most of the costermongers obliged her, and chanted out their equally vulgar responses, much to Miller's delight. On that last occasion I saw Miller cavorting around the stage, having abandoned her Aëolian Pianola, which was still playing sonorous chords. I had to turn my head away as she approached the finale to her questionable behavior and singing on the stage.

I was grateful therefore, that at least on this occasion at the party, I did not have to converse with the woman, or worse, be compelled to make small talk with her. Lodge, I just noticed, had no such reservations or scruples regarding Miller's overt and questionable act and was at this very moment happily engaging her in deep conversation.

My attention was then captured by the sound of a full-blown argument, which was erupting between Millie Hylton and Fanny Robina, though neither seemed to be in full possession of their faculties.

Undaunted, this incident was followed by an outburst of song by Gus Elen, who also called to life the highly varnished pianoforte by playing it. At the same time, it had the effect of causing a migration of people scattered around the large drawing room to congregate around him and join in the singing of his famous costermonger songs encouraged by Harry Champion. In the wake of this movement of people I noticed several inert bodies who were either sleeping or had simply passed out.

Whilst I was contemplating this strange scene and listening to Harry Champion sing a song called, *'Boiled Beef and Carrots,'* a ballerina, name of Pavlova, and looking, at least on this occasion, rather embonpoint,[3] came tip-toeing on her arched feet, up to me. Within moments of her having done so she was talking interminable nonsense about feelings of rejection or pain especially each time she contemplated doing something, such as making a cup of lemon tea, whilst in fit of pique or in the grip of chronic ennui.

"Do you ever experience episodes of feeling rejected, or of mental pain every time you do something you ought not to Theo?" she asked, looking directly into my eyes without blinking.

"No," I retorted, diverting my gaze to the empty glass that I was holding.

"I have it on good authority from my psycho-analyst, as I call him, and who remains eminent in his field, that this is a condition where my brain is trying to learn how to re-act to an unpleasant experience. Listening to a piece of music might invoke bad memories or experiences, which can produce feelings of vulnerability, despondency or anxiety," Pavlova informed me.

"Really," I replied, still looking into my empty glass.

"Do you discuss your feelings of vulnerability with your psycho-analyst Theo?" inquired Pavlova, still staring directly into my eyes.

"I do not, since I neither possess such feelings, nor can I afford such reckless and misplaced philanthropy," I answered, regretting being in her presence and having to experience her tormented soul being bared in my presence.

"You are indeed fortunate; either that or you are unable to appreciate reality Theo, if you do not suffer, as I do continually, from profound feelings of despondency, anxiety or vulnerability. In this respect, I simply cannot believe your good fortune," she said.

"Well sometimes I do experience mild symptoms of those emotions you describe," I replied.

"Oh really," she said, with a facial expression of exultation and victory at her intuition, "when do you experience these feelings, please do reveal all?"

"Now," I answered, "particularly right at this moment."

Her response to me was predictable as it was welcome. She put down her small glass containing aërated water on a tray held by a nearby wooden tallboy. Looked at me and burst into tears. She then turned on her toes and tip-toed away on her high arched feet towards the open drawing room door, through which she left the room.

A few moments later a commotion of considerable magnitude was heard by those of us in the room. This disturbance caused most people in the drawing room; or at least those of us able to appreciate the situation, to turn our heads and look in the direction of the door.

Thinking Pavlova had gotten herself in some sort of emotional difficulty, intentional or otherwise, I continued looking at the doorway in the expectation of being furnished with an explanation for the commotion. It was not long in coming, for at that precise moment, Little Bo Peep, dressed in her impoverished shepherdess' costume complete with frayed matching bonnet and her long crook came marching into the drawing room shouting and waving at all and sundry, including me, in an overt and conspicuous manner.

"Hello Theo, where is Jack?" she shouted at me.

"I think he is at the pianoforte sorting out the songs to be sung with Harry Champion," I replied.

Bo Peep came up to me.

"I noticed just before I came into this room," she said, "that you were talking with Pavlova. She can be a bit of a handful to deal with, especially if it is one's intention to have some fun and drink irresponsibly. It is her mission, unfortunately, to convert as many people as possible to her way of thinking, in endeavoring to understand a perceived problem within the human condition or tortured soul. That is, if one is able to cope with all that Schopenhauer propositional thinking about delaying a pleasure, and deriving a peculiar pleasure, by doing so!"

"I term it flexible emotional response to a series of circumstances, the existence of which is called life," I responded, "and should not be influenced by Pavlova's psycho-analyst, who presumably is intent on finding fault in anyone, including I imagine an inanimate ventriloquist's dummy!"

This last remark elicited an ear-piercing high-pitched giggle from Little Bo Peep, which not surprisingly, attracted the attention of others in the drawing room.

"Well," Bo Peep responded eventually, "what do you expect from Pavlova's psycho-analyst, who spends the majority of his time in the company of blabbering lunatics, the vulnerable at large or hypochondriacs? It can only be expected that a person who deals exclusively with the hyper-loquacious mental wreck and tortured soul is going to have a somewhat warped view of humanity in general and a jaded view on ventriloquists' dummies in particular?"

"It is possible" I replied, "that our Anna Pavlova wishes to induce doubt into other peoples' minds about their own so called fragile emotional re-action to living, and thus get them to visit her eminent psycho-analyst, as she terms him. And perhaps in bringing new clients in; she will have her considerable fees remitted altogether," I offered jokingly.

"The thought was upper most in my tortured mind!" responded Little Bo Peep.

Suddenly the sound of broken glass was heard followed by a loud thud, as if an inert body had fallen to the floor of the drawing room. It had, and it was Jules Léotard, the accomplished aërial trapeze artiste and gymnast who had lost his footing whilst standing up and had fallen to the floor dropping his wine glass in the process.

Immediate help was at hand in the person of Vulcana, who with one hand lifted the hapless gymnast back on to his unsteady feet. Whilst helping Léotard, she was not in any way distracted from the audible argument she was conducting with Rosa Richter, otherwise known as, 'Zazel.' She was another aërial acrobat and human cannonball, working the Royal Aquarium & Winter Garden in Victoria and about whom a song was composed by George Leybourne, the manager there.

Vulcana, whose real name I knew to be Katherine Williams, was of course a close friend and confidant of the recently deceased Bella Elmore. In fact it was she who alerted Inspector Walter Dew, of the Criminal Investigation Department at Scotland Yard as to her suspicions regarding the murder of Bella. I recalled vividly when Jack and I were waiting on Lodge in Kettner's Restaurant.

At the time he came staggering into the bar, clutching, *The Daily Telegraph* newspaper, bearing the terrible news that his Bella Elmore, one of his beloved *Three Graces*, had been quote, 'done in!'

Much of the credit for initiating this investigation lies with Vulcana and John Nash and Lil Hawthorne his wife. I remembered that newspaper report which stated further that the police were summoned to an address at Hilldrop House, near the vast expanses of Hampstead Heath. The very same Hilldrop House, I recall, in which Jack and I stayed overnight when we were guests of Bella and her murderous husband, the good Doctor Crippen. It seemed at the time that these friends of Bella's, whose real name was Cora Crippen, reported her missing when she failed

Imperial Music Hall

to turn up for crucial rehearsals at the Imperial Music Hall in Victoria.

Later, when Bella did not appear at the Royalty Music Hall in Soho, as expected. Her stage colleagues alerted both the manager of the Royalty Music Hall, Mr. Arthur Bourchier and other co-artistes who became concerned. They then became increasingly suspicious, and rightly so, when, Kate Williams, the professional strong woman known as Vulcana and close friend of Bella Elmore, informed them that she had met Bella's husband, Crippen at a ball recently. There, Crippen is said to have informed Vulcana that Bella had returned to the United States.

Vulcana did not in any way accept this explanation from Crippen because Bella Elmore had never mentioned this planned trip. Williams' suspicions were increased further when she noticed that items of jewellery belonging to Bella, and of which she was inordinately proud, were being worn by a woman, with a fondness for large hats, standing with Crippen, whom he subsequently introduced as his niece, Ethel Neave.

The rest of course is history and subsequently they discovered Bella's remains in the cellar after Crippen and his mistress, Ethel Neave, bolted to Antwerp and eventually boarded the Canadian Pacific liner, *SS Montrose*, bound for Canada, as fugitives from the law. Who was it said the world is but a stage? Possibly Lodge; though it has always appeared to me that there is more drama off the Music Hall stage than upon it.

I then came back down to earth somewhat, when Maud Darling made her entrance, as she staggered into the parlor screeching and screaming at all who cared to turn their heads and look at her. Eva Carrington fresh from her recent marriage to Lord de Clifford at the St. Pancras registry office closely followed her. Phyllis Dare with her sister Zena Dare in turn marched in to the room. It was evident to see that all four had been drinking heavily; somehow, somewhere and for sometime. The repercussions of this would soon, no doubt, make themselves manifest upon the rest of us.

"Obviously another char à banc has just arrived and delivered these Bacchanalian thespians to infuse the reception with yet more fresh blood and vigor," I remarked to Bo-Peep, who had just returned from the bar.

"Fresh blood, did you say Theo? That is rather optimistic, I would have…" said Bo Peep.

"Good evening," interrupted a person without any encouragement from either Bo Peep or me, "the name is Terry, Ellen Terry, married to the famous painter George Frederick Watts."

"Who, did you say? I thought Watts invented a steam engine attached to a locomotive," inquired Bo Peep.

"Was he not a Pre-Raphælite?" I interjected.

"He never had the wish to be part of the Pre-Raphælite Brotherhood, which he considered were obsessed with an impossible historical past. Complete with damsels in distress, looking as though they had had their fill of chloral hydrate 4 and somehow staggered out of the fourteenth century and in to this twentieth century by mistake," said Terry.

"Did not Watts paint you in the rôle of, '*Portia from the Merchant of Venice*,' resplendent in your stage costume? I ask this because up until recently. I had always thought that precious painting of you was done by the confirmed lunatic, Gabrielle Rossetti!" said Bo Peep.

"My husband, who, as you know, was besotted of me, did not paint me, my dear," answered Terry, "he simply immortalized me for all of posterity to wonder at in a work called, '*Portrait of Ellen Terry,*'"

"Oh you mean similar to the image or concept in Oscar Wilde's, '*The Picture of Dorian Gray*?'" retorted Bo Peep, "but surely when Watts painted you, during your one year of marriage to him, he did so making you conform to the Pre-Raphælites' concept of a woman. He painted you typical as a typically romanticized image of femininity. That is to say looking like an androgyne with a dream-like vacant expression upon your face, represented on canvas.

"Especially in the painting of you he knocked off about 1865 where you are represented in oils as though you yourself have ingested laudanum or indeed an excess of choral hydrate. Whilst, staggering, almost by accident, from that fourteenth century and into the mid nineteenth century. Avoiding reality is symptomatic of those retrogressive dreamers called the Pre-Raphælites, including your man Watts. And, typical of other Pre-Raphælites, he was obsessed with the female form, in all its stages of health or decline.

"This is instructive here Terry, because it shows, unequivocally, the Pre-Raphælites' ego-centric obsession with looking into the body – themselves; as distinct to their looking out from the body away from themselves and into a world full of challenges and opportunities. Especially, looking at society of which we all form a part and being fully aware of developments across the social spectrum, or divide..." said Bo Peep, then drinking deeply from her champagne glass.

"Let me remind you Bo Peep..." interrupted Terry.

"I have not finished yet," continued Bo Peep, regaining control of her speech and leaning on her shepherdess's crook. "The Pre-Raphælites' failure to lead society into accepting a new order, have instead, by their innate aversion to change, created a nightmare. This apocalyptic syndrome has now been given frightening reign, let loose, by that moribund state of mind. It is further augmented, and given credence and cultivated by Rossetti, Morris and other living fossils existing in that doomed Avalon called the Red House. The Pre-Raphælites represent nothing more than bankrupt, defunct ideals and wrecked dreams. That they are destined for oblivion, from whence they originated, is a surety. Would you not agree Ellen Terry?" asked Bo Peep.

Terry's re-action was unexpected.

"Yes, I do agree with you Bo Peep," said Terry, who then turned on her dainty ankle and left the room.

"If Ellen Terry thought she was hard done by, then she ought to have engaged with those *Three Graces* who at the moment were anything but," said Bo Peep, pointing with her empty champagne glass at Mabel Green, Dot Hetherington and Katie Lawrence, all of whom were having a turbulent time of it.

It was, in fact, the first time I had seen Mabel here at Lodge's drinks reception. But she was clearly becoming drunk on the copious amounts of brandy and the Coca~Cola she had evidently been drinking. She was not quite at the stage of slurring her word, but that condition was predictably not far off, given her current behavior and consistent rate of consumption of alcohol.

"You, Katie Lawrence, cannot sing to save your life let alone for your supper," stated Mabel, whilst steadying herself against a heavy ornately carved mahogany sideboard, upon which was a further generous supply of drinks.

"I beg your pardon," retorted Lawrence, "what did you say?"

"You heard me; unless are you deaf as well as being tone deaf?" continued Mabel, verbally limbering up for an inevitable final showdown with the two other *Graces*.

"You were only invited to join us, as the third *Grace*, because of your friendship with Lodge," interjected Dot Hetherington. "It is you who cannot sing, as witnessed by your peculiar voice!"

"Do not be ridiculous. There was no nepotism involved. You were there when I performed gracefully with the other contestants. I was chosen by Michael Lodge, because unlike you two, I have a talent in being able to sing. In short, I was brought in to bail you two out and lend credence, dignity and ability because of my fine voice and exceptionally wide tessitura," resounded Mabel, lighting up another Trichinopoly cigar, "and, it is I who brings easily that much needed nobility of purpose and gravitas to the elegiac Choral Anthem Symphony."

"Really," said Katie Lawrence, after which she threw the entire contents of the glass she was holding down her throat.

"And, I will have you know," continued Mabel, brandishing the newspaper cutting from her hand-bag, "that at least I have made the reviews in the national newspapers for my acclaimed singing, dancing and acting abilities. Witness my unbridled success continued in the production of the '*Little Michus*,' which was performed at Daly's Theater in Leicester Square.

"It was hailed as an unmitigated disas... triumph for the West End! In particular, one review went on to say, there were stunning performances by Huntley Wright, Miss Mabel Love, Robert Evett and by no means least, Mabel Green. The *Daily Mail* newspaper mentioned my name; Miss Mabel Green, not Dot Hetherington or Katie Lawrence!"

I was watching this encounter when Jack came up to me with May Yohé on his arm.

"Hi Theo," said Jack, "how are you doing? Enjoying the impromptu cabaret act with Mabel and friends? You remember May, May Yohé."

"Theodor, Theodor Houston, how are you? I heard you were both over here working the halls. I am pleased to eventually meet up with you two!" said Yohé.

Jack and I remembered working with Yohé some years back in New York. But we had lost contact with her since she moved away from eastern cities as New York,

Atlantic City and even the Coney Island resort. I recalled her being out of Bethlehem, Pennsylvania and that she was was fortunate to marry into the English aristocracy by accepting the hand of Francis Hope-Pelham-Clinton, his grace the Duke of Newcastle.

She may have married a duke; but she had the reputation of being the, *Queen of the Naughty Nineties*! The duke, I understood, was the hapless owner of the infamous Hope Diamond reputedly the bringer of adverse fortune. Still she did not appear to be suffering from any outward display of bad luck as she spoke with Jack and me.

"Jack was just telling me Theo, about how you both have endured a baptism of fire, as it were, over trying to figure out Music Halls in London," said May.

"Too right," I replied, "Jack and I came down to earth with a crash when we were performing at the Imperial Music Hall, which as you know May, is situated in a peculiar place called The Royal Aquarium & Winter Garden in Victoria, here in London."

"What was it that George Leybourne, the manager of the Imperial reminded us of just before we hit the floorboards there, Theo?" said Jack.

"His advice was good, if a little too late, "I replied, "Leybourne informed us, that firstly, Music Hall in England is not the same as Vaudeville is in America. Secondly, what we from the States, term as Vaudeville in America is not the same as Variety Theater is in England. And thirdly, what in England might be considered Burlesque would be termed Vaudeville in America."

"I guess he is right," said May Yohé.

"He was trying to advise us of those crucial differences amongst the various types of theaters in England. He then wished us good luck. He probably knew that we would make absolute imbeciles of ourselves during our début, which predictably, degenerated rapidly into spectacular débâcle within seconds of beginning our performance on stage. We did not disappoint him!" I replied.

"But, having undergone that baptism, we learned soon enough how to differentiate between the types of audiences," offered Jack.

"How are you finding it May?" I inquired.

"For the main part, not too bad but I agree there are finite differences. Though to be honest I find, being married to Francis, the Duke of Newcastle and attending various salons in Marylebone or Mayfair more intimidating than any Vaudeville or Music Hall stage could ever be. Why only last week we were invited to a reception at Chandos House, the embassy of the Austro-Hungarian Empire. You know, near Cavendish Square, It is also the residence of the ambassador, Prinz Paul Anton Esterhazy, who has a well-deserved reputation for his lavish and extravagant entertainment and receptions which are usually done on a monumental scale.

"When I eventually met with the ambassador, it was all I could do to remain standing. Never in my life have I ever encountered such concentrated snobbery and on such a vast scale as I did there in that embassy. The kind of snobbery, which in my opinion, we simply do not experience back home in America. I say this because I have, and so have you two, been to receptions in New York given by seriously wealthy people, such as the Astors, the Morgans or the Fricks. And even at the Vanderbilt's mansion at the Breakers on Long Island!" said May Yohé, smiling generously.

At that moment Queenie Leighton came up to us and offered her hand to me.

"May I introduce Queenie Leighton to you May," I said, "Queenie is an accomplished practitioner in the art of galvanizing into re-acting with her any audience that a theater may have sitting in its auditorium!"

Having shaken hands, the two ladies greeted each other as though long lost cousins reunited again. We left them hugging each other and laughing for all to see and hear.

"Have you noticed anything about this evening's reception Theo?" asked Jack, when we had arrived at the makeshift bar to refill our glasses.

"Nothing other than the fact Aloysius, Lodge's man-servant, seems terribly put out at this interruption to his quiet, orderly and inflexible routine," I replied, pointing to the hapless man-servant engaged in remonstrating with yet another guest who had elicited his eagle-eyed attention for some unspecified misdemeanor.

"In that case perhaps you ought to leave now madam, whilst you have the capacity to do so," I distinctly heard Aloysius suggest to Nellie Melba, who for reasons I simply could not figure out, was toasting bread speared on to the end of an ornately fashioned brass poker against a blazing fire in the grate. [5]

"It is obvious," Jack continued, "that Lodge has invited a large contingent of male and female impersonators without his realizing it. Or perhaps, Theo, he does; I wonder?"

Before I could give a considered reply, our attention was then diverted from Nellie Melba's odd behavior when suddenly the drawing door burst open and in danced Cinderella, yelling at everyone and waving her arms about in an abandoned carefree manner. In so doing one of her arms came into contact with the back of Aloysius's head. Paying no attention to that, she came prancing over to where Jack and I were standing.

"Good evening Cinderella," said Jack, "always a pleasure to see you. Tell me when might we expect Marmeduke to make an appearance; I take it he has been invited?"

"I believe so Jack. I saw him step out of a Hansom carriage as I arrived in mine," responded Cinderella, with a smile.

"Both Jack and I are very pleased with our new act and look forward to working with Marmeduke. We now feel that we have reached our métier," I said, whilst pressing a glass of Henri Cachet Brut NV Champagne into Cinderella's hand.

"Do you have any further thoughts as to how you might wish Marmeduke's act to develop?" asked Jack.

"There is an idea I think Marmeduke has been playing with, or at least so he told me, that might be of interest. But why not ask him when he arrives. He is sure to be here soon…" replied Cinderella, with a smile.

"Cinderella, Cinderella," interrupted a person who was quite clearly drunk.

We all instantly recognized the drunk as being Billy Williams and he was obviously enjoying himself. I remember him as being from Melbourne and was known as the, *'Man in the Velvet Suit,'* for visually obvious reasons. He also had a reputation of being quite the natural comedian, debonair and for imposing his humorous personality on people involved in Music Hall, including us at this very moment.

"Cinderella," he continued unabated, "I have been searching this house looking for you. Somebody told me you had arrived earlier. What good fortune because I need to speak with you. Are you busy at the moment?"

"Yes, I am going over there to join in some fun with Dan Leno at the pianoforte," answered Cinderella decisively. And then promptly marched off to where Leno was launching into yet another of his songs.

Jack and I decided to accompany her to the renowned Dan Leno, known as, *'The Funniest Man on Earth.'* With good reason; given his acclaimed and various rôles as a pantomime dame, albeit laced with a noticeable misogynistic trait. Unfortunately Billy Williams also decided to join us, and upon reaching Dan Leno, launched into him verbally.

"George, I have not seen you in ages!" announced Williams to Dan Leno.

"Dan, my name is Dan, Dan Leno."

"No it is not, it is George, George Wild Galvin," replied Williams.

"No, no, you got me all wrong," riposted Leno, whilst sorting out the sheet music on the brass music stand, "it is Dan, Dan Leno."

"No George, I have known you and that other Music Hall artiste, Topsy Sinden since we were all street urchins roaming around the Somers Town neighborhood, at the back of the St. Pancras Hotel and the station. Your father was called Galvin, John Galvin and I certainly do remember him!" insisted Williams.

It was Cinderella who began the song, *'The Hardboiled Egg and the Wasp,'* [6] in response to Dan's introductory bars on the pianoforte, of which he is an accomplished player.

> *But not one word said the hardboiled egg,*
> *The hardboiled egg*
> *The hardboiled egg*
> *And what a silly insect the wasp to beg*
> *If you can't get any sense out of a hardboiled egg!*

Vesta Victoria instructed Leno next, to give her the opening bars for her famous song, *'Now I have to call him Father.'* [7] And to which we all joined in the lascivious chorus.

Her rousing song attracted several other guests to join our group gathered around the pianoforte, including the distinguished looking George Lashwood, who was known, for some unknown reason, as the, *'Beau Brummel of the Halls.'* He immediately engaged Billy Williams in some mindless idiocy, the effect of which occupied their minds in vacuous isolation.

"Perhaps the Williams and Lashwood characters will cancel each other out and leave the rest of us in peace to sing," said Clara Butt, as she elbowed her way to the center of the group to demonstrate her vocal range as a soprano.

Clara Butt, after virtually exhausting her considerable repertoire, finally yielded to Wilkie Bard, the singer of such favorites as, *'I want to sing at the Opera,'* and *'The Night Watchman.'* both of which he sang with an unusual clarity of diction and sustained melodic intensity.

He then sang a song called, *'She Sells Seashells.'* [6] A song that neither Jack nor I was familiar with; but would be difficult to sing on stage in front of an audience.

This song is guaranteed to defeat the most accomplished of singers, in getting the right words in the right sequence! The first verse runs typically;

> *'She sells seashells on the seashore*
> *The shells she sells are seashells, I'm sure*
> *For if she sells seashells on the seashore*
> *Then I'm sure she sells seashore shells.'*

Needless to say, Bard sang his song perfectly, I think, and again with clear unconfused pronunciation.

What then happened surprised us all, gathered around the pianoforte. It involved Mabel Green, no less, Lodge's third *Grace*. She had clearly just abandoned her argument with the other two members of the *Three Graces*, Katie Lawrence and Dot Hetherington. But judging by her flushed countenance, had not abandoned her brandy with the Coca~Cola.

This fact in no way distracted Mabel from the intention she had obviously formed in her mind as she staggered to our group standing around the pianoforte. With her rolled up white cotton lace parasol, which she carried about with her at all times, prodded Dan Leno in the shoulders.

"Well, get on with it then," she spluttered out.

"Get on with what?" inquired Leno.

"That song, the music to which, you have just played. Lead me in," retorted Mabel, as she rested her burning Trichinopoly cigar on the top of the highly varnished mahogany keyboard bracket.

Leno duly obliged Mabel and commenced playing the introduction bars for, '*She Sells Seashells!*' We all of us, gathered around the pianoforte, braced ourselves in readiness to witness a spectacle of Titanic proportions, a débâcle to end all débâcles, the mother of all disasters, as it were. I was about to leave the group and avoid what could only end in tragedy and embarrassment, perhaps possibly unpleasantness or indeed dire consequences for Mabel. Especially now that Lodge, having spotted us, was walking determinedly towards our group interested in the expressions upon our faces, as Mabel prepared to sing the song.

Predictably, the first line of the verse was delivered in a hesitant manner. In that she differentiated between the words, '...she sells *sea-shells*, as opposed to *seashells,*' as sung by Wilkie Bard minutes earlier.

Amazingly Mabel, clearly inebriated, sang two verses word perfectly and with a sustained moderation in her vocal delivery guided by Leno's accomplished playing at the keyboard. The end of her recital was met by thunderous applause. I was astounded at what I had just witnessed and turned to Cinderella to register my reaction, but noticed she had left the group. None the less I continued with my applause for Mabel in her triumphant lyrical delivery.

Mabel then picked up her burning Trichinopoly cigar from the timber frame of the pianoforte. Having done so, she then staggered out of the group fresh with her resounding achievement at the pianoforte and flush with her obvious success. Now suitably imbued with verisimilitude which added an undeniable credence to her status, approached the other two members of the *Three Graces* and having done so, Mabel then resumed her argument and trading insults with Dot Hetherington and Katie Lawrence.

"You can now perhaps now see why I engaged Mabel Green as the third *Grace*. My decision was based upon a perceived ability in her and an unbreakable faith I have in that evident talent she possesses in order to acquit herself in the rôle of *Courage*. And do justice in espousing the profound sentiments therein."

I turned around to see Lodge standing next to me. He was evidently pleased with what he too had witnessed in confirming his decision to elevate Mabel to the Pantheon of his *Three Graces*. They would, according to Lodge, with the effortless ease of goddesses, sweep all before them as they attained for him new heights in box office receipts.

1. Utter boredom
2. Performing dancer to song

3. A person of plump proportion
4. An invigorating solution inducing ecstasy especially when dissolved in alcohol.
5. A type of thin toasted bread, created by Auguste Escoffier, used a staple diet for Melba when ill in 1987.
6. Written and composed by Dan Leno from *Mother Goose* 1903
7. Composer by Terry Sullivan and Harry Gifford and sung by Bard

Chapter 39

The Servant and the Impresario

Lodge's drinks reception, held ostensibly to celebrate his having been offered the Royal Albert Hall in which to perform the mighty Choral Anthem Symphony. This monumental oratorio, in which powerful orchestral forces are summoned in order to augment the choral attestation to the noble ideals of *Courage*, *Aspiration* and *Hope*, especially in the face of adversity. A noble quest indeed; but Lodge had not sought nor obtained approval from his man-servant Aloysius. The party was also interesting, in that it provided a perfect opportunity to witness, first hand and off stage, the antics of some of the leading Music Hall artistes from America and London.

I was talking with Lodge on precisely this observation, but became distracted as we both witnessed Sir Augustus Harris make an entrance in to the drawing room. As Harris did so, he staggered into various items of furniture ranged around the place and of which he seemed totally oblivious. Typically, within a matter of a few moments of arriving, he had walked, as though blind, into several objects, knocking them down to the floor, without any realization that he had done so.

Unfortunately, for Sir Augustus, that was enough to elicit the attention of Aloysius, the man-servant, who by his facial demeanor, was clearly looking for a victim upon whom he could revenge himself and vent his wrath. For such was his profound annoyance at this party taking place, in his home and, without his consent. He had now found a victim in the person of Sir Augustus Harris, manager of the esteemed Theater Royal at Drury Lane and pantomime impresario extraordinaire.

"Sir, might I assist you in regaining your carriage?" asked Aloysius, in an officious manner.

"Do not be ridiculous my good man, I have only just arrived. But, if you do want to make yourself useful you may supply me with a large glass of your best champagne," replied Sir Augustus, whilst leaning for support, in an attempt to steady himself, against a nearby limestone jardinière supporting a red glazed urn containing an inordinately large plant of the aspidistra species.

Alas, this laudable intention failed disastrously, as baronet, red glazed urn, aspidistra and limestone jardinière tumbled down to the silk red broadloom-carpeted floor of Lodge's drawing room, much to Aloysius' evident disgust.

Immediately several in the room went to Sir Augustus' assistance, motivated not by altruism, one suspected, but rather by the hope of potential employment by the fallen impresario. Aloysius merely stood there in his glorious, if ostentatious, powder blue uniform complete with gold braid and epaulettes looking at Sir Augustus in disbelief. Presently Aloysius put a cigarette to his lips. He then produced a match from a box of Bryant & May improved phosphorous matches. To my utter amazement Aloysius struck one on the sole of his boot and offered the flame to his cigarette.

He then managed to bring himself to speak.

"Just what do you think you are doing charging about

my house like a bull in a porcelain store?" asked Aloysius, beside himself with anger. "Have you no respect for other people's property? This house here in the Bergen Avenue is not an extension of your disreputable saloon theater in Drury Lane. Where, I might add, all manner of disrespectful behavior is not only tolerated but enthusiastically encouraged by you and the management of that God-forsaken emporium of vice. Now where is your coach-man, because I shall get him to carry you off these premises?"

"I beg your pardon, whom do you think you are addressing?" asked Sir Augustus.

"I am addressing a person who is incapable and..." replied Aloysius.

"How dare you!" interrupted Sir Augustus, "how dare you address me, a flunky, in such a confident manner and accuse me of being incapable..."

"I had not finished," started in Aloysius, "I was about to say, being incapable of respecting the property of other people; but as it happens you took the words out of my mouth. Irrespective of your destructive behavior; you are, sir, quite drunk and incapable by virtue of the alcohol you have clearly consumed. And now you should leave. I will accept your apologies confirmed in writing at a later date."

"You are addressing Sir Augustus Harris, impresario, manager of the Theater Royal and friend of your master, Michael Lodge. Would you prefer that we continue this discussion in his presence?" demanded a flushed faced Sir Augustus.

"To me" replied Aloysius, "you are none of those and as to continuing this discussion. I would prefer that you did so with your coach-man whilst he endeavors to deliver you to your own house. There you may, with reckless abandon, behave in a disrespectful manner. And as to who is my lord and master; I am master in this household with no other above me."

"Do I have to tolerate this impertinence from a flunky, including one who is dressed in a conspicuously preposterous uniform looking for all the world as if he were on his way to a fancy dress ball?" asked Sir Augustus, addressing those guests in his immediate vicinity.

"My sartorial preferences have very little to do with you sir," retorted Aloysius, "and in fact if there is anything ridiculous here it is certainly not me, but, rather, you and those absurd pantomimes you force an unsuspecting audience to have to endure, in that den of iniquity you call the Theater Royal. The Royal aspect in the title deserted the place years ago when you decided to trivialize the noble art of theater interpretation to that of pantomime."

Jack and I exchanged glances, whilst shrugging our shoulders. We both of us knew where this was going. We had in the past witnessed in this very town house in the Bergen Avenue, such an encounter with Aloysius. On that occasion, if I recall correctly, Aloysius had triumphed convincingly in his resounding victory over Lodge. Just how Sir Agustus Harris would fare in this encounter, remained open; but experience would suggest however, that it is a cardinal mistake to take on Aloysius, unless one possesses two basic attributes; sobriety and an inordinately high level of intelligence. Anything less will simply not suffice.

Only recently whilst we were taking luncheon here Aloysius, the impudent, and now very much loquacious man-servant, had spent the entire time contradicting Lodge's every statement. Typically Lodge would make a disparaging remark about the on-going activities of the interfering and pettifogging Metropolitan Board of Works. An unelected government body which endeavored remorselessly, to regulate, through the imposition of strict licenses, those who operated Music Halls, including the Theater Royal run by Sir Augustus. It was their avowed intention to put Music Halls out of business and quite simply, to legally bankrupt their operators.

To this remark by Lodge, Aloysius retorted by insisting that the Metropolitan Board of Works remained a laudable organization dedicated to protecting the public. Especially, Aloysius insisted, from the excesses emanating out of those Music Halls, which, if unchecked, would have audiences degenerating back into the gross immorality which was extant and all pervasive in those *Pleasure Gardens*. Together with decadent activities that were carried on in such outdoor places. They were known for their reckless *Unbecoming Behavior*, to say nothing of the licentiousness and debauchery, which took, place there, on an unimaginably vast scale.

In addition, Aloysius had said to Lodge, his lord and master, whilst serving luncheon to him and his guests. That alcohol, without doubt, made the audience, which comprised nothing more than the inherently disrespectful and their brethren, the pervasive *Undeserving Poor*, obstreperous and contemptuous of authority, temporal or spiritual. Free from any moral constraints the audience was given to behaving in an inordinately confident manner, oblivious to those inhibitions imposed on them by moral considerations especially, when they are sitting in their comfortable, red plush velvet, upholstered seats with brass division rails, totally unaware of the decent things in life.

I remembered at the time, what made the encounter with Aloysius and Lodge over luncheon then. And now again this confrontation with Sir Augustus Harris particularly enjoyable, was the total absence on both occasions of any deference, subservience or even basic respect, shown by Aloysius. In fact, an inherent respect one might expect to see in any servant's attitude to their master, in the case of Aloysius, was totally lacking.

Indeed Aloysius's inordinate confidence, not only with his master, Michael Lodge on that previous memorable occasion at luncheon, but now with this baronet of the theater, was remarkable. He was, in fact, of course, Lodge's actual man-servant; even though he seemed to display an extraordinary and deep contempt for someone who was supposed to be his master.

However, we all of us standing in the drawing room witnessing this current encounter, could detect quite clearly Sir Augustus Harris's mounting exasperation. Especially with the unchecked confidence, if not mounting disrespect, which the powder blue tunic wearing bewigged Aloysius felt, at his convenience and liberty, free to extend, in a forthright manner, to Lodge's guest in the person of Sir Augustus Harris.

I remembered talking with Jack some time ago when we were guests of Lodge and being served luncheon by his man-servant. Could it be, I recalled asking Jack at the time, that Aloysius retained an unbreakable hold over Lodge and any of his colleagues, friends or guests. I would dread to think of the ramifications resulting therefrom. None the less, Jack and I concluded that it was highly probable, and we remained convinced, that Aloysius did indeed have an inflexible hold over Lodge!

Who was this Aloysius? I again asked myself. Where did he come from and how came he to be working in a domestic capacity in Lodge's town house in Bergen Avenue? I looked again at Aloysius and studied him; and concluded that he was without doubt a seasoned practitioner in copralalia.[1] Especially with his ready and compulsive profanity bordering clearly on Tourette's syndrome, together with his also being a prime candidate for copropraxia.[2]

Before I could consider any other of his social failings, I was acutely aware that Aloysius was intelligent. That fact could never be in doubt. That he possessed inherent humility and politeness certainly could. I remembered when we came here previously for that infamous luncheon, his manner, personality and characteristics were less than one would expect from a servant of the household, in which we found ourselves and as personal guests of his master.

Again, I was compelled to look at the man-servant berating Sir Augustus without any inhibition or fear and, in full sight of Lodge and other guests assembled in the drawing room. Who was this man-servant, I kept asking myself whilst viewing him.

He was tall and had a shuffling gait exaggerated by his obvious and conspicuous affliction of St. Vitus' Dance. A debilitating shaking nervous disease, similar to that of Parkinson's, but which was in perfect synchrony with a defective eye that twitched almost constantly. His greasy hair, though thick, was dark and unkempt. His face was pocked-marked and blotched, as were his hands, as though he had, at some stage in his life, handled vast quantities of acid.

His eyes, when not twitching, were of a dark brown and set deeply beneath a bulbous forehead. He often looked into the middle distance with eyes that conveyed sadness at times, as if they had witnessed great sorrow in the past. His ability to return wit, instantaneously and succinctly with unerring rudeness and devastating accuracy was remarkable and astounding to say the least.

He could in my experience of over thirty years treading the floorboards on stage, earn himself an enviable reputation in Vaudeville, or indeed in any English Music Hall as a monologist, or in some similar rôle which demands a quick and facetious return of wit or observation of other people's weaknesses or character defects. He would certainly be of equal standing with such acclaimed *Improvising Monologists* as Heywood Broun or even Charles Sloman. On numerous occasions, because of this talent, Aloysius had elicited a surprised re-action from both Jack and me, and other guests including the hapless Sir Augustus Harris, now at his mercy.

I had been entertained in houses across the United States, and in such places, any flunky of the household, be they a humble housemaid or senior butler, paid unceasing deference to their masters and his family and visiting friends or guests, demonstrating respect and obedience. Clearly in the case of the man-servant Aloysius, unerring deference was but a concept to him; but innate rudeness an accomplished skill, which he deployed to devastating effect. This situation in itself would not normally have engaged my attention, or that of Jack, I would suspect, but knowing Jack as I do, he would be thinking thoughts similar to mine.

At length, Lodge intervened and endeavored to establish his precedence over his mercurial man-servant. That attempt failed miserably from the outset, as I remain convinced that both Jack and I distinctly heard Aloysius denounce Lodge under his breath, and then continued to harangue Sir Augustus Harris.

"You claim to be the manager of the Theater Royal. The only thing you can manage is to mock the decent, the respectful or the dignified. By allowing your audiences to become drunk whilst in your den of iniquity, you ply them not only with cheap alcohol but with the ridiculous and the inane too; for what else could a pantomime be? With men dressing as women and women dressing as men; disgusting if you were to ask me. And, not only that, but you trivialize everything respectable down to the lowest level of farcical debauchery.

Is it any wonder the Metropolitan Board of Works seeks to regulate your activities and avenge themselves upon your lewd establishments? You have brought their attention upon yourselves by your unceasing acts of wanton disrespect and frivolity set in obscene idiotic scenarios, fit more for the circus presumably from whence they originally came," concluded Aloysius.

We all turned to Sir Augustus Harris for a riposte, or at least a rebuttal to this scathing attack.

"I give my audiences what they desire," Sir Augustus Harris remarked, though feebly, "if they want such entertainment in the form of pantomime, then so be it. It is their choice and they are free to spend their money on whatever form of entertainment they see fit to do, and not have decisions made on their behalf by an unelected bunch of sewage engineers by the name of the Metropolitan Board of Works – a misnomer if ever there was one."

"We do not receive complaints from our loyal audiences; and as far as we impresarios are concerned, the public, and its tastes, come first and not the pettifogging interfering Metropolitan Board of Works!" interjected Lodge, who had moved to Sir Augustus's side in order to lend support, albeit, I suspect, in defense of mutual box office receipts.

This remark predictably elicited murmurs of approval from the various Music Hall artistes gathered around and now looking at Aloysius accusingly and with smouldering eyes.

I do not think for one moment that the phlegmatic Aloysius was in the least bit bothered by their re-action.

"The Metropolitan Board of Works," continued Lodge, "remains nothing more than an unelected, interfering, public body. Motivated by a misguided inclination, from which they intend to impose their moral tyranny and crusade on to the public. Especially, in what the public may wish to see and enjoy on the stage; or what they may not want to enjoy. As I have said before, the Board should limit their activities to commissioning and constructing deep level sewers, at which they eminently excel, and, for which they have an unenviable reputation. They should not try to govern our great British Music Halls of which we can all be justly proud!"

Lodge had uttered those words in all honesty whilst still indulging in his habit of looking over his shoulder, which I still found somewhat unnerving.

"That does not detract from my presupposition; in that both your remarks and those of Harris' too; merely confirm the unalterable truth that the so called discerning public do not choose what will be playing in a particular Music Hall anywhere in the metropolis, or indeed in the provinces. They attend, in their droves the lesser of the various evils available to them and also..." said Aloysius, contemptuously, in trying to establish an inflexible *à priori* to conclude his proposition.

"I cannot accept that," interrupted Cinderella, before Aloysius had an opportunity to complete it, "I cannot accept such a warped and uncorroborated defective presupposition! It simply fails to take into account the very important concept of free will and its implication in establishing that we are not automatons. Neither are we puppets; controlled by hidden wires. Nor are we dolls or dummies, with the exception of at least one person standing in this room. We are not, as you suggest Aloysius, devoid of a mental capacity to think when discerning amongst choices presented to us."

"Let me augment Cinderella's remarks. Music Halls represent a vital aspect and essential altruistic rôle in society during our all too brief tenure on this earth. They lend dignity and, by their virtue, are able to imbue the soul with a nobility of purpose, including, in the face of adversity such noble ideals as *Hope, Aspiration* or *Courage* of which I remain the greatest exponent, especially with my wide tessitura!" added Mabel Green, of the esteemed *Three Graces*.

"Might not the Music Hall," Sir Augustus suggested, "be used to convey such ideals as our being British or American, and indeed encourage that social mobility we all of us desire?"

"I speak from personal experience," said May Yohé, stepping forward into the fray, "the advent of the Music Hall has broken down those barriers which hitherto prevented those talented individuals amongst us from going forward for the benefit of all mankind in its diverse and fascinating manifestations. I myself, although born and raised in Bethlehem, no, no! The one in Pennsylvania, but was fortunate in being offered the hand of Francis Hope-Pelham-Clinton, now his grace the Duke of Newcastle!"

"Music Hall, Aloysius, if that is your real name, is not just about songs and anecdotes; it provides a social cohesion from which anything a society wishes to fashion may do so. We all hear stories of where Music Hall artistes are able to progress through society and often become ennobled in the process. Can this be an example of your so-called various evils available from them, as you stated a few minutes ago?" inquired Jack Mitchell, out of Jersey City.

"In addition," interjected Katie Lawrence, "our glorious Music Halls and Vaudeville have facilitated the ability for us women, often disparagingly known as, *'Angels of the Home,'* to escape the drudgery of the house and instead to apply our welcomed talents to the stage. I need only mention, my friend Dot Hetherington and even the redoubtable Mabel Green."

"Not to mention our sweet little Sarah Fairbrother who worked tirelessly with us at the Theater Royal in Drury Lane before she was swept off her feet to the altar by, a cousin of our late Queen Victoria, his grace the Duke of Cambridge. And our dear Harriet Mellon, also of Drury Lane, is now her grace the Duchess of St. Albans," remarked the Sir Augustus Harris, manager of the same Theater Royal in the Drury Lane at Covent Garden.

"Is this not the same Duke of Cambridge who is a regular patron of the Music Halls? He was also the Commander in Chief of the British Army for over forty years? Hardly worthy evidence to submit in one's endeavor to denigrate the laudable and purposeful rôle Music Halls continue to play in today's society.

"And we all know of the wager of the Earl of Clancarty and his being besotted with Bella Bilton, who at the time was appearing at the Oxford Music Hall, in Oxford Street, but which resulted in a blessed marriage. Music Hall, Vaudeville, Burlesque or Variety Theater, all are in existence, simply because there remains a requirement for them. They have evolved with society.

"It is not for you Aloysius, or that sanctimonious Metropolitan Board of Works, to instruct us or even suggest how we might wish to conduct ourselves in a public place such as a Music Hall. We the people decide; not sewage engineers," stated Cinderella, delivering her unerring coup de grâce, as she left the drawing room.

"Indeed, taking up what Cinderella has just alluded to, not only have some of us performers and Music Hall artistes become famous on the stage, but away from it too. One need only look at the successful alliances between the Music Hall artistes and nobility, the finest nobility in the land. Take Anastasia Robinson and her marrying the Lord Peterborough, or Lavinia Fenton, becoming the wife of the Duke of Bolton. Who here in this drawing room could not express absolute joy at knowing of the union between our Frances Braham and the Earl Waldegrave?" said a recovered and confident Anna Pavlova, looking unblinkingly into Aloysius's twitching eyes.

"Even the Prince of Wales would attend alongside the ordinary subjects of the realm. Why, even in more recent years, the Prince of Wales, before being crowned Edward VII[th.] attended the Canterbury Music Hall with their graces the Dukes of Cambridge and Teck with his Duchess. And, as we have just heard, nobility and the Music Hall go hand in hand – well literally to the altar," retorted Lodge.

"The whole rationale of censorship, at least in England, is built upon a defective premise, which has no real relevance today. Henry VIII[th.] introduced draconian censorship, not as a means of preserving public morality, but rather to control what was said on stage. Religious or political sentiments had been expressed previously, but which may not have been conducive to the the Crown's interests.

"Hence, the office of censor has always been filled by a member of the royal household; in the person of the Lord Chamberlain. The Metropolitan Board of Works, this usurper, now wishes to continue those outmoded and draconian concerns involving censorship today!" said Sir Augustus.

"This is about freedom, a freedom of choice and the inalienable right of the great British people to choose for themselves and not to be censored at every step by an unelected, atrophied Metropolitan Board of Works, which with its abuse of powers wishes, to ban our precious Music Halls or theaters and return us all to a Cromwellian tyranny of puritanical killjoy and grim existence!

"We all know what that entailed, especially to our freedoms and right to entertain ourselves. After that dreadful Puritan Interregnum which lasted for an unimaginable eleven miserable years. Talk about enduring the unendurable. But during the course of which pastimes, regarded as irreverent or indeed frivolous, including our beloved theater, were banned. However, thankfully, they were re-instated with the return of Charles II nd to the English throne during the Restoration of 1660.

"Now this unelected Metropolitan Board of Works together with that venal woman Mrs. Ormiston Chant seek to reimpose this tyranny upon us yet again. Their censorship is not restricted to the Music Hall; it extends into the concert hall too," stated Dot Hetherington, lyrically, as if she were about to burst into song.

"Even I," said Clara Butt, slurring her words slightly, "was prevented from singing Saint Saëns's opera, '*Samson and Delilah,*' simply because representations of biblical subjects are banned on the British stage. Not to mention my good friend Maud Allan's courageous portrayal of, '*Salomé*,' what with John the Baptist's head rolling about the stage."

"Rather like Judd, our ventriloquist's dummy's head!" offered Jack.

"And, let me say, even fortitude in the face of adversity, and such magnanimous intent should be conveyed in the idiom of music, song and acts for the whole of humanity, in its diverse forms, to enjoy. It is not just for clever people, more or less similar to us, standing now here in my drawing room," riposted Lodge, holding his guests enthralled by his acute observations.

I had witnessed this phenomenon before, and still found disquieting the undoubted certainty that Lodge was living proof that a little knowledge was a dangerous thing. I watched him as he stood there, attempting to persuade with an unswerving passion, those guests assembled in his drawing room to his way of thinking about the efficacy of box office receipts. He remained though, and without doubt, s*ans pareil!* [3]

I thought Aloysius might verbally explode or retaliate in some other way as he looked menacingly at Sir Agustus Harris and those assembled around him.

"You may decry that which I have stated," he said whilst moving his head in an arc, "but connections to nobility, by whatever means, are no guarantee of correctness in behavior. Indeed such licentious *Unbecoming Behavior*, has in the recent past been on numerous occasions condoned by royalty. You yourself Harris, mentioned the Prince of Wales' regular attendance at the *Pleasure Gardens*, such as those at Vauxhall, Marylebone, Ranelagh or Cremorne.

"Even the words, *pleasure gardens,* are euphemistic; in

that they indicate or evoke a contrived innocence, based on the notion of strolling around a formal garden admiring the foliage. But as I have stated, those words are deliberately contrived; and in fact a euphemism and a disguise for a place where unbridled and wanton behavior are not only condoned, but enthusiastically encouraged.

"And the fact that you mention royal connections with *Pleasure Gardens*, does not itself lend verisimilitude to those places or the behavior extant in the advent later of Music Halls. They simply replaced one moral corrupting destination with another and where moral sensibilities are still relegated with ease to oblivion. This cannot come as a surprise, given the continuous onslaught of innuendo or euphemism in tainted verse coming from those degenerate artistes on the stage. Who themselves are certainly not above exhorting their audience to even higher levels of lewd debauchery, together with an unceasing disrespect for decency, religion or authority.

"Those places were infamous in what was allowed in full sight of God. The fact that members of the nobility were inveigled into forming matrimonial alliances with performers at those *Pleasure Gardens,* or with artistes from the Music Halls, and all which they represent, only goes to establish my conjecture. But there it is," declared Aloysius.

"Ah, but you Aloysius, make the mistake, in my humble opinion, of viewing something superficially and allowing your own emotions and preferences to dominate in defining that which is nothing more than innocent entertainment to be enjoyed by all. Otherwise you are reading too much into it. Rather as the Metropolitan Board of Works do in their consideration of Music Halls in general and a few in particular, but which they have never really understood.

"The reason is that the Metropolitan Board of Works is blinded by an *à priori,* which simply prevents them opening their closed eyes. This explains their inordinate enthusiasm for promoting Theaters of Variety complete with all their smug homogenized safe entertainment endured in the absence of alcohol.

"Aloysius, you must know as we all do, that the Metropolitan Board of Works is an unelected board of sewage engineers, a board which is moribund and evidently corrupt at worst, or inept at best, usurping powers from the Theatrical Regulations Act 1843. An act, no less, that was passed sixty nine years ago in 1843 and under it, still attempting to pass moral judgment upon us today, in what we may show on stage in our great British Music Halls and in how they are managed.

"We the great British people; did we not defeat Napoleon or more recently the Boers in the Boer War, only to become enslaved by a board of deep level sewage engineers? Rather, those same engineers ought to go back to tendering their steam engines and pneumatic sewage pumps and leave the business of running the Music Halls to those such as Sir Augustus and even Lodge there.

"For whilst Sir Augustus is motivated by popular stage shows and Lodge by box office receipts, they together represent a formidable and potentially lethal combination which sympathizes with the public in understanding what it is they want in terms of stage entertainment and…," insisted none other than Marmeduke, who had just arrived, albeit a bit worse for wear.

Marmeduke was then prevented from continuing his speech. This was as a result of the spontaneous and unanimous outburst into tumultuous and sustained applause, from those gathered in Lodge's drawing room that evening. This included those passive witnesses who had been observing this impromptu encounter from the comfort of their Chippendale chairs, the seats of which were covered in resplendent pink and white striped moiré silk.

I was truly astonished to see and hear Marmeduke make such an impassioned plea, which he aimed directly at Aloysius, who looked defenseless against this well-thought out presupposition and resounding tour de force executed by Marmeduke.

Lodge's employé Aloysius, looked defeated and his hunched shoulders encased in gold epaulettes showed his inner turmoil. If there could be such a concept, Aloysius appeared to take this coup de grâce, delivered with unerring accuracy by Marmeduke with a certain degree of dignity, even humility. That may have appeared to be a satisfactory end of the matter, with Aloysius being despatched forthwith down to the servants' quarters, where he justifiably belonged. However, experience in these matters and those more recently, especially in this very town house would suggest something very different would probably be the outcome.

Whilst those and I gathered in Lodge's drawing room, witnessing the polemic, were truly impressed with Marmeduke's effective a coup de grâce, I could not help but think that while he may have vanquished Lodge's man-servant on this auspicious occasion. Aloysius did not strike me as a person who would forgive, nor indeed forget.

It would be only a matter of time before that inevitability manifested itself, probably at some later date and at a most inconvenient time for his master, Michael Lodge. Then, almost certainly, Aloysius would revenge himself upon Lodge's person, and consequently, when he had him alone, would therefore be able to reëxert his hold over him.

1. Involuntary swearing and utterances of obscene words or inappropriate derogatory remarks
2. Performing obscene gestures
3. Without compare

Chapter 40

The Inglorious Commiseration

It was difficult to grasp just what kind of bizarre household Lodge was running at his town house in the Bergen Avenue. The household seemed to comprise the singular and extraordinary at every turn, reflecting Lodge's predilection with the unusual, to say the least. As to his man-servant, the loquacious Aloysius, he appeared indifferent to Lodge or his instructions and displayed a profound contempt for Lodge in general. However, the drinks reception was rapidly degenerating into something unexpected. And even Lodge's man-servant, had gotten above himself and was subjected to a comprehensive admonishment by those guests, including several Music Hall artistes, present over his views on the rôle of Music Hall in society.

"I tell you what Theo," said Jack, "you and I have been playing Vaudeville for over thirty years each, and I swear to God I have never seen Music Hall artistes come together in such a effective way to protect and defend their profession or themselves. Protagonists, even enemies have come together spontaneously to form mutually beneficial alliances for this specific purpose, only to dissolve as quickly! I began to feel sorry for Aloysius and his cause, but set against Music Hall artistes, en-masse, his was a lost one, and inevitably doomed to failure."

"I did not agree with Aloysius's views on Music Halls," I responded, "which he holds and is eager to express to all and sundry at every opportunity presented. His opinions, like him, stem from bigotry and a frightening misunderstanding of what Music Hall and artistes are about. In this respect Lodge's is correct. Box office receipts are a sure indicator of what the public want. It is not up to presidents, kings, queens or the Metropolitan Board of Works and similar bodies including self-appointed agitators like Ormiston Chant, *et al*, to tell, us, the people, what to do, enjoy or accept. We have of course in the United States enshrined this approach in our Constitution. We the people decide.

"If I understand what was happening in those *Pleasure Gardens,* to which Aloysius alluded to," continued Jack, "then it would seem to me those who attended, including the Prince of Wales, thoroughly enjoyed themselves. Dot Hetherington remarked upon that Cromwellian tyranny which held England in its grip for eleven years and during which frivolous innocent entertainment was outlawed! Christmas was abolished and anybody seen laughing was held in high suspicion."

"In this respect Jack, no one person, group or government has the right to impose their views, however derived, upon others. For the simple reason; they may prove to be wrong and that is why our Constitution back home endeavors to enshrine these basic principles, despite the occasional incursion by narrow minded or over-zealous senators. There is only one judge in this business and that is, as Lodge is forever reminding us, box office receipts!" I retorted.

"I think that what you propound is correct Theo. I am also beginning to appreciate Loge's way of thinking. In the time we have gotten to know him, he has never imposed his views on you, me or others to my knowledge. Rather, he has sought to find what it is people want; hence his meeting with us in Chicago in order to persuade us to accompany him back to London and to hit the floorboards there," said Jack, pensively.

"I agree, and, do not forget Jack, you and I are carved from the same block as JP Morgan, Vanderbilt or Carnegie; we live, breathe and survive by the dollar. In this respect Lodge is absolutely correct; box office receipts are not just indicative, they are vital. Without them we none of us would be plying our trade and nor would Vaudeville, Burlesque, Variety Theater or Music Halls exist. And I will tell you something else Jack, and that…" I replied

Alas that something else would have to be held in abeyance until another time, for at that inopportune moment Edna May almost fell into our conversation.

"Jack Mitchell and Theo Houston; well, well, I sure did not expect to see you here, let alone in London. Are you on vacation?" she inquired.

"If you were still working Vaudeville you would know what we are doing here. And no, we are not on vacation. We have taken up residence in London, at least for the time being, whilst we make our way around the various Music Halls in this here metropolis. But then I might ask the same of you. I was under the impression that since you managed to escape out of Syracuse and get your hooks into that millionaire a few years back, what was his name? Ah yeah, Oscar, Oscar Lewisholm, that you did not have to work anymore. So, what are you doing here; are you on vacation?" asked Jack, with deliberate asperity in his voice.

"I and my devoted husband, who is bessotted of me, are doing Europe. We came over on the RMS *Titanic* a few months back…" replied a phlegmatic Edna May.

"Are you saying that you were one of the few lucky women to have gotten off the *Titanic* into a life boat and survived the tragedy?" interrupted Jack.

"No Jack, we sailed on the *Titanic* months ago before she sank," replied May.

"Were you performing on the stage whilst doing Europe," inquired Jack.

"No, much to the chagrin of my adoring followers, I have no need to perform on stage now that I am a pecuniary emancipated woman. No we attended the opera in Berlin, at the glorious Schauspielhaus Theater. That was an experience in itself. That Schauspielhaus Theater in Berlin represents the apotheosis of classical buildings but with clear geometric lines as it was constructed in the early part of the nineteenth century. Do either of you know the Schauspielhaus in Berlin?" asked May.

"I guess not. Since neither Theo nor I have had the pleasure of going to the Prussian capital," answered Jack.

"Oh! You do surprise me Jack. Really you ought do more travelling and see more of the world. After all there is more to life than Jersey City. The Schauspielhaus might possibly be of interest to you, given the fact that it was created by Karl von Schinkel in 1819 as a powerful exposition of the Greek Revival style. The building expresses a series of rectangular masses which are reflected in a classical profile representing a double Parthenon, similar to the famous Parthenon to be found in..." May informed us.

"Which Parthenon are you talking about," interrupted Jack, "the one in Athens or the one in Nashville, Tennessee?"

"Why, the one in Nashville of course!" replied May.

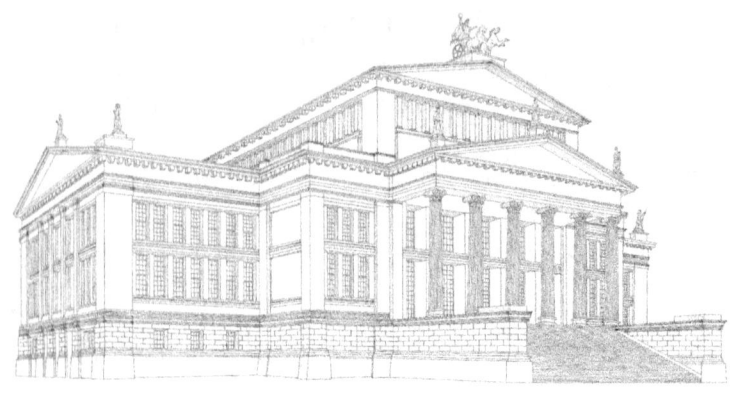

Schauspielhaus, Berlin

Really, Edna, you do surprise me about your architectural appreciation of the Schauspielhaus," responded Jack.

"Oh, do I? But, whilst we were there," continued May, "my husband and I also witnessed a divine performance of Wagner's glorious opera, *'Das Rheingold.'* You possibly have not heard of it."

"*'Das Rheingold,'* not *'The Rhinegold,'*" I inquired.

"Is there a difference between the two?" Edna May asked.

"Only in the spelling," answered Jack.

"Before Berlin we toured Italy and then intercepted the Orient Express via Paris for London. And here we are attending a drinks reception given by my husband's new best friend, the impresario Michael Lodge. Do you know Michael Lodge, the famous impresario?" asked May.

"Please, do tell us about him," replied Jack.

"When dealing with Mr. Michael Lodge, one needs to bear just one thing in mind and that is…" said Edna May.

Alas, we were not to be advised of that one thing one

ought to bear in mind when dealing with Mr. Michael Lodge. For at that precise moment Albert Chevalier, famous for his *'Coster'* songs, burst out loudly with the pianoforte, into a rendition of, *'My Old Dutch,'* to which most of the guests in the parlor joined in. In the meantime we watched Gertie Millar falling over backwards on to a chaise longue covered in yellow and white striped moiré silk.

Nobody went to her aid. After a few minutes Katherine Williams, Vulcana the strong woman, staggered over and attempted to lift the now dishevelled Millar. But either as a result of being overcome with emotion, weakness or alcohol, she too collapsed on to a hapless Millar.

Marmeduke, acting as though he were a lower ranking aristocrat, went lumbering around the drawing room in a loose-limbed manner, as though being controlled by hidden wires. In the next minute he had walked over to where Mabel Green was reclining on a blue watermarked silk upholstered sofa, with what looked like a generous brandy with the Coca~Cola in one hand and a large Havana cigar in the other.

She was obviously drunk. That fact in no way prohibited Mabel from conversing with Marmeduke, or rather their shouting at each other for all those in the drawing room to hear, even over the noise being created by Mark Sheridan's singing of series of risqué seaside songs including, *'Brighton the Best of the Spas,'* whilst playing the pianoforte with his fists.

Mabel looked a sight with her bulging big eyes, rouged cheeks and deep red colored lips. She was dressed in a Buckingham Green satin dress, the type that billows out, similar to what we in America call the southern belle presentation look. Around her shoulder, she wore a short red cape of crushed velvet complementing the red satin ribbons with which her dark auburn hair was held in place. Around her neck she displayed a black velvet choker impressed with a deep green colored diamond.

Her high heeled red boots, which were immediately visible, contained miniature silver colored sequins sewn into the leather. Her sartorial preferences seemed incongruous with the drink in one hand and her cigar in the other whilst laughing and screaming at Marmeduke. She was reclining or, had collapsed; it was difficult to determine which. As I viewed her I became aware that Lodge was, looking at her too.

He was doing so from the far corner of the parlor, behind a limestone jardinière supporting a green glazed urn containing an inordinately large plant of the rampant *Mother in Law's Tongue,* species. He appeared somewhat mystified at Mabel's behavior. It was Mabel voice in particular that I could see had attracted his attention, even from the distance he was away from her. I became intrigued and moved towards Mabel and Marmeduke, neither of whom acknowledged my presence.

"Sometimes of an evening, I prefer to smoke from a meerschaum pipe; but only to gain that essential horsy voice. I find that my audiences adore it," I overheard Mabel inform Marmeduke.

"When did you first learn how to reach those sublime notes that only true sopranos can reach?" asked Marmeduke.

"When I was a young I had a natural talent that my mother recognized. But whilst I can reach those notes, I prefer doing a Vesta Tilley and getting into a sailors outfit or that of the *Rough and Ready*. Then doing the public houses down the Whitechapel Road, Mile End Road or even as far out as Limehouse, especially at the infamous Waterman's Arms in Newcastle Street the landlord of which is a fellow called Daniel Farson. He likes a sing song any time of day or night! But, Marmeduke, I can pull more money in one night doing the East End public houses than Lodge pays me to screech my head off in that cholera ridden Anthem Symphony of his!"

"Does he know of your moonlighting activities Mabel?" asked Marmeduke.

"No more than he really knows who you are; may I call you Cinderella?" inquired Mabel, with a warm smile on her rouged lips.

"Of course you may Mabel," replied Marmeduke, laughing, "of course this cross-dressing came about because of the *Exclusivity Clause*, which was in force at the time. Perpetrated by no lesser person than our intrepid impresario standing over there and whilst we know it has just been rescinded, at the time it caused real hardship. It was one of the reasons I decided to disguise myself within differing characters. Cor, what an act I had to perform; literally worthy of Music Hall!" replied Marmeduke.

"It was the same with me prancing around the stage a member, an esteemed member of the *Cremorne Belles* Troup. Much as I enjoyed working with them, the pay was minimum and simply insufficient to stay alive. Same when I took work as a singer in the *Little Michus* which got me good reviews but very little money!

"The reason I smoke these infernal cigars is to deliberately subdue my soprano voice. I need to husk it up on an all too regular basis if I am to do justice to my boyish voice with a cockney accent, and acquit myself with distinction, singing cockney songs in the East End boozers. That is, if I am to earn my supper, which incidentally I normally take at the Café Royal, each evening, when I have finished singing!" said Mabel, downing her brandy and the Coca~Cola in one go, before making to get up, but thinking better of it and collapsing back into her seat.

"I can disguise myself with clothes but never with my voice. I wish to God that I could. That is why I say very little to people I know but only as acquaintances. Our erstwhile host this evening thinks I am only two distinct characters; Little Bo Peep and Cinderella. He did not recognize me earlier when I changed into my Marmeduke garb and said hello whilst walking by him!" admitted Marmeduke.

At that moment Florrie Forde, the talented Australian singer from Richmond in Melbourne, singing softly to herself, came waltzing by. Fortuitously, because in her right hand she held a full bottle of Laurent Perrier 'Sans Sucre' Champagne that Mabel deftly intercepted and filled our empty glasses with its sparkling contents.

"I too," Mabel advised, "came in to this party earlier wearing a robust herringboned pattern blue serge suit, light gray shirt and necktie of blazing red satin and black boots and sat and spoke to Lodge for quite some time. He did not suspect anything!"

"Do tell me, how can you hide your curly locks of luxurious auburn hair when acting as a man?" inquired Marmeduke.

"Quite, quite simply Marmeduke," Mabel said, "this is but a wig!"

"Why is it Mabel we and half the guests at this party are all confirmed cross-dressers? I can point out at least eight such persons within a few feet of this sofa. The Texan born Mr. Vander Clyde Broadway is in attendance as Barbette, dressed as a girl trapeze artist and over there is our Bessie Bonehill. Not to mention Walter Bothwell

Bruhn who prefers to be known as the female, Bothwell Browne. Hetty King, Millie Hylton, Fanny Robina and Bessie Bellwoood, you of course know. But let us not forget, or forgive, Ella Shields and Vesta Tilley, both of whom look as though they have argued each other into a stalemate!" said Marmeduke, pointing with his cane to the two combatants in question.

"Because in my experience," answered Mabel, "I think some people like to experience being another person and getting into the appropriate clothes to facilitate that desire. What does the popular press describe it as? Ah yes *Drag*, on account of our supposedly *dragging* our long dresses behind us!" [1]

"I think so," answered Marmeduke.

You and I cross dress because our Music Hall acts or turns demand that we do so. When I danced with the *Cremorne Belles*, I will have you know," said Mabel in a high pitched grandiose voice, "I was amazed to discover that more than half of the dancers which made up the troupe, were in fact boys! That in itself did not bother me in the slightest. Rather, I felt privileged in being a valued member of the *Cremorne Belles* for whom I have highest respect and the greatest admiration, especially when they execute their complex routines involving, as they do, an incredible coördinated precision."

"I too like to swagger down the Strand, dressed as a toff in a black morning-coat, silver colored waist-coat, striped trousers, highly varnished boots and a shiny black silk top hat and push people out of my way!" replied Marmeduke.

"I wonder how long we could keep this charade up without our being discovered. Because whilst I like Lodge, and he is a good man, he still thinks of me as though I were the sole depository of being prim and proper. Full of sweetness and light," announced Mabel.

"Well are you so?" ask Marmeduke.

"Certainly not," replied Mabel, smiling.

"May I refill your glass Mabel and your friend's here too?"

At the same time Mabel's attention was taken by Little Tich as he passed wearing his long boots and gently singing to himself his acclaimed song, *'The Gas Inspector.'*

The person offering such reckless and conspicuous generosity was dressed soberly and wearing a frock-coat made with the finest of silk and matching trousers as well as highly polished boots which showed a degree of self esteem. His shirt too was of the finest silk the wing collars of which were fastened with a blazing red satin neckerchief secured with a purple stone of purist amethyst.

You may indeed my good man. By the way where is your lord and master; for we should like to make his acquaintance?" inquired Marmeduke, of the person pouring out Heidsieck Brut Champagne into his glass.

At that moment Mabel returned her attention to the person now filling her empty glass with the Champagne.

"Thank you Michael; you do of course know Marmeduke, he has in the past worked with your two protégés in Theo and Jack," Mabel said, as Marmeduke got up to shake Lodge's outstretched hand of welcome.

"Oh, I assumed you to be the butler," Marmeduke said, turning his head away in embarrassment.

"These simple mistakes can happen," rasped Lodge, "might I join you?"

"Of course you may," replied Marmeduke, as Lodge manhandled with one hand a nearby Chippendale chair the seat of which was covered in a resplendent pink and white striped moiré silk. He sat down in front of us.

"An easy mistake to make Marmeduke," said Lodge,

with the ease of Proteus changing shape, "an easy mistake to make. I am in fact the host of this party and I am an impresario. Though we have never been formally introduced until now of course, I have seen you with Jack and Theo, I think from memory at the Empire Music Hall only recently. But alas, we have not been formally introduced; I am delighted to make your acquaintance."

"We were just discussing the extent of the phenomena of the fashion to cross-dress," Mabel said to Lodge, whilst pointing with her white cotton lace parasol vaguely in an arc around the drawing room. "Marmeduke retains some very interesting views on this matter which I am sure he is anxious to share with you. But forgive me, I see that Marie Lloyd has deigned to show up and join our little soirée. Please excuse me for a few minutes."

"I confess I do not hold with such outlandish conduct on stage, though I know perhaps one person possibly even two, who indulge in that abandoned and reckless behavior, though for the life of me I cannot imagine why. Imagine if you will Marmeduke, the consequences, were the public to find out that a particular favorite artiste of theirs was not what he or she purported to be.

"Consider Marmeduke, the dire consequences; the indignity that could only attend a penchant for such misplaced sartorial preference, together with the shame, the humiliation, along with the vicious whispers including having to wear a large hat to cover one's eyes!" warned Lodge, as Mabel staggered up with difficulty from the blue watermarked silk covered sofa. She made off, screaming at Marie Lloyd, who immediately left the room unaware of the fact that Mabel was calling her.

"I think one only has to be one's self to fulfil one's destiny; would not you agree Mr. Lodge?" asked Marmeduke, in a lugubrious voice.

From where I was standing, I could see that Lodge was looking at Marmeduke intently, as though something was stirring in the back of his mind. At length he enunciated precisely what he was thinking.

"No, no, no Marmeduke, this, this simply will not do!" uttered Lodge, in voice, a pitch higher than normal, whilst he laid down his fluted champagne glass on a nearby occasional table made of polished satinwood.

He then looked at Marmeduke closely.

For myself, watching this encounter, I could feel that certain uncomfortable presentiment about to manifest itself.

"As I said Marmeduke, this simply will not do; my close acquaintances address me as *Loge* in recognition of the only honorable character in Wagner's opera, '*Das Rheingold*.' Please, please feel free to address me accordingly," begged Lodge reverting to his glass again.

At the same time there was a commotion near the pianoforte, which from where I was standing, involving Vesta Tilley, behaving rather as a fellow might, in physically remonstrating with her arch rivals Ella Shields and Hetty King.

"Well Loge, Mabel and I were just talking about those cross-dressers, who continued to do so, even when not performing on stage in the limelight and possible derive some perverse pleasure in doing so!" advised Marmeduke, with an inordinate confidence in addressing Lodge.

"Do not be ridiculous; off the stage! For what reason would one want to go around in the clothes appertaining to the opposite gender? It remains inconceivable. Just look around you here in my drawing room. Could you possibly imagine anyone here would resort to such a desperate course of behavior in conducting themselves;

the idea is preposterous?" said Lodge, with a questioning look through his monocle affixed to his suave face.

"Well in actual…" began Marmduke.

"Sorry, but I have been involved in Music Hall for over thirty five years, "interrupted Lodge, "and I have never in all those years come across more than two very sad cases. It is a myth I tell you, a myth perpetrated almost certainly by the Metropolitan Board of Works or that venal Mrs. Laura Ormiston Chant. Or even worse, the Salvation Army.[2] All three of them are but eager to assert their repellent and insidious views and seek the destruction of our precious Music Halls. They may well hope to spread these vicious and unfounded, slanderous statements about the efficacy and wholesome entertainment we offer in our Music Halls."

"What do you mean by that remarkable statement?" asked Marmeduke, looking incredulously at Lodge. "Please do explain to me, how the devil the Metropolitan Board of Works, that venal Mrs. Laura Ormiston Chant or the Salvation Army are able to become a threat to you and the operation of your Music Halls?"

"Quite, quite simply," replied Lodge, moving his Chippendale chair nearer to Marmeduke, "in London, there are but three perennial enemies, *Three Apocalypses of Doom*[2] as it were, of Music Halls and, by implication, of drink. The first apocalypse, so to speak, concerns the on-going activities of Metropolitan Board of Works, a venal organization, with a seemingly innocuous name, which has begun the remorseless process of trying to impose draconian regulations on our popular Music Halls. They have also antagonized the fraternity of street costermongers who inhabit large swathes of the East End of London.

"The second apocalyptic threat emanates from that

malevolent Mrs. Laura Ormiston Chant, especially from her cohort of malcontents, called the Social Purity Alliance which wages constantly an unceasing campaign against what they see as the immoral style and bawdy operation of our revered Music Halls. She in particular thinks they are attractive to prostitutes and the like! Yet their claims lack validity and are, of course, totally without foundation. That woman, that woman Chant and other meddling crusaders have convinced the puritans who run the Metropolitan Board of Works, of the efficacy of banning drink in all new Music Halls constructed after 1909. Can you simply imagine that unmitigated horror ever coming to pass; a functioning Music Hall devoid of alcohol?

"But the third apocalypse, and by far the more destructive of the three, is without doubt that all pervasive and interfering organization and scourge of mankind; the Salvation Army. By comparison, the two other *Apocalypses of Doom* pale into insignificance by the actions of that venal organization, which constantly endeavors to drive our patrons away from exercising their inalienable rights to attend Music Halls and drink. However, that vile organization has actually managed to close down one or two Music Halls, including the famous and legendary Eagle in the City Road.

"Regarding that inestimable loss to civilization of The Eagle public house, in the City Road, it was frequented by leading literary figures, including someone called Charles Dickens; I think who wrote of his experiences there in his, *Sketches by Boz*. A fourteen-year-old Marie Lloyd made her stage début there in1884. Despite this apparent fame The Eagle which became the *Grecian Saloon* was acquired by that preposterous and sanctimonious, abstemious Salvation Army in 1899.

"Accordingly, they purchased the premises and then

promptly closed the public house down on the premises of moral turpitude, causing widespread anguish throughout London and indeed our Empire, on that terrible day; a terrible day that will live on in infamy.

"Though the closure of The Eagle public house was an irreplaceable and indeed an inestimable great loss to humanity, it was as a direct result of the Salvation Army concentrating all its resources for an all-out campaign to discredit it. We still live under this constant threat, this real and perceived threat to our very survival, our way of life, under this *Sword of Damocles,* as it were, even to this very day.

"Why only the other day, as it happens, I learned of some disquieting news. The famous and well respected Royal Aquarium & Winter Garden, which also houses the resplendent Imperial Music Hall embedded within its magnificent metallic halls, has been sold to the Wesleyan Methodists. And, it is their avowed intention to demolish that magnificent structure and hallowed place of entertainment as soon as they are able to. And replace the building with a temple of sobriety and temperance to be named the Methodists Central Hall. This building, they insist, will be a beacon to those who have fallen and provide inspiration to the faint-hearted. Work is to commence on this huge undertaking as soon as funds are in place."

Lodge said these words with an audible timbre in his voice. His moist eyes reflected that inner turmoil wracking his heart on learning about the inestimable loss of the Royal Aq. Presently he pulled himself together.

"But they shall not have their way, they shall not!" replied Lodge, now working himself into a state. "They may win a battle here or there; but not the war."

Such was Lodge's commitment to his vocal delivery

that he was unaware of a gentlemen standing next to him, holding out his hand.

"I did battle with those apocalyptic creatures," continued Lodge, "when I addressed the Fourth Estate at the Charing Cross Hotel recently. And, let me tell you; I defeated them convincingly. They invite swift retaliation from me, and others of similar thinking, if they dare encroach into our private domain and…".

At length Lodge looked up and acknowledged the gentleman who was standing next to him.

"I just wanted to thank you for a very enjoyable evening Mr. Lodge and to thank you, before I leave, for inviting me to your beautiful town house. I have enjoyed myself immensely and particularly liked your robust defense of Music Hall against that loquacious fellow afflicted with the St. Vitus's Dance…" said the gentleman.

Royal Aquarium and Winter Garden

"His name is Aloysius, and he is my man-servant," interrupted Lodge.

"Oh really, I must say rather, he did seem very confident and quite learned for a man-servant, in his replies and indeed suggestions to yourself. But none the less I came over to bid you good bye and thank you for your reckless hospitality," said the gentleman shaking Lodge's outstretched hand.

"Have we not met before? Because for some reason I feel certain that I know you?" asked Lodge, with a questioning look upon his face.

"I confess. We have indeed met before, when I arrived at your party seven hours ago. I was one of the first guests to arrive with others in the char à banc we hired to convey us here to your drinks reception," replied the man.

This same person wore a robust herringbone pattern blue serge suit, a light gray shirt and necktie of blazing red satin and black boots!

"I am sorry if I have interrupted your conversation," he said, turning and facing Marmeduke.

"Jack and Theo," shouted Lodge suddenly, gesticulating wildly at us, "come and meet my new best acquaintance and say hello to your friend Marmeduke too."

We obliged and came around the blue watermarked silk covered sofa to join them.

"Jack, Theo you both of course know Marmeduke your new erstwhile stage partner. But do you know Mr...?" asked Lodge.

"The name is Smith, Franklyn Smith. People who have gotten to know me kind of call me Frank, which I dislike immensely. I prefer to be called by my proper name, that of Franklyn," replied Smith.

Jack offered his hand to Smith who took it and shook

it heartily. He then did the same with mine, after which my hand hurt.

"Theo, Jack," announced Marmeduke, "we were just discussing, at Lodge's insistence, people who prefer, and indeed, feel more comfortable in the clothes of the opposite gender."

"Really," said Jack, rubbing his hand that Smith had shaken earlier, "whatever got you to discuss such a subject? Was it because this house is full of such people?"

"What people Jack, what are you driving at and who are these people about whom are we talking?" asked Lodge, with a startled look upon his face.

"These people Loge, your town house is full of Music Hall artistes," replied Jack.

"Lodge here was saying earlier that he found it surprising that people would even consider getting into the clothes usually worn by members of the opposite gender. He asked us to consider the indignity that could only attend such a reckless sartorial preference, together with the shame, the humiliation, along with the vicious whispers including having to wear a large hat to cover one's eyes! He added that in his thirty five years in the Music Halls business, he had yet to meet such an unfortunate a person afflicted with such a debilitating condition. What do you think Franklyn; do you hold *views* on this matter?" asked Marmeduke.

"A person who feel compelled to dress as though they were of the opposite gender, as it were, I find utterly remarkable and can only assume they suffer from a particular idée fixe, which propels their monomaniac condition to undertake such an extreme conduct. What could possibly drive a person to such drastic, or indeed, draconian lengths, one can only ask?" offered Franklyn, to Marmeduke's polite inquiry.

"Possibly that they are camp?" offered Jack.

"What do you mean camp; camp as in a row of tents?" inquired Lodge, tentatively.

In reaction to Lodge's faux pas, Jack looked up to the ornately decorated ceiling of the drawing room. Franklyn looked into his wine glass. Marmeduke looked down onto the red silk broadloom-carpeted drawing room floor, I looked at my steel case watch and Lodge looked like a fool. Even so, Jack was magnanimous in his disposition to let that faux pas, pass without a well-deserved acerbic comment. Probably, I thought, because Jack was after all, a guest at Lodge's reception party, and to have done so would not have served any purpose.

"In my day, one could go to prison for such wanton and outrageous behavior, and I am not talking about *Unbecoming Behavior* either!" said Marmeduke.

"Here in London you still can," replied Lodge, pensively, looking into his nearly depleted glass, still oblivious to his continuing faux pas.

We all of us paused to drink deeply from our various glasses.

I have known Jack for over thirty years and thought I had seen all the range of facial expressions he has at his command. I was wrong. The expression upon his face as I looked at him was one I had not seen before. But, it could certainly re-define the word incredulous.

Jack looked into his half filled glass and then poured the entire contents of neat whisky down his throat. Having done so, he then breathed out noisily.

"Theo, assist me in my choice of a refill at the bar," he said.

I accompanied him to it.

"Do you know Jack, I possess no clue as to whether Mabel, Cinderella, Bo Peep and Franklyn are for real. All in fact are just too convincing," I said, to Jack whilst standing at the makeshift bar in Lodge's drawing room.

"Your passing observation has fooled Loge convincingly, but I am though, surprised at you Theo." responded Jack, "this party could just as well just be a cross-dressers' convention. And, I might add; either Loge is extremely clever or he is very clever!"

"Yes Jack, I agree with you. Lodge does know that typically Hetty King, Ella Shields or Vesta Tilley or to name but three in this room alone, cross-dress and make a living out of doing so..." I said.

"No, Theo," Jack said, interrupting me, "it not what they do, when performing on stage, in whatever manner they are dressed and it is not about Tilley strutting around a stage in the uniform of a belligerent sergeant major. Rather it is about what they do *off* stage, that Loge is in total denial."

"Typically then, take Vesta," I continued, "everybody knows, including Lodge, that at the age of six, Vesta Tilley first donned male clothing when she appeared on stage as, '*The Pocket Sims Reeves.*' Her act was based, I think, upon impersonating Sims Reeves, who at the time was a renowned opera singer and from whose operatic repertoire she sang songs.

"When asked why she preferred dressing in male clothes and performing male rôles, she replied, and I quote her response, 'I felt that I could express myself better if I were dressed as a boy.' In fact the public at large know this and buy tickets in order to see her and others such as King, Shields or the Texan, Mr Vander Clyde. Especially when he is dressed as the girl trapeze artist, commonly known as Barbette," I said.

"You surprise me Theo. Normally you are an excellent observer. As I have just told you. It is what these artistes do *off* stage not upon it," replied Jack.

"Yes but Jack, Tilley later married her song writer, Abraham Walter de Frece," I retorted.

Jack did not reply immediately to my statement; rather he was occupied looking in the direction of Sir Augustus, who was now sitting on the red silk broadloom-carpeted floor. Eventually, Jack responded to my remark with a suggestion.

"Come on Theo, let us help Gus back on to his feet, for clearly he is having difficulties doing so himself," suggested Jack

After a rather undignified struggle, we at last managed to lift Gus to his feet. However, he insisted on being left next to a *Verde Vecchia Chiesa* marble jardinière, which supported a large gilded cherub, one with a look of concentrated malevolence in its chubby facial features. The particular one had some of its fingers missing, but none the less Sir Augustus held on to it with a grim determination in order to support himself.

Both Jack and I, in the meantime, made our way to the pianoforte where Marie Lloyd was in full voice, but stopped for breath when we arrived.

"Jack," she said, "if you are here, then that mausoleum buying Lodge cannot be far away."

"Marie, he lives here, this is his home," Jack replied.

"I have not a clue. All I know is that I am attending a party given by some theatrical impresario the name of whom eludes me," replied Lloyd, before reverting to her song about, *some geezer up there in a balcony*.

Jack, I noticed, had assumed the rôle of pianist in order to accompany Lloyd. I began to move away from the pianoforte as I did not feel able to sing songs, most of which by now had taken on a cockney idiom which was beyond my ability to understand, let alone sing in tune.

I was about to turn and head off to the bar when Marmeduke appeared in front to me

"Can I get you a drink Theo?" he asked, as we walked to the bar.

"That is very civilized of you Cinderella, sorry I should say Marmeduke! You are such an accomplished performer it is difficult remembering what to call you!" I said, feeling slightly stupid.

"Call me by what I wear Theo. I am hardly dressed as Cinderella wearing this Prince of Wales checked patterned suit. Would you not agree?" asked Marmeduke as he poured whisky into my depleted glass.

"Where is Mabel with whom you were speaking?" I asked.

"Oh Mabel has only gone momentarily, in order that she might speak with someone she knows but had not until now an opportunity to talk with," answered Marmeduke.

"I do declare Marmeduke, Mabel intrigues me in that she argued very persuasively against Aloysius in defense of Music Halls, which I would not have thought to be her forte, especially given her overtly dainty prim and proper sensibilities. One imagines the sight of a crushed rose would reduce her to a flood of tears worthy of Little Bo Peep's!" I responded.

"What else do you find intriguing about Mabel?" inquired Marmeduke.

However before I could answer that polite inquiry we both of us turned simultaneously in response to the sound of an event unfolding before our very eyes at the far end of the drawing room.

Jack and I had only just lifted Sir Augustus Harris from the floor upon which he was sitting and helped him to his feet. We left him hanging on determinedly to a particularly ornate three feet in height *Verde Vecchia Chiesa* marble jardinière upon which was a full sized gilded cherub with a look of concentrated malevolence in its chubby facial features. In addition it had some of its fingers missing on one hand; whilst in the other it held a bunch of ornamental grapes which appeared intact.

Having been alerted by Sir Augustus' outcry, we were in time to be able to witness him fall again, this time in slow-motion, as it were, on to the limestone jardinière and in the process, push it over along with the gilded cherub. A few seconds later we saw the cherub disintegrate on impact with the floor, with part of its distinctly ugly face moving through the aëther in our direction, causing both Marmduke and I to duck to avoid it.

The remains of the cherub formed a mass of shattered gilded parts, which were then convincingly flattened by the impact of the heavy *Verdi Vecchia Chiesa* marble jardinière. Closely followed by the not insubstantial frame of Sir Augustus' person joining the masonry heap comprising a disintegrated gilded cherub, a shattered marble jardinière and not least Sir Augustus' inert body laid on top of the pile.

Oblivious to this event, Jack continued playing the large highly varnished mahogany panelled pianoforte to the accompaniment of manic laughter by those who saw the accident. Marmeduke and others went to Sir Agustus' aid.

"That malevolent looking cherub was doomed to permanent oblivion the moment this drinks party began," I overheard somebody say. "Aside of which that repulsive cherub was on its last fat legs anyway. I might add, it had never really recovered since the fall it sustained some months past. Then it had to have its fingers amputated in order to save its hand."

I turned around to see who it was that had uttered these prophetic, if facetious, remarks. To my surprise it was Queenie Leighton.

"Would you not agree with me Theo?"

"Rather," I replied, "how did you get on with May Yohé?"

"You mean her grace the Duchess of Newcastle," Leighton responded, with a smile.

"She is still a girl out of Bethlehem, Pennsylvania, Queenie. Jack and I knew her some years back when she played the Vaudeville circuit in New York. But she is an excellent person and very good fun to be with and will almost certainly carry her gracious title with dignity and aplomb," I offered.

"How are finding working the London Music Halls Theo? Is it better fun than New York?" inquired Queenie.

"I do not think it is better fun Queenie. Music Hall in London is different from Vaudeville in New York. I might add, that in New York, Vaudeville is more obvious and wild. In London it is much more polished and refined. Music Hall here is a product of history starting, I think, with the *Pleasure Gardens,* such as those of Cremorne, Vauxhall, Ranelagh or indeed Marylebone. In those *Pleasure Gardens* debauchery and licentiousness were almost de-rigueur. But that in itself not surprising, given the fact the entertainment consisted of cock fighting, overt gambling, bull-baiting and boxing matches with both male and female contestants!

"However, those *Pleasure Gardens* retained public houses, from which such humble establishments as your Song and Supper Rooms originated during the eighteen thirties. One such famous one was of course, Evans's Music-and-Supper Rooms, located in Covent Garden." I said.

"It was called 'Evans Late Joy's' that was the name most people referred to it by," Queenie informed me , "and two other notable Song and Supper Rooms were the Mogul Saloon in Drury Lane and the Cyder Cellars in Maiden Lane. Both are located in Covent Garden."

"I think that I may have asked this question before; but did Covent Garden or Hatton Garden start out as *Pleasure Gardens,* similar to the more well known ones as Cremorne Gardens, Vauxhall Gardens, Ranelagh Gardens or Marylebone Gardens?" I inquired of Queenie

"No Theo. Covent Garden started out as a fruit and vegetable garden for a convent. The name has been corrupted over the years into Covent Garden. Hatton Garden was simply a large garden to Hatton House the home of Sir Christopher Hatton, Chancellor to Queen Elizabeth I$^{st.}$" related Queenie, before drawing deeply from her glass of champagne.

"From such *Pleasure Gardens* two distinct strands developed, I think Queenie. The first involved the origin of Music Halls, as we know them now. They really started out from the *Pleasure Gardens* that retained public houses and from such humble establishments some Song and Supper Rooms originated during the 1830s. They did so by either extending the existing public houses or constructing new and larger ones.

"Typical was the development of the Canterbury Tavern into the Canterbury Music Hall at Waterloo The New Bedford Music Hall in Camden Town was originally the Bedford Arms public house, the London Pavilion began its existence as the Black Horse public house. Even the fabled Criterion Theater was built on the site of the White Bear Inn, and the Oxford Music Hall was originally built out of the Boar and Castle public house in Oxford Street. The so called first Music Hall, Wilton's in

Whitechapel, started out as the Prince of Denmark public house.

"In order to attract a smaller but wealthier middle class clientele, other public houses were converted into respectable Song and Supper Rooms, such as Evans Late Joy's in the Covent Garden, as you say Queenie, serving hot food as supper clubs, whilst providing entertainment. Such establishments began to appear from about 1835 onwards and stayed open until the early hours of the morning. Of course these modest song and supper rooms soon developed into the lavish red plush establishments, indicative of the interior decorative and ornate appointment of the Music Halls we know and love today.

"In those song and supper rooms, proceedings were 'chaired' by a vocalist, such as the legendary John Caulfield. Later that rôle developed into that of compère. Acts or turns were performed on an elevated platform – a stage, located at one end of the hall. Those places evolved into the Music Hall we recognize today.

"The second development out of the *Pleasure Gardens* was into something resembling, typically the Coal Hole, a public house and combined small theater located, I think from memory, in the Strand, near the Thames at Charing Cross in London and still retains a scurrilous reputation, deliberately to attract a certain type of audience, that of *Rough Trade.*

"One is not going to persuade the affluent or wealthy middle classes into hanging around with the coarse *Rough Trade* in such a utilitarian establishment as the Coal Hole, unless of course, one is an Oscar Wilde or some other such sybarite or copralaliac. Even the very name, Coal Hole, betrays its origins and is symptomatic of its approach to entertainment of the lower variety, especially for the *Undeserving Poor.* In this respect, Music Halls have come a long way from the Penny Gaffe. There persons could clown around and dance, but which were popular in earlier times before the advent of the Salvation Army which viewed them with unrestrained hostility.

"There was of course, as you probably know, Queenie, a difference between song and supper rooms evolving into public houses with a theater attached turning into Music Halls and established theaters. In the former one was permitted, whilst watching an act or turn from a table in the auditorium, to smoke tobacco and drink alcohol. By contrast, in theaters at the time, one would be seated in stalls focusing on the stage. Any drinking allowed on the premises was restricted to the aptly named Crush Bar away from the auditorium.

"Accordingly to Lodge, the Music Hall is evolving into yet another guise as a result of the activities of the Metropolitan Board of Works and that Valkürian woman, Lily Langtry. There is now what they call the emerging smug Theater of Varieties, complete with red plush, glass chandeliers and brass fixtures and fittings, including division rails, on what one might call, on a pervasive and grand scale. This, of course, is to give the impression of the utmost respectability and lend verisimilitude to these new establishments," I completed.

You are well informed Theo," said Queenie, after which she poured the entire contents of her champagne glass down her throat, and breathed out noisily.

"That is why Music Hall artistes in London, including you Queenie, are a very special group of talented people. Well just look about this room" I invited.

We both did so, just in time to witness Hetty King falling against one of the drawing room walls - which were covered in purple silk flock wallpaper with raised velvet intricate designs - and slide down gracefully to to the floor. Our attention was then focused on the inert body of the baronet Sir Augustus Harris recumbent over the toppled *Verdi Vecchia Chiesa* marble jardinière and busted gilded cherub.

We noticed Gertie Millar of, *'The Rhinegold,'* fame now laid out and comatose, having fallen over backwards on to a chaise longue tastefully upholstered in yellow and white striped moiré silk. We also were able to experience Anna Pavlova crying her eyes out over absolutely nothing. In addition we could hear quite audibly Phyllis Broughton still slightly slurring her words, but arguing passionately with Sarah Bernhardt as to her real name of Rosine Bernardt. Whilst Vesta Tilley was still squaring up to Ella Shields in a way that could only end in tears in a physical attempt to resolved their thespian differences.

We were also treated to an impromptu display of intricate ballet dancing by Clara Butt and Dan Leno, before Dan lost his footing and both dancers, inextricably linked arm in arm, fell back on to a particularly elegantly carved satinwood occasional table which in the next moment was reduced to smithereens. That event attracted the attention of the distinguished looking George Lashwood, who endeavored to go to their assistance. He managed to walk a few feet towards the stricken Butt and Leno, then stopped, wavered for a few moments and collapsed into a heap on the drawing room floor.

Queenie and I looked over to our left, to the far side of the drawing room, in the direction of the intricately carved ochre colored *Rosso Collemandina* marble chimney piece, which I now noticed was without its Ellis & Lloyd brass carriage clock.

However, we were just in time to witness Jules Léotard,

the accomplished aërial trapeze artiste, attempting to balance his body on one toe on a red velvet upholstered footstool to demonstrate his talent to Billy Williams who was standing nearby. Unfortunately, in Léotard's endeavors to do so, he succeeded only in failing catastrophically, when he lost his footing yet again and fell on to Williams, thus propelling both Williams and himself into the open fire place, causing Nellie Melba to lose her toast and drink to the rampant flames leaping out from the fire grate.

"You were saying Theo something about why Music Hall artistes in London are a very special group of talented people. Well, just look about this room in order to observe them!" said Queenie.

I did as Queenie suggested and took in various characters and individuals disporting themselves.

"As I was saying Theo," said Queenie refilling her depleted fluted glass, "you seem very passionate and knowledgeable about London Music Halls; their history, architecture and the artistes who play in them."

"Most of what I know about London Music Halls I have learned from Lodge. It is he who is passionate and knowledgeable about London Music Halls. It is his continuing and abiding interest in them, which I find contagious. He is in his element when describing a Music Hall. He lives and breathes them. London Music Halls are indeed fortunate to be of abiding interest to Lodge. And further, I know that both Jack and me are beneficiaries of his largesse," I declared.

Queenie looked at me without blinking and for some time. Then with the determination of someone who has made up her mind on a decided course of action, opened her mouth and spoke to me softly.

"You do not know Lodge as I used to," said Queenie

Leighton, "what you say about him is true. Also, what you do not know about him may equally be so. There are very few people in this room, including those who were here earlier, as guests to his drinks reception, that in some way or other do not owe their successes or even livelihood to Lodge. They may not know it; and they may not want to know it, but there it is."

I remained silent, since no answer was required from me.

"Theo," continued Queenie, "follow me. I will show you something that will define Lodge for what he really is. But I must swear you to absolute secrecy. May I take that as being the case Theo?"

I answered in the positive and duly followed Queenie as we negotiated our way through the drawing room over inert bodies and avoiding people staggering around as though they were sleepwalking.

We left the drawing room to its occupants in various states of mental decay. Opening the door of the dining room, that we knew gave egress into the hallway of the *piano-nobile*, we walked through this room. We then found ourselves in a dimly lit passageway, illuminated only by the weak, blue, gas light emanating from the two wall-mounted bronze appliqués, in the form of angels holding forth fire brands. After our eyes had adjusted to the low light, we made our way along the gloom of the hallway.

As we closwed doors behind us, an eerie silence now pervaded the town house.

At length we came to the staircase addressing the *piano-nobile* and peered over the balustrade. We looked up into the upper floors of the house and then down into the depths of the building. Both were in darkness and in silence, with not a trace of activity or noise. We both gripped the staircase banister to steady ourselves whilst we ascended the rickety bare timber stairs, creaking our way up to the upper floors of the house.

We continued through various corridors making our way to into the upper reaches of the house with Queenie leading me and who evidently knew her way round what appeared to be a labyrinth of corridors. Eventually, we ascended another flight of narrower stairs, which led to the garret floor of the house and into the attic. At the top of these stairs we came to a landing that gave out into the beginning of a corridor that was lined with a strip of coconut matting along its length. As we made our way along the corridor, the elm floorboards creaked remorselessly

At the same time we began to detect even more singular sound. It was coming from a room in an adjacent short corridor. This peculiar sound, very faint at first, but increased in loudness as we approached the closed door. It was the sound of a pianoforte. We made our way, in the dim light, towards what I thought was the origin of the sound of the music. I did not know what I expected to see; perhaps Lodge at the pianoforte, or perhaps even the loquacious Aloysius playing for his own amusement.

At the far end of the corridor was a heavy, highly varnished, solid-looking mahogany door that led to even further recesses of the house. We continued towards this closed door from whence the sound of the pianoforte was coming and upon reaching the threshold, attempted to open it. Queenie had difficulty pushing it open, but when I applied my shoulder to it, I overcame the door's resistance and it swung open on its creaking hinges.

Queenie entered the chamber and so did I, though with some hesitation, for I neither wished to disturb Lodge at the keyboard, or indeed be an over inquisitive guest in someone else's house. Queenie suffered from no such inhibition, and continued on into the chamber. When I did eventually follow her in through the open doorway, I could not quite believe what I was seeing or indeed, experiencing. The room was still in keeping with the rest of the house, in that it had its allocation of odd if incongruous eclectic collection of furniture.

What we found was neither Michael Lodge, in rapture over the keyboard, nor his man-servant Aloysius, but rather, an expensive, very grand looking Aëolian Pianola playing quite contentedly to itself. It also appeared that the mechanism operating the keys was being powered by electricity.

I began to examine the perforated roll operating the Aëolian Pianola and was gratified to note that the music being played, albeit mechanically, was a piece especially written for the pianoforte called, *'Echoes of Valhalla.'* I am familiar with, and remain very fond of, this elegiac and sensuous musical work by the composer, Edward Plesse.

However, it was not Plesse's elegant and sonorous music complete with arpeggios emanating out from the Aëolian Pianola which had arrested my attention. It was the way Queenie was looking at me.

"Why have you brought me here Queenie; and why am I listening to this rapturous and sublime music?" I asked.

"Think back Theo to when you and I took tea at Claridges's Hotel. You related to me your experiences of being locked in Wilton's Music Hall as a result of your having a fall and being unconscious for a while before coming to in the dead of night. In that Music Hall you wandered around in a daze. Eventually you collapsed into a seat in the Dress Circle," said Queenie.

"Yes I remember that event with horror. But previously I had fallen down a staircase and become

Wilton's Music Hall

unconscious as a result of my fall. I was still concussed to an extent when I came to in the locked Music Hall in the middle of the night. And, I figured I must have imagined more than I really experienced as a result of being semi concussed. At that particular time, I was trying to find sleep, whilst sitting in the upper balcony, but was awakened by a loud squeaking sound and found myself instead experiencing a kind of activity being enacted on the stage in front of me.

"It involved two characters, one of whom was a gentleman and he wore a dark purple fez made of felt with a gold tassel to one side. In addition he wore greying voluminous trousers, which tapered at the ankles. His shirt was of flaming red in color over which he wore a purple waist-coat, with gold piping, which matched his purple fez.

"The other, his companion, was a woman, of inordinate striking beauty, wore a rather peculiar dress, resembling a layered petticoat, above a pair of exposed horizontally differently colored striped knickerbockers. She too wore a flaming red, in color, shirt and a purple waist-coat with gold piping. But upon hers, silver sequins had been sewn into the fabric.

"What made this double act peculiar was the fact that both were blindfolded and she was tied to the revolving Catherine wheel. It was from such a wheel that I had heard that squeaking sound. In the meantime, he was holding in his left hand, five sharpened knives, glinting in the subdued light. The final destination of those knives was evident to me, and would no doubt be thrown at the woman.

"The fez-wearing individual was swaying, as though he were in a breeze, positioned himself in readiness to perform his death-defying feat. In the next instant he had thrown all five knives in rapid succession, whilst still blindfolded. But then to my horror, in the gloom of the auditorium and stage, I had come to realize something. The squeaking noise from the Catherine wheel, that had awakened me, was now audible no more, and in fact had ceased. Subsequently, the Catherine wheel, upon which the woman was tied, had stopped revolving altogether.

"Then to my unfolding horror, the awful realization dawned upon me. The Catherine wheel, upon which the woman was lashed, had not been able to revolve in sequence with her erstwhile partner's knife throwing act. Consequently, unable to revolve, she had remained motionless, and thus was unable to avoid receiving all five sharpened knives straight into her chest, each one piercing her heart!" [3]

I stopped to think about that momentous remark I had just made; but as to why, I simply am unable to answer. Presently I continued.

"But then Queenie, come to think of it, for some reason, Lodge told us about Wilton's Music Hall and some of the other tragic incidents which have occurred there in the past. Including this one a few years ago about a blindfolded knife throwing double act involving a revolving Catherine wheel, to which a female artiste was strapped, going horribly wrong. So I guess in my concussed state I was partially dreaming at the time," I said.

"Did you dream those experiences Theo?" said Queenie, "Or did they happened in front of you! Theo, please look at this painting."

Queenie then pulled a purple cord, at the end of which, was a bulbous tasselled gold-braided ball and immediately two heavy red velvet curtains parted revealing a tripod easel. Resting upon this easel was full size painting of a woman contained within an ornately decorated gilded frame.

The woman depicted in the painting had been created by an accomplished artist. Upon closer examination I realized that the painting had in fact been painted expertly by no less a painter than a famous society painter. The woman he had immortalized in oils, was of striking beauty, and wore a rather peculiar dress, resembling a layered petticoat, above a pair of exposed horizontally differently colored striped knickerbockers.

In addition, she wore a flaming red colored shirt and a purple waistcoat with gold piping with silver sequins sown into the fabric. Her face was one of profound beauty and reflected intelligence and sensibility. Her dark luxuriant hair was tied back on top of her head. The picture had a radiance emanating from it, which very few portraits are able to create.

I then realized that the painting of the woman on the canvas was the same as the image of the woman I had seen during my delirium whilst locked in Wilton's Music Hall during the night! A cold shiver went through my spine, as I asked the inevitable question, knowing already what the answer could only be.

"Who is that woman depicted on the canvas Queenie?"

"She, Theo, was Michael's wife; it is her image that you see painted upon the canvas before you. It was she who died on the Catherine wheel, albeit, some years ago. He keeps her memory alive in this room," said Queenie.

"What, by occasionally looking upon this image of her?" I asked.

"No Theo he does not. Nor will he ever look upon this painting. But he will sit here for hours!" said Queenie, with moist in her soft brown eyes.

"Doing what; if he does not gaze upon her image?" I inquired, filled with curiosity.

"He will listen to this Aëolian Pianola," Queenie said, "playing over and over again on a never-ending perforated pianola roll of this music called, '*Echoes of Valhalla,*' composed by Edward Plesse. It was, alas her favorite piece of music for pianoforte which she enjoyed playing when she lived. And, this Aëolian Pianola, which is powered by electricity, has been playing only this piece of music, '*Echoes of Valhalla.*' It has been doing so on this non-stop loop ever since she died on that Catherine wheel some quite years ago now."

I looked down on to the highly varnished mahogany panelled Aëolian Pianola and to the ivory keys responding to the continuous perforated roll, which was creating the music. Except now, the music was filled with an indescribable sadness; compounded by a deep feeling of regret, as the arpeggios emanating from the heart of the Aëolian Pianola continued to fulfil their melancholic duty and destiny in playing perpetually.

An overwhelming surge of sadness enveloped my being and found that I had to lean against the bare undecorated wall for support. Queenie noticed my discomfort and emotional re-action to this revelation. Immediately, she closed the velvet curtains upon the portrait, and in so doing, released me from the turmoil, which had gripped my heart.

"Come on Theo, I will take us home," said Queenie, taking my arm in hers.

I fell in eagerly with her welcome suggestion.

A few minutes later, Queenie and I were walking slowly down the various staircases, but in deep thought. I could still hear those sublime and sonorous chords of, *Echoes of Valhalla,* by Plesse, still emanating from the Aëolian Pianola. But to my regret, the sound from which, became fainter gradually as we descended down the stairs.

We returned to where the party had been held, only to find the place deserted and replaced by an eerie silence. We could detect neither the sound of laughter or argument. We took one look about the carnage and so having gathered our coats, canes and what wits we still possessed; Queenie and I made our way to the front door of the house. That door, through which we had entered Lodge's town house some hours previously, I knew allowed access down on to Bergen Avenue. And there in the carriageway, hopefully, we might avail ourselves of a passing carriage to convey us to where Queenie considered home to be.

Having gotten to the front door however, and tried opening it, we were confronted by a vast array of locks. We both of us figured this was not going to be an easy task but did in fact persevere. Eventually, but with some difficulty managed to release a series of catches and locks, more appropriate to a bank vault than a house. But, I supposed, typically in keeping with the general peculiarities of Lodge's town house.

Having released the locks, we finally opened the double-leaf front door, and stepped outside on to the stone landing at the top of a flight of steps leading down to the carriageway. We paused for a moment on the landing peering into the fog. There was no sound in the fog, not even a solitary carriage plying the avenue for a late fare, such as ours. None the less, we possessed our souls in patience and descended the stone steps leading down to the roadway.

In so doing we noticed, with a degree of not totally unexpected amazement, a powder blue tail-coat with gold braid emblazoned on the front and epaulettes to match, together with a powdered grey horsehair wig abandoned on the stone steps. We continued on descending the steps to the carriageway.

Having gained the sidewalk we stood and just looked at each other. Then spontaneously, we both looked back at the discarded powder blue uniform on the stone steps. Whether it was the sight of that abandoned uniform and wig, I could not say, but in the next moment, Queenie and I fell about into uncontrollable fits of laughter whilst we attempted to stagger down Bergen Avenue and into the swirling acrid fog and oblivion.

1. The acronym *drag*, 'Dresses Resembling A Girl,' is a theatrical term in use from 1870s, describing a male posing as a woman
2. For a more detailed account of the Apocalypses refer to, Music Hall - The Saga Goes On. Chapter 5
3. For a more detailed account refer to, Royal Aq – Queen of Music Halls. Chapter 25

Index